FLIGHT
OF the
RENShAi

DAW Books Presents
the Finest in Fantasy by
MICKEY ZUCKER REICHERT

FLIGHTLESS FALCON

SPIRIT FOX (with Jennifer Wingert)

The Novels of Nightfall:
THE LEGEND OF NIGHTFALL (Book 1)
THE RETURN OF NIGHTFALL (Book 2)

The Books of Barakhai:
THE BEASTS OF BARAKHAI ((Book 1)
THE LOST DRAGONS OF BARAKHAI (Book 2)

The Renshai Chronicles:
BEYOND RAGNAROK (Book 1)
PRINCE OF DEMONS (Book 2)
THE CHILDREN OF WRATH (Book 3)

The Renshai Trilogy:
THE LAST OF THE RENSHAI (Book 1)
THE WESTERN WIZARD (Book 2)
CHILD OF THUNDER (Book 3)

The Bifrost Guardians Omnibus Editions
VOLUME ONE:
GODSLAYER
SHADOW CLIMBER
DRAGONRANK MASTER
VOLUME TWO:
SHADOW'S REALM
BY CHAOS CURSED

FLIGHT OF THE RENSHAI

Mickey Zucker Reichert

DAW BOOKS, INC.
DONALD A. WOLLHEIM, FOUNDER
375 Hudson Street, New York, NY 10014
ELIZABETH R. WOLLHEIM
SHEILA E. GILBERT
PUBLISHERS
www.dawbooks.com

First Printing September 2009
1 2 3 4 5 6 7 8 9

 DAW TRADEMARK REGISTERED
U.S. PAT. AND TM. OFF. AND FOREIGN COUNTRIES
—MARCA REGISTRADA
HECHO EN U.S.A.

PRINTED IN THE USA

To Jackie Moore,

the very definition of teenage boy

ACKNOWLEDGEMENTS

Sheila Gilbert, for her always invaluable assistance, and Jody Lee, for her always invaluable cover art.

Also, Foxy Moore, who keeps me almost sane.

CHAPTER 1

A SEA BREEZE RIFFLED the black bangs of Prince Arturo of Béarn, carrying the rich, salt aroma of the Southern Sea. Overhead, the mainsail fluttered restively, and a cleat drummed against the mast. The young prince rested a booted foot on the gunwale, and his two-man Renshai escort shifted with immediate and effortless grace to the rail. Should the ship lurch, should Arturo slip, should some inexplicable madness drive him to leap overboard, they would rescue him with the same swift and bold dexterity that characterized their legendary swordcraft.

Arturo studied a sea glazed with calm, the occasional puff of air chopping foamy wavelets into a rich blue span that might otherwise have passed for woven tapestry. The sailors aboard the warship worked with a leisureliness that suggested boredom, and the soldiers sat in conversational groups as they routinely sharpened and oiled their weapons. Two weeks upon the Southern Sea had revealed no sign of the pirates that had been plaguing the trading ships over the last several months. They had seen only one other vessel while guarding the docks, a cautious freighter from the East that had successfully delivered a load of spices, cosmetics, and fine fabrics to Béarn's port.

The Béarnian ship, numbered *Seven*, might have seemed a dull prison to most of the men aboard her; but Arturo savored the dense salt tang of the ocean that flavored every bite of food and every breath, the rock and toss of the deck even at its most extreme, and the looming sky, whether bright sapphire and full of fiery sun or dark slate beneath a threatening network of clouds. At sixteen, he appreciated any real-life activity that rescued him from the monotonous lectures of his many tutors, the seemingly endless parade of hangers-on and malcontents through his father's courtroom, the pretty manners of the courtiers, and the delicate, fawning tiptoeing of servants in his presence. Here, the sailors mostly ignored him, not even bothering to curb their jargon laced with saucy talk well beyond that which would gain him a severe scolding from his nursemaids and mother. The soldiers accepted his presence among them, their hygiene nonexistent and their bodily noises loud, crude, and unpardoned.

Only the Renshai maintained proper decorum, their demeanor professional and their competence unquestionable. The larger, Trygg, bore the classic blond hair, fair skin, and blue eyes that betrayed the Renshai's Northern origins. He carried more bulk than most of his kind, all of it muscle, though it seemed not to hinder the lightning refinement of Renshai maneuvers that relied on quickness and dexterity rather than strength. The smaller warrior fit the body image of Renshai better: thin and sinewy, fine-boned, his muscles totally defined but utterly lacking in bulk. Named Gunnhar, he had hazel eyes and sandy hair, hacked functionally short. Not a strand ever fell into his eyes. Each wore a sword at his hip, the leather of the sheaths and hilts smooth with use but without a hint of dirt or darkening. Renshai tended their swords with a fanaticism most men reserved for family.

Prince Arturo considered moving to ease the watchful burden from his escort, then decided against it. The Renshai probably appreciated the need for some attentiveness. Though he knew they would have preferred charging into an army, mowing down enemies like wheat stalks before a scythe to protect him, he supposed worrying over his position and mental state proved more interesting than staring at him while he read or groomed or slept.

Arturo blinked salt-rime from his brown eyes, then ran his hands over his coarse features and generous nose, glad he did not have to worry about his appearance on board. The hems of his blue-and-gold cloak had come undone in the drenching winds of the previous day, and his broad knees poked through tears in his britches. His thick, dark hair now lay in a thick, dark snarl. At the best of times, he barely resembled the massive, well-groomed bear of a man who was King Griff of Béarn.

A shout wafted from above and forward. "Ship off the port bow!"

The conversations in the stern cut off in mid-sentence. Every man whirled toward the sound, and several rushed forward. Gunnhar and Trygg displayed no reaction, other than to look askance at their charge. When he moved, they would also, far fleeter and with a natural, delicate grace that would make all the accompanying Béarnides, including Arturo, seem massive and lumbering in comparison.

Heart pounding, Arturo lowered his foot. He turned, eager for more news from the forecastle.

The lookout did not disappoint him. Over the deck-level rumble of new conversation, he cried out clearly, "Dark sails. No standard." His voice sank as he shinnied from the riggings, and his tone held admiration as well as a hint of fear, "Coming at a right goodly clip." Their own sails could scarcely find wind, moving at a snail's pace, if at all, in the quiet calm of the morning.

Footsteps pounded from below, and the night crew spilled onto the deck. Captain Jhirban waited until the last man had joined them before slamming the hatch closed with a sound like thunder. Having seized every man's attention, he sprang onto an overturned crate with a spryness that belied his Béarnian bulk and his advancing age. Curls cascaded to his shoulders, a wind-tousled mixture of silver and black, and he wore Béarnian blue and gold, with the rearing grizzly on his chest.

Arturo glided forward to join the rest of the men, the Renshai dogging his every step. He noticed that most of the soldiers' hands had instinctively drifted to their sword hilts and cursed his own inexperience. He mimicked their stances, but his hand fell on empty air. Three times, he reached for his broadsword and, three times, he missed. Finally, he took his eyes from the captain to look at his sword belt. No blade hung there; he had removed it while seeking a more comfortable sitting position earlier in the day.

An icy bolt of fear spiked through Arturo. He tensed to turn, when something cold poked the back of his hand. He glanced at it, recognizing a familiar engraved hilt with a brilliant sapphire in the pommel. The split-leather enwrapping it looked stiff, unhandled. He followed the bright scabbard, its tooling still deeply fresh, to the pallid long-fingered Renshai hand that cradled the sheathed blade.

"You might need this, Sire," Gunnhar whispered, making no mention of the prince's antics, though they surely amused him.

"Thank you." Prince Arturo accepted the sword without a glance toward his benefactor. The Renshai's tone was flat, but Arturo dared not face the judgmental hazel eyes. A Renshai would rather enter a courtroom stark naked than unarmed. Their parents thrust swords into their fists the instant their pudgy baby fingers could close around a hilt, and they demonstrated the same respect for their chosen weapons, always swords, that other men reserved for royalty. If a man toppled overboard at the same time as a Renshai's sword, Arturo suspected the weapon would get rescued first.

"Sailors." Captain Jhirban glanced around the gathering, his features squinted into wrinkles and crow's-feet. Salt crusted his cheeks, and the sun had baked his skin into leather. "Man your positions and prepare to back up anyone who needs it, but stay out of the soldiers' way should battle become necessary. Friendly deaths and hampered sword arms can turn the tide of a battle."

"Aye," the fifteen sailors chorused, scurrying to the lines and tiller, attentive to the fighting men.

"Your Majesty . . ."

Still fastening his sword to his belt, Arturo froze, cheeks reddening. He wished the captain had not chosen that moment to draw every man's attention to him.

If the captain noticed Arturo's unpreparedness, he gave no sign, continuing his speech without a hitch or interruption in the flow, ". . . I think you should go belowdecks. It's safer."

"No!" Arturo wished he sounded more like a warrior than a terrified adolescent. His maturing voice cracked at the most inopportune moments. "If that ship is manned by pirates, every sword arm is needed, including my own."

The captain frowned, clearly preferring to continue his speech rather than wasting time arguing, yet constrained by protocol. "Your Majesty, I must insist. You're too important to risk."

Haunted by his earlier lapse, Arturo refused the demand. "Captain, I will not hide belowdecks like a coward while men . . ." He added emphatically, ". . . *my* men are fighting." He finished clipping on his sword and gave the captain his full attention. "Go on." He made a formal gesture that bade Jhirban to take his thoughts in another direction. "Command the soldiers."

Captain Jhirban scowled. "Prince Arturo, you aren't welcome on deck during this exchange. If I brought you home dead, King Griff and Queen Matrinka would have my head, not to mention my title. You *will* stay below."

Arturo planted his feet firmly on the planking. "When they sent me on this mission, Captain Jhirban, my parents knew the risks. I'm trained in warfare, and I will fight." His words and tone left no room for argument. No one knew if he would inherit the throne of Béarn; a magical test created by the gods chose the king's successor after the ruler died or stepped down. Though Arturo studied decorum and protocol, watched his father's judgments, and trained in policy as well as warcraft, he secretly hoped one of his sisters or half siblings would fill the future role. He preferred the outdoors to the stifling inner chambers of the mountain palace, and even the courtyard walls seemed too constraining. If he could prove himself as a warrior, they might groom him for a command position in the army or guard force instead.

"Your Majesty!" the captain admonished, tone tinged with parental authority. "I cannot allow—"

Arturo interrupted, "You can, and you will. This discussion is over."

The captain's jaw clamped, and scarlet tinted the sunburned cheeks.

The lookout shouted, "Captain, they're heading to our broadside."

Captain Jhirban's nostrils flared. Several men ran to the gunwale to confirm the position and startling speed of the other ship. "How can it . . . ?" he started, standing tall on his crated dais to look over his followers: soldier and sailor alike. His aura of command returned. "Come about, men! Quickly. Bring us bow to bow."

The sailors scurried to work, attempting to move the ship though there was barely a hint of wind.

"To the oars!" Jhirban shouted.

His men responded instantly, several pounding belowdecks to obey his command.

Captain Jhirban spared only a moment to scowl at Arturo before addressing the soldiers. "Bowmen, prepare your flights at the bow and port rail. Don't volley until I give the order." He dashed toward the prow and its massive carved bear. "The rest of you, stand ready for a boarding. Do whatever you must to keep yourselves safe, but take a prisoner if you can do so without too much risk. We need to know who these pirates are." He clambered onto the bear masthead while the warriors prepared. "I'm going to parley." He added, under his breath, "Mistaken us for a merchant vessel, the gluttonous fools."

Arturo wondered how such a thing could happen. *Seven*'s sails clearly identified them, with Béarn's colors as well as her name. Even the most illiterate pirates must know the familiar blue and gold of the West's high kingdom.

The ship lurched sideways, sweeping Arturo's feet out from under him. He scrambled for balance, assisted by Trygg's steadying hand. The sailors remained upright, though some stumbled, and several of the fighting men went down.

"Arturo," Jhirban shouted, without looking in the prince's direction, his attention glued to the sea and approaching danger. "Go below!" He did not turn to see if his command had any effect this time.

Arturo remained in position, more from adolescent stubbornness than courage, the Renshai stepping in front of him. Though not yet fully grown, he was already taller and broader than his escort and had no trouble seeing over them. The sailors scrambled to bring the ship into better position. They could not risk a broadside hit. Their eight bowmen found positions at the rail, while the swordsmen shifted uneasily at the perimeter, waiting. Captain Jhirban stood firm upon the figurehead, despite the jerky movements of the ship, appearing composed and controlled. Though fully exposed to the other ship, he was in no current danger, so long as his balance did not fail him. Every country, no matter how hostile, obeyed the rules of parley, absolutely assuring the safety of any man who came forward to talk.

Arturo studied the other ship, surprised to find he could not identify its construction. His schooling had included the crests, crafts, and colors of every country in the world, the designs of their buildings and ships among them. This ship looked like nothing he had seen before, its hull oddly angled, its planking so tight he could not identify the seams between them. A plain iron spike served as its masthead, and it carried three taut brown sails to *Seven*'s two.

As the ships settled into a skewed prow-to-prow position, Jhirban cupped his hands around his mouth so that his voice would carry forward. The bowmen tensed, arrows nocked but not drawn, equally constrained by the laws of the parley, unbroken for millennia.

"Hail the other ship!" The captain's voice emerged in a deep and carrying tenor. "Are you friend or foe?"

No answer came, though the unstruck ship continued forward at its tremendous speed. The captain tensed, prepared for a retreat. If the vessel rammed them, he would surely lose his perch and, possibly, the structural integrity of his own ship.

Arturo tensed, hand tightening around his sword hilt. Bits and pieces of previously dismissed conversations drew together in one moment of stark and ugly terror. He suddenly realized that his parents had allowed him aboard only because no one expected the *Seven*'s voyage to be anything more than a routine patrol. Upon spotting anything suspicious, the ship had orders to return to Béarn for a hasty report. The soldiers were merely a precaution.

Apparently, the shocking speed of this encounter had caught even Captain Jhirban, a thirty-five-year veteran of the sea, by surprise. Now Arturo understood why no one had directly seen the pirated trading ships go down, despite ever-increasing onboard security. No vessel had come through an encounter intact; no man had survived to tell the tale.

The urge to scuttle belowdecks struck Arturo hard and low in the gut. His legs felt rubbery, unable to obey the sudden compulsion, and that gave him time to screw up his courage and force himself to remain boldly in place. *You can do this, Arturo. You can do this.*

Then, an insectlike whine filled Arturo's ears. The captain staggered backward with a strangled noise. Something skittered across the deck, splashing scarlet droplets on the planking. Jhirban tumbled from the figurehead and collapsed, with breathtaking force, across the railing.

The prince stopped breathing.

Soldiers and sailors swore viciously, screaming their rage toward the approaching ship. Someone shouted, "Loose, gods damn it! Kill the dishonorable bastards!" A volley of arrows peppered the sea, falling short of their target. The bowmen hurriedly reloaded as the first mate screamed orders at the sailors and the second-in-command stepped in to bunch the soldiers as well.

Trained in healing by his mother, Arturo tried to run to the fallen captain, but his path was blocked by the Renshai who forced him backward with the precision of herding dogs.

Arturo froze, staring at the captain's body, hanging utterly still across the railing except for the relentless patter of blood from his neck to the gunwale. One of the sailors picked up an object from the deck that resembled a slender arrow but glinted like silver in the sunlight and bore no fletching. The captain's blood smudged the sailor's hands.

"Let me help him." Arturo attempted to slip around the Renshai. "I know some healing." Though true, it seemed moot. He had no herbs, and every soldier knew enough to hold pressure on an open wound. Yet no one appeared to be doing so.

Trygg nimbly shifted to block Arturo again. "He's dead."

"Maybe not." Arturo lunged for a hole, even as Gunnhar closed it. "I have to try."

"He's dead," Gunnhar repeated. "Believe me, Sire, Renshai know dead."

A cry sounded from the other ship, a single indistinguishable word.

"Loose!" shouted Béarn's second-in-command.

A hail of unfletched metal shafts whined onto the *Seven* as the bowmen's strings twanged. Four Béarnian bowmen collapsed as the arrows left their strings. Trygg and Gunnhar jerked Arturo nearly off his feet, Gunnhar swearing vehemently.

At the mishandling, rage flashed through Arturo, but a glance at the smaller Renshai squelched it. Blood stained his tattered sleeve, and the fingers, still clutching his sword hilt, had turned ghostly white. Despite the wound, he had managed not to drop it. Without bothering to assess the damage, Gunnhar effortlessly shifted the hilt to his left hand. "Cowards!" he screamed. "Fight fair! Face-to-face! Sword-to-sword!"

Arturo grabbed for the Renshai's arm, intending to wrap the sleeve into a makeshift bandage. Gunnhar moved faster, charging toward the port rail, where the clang of metal striking metal filled the air. Once again, Arturo's fingers closed on empty air, and he jerked his attention to a line of grapples hooking *Seven*'s rail. The remaining bowmen retreated, and the swordsmen rushed in to sever boarding lines. Heart hammering, fear balling in his throat, Arturo chased after the warriors, intending to assist.

More enemy missiles whined through the air, and the front line of *Seven*'s warriors collapsed, tripping up some of those behind them. Both Renshai managed to keep their feet, flying over their own men to slash down boarding enemies with perfect sweeps of their swords. Arturo ducked in, treading more carefully, intending to unhinge grapples; but the Renshai wove a web of steel in front of him, blocking his advance even as they dispatched enemies.

Others did not prove as swift or lucky. As Béarnides fell, to the volley or tripped up by falling companions, the enemy swarmed over the side. Arturo managed a glimpse through the whirling blur of Renshai steel, his own sword incapable of penetrating the protective barrier. The few enemies he saw wore tight leather helms, clots of thickly curled reddish hair escaping in places. Between leather gloves and long cotton sleeves, Arturo caught glimpses of medium-toned flesh with a hint of olive. Their swords were short, curved and serrated, and they spoke in a language he did not recognize.

Battles broke out over every part of the ship, and the commanders' orders became lost beneath the strange war cries and shouts of the invaders, the clamor of steel, and the screams of the injured. Arturo tried to watch every direction simultaneously. He slashed at a pirate behind him, only to have a Renshai appear suddenly between them. Forced to pull his blow, he watched as Trygg effortlessly cut down the enemy, immediately moving on to the next.

Strangers and companions flopped to the deck, screaming in unmitigated agony or lying in an ominous silence. The deck became slick and crimson, every step a hazard. Arturo lunged for an enemy, only to find himself nearly skewering one of his escort. Again, he pulled the blow, this time howling in fury. "Let me fight, damn it!"

Men surged around him, locked in a combat he seemed incapable of joining.

The Renshai gave no reply, hard-pressed to their own defenses. Gunnhar's sleeve had turned completely scarlet, and gore filled his hair. Blood ran freely from his nose and right ear, and a limp marred his once graceful movements. Trygg had lost his shirt, and his pants hung in tatters. Bits of flesh and hair speckled every part of him, and crimson rivulets trickled down his back.

Twice more Arturo attempted to join the battle, and the Renshai beat him back, tending his defense with an obsession that made them careless of their own.

"Let me fight!" Arturo howled, cringing every time a Béarnide fell. "Let . . . me . . . fight!"

Heedless, the Renshai herded him toward the hatch as the battle surged around them.

"Get . . ." Trygg gasped out. ". . . below . . . decks . . . Sire."

It was no longer a matter of adolescent pride. Arturo knew he was going to die. They all were. Only a handful of Béarnian soldiers remained standing, fighting, and the pirates were cutting down the regular sailors with barely an effort. "No!" Arturo preferred to die hacked down by an unseen opponent in battle rather than cowering behind a barrel or a stack of unused lines.

Trygg shoved him.

"Stop it!"

The hatch creaked open, and Trygg pushed Arturo again.

Arturo staggered toward the opening. "No! I don't want to die a coward!" He spoke words he knew the Renshai could not ignore. No insult was more vicious to them, nothing more shameful than a coward's death.

"You're a prince. They'll take you alive—for ransom."

Though true in ordinary circumstances, it seemed unlikely here. These strangers came from no known country on the continent, spoke no recognized language. Barbarians, even pirates, would not understand royal protocols and conventions any more than they had parley or colors. Soon enough they would discover that a realm warship, unlike their previous targets, carried little worth stealing; and they would likely vent their frustration on any Béarnide who survived the battle. *Such as a hidden prince.* Death in battle seemed far preferable to the torture fueled by the pirates' frustration.

Without the time to explain the complexities of his thoughts, Arturo turned his stumble toward the open darkness into a deft leap over the hatch. An enemy sword slashed open his sleeve, drawing a stinging line of blood along his forearm. Arturo riposted, more from training than intent. His sword struck something hard with an impact that ached through his hands, followed by a grunt of agony. The blade stuck fast. A glint of light touched the corner of his vision, a raised, serrated blade plunging toward him. Ducking, Arturo ripped his blade free, splashing warm pinpoints of blood. An enemy collapsed in front of him, and he spun to avoid tripping over the body. Air whooshed by his cheek, as an enemy blade passed dangerously close.

Arturo waved his sword wildly in front of himself—protective chaos—while he tried to regain his bearings. Bodies littered the deck in grotesque positions, and he did not waste time with identification. Men surged around him, most red-haired invaders; and their strange blades capered through the sunlight. Several rushed to engage him at once.

A cry rose over the deck in a Renshai accent, "Modi!" It was a desperate call for the god of wrath, one Renshai usually reserved for a severe or mortal injury. "Modi!"

Arturo turned toward the sound, baring his throat to an enemy sword. Before he could think to dodge, someone flew through the clot of battle, slamming against Arturo with a force that sent him sprawling. Cold steel bit through the top of his shoulder instead of his neck, the searing pain all-encompassing. He screamed, losing track of direction, stumbling into a solid rail that drove the breath from his lungs in a sudden gasp. Beside him, Captain Jhirban's body dangled, a ragged hole through his neck, his face bloodless, his dark eyes wide open and empty.

Panic seized Arturo in a grip like ice. *I'm going to die. We're all going to die.* He had known it for some time now, but the deeper realization of all that death entailed had not struck him until that moment. Another enemy sword sped toward him. He dodged, and the blade slammed the rail with a ringing clout, the vibration aching through his body. He raised his own sword, his elbow thumping Jhirban's corpse and rendering his movement awkward, useless. Again a sword jabbed toward him. Caught between the press of battle and the corpse, Arturo leaped to the gunwale. The sword stabbed beneath him, opening its wielder's defenses. Arturo swept in, slamming his blade down on the man's leather-helmeted skull.

The impact shuddered through his arms. The pirate collapsed, and the momentum knocked Arturo off-balance. He teetered on the gunwale, certain a fall in either direction would seal his doom. Swords seemed to spring at him from every direction. His equilibrium lost, he knew he would fall on all of them, skewered like a target on an army of pikes. Fear left him awash in ice, then disappeared abruptly, leaving relieved acceptance in its wake. *It's over.* The pain, he knew, could not last long.

"MODI!" Trygg appeared suddenly, soaring between his charge and the sea of blades.

"No!" The sacrifice shocked and horrified Arturo. "No! No! No!"

Trygg's body crashed into Arturo, rolling onto the waiting blades. The impact drove Arturo backward. He fell into empty air, catching a glimpse of the brilliant blue of the water before his head struck the *Seven*'s rail and he knew no more.

CHAPTER 2

Skill has no limits, and anything will come with practice. If it does not, look to your own dedication and will.
　　　　　　　　　　　　　　　　　　—Colbey Calistinsson

THE SUN BEAMED DOWN upon the Fields of Wrath, glazing the thatch roofs of the simple Renshai cottages. In a patch of ground trampled to mud, Saviar Ra-khirsson practiced the complicated maneuvers he had learned that day in a wild flurry of *svergelse*. His swords pranced and twined through the air with a speed that made them appear liquid. He whirled on well-muscled legs, oblivious to the sweat trickling over his entire body. His red-blond hair grew moist, sheened with golden highlights, and droplets flew with every motion. His deadly dance was as much prayer as practice, a tribute to Modi, god of wrath, and his mother goddess, Sif. Six months past his eighteenth birthday, Saviar had finally nearly mastered the sequence of training that would allow him to be considered a man among Renshai. He had only to demonstrate his skills to his *torke,* his teachers, to achieve his goal; and he begged the gods for the agility and focus to pass this vital test in the next few months.

The comings and goings of Renshai around him seemed to disappear as Saviar concentrated on his task, but a nearer movement caught his attention. Something threatened off his left flank. Immediately, Saviar spun to meet another sword in the hand of his brother, Calistin. Steel chimed against steel, live and sharp. Renshai never lowered themselves to dulled or wooden practice blades. A Renshai who could not dodge quickly enough deserved to die. Renshai defense relied wholly on speed and dexterity. They shunned armor as cowardly, and even clothing or jewelry that might accidentally help fend off a blow had no place in their society. Life consisted of thrust and parry, the lethality of a blade, the music of clashing steel.

The impact vibrated through Saviar's hand, and he found himself face-to-face with Calistin. Though only nine months younger, his brother stood a full head shorter than Saviar. Yellow hair in need of cutting flashed around childlike features that wore an expression of calm intensity. As fast as it had woven into battle, Calistin's sword retreated and reappeared. Saviar sprang to the right, barely catching the other blade on his own. It scratched down the length to his hilt. Anticipating a disarming maneuver, he bullied forward, attempting to off-balance his smaller opponent. Calistin gave no ground, instead leaping nimbly aside. The tip of his blade flicked under Saviar's crossguard to tap the hilt. Saviar tightened his grip, too late. The sword flew from his hand.

Saviar drew his other sword, even as he dove in to catch the weapon he had lost. Allowing it to touch the ground would gravely dishonor it. Calistin wove a silver web of steel in front of Saviar, forcing him backward, then snatched the hilt from the air himself. Now, with two weapons to one, Calistin charged his brother, his own second sword still in its sheath.

Though accustomed to his little brother's superior skill, Saviar still found it irritating. Rejecting the mistake that had lost him battles in the past, he did not charge in anger. Instead, he focused on Calistin's every precise, lightning movement, prepared only to defend himself. Calistin kept his own sword high, Saviar's captured one low. His attacks came so swiftly, Saviar found himself losing track of the blades despite his concentration. He met the first blade with his own, ducking the second. Sword against sword, he used his superior strength to shove Calistin backward. The younger Renshai caught his balance with a single, delicate step. He did not even seem to shift his weight before diving in again, a blurred whirl of motion. As always, he moved with the speed of a tornado and with deadly accuracy. One sword disarmed Saviar a second time, while the other ended its course at the redhead's neck. Bested, Saviar froze, glaring at his brother through eyes so pale blue they were nearly white, a perfect match to those of their paternal grandfather, Knight-Captain Kedrin.

"Got you," Calistin said with maddening smugness as he easily caught the flying weapon in a hand already burdened. He now held three swords to none.

Saviar shoved aside the hovering blade at his throat and wished he could bury a fist in his brother's self-satisfied face. Even if his parents had allowed it, he would miss. Calistin's swift grace would make him look like a lumbering fool in comparison. "Sure, okay. You got me. Hurray for you." He glowered at features that barely resembled his own, baby soft with blunt cheekbones and long lashes. Calistin had blue eyes, too; but his were darker, like their mother's, and held a hint of stony gray. "Now give me back my damned swords."

Calistin tossed the weapons, and Saviar caught their hilts as he had practiced so many times, nearly since birth. He slammed both blades back into their sheaths, his ardor for training lost.

Calistin watched his brother's every movement. Even standing still, he seemed to exude a grace that Saviar tried his hardest not to covet. The gods had bestowed on the youngest of three brothers every possible gift that might make him the consummate Renshai. He personified quickness and agility and had achieved the sequence of skills that earned him adult status at the youngest age of any Renshai, just thirteen. He sported the sinewy, light-boned figure, the classical golden hair, fair skin, and pale eyes; and his features even bore some resemblance to the greatest Renshai in history, the hero, Colbey, who now lived among the gods. Like all Renshai, Saviar and Calistin were each named for a brave warrior who had died in battle and earned a place in Valhalla among the *Einherjar;* but Calistin had received the honored name of Colbey's own father. Calistin was the best; worse, he knew it. "Renshai maneuvers rely on speed, never strength."

Saviar continued to glare. It was an oft-quoted truth every Renshai appreciated. "I know that."

"But you're still trying to defeat me with size and muscle, Savi."

It was true, which only made the words sting more. Saviar had inherited their father's strapping build, as well as his stunning good looks; but those things seemed more curse than blessing to a Renshai. The Renshai leaders had found them worthy of the tribe, despite being half-breeds; but Saviar often thought he would have done better following his grandfather and father into the Knights of Erythane instead. His bulk fit their ranks better, and the constant attention of women embarrassed and distracted him from the swordwork that was supposed to be the only thing in life that mattered. Saviar often wondered how two boys with the exact same bloodline could wind up looking so completely different. "You're my brother, Calistin, not my *torke.* My *baby* brother, at that."

"*Baby* brother?" Calistin's features screwed, and his hands blanched around his hilts. "I've been a man for nearly five years now. You're still just a boy."

Calistin might just as well have buried a blade in Saviar's gut. Anger flashed through him, and it took strength of will to keep from attacking his brother. The urge to draw both weapons and fly into a battle to the death seized him, and only the words of their wise father rescued him: "A man of honor never allows emotion to control him." Instead, he turned on a heel and stalked toward home.

Calistin's taunts chased him, "Come on, *baby* brother. Have at me!"

Saviar did not look back, quickening his pace and gauging Calistin's location by his voice. To his relief, Calistin did not follow.

"You know you want to! You're acting like a big, old *coward*."

It was the worst insult in the Renshai vocabulary. Saviar's hands clenched to fists and his nostrils flared, but he resisted looking behind him.

"Coward! Coward! Coward!" As the chant faded into the distance, it sounded more like an echo.

Ra-khir would never allow his son to vent his rage on family, so Saviar veered away from their cottage, seeking a quiet corner where Calistin might not think to look for him. He found his solace in a sandy clearing filled with stones, shattered crates, and other bric-a-brac meant to simulate a city battle. Many a misstep had claimed the lives of otherwise competent warriors, and the Renshai practiced in all weather conditions, in darkness as well as light, on hillsides and in the thickest of forests. They spurned any weapons but swords, those forged to demanding specifications, and they learned to use either hand with equal ability. Now, Saviar lashed back into a *svergelse* fueled as much by fiery rage as necessity. Like all Renshai, he had learned to channel his emotions through his sword arm, skewering and slashing imaginary enemies with a speed his size belied.

But the world refused to narrow wholly to self and sword arm. Saviar found himself thinking about his other brother, Subikahn, his twin, now visiting his father in the Eastlands. It seemed a cruel twist of irony that the brother Saviar loved without reservation had shared a womb but only half his parentage, while the one who provoked him to frenzies shared every droplet of blood.

As a child, Saviar had never questioned this oddity. For the first seven years of his life, the journey to the Eastern high kingdom in Stalmize to visit Subikahn's father had seemed like a normal and expected vacation. The entire family had gone, Kevral taking over her sons' weapons training en route and while they stayed at the castle.

Saviar remembered it as a paradise. Though sparsely furnished compared to Castle Béarn, and lacking the murals and carvings, it felt huge and strangely homey. Subikahn's father, King Tae Kahn, was a small, dark, wiry man with the dexterity and speed of a Renshai who enjoyed romping on the floor with the boys. He seemed more like a friend than a father and indulged them with sweets and toys. He had a constant companion, a silver tabby cat who put up with the children plucking at her ears and yanking her tail without clawed retaliation. When his family's responsibilities to the knights and the Renshai forced Subikahn to make the trips alone, with only his *torke*, Saviar found himself missing the Eastern king and castle nearly as much as he did his twin brother.

Now, Saviar launched into a wild sequence of thrust, slash, and parry, his mood evened by exertion as well as his memories of happier days. Later, he had learned Tae had a dark and dangerous past, upon which his parents refused to elaborate. Only then, Saviar began to wonder about the numerous scars the king carried on his body, including lethal-looking gashes on his forehead, across his chest, and directly over his heart. "Scars are a warrior's badges of honor," the Renshai often stated, yet Tae never considered himself a competent or deliberate fighter. He dodged questions about old wounds with self-deprecating humor and tried to hide them beneath his clothing.

A blur of gray was Saviar's only warning. He barely twisted in time to rescue his hilt from another disarming. Instead, the tip of Calistin's blade tore his sleeve and cut a fiery line along his forearm. *Damn that little bastard!* The curse rose to Saviar's mind without thought or reason. In truth, Calistin was the only brother of the three who was legitimately born.

Calistin drove in without apology. "Pay attention, Savi!"

Saviar retreated, mindful of the practice field debris. He needed a moment to get his bearings, to measure an opponent he already knew too well. "Leave me alone, you annoying little—" Forced to defend another lightning strike, he let the insult go, weaving both swords around Calistin's one to protect his throat and chest.

Calistin laughed. "You should be prepared for anything, anytime." His blade skipped circles around Saviar's, then drove through a nonexistent opening. "Enemies don't wait until you're in the mood."

Saviar managed a hasty riposte that saved his gut. "You're . . ." He slashed for Calistin, swords cutting empty air, only to find the tip of his brother's blade in his face. ". . . my only . . ." He batted the sword downward. ". . . enemy!"

Calistin's sword blazed up faster than Saviar could block, straight for his groin. *Demons!* Saviar dove, rolling. Stones and rubble jabbed his back, aching through his right hip. He came up in a crouch, still clutching his swords, barely fast enough to bat aside Calistin's next attack in time.

"You're already dead, by rights." Calistin let Saviar know he had pulled at least one blow. Though Renshai sparred with live steel, it was the better warrior's job to weigh his opponent's skill and pull life-threatening strikes. It would humiliate a *torke* to kill a student by accident. Every Renshai strived for complete control of every motion, and the sword was merely an extension of the arm. "I let you live."

Enraged, Saviar lunged at Calistin. "Don't do me any favors!" He chopped for his brother's neck, and the left leg a moment later.

Calistin spun aside with ease, dodging both attacks and returning one of his own. This one touched Saviar's chest in clear warning. With any power behind it, the blade would have cut bone like butter.

Fatal, Saviar realized. Seething, he came to an abrupt halt. "All right, you killed me. Happy?"

"No." Calistin performed a swirling *svergelse* with the grace of an angel, a golden blur of lethal power. Even Saviar found himself staring wide-eyed until the blade licked free from its pattern and sped toward him once again.

Believing the battle finished, Saviar scrambled backward in time to redirect the strike. As he swept in for the riposte, he pleaded. "Please, Calistin. I want to be alone."

Calistin wove between the two blades. "Your enemies won't care what you want." He managed three perfect strikes as he spoke.

Saviar sheathed his right-hand blade, blocking only with the other. He was a competent swordsman, capable, like nearly all Renshai, of taking on three warriors from any other culture. Against his little brother, however, he felt like a hopeless clod. He set himself strictly to defense, fending each blow with his sword and biding his time for an opening. When it came, he lashed through it with his bare hand, intending to surprise his brother with a clout on the ear. Instead, his fist glided through empty air, and Calistin used Saviar's own momentum and a well-placed foot to send him sprawling onto a deadfall. Breath dashed from Saviar's lungs, bark scraped his lips and knuckles, and the flat of Calistin's sword crashed across his shoulder blades.

"Once again, Savi, you're dead."

Pain ached through Saviar's mouth, and he tasted blood. As he fought to suck air into his suddenly empty lungs, the urge to throttle Calistin became an all-consuming obsession.

"Get up," Calistin demanded.

Saviar's throat finally spasmed open, admitting air. Through it all, he had managed to keep hold of his sword, the pattern of the knurling ingrained against his palm. He did not yet trust himself to speak.

He drooled out a mouthful of scarlet spittle. "Leave me alone," he finally managed.

"Saviar, it's important you know—"

Saviar rose, whirling on his brother. "By Sif and Modi, go away, Calistin. Leave me alone, or I'll . . ." He could not finish. A thousand possibilities whirled through his mind, but he had to discard all of them. Violence would never succeed against Calistin, and the only things the younger man owned that mattered to him were his swords. Saviar could do nothing to harm his little brother in any way, and that had nothing to do with honor, morality, or even love.

"But . . ." Calistin sheathed his sword and stared at his brother. The last dying rays of sunlight struck golden highlights from his hair, and he appeared tiny, almost frail. Though nearly eighteen, he still had the proportions of a young boy: skinny with an oversized head, short torso, legs, and arms. Large, blue-gray eyes studied Saviar from baby-round features. He looked more like a lost child than a Renshai warrior. ". . . I'm just trying to help you . . ."

Saviar wiped his mouth on the back of his hand, smearing a line of blood across his sleeve. He sheathed his second long sword and emphasized each snarling word, "Just. Leave. Me. Alone!" He turned his back on his brother, a sign of grave disrespect, a gesture Renshai used to convey that an opponent had so little skill that even a surprise attack from behind was no threat. At the moment, Saviar would rather die than turn, even if Calistin did assail him again. He strode blindly toward the family cottage, not caring if his brother followed.

The sun crept further toward the horizon, leaving a spray of colors across the sky that Saviar ignored. For the moment, anger would not allow him to enjoy anything, no matter how magnificent. He wove through the crude dwellings to his own, then crashed through the door and into the common room and its familiar sparse furnishings. He slammed the door behind him. Only then, he verbalized his rage, "I swear from the highest mountaintop, to every god listening: *I am going to kill my little brother!*"

Kevral appeared in the doorway separating the two main rooms. Though in her mid-thirties, she appeared a decade younger. If any silver had entered her short-cut locks, it remained hidden amid the white-blonde strands. Despite two pregnancies, she still had a thin, almost boyish, figure. She held a cleaning rag in one callused hand and a vial of oil in the other. "Really, Saviar? So you've mustered an army?"

Startled silent, Saviar flushed. "Sorry, Mother. I didn't know you were home."

"You're bleeding." It was a statement of fact, devoid of concern. Kevral tossed the rag in a perfect arc. Saviar snatched it from the air and held it against his mouth. It smelled oily and tasted sweet and metallic. She had clearly used it to clean at least one of the swords strapped always to her waist, and Saviar could not help feeling honored. Renshai revered their swords, none more so than Kevral. She owned a weapon given to her by the immortal hero, Colbey. The other blade seemed just as extraordinary to Saviar, handed to her by an *Einherjar* warrior in Valhalla named Rache. The latter blade even had a name, *Motfrabelonning,* meaning "Reward of Courage," though it had once borne the name *Tisis,* "Vengeance."

Saviar explored the wound as he staunched the bleeding. It seemed to originate from his lips, which now felt torn and puffy. Blood also welled from the slash across his forearm, staining his opened sleeve.

"You *were* talking about Calistin, right?"

Saviar blew his nose into the rag, glancing at the result to ascertain that it was not also bloody. He was the oldest, by only a few moments in Subikahn's case, and definitely the largest of the three brothers. "Who else?"

Kevral smiled. "Then I was right. You would need an army to kill him."

"I suppose." Saviar had no wish to discuss Calistin's prowess with his proud mother. "Where's Father?"

"Drilling." Kevral referred to the knight training.

Saviar tried to sound casual. The Renshai considered Ra-khir a mediocre swordsman, but Saviar had watched his father duel on the Bellenet Fields with many different weapons and impressive skill. It was a guilty pleasure. Most Renshai disdained the Knights as semi-competent warriors wedded to a rigid and foolish code of honor, even as the rest of the Western populace admired them. Subikahn smiled tolerantly when Saviar spoke of his father's ability and passion, listening politely though he clearly did not share Saviar's ardor. Since the Renshai leaders had recognized Calistin's skill at age six, they kept him so immersed in Renshai swordwork that he had lost all interest in anything else, including his father's talents. By decree, no one bothered Calistin. He had no responsibilities, no chores, and no distractions. He was expected to practice sword form and craft every waking moment, with or without the guidance of the best Renshai *torke.*

Rag still clutched to his face, Saviar ran back outside. The sun had set, leaving the Fields of Wrath awash in gray; but the sounds of clashing steel still dwarfed every other. Though anxious to reach the

Knight's tourney field in time, Saviar kept his step careful and attentive. To blunder into a mock battle might result in an ignoble death, and he also worried about Calistin finding him again. One more encounter with the arrogant, little brat might set Saviar over the edge into a madness he could not control.

But no one accosted Saviar as he dashed across the Road of Kings, lined by flawless carvings of bears and statues of the legendary, ancient King Sterrane. Moonlight lit glimmers of quartz in the stonework, making them appear to glow, and Saviar shivered in the cold evening air. Renshai never admitted fear, but Saviar and Subikahn had whispered their childhood trepidations to one another and once avoided those massive memorials. Béarnian carvers had a talent for making their creations eerily lifelike; and, in the darkness, they seemed to move.

Saviar needed only to cross a farm field to enter the town proper, but he chose a shorter route to the Bellenet Fields that took him through the forest. Leaves sloshed beneath his feet, saturated into soup by winter snows, now melted by the thaw. The first green buds graced the tips of some of the otherwise naked branches. The birds had gone to nest, but a strident hoot cut the air directly over his head, warning the animals of a human intruder.

Saviar looked up, at first seeing nothing. Then, suddenly, a massive feathered head whipped around to reveal two glaring eyes, like freshly washed dinner plates. A ghostly form rose soundlessly into the air, resembling a small boy in size and shape. *An owl*, Saviar realized, watching it disappear into the darkness. He had often considered owls the Renshai of the animal world: swift and graceful, silent and deadly. He quickened his pace. If the night creatures had come out of hiding, it seemed unlikely he would reach the practice grounds in time.

Saviar raced from the forest onto open ground, startling a ground dove into whirring flight. There, he found only the hulking figures of tourney fences. No man or animal stood upon the fields. *Damn.* He started to turn to leave, but need held him in position. He could not return to the Fields of Wrath now, not with Calistin waiting to pounce on him and his mother still lauding her youngest son's skill. Saviar could never admit to Kevral that, sometimes, not too often, he wished he were anything but Renshai. To speak such words would wound her deeply.

Instead, Saviar headed toward the Erythanian stables where the Knights of Erythane kept their horses. Since the day he had earned the title Apprentice Knight, Ra-khir had insisted on tending to his own white charger. He trusted no groomsman to do as thorough a job on his beloved and hard-earned Silver Warrior.

Unlike the Fields of Wrath, the streets of Erythane lay deserted after sundown. Smoke rose from the cottage chimneys, and the savory aromas of cooking meat, grains, and breads filled the empty spaces. Saviar's gut churned with excitement. Renshai practiced hungry and thirsty or on a full stomach, all conditions that might exist in a real battle. They rarely ate as families, instead snatching mostly raw foodstuffs from communal stocks as the urge struck them. No Renshai knew how to hunt or fish, how to tend vegetables in small plots or massive farms. It was all time better spent honing swordcraft or cleaning and sharpening blades. Every moment dedicated to swordplay meant an improvement in ability or endurance. Every one given to cooking, sleeping, talking, playing, or resting was considered wasted.

At length, the familiar shape of the stable came into Saviar's view. Not much farther along, he saw the Knight's Rest, a high-scale tavern that catered to the upper class. Many of the unmarried knights gathered there after a grueling day of drills, and Ra-khir sometimes joined them. If Saviar could not find his father in the stable, he might at the Knight's Rest. At the least, they could walk home in the darkness together.

Upon reaching the stable, Saviar poked his head inside. The sweet, distinctive odor of horses wafted to him, and the snowy forms of the knights' chargers showed vividly against the darkness. One of the animals nickered and snorted, the sound rising over the background din of crunching hay. Letting himself inside, Saviar walked quietly down the row, stroking whichever heads rose to look at him over the half-doors of their stalls. He paused longest in front of his grandfather's mount. Ten years old, Snow Stormer bore the same name as his predecessor, a tribute the mischievous stallion had not yet earned. Saviar had watched, fascinated, as Knight-Captain Kedrin mourned the loss of the animal that had borne him through so many journeys, practices, and battles during his then-twenty years as a Knight of Erythane. Accustomed to Renshai, Saviar had never before seen a grown man cry.

A shrill whinny shattered the near-stillness from halfway down the second lane, followed by Ra-khir's voice. "Give me that, you rascal!"

Saviar smiled and quickened his pace, tucking the bloodstained rag into his belt and knotting his tattered sleeve. As he turned the corner, a lantern lit Silver Warrior prancing an excited circle, a fancy hat with an arched plume perched precariously upon his head. Ra-khir watched the horse's antics, still dressed in his practice uniform, damp and covered with dirt. He held a brush white with horsehair in one hand and a rag in the other. His red-gold hair lay in hopeless disarray, sweat-plastered and smashed in patches where the hat had once perched jauntily. Even the look of consternation could not mar the rugged handsomeness of his features: eyes the green of polished emeralds, his features bold and chiseled, his cheekbones high and fair. Saviar never considered himself good-looking; yet, when he took the time to study his father's features, it startled him to think he closely resembled this paragon.

"You're a bad, bad horse." Ra-khir's gentle admonishment held none of the seriousness of his words.

"Either that," Saviar said, leaning against a nearby stall, "or he's an embarrassingly disheveled Knight of Erythane."

Ra-khir jerked toward his son, and his cheeks flushed visibly, even in the darkness. He smiled warmly, revealing a row of teeth that matched the brilliant fur of his steed. "That description would fit either of us." He indicated his muddy, crumpled uniform with an all-encompassing gesture. "My father would kill me if he saw me this way."

Saviar grunted, knowing better. "If that were true, we'd have burned your pyre long ago."

Ra-khir snatched for his hat, caught it, and placed it on his own head, apparently oblivious to the hay stalks this added to his locks. "You're right." He sighed, then shrugged. "Can't fathom how all the others manage to look perfect all the time."

Saviar helped his father back Silver Warrior fully into his stall and close the door. "Well, for starters, they don't roll around in straw and feces playing with horses." The conversation remained at the level of shallow banter. Saviar noticed that happening a lot more in the last year. As a child, he had never worried about looking foolish or silly in front of his father; he had plunged into the most embarrassing topics without a moment's hesitation. Now, as a budding adult, he tended to weigh his words and worry about their effect. It felt like everyone, even his parents, was judging his every utterance and action. Saviar pulled a stem from his father's hair and handed it to him.

As Ra-khir claimed it, Silver Warrior arched his neck over the partition and delicately wrested it from Ra-khir.

Ra-khir shook his head as the stalk disappeared into the horse's mouth. "That's right, Warrior. That particular piece of hay is the best one in the entire barn."

"Apparently." Saviar also watched the horse eat, loath to allow his thoughts to return to the Fields of Wrath. He loved these moments alone with his father and wondered why he could remember so few from his childhood. "Are you finished here?"

"Just." Ra-khir wiped his hands on the rag, then hung it, and the brush, on a nail outside Silver Warrior's stall along with his halter, comb, and curry. He turned to face Saviar directly, showing no sign that he missed the opportunity to relax with his peers in the Knight's Rest. "Now what can I do for my beloved oldest son?"

Saviar shrugged, not certain himself what he had expected. More than anything, he just wanted some alone time with his father. "Nothing, really, I—"

Ra-khir gave his full attention to Saviar. He would allow no horse or human to steal this moment. He nodded for Saviar to continue.

Uncertain how to phrase his thoughts, Saviar blurted out, "Is it immoral to hate one's own brother?"

Ra-khir's lips went tight, as if he fought a smile. He would not belittle his son. "Is this a general ethical question? Or are we talking about Calistin?" As Silver Warrior reached for his hat, Ra-khir stepped aside, then moved several paces toward the front of the stable. There, he found a hay pile protected from the floor's dampness by a hatchwork of crate slates. He motioned for Saviar to sit.

Saviar walked to the indicated spot and crouched amid the slats. His Renshai training would not allow a less defensible position, even in the presence of no one but his father. "How do you know I didn't mean Subikahn?"

"Lucky guess." An unusual hint of sarcasm touched Ra-khir's tone. He sat beside his son. "What did Calistin do . . . this time?"

Now the words came pouring out. "He won't leave me alone. He's constantly badgering me, acting like my *torke* instead of my smug little brother." Saviar knew Ra-khir would not approve of his insulting a loved one, but he found himself incapable of stopping, "He's so damned conceited. He thinks he's the best swordsman in the world."

"Isn't he?"

Saviar scowled. "Are you taking his side?"

Ra-khir's brows rose in increments. "As far as I'm concerned, there are no 'sides' in this family. I'm only asking for a simple truth."

"Maybe," Saviar grumbled. "But he doesn't have to keep shoving it in my face." He mimicked Calistin's childlike voice, "Stop trying to use your strength against me . . . Renshai don't do that . . . you're doing this wrong . . . I'm a man, and you're not . . ."

Ra-khir nodded sagely. "That's what it really comes down to, doesn't it?"

"What?" Saviar said guardedly, suspecting he would not like his father's next words.

"You're . . . jealous?"

"No," Saviar said, too quickly. Then, after a moment of contemplation, "Well, maybe." He added in his defense, "I wasn't. Not at first. I was really proud of my little brother. I mean, a man. At just thirteen." He shook his head in genuine admiration. "He's amazing."

"Yes, he is." Ra-khir encouraged, "What changed your feelings?"

"Calistin." Saviar could not take the edge from his tone as he spoke the name of his tormentor.

When nothing followed, Ra-khir said, "I need more."

Saviar bit his upper lip, suddenly ashamed about raising the subject. Ra-khir was as much Calistin's father as his own. An attack upon one's child required a defense, regardless of the accuser. "I'm sorry, Papa. I'm putting you in a difficult position."

Ra-khir smiled. "I'm a Knight of Erythane married to a Renshai. I live for difficult positions."

Saviar also grinned. "Clearly." He loved his mother with all his heart, but he also knew how challenging she could be, especially for a man of such high and exceptional honor. As his own thoughts began turning to women, Saviar had taken to wondering how Kevral had managed to entice not just one good man, but two, to care so deeply for her. Subikahn's father had also once proposed, and the rumor was that she had so badly broken his heart that he refused to court again. Only the Renshai trained its women, as well as men, to warcraft; and the ferocity of Renshai women confused and frightened most *ganim*, the word Renshai used to refer to outsiders.

The enduring relationship between his parents confounded most people, but never Saviar. Usually a relentless taskmaster of a *torke*, Kevral softened visibly in Ra-khir's presence, and he never failed to make her smile. In the privacy of home, and on voyages beyond the Fields of Wrath, they held hands like adolescents in the throes of first love. The knight still called his wife the most beautiful woman in the world, with clear and undisputable sincerity, no matter how sweaty and dirt-streaked she appeared. The looks they gave one another defined love in its purest, rawest form; and it spilled out to encompass their entire family.

"So," Ra-khir pressed, not as easily sidetracked as his son. "What about Calistin changed your feelings?"

Saviar knew generalities would not suffice. His father would need some indication that he had thought through the matter and had a legitimate concern. "I guess it's his decision to keep smacking me in the head—and not just with the flat of his sword. He actually uses his accomplishments to . . . to demean me."

"Is it possible you think Calistin does well only to make you look bad?"

Saviar did not believe it had become so specific and personal. *Sometimes I wonder if he doesn't do well just to make everyone look bad.* He kept the thought to himself. Voicing it would make him sound petty and childish. "Not at all. I don't even mind him crowing about his achievements. It's not modest, it's not what an honorable man does, but he earned them."

Ra-khir leaned forward and nodded encouragingly.

"But does he really have to tack on how little I've accomplished in comparison?"

"Of course not."

"I'm trying to concentrate on the maneuvers I need to know for my testing. If he would at least distract me in ways that help me perfect what I need to know, instead of constantly trying out his new inventions and interests or things to improve his own swordwork." Saviar studied his father's features to ascertain how Ra-khir was handling this information. As he appeared reflective and interested, Saviar continued, "Under the guise of helping me, he's only helping himself. And undermining my confidence."

Ra-khir wiped his forehead with the back of a gloved hand. Like all of the knights always did, he wore the blue and gold of Béarn as well as the black and orange of Erythane. "Have you told Calistin this?"

Saviar turned his gaze to his own hands, the nails filthy and broken. Blood traced the creases of his right palm. "I've tried." He sighed. "Papa, I love him because he's my brother. But, if he weren't, I don't think I'd even like him."

"Does anyone? Outside of our family, I mean."

The question caught Saviar off his guard. He looked up to meet his father's emerald gaze. "They all think he's awesome. The ultimate Renshai. The Colbey Calistinsson of our time."

"But do they like him?"

"I . . ." Saviar did not know how to answer. "I . . . don't . . . really know." He tried to divine his father's purpose in asking such a question. "Does it matter?"

Ra-khir's brows rose. "To Calistin, it probably does."

"Maybe." Saviar was not so sure. Calistin did not seem to care what others thought of him personally, so long as they envied his sword skill. "Papa?"

"Hmmm?"

"How can two brothers be so completely and utterly different?"

Ra-khir laughed. "How similar are you and Subikahn? And you're twins."

Ra-khir had essentially made Saviar's point. "Subikahn and I are half brothers, actually. And, yet, we're still more alike in personality than either of us is to Calistin. And we're close enough in age to practically be triplets."

Ra-khir shrugged. "Look at the princes and princesses of Béarn. They're as disparate as Béarnides get."

Once again, Ra-khir appeared to be arguing the wrong point. "But, Papa, they have three different mothers. And some have a different father, too."

"What?" The word was startled from Ra-khir.

"Prince Barrindar and the princesses, Calitha and Eldorin are King Griff and Xoraida's children. Princess Ivana Shorith'na Chatella Tir Hya'sellirian Albar . . ." Saviar prided himself on knowing and pronouncing the full elfin name, though the populace knew her only as Princess Ivana. ". . . is the offspring of King Griff and his elfin wife. Princess Marisole, Prince Arturo, and Princess Halika are Queen Matrinka's children. All three of them were clearly sired by Bard Darris."

Ra-khir's tone turned stiff. "That's not common knowledge, Saviar."

"I'm not speaking it commonly."

"You won't?"

"Of course not. Was I raised by fools?" Saviar turned his father a wicked grin.

Ra-khir released a pent-up breath, ignoring the question. Addressing it would require him to defend or damn his own intelligence. "Who told you?"

Saviar rolled his eyes at the ridiculousness of the query. "Anyone with a reasonable education knows how the bardic curse gets passed. The bard's heir is always the firstborn child of the bard. In this case, Marisole." He shrugged. "Once I realized that, I started looking. Only Halika didn't inherit Bard Darris' snout—"

"That's not nice, Saviar."

Saviar ignored the interruption to finish his reasoning. "—and she's too normal-sized to be the product of two massive Béarnides."

"Queen Matrinka is not massive. She's—"

"—big-boned and curvaceous," Saviar finished. "My point stands." Suddenly realizing his father had sidetracked him, Saviar added, "Both of them. Brothers of full blood should not be as different as Calistin and me."

Ra-khir said nothing for several moments, which surprised Saviar. The older man could easily argue that the physical resemblance between Saviar and Calistin was real enough that complete strangers sometimes recognized them as relatives. Saviar knew plenty of examples in his own life of siblings who bore few or no similarities in appearance or temperament. An intelligent boy with a dupe for a brother. A runaway-wild girl with a painfully timid sister. Saviar even knew a set of twins, one with striking dexterity, the other laboriously clumsy. Mothers seemed to love comparing their children to one another, sometimes labeling them as the pretty one, the obedient one, the nice one. Siblings often turned out remarkably different, yet Ra-khir did not resort to these familiar examples. Either Saviar's deduction about the royal siblings utterly disarmed him, or he was hiding something else.

The latter thought raised Saviar's suspicions. "You know something about Calistin, don't you?"

Ra-khir answered with a touch of defensiveness. "I know everything about Calistin. He's my son."

"Something," Saviar pressed, "that you haven't told either of us."

"I have told you," Ra-khir said in a flat tone, "everything I can tell you."

He was hiding something, yet Saviar knew no amount of weaseling or cajoling would bring it to the fore. Ra-khir's honor would never allow him to do anything his word bound him against. Continuing in this vein would only upset Ra-khir at a time when Saviar wanted his father's assistance and empathy. Instead, he found himself uttering a self-imposed secret he had never spoken aloud, "Papa, sometimes I wish, I mean, I think I wish, I wasn't . . . Renshai."

Ra-khir closed his eyes. The words clearly hurt him.

"Are you all right?"

Ra-khir's lids snapped open, and he smiled, though it looked forced. "I'm fine, just worried about you. You're unhappy with the life your mother and I chose for you?"

Saviar hurried to undo the damage. "Not unhappy, Papa, no. I mean I love the swordwork, the religion, the history. I just . . . sometimes . . . I'd just like to do . . . other things." He added belatedly, ". . . too." He laughed at his own suggestion, dismissing it. "Ignore me. It's the intensive training that's made me what I am. I just want it all, I guess. No one could become a knight *and* a Renshai."

"A knight?" Ra-khir's forced grin turned genuine, almost wistful. "You want to be a Knight of Erythane?"

Saviar laughed again. "Silly, huh? The huge amount of training involved in either would preclude the other."

Ra-khir gave no answer.

"Right?"

"Well," Ra-khir said hesitantly. "I would think so. And yet . . . ?"

"Yet?" Saviar encouraged.

"There is someone who is both."

Startled silent, Saviar stared. He knew of no other Renshai who would even consider the staid, stuffy life of a knight, filled with long-winded ceremony, multiple weapons' training, and stifling ethics. His father's use of the present tense, however, suggested the man he spoke of currently lived. It was not some hypothetical historical figure. "Who?" he finally managed.

"You've clearly studied," Ra-khir said, finally regaining the upper hand. It was also a subtle, probably unintentional insult to Calistin. The youngest son, bound to a life of relentless swordwork, would never manage more than a basic education, mostly Renshai language, history, and tradition. "This one, you'll have to figure out for yourself."

CHAPTER 3

Biases are always justifiable when they're yours.
—*Sir Ra-khir Kedrin's son*

BARD DARRIS SQUIRMED in his seat at King Griff's right hand, attentive to every movement in the courtroom yet bored by the seemingly endless procession of nobles, merchants, and complainants down the woven-wool carpet. The inner court guards surrounding them managed to look fresh and eager despite the length of the proceedings. Darris envied their ability to at least appear to maintain their alertness indefinitely, even if it was a farce. He wished he could have retired with Queen Matrinka hours earlier; but his main duty as bard was to serve as primary bodyguard to the king of Béarn.

At Griff's other hand, Guard Captain Seiryn stood as often as he sat, assisting in those matters that involved the guardsmen of Béarn no matter how tangentially. His gaze swept the dwindling audience of nobles and commoners seated on chairs on either side of the aisleway. His watchful eye kept the inner court guards vigilant and the sentries escorting the various visitors and prisoners mannered and within protocol. He had no authority over Béarn's bard, however, and paid no attention to Darris' progressively drooping posture.

That left Darris free to brood and dream, his mind slipping always to Queen Matrinka: her soft brown eyes, the thick ebony hair that his fingers captured, her gentle loving features, and her plump Béarnian body still soft from the three children she had borne. Darris had loved her since adolescence first turned his thoughts toward women; and she loved him, too. When the populace demanded she wed her first cousin, King Griff, to keep the bloodline strong, Darris had thought his heart would shatter like a glass figurine. As always, Griff had found the simplest solution, one designed to keep everyone happy. It was Griff who married Matrinka but Darris who shared the queen's affection. The resultant offspring, Marisole, Arturo, and

Halika, though sired by Darris, belonged to the king and queen by law. Ignorant of, or deliberately blind to, the arrangement, the people of Béarn accepted the prince and princesses without question.

Béarnian law allowed and encouraged its kings, and only its kings, to wed many times to assure the birth of at least one heir who could pass the gods' test. Griff next married his elfin sweetheart, Tem'aree'ay. Darris smiled at the memory. He had played an important role in that. Obsessively rereading and reinterpreting ancient Béarnian law, Darris had found what was needed to allow that union despite the many strict rules that governed who could marry an heir to Béarn, the same ones which had kept Matrinka and himself apart. With help from the populace and his Council, Griff had selected a third wife, Xoraida, who met the bloodline criteria for royalty. She, too, had borne him a son and two daughters.

The double doors at the end of the room crashed open, sending the banner behind the thrones into a fluttering dance and drawing Darris' full attention. A Béarnide entered the courtroom without escort, wearing the on-duty uniform of the guards. A blue-and-gold tabard speckled with dirt lay twisted over his mail, the rearing grizzly on the front still vividly clear. His thick, black hair sat on top of his scalp in a frizzy, uncombed ball, and he clutched his helmet in his hand. Every eye followed his walk down the golden carpet, and Darris noticed that he left muddy footprints in his wake.

As he approached the dais, the guard looked nervously at Captain Seiryn, then bowed deeply.

Griff studied the guard with a kind expression devoid of the curiosity that plagued Darris and every other member of the audience. Like all of the god-sanctioned rulers of Béarn, Griff was neutrality incarnate, the very fulcrum of the world's balance. Enormous, yet uncomplicated, the ruler of the West's high kingdom seemed more like a massive, bearded child than an absolute commander-in-chief. He looked at the guard through coarse, ebony bangs and smiled. "Hello, Lazwald. What news have you brought me?"

The guard rose, dark eyes darting nervously, clearly startled that the king knew him by name.

Darris nodded encouragingly. The king made it a point to recognize as many of his citizens as possible.

"Sire, your presence is requested in the Council Room as soon as possible."

The corners of Darris' lips slid downward, though the king's expression never changed. The Council rarely interrupted court. Most of their affairs involved protocol, law, and state, matters that required mulling. It also bothered Darris they had sent a guardsman rather than a page, which suggested they had gathered hastily and dispatched whoever had brought them the news that resulted in their sudden need for a meeting. Information from guardsmen, when important enough to disturb the king, was rarely good.

King Griff gave no sign he had made the same intuitive leap as his bard. "Very well, then. Court is dismissed for the day. Anything remaining will hold over until tomorrow."

The audience rose from their seats, muttering amongst themselves as they headed down the carpetway toward the double doors. Darris leaped to his feet, pausing to execute a bow before stooping to retrieve the lute beside his chair. His liege rose stiffly from his padded throne to tower over his escort. The inner court guards filed out the back exit, leaving only the king, his captain, and Darris.

Béarnian big, burly and massively boned, the other two men towered over Darris, whose Pudarian origins seemed obvious in their presence. Pure-blooded Béarnides sported thick bristly black hair, coarse features, fair skin, and brown eyes. A tall, sturdy lot, nearly all the men wore heavy beards. In contrast, Darris had a slender, average build. Soft, mouse-brown curls framed a delicate face with thin brows, an overly large straight nose, and broad lips.

Those differences might have singled him out enough, without the bardic curse, passed to the oldest child of his line for millennia. Though imbued with insatiable curiosity, he could impart what he learned only through song. As such, he usually carried a mandolin or lute in addition to the sword at his belt. Now, he slung his instrument onto his back, running verses of courage and hope through his mind. He might need them at the Council meeting.

As they trod through castle corridors replete with animal-shaped torch brackets trailing strings of gems, carved and painted statues, and vast murals encompassing the doors and windows into their art, Darris mulled the possibilities through his mind. He had practically memorized the artwork; his inhuman inquisitiveness had forced him to study every nuance in the past. Now, his focus narrowed to the reason for the abrupt meeting. Surely, it had something to do with the pirates on the southwest coast. Béarn currently had no other significant enemies. Friends now ruled the vast Eastlands, and trade with the reclusive Northlanders had become one-sided in the North's favor. The many and varied countries that made up the vast territories of the Westlands, though essentially under Béarn's rule, were mostly left to govern themselves. King Griff kept his touch and taxes light; and, consequently, heard few complaints.

A pair of guards clutching polearms stood at the Council Room door. Both bowed as the trio approached, and one opened the door with a grand and practiced gesture as he did so. Darris peeked around him into the familiar, austere room. It contained nothing but a long, rectangular table, and the members of the Council seated around it, who rose at the king's approach. The walls were kept symbolically bare, to emphasize the importance of the discussions occurring there. As the three men stepped through the entrance, the door whisked closed behind them.

Darris assessed those present with a glance, nodding at each in turn as the king claimed the head seat, leaving the one at his right hand for Darris. As usual, Captain Seiryn chose a position standing near the door. Though an official member, he carried no noble blood and deferred to the men and women he considered his superiors. The oldest, seventy-nine-year-old Minister of Courtroom Procedure and Affairs Saxanar, looked grim. Fanatical about protocol and grooming, he wore his colors fastidiously. Not a single white hair lay out of place, and his deep brown eyes held a glaze of pain.

Beside him, Prime Minister Davian kept his head lowered, hiding his scarred features beneath a curtain of salt-and-pepper hair. Once a peasant carver, he had earned his title by leading the band of renegades who had helped reclaim Griff's throne from usurpers. His no-nonsense cleverness had won over even stodgy Saxanar, who had made it known in the past that he believed only blooded nobility made for proper councillors.

Another former leader of the renegades, Minister of Internal Affairs Aerean, also held an honorary title. Though rapidly approaching forty, she still maintained the boundless energy and enthusiasm that had irritated Saxanar since her appointment. Though primary nobility, Minister of Household Affairs Franstaine had a habit of vexing the staid, older ministers nearly as much as Aerean. An in-law uncle of Griff's mother, he was as notorious for his strange sense of humor as his seemingly limitless patience.

Only a year or two older than Aerean, the Minister of Foreign Affairs, Richar, handled the visiting dignitaries, usually Western merchants and disputants in claims too difficult for local kingdoms to handle. Fair and tactful, he grew positively exuberant when his charges became more exotic. Though greatly contaminated, by Saxanar's standards, his line did contain royal blood in its distant past.

Though essentially devoid of noble blood, Zaysharn never seemed to bother Saxanar at all. The Overseer of Béarn's livestock, gardens, and food had a quiet attentiveness that made him nearly invisible, despite his Béarnian sturdiness and size. He dwarfed the tiny woman at his side, the Minister of Local Affairs, named Chaveeshia. Her size alone revealed her mixed heritage, but she also had brown hair and a tinge of green in her eyes. She tended the relationships between Béarn and its close neighbors, mostly Erythanians and Renshai. Her commanding manner and sharp tongue made her a natural for the position, despite her lack of size.

This time, her usual charges were conspicuously absent, apparently because of the suddenness of the meeting. The Captain of the Knights of Erythane and the leader of the Renshai also held regular seats at the Council table. Queen Matrinka, too, had a right to attend, though she frequently waived it. Darris appreciated that no one had fetched her to the Council Room this time. She did not need to hear bleak news until after wise heads had pondered meanings and crafted solutions.

King Griff took his seat, and the others followed suit. Only Captain Seiryn remained standing. Prime Minister Davian called the meeting to order. The years had not treated the ex-carver's face kindly, adding wrinkles to the mass of scars that already marred it. It now appeared more homely than heroic. "Your Majesty, I apologize for calling you here so abruptly."

Griff waved off the need for explanation, though Davian continued in the same vein.

"This news cannot wait." Despite his bold words, the prime minister cleared his throat in obvious delay. He glanced at Saxanar, who relinquished the necessity for protracted protocol with a gesture, clearly to Davian's dismay. "Sire, it seems the pirates have struck again, this time in two attacks. The first was against our forces on the shore, the second against ship number *Seven*."

Seven? Darris' throat seemed to close; breathing became all but impossible.

Griff jerked up his head, his lips pursed into a bloodless line, his gentle eyes wide. "What . . . what . . . was the . . . outcome?"

Darris forced a tight swallow, allowing air to wheeze into his lungs. It was not the first time the pirates had led a minor assault on the coast; they seemed to be carefully testing Béarn's defenses. But *Seven* had gone on a routine mission; its presence alone was supposed to keep the pirates at bay. Jhirban had assured them that mere thieves would never dare attack a Béarnian warship, especially in her own waters; and, thus far, the pirates had limited their conquests to merchant vessels. *Arturo was on that ship.* Darris stared at Davian, needing to know the details for reasons far beyond bardic curiosity.

"The onshore army repelled the invaders, Sire."

Though good, that was not the news Darris awaited. Seiryn allowed himself a small, self-satisfied smile.

"Fifteen casualties, twenty wounded on our side, Sire." Davian read the numbers through gritted teeth. He fairly spat the rest, "All thirty-seven invaders dead."

The ship. Darris needed to know the fate of his biological son. His only son.

Though surely just as concerned for Arturo, Griff asked the necessary questions first. "No enemy prisoners?"

"No, Sire."

For once, Zaysharn did not hold his tongue. "There were Renshai among the troops, Sire." His tone held an odd note of disdain that bordered on anger. "Renshai do not take prisoners."

The words shocked the room silent. Zaysharn rarely spoke; when he did, he nearly always made a point of great import. It was not like him to blurt out anything, especially so clearly imbued with emotion.

Davian's blemished cheeks barely allowed a tinge of red. He spoke with the evenhanded patience Zaysharn had discarded. "Your Majesty, once Renshai become embroiled in battle, it is difficult to . . . er . . . unembroil them."

Zaysharn broke in again. "They kill everyone in sight."

"Not everyone." Darris could not help entering the discussion. One of his closest friends was Renshai. "Not companions." It was not a wholly fair defense. He had traveled with Kevral on several serious missions, and she had, on occasion, threatened the lives of allies. Friends less skilled or quick might have lost their lives.

"Even companions, sometimes, Darris." Captain Seiryn entered the discussion. Though negative, his assessment did not seem judgmental. "I've seen it. Renshai are highly skilled, brave warriors; but commanding them is a challenge. Rather like commanding a palace full of cats."

The seriousness of the circumstances kept anyone from laughing, but they all understood the reference. Béarn Castle had become nearly overrun with the offspring of the queen's favorite pet, a calico named Mior. The mother of these multitudes had passed away a couple of years earlier, at the ripe old age of twenty-seven. Only Darris and a handful of friends knew how severely her passing had affected Matrinka. She had had a bond with the cat that went far beyond mistress and pet. With a process no one seemed capable of explaining, they had exchanged a form of mental communication. Matrinka kept hoping she could create a similar attachment to one of the kittens, but every attempt had failed so far.

When no one laughed, Seiryn clearly felt obligated to explain. "Renshai don't use strategy or repeat patterns when they fight. Their only driving goal is glorious, *individual* death in battle. They are not only impossible to hold to a plan, they are also unpredictable." He shrugged in clear apology, not wishing to speak ill of a group of people the king admired. "Furthermore, a mortally ill or injured Renshai will attack anyone to assure himself or herself a death in combat. Any other death they scorn as cowardice."

Griff turned his attention directly on his captain. "Are you saying we shouldn't have Renshai among our troops?"

"No, Sire, I—" Seiryn started, interrupted by Zaysharn, who seemed to have completely abandoned his quiet persona.

"That, Your Majesty, is exactly what he is saying."

A scowl pinched Seiryn's face, and he glared at the overseer. "I am perfectly capable of making a point, Lord Zaysharn—and that was not it."

Zaysharn stood, presumably to level the argument. "Your men would agree with me."

"My men," Seiryn said through clenched teeth, "are not your concern."

Though wild with worry for Arturo, Darris could not help getting swept up in the discussion. His bardic curiosity demanded it.

The king swallowed hard, looking pained. "Is that true, Captain Seiryn? Are the soldiers unhappy about serving with Renshai?"

Seiryn backed down from Zaysharn with clear reluctance to face the king directly. "Sire, there is some discomfort in the ranks. Nothing I can't handle."

Saxanar made an archaic gesture indicating that he wished to speak, and the others yielded to his preeminence. "Some of the soldiers have threatened to quit."

"Let them," Seiryn grumbled. "I've enough real men among them; I don't need defeatists."

Saxanar ignored the interruption. "Others have simply expressed concern, and more just want reassignment. Perhaps if we went back to separating the Renshai into their own platoon—"

This time, Seiryn refused to allow the old minister to talk over him, "That didn't work. The Renshai need oversight, and we need their sword arms."

Zaysharn broke in again, "Instead of our own?"

"In addition to our own." Seiryn turned the overseer of livestock another pointed glare.

Aerean bounced to her feet. "I've heard a lot of talk in recent weeks about Renshai. Even the servants and commoners are talking about how fierce they must have been to become exiles from the Northlands for . . . for violence. How they slaughtered a path through the West and East before seizing the Fields of Wrath.

Though silent to this point, Darris could not help adding the perspective his studies gave him. "But that was hundreds of years ago!" He wanted to add more, that the Fields of Wrath had been considered uninhabitable wasteland when the Renshai settled there, but it seemed an insignificant point. The Renshai thrived on a barren plain because they did not need proper growing or grazing land. They dedicated every moment of their lives to learning warcraft and purchased their necessities by selling their one and only talent, mostly to the kings of Béarn. For far longer than the memory of anyone living, the Renshai had served as guardians to the princes and princesses of Béarn. Even the king had a Renshai who guarded him obsessively whenever business took Darris from his post.

Zaysharn turned on Darris. "Hundreds of years have not bred the ferocity out of wolves, nor out of Renshai either."

Aerean seemed not to realize the tangent the discussion had taken. "It's said they burn off horn buds at birth and hide the scars beneath golden hair. That some have seen tails tucked into their trousers."

A sudden silence gripped the room, and every eye turned to Aerean.

Aerean's cheeks flushed a brilliant red. "I'm just saying what I've heard, not whether I believe it."

Golden-haired devils from the North, the Westerners had called them in the years when Renshai ravaged the countryside. The prejudice lived on, long after a coalition of Northern tribes had all but obliterated the Renshai and the last surviving few had proven themselves reliable heroes in the Great War against the East. In the more than three centuries since, hatred for the Renshai had come and gone in cycles; each time, the legends grew more odious and, now it seemed, more literal.

Chaveeshia finally broke the silence. "They're not really demons." As the diplomatic link between the Fields of Wrath and Béarn, the diminutive woman voiced an opinion that carried the weight she did not. "I've seen bald Renshai without scars and Renshai newborn. No horns. No tails."

King Griff cleared his throat loudly. "No one believes the Renshai are actual demons."

Aerean shrugged but did not gainsay her liege. Darris doubted she personally expected to find horns and tails, but the common folk might. Since elves and their magic had come to Midgard, the populace had reason to believe in legends once dismissed as utter nonsense.

"What matters is keeping our troops strong and focused, especially given the enemy at our ships and coastline." Griff turned his attention fully back to Prime Minister Davian.

Though clearly reluctant, Davian returned to his report. "Your Majesty, I recommend we table the discussion on Renshai for another time. I . . ." He swallowed so hard, his words faltered. His eyes became a blurry smear of black. "I regret . . . to inform you . . . that . . ."

Torn between wanting to tear the words from Davian's throat and never having to hear them, Darris waited in the same breathless hush as the others.

". . . the ship called *Seven* . . ." Davian lowered his head.

The wait had become intolerable. Darris felt tears forming in his own eyes, though he had not yet heard the words spoken. *By all the gods, please let Arturo be all right.* He felt selfish for the thought. The others aboard the ship also had kin, but he could only concentrate on the fate of his boy.

Davian tried to finish, his voice a gasp, ". . . and all aboard her . . ." He lapsed into a silence no one dared to break. A tear coursed down one cheek.

". . . were . . . lost."

Horror gripped the room. His vision blurred, and Darris realized he was also crying.

King Griff clasped his hands over his lowered face, his cheeks seeming to melt into his palms. His voice emerged muffled. "All?"

Agony spiked through Darris. He wanted, needed to console his king, but he found himself unable to move. His thoughts remained frozen in place, incapable of further contemplation.

Davian addressed the hovering question. "It appears so, Sire." He glanced around the room, as if for help, but no one leaped in to rescue him from the words he needed to speak. "We have ships recovering . . . remains, Sire. We have found . . . no . . . survivors." He studied the king as he spoke, clearly weighing the effect of every word before allowing it to leave his lips. "I'm so, so very sorry, Your Majesty."

"As are we all," Saxanar said, tone made gravelly by grief. "This is a sad day for Béarn."

His fervor spent, Zaysharn disappeared back into his usual quiet position, his head bowed.

King Griff looked up from his hands, tears freely flowing and a line of moisture stringing from his mouth to his palms. "Did they . . . find Arturo's . . . ?"

Davian did not force him to finish before replying, "No, Sire."

"Then there is hope."

"No, Sire. No hope." The prime minister dashed the last pretext. "We recovered both of his . . ." He avoided the word "Renshai" in light of the previous conversation. ". . . guardians. They clearly fought to their deaths, Sire. The water—frigid, and sharks . . ." Caution kept Davian's speech choppy. He struggled to make his point without provoking images of Arturo's mangled corpse.

Hacked by blades, eaten by sharks, freezing, none of those seemed pleasant ways to die. Darris tried not to speculate.

Aerean wrapped her arms around the massive king, rocking him ever so slightly to remind him of her presence without shoving him out of his seat.

Griff's face returned to his hands. His body shuddered rhythmically. "My son," he whispered. "My son."

Darris suffered a pang of jealousy he had long ago convinced himself he never harbored. *Not Arturo.* He could not help feeling responsible. Matrinka had protested, but Darris had backed the boy's decision. Griff had allowed Arturo to sail, mostly on the advice of his bodyguard and bard. *What have I done? What have I done?*

The king looked up abruptly, his face a wet mask of grief. "And so many other sons. Has anyone informed the families of those aboard the *Seven?*"

"Not yet, Sire," Davian said, looking around the room. "We thought you should know first."

"Yes. Yes, of course." Though obviously sad, the king never fully lost his composure. "I will leave it to you to inform them and to provide proper compensation for heroes lost in the line of duty to Béarn."

Davian bowed, "Yes, Sire."

The exchange passed in an incoherent fog. Darris found himself staring at his fingers and seeing nothing until the king seized his hand.

"Come, Bard Darris. We must inform the queen."

"The queen," Darris repeated dully. He rose, dazed, the word defying meaning. He wrestled with it until the single syllable found definition, *the king's wife*. He moved toward the door, more from Griff's steering than any intention. *The king's first wife*. He was through the door before he noticed it opening, and its closing became equally lost. *Matrinka!* That realization cleared Darris' mind in a terrified rush. "We're going to tell Matrinka . . . ?" he managed breathlessly.

The king finally released Darris' arm, speaking in a low whisper, "You're going to tell her, Darris. You're the one she's going to need."

"But . . ." Darris kept moving without memory of a single step. Before he knew it, they stood just outside the queen's bedchamber. "But . . ." He could think of no way to finish the sentence he had now started twice. All envy vanished, replaced by an intense fear bordering on panic. By law, Arturo was Griff's son; and their bond was as real as any father's and child's. Arturo had gone to the grave believing himself the product of the king's seed. Yet, Darris, Griff, and Matrinka knew otherwise. The king was right, as always. Matrinka needed her one true love. At a time like this, she needed Darris.

Darris found himself alone, staring at the familiar teak door emblazoned with the royal crest, a bear with ruby eyes rearing in a circle of emeralds. Griff had neither the build nor inclination for sneaking, but he had managed to disappear without his bard's notice. *Some great guardian I am*, he thought. Then his mind narrowed to Matrinka. He would do anything not to hurt her.

Darris put a hand on the latch, closed his eyes, and twisted.

CHAPTER 4

Only a Renshai could find entertainment in charging toward death.

—*King Tae Kahn, Weile's son*

STARS GLIMMERED IN the dark expanse of sky, partners to a blazing sliver of moon. Calistin Ra-khirsson perched on a hill overlooking the Road of Kings, a freshly oiled sword still balanced on his knees, the perspiration of a satisfying workout still cooling his scrawny, childlike limbs. He loved sitting alone late at night, after all his *torke* had gone to bed, seeking patterns in the lights overhead. It had surprised him to realize that, unlike clouds, each star held a steady and predictable place in the sky, varying only with the seasons.

Calistin knew that certain of the Renshai maneuvers, such as *stjerne skytedel,* "the shooting star," or *musserende,* "sparkling", took their names from these heavenly bodies. Over the last year, he had begun to wonder if others also did so, in less obvious ways. One of the most advanced techniques was called *åndelig mannhimmel,* which literally meant "spirit man of the sky." Calistin had identified a figure in the autumn heavens that reminded him of the maneuver in its pose as well as the pattern of its gradual motion across the sky. He thought of more subtle ones, too, such as *krabbe,* "the crab" and *mulesl om natten,* the "night mule."

But it was not Calistin's job to seek the details of history or the reasons behind the realities, only to plumb the physical and mental skills necessary to make him the most capable swordsman in existence. Every thought, every movement, every action should bring him closer to this goal and no other. He rose, sheathing his weapon, and stretched with leisurely grace. Right now, he needed sleep most of all.

A sound from below claimed Calistin's attention, and he dropped to an instinctive crouch. Figures appeared on the Road of Kings, a group of young men or boys by their movements. Calistin counted seven, one smaller than the rest and clearly resistant. The other six remained clustered around him, driving him forward with occasional jabs that sent him stumbling. Their voices wafted to Calistin as an indistinct rumble pierced by occasional laughter.

Curious, Calistin watched. He had not left the Fields of Wrath since early childhood, and nothing in his Renshai experience explained this situation. The larger ones formed a crooked ring around the smallest. Then, suddenly, one slammed a fist into his face. His victim crumpled. As he collapsed, moonlight glimmered from his orange mop of hair. The darkness otherwise limited Calistin's vision to dull black and white, and a vast spectrum of gray.

Redhead. Calistin knew the majority of Westerners sported locks in colors that ranged from wet sand to a deep ebony black. Blonds and redheads predominated only among those of Northern origin, and just one Northern tribe lived in the Westlands. *Renshai.* Idly, Calistin wondered how this young member of his tribe had come to be on the Road of Kings so late at night and unarmed. No Renshai would willingly travel anywhere without at least one sword.

Another blow followed the first, then the six young men fell upon their quarry like hounds on a rabbit. Arms rose and fell, fists flew, then the action disappeared beneath the press of flailing bodies. Their conversation degenerated into jubilant shouts and desperate screams.

Calistin found himself halfway down the hill before he realized he had moved. He knew some prejudice existed against the Renshai, but he could not imagine anyone finding glory in a battle of six on one, even against a master swordsman.

The group seemed to take no notice of Calistin's approach. He could see and hear them clearly, aside from the child on the bottom, concealed and muffled by his attackers. They shouted curses and insults in the Western tongue with Erythanian accents.

Slowing to a walk, Calistin stepped up to the roiling mass of bodies and tapped one youngster on the shoulder. "Who's winning?"

Four of them disengaged to whirl toward Calistin. The other two remained in place, pinning the struggling boy. Calistin could no longer discern the color of his hair through the darkness, but he could see liquid smeared across the child's face. He looked about nine or ten years old, which was not terribly helpful. Well-blooded Renshai appeared much younger than their ages, including Calistin himself.

"Git 'way, boy!" one snarled, features close-set and sneering. "Or ya's next."

Calistin ignored the threat to continue studying what remained of the battle. The young men all wore stained and ragged clothing, their expressions fierce, aside from the one on the bottom. He turned Calistin a pleading look with large, light-colored eyes.

"All right," Calistin finally said. "I'm game. But I think you'll need a few more punks to make it interesting." He met the child's frightened gaze. "Your current fight doesn't seem very challenging. Why not use this one against me, too?" He gestured at the cowering boy, still pinioned beneath his attackers.

The biggest of the young men rose, towering over Calistin by a head and a half. "Ha, ha, ha. Thinks lots a yasself, don't ya, boy?"

The question seemed ludicrous. "Of course. Why wouldn't I?" Calistin smiled. "And I'm not a boy. I'm a man, by Renshai law."

The largest paled visibly in the moonlight. The others looked at him for guidance. Then, one of the ones holding down the boy, a powerfully built youngster with a wicked scar along one cheek spoke up, "Renshai or no, Parmille, we's kin take him."

The one assisting him hissed, "But he's blooded, Avra. Blooded."

Calistin waited with calm patience while the group discussed whether to attack him. He did not bother to correct their misconception. Hundreds of years before his birth, when the Renshai spent most of their time battling Northern neighbors or slaughtering their way across the Westlands, they achieved adulthood at the time of their first kill rather than by testing. Western beliefs remained rooted in the ferocity of those long-ago days. If these young men chose to believe a myth that made Calistin seem more dangerous, he saw no reason to dissuade them.

The one called Avra rose, revealing a lean, muscular figure as tall as Calistin's father. "Blooded's he?" He jerked a long knife from the folds of his ragged tunic. "Then let him bleed."

Other knives in other hands joined him, some with clear reluctance. The remaining youth still holding down the boy looked from his charge to his leaders, clearly uncertain whether to join the fight. Calistin judged their competence in that moment and found it lacking. Avra had strength and Parmille a hint of dexterity; but the others looked slow, cloddish, and weak. Calistin did not worry about any of them, even en masse. He wondered only why the redhead did not seize this moment to disarm his last tormentor. *Perhaps he has serious injuries.*

Calistin anticipated a sudden attack that never came. Instead, the young men gathered just beyond the range of a sword stroke, leading with their knives. They clearly had experience working together.

Leisurely, Calistin watched their every movement, more bored than excited or amused. He did not yet feel threatened, so did not bother to draw a weapon.

"C'mon, Renshai," Avra sneered, his stance low and his movements measured. "Ain't ya even gonna defen' yasself?"

"Defend myself?" Calistin addressed Avra, though his gaze followed every man. "Against what?"

The last of the toughs released the boy on the ground. He slammed his heel into the boy's gut, driving breath from his lungs and sending him into a curled knot of pain. Only then, the last punk joined his friends. He hurriedly produced a short, crude blade.

Avra made a curt gesture. " 'gainst this!" All six lunged at Calistin in a ragged semicircle.

Calistin drew and cut. His blade wove between his adversaries, now licking through a grip, now tapping a hilt. He finished in the same fluid motion, his sword back in its sheath, their knives thumping to the ground, and every young man staring at his hand. Most disarming maneuvers would have claimed two or three fingers, and the Renshai finesse left them too startled to move or speak.

"More?" Calistin suggested as the group backed carefully away from him.

As one, they turned and fled, abandoning their knives, and their victim, in the dirt.

Calistin could have caught at least one hilt before it fell, but he had chosen not to do so. Renshai honored the blades of sparring partners and respected enemies, but these rowdies deserved none of his consideration. Instead, he stomped their blades into the dirt.

Finally, the redhead stood, face smeared with a sticky combination of blood, tears, and snot. A snarl of carrot-colored hair fell over one large eye to a mass of freckles on his cheek. A crooked nose gave his face an odd, lopsided look. Remarkably skinny, he looked more like a straw doll or scarecrow than a living boy.

Calistin spoke to him in the Renshai tongue, "My name is Calistin." Any tribesman would already know of him, but he could think of nothing better to say.

The boy took no notice of the words, though he apparently accepted them as a show of friendship. He ran to Calistin.

It was clearly a nonthreatening gesture, yet Calistin did not know how to react. He remained still as the boy hurled himself at Calistin and wrapped scrawny arms around him. "Thank ya's, thank ya's, thank ya's! Ya's 'mazin'! M'hero, thank ya's, thank ya's thank ya's!" He spoke Western with the same Erythanian accent as Parmille.

He's not Renshai. Calistin's interest in the boy evaporated. He tried to walk away, but the death grip on his legs made that impossible. "Go away."

The boy's grip tightened. "I owes ya m' life! M' life! Thank ya's so much, m'lord. M'savior!"

Calistin blamed exhaustion for causing him to make such a ridiculous assumption. His own father had no Renshai blood at all yet sported the reddish-blond hair usually associated only with Northmen. He wondered why it had never occurred to him to ask about Ra-khir's coloring in the past. Not that it bore any significance; nothing mattered to Calistin but his swordwork and becoming the best. "Let go of me."

The boy's voice muffled as he buried his face in Calistin's tunic. "I owes ya ever'thin'."

Calistin tried to pry the boy loose without aggravating his injuries. "You owe me nothing. Go away."

"Ever'thin'. I owes ya absolutely ever'thin', m'savior."

Tact and politeness had failed, so Calistin went for shock. "I only saved you by mistake."

"By mistake?" The boy looked up suddenly. "It don't—I means it shouldn't matter if—" A light dawned in his pale eyes. "It's 'cause a m'orange hair, ain't it?" He smiled broadly, his mouth enormous. "Ya's thinkin' I's . . . thinkin' I's . . ."

". . . Renshai. Yes," Calistin admitted, managing to free one leg. "But you're not, are you?"

"Don't know. I's might be bein'."

Calistin rolled his eyes. He would not ordinarily waste this much time on anyone. "You'd know if you were."

"Mebbe not." The boy kept a death hold on Calistin's left leg, and the Renshai finally noticed the crimson mess the boy had smudged along Calistin's clothes where he had buried his face in gratitude. "I's been 'lone 'long's I kin 'member. Avra an' them ones ain't likin' me 'cause they says redhead Er'than'yans gots Renshai blood in 'em." He grinned. "An' 'cause I's taked this off 'em." He held up a wad of something white and green that reeked of rot and foliage.

Calistin made a mental note to ask Ra-khir about red-haired Erythanians when he found a chance. It might explain how Calistin had inherited so many of the ancient Renshai features despite his father. "What in Hel is that thing?"

"Cheese," the boy said triumphantly. "Want some?"

Calistin shoved the proffering hand away. "I'd rather eat my own puke."

The boy shrugged and raised the mass to his mouth.

Torn between revulsion and morbid curiosity, Calistin waited a full beat before slapping the moldy, unrecognizable lump from the boy's hand. "Don't eat that. It's disgusting!"

The redhead yelped and finally released Calistin. He hesitated, clearly torn between obedience and hunger.

"Leave it there." Calistin sighed, not wishing to further bind himself to the irritating child yet feeling responsible for at least a decent meal. "I'll get you some real food. All right?"

The boy's face lit up, and he lunged for Calistin again.

Calistin shifted into agile retreat, and the boy missed; but the gratitude still tumbled out, "Thank ya's, m'savior. Ya's most most grashus, m'savior."

"Quit calling me 'savior.' " Calistin started back up the hill, not bothering to see if the boy followed. "It sounds too much like my brother's name, Saviar."

Grass crunched as the boy scurried after Calistin. "Then what's I s'posed ta call ya, hero?"

"My name is Calistin."

"M'name's Treysind, Calis . . . Calitsan . . . Calee."

Calistin winced as Treysind repeatedly mangled his name. "Calistin."

"Caleetsin," Treysind tried. "Caliti. How's 'bout if I's jus' callin' ya's Cali?"

Calistin wanted to say he did not care, that the boy could call him anything since they would soon part and not see one another again; but he knew he would never hear the end of it if Saviar heard the child call him Cali. "Let's just stick with 'hero.' "

Saviar Ra-khirsson dashed from the cottage after a cursory breakfast from family stores, hoping for a few moments of practice before facing his *torke*. Though spring had already arrived, the early morning air still held a winter chill. Dressed only in his short-sleeved tunic and breeks, he shivered beneath an onslaught of goose bumps but gave no thought to his cloak. Exertion would warm him even before the sun's rays thawed the ground, and extra folds of fabric would only hamper his sword arm.

As Saviar raced toward his first lesson, he collided with a boy. Breath huffed into his face, and the child collapsed beneath him, tangling his legs. Unable to save his own balance, Saviar tumbled, rolling as his *torke* had taught, and coming up in a wary crouch.

With a peep of surprise, the boy scrambled to a secure position as well.

Saviar did not recognize the small redhead, who did not carry a sword. Mortified, he berated his own clumsiness with flush-cheeked apology, speaking Renshai. "I'm very sorry. I didn't see you."

The boy waved a hand toward the cottage Saviar had just vacated. He used the Western tongue. "I's sorry I's gots in ya's way. I's jus' waitin' for Hero."

"Hiro?" Saviar rose, confused. It was not a Renshai name, not even an Erythanian one. He switched to the same language as the boy. All but the most dedicated and reclusive Renshai knew Western and the Common Trading tongues in addition to their own. "Who is Hiro?"

The boy smiled, eyes glazing like an adolescent girl in love. "He's *my* hero. He rescueded me from bullies an' gived me food good 'nough fors a king. I's so full I couldn't even eat m'breakfast." He held out a lump of something reeking and greenish, displaying it like a trophy.

Saviar's nose wrinkled, and he sucked air through his teeth. "You're going to eat that?"

"It's cheese."

"Was it?" Saviar made a dismissive gesture, suddenly guilty for the scraps he had left on his plate. "So, does this hero of yours have a name?"

"Cali—" the boy started and stopped, brow furrowing. He returned the moldy parcel to his pocket. "Cali . . . something."

Saviar could scarcely believe it. "Calistin?" he tried.

The boy's face brightened. "Tha's it! Cali . . . Cali . . . what ya's sayed. Ya's *knowin'* Hero?" He made it sound like just having made the acquaintance of the excruciatingly irritating blond was a god-sanctioned honor.

Unfortunately. "He's my brother," Saviar admitted.

The boy pranced in an excited circle, clearly unable to contain his enthusiasm. "Ya's must be Sayvyar."

"SAV-ee-ar." Saviar restored the inflection of his name.

"An' ya's gots orange hair, jus' like me!" the boy finished in an animated squeak. " 's no wonders Hero thinked I's Renshai."

The boy had only one thing right: his tangled mop bore the brilliant hue of a pumpkin or carrot, accompanied by a wild wash of freckles. Though a mix of wheaten and burgundy that passed for a light gold-red, Saviar's locks in no way resembled the boy's. No one could mistake the two for relatives. "When it's hair, most people call it red or strawberry, not orange."

"Red, then." The boy accepted the correction easily. "M'name's Treysind."

"Saviar," Saviar repeated from politeness. Though he had lost much of his solo practice time to the encounter, curiosity held him in place. "Did Calistin really save your life?" Calistin always said he firmly believed anyone incapable of defending himself deserved to die. Saviar could not imagine Calistin troubling himself to rescue one of his own brothers, let alone an Erythanian.

"Yup."

"Really?"

Treysind closed his eyes and sighed. "He's tha greatest hero ever. I's owin' him m'life."

"Did he ever figure out you aren't Renshai?"

"Yup."

"And then?" Saviar could picture Calistin chopping the boy to pieces, along with the bullies, simply for wasting his uniquely valuable time.

"An' then he tooked me home an' feeded me."

Saviar blinked. "*Calistin* did?"

"Lots an' lots an' lots." Treysind patted his stomach. "I's still filled. Too filled ta—"

Saviar interrupted, not wanting Treysind to display his vulgar prize again. "Yes, yes." He stroked his chin, feeling the first soft wisps of beard. "And you're absolutely sure it was Calistin?"

"M'hero, yup. Tha's tha name he gived me." Treysind seemed incapable of not smiling anytime he heard the name, the same one that jarred Saviar into scowling exasperation.

Knowing better than to arrive late for his lesson, Saviar finished a conversation he preferred to dissect. "Well, then, you should know. His highness, I mean his 'heroness,' got in quite late last night. He'll probably sleep till midmorning."

"I's gonna wait." Treysind stood as tall as possible, which barely brought him up to Saviar's chest. " 's long's it takes."

"Very well, then," Saviar saluted Treysind as he headed toward his lesson. "I wish you good day." He broke into a trot, bewilderment not yet sorting itself into wonder or amusement. If Calistin had a softer side, he kept it well-hidden; yet, confronted with direct evidence of his brother's generosity, Saviar could not refute it. *Perhaps, just perhaps, there is some good in Calistin after all.*

For reasons Saviar could not explain, the idea that his savage, perfectionist brother had done something charitable buoyed him through another grueling day of lessons. Though bulky compared with his classmates, he felt nearly weightless. His maneuvers came intuitively, requiring little thought; and he managed a quickness that pleased his *torke* enough for several to insist he test again for manhood in the coming months.

Late into the afternoon, Saviar still found himself too interested and busy to notice the exhaustion that usually enveloped him. Even his mother, his last *torke* of the day and his harshest critic, found nothing to complain about in his performance. She had won her own Renshai womanhood at fifteen, and it clearly pained her that two of her sons remained children three years longer.

Kevral's class froze in the last position of its current *svergelse,* and she moved around them making miniscule corrections to the positions of arms, swords, and stances. At last, she came to Saviar and clapped her hands. Her expression gave away nothing, but joy sparkled in her pale eyes. She did not speak and made no changes to his positioning, a true compliment.

In that moment of satisfied silence, Saviar heard distant hoofbeats, drumming nearer.

Kevral returned to the front of the class. "All right, then."

Swords whisked back into sheaths. All eyes pinned their *torke* to see whether she would move on to the next maneuver or drive them to another performance of the same. Every boy and girl forced his or her breaths to emerge evenly, quietly. To appear winded would assure a longer and more difficult session.

Two white horses topped the rise above the practice field. *Knights' horses.* Saviar stared, filled with awe and joy. He loved the strong movements of those well-muscled steeds, the crisp authority of their riders. The other students also took their gazes from their *torke.* Kevral frowned but turned to see what interested her pupils behind her back.

Slowed to a walk, the stallions approached. As they drew nearer, Saviar could make out the familiar uniforms and plumed hats. A moment later, he recognized his father and grandfather. From a distance, they appeared like twins, both tall and stolid with straight, handsome features. As they drew up to Kevral, Knight-Captain Kedrin's age became more obvious. His hair matched his mount's pure white fur, equally clean and bright; while Ra-khir's reddish-blond locks showed only a hint of silver at the temples. Kedrin's features had grown craggy while Ra-khir's still held their youthful smoothness. The grandfather's eyes, however, betrayed no age at all. An uncommon whitish blue, like Saviar's, they gave away nothing.

Kevral walked to the knights. Usually, any interruption of her instructions left her scowling and irritated. Now, a ghost of a welcoming smile traced her lips, overwhelmed by growing furrows of concern. Saviar knew what cued his mother; Ra-khir knew better than to intrude on a Renshai practice without grave reason.

Ra-khir spoke first, clearly worried Kevral's impatience might drive her to say something unbecoming. "Good evening, my darling." He flourished his hat with a grand gesture befitting a noble lady. "I deeply apologize for interrupting your lesson."

Kevral gave him only an expectant, "Yes?" She hated the knight's formality and forbade it within the confines of their home; but Knight-Captain Kedrin's presence and Ra-khir's official garb required it. They were on duty.

"I'm afraid the Knight-Captain and I have been called away to Béarn." Ra-khir added in a less formal tone, "Prince Arturo's gone missing."

Kevral's demeanor softened abruptly. The trace of a smile vanished. "Missing?"

"Presumed dead."

Fear clutched Saviar's heart, and his hands went suddenly cold. He remembered Marisole's little brother from freer days when they had had more time for play away from the grueling sword training that tied them always to the Fields of Wrath. Two years younger and in awe of his older sister, Arturo had toddled in her wake, his enormous brown eyes sweet and irresistible. Any attention from her friends made his face glow with pleasure and his toothless mouth open into a broad smile.

Knight-Captain Kedrin gripped Ra-khir's arm in warning. Such matters did not warrant discussion in front of children, usually; though nothing about death startled or bothered young Renshai. So long as it occurred in battle, they welcomed and glorified it, their goal since infancy. Even Saviar had every intention of dying in fevered and magnificent combat, freeing his soul for the perfect afterlife in Valhalla.

"Oh . . . no." Kevral glanced at the ground, then kicked it savagely. "Oh, no." She seemed on the edge of asking about Matrinka, about Griff, Darris, and Marisole, all of whom must be crazed with grief. Instead, she took the tack of a true Renshai. "His escort? Where were they? They should have kept him safe." A hard edge of disdain and anger entered a tone that, only a moment before, had displayed all-too-human concern.

"They're dead, my lady," Ra-khir defended the prince's Renshai guardians.

Before Ra-khir could explain further, Kedrin spoke sharply, "Sir Ra-khir! That is not an appropriate topic for youngsters." He made a gesture that encompassed Kevral's entire class, advanced boys and girls ranging in age from fifteen to twenty-two.

Kevral's cheeks darkened, and Saviar grimaced, prepared for a barrage of maternal anger that never came.

Ra-khir held her at bay with a pleading gesture, then turned on his own father. "Captain, I beg to differ. For Renshai, this is not only an appropriate topic, it is a necessary one."

Kedrin's lips clamped closed, but he gave his son permission to continue with a brittle nod.

Ra-khir obliged. "They died in battle, defending Arturo to the end."

Kevral managed a smile, tempered by the gravity of the situation. The slain Renshai would surely be celebrated that evening, their names added to the roles of heroes for use in naming newborns. It was this practice, Saviar knew, coupled with the Renshai propensity to look younger than their ages that had once made them seem invincible, demonic. The other Northern tribes had referred to them as *djevgullinhåri*, the "golden-haired devils."

Kevral took Ra-khir's hand, speaking so softly Saviar could scarcely hear her. "Please give Matrinka my condolences. And do what you can to help her through this."

Though upset by the situation, Saviar enjoyed his mother's rare moment of softness. Though Renshai through and through, she could still place herself in the position of an anguished, kind, and gentle queen who was also her friend.

"I'll do my best," Ra-khir promised. Saviar could tell he wanted to say more, perhaps to remind Kevral that others more appropriate were already at the queen's side; but he stopped with those words. Saviar wondered if his father hesitated to mention Darris and Griff because of their conversation the night before. Ra-khir would not want anyone else to divine Arturo's blood parentage on account of his words.

Memory of that talk brought a sudden idea to Saviar's mind. As the knights turned to leave, he spoke it aloud. "*Torke?*" He knew better than to refer to Kevral as "Mama" during lessons. "May I go with them?"

Ra-khir froze with his mount half-turned, and Kedrin stiffened. Kevral glanced at Saviar. "I wasn't aware that you were invited." Ra-khir turned his attention to his own father. Clearly, he wished to extend that invitation, but the hierarchy of the knights gave him no right to do so.

Kedrin rescued his subordinate son. "Of course, Saviar may accompany us. We'd be delighted to have him, with your permission, good lady."

Kevral continued to study her son. Saviar remained in position, not even daring to breathe. She would see pleading as weakness and surely deny him. Until he became a man, however, Saviar could not make this decision without her.

Kevral turned away from Saviar, and his heart sank. She curtsied in the general direction of Kedrin, more in deference to his status as father-in-law than Knight-Captain. Saviar bit his lip, forcing himself not to cringe. No telling what a Renshai as committed as Kevral might say to any man who interrupted her practice, especially when she considered him her martial inferior. "Excuse me, Captain. Might I borrow your companion for a few moments of private conversation?"

Saviar released a pent-up breath. Whatever irritation his request had inspired, Kevral intended to vent on her husband alone. *At least, for the moment.* Saviar tried not to consider the punishment she could heap on him under the guise of training. *Sorry, Papa. I didn't mean to involve you, too.*

———✠———

Once properly dismissed by his superior, Ra-khir eagerly followed Kevral beyond earshot of her students. Even after all these years, he still enjoyed watching her from behind. Every tiny movement, from her rare curtsy to her confident strides, held a grace trained into her nearly since birth. The most seductive dancers could not compete for his attention. For all their girlish dexterity, their motions lacked the absolute power and commitment of Kevral's; and few could boast such tightly muscled buttocks.

Kevral turned suddenly, and Ra-khir had to stop short to keep from running into her. She opened her mouth to speak, then closed it, staring at him instead. "You're grinning like a lunatic."

Ra-khir's smile turned wolfish, and he crooked an eyebrow. "I like what I see."

Kevral clearly could not suppress her own grin. "Gods, that really is all you men think about, isn't it?"

"Not *all*." Ra-khir mocked defensiveness. "Just nine times out of ten, give or take one."

"Still?" Kevral shook her head, eyes rolling. "We've been married for like a hundred years. Granted, I only had two pregnancies, but I've given birth to three sons." She indicated her lower regions with an agile gesture. "What's left to leer at?"

Ra-khir could scarcely believe the question. "Eighteen perfect years, not a hundred, and it seems more like eight. You're more beautiful now then ever." He drew her into his arms, her body like taut bundles of wire. "I'm the luckiest man in the world."

Kevral kissed him, the touch of her lips deliciously soft and yielding. She was a fierce, and strangely gracious, lover.

Ra-khir returned her kiss and tightened his embrace. Sinewy and more potentially lethal than a serpent, she still felt small and helpless in his massive arms. His desire to protect her, though misplaced, consumed him. He might have stood there all day if Kevral had not gently disengaged.

"I didn't bring you here to . . . slobber and tickle."

I'll be quick, Ra-khir nearly quipped before seeing the serious look on Kevral's face. Instead, he stepped back and waited patiently for her to explain.

"Ordinarily, I'd never let a student travel this close to his manhood testing, but it seems important to Saviar."

Ra-khir had to agree. "He's never dared asked before." When it came to Renshai training and the boys, Kevral outranked him as fully as Kedrin did among the knights. "It's obviously something he feels strongly about."

"Why?"

Ra-khir hesitated, confused. "Are you asking *me*?"

Kevral shrugged. "Even if Saviar knows why, and he probably doesn't, he wouldn't tell his mother."

The words made no sense to Ra-khir. "Why not?"

Kevral studied Ra-khir as if he had grown wings. "Because he's an adolescent boy, and all adolescent boys hate their parents."

Stunned, Ra-khir could do nothing but stare. They stood in silence for several awkward moments before he finally managed to stammer, "Th-they do?"

Apparently mistaking his surprise for an act, Kevral laughed. "Of course they do. You know that. You were an adolescent b—" She broke off abruptly and ended with a simple "Oh."

Ra-khir's thoughts drifted back to a bitter childhood he rarely consulted when raising his own sons. When Ra-khir was quite young, his parents had separated. His mother had remarried and insisted that her new husband was his father. She had held Kedrin at bay with threats and trickery, lied to Ra-khir about his origins, and the fool she married assisted her deception. Ra-khir had not learned the truth until his teens. When his mother gave him an ultimatum, he chose his father over her and started the relationship he should have had throughout his childhood. "When I was an adolescent boy, I was just getting to know and love my father. And I had every reason to dislike my mother."

Kevral turned him an apologetic look. She had clearly not intended to dredge up those memories. "Adolescent boys who grow up with loving parents reach a stage where they sort of . . ." Kevral cocked her head, as if trying to quote someone verbatim and not quite finding the correct words. ". . . distance themselves from their parents in order to find their own place in the world."

Ra-khir guessed at the source of Kevral's words. "Matrinka?" Usually, she quoted Colbey Calistinsson, but child rearing was not the purview of the consummate Renshai.

Kevral smiled sheepishly. "Darris, actually. He was in Erythane several months back doing . . . something diplomatic . . ."

Ra-khir marveled at how such brilliance with martial training could be accompanied by such complete ignorance about anything political.

". . . and I asked him why my boys went from treating me like a fount of wisdom to treating me like a humiliating and utter moron."

Ra-khir huffed out a relieved sigh. "So it's not just me?"

"No, it's all parents. Apparently, we're all morons. For a while, at least."

Glad to find a logical and less personal reason for the change in his relationship with Saviar, Ra-khir glanced back toward the class. It did not appear as if the Knight's-Captain, or any of the Renshai students, had moved a muscle.

"So, do you think Saviar had a reason for wanting to accompany you? Or do you think he's just avoiding his lessons?"

Ra-khir pursed his lips, giving Saviar the benefit of his doubts. The boy did not have a history of dodging work or even difficult situations. Ra-khir suspected Saviar's newfound interest in the knighthood had more to do with the boy's request, but Ra-khir could not tell that to Kevral. It would upset her, probably wholly without cause. Likely, Saviar's attraction to the knights was merely part of the aforementioned "finding his place in the world." Eventually, his curiosity would wane, and it seemed beyond foolish to worry Kevral or give

Calistin another point on which to harass his already beleaguered older brother. "I trust Saviar's judgment, and he's not a shirker." Ra-khir added wistfully, "The boys spend so much time honing sword-craft, I rarely get to spend time with any of them. I'd really like him to come, if you don't mind."

Kevral nodded. Saying nothing, she drifted back toward her students, Ra-khir following in her wake, as always enjoying the view.

When Kevral returned, her expression gave away nothing. She pinned Saviar with her gaze. "You will practice."

Though not a question, Saviar replied as if it were, "At every dismount. I won't sleep until I've worked hard enough to satisfy you." Saviar knew it helped his case that he had performed so well in class that day.

"I'll see to that," Ra-khir promised, mounting Silver Warrior.

Kevral drew in a deep breath and released it.

Saviar felt as if his heart stopped beating for that moment, as if concerned to make noise and drown out his mother's decision.

"See that he does." Kevral made a dismissive gesture toward her eldest son before turning her attention to the rest of her class. "Again!" she commanded, sending the Renshai scrambling to repeat their last maneuver. From that moment, she showed no further interest in the knights or her son, though she surely kept track of their every movement by sound. No Renshai could remain entirely unaware of any nearby human, friend or foe.

Ra-khir reached out a hand, and Saviar caught it eagerly, before his sword-dedicated mother had a chance to change her mind.

CHAPTER 5

My actions vary with circumstances, but honor itself is not situational.
—*Knight-Captain Kedrin Ramytan's son*

A HEAVY BREEZE, wet with frost, caressed Saviar's sweat-soaked body, a cool and pleasant contrast to his overtaxed limbs and muscles cramped by hours astride a shared horse. Silver Warrior had a smooth, rolling gait; but that barely diminished the discomfort of bouncing on withers instead of settling into the comfortable hollow worn by nearly two decades of riding and softened by the stallion's age. Accustomed to free movement, and understanding that his life might depend upon his speed and agility, Saviar had cursed the stiffness that assaulted his backside upon dismounting. Nevertheless, he had forced himself to give his all to the sword practice he had promised his mother. Now, finished with both, he refused to limp as he approached his father and grandfather.

The knights perched on a deadfall, conversing softly. Both wore the requisite colors, their cloaks immaculate, their swords sheathed, and their hats perched at the proper, jaunty angle. Travel foods lay spread in front of them, but neither man had touched a morsel. Half-starved, Saviar marveled at their self-control as he crouched across from them, his own ardor for the meal unhidden. He could not keep his stare from the journey bread, dried fruit and jerky, the waterskins. Though nothing special, at the moment it seemed like an irresistible feast.

"You didn't have to wait for me," Saviar asserted, sucking back welling saliva before it emerged as drool.

"We did." Ra-khir gestured at the bounty. "To do otherwise would be impolite."

Saviar shook his head without argument. He had told them to start without him, but the knights' unmitigated honor would not allow them even then. Saviar wanted to tell them that he would have found no rudeness in their eating while he practiced, and that they could abandon formality in his presence; but either comment seemed unnecessary, perhaps even insulting. The knights' honor had nothing to do with Saviar and everything to do with the code by which they chose to live.

Saviar scooped up a piece of jerky and a hunk of bread, not wishing to delay their meal another moment. In the future, he decided, he would practice on a full stomach. He would find it painful and would, likely, vomit; but it would save his father and grandfather from suffering. In addition, it would please his mother who insisted they practice on all terrains, in twilight and high sun, in blizzards and even states of fever. "An enemy," she often reminded him, "will not plan an attack based on your comfort."

Though driven to shove everything into his mouth and swallow, Saviar forced himself to chew. Kevral had a point, though it seemed a bit excessive and silly at times. Other than the pirates on the Southern Sea, Saviar knew of no one poised to battle any of them, except perhaps his own brother. If Renshai went to war, they did so by choice, to aid the Béarnides in the pirate skirmishes. Until Arturo's disappearance, however, those had not seemed much of a threat.

Saviar waited until he had consumed the food in his hands at a reasonable pace before swallowing the last bite and speaking. "So what happened to Arturo? How did he go missing?"

Ra-khir washed his last bite down with a swallow of water. "He was aboard a harbor warship. Pirates slaughtered the entire crew." He lowered his head respectfully. "There were no survivors."

Saviar caught himself wiping his hands on his britches. Though they said nothing, he knew the knights did not approve. "Including Arturo?" He shook his head as he reached for the fruit. "Then why do they say he's just missing?"

"The ocean has sharks and scavengers." Kedrin spoke plainly, as if to an adult. Though he had wanted Ra-khir to temper his words around the other Renshai youths, he made no attempt to do so now with his grandson. No matter the Renshai definition, Kedrin clearly considered Saviar a man. "Not every body returned intact or at all. It would not be prudent to put a prince to pyre until his identity is certain."

Saviar seized a piece of dried fruit and put it in his mouth, chewing as he considered. Kedrin had basically said that Arturo's body might have floated ashore in pieces. The reality of that image leaped suddenly to the fore: sharp, jagged teeth ripping into the young man's flesh, streaming blood that attracted more of its ilk, tearing him to pieces. Saviar could only hope the prince was dead when he hit the water. He gave no thought to the young man's escort. The Renshai would have reveled in the battle, earned and celebrated their deaths against superior warriors or numbers. Saviar had enough experience to realize the rest of the world thought differently. Savoring the sweet aftertaste, he swallowed the fruit. "What was a young prince of Béarn doing aboard a ship facing off with pirates?"

Ra-khir smiled ever so slightly. And, though it seemed an odd reaction to their current conversation, Saviar believed he understood. His father always appreciated when Saviar thought beyond the mindset of a Renshai.

Kedrin responded again, "Until then, the pirates had taken only merchant vessels. *Seven* was supposed to sit in the harbor to protect the incoming tradesmen and scare the pirates from making landfall. No one imagined a bunch of thieves would dare attack a Béarnian warship directly. Even if they did, the defenses seemed impenetrable."

Saviar knew little about pirates other than that they stole from ships. For most of his life, they had worried the coast of Béarn, though in small numbers and infrequently. They seemed more of a nuisance than a clear threat. Yet Kedrin's expression told Saviar otherwise. Once a mere annoyance, the pirates had now grown into a serious problem. There was clearly more to Béarn's calling of the Knight's captain than just a mission of comfort to a grieving king and queen.

Saviar sat back on his haunches without reaching for more food. "This is critical, isn't it?"

Ra-khir pursed his lips. "The loss of a royal always is."

Saviar dismissed his father's words with a gesture. "I mean beyond that. Who are these pirates?"

"No one knows," Kedrin admitted. "Once dismissed as a greedy band of malcontents, they now seem to have become large and organized. They're clearly testing Béarn's defenses, not just stealing treasure."

"Someone is backing them," Ra-khir agreed. "A country at least. The question is who?"

Saviar froze, not liking what he heard. Neither his father nor his grandfather became distressed easily, and he had never heard either overstate a threat.

Kedrin shrugged. "Who, indeed?"

As the knights no longer seemed to need him as part of the conversation, Saviar returned his attention to eating. He did not have enough experience or knowledge to solve such a mystery, nor even to fully and clearly understand its significance.

Ra-khir rose, brushed crumbs from his lap, and bowed to his father. "Excuse me, please, Captain."

Kedrin dipped his head and made a majestic, but offhand, looping gesture that clearly granted the request.

Saviar smiled. These were the moments he loved, watching the knights perform routine acts with grandeur that made even tiny details seem important. He watched his father disappear into the brush, surely to relieve himself, then turned his attention to his grandfather.

Captain Kedrin grinned broadly at his grandson, showing teeth as brilliant as pearls that made a strange contrast to the dull, gap-toothed mouths of most of the populace. Like all knights, he cared for his body meticulously. "I'm proud of you, Saviar. Not every young man would volunteer for a mission this difficult. It won't be easy to face a friend who just lost a beloved brother, especially trained by a culture that doesn't look upon death as tragedy."

"Death in *battle*," Saviar corrected. The Renshai deemed succumbing to age, accident, or disease the direst of catastrophes, for it doomed one's soul to Hel. Only brave warriors killed in glorious combat could be chosen for Valhalla. "Though, in this case, your point stands. Prince Arturo did die in battle."

"Surely." Kedrin's blue-white eyes sparkled. "My point stands."

Cued by his grandfather's look, Saviar directed his thoughts back to Kedrin's original statement. His cheeks turned warm. "And I'm not sure I deserve your respect. I do plan to console Princess Marisole, but that's not the real reason I asked to come along."

"Oh?" Though an expression of interest, the word also carried a clear note of understanding. Kedrin, Saviar suspected, had known that all along.

The flush on Saviar's cheeks grew deeper. "Well, I . . . was hoping I might . . ." He spoke slowly, weighing his grandfather's reaction. ". . . get a chance to do some research." As the Knight-Captain showed nothing but curiosity, Saviar continued more boldly. "In the Sage's library."

"Ah." Kedrin encouraged his grandson to continue. He seemed to have wholly forgotten his dinner. "Well, this thing you need to know must be important for you to risk facing the Sage. He guards his scrolls and books with the ferocity of a she-bear with cubs."

Saviar winced. He had heard as much, but he had never directly faced the Sage in his tower. Charged with keeping all the knowledge in the kingdom, the Sage had an army of pages granted access to every event or occurrence, no matter how embarrassing or secret. To deny them would incur the wrath of ancient law, a crime as unthinkable as slaying a messenger or a man calling parley in battle. He lived in the tower with his many chronicles, writing them into history and rewriting the oldest, crumbling pages. "Well . . ." Saviar kneaded a dried apple between his fingers. "I'm just wanting one piece of information. The Sage might know it without me having to touch any of his treasured papers."

Kedrin shifted, leaning toward Saviar. "What is it you want to know?"

It suddenly occurred to Saviar that he had found the perfect source for his answer, and he felt like a dullard for not considering Kedrin sooner. If anyone knew the answer, the captain of the Knights of Erythane would. "Papa said there's a man who is both Renshai and Knight, and I'm trying to find out who this remarkable fellow might be."

Kedrin sat back with a wry laugh. "Well, you needn't trouble the Sage at all. If your father told you it was a man who held this distinction, he misled you."

Startled, Saviar tried to recall Ra-khir's exact wording. When it did not come, he leaped to his father's defense. "I don't remember exactly how Papa put it." His exoneration could only go so far, however. "He may not have said 'man,' but he certainly didn't say 'woman.' I would have remembered that." Saviar turned his attention directly on his grandfather, the apple forgotten in his hand. Renshai women fought alongside their men, learning the same sword techniques from birth; but theirs was a society much misunderstood and maligned. Even the other Northern tribes would never think to send their women to war. Not that it never happened. Every civilization seemed to have a story about one woman who distinguished herself in swordsmanship, either while disguised or against the comprehension or wishes of her people.

"Oh, dear." Kedrin screwed up his features self-deprecatingly. "Now I've misled you further. As you know, the Knights of Erythane have strict codes of honor. Only males may serve the kings in this manner."

"Male, but not a man." Understanding dawned slowly. "It's Colbey, isn't it?"

Kedrin nodded with a smile.

As he contemplated his own words, Saviar's brow gradually lapsed into wrinkles. "Colbey Calistinsson? An immortal, so not a man. The ideal Renshai, certainly. But a Knight of Erythane?" Saviar shook his head in disbelief. From what he knew, Colbey had little tolerance for *ganim*. He found them slow and awkward, focused on the superficial and easy. "How can that be?"

Kedrin ran a hand through a thick head of silver hair, speckled with strands of its previous red-gold. He straightened his tabard, adjusted his sword, and settled into a position better suited to comfort than defense.

Though it bothered his Renshai sensibilities, and Saviar found himself locked into a crouch unable to buck his own training, he did not judge his grandfather. He stuffed the chunk of dried apple into his mouth and chewed.

Ra-khir returned from his errand, his clothing and grooming immaculate. Though he had brushed through weeds and trees, not a bit of leaf, twig, or seed marred the image. He studied his father and his son briefly, clearly to ascertain whether or not he could speak without interrupting. As both men fell silent at his entrance, he uttered the first words, "Did I miss anything?"

Suddenly feeling guilty for finding such an easy solution to his father's challenge, Saviar dodged Ra-khir's gaze.

Kedrin nodded toward Ra-khir, then Saviar, in turn. "I was just preparing to tell the story of Sir Colbey Calistinsson."

Ra-khir turned his son a searching look that held a hint of disapproval. "This isn't exactly what I meant when I said you should use your studies to find the answer."

Staring at his boots, Saviar sought words to explain. His father had not expressly told him not to ask Kedrin, and he had planned to get the information from the Sage before the Knight Captain volunteered it.

Kedrin rescued his grandson. "Sir Ra-khir, what better way to research than to ask the person most likely to know the correct answer?"

Ra-khir back stepped with a majestic gesture of respect directed at his captain. "Well, yes, Captain. Of course, sir." He bowed. "I only meant that running to one's grandfather for help does not require the same intensity and effort as finding the information on one's own."

Saviar watched the exchange in quiet amusement. For most of his life, the paternal side of his heritage had hampered him. His physical size and broad musculature hindered his agility, and many Renshai considered the Knights of Erythane stiff, stodgy objects of ridicule. For once, it felt good to have a man of Kedrin's rank and experience on his side.

"Well, Sir Ra-khir, when one's grandfather also happens to be the best source of information about a certain topic, why should one be penalized simply because he happens to be one's grandfather?" Kedrin's pale brows arched. "Any other man's child would be considered brave and wise to bring such a question to me."

Saviar considered mentioning that he had not actually asked Kedrin, only informed the captain that he planned to research the answer in the Sage's library. Instead, he held his tongue. Kedrin was handling the matter quite ably without his meddling.

Ra-khir opened his mouth, then closed it. He raised a hand as if making a point, started to speak, then stopped again without a sound emerging.

Saviar continued to study his feet. It might humiliate Ra-khir if Saviar seemed to take too much amusement from his father's obvious discomfort.

Finally, Ra-khir heaved a sigh. "Captain, I request permission to speak freely."

Kedrin did not hesitate. "Granted. Consider yourself off-duty, my son." His brows remained high, showing curiosity for the words Ra-khir had not managed to find a polite way to speak.

Ra-khir's shoulders relaxed. Though his dress remained fastidious, as always, the transition to a looser, informal stance was obvious even to Saviar. "Why is it when I bring you a question, I get riddles and enigma? When Saviar asks, he gets instant solutions and entertaining stories."

Kedrin laughed, and Saviar found himself smiling despite his best intentions. His grandfather spent so much time immersed in formality and vital matters of country that Saviar rarely saw or heard him relax. "First, Ra-khir, perhaps Saviar asks better questions." He winked, though whether at son or grandson, Saviar was not sure. "Second, he's not training to become a Knight of Erythane. And third . . . well, you'll understand when you become a grandfather."

Ra-khir shook his head with a grin, looked away from his captain and rolled his eyes. "As to your third point, Father, more riddles. I won't argue the first because I think it pertains to the third. But I will take exception to the second." He turned his attention to Saviar, much to the boy's chagrin. "It is exactly because Saviar is considering becoming a knight that he asked about Sir Colbey in the first place."

A light seemed to fill Kedrin's face, and his eyes sparkled. Saviar expected his grandfather to ply him with questions about the seriousness of his intentions. Surely he wished to do so, but he remained true to the conversation instead. "It would seem to me, then, that

Saviar should know the extraordinary details of Colbey's story before he makes such a difficult and momentous decision."

Their discussion forced Saviar into consideration. Many times he had wished he had pursued knighthood rather than the intense and single-minded Renshai training. Until his recent discussion with his father, however, he had accepted the lot his parents had given him. It had never occurred to him that becoming both was possible. The fact that Colbey had done so barely seemed reason to change his mind. The immortal Renshai had performed many feats no one else had accomplished, before or since.

Uncomfortable beneath the sudden scrutiny of father and grandfather, Saviar cleared his throat. "So, Grandpapa. Tell me about Sir Colbey."

Ra-khir sat, Kedrin resumed his position of comfort, and Saviar remained in his Renshai-wary crouch.

"It all began more than three hundred years ago, in the reigns of King Sterrane of Béarn and King Orlis of Erythane. Though nearly eighty, Colbey Calistinsson appeared much younger, with an agility and speed beyond even those one usually associates with men your age." Kedrin waved a hand in Saviar's general direction.

Saviar seized upon the pause. "Because he was immortal."

"Yes," Kedrin said, though a twist in his tone suggested it was only half an admission. "And because he kept himself as well as any man can. At the time, he did not know the blood of Thor ran in his veins. No one did."

Saviar nodded, understanding those details well, as all Renshai. As it turned out, Colbey had not known either of his blood parents. His Renshai mother had died in battle, the baby plucked from her womb by Sif and placed in one otherwise barren. He had no siblings; and Colbey still considered the man and woman who raised him, Ranhilda and Calistin, his only true parents.

Kedrin continued, "The Great War was over, the West victorious over the mighty armies of the Eastlands. The scourge of the North had left the Renshai tribe with only two living members; and, of the two, only Colbey survived the War."

Saviar spoke from his Renshai history lessons, "The other was Rache, right? The *Einherjar* who gave Mama her sword."

Kedrin nodded. "And Colbey was traveling through Erythane with a boy about your age, also named Rache as I recall." He looked askance at Ra-khir, who bobbed his head in assent.

Again, history filled in the gaps for Saviar. Modern Renshai consisted of three tribes, each descended from a couple from the era of Kedrin's story. The first, the tribe of Modrey, his mother's tribe, carried the most ancient Renshai blood. The tribe of Rache, the boy in Kedrin's story, initially carried no true Renshai bloodline. Rache's mother, Mitrian, had married Tannin, the patriarch of the third, half-blood tribe. As this information did not seem significant to the story, however, Saviar kept it to himself and gave his grandfather an encouraging look.

"Rache wound up dueling with and killing a young apprentice knight named Shalfon."

"Killing?" The word startled out before Saviar could think to stifle it.

"Killing," Kedrin repeated. "Duels to the death were a lot more common in those days, and it is likely that Shalfon set that end point as a condition of the challenge."

Kedrin's open-mindedness pleased Saviar. Most would automatically condemn the outcome as a Renshai succumbing to his violent nature.

"In the process of cheering on his charge, Colbey insulted the boy's father, Brignar, resulting in a second duel. There is ambiguity over who actually initiated the challenge, but history records that it was fought immediately and with swords, which suggests that Colbey did."

Saviar had to agree with the assumption. Knights displayed far more patience than Renshai, and ancient knights, especially, preferred mounted combat with pikes.

"In any case, there is no doubt that Colbey won the battle handily, badly humiliating his opponent in the process." Kedrin looked at Ra-khir, who frowned sourly.

Sensing a scandal, Saviar understood his grandfather's hesitation. Yet his own Renshai impatience won out over courtesy. "What happened next?"

Kedrin sighed but dutifully continued, "I'm afraid Brignar did something . . . unchivalrous."

Knowing Colbey as every Renshai did, Saviar guessed. "Colbey taunted Brignar, didn't he?" A likely scenario came to the fore. "Oh! He turned his back on his enemy."

"The ultimate gesture of a warrior's disdain, yes."

Saviar presumed the rest, gasping at the enormity of Brignar's infraction. "And Brignar attacked him? From behind?"

Kedrin grimaced. "I'm afraid so."

The rest was obvious. Colbey would not have forgiven the crime. "And died." Saviar's brow furrowed. After that, the trail of understanding broke. "But how . . . ? Why would the Knights of Erythane want Colbey to . . . after he just killed . . . ?" He studied his grandfather's striking features, sucked in by the utter pallor of those white-blue eyes. *Do my eyes really look like that?*

"It was old law," Kedrin explained. "Long established and only changed within my lifetime." He casually fixed a crease in his sleeve. "When a man bested a knight in fair combat, he earned the knight's position. Once he pledged himself to Erythane and Béarn, he received the position, title, and steed."

"Frost Reaver." Saviar had long known the name and color of Colbey's beloved stallion. It had always seemed strange that a Renshai would choose to ride a beast of such standout brightness, yet Saviar had simply dismissed that as one of the many oddities of Colbey Calistinsson. "Could that be the same horse?"

"It is." Ra-khir blurted, then covered his mouth, eyes wide.

Kedrin only laughed at the interruption. "You're off-duty, Ra-khir. Feel free to speak your mind, even if it is ill-timed."

Ignoring the obvious sarcasm, Ra-khir obeyed. "Like the gods, he eats the apples of Idun to stay forever young. I've ridden him."

Now it was Saviar's turn to barge in without thinking. "You've *ridden* Frost Reaver! You've ridden *Colbey Calistinsson's* horse!" Kedrin's story no longer mattered. Saviar had to know. "When? How?" He did not leave time for answers before adding accusingly, "How come you never told us?"

Ra-khir shrugged and flushed and smiled simultaneously. "The time was never right."

"And now?" Saviar could not let the matter rest. He wondered how many other incredible things his father had never found the right time to tell him.

"If you wish." Ra-khir studied his own mount, grazing pleasantly on moss and leaf sprouts. He had not bothered to tie the stallion; Silver Warrior would not stray. "When Colbey embarked on his mission to save the world, he gave me Frost Reaver."

"*Gave* you . . . ?" Saviar's voice cracked.

"When Colbey survived despite even his own expectations, I gave him back his horse." Ra-khir winked. "There're few things more pitiful than a pleading immortal, especially a Renshai immortal."

Saviar dropped to his haunches, shocked silent. He had heard about his parents' exploits, their missions to rescue the West, his mother's visit to Valhalla. He also knew that Kevral and Ra-khir had fallen in love during these deadly excursions. But he had never heard that his father had a personal relationship with the Renshai's most cherished hero. Unable to wrap his mind around this stunning admission, he pushed his thoughts back to one he might. "So Colbey . . . pledged his allegiance . . . to Erythane and Béarn?"

"Shocking, isn't it?" Whether Kedrin referred to Ra-khir's admission or Saviar's question, he did not know. "Colbey did so swear in an informal ceremony before the King of Erythane. Remember, at that time, he was pledged to help protect the Westlands anyway, and he trusted the man who became Béarn's greatest king. Sterrane and Colbey were close friends."

Saviar took the information a step further, "And Colbey was nearly eighty years old. He couldn't possibly have guessed he would go on to live another three hundred years." The implications seemed staggering. "So . . . has anyone ever called him in to fulfill his knightly pledge?"

Ra-khir grinned viciously. "He's never taken guard duty, if that's what you mean. Colbey's title is not commonly known, even among the Knights of Erythane."

"To my knowledge, no one has called Colbey in for any reason, then or since." Kedrin put a more serious spin on the question, "Who would dare?"

Who, indeed? Saviar wondered, yet he also knew that in times of great trouble men sometimes resorted to desperate measures.

CHAPTER 6

Leadership can be taught, and wisdom can be gained; but character comes only from the heart.
—*Knight-Captain Kedrin Ramytan's son*

THE STORY OF SIR COLBEY Calistinsson consumed Saviar's thoughts as the three men traversed the highway between Erythane and the mountain kingdom of Béarn. It seemed odd to the young Renshai that he continued to mull the details long after reality sprang to the fore and begged dismissal of the whole idea. The fact that Colbey had accomplished some feat made it no less impossible, and even the great hero of the Renshai had fallen into this situation wholly by accident.

So, Colbey had killed a man, one of hundreds or, more likely, thousands. He had lived in a much different era: when a Renshai's adult status was determined by a kill, not competence with a test. History spoke of a time when, banished from their Northern homeland for barbarism, the Renshai had wandered through the West and East, slaughtering for supplies or, merely, for fun. War was a Renshai's life, his satisfaction, and his glee. And it had stoked a hatred that existed even to this day, centuries after its inception and long after the Renshai had turned to more peaceful means of obtaining their necessities.

It was during this period of isolation and exile that Colbey had been born and raised, and he brought the flavor of his upbringing into his adulthood. With a bargain and a battle, the Renshai tribe had regained a piece of the North, from that point on referred to as Devil's Island. Bitter about their loss, the combined armies of the North had attacked the island in the dead of night, slaughtering nearly every Renshai. Only much later, the shattered remnants of the Renshai had re-formed in the West from the three tribes, only one of which had a full complement of original Renshai blood. *The tribe of Modrey. My mother's tribe.*

Now riding behind his father, on Silver Warrior's broad rump, Saviar strained new muscles and let the scenery scroll by without notice. His swords tapped his legs with every stride in a steady pattern: left, right; left right. He appreciated their touch; without them, he felt as naked as any Renshai would. He sighed, understanding the improbability of his double dream yet unable to let it go. He wondered why Ra-khir had fueled his desire by using Colbey's status as both Renshai and knight to whet his son's curiosity. Even the immortal Renshai had not undergone the intensive training currently required by the Knights of Erythane.

Kedrin, Ra'khir, and Saviar had passed several other travelers on their way to Béarn. Most stepped aside with courteous bows for knights as respected as the Renshai were reviled. Now, as they topped a low rise, Saviar glimpsed a wagon around his father's broad back. It sat, lopsided, by the roadside. Freed from its traces, the horse grazed the ditches. Two ragged men stood in the center of the roadway, waving at the knights.

"What's this?" Ra-khir whispered.

Knight-Captain Kedrin murmured just as quietly. "Someone appears to need our assistance."

The knights reined their steeds in front of the men, who immediately started bowing and bobbing, as if facing royalty.

Saviar's troubling thoughts disappeared, replaced by sudden curiosity. He said nothing, taking his cues from his father and grandfather. They had a job of vast import awaiting them in Béarn, a summons from the king to obey. They could not afford to allow a simple broken wheel to delay them, yet they seemed prepared to do so. Curious where the path of honor would lead them, Saviar watched in silence.

"My lords," one called, a tall lean man with a mop of sand-colored hair and skin darkened by the sun.

Before he could finish, the other cut in. "My lords, my lords." He bowed deeply, his arms scarred and thick, his face craggy. Though better than average height, he still fell short of his lanky companion; and he sported tightly trimmed dark hair.

Perhaps to forestall an endless stream of greetings, Kedrin did not wait for the men to make a request. "Do you need help fashioning another wheel?"

"No, sir!" the second one said swiftly, with a tone akin to horror. "We would not ask your esteemed selves to assist with such a menial chore—"

"Rather," the first interrupted, his Adam's apple bobbing in his slender throat. "We wondered if you could save us the full trip to Béarn."

The second cut in again, his tone suggesting that he found the other man's gall upsetting. "Not that we deserve such consideration . . . but we understand the Knights of Erythane . . ." He paused with a deep swallow, as if prepared for his companion to leap in before he finished, just as he had done.

The sandy-haired man went quiet and allowed the other to complete his thought. Saviar forced himself not to smile. Their juggling act between desire and concern for offense amused him.

". . . are wise and fair judges of conflict." He added swiftly, sweat visibly beading on his face, "We understand that we are not worthy of those most beloved and trusted by kings, but . . ."

Kedrin tried to help. "But our time is less valuable than King Griff's, and you're hoping to spare him the need to listen to your dispute in the royal courtroom."

The dark-haired man pulled at his collar, and his grimace softened to a hopeful grin. "Well, yes, sir. Only if you agree, sirs. Despite my neighbor's words, we're not concerned for our need to travel, only for wasting His Majesty's precious time." A flush covered the tips of his cheekbones. "Not that I think your time isn't of great import, sirs, as well."

Kedrin replied agreeably. "Only less so than that of the king." He did not await an answer. "A fine and noble thought that does not require explanation." Removing his plumed hat, Kedrin performed a grand flourish. Saviar finally allowed himself a smile, this time in admiration. He had seen both knights make gestures of this magnitude before, but they never ceased to amaze him. "I am Captain Kedrin, son of Ramytan, Knight to the Erythanian and Béarnian kings: His Grace, King Humfreet, and His Majesty, King Griff."

The peasants executed bows that looked awkward after Kedrin's display. The dark-haired one with the scarred arms answered first, "Honored captain, my name is Eshwin, and I'm a breeder of fine horses." His gaze drifted to the white chargers for the first time, and he gave a nod of appreciation.

"Tirro," the other said, giving another long-legged bow. "I'm his neighbor, a farmer."

Saviar watched intently, uncertain where to expect the proceedings to go and glad he did not have to make the decision. Though dismissed as simple by most Renshai, the honor of the knights was filled with ethical conflicts and dilemmas on a daily basis. It seemed ignoble to discharge the problems of even a lowly peasant without fair hearing, yet the captain of the Knights of Erythane could not spend his every waking moment judging every decision of the underclass. Glad he was not the Knight-Captain, Saviar felt content to watch without preconceived notions or expectations.

Unlike Saviar, Kedrin seemed unburdened by doubts. "I will grant your request," he said, "but only if you agree to two conditions. I will cite them, and you both may decide whether you will abide by all or none. If either of you refuses, no judgment shall be rendered."

The peasants glanced at one another with a mixture of excitement and trepidation.

"First," Kedrin said, his voice booming, his presence strong and overwhelming, "You will both agree to accept whatever decision we make, without stipulation or question."

The men nodded swiftly but said nothing. Tirro shuffled nervously from foot to foot.

"Second," Kedrin said, in the same grand voice, "this is not a matter worthy of a captain or a well-established knight, so I will put the matter before the youngest of us. Our knight-in-training."

Shocked as much by the title as the realization that his grandfather had just put the onus on him, Saviar felt a wave of terror strike him. He froze, unable to speak, his mind stammering denials that never made it into words.

Tirro's gaze went to Saviar. "I agree to these terms."

"As do I." Kedrin's proclamation clearly did not bother Eshwin. Neither seemed to notice the abject horror that held Saviar dumb and unmoving.

"Very well." Kedrin motioned to the men again, not bothering to look at the effect his words had on his grandson. "State your cases. Eshwin first, please."

It all happened so quickly, Saviar had no time to think or protest. Before he knew it, the short man cleared his throat and began: "Three years ago, I bought a well-marked mare of sound confirmation and quality at a rather hefty price. I had obtained a magnificent stallion previously, and I intended to become a breeder. After the second season without a foal, however, I declared my only mare barren."

Kedrin looked at Tirro. "Do you agree so far?"

Tirro gave one long nod. "I do, sir."

Saviar's mind raced. He forced himself to focus on every word and tried to ignore the pounding of his heart, the worry that turned his mouth dry as cotton. He had no time to consider his grandfather's motives, only to concentrate on the details coming at him at galloping-horse speed.

Eshwin continued, "My neighbor had recently lost his elderly plow horse and asked where he could find a replacement. My mare seemed worthless to me, so I sold her to him at a pittance . . ."

Tirro frowned and shook his head.

Apparently catching his neighbor's reaction from the corner of his eye, Eshwin amended. "Well, a pittance compared to her initial price, anyway. A quality broodmare is worth so much more than a plow horse, but nothing if she can't conceive."

A pause ensued, and Kedrin filled it. "You were both content with this initial agreement?"

"Yes, sir." Tirro bobbed his head dutifully.

Eshwin's lips twisted. "Not exactly thrilled, Captain, but resigned. A horse breeder is nothing without foals, and it would take me years of odd-jobbing to raise the money for a new broodmare. At least, this gave me a start."

"So," Kedrin clarified. "Not a happy contract, but a legitimate one."

This time, they both shrugged, nodded.

Saviar clung to each word, nuance, and demonstrated emotion. Thus far, he had heard nothing that required judging. He hoped his silence made him look wise and pensive rather than terrified.

"Until the birth of the filly," Eshwin said.

"Ah." Apparently, it all became clear in that moment to Kedrin.

Saviar needed more. "So she was not barren after all."

"No, sir." Eshwin glanced sidelong at his neighbor. "I feel the foal should be mine. Without my stallion, she would not exist; and I sold the mare for the price of a barren horse."

"She's mine," Tirro said. "I bought her mother for a fair price we agreed upon. I owned the mare at the time of the birth, and the filly was born on my farm."

"At the least," Eshwin added, "he should pay a studding fee."

"Should I pay a studding fee when I never contracted for a foal? I didn't want her."

"Then give her to me."

The neighbors glared at one another as they veered onto old ground. They had clearly argued these same points, without acceptable compromise.

Replacing his hat, Kedrin turned his attention to his grandson. "It would seem, Saviar, that the time for judgment has arrived."

Saviar swallowed hard and dismounted. He executed both gestures as delay, but they gave him too little time to think. His legs ached from the long ride. He wanted to make a just decision, to please his father and grandfather; yet he also worried that he might thwart the law or make a grave mistake. "I . . ." he started, pacing to avoid looking anyone in the eye. ". . . believe the law sides with Tirro. With ownership of the mare goes possession of every internal working part of her." He stopped to glance at Eshwin. "One does not sell a chicken and expect to get back the eggs."

"But . . ." Eshwin started, forestalled by Kedrin's frown and Saviar's raised hand.

"However . . ." Saviar felt sweat trickle down the front of his tunic. "Laws are constructed to handle general cases and cannot consider every specific to which they might apply." He finally dared to look at Ra-khir who showed him nothing. At least, he did not look aghast. Saviar stopped in front of Tirro. "You care for your neighbor, don't you?"

Tirro's eyes widened, and he nodded vigorously. "Oh, yes, sir."

"You know Eshwin sold you the mare only because he believed her barren. Can you not forgive him his mistake?"

"Forgive?" Tirro blinked, clearly befuddled by the wording. "It is not a matter of—"

Saviar did not allow him to finish, turning instead to Eshwin. "And can you understand why your friend claims the foal as his?"

"Of course." Unlike the farmer, Eshwin showed no confusion or hesitancy. "She's valuable. An unexpected windfall."

Saviar turned his back for a moment to consult the knights. Both watched with expressions of mild curiosity and nothing more. Apparently, they wanted him to handle the judgment on his own; and they would not interfere, even with subtle hints.

As Saviar expected, the farmer defended himself from the suggestion of a selfish motivation. "No. He has it wrong. It's not the money I'm after, not really."

Like Saviar, Eshwin turned his full attention to the farmer. Clearly, the breeder had either never heard the upcoming explanation or had never truly listened.

"It's just that giving birth puts my plow horse out of commission for at least six weeks. I'll need the money I get selling the filly to rent another plow horse."

Saviar started to speak, but Eshwin interrupted. "Is that what's bothering you?"

Tirro stiffened, clearly startled by the question. He turned toward the horse breeder. "Of course."

Saviar glanced at the broken wagon, then at the horse, grazing placidly on roadside brush. Sunlight sheened red highlights from well-groomed chestnut fur, and its long tail and clipped mane looked combed and clean despite the journey. It had a thick chest and muscled legs. "Whose horse is this?"

The two men's gazes followed Saviar's.

"That's my stallion," Eshwin said with clear pride. "Beautiful, isn't he?"

"Yes," Saviar agreed, an idea coming to him suddenly. "Handsome. And mannered, too."

Eshwin fairly beamed.

"Can he . . . pull a plow?"

Eshwin made a dismissive noise. "Of course he can pull a plow. He can do anything." Suddenly realizing where Saviar was going, he smiled at Tirro. "Would you . . . ? Would you like . . . to borrow him?"

Tirro continued to study the stallion. "You . . . would let me? He's your pride and joy."

"I can spare him for six weeks or so. He's a good, calm horse who will do as you ask."

Saviar glanced at Ra-khir and thought he saw a slight smile playing at the corners of his father's lips. *Is it a grin or a grimace?* Doubt assailed Saviar, but he refused to show it to the strangers. "It seems we have found an equitable solution, then. The filly belongs to Eshwin at the moment of its weaning, and he will provide for any upkeep beyond mother's milk prior to that time. In exchange, Tirro will get full use of the stallion for his farm until the mare can return to work. In the future, you may wish to make mutually agreeable arrangements for breeding the stallion and mare again."

Saviar waited in a tense silence that seemed to stretch into an eternity. The solution appeared fair to him, but he might not truly understand enough details of farming or breeding to see a glaring problem.

"Thank you, young knight-in-training!" Eshwin said with clear enthusiasm.

Tirro took a bit longer to decide whether or not he liked the compromise, then finally smiled crookedly. "Supremely fair, young man. You'll make a fine knight some day."

Saviar's cheeks reddened at the compliment. "You're welcome, kind sirs." Uncertain what to do next, he half-walked, half-backed to his father and accepted a hand up to the charger's rump.

The knights' horses took off at a gentle lope, soon leaving the farmer and breeder behind. Saviar cringed, awaiting his father's assessment. The neighbors were happy with his ruling, but he had no way of knowing whether or not he had found the right solution by the rigid moral code of the Knights of Erythane.

Ra-khir gave his son nothing. They traveled in a silence broken only by hoofbeats, birdsong, and the occasional animal snort. Finally, Saviar could stand it no longer. "Did I handle that . . . well enough?"

"You did fine, Saviar," Ra-khir said without zeal. "You did very well."

Kedrin cut in, his tone filled with all the excitement Ra-khir's lacked. "What your father means, Saviar, is you did a magnificent job."

"Captain," Ra-khir said warningly.

But Kedrin ignored his own son to continue lauding Ra-khir's. "You knew the law and cited it, but you also realized that the men in this case were bound by it only if they could not agree on another solution. Then, you steered them toward one that worked."

Ra-khir spoke his piece, "A bit too directly, though, Captain, don't you think?"

Kedrin laughed. "Maybe. But this was Saviar's first judgment, and he handled it very well. Had this been a test, he would have passed."

"Yes." Ra-khir's tone remained flat. "Had it been."

Saviar remained as quiet as possible, certain he had no direct role in this discussion, even though he was the subject of it. The two older men had always seemed perfect friends as well as father and son, closely allied in word, thought, and deed. He had never heard them argue.

Kedrin went straight to the point, "What's bothering you, Ra-khir?"

Ra-khir considered his reply. Behind him, Saviar saw the stiffening of his back and shoulders while he thought. Then, Ra-khir spoke with measured caution, the hostility leaving his tone. "Are we talking captain to subordinate? Or father to son?"

Kedrin reined his mount directly beside Silver Warrior, and they walked along in tandem. "Father and son, then?"

"Fine." Ra-khir continued to look straight forward, toward the mountains that defined the city of Béarn. "Papa, with all due respect, I don't wish to talk about it now."

"Ah." A smile played across Kedrin's lips, and he winked at Saviar. "Then, perhaps, *Sir* Ra-khir, we had best go the captain to subordinate route."

Ra-khir finally turned his gaze to Kedrin, and his posture further stiffened. Saviar wished he could see his father's expression. "Captain, with all due respect, I don't find this subject appropriate for children."

Kedrin threw glances in every direction. "And I, Sir Ra-khir, don't see any children."

"Saviar—"

Kedrin interrupted, a rudeness he rarely indulged in. "—is of age, Sir Ra-khir."

"Not by the tenets of his own people."

Saviar bit his lip and scowled. The reminder hurt.

"We," Kedrin said with clear warning, "are not Renshai. By our standards, and those of the kingdoms we serve, Saviar is a man."

Ra-khir did not argue. Not only was Kedrin's point undeniable truth, it would gain him nothing. "Yes, sir. But I don't feel this is a topic appropriate to discuss in his presence."

"I want to hear it," Saviar blurted out, immediately cursing himself for the indiscretion. His best strategy was to remain silent. *Better to look the fool,* an old Erythanian proverb stated, *then speak foolishly.* He tried to fix the damage. "If it involves me, I should know."

Kedrin inclined his head toward Saviar without losing the rakish angle of his hat. "The young man has a point, has he not?"

Ra-khir's words emerged stilted, clearly spoken through gritted teeth. "It is not always in a man's best interests, Captain, to know every word spoken about him."

Saviar no longer thought it best to keep quiet. He knew he could gain the advantage with appropriate outrage. "You mean you're going to speak ill of me? My own father?"

"No, no," Ra-khir cringed, half-turning in his saddle. "Saviar, I wouldn't ever speak ill of you. There is nothing ill to speak. You're a boy . . ." He amended, "A man of great talent and caring nature. I am proud of you every moment of every day."

Saviar hammered the point home. "Then why can't you speak freely in front of me?"

Cornered, Ra-khir groaned politely. "Very well, Saviar. Captain." His shoulders slumped ever so slightly, as if he wanted to collapse but could not because it might belittle the uniform of the Knights of Erythane. "I just feel Saviar gets enough pressure from his mother without us adding to his burden."

Kedrin urged gently, "What do you mean?"

"I mean she's always after him to perform his best, rain or shine, day or night, well or sick."

"What's wrong with that, Sir Ra-khir?"

It was not the question Saviar expected. He stared at his grand-father, who presented him with another wink.

"Nothing, in theory, Captain. But it's a lot of stress for a child, especially when he's always getting compared with a brother who has the—" Ra-khir stopped with an uncomfortable suddenness. "—who has a unique amount of . . . uncanny . . . natural . . . ability."

"It is the life you chose for him, Ra-khir."

Saviar mulled his grandfather's words, his brow knitting. They seemed to hold an inordinate meaning for the knights that he did not understand. He supposed it referred to his father's decision to marry a Renshai, yet Ra-khir's prolonged hush made it appear to carry even more weight.

"Yes," Ra-khir finally said. "And I knew there would be times when I regretted it. Yet . . ." Now he gave Kedrin his full attention. ". . . I don't think, Captain, that we should add to the boy's . . ." Again, he corrected himself, ". . . the young man's burden by expect-ing him to mimic the accomplishments of an immortal."

"Ah."

"Especially Colbey Calistinsson, who didn't even undergo the in-tensive training of the Knights of Erythane, in addition to those of the Renshai."

"Do you think he couldn't have?"

"I don't know, Captain. I doubt he would have spared the time; but that's not my point." Ra-khir dropped a hand from the reins to smooth the fabric of his knight's tunic. "I just think we should allow Saviar to relax on the rare occasions we manage to pry him off the Fields of Wrath."

Kedrin chuckled.

The sound seemed so out of place, Saviar jerked his attention fully to the Knight-Captain.

Ra-khir tensed again, looking askance at his father. "Did I say something amusing, Captain?"

"Indeed, Sir Ra-khir. Did you think a journey to console the sib-lings of a lost young prince could be seen as a pleasure outing?"

Saviar saw the grim humor in the situation, and he knew Ra-khir must, too.

"Well, no, Captain," Ra-khir admitted. "There is that aspect of the trip. But I rather thought . . . I mean I wanted . . ." He seemed unable to complete the thought.

So Kedrin helped him. "We can learn from every experience, no matter how small. Don't you want the chance to guide your son on different paths than just the one his mother chose for him? You lose that if you decide only to play with him, to avoid the difficult events and discussions in his presence."

Saviar realized the conversation had progressed to levels he did not quite understand. The words conjured only images of Tae's relationship with Subikahn. In his youth, Saviar had envied the playfulness of his twin's father, how Tae had turned every interaction with the boys into a merry game. In the Eastlands, they had had no worries, no responsibilities. If anything negative ever happened in that kingdom, the twins remained blissfully ignorant. Tae seemed steadfast in assuring that nothing of import ever troubled his only son, nothing disagreeable ever marred their perfect bond. Now, Saviar eagerly awaited Ra-khir's response; but, when it came, it surprised him.

"This isn't about me and Saviar anymore, is it, Captain?"

Saviar's muscles locked in spasm. *They read my mind.*

Kedrin, too, looked taken aback momentarily, then smiled. "I suppose there is a bit else mixed in there, Ra-khir. We are a product of our experiences, no matter how hard we try to escape them."

His grandfather's words cued Saviar to the realization that they were referring not to Tae, but to Ra-khir's clownish stepfather.

"Biased or not, my point is still valid," Kedrin insisted. "Every life experience changes us. Why shouldn't I want the best for my grandsons?"

"You should, Captain." Ra-khir continued to emphasize the knightly relationship long after they had already reverted to a father/son conversation. "But is overburdening him with options and decisions really 'best'?"

Saviar felt the need to cut in. "I'm not overburdened. I want to know what it's like to be a Knight of Erythane in training."

"Did you like it," Ra-khir said stiffly, "when your grandfather asked you to make a judgment in the king's place?"

Saviar flushed, then told the truth. "It scared me to death." He added quickly, "But I'm used to getting put in difficult situations, and I felt great when I realized I actually . . . handled it . . ." He turned to doubtful questioning. ". . . all right? Didn't I?"

Kedrin reassured. "You handled it very well. In fact, you demonstrate an impressive natural kindness, empathy, and sense of fairness. You have great potential for knighthood."

Ra-khir's stiffness became so intense it looked painful. He might gainsay his father but never his captain. "Please, Captain. Don't encourage him."

"Why not?" Saviar and Kedrin said in tandem, though the knight tacked on a "Sir Ra-khir."

Ra-khir sighed deeply, then shook his head. He drew breath, and Saviar awaited a lecture. Surely, his father would remind him how exhausting Renshai or knight training was on its own, how few managed either. He would have to pass his Renshai testing before he could even consider becoming a knight-in-training, and none of his Renshai peers could possibly understand why he would attempt both. They would tease him viciously; and even the knight-apprentices might ostracize him.

But Ra-khir did not lecture; he did not need to. "You say I'll understand when I'm a grandfather? I'll truly understand?"

Kedrin only laughed.

CHAPTER 7

Babies are born innocent, without preconceived notions or preju-dice. They have only needs. They love the ones who satisfy their needs, their parents. Blood does not become significant until their minds become warped by societal bigotry.

—Sir Ra-khir Kedrin's son

DEW COATED THE HEDGE of prickles, the sawgrass, and the random array of rocks and twigs that littered the central courtyard of the king's palace in Stalmize. Prince Subikahn leaped and danced through obstacles that made the gardeners shudder every time they had to tend the area. His sword cut bold arcs through the air, leaving a wake of flashing silver. Silently, his *torke,* Talamir, watched every movement, his expression unreadable.

Subikahn drove into the last maneuver, his sword low, his legs flexed. Silky black hair spilled into eyes nearly as dark, with just a hint of his mother's blue. The sword made a shining contrast against the deep olive of his skin. He held the position for what seemed like forever, waiting for his *torke* to speak.

"Beautiful," Talamir finally said.

"Thank you." Subikahn slammed his sword back into its sheath. "Now what did you think of my *svergelse?*"

Talamir laughed. "You did a fine job, Kahn. You'll definitely pass."

"You're sure?" Though he knew he had performed well for several months now, Subikahn still worried about his manhood testing.

"No doubt. They'll pass you."

A man. The words sounded wonderful from the mouth of one who would certainly know. "You're not just saying that because—"

Talamir interrupted, his tone gaining a note of irritation, "I would never say something that important just to please anyone. You know that."

"Of course. I'm sorry." Subikahn could not stop grinning. "I didn't mean to impugn your character. I'm just so excited." Suddenly seized by the desire to share, he raced toward the gate. "Let's tell my papa. Everything."

"Everything?" Talamir scurried after his student. "Subikahn, wait. What exactly do you mean by *everything*?"

"I mean everything." Subikahn tripped the latch and yanked on the heavy portal. "He's a wonderful man who deserves to share my every delight. The most understanding father in the world will find joy in whatever makes me happy."

"I'm not so sure," Talamir said, his soft reply lost beneath the squeal of massive hinges. Closing his eyes, he followed Subikahn into the castle.

Sunlight glinted from bits of quartz and mica in the mortared stone construction of Stalmize Castle. King Tae Kahn clung like a spider to the courtyard wall, directly below the library window. Above him, his constant feline companion, Imorelda, watched him through the window, tail twitching daintily, her paws tucked calmly beneath her. *You have a visitor,* she said in the mental voice only he could hear.

Who's there? he sent back.

Not here. Down there. The silver tabby glanced past him to the ground, five stories below.

Tae followed the animal's gaze to a plump maid arranging blankets on the ground beneath him. *Alneezah.* He knew her at once, from her actions alone, and he could not help smiling. The servants had grown used to their king's strange antics. The son of a crime lord who had survived his youth by his wits, quickness, and wiles, he suffered from a restless need to know the location of every exit and to practice using them on a daily basis.

Tae's guards and butlers had requested the right to cushion the entire base of the castle, in case their king lost rooftop footing or a grip on a window, niche, or ledge. Afraid to lose his edge, Tae had dismissed their requests as unnecessary. Still, Alneezah always found an excuse to keep Tae safer. She also knew Imorelda's favorite treats and somehow always had them on hand for chance meetings in the corridors.

"What are you doing down there?" Tae called to the maid.

Alneezah did not bother to look up, though she did grant the king a respectful curtsy. Tae hated formality, but his advisers assured him of the necessity. Without it, they told him, he could not command the respect required to run a single country, let alone the entire East-lands. "I'm airing out some quilts, Your Majesty."

"In the central courtyard?"

"Yes, Sire."

"On the ground?"

Alneezah finally glanced up. Though not traditionally beautiful, her features were becoming in their own way. Shiny black hair fell in waves past her shoulders, hiding her ears, and bangs eclipsed her gentle, brown eyes. The pink circles of her cheeks gave her a look of constant coyness, and her small nose seemed to disappear above full, heart-shaped lips. "Yes, Sire. On the ground."

"Directly beneath my dirty feet."

Alneezah bit back a smile. "Oh, I hope they're not dirty, Your Majesty. Some dignitary may wish to kiss them."

Caught off guard by the unabashed banter, Tae had no retort.

★She's good. You should marry her.★

Tae felt his cheeks warm. When Kevral had chosen Ra-khir as her husband, she had devastated Tae. It was not that he had expected anything different. At that time, Ra-khir had everything he did not: striking good looks, impeccable honor, and a romanticism Tae could only watch and envy. Also, Ra-khir had just single-handedly gone to war against the entire country of Pudar to win Kevral back from their custody. Since then, Tae had devoted himself entirely to their son and never considered courting another woman.

Not that Tae had had no opportunities. The lesser kings of many countries had offered their daughters to him, and nearly every un-attached woman in his own kingdom batted her eyes and giggled around him. He had a trove of barren concubines who happily shared his bed to satisfy their urges as well as his own. But, his deep love, and most of his attention went solely to his son; and only Imorelda consumed as much of his time. He had brought the boy into the world and swore to any gods that might exist that he would do a far better job raising Subikahn than his father had done with Tae.

Tae reached for any excuse to silence the cat. *★Alneezah? She's too young for me.★*

★She's nearly thirty. You're thirty-seven.★ Imorelda rose casually to poke her furry head out the window. Shed hairs swirled through the sunbeams, making her appear to grow an unearthly halo. *★Close enough.★*

Tae ignored the animal to call down to the maid again. "You don't need to protect me, you know." His toes wedged into comfortable ledges in the mortar, and his fingers looped around irregularities in the stone.

Alneezah continued spreading blankets as if Tae had never interrupted. "Who said anything about protecting you, Your Majesty? You have two competent guard forces for that."

It was true. In addition to the main army, his father commanded an elite group of men. Organized criminals, they penetrated every area of the world with ease and acted on information with a swift efficiency the guards would not dare to emulate. Though no one other than Tae knew it, Imorelda acted as a third line of defense. Only four other people in the world would even believe he could communicate with a cat. Queen Matrinka had had a similar relationship with Imorelda's mother, Mior, and only Darris, Kevral, and Ra-khir knew about it. All three of them, as well as Tae, had needed serious convincing despite trusting Matrinka implicitly. Eventually, Tae's uncanny knack for languages had allowed him to communicate with Mior also and, later, with the kitten she had gifted to him. Few humans seemed able to resist Imorelda's charm, and they all spoke openly in her presence.

She's cagey and cheeky. Qualities I adore.

Then you marry her. Tae shifted fingers that had begun to cramp. *Most humans look upon those as character flaws, not qualities.*

Most humans wouldn't know quality if it scratched their eyes out and batted them around the floor.

An interesting turn of phrase.

Imorelda sat on the window seat and licked one gray paw. *Yes, isn't it? I made it up myself.*

I would never have guessed.

Imorelda stopped her bath suddenly, and her head disappeared from the window. *Subikahn's here.* Her face returned, her little black nose crinkled. *And that yellow-furred one who always smells like metal and oil.*

By "yellow," Tae knew she meant blond. She always identified humans by the color of their hair, which she interchangeably referred to as "manes" or "fur." *You mean the Renshai. Talamir?*

Yes, that one. They're looking for you.

Tae skittered back up the wall to the window ledge.

Imorelda yawned and stretched before moseying out of Tae's way and allowing him to duck inside.

"Ah, there you are, Papa." Subikahn showed no surprise at finding the king of Stalmize dangling out of a tower window. His thin black hair was disheveled, like his father's always was, his cheeks still pinkish from exertion. His olive skin always seemed darker in the presence of his pale Renshai *torke*. Subikahn's lips held a smile that seemed permanently glued there, while the Renshai looked more nervous than excited. He shifted from foot to foot, his hands hovering above his swords. He would not touch a weapon in the king's presence, but he seemed incapable of putting his hands calmly at his sides.

Tae spun toward them on the window seat, preparing to dismount; but Imorelda stomped into his lap before he could drop his feet to the floor. Effectively trapped, he sat. "Hello, Subikahn." He nodded toward the other Renshai, "Talamir."

"Your Majesty," Talamir executed an awkward bow. "Thank you for seeing us without notice."

It seemed a strange statement. Tae had never denied either of them audience, any time or anywhere, in the past. "Well, I could hardly have declined, could I? I simply entered the room, and there you were."

Talamir bowed several more times. "I'm sorry, Sire. Were we disturbing you, Sire? We can come back later, S—"

Subikahn seized his teacher's arm. "He's kidding, Tally." He turned Tae a pleading look. "Papa, tell him you're kidding."

"I'm kidding," Tae admitted, petting the cat hand over hand, until tiny hairs danced through the sunlight. She had a circular pattern of black stripes against a grizzly silver-gray and only one spot of white, at the very tip of her tail. "What can I do for the two of you?"

Subikahn looked like he might burst. "Talamir says I'll definitely pass my testing. When I return from the Fields of Wrath next time, I'll be a man!"

A wave of excitement passed through Tae, and he could not help grinning. The testing of the Renshai meant little to him, but it would make his son, and Kevral, happy. Nothing else mattered. "That's great news! On your return, we'll have to celebrate." A strange idea came to him suddenly. His advisers had bothered him for years about hosting a dance or massive party, a way to interact with lesser royalty and get to know them better. He was already popular with the peasantry, who saw the king as one of them. He often came across as shockingly down to earth. He kept their taxes low and allowed those with more experience and intelligence to make judgments and preside over his court.

The nobility, however, remained suspicious of the family who appeared to have no history before wresting power from the previous king of Stalmize, even nearly twenty years later. Tae suspected his advisers also hoped he would finally find a queen when he became lost in the romanticism of the event. "Perhaps a ball? We've never had one of those before."

Subikahn's smile seemed to encompass his entire face. "Thanks, Papa. That would be wonderful." He turned an adoring look upon his swordmaster.

Talamir remained stonily silent.

Imorelda butted Tae's hand with her head, and he scratched around her cheeks and ears. He could not imagine a more perfect moment: his only son deliriously happy and his cat purring mightily in his lap.

"Papa, there's more."

Still grinning, Tae inclined his head toward Subikahn to encourage him to continue.

Talamir closed his eyes and lowered his head.

"Papa," Subikahn blurted, his words nearly tumbling over one another. "I'm in love."

Though he did not stop grinning, Tae sucked in the sides of his mouth. Amused by the admission, he continued to stroke the cat. He had waited a long time for his son's first crush, glad the boy trusted him enough to share it. "Really? Who is she?"

"I've fallen for a Renshai, Papa. Just like you."

Just like me. Tae's grin wilted, and he shrugged. "I wouldn't wish my love life on anyone, Subikahn. Especially you." *So it happened on Kevral's watch.* He wondered why she had not mentioned it, or if she had been too busy training to even notice. Her intense and one-sided devotion to sword work might make her oblivious, even to her son's distraction. He wondered if she truly loved her children as much as her swords, her husband as much as her devotion to the Renshai techniques that made them the best swordsmen in the world.

Tae found himself shivering, filled with a sense of foreboding, and wondered why. It would fall to his long-suffering and able advisers to get the populace to accept a Renshai princess. If Subikahn had waited this long to mention her, he could not miss her too much, which meant their relationship could not have gotten serious yet.

Subikahn's excitement, however, told a different story. It was fresh and strong, beyond the level of a budding crush. In his excitement, he seized his *torke's* hand.

"So," Tae continued carefully. "When do I get to meet her?"

Subikahn laughed with the wild abandon of someone so madly in love it springs forth from every pore. Though playful at times, the young prince rarely became so giddy he could not contain himself.

This time, the words practically spilled from his mouth. "You know my lover, Papa. Very well. It's . . ." He squeezed his teacher's hand. "It's Talamir."

Few things could have surprised Tae more. He sat in stunned silence, his hand stilling on the cat, his expression exposed. Unbidden thoughts jolted into his mind, among them the dire realization that his son had just blithely confessed to a capital crime.

For several moments, no one moved or spoke. Then, cautiously, Talamir freed his hand from Subikahn's, apparently anticipating a fight. Any difficult situation sent a Renshai to his sword.

Subikahn finally broke the hush. "I've found true love, Papa. True love! Aren't you . . . happy for me?"

What's wrong? Imorelda stopped purring.

For once, Tae ignored her. "But . . . he's a . . ."

". . . Renshai?" Subikahn finished.

". . . man," Tae corrected. "Talamir's a man." He turned his son a confused look. "Right?" He wondered if he had missed something. Renshai women worked so hard, they often developed musculature in ways other females never did. Hard arms and thighs, tight abdominal musculature, were the norm for Renshai. Even Ra-khir had mistaken Kevral for a boy the first several times he met her. Yet, she had eventually developed enough breast and curve to look like a hardened woman rather than a man. And Talamir was clearly no youngster. He appeared to be in his twenties, and Renshai routinely looked younger than their ages.

"Yes, Papa. Tally passed his testing ten years ago. He's definitely a man."

Tae did not know what else to say. He and his son were talking at cross-purposes. They might just as well be using different languages, except the conversation would still make more sense. Tae spoke every known tongue fluently. He did not care when or if Talamir had ever passed beyond Renshai adolescence. He wanted to know why his son was calling a grown man "lover" as if gender meant nothing. He could not understand how two males could confess to a hanging crime with enthusiasm and excitement. *Execution.* Dread enveloped him. *Not Subikahn. Not my only son.* Tears pressed Tae's eyes, and he did not trust himself to speak.

What's wrong? Imorelda asked again; and, again, he ignored her.

Subikahn and Talamir exchanged serious glances. "I told you we needed to keep it secret," the older Renshai whispered. The acoustics of the room carried it to Tae's ears anyway. "I warned you not to say anything."

"He's my father," Subikahn hissed back. "The best man in the world, and he loves me."

The best man in the world. It was exactly what Tae had always wanted to hear his son say, yet it did not warm his heart this day. Something inside him had died, and he worried that he might never know another moment of joy in his existence. He forced himself to speak, saying the only words he dared. "Go to your quarters. I need some time alone to think."

Talamir bowed and left the room faster than decorum dictated. Subikahn opened his mouth to speak, then closed it. He started again, stopped, and sighed deeply before shuffling from the room as well.

Assailed by all the emotions shock had kept at bay, Tae buried his face in the cat and let them overtake him.

Grimly, King Tae Kahn walked the night hallways of Stalmize Castle, blind to the minute details he usually registered from habit. As a young man, survival had meant remaining attentive, even in sleep; and the need had stayed with him every moment of every day since. His torch threw wild shapes on the stonework, bringing shadows into vivid relief as he moved. That made him wildly uncomfortable. He would have preferred creeping through the darkness, unseen and unheard; but to do so, he had long ago learned the hard way, risked attack by his own guards. He noticed their every movement as they shifted to allow him free access, recognizing him in the hated, but necessary, torchlight.

Tae reached Subikahn's bedroom door sooner than he wanted. He stood there several moments in indecision. He had not eaten or slept since their conversation that morning. Nothing but his son's confession had found a toehold in his thoughts, and formulating his plan had taken precedence even over bodily functions. He believed in the choice he had made, yet he still hesitated. No course of action seemed right; yet doing nothing would be the worst decision of all.

Tae studied the door without seeing it, knowing the teak outline as well as the palm of his own hand. He had memorized every line in the grain, every knothole in the pattern, every stain. He had spent the happiest times of his adulthood here, cradling and singing to his infant son, romping with the boy he had become, listening to the details of his adolescence. No friendship had ever been forged more solidly. The world had never known a love so genuine and deep. Yet, soon, for the boy's own good, Tae would have to do the most hateful thing he could ever have imagined.

Tae's hand rose, as if of its own accord, and knocked solidly on the teak door.

For several moments, nothing happened. Tae had just released a pent-up breath when the panel edged open a crack and one sleepy brown eye peered through it. "Papa?" Subikahn said through a yawn. His black hair lay in a tangle around his face, and he wore only his blue satin sleeping pants. His chest looked sinewy, muscled but lightly built, like his father. "What time is it?"

"It's late," Tae admitted. "I need to talk to you. Please come."

Subikahn yawned again. "Just a moment." The door swung shut.

Tae heard muffled voices through the wood. Subikahn had always shared his room with his Renshai *torke*, even as a toddler. For the first time, Tae found himself despising the arrangement. *Was this the first time a Renshai took advantage of my son?* The idea enraged him. He had obliviously allowed adults to share a room with his boy; that made it partially his fault. That Kevral and the other Renshai trusted those teachers should not have been enough. Teeth gritted, Tae waited until the door finally swung open. A now-robed Subikahn scooted out and pushed it closed before Tae managed to catch a glimpse of Talamir.

Subikahn shook his head, worsening the tangle that comprised his hair. "Where are we going?"

"The library." Tae wanted to take the young prince as far from his bedroom and the court as possible. He did not want any sound to betray the other part of his plan. "We're going to the library." He headed off in the proper direction.

Subikahn followed, clutching his robe. "To talk."

"To talk," Tae confirmed.

"In the middle of the night."

"Apparently."

That shut down the conversation. Subikahn continued to trail Tae's brisk pace without speaking, and they both moved with a delicate, silent step down the hallways, up the tower steps, and to the heavy oak door to the library. There, they paused, while Tae tripped the latch.

"Is this about Talamir?" Subikahn said as they entered.

The library appeared different in the darkness. The window seat lay empty, striped by the light of moon and stars. The shelving looked like animals hulking in the shadows. As much from habit as concern, Tae scanned the area to ascertain that they were alone, using the torch to banish shadows from every corner and cubby. He saw nothing out of place, every book as he had left it, every shelf as it should appear. Finally, he extinguished the torch, laid it aside, and claimed the window seat. He motioned Subikahn to the chair from the reading nook.

The boy accepted the seat, spinning it around to face his father. "You know I love you, Papa. I didn't mean to upset you." He sat, ramrod stiff and clearly nervous.

"I know." Tae stared through the window. He could see the empty courtyard clearly in the light of the half-moon. He was obsessively cautious by nature and would not allow anyone to overhear this conversation.

"You like Talamir. Don't you?" Subikahn's face looked childlike in the moonlight.

Tae sucked in a deep breath and let it out slowly. "Not at the moment, no."

"Papa, it's not his fault—"

"Subikahn—"

"I'm as much to blame—"

"Subikahn! Listen to me."

The young prince fell silent.

"We're not here to talk about Talamir. We're here to talk about you."

Subikahn nodded, lips tightly pursed.

Tae glanced at his own scarred and callused hands, knowing he had to broach subjects with which he never wanted to burden his son. "Subikahn, I grew up much differently than you did."

Subikahn bobbed his head again. That much, he knew.

"My father . . ."

"Granpapa Weile."

"Yes." Tae wished his son would stop interrupting. He had never enforced manners or formality, despite his advisers' suggestions. "Granpapa Weile . . . didn't have time for play. He only asserted how I had to stay tough, stay alert, stay quick to stay alive."

Subikahn tossed a glance around the room. "I know what you're trying to say, Papa. That it's a great privilege to grow up as a prince. And a great responsibility."

Tae went quiet a moment. Those words had not come from him. As king, he mostly delegated. He did not have the patience for long-winded noblemen, and he found their problems too petty to consider. He served mostly as a figurehead, and his advisers and elite warriors equated the positive things in the kingdom with him and the negative with other people or factors.

"That's true, Subikahn." Tae gave the boy an intent look, hoping to silence him. "But it's not what I planned to say."

"Are you going to tell me about . . . the scars?" Subikahn had pestered his father mercilessly for stories about the myriad and often fatal-looking wounds that covered Tae's scrawny body.

Tae caught himself self-consciously plucking at his garments to cover any bared flesh. Usually, he did not think about his many disfigurements. Scarcely anyone knew the cause of most of them, and he alone knew where every one had come from. He had laughed off or dodged his son's questions in the past. A child did not need to know the terrifying details. At only ten years old, Tae had found himself at the mercy of his father's enemies, forced to watch his mother raped and murdered before suffering sixteen stab wounds and being left for dead himself. It was not the last time enemies of Weile Kahn would leave their mark upon him, and he had honestly earned many of the other scars without his father's assistance.

"Not yet," Tae said, disappointing Subikahn once again. "My father and I have not always gotten along." It was gross understatement. Weile was a born leader with a knack for gaining followers and a grandness to his every action, while Tae preferred to live his life in the silent shadows. The worst and best things in his life always bore a direct connection to Weile Kahn. "And I swore that, when I had a son, things would be different. I would treat him with honor and respect. I would assure that he always knew his father loved him and would do anything for him. I never wanted him to feel alone."

"And I know that, Papa. I truly do." Subikahn seemed sincerely eager to quell his father's doubts. "No child has ever had a happier upbringing. Even Saviar is jealous."

Tae smiled, but the circumstances made it forced and crooked. "I'm glad to hear that. But, in the process of making you happy, I made a serious blunder."

Now, Subikahn finally fell into a hush, clearly focused on his father's next words.

"I coddled you too much, Subikahn. I was so intent on keeping your childhood happy that I shielded you from the necessary experiences that keep a young man from becoming a mark."

"A . . . mark?" Subikahn clearly did not understand, which was exactly Tae's point.

Tae leaned forward, his heart pounding. He still had a chance to retract his plan, to send his son back to bed confused but whole. Then, an image of his son's lifeless body swinging from the gallows filled his mind's eye, and he forced himself to continue, "It's the horrific things in life that make a man careful, wiser."

Subikahn laughed.

It was the last reaction Tae expected. He stopped speaking. And stared.

Subikahn explained. "Are you worried I'm too innocent to defend myself?"

Apparently, Subikahn had grasped the point. "Well . . ."

"Papa . . . I'm Renshai." Subikahn opened his robe to reveal a sword at his left hip, and little else. He had not bothered to put on clothes, but he would never go anywhere without his weapon. "And you've taught me plenty about climbing and hiding and dodging. Hel's ice, some of what you've told me overlaps eerily with the Renshai training. And don't get me started on languages . . ."

In that light, Tae's concerns did seem a bit silly. Subikahn was not exactly the classic prince, lounging around the castle getting dressed and flattered by servants and eating too many peeled grapes. While Subikahn did not have his father's uncanny skill with languages, he did read and speak Eastern, Common, Western, Northern, and Renshai. Though Tae appreciated the ability to communicate with anyone anytime, his skill had often seemed as much a curse. Weile Kahn had exploited his son's talent at a very young age, using him to spy on strangers and enemies. No one ever suspected a child could understand so much.

"Those things will help you," Tae admitted. "But you can't become street-smart without challenging the street. And you can't become world-smart without facing the world."

Subikahn's brow furrowed. "So you want me to . . . travel?"

Tae remembered his own odyssey, fleeing the Eastlands with his father's most lethal enemies on his heels. He had had little combat training and nothing but the clothes on his back. Rarely eating, never sleeping, he had tried desperately to keep just a step ahead of death, his only goal one more moment of survival.

"But I've already gone to Erythane and back many many times."

Tae sighed. The situation had utterly changed since his father had banished him, at fourteen, with the words, "Come back when you're twenty. If you're still alive, all this will become yours." Weile had waved a hand toward Stalmize. At the time, Tae had believed his father meant his current business: organizing and leading bands of murderers, thugs, and thieves. Never had Tae imagined Weile would take over the kingdom itself and pass it along to his only child. As promised, at age twenty.

In less than two years, Subikahn would reach that same crucial age with little to show for it other than the Renshai training.

Tae cleared his throat, making the pronouncement he had dreaded. "Subikahn, for your own good, I am hereby banishing you from the Eastlands until you reach the age of twenty."

"What?" Subikahn's features lapsed into confusion. He seemed uncertain whether to be shocked or amused.

"You are not to run to your mother but to seek out every part of the world and bring back some unique item as proof of your travels."

"What?" Subikahn seemed stuck on the word, his features open, registering real surprise now.

Tae could feel his resolve wavering. He hardened his heart, imagining himself as Weile Kahn. He had despised his father's business and techniques; yet Tae now, finally, saw the wisdom in the way Weile had tossed his son into the fire. Without that ordeal, Tae would never have survived his trials with Kevral, Ra-khir, Darris, and Matrinka. "I expect you to visit the entirety of the Westlands, even the parts farthest north and east. I expect you to weather the Northlands—"

"But I'm Renshai!" Subikahn shouted in horror. "The North? They'll slaughter me!"

Tae lowered his head. The differences between his own test and Subikahn's were enormous. Even sent to a land of enemies, his son would never be recognized. Tae saw no reason to give the obvious advice, that Subikahn not bother to mention his mother's heritage or his training. He would easily pass for a full-blooded Easterner if he kept his swords sheathed and his mouth shut. If the boy could not figure out something so simple, he truly did deserve to die. "You'll find ways to cope. We all do."

Subikahn considered the words in silence for several moments, nodding, clearly finding the positives inherent in having no responsibilities while exploring the entire world. "Very well, Papa. If you think that's best. Talamir and I will pack—"

"No!"

At the sudden, forceful shout, Subikahn jumped.

"You will go alone."

Now the horror that had previously escaped the prince appeared, stamped across his features. "But, Papa, Tally and I—"

"No!"

"We're a couple—"

"No!"

Subikahn's voice turned pleading. "Please, Father. I can't go two years without seeing my—"

"You can." Tae could not allow Subikahn to finish that sentence. Whatever word the boy used would enrage him. "And you will." Softened by his son's pain, Tae lowered his voice. "Subikahn, this will give you a chance to experience . . . other things. If your love is real and strong, it will survive two years of separation." It was all platitudes. Tae felt certain Subikahn's youth and inexperience explained how he had fallen for the first non-related person, man or woman, who had invoked feelings of accomplishment, closeness, and security. Surely, Subikahn would meet attractive young women on his journey, and their tribulations would bring them closer. Until Subikahn experienced the kind of love Tae still suffered for Kevral, until he opened himself to new and different circumstances, he would never know what he really needed, what he really wanted.

"You don't understand—"

Tae glowered at the insult. "I love your mother now as much as I did the night you were conceived, even though I have seen her only once or twice a year in the last eighteen." He gave Subikahn a pointed look. "That, my son, is love."

Subikahn's shoulders sagged. "Yes, Papa. You're right." The corners of his lips twitched but never made it into a smile. "I trust your instincts and your devotion to me. If you feel this is right, then I will leave in the morning. Alone."

Tae gritted his teeth. Nothing had ever felt less right. Subikahn meant everything to him: his beloved son, the lone product of his infinite and ill-fated affection for Kevral, the only future of family and kingdom. But Tae knew that to back down from his decision would condemn Subikahn to execution. The boy's raw enthusiasm, his ignorance of Eastern law, his emotional innocence would assure that other people, dangerous people, discovered his lethal secret. And used it against them. "You will leave now, Subikahn."

"Now?" Subikahn looked up at his father through a long fringe of bangs. He appeared so young, so childlike. "But I need to pack. To tell Tally 'good-bye.' To explain—"

"Now," Tae repeated, fighting the tears forming in his own eyes. "No packing. No good-byes. No explanations. Just outside the door, my men have clothes for you and as much food and money as I'll allow you to take." Tae avoided Subikahn's judging stare. "It is best."

Subikahn stood in silent misery.

Tae resisted the urge to gather his son into his arms. A tearful separation would destroy his will and drive him to rescind what he knew in his heart was the proper course of action. "Farewell, Subikahn. I'll see you in two years." He smiled wanly, "I only hope I'll recognize you as a man."

Slipping past his son, Tae opened the door and disappeared into the hallway with his waiting guardsmen. He did not instruct them. They knew what to do. They would see Subikahn safely off into the world.

Meanwhile, Tae had other pressing business.

CHAPTER 8

When you corner a lion, expect a fight to the death.
—Queen Matrinka of Béarn

THE SECOND KNOCK on the teakwood door did not surprise Talamir, already dressed and ready. His hand fell to his sword hilt, and he called out, "Who is it?"

No answer followed, just another, harder rap at the door.

With a sigh of resignation, Talamir rose and headed cautiously toward the door. He had no idea what to expect, other than knowing he would not like whatever the king had planned. The look on his face after Subikahn had made his announcement combined surprise, horror, and abject rage. Talamir felt certain the king would vent that squall of emotion on him. *Subikahn's gone.* Talamir knew it. *The best thing to ever happen in my life is over.*

Talamir tripped the latch, opened the door, and assumed a warrior position, anticipating a fight. Instead, he faced three men dressed in the kingdom's colors: black and silver. These were not standard guards; they wore no visible armor, nor the kingdom tabards. Dressed in close-fitting black, they stood with faces swathed in a silver gauze that identified them as the king's elite protectors. No one ever saw their features, at least not while in Tae's employ, yet the covering did not seem to hamper them in any way.

The tallest of the three stepped forward, a sinewy giant lost in the folds of his all-concealing robe. "Talamir Edmin's son?"

Talamir gave a barely perceptible nod. His mind and heart raced, trying to anticipate King Tae Kahn's intentions.

"The king wants you in his court. Come with us, and leave the sword."

Talamir would sooner leave his eyeballs. "No."

All three men paused, facing Talamir. Apparently, they studied him through the gauze. Finally, the tallest spoke again. "You won't come?"

"Oh, I'll come." Talamir knew that to refuse would guarantee his execution. "But the sword goes with me."

"It stays." The same man continued to speak.

No good could come of arguing the point. Talamir stood his ground and made no move to remove the weapon. Anyone who reached for it would lose his hand.

Wisely, not one of the three made any motion to disarm him. The smallest of the trio, a man of average height and bulk, finally spoke. "You are a warrior of honor?" he asked.

"I am." Talamir raised his chin. Many around the world considered the Renshai demons, but few deserved the insult. Renshai had a distinct code of honor that relied on personal speed and skill.

"Then you will not bare steel in the presence of the king."

It was as much statement as question, yet Talamir knew he would have to answer. "Very well." He had no intention of killing Subikahn's father, yet his honor did not forbid him from pulling the weapon in defense of self and loved ones, with or without the promise.

"Come with us, please." The same man gestured to Talamir, and the Renshai went to him. He had a sophistication about him that the others did not share. Accustomed to judging others by physical form and movement, Talamir found their swathing disconcerting. Nevertheless, he guessed that the smallest of the group was the leader, though he had not originally spoken. He had an aura of charisma about him that came through in motion, in speech timbre and pattern, in the way he carried himself beneath the robes and mask.

Talamir walked with this man, the one he labeled the Shadow Leader. The others fell into step around them, the tall man in the back and his companion leading the way. Talamir studied the man in front of him, the only one who had not spoken. Though not impressive in height, he carried himself like a warrior, either stout, massively muscled, or both. He had a waddle to his walk, but he carried his head high and unconcerned. Either it never occurred to him that the Renshai might attack from behind or, more likely, he believed he could handle any threat. Talamir doubted it was all foolish bravado.

The walk continued in silence until they stood several strides outside the courtroom. At that moment, the man beside Talamir whispered, "Pay attention if you want to survive."

Talamir had no idea whether or not to trust this stranger, but he saw no reason not to listen. He knew homosexuality was a crime in the Eastlands, but to punish Talamir, Tae would have to reveal his partner. It seemed unlikely the king would allow Subikahn to undergo life-threatening punishment. He nodded once to indicate he had heard.

The squat man in the lead opened the courtroom door on an enormous, empty room. Benches lined the middle in two rows, and a massive chandelier hung over them, the candles currently unlit. A string of torches along the wall flickered, bathing the walls but leaving the central areas mostly shadowed. No one sat upon the dais at the front.

Talamir stood between the lighter two men as the squat one closed the doors behind them. He chose to remain there, arms folded across his chest, massive broadsword outlined against the thin black linen of his costume.

Though it felt long in the self-imposed silence, the wait was only a few moments. Tae appeared through a curtain behind the dais. He did not sit upon the throne but stepped down to the level of Talamir and the guards, walking within speaking range though still a finely-measured distance from a sudden lunge and sword stroke. Even more wary than usual, Talamir could not help but notice that Tae chose the perfect position for foiling a Renshai. Either he had gotten spectacularly lucky, or he had learned much from traveling with Kevral. Not that it mattered. It only meant an extra step, an extra lightning instant, for Talamir to kill the king should such action become necessary.

Talamir shook the thought from his mind. He had promised not to bare steel in Tae's presence, and he had no intention of doing so unless cornered. Even then, he would not murder Subikahn's father, a man his lover adored and respected.

Tae did not bother with preamble. He glared at the Renshai with a hostility Talamir had never seen from the playful king before. "Your job was to teach Subikahn Renshai maneuvers, not how to become a *bonta.* He used the Eastern vulgarity for a man who sleeps with other men."

Talamir gritted his teeth but refused to take offense. He could not afford to lose his composure. "The prince is a competent Renshai, Your Majesty. He will pass his tests of manhood when we get home."

"Home?" Tae's brows shot up. "The prince's 'home' is here. In Stalmize."

Talamir flinched. "I—I meant no insult, Sire. When I said "home," I meant *my* home." He glanced into Tae's eyes and read a deep, primal anger. His own hand slunk inexorably toward his hilt despite his best efforts to keep it still. Renshai fought with blades, not words.

"Talamir Edminsson, you are charged with raping the crown prince of Stalmize."

Shocked, Talamir took a physical step backward. His mouth fell open, but no words emerged. He pictured Subikahn, an olive blur of movement, his fine black hair a rich indigo in the sunlight. By looks, only a hint of blue in his eyes betrayed the Northern side of his heritage, but his quickness and agility would reveal him to any Renshai in an instant. Warmth suffused Talamir at an image he found strikingly handsome, and he forced himself to speak. "I didn't rape anyone, Sire. Subikahn is a willing lover."

"How dare you." Tae fairly hissed. "He's a child; you're a grown man of . . . of . . . How old are you, Talamir?"

At the moment, Talamir could scarcely remember. "I'm . . . twenty-seven, Sire. And Kahn is nearly also a man, by Renshai standards. He only needs to complete—"

Tae exploded. "His name is Prince Subikahn to you!"

"Prince Subikahn," Talamir corrected. "Yes, Sire. Prince Subikahn only needs to—"

Tae gave no ground. "Shortening an Easterner's name is grave insult."

"I'm sorry, Sire. I didn't know." Talamir added before thinking, "You go by Tae, not Tae Kahn, Your Majesty. And Prince Subikahn often calls me Tal or Tally."

"I go by 'Your Majesty,'" Tae reminded through gritted teeth. "And you, Tal . . ." He pronounced the nickname with a tone that made it sound oddly filthy, grotesquely evil. ". . . are not an Easterner."

"Well, yes, Sire. I mean, no, Sire, I'm not, but . . ."

"The name I choose for myself is none of your business."

"Yes, Sire." Talamir wished he had never broached the subject. It did not matter, and it only seemed to further enrage the king. "Of course not." As he understood it from Subikahn, Weile and Tae used "Kahn" as a separate surname that served the same purpose as Talamir's own "Edminsson." As a Renshai, the prince went by Subikahn Taesson, so they had incorporated the "Kahn" directly into his given name.

"What do you have to say for yourself?" Tae finally demanded.

Words failed Talamir. He had never seen Tae angry before, and it unnerved him. "Sire, I'm worried to say anything. Every word from my mouth seems to further upset you."

Tae folded his arms across his chest, a seemingly indefensible position. He carried no visible weapons either, a dangerous way to confront an armed Renshai who, ordinarily, would take such disdain as a challenge. "It's your actions, not your words, that enrage me, Talamir."

Talamir had barely moved since entering the courtroom. "My actions, Sire?" He became acutely aware of the location of his right hand and was glad to find it at his side, not on his hilt.

"You . . . raped . . . my . . . son!"

It was the second time Tae had spoken the accusation, yet Talamir found himself equally stunned and horrified. "No!"

"You were in a superior position, and he trusted you. You used your power over him to coerce him into . . . unspeakable acts."

"No." Talamir dropped his voice nearly to a whisper. "No, I—" His mind raced to his relationship with the man he loved, and he could not forget the turmoil he had suffered at the same age. Always, he wondered when his interest in women would come, long after his peers already talked about little else. He even forced himself to consummate a relationship and managed it only by avoiding the parts other men craved, picturing the handsomest of his male peers in her place. Like nearly all Renshai trysts, this had not resulted in a child. The Renshai testing began before birth; hard-bodied women found conception far more difficult. An infant who could not last through the grueling workouts of its mother could never survive Renshai training. They even rushed into battle in advanced states of pregnancy.

Hailed as a hero for his unwavering dedication to his swordwork that allowed him to forswear the temptations of the flesh, Talamir endured in silence. He had gained the status of *torke* at a young age, his devotion to the Renshai maneuvers paying off, though he hid the secret of his passions in shame and fear. He was a true man's man, a warrior with few equals, yet nothing but a *bonta* to the King of Stalmize, the one man whose blessing he needed.

Talamir had not meant to fall in love with Subikahn, nor to encourage the youngster's devotion to him. It had happened in the quiet nights of desperation when the prince confided his fears and his pain to his teacher, trials that sounded all too familiar. Talamir had meant only to soothe the agony, to help the boy find enlightenment, understanding, and joy in a world stacked against them. But the closeness of their experiences, the sharing of their darkest secrets, and the heartfelt depth of knowledge that few could understand had brought them irrevocably closer. He loved Subikahn with a profundity and passion he had never before known in his life. And he knew the young prince felt the same way. "I didn't rape anyone. I never would."

"Remember," the black-clothed figure beside Talamir hissed. "The penalty for willing participation in a homosexual act is death."

Death. The warning made no sense to Talamir, who had already realized he stood in mortal peril. The Shadow Leader had promised to help him spare his life, not lose it. Being reminded of the gravity of the situation only made Talamir more nervous, more certain to make a fatal mistake. Again, he found his fist nearly on his hilt and forced himself to move it. "Sire, your son . . ." Talamir started.

"Yes."

"Your son . . ." Understanding suddenly struck Talamir. If he pressed his current point, if he made the king believe the truth, he condemned both Subikahn and himself to execution. Two willing participants equaled two killings. One rapist meant only one. "Sire," Talamir restarted, his tongue feeling suddenly swollen. He was about to condemn himself to a brutal death; yet, doing so seemed the only way to rescue his lover. "Sire, you're right. I am solely at fault; Prince Subikahn Taesson is an innocent victim of my . . ." The last word clung to his tongue, and he had to shake it loose. ". . . depravity."

Tae seemed nearly as surprised by the confession as Talamir had by the accusation. "You . . . you admit . . ." His tone abruptly changed. "I knew it. You bastard! You brutalized my son. You ruined him for any woman! You . . . !" He gestured inarticulately for a moment before regaining his composure. "Talamir Edminsson, you are hereby sentenced to death by torture." He made a clear, broad gesture to the three men near Talamir. "Take him to the dungeon."

"Don't fight," the Shadow Leader said.

He might as well have been talking to the wall stones. Talamir had his sword free and slashing before anyone could move to stop him. Tae flew up the spectators' seats to the chandelier in a heartbeat. The other three moved almost as quickly, but their nearness to Talamir hindered them. The tip of one's glove followed the path of the sword, trailing blood. Another clamped a hand to his ear, swearing. The third, the one who had advised Talamir, managed to completely avoid the stroke, disappearing into the shadows of the court.

Though injured, the other two put themselves between Talamir and the exit. Both suddenly clutched blades, though Talamir had seen neither carry one. He crouched into a ready position. The rumor that one Renshai was equivalent to any other three competent warriors was not exaggeration. He had trained to take his enemies in packs as well as individually, to even expect treachery from those who initially battled with him, as friends. "If I am going to die, it will be in battle, not slung from a gallows." He lunged toward the largest of Tae's guards.

The man caught the strike on his blade with a firmness that sent vibrations rippling through Talamir's fingers. He withdrew, then sliced in again, whirling to face his second opponent.

The first recoiled, barely rescuing his chest from a fatal tear. The second sprang in as Talamir cut for him. He managed an awkward riposte that spared his life but opened his defenses. Talamir jabbed for the kill.

Something slammed into Talamir's legs, sprawling him. The Renshai madness caught him then. "Modi!" he swore, twisting like a *wisule* to face this new threat. The Shadow Leader clutched his ankles in a death grip, and a dagger in his fist jumped for Talamir.

"No!" The Renshai kicked and rolled. A sword swept toward his face, and he met the attack with his own blade, surging free. He saw movement overhead. At the same time, the two remaining elite guards sprang as one.

"Modi!" Talamir shouted, this time in wild abandon. He was going to die, but he would do so bravely, as a Renshai man. He redirected the first stroke, wove under the second. Something pricked his hip, even as he raised his sword to impale the figure flying toward him from the chandelier. *The king!* he realized suddenly. *Subikahn's father.*

The tear in Talamir's hip burned, a shocking agony for a Renshai immersed in battle, a Renshai whose battle rage should have driven him past all pain. He could feel its every motion through his veins, tearing, blazing, coursing through his body. "Poison," he gasped out, staggering. His blade missed its mark. Tae landed on him with enough force to bear him to the ground.

Still Talamir fought, writhing and kicking, spewing out words that ceased to make sense, even to himself. Someone jerked the sword from his hand. He lunged after it, howling like a beast. His thoughts swirled, wildly unfocused, and he groped for them with the same intensity with which he would wield his sword. "No! No! No!" He had to die with it in his hands. Die with it to go to Valhalla. And take the lying bastard who stooped to poison with him.

Oblivious to Tae expertly securing his limbs, sparing no attention for the two armed men trying to pin him with threats that no longer mattered, Talamir turned his gaze directly and accusingly on the smallest of the elite guardsmen. "You coward." He spat out the worst insult in the Renshai vernacular. "You filthy, shit-stinking coward."

Then, darkness descended on Talamir, and he knew no more.

Saviar Ra-khirsson slipped quietly into the Béarnian guest quarters he shared with his father and grandfather, undressed in the dark, and crawled into bed. The sheets felt lavishly soft, silky, and cold against his flesh; and he detected a hint of lavender amidst the sword oil, leather, and horse dander smells that defined the Knights of Erythane. Saviar felt himself drifting almost immediately; exhaustion from a grueling practice, combined with the plushness of his bed, dragged him rapidly toward sleep.

Kedrin's voice jarred abruptly through Saviar's muddling thoughts. "Savi?"

"Mmmm?" Saviar returned, unwilling to abandon the welcome comfort of drowsiness. If he focused too hard on his grandfather, he might come fully awake and have difficulty relocating this fine and comfortable place.

"They've called a special Council meeting for the morning. A Nordmirian ship docked this evening."

That fully roused Saviar. He propped himself onto an elbow, though he could barely discern Ra-khir's and Kedrin's beds through the darkness. Ra-khir slept between them. "A *Nordmirian* ship?" The Northlands consisted of a vast, frozen territory supporting several tribes who seemed constantly at war with one another. Aside from traders, they interacted rarely with the West. They also held a deep-rooted and deftly taught hatred for the Renshai tribe, once a part of them. Saviar could not keep suspicion from his tone. "Why?"

"We'll find out tomorrow." Kedrin peered across Ra-khir. "If I had to guess, I would venture it had something to do with ore."

"Ore?" Still leaning on his elbow, Saviar crinkled his forehead, though Kedrin could not see his confusion through the darkness. The chill of the sheets gave way to the trapped warmth of Saviar's body.

"Iron ore," Kedrin explained. "The West's great mines are nearly tapped out. The East has never been a good source, but the North has the most productive mines in the world."

"Really?" Saviar wondered how he had gone through his entire childhood obsessed with steel and yet had never known this fact. *It's because Renshai care only about ability and maneuvers. When they need supplies, they buy or, in the past, take them.* In that context, it made sense that the Renshai would pay little attention to such details. They also knew nothing about hunting or fishing, about clothing or adornments.

"Really, Saviar. And I thought you might want to attend the Council meeting."

Ra-khir stiffened suddenly, apparently jarred awake. He stretched beneath his covers, politely quiet.

"Really?" This time, the word emerged as a squeak. Saviar could scarcely believe the invitation. At only eighteen, he might become a part of kingdom politics, of an affair with vast significance.

Apparently misinterpreting Saviar's question, Kedrin added, "All right, I admit it. They're dead boring. But I thought someone who had never seen the Council Room might find even the regular goings-on of some interest. Also, I know you've never met a live Northman. I've always felt it better to form opinions based on reality rather than stereotypes and stories."

Saviar understood the underlying point. His mother held an entrenched disdain for all things Northern and tended to voice her opinion at any opportunity. Usually, Renshai remained aloof from discussions of their Northern cousins; but there was clearly no love lost and some actual hatred on their side as well. "I'd like to come, Grandpapa. Thank you for inviting me."

"You're welcome," Kedrin said sincerely, settling back beneath his covers. "Dress appropriately, and I will expect you to remain a silent observer."

The mere thought of speaking out in front of diplomats and royalty made Saviar quail. "Silent, of course. I would very much prefer it." He rolled to his side, prepared to fall asleep. Before he had a chance to settle in, however, Ra-khir finally spoke.

"Pardon me for overhearing the end of your conversation, Father, but did you just invite Saviar to the Council meeting?"

Kedrin sat up. "Indeed I did. Is that a problem?"

Saviar closed his eyes. He seemed to be the cause of a lot of friction between his father and grandfather these days. Nothing he could say would seem anything but rude, so he remained utterly silent and chased sleep.

"Not per se." Ra-khir's tone remained neutral, with just an edge of discomfort. He did not seem angry. "I think everyone should have an idea of how a kingdom operates, and Saviar is lucky to have some of the same opportunities I did to learn. However, under the circumstances . . ."

Saviar assumed his own curiosity seemed to lengthen Ra-khir's pause until Kedrin spoke to fill the gap.

"Yes, Ra-khir? What about the current circumstances bothers you?"

"It's just that Thialnir arrived last night." Ra-khir referred to the Renshai's representative at the conference table. "A Nordmirian captain and a hardheaded Renshai in the same small room? Why not just hand my son a burning brand to snuff in a barrel of oil? The king's guards will have enough to worry about without an extra Renshai."

Kedrin sounded affronted. "My grandson wouldn't engage in any violence that might endanger the high king."

"Your grandson," Ra-khir replied stiffly, "is Renshai."

Saviar was speaking before he could stop himself, "His grandson is in the damned room!"

Both men fell silent and turned toward the boy.

"First, I'm highly offended that you think because I'm Renshai I can't control myself."

Ra-khir recoiled, his tone turning defensive. "That's not what I meant, Savi."

Saviar continued, "I can't say for sure how I'll react in a situation I've never been in before." He sat up, now fully awake. "I certainly hope I would never engage in any behavior that might put King Griff in danger. But you're right about one thing." Saviar made a vague gesture toward Ra-khir in acknowledgment. "Regardless of what I would or wouldn't do, having a second Renshai in the room will alarm the guards and make their job harder. I don't want to be responsible for that."

Kedrin's voice seemed soft in comparison. "A good point well made. I concur and surrender to you both." He addressed Saviar directly. "Perhaps another time?"

Saviar liked that his grandfather could admit defeat with extraordinary grace. It was an important lesson his *torke* would never teach him. "I would like that very much, Grandpapa. One day very soon, it will happen."

Talamir awakened to a deep inner pain that seemed to stretch through his skin, and a throbbing headache. He rolled to his stomach. The biting cold of this new portion of the stone floor seeped through him. An odd, bitter taste filled his mouth. He forced himself to hands and knees, the movement telling him two things. First, he was unarmed; and, second, he had to vomit. He did so in a mucousy pile, then recoiled from it, wiping his lips with the back of his sleeve.

"You're up," a voice purred behind him.

Talamir whirled with a speed that stole his balance and sent him retching again. He vomited for a long time, unable to gain control of his heaving gut until well after the last watery contents of his stomach trickled onto the floor. Two more things entered his consciousness in that time: he lay in a barred cell, and the man who had addressed him was the same one who had whispered to him in the court. Again, the Shadow Leader wore the black swirl of garments, silver around his covered face.

Talamir wanted to turn his back but worried about his self-control and balance. "You poisoned me, you ignoble bastard. You poisoned me."

"I didn't poison you."

The composure of the response incited Talamir. "You did! You poisoned me."

"If I poisoned you, you would be dead."

Talamir sank to the floor again, taking care to miss the disgorged contents of his stomach. He clamped his hands to his head. "I wish I were dead."

"If you really mean it, Talamir, that can be arranged. You are under order of execution."

The words only angered the Renshai. At least, if the poison had finished him, he might have died in battle. He had had a chance to find Valhalla. Now, he would die a craven, a coward executed by a king who claimed to love his son but had chosen to torture him in the worst possible way. "You should have killed me in the courtroom. I could have died a—" He made the most vigorous hand gesture he dared. "You wouldn't understand."

"To the contrary, I understand completely." The elite guardsman unwound the material from his face to reveal the familiar features of Weile Kahn. He bore a striking resemblance to Subikahn, more so than Tae, and Talamir found those features breathlessly handsome. Weile's eyes were dark and depthless, his hair like midnight with patches of gray at the temples and gently distributed throughout. Though coarsened by maturity, his face bore no notable wrinkles. His stance completed the picture, commanding respect. "My grandson is Renshai. I know what it means to die in battle."

"Sire." Though already on his hands and knees, Talamir attempted to stoop lower.

Weile followed the movement, though slight. "None of that formal crap. I'm untitled by choice." Though true, he had been king only seventeen years earlier, when he gave the crown to Tae and slipped into relative obscurity.

"You told me you would help spare me."

"And I kept my promise." Weile glared at Talamir with an intensity that cowed him, despite being Renshai. "You were on your honor not to bare steel in the court."

"But I had to—"

"And I told you not to fight." Weile's expression became stonier, and Talamir found himself unable to talk, unwilling to further defend his actions. "You scarred two of the best men in the world, bodyguards I've trusted for over forty years. Men who would gladly give their lives for me and have forsaken all other pleasures, including those of women, to remain at my side when I need them."

Talamir lowered his head, suddenly awash with guilt for resorting to unnecessary violence. The remorse seemed wrong, out of place in the repertoire of a man trained lifelong to react to threats with a sword; yet it remained no less powerful and real. He could not understand why Weile's words had such a profound effect upon him. Yet, as he sat in the deep and meaningful silence that followed Weile Kahn's pronouncement, Talamir's mind focused on a single phrase: "forsaken all other pleasures, including women." Weile's bodyguards, men feared and respected throughout the Eastern kingdom. *Could those two be lovers?* Only that, as well as a vast love for his grandson, might explain why Weile had taken a personal interest in Talamir's situation.

"If you want my help, you have to do as I tell you."

Talamir forced himself to raise his head. He could not quite manage his usual wary crouch, but he did clamber to his haunches without vomiting. "You can . . . you can still . . . lighten my sentence."

Weile blinked deliberately but otherwise did not change his expression. "Talamir, I believe I could have gotten you off just by talking to my son had you not compounded your simple offense with . . ." He added with significance, ". . . high treason."

Again, Talamir suffered the intense regret that had assailed him earlier. He understood its source better now; he had discarded honor and common sense. He had attacked his lover's beloved father after vowing to himself that he never would. "I made a huge mistake." He looked up at Weile, eyes welling with tears beyond his control. "I'm a Renshai *torke,* I'm supposed to shape young sinews and minds. Yet, when it came to saving myself and the one I love most in the world, I did everything wrong."

"Not everything."

Awash in anguish, Talamir barely heard. "Why didn't you kill me in battle?" The prison cell blurred to bars and granite, an endless gray reeking of sweat, urine, and sickness.

"Talamir, you went against your honor by baring steel in the court. But you proved yourself to me when you lied to protect Subikahn."

Talamir saw no virtue in that action. "I said I raped my lover. I claimed to have hurt the one person I never would. What if Subikahn comes to believe it?"

Weile snorted. "I don't even think Tae believes it."

Talamir jerked his head up and immediately wished he had not. His stomach protested emphatically.

"I was testing you. I just wanted to know whether you would sacrifice yourself for Subikahn." Weile spoke of such things without a trace of self-consciousness, as if they were chatting at the local tavern. "You've proved your worth."

"But at what price? I'm going to be tortured to death, and Subikahn . . . ?" Talamir scarcely dared to ask. He had avoided the question thus far, desperately worried to hear the answer. "Is he . . . ? Will he be . . . wholly spared?" A worse thought struck him. "He won't have to . . . watch my execution, will he?" The very thought seemed worse than anything the guards of Stalmize could do to him.

Weile Kahn closed his eyes, shook his head. He seemed slightly amused. "You're not the only one who loves Subikahn. His father coddles him."

"Usually." Now that he had broached the subject, Talamir had to know. "But this time?"

"Banished till his twentieth birthday and charged with visiting every continent in the world."

Talamir's eyes widened, no longer teary. "He doesn't have a lick of street smarts. The world will eat him up."

"Which is why he needs a dedicated bodyguard." Anticipating the argument, Weile raised a hand. "Not because he's not a skilled swordsman, already far more so than his father. But because he lacks experience, wisdom."

Talamir knew exactly who Weile meant. "So . . . you can still . . . get me off?"

"Not for high treason, Talamir."

The Renshai slumped. He had, apparently, misunderstood.

"But I can help you escape." Weile raised an arm to reveal a key dangling from his fingers. He unclipped his own sword and passed it through the bars.

Despite the residual effects of the toxin, Talamir leaped for the offering. He pulled it through with the enthusiasm a starving beggar shows a fresh baked pie.

"And wear this." Weile stuffed his black robes and silver gauze through the bars. "I'll help you put it on properly; my men will easily spot a fake. And make absolutely certain you leave it with one of us once you're out. Otherwise, we will have no choice but to hunt you down ourselves."

Talamir clutched the sword like a lifeline, forcing himself to listen even as he studied the line of the blade through its sheath. He would not know its quality until he drew it but knew better than to do so with the king's father standing so near, unarmed, and still in possession of the key. He owed Weile more than his life.

"Don't do anything stupid." Weile separated that piece of advice from everything before and after.

Talamir did not know whether to resent the implication or agree with it. Thus far, he had not conducted himself well, and Renshai were not known for their caution or strategy. Even in war, they fought without plan, their sole focus to win each individual battle or die fighting.

"My men know and will not bother you unless you force their hands." Weile added with intensity, "That will irritate me, and you don't want me irritated."

Talamir believed it.

"The regular guards, however, do not know. They're good men, just doing their jobs. If you act as if you belong and walk right past them, you should get free without violence." It was warning as much as information. "I gave you that sword because I know Renshai. You're more secure and, in a strange way, safer with it. I would appreciate it, however, if you didn't kill anyone in the employ of the king."

"I promise."

Weile raised a brow.

"I mean it," Talamir said. "I won't bare steel, this time. Not unless there is no other option."

"And you will commit to attending my grandson until his return."

"Gladly."

"Even if your relationship fails."

Talamir could not imagine such a contingency. Nothing had ever felt so right to him. Nevertheless, he hesitated to show that he had appropriately considered the words. He was old enough to realize that no relationship of love was ever entered into to fail, yet they so often did. "Even should we become the bitterest of enemies, I will do as I have promised you. I will gladly lay down my life for Subikahn."

"See that you do, Talamir." The words were simple, the threat implied. "See that you do."

CHAPTER 9

One lie is enough to undo a man.
—*Queen Eudora of Pudar*

EXHAUSTION HOUNDED SAVIAR as he stumbled over the threshold to the practice courtyard set in the middle of the castle grounds. It had become familiar over the past few days, yet Saviar still marveled at its size and scope. Constructed for multiple uses: guards, members of the royal family, visiting dignitaries, and the Renshai who guarded the heirs, it seemed well suited to their many styles of combat.

An enormous rack near the door held a variety of weapons, the like of which Saviar had never seen. Swords of myriad types alternated with axes, lances, and spears. Staves and hammers held their places, along with incomprehensible polearms that combined loops, scoops, and points with blades. Shields and helmets, sticks and bones, lumpy wooden-and-iron implements that seemed little better than clubs: everything had a place in the practice courtyard of Béarn. They all had one thing in common to Saviar's mind; only the most desperate warrior would use them. The blade edges were notched, cracked, and blunted, the points worn down to bruising nubbins.

The terrain also ran the gamut, mostly vast open space. In one area, someone had built a crude series of ceilingless rooms, including a spiral staircase, apparently as preparation for indoor battles. Another area, the one Saviar had thus far chosen, had sticks and stones strewn over it in random patterns, along with a tattered pack spewing rotten boots and clothing. The left boot sole had become a convincing nemesis, having already turned his ankle twice.

For a change of pace, Saviar chose an open area, though many of his *torke* would have admonished him. "Tiredness is not an excuse for laziness," Kyntiri often told them. "When you're sick, shy of sleep, or injured is the best time to push yourself past any limits. Your enemies will not give you quarter for weakness, and the worst of them will target those most-vulnerable moments." Driving the words from his mind, along with the accompanying guilt, Saviar drew his sword, parried an invisible blade, and cut for his nonexistent opponent all in the same smooth motion.

Fatigue seemed to lift from Saviar's body as he launched into a complicated *svergelse*. He spent hours performing sword maneuvers daily, yet he never tired of them. At times, he did not want to start; but, once he did, he always found that strange, soaring pinnacle of joy that his *torke* so often lauded. His sword dipped, cut, and wove through the air, the breeze of its motion cooling limbs swiftly bathed in sweat. His sword became an extension of his arm, moving swifter than the eye could follow.

Saviar leaped and parried, thrust and slashed through an army of enemies, his pace never faltering and his mind never budging from his *svergelse* and imagined foes. He cut through a dozen, then a score, battling them in pairs and trios, midgets and giants, fast and slow. His defense was movement; Renshai relied on nothing else. Battle was life, was death, and everything between them.

The door creaked open. Alert to movement, Saviar knew it at once, pausing in his lethal dance to gauge the intruder. In battle mode, his mind sought clues as to the intention of the other, cautious friend or lethal foe. He had wholly forgotten his location, the inner sanctum of Béarn, where no enemy could enter without first undergoing the scrutiny of an entire force of kingdom guards.

The newcomer was a stranger, an adolescent male with pale, rugged features, blond braids, and alert, blue eyes. He wore an emerald-colored tunic of odd design, cut low in the back, and heavy woolen leggings. Leather, thick-soled sandals hugged his feet, the laces criss-crossing up his britches to disappear beneath his skirting. A broadsword that looked too big for him swung at his side, and he clasped a huge, studded shield in his hand.

Saviar caught himself staring. By coloring, the youngster could easily have passed for Renshai if not for his bulk and the shield. Blocking blows with anything but one's own blade was considered cowardice by Renshai. *Could this be a Northman?*

The newcomer met Saviar's stare with a smile. "Hullo." He spoke the Common Trading tongue with a heavy, musical accent. "My name is Verdondi Eriksson."

Saviar did the only polite thing. "Saviar." He lowered his weapon. "Uh, Ra-khirsson."

"Uhlrrakirsson?" Verdondi's eyes narrowed in clear confusion. "That sounds like a Northern name."

Saviar grinned at the misconception. "My father is Ra-khir, not Uhlrrakir. The "uh" part was just my incompetent stuttering."

Verdondi laughed, then his lids drooped further and his fair brow crinkled. "So, Ra-khir is a . . . an . . . Erythanian name?"

Now it was Saviar's turn to laugh. "Not exactly. His father named him Rawlin; his stepfather, Khirwith, called him Khirwithson and tried to lose the original name. As I understand it, my child-papa got it all blended together and the new mess stuck."

"So his stepfather would have had him being Khirwithson Khirwithsson?"

"Apparently." Saviar had never thought about it in detail. In Verdondi's voice, though, the name sounded stupid, which seemed appropriate. Ra-khir rarely spoke of his stepfather; but, when he did, Khirwith came off clownish and dull. "Ra-khir even has a hyphen in the middle."

This time, they laughed together.

Verdondi pulled at his leggings, bunched beneath the leather straps. "So, Saviar Rah-hyphen-khirsson. How about a spar?"

Saviar accepted in a heartbeat. He had often longed to try his hand against a stranger, especially one his own age.

Verdondi unsheathed his sword, laying it gently on the rack. He sifted through the Béarnian weapons, choosing a similar sword and cramming it into his emptied sheath. When Saviar made no similar move, Verdondi eyed his opponent's more slender sword, then picked one of similar size. He headed toward Saviar, offering the hilt. "Here."

Saviar accepted the inferior weapon, staring at the blunted edges, the notches, the broken tip. No Renshai would be caught dead on his pyre with such a pitiful excuse for a sword. "What's this?"

Verdondi stared. "Your practice weapon, of course. You didn't think we were going to spar with live steel, did you? Someone might get hurt."

"Um." Saviar recovered quickly, cheeks hot with embarrassment. He should know better. Though Renshai never stooped to using blunted weapons, the Knights of Erythane considered them a normal and safe part of training. "Of course. I'm sorry. Stupid of me." Reluctantly, he placed his regular sword on the rack and replaced it with the practice blade. "So, where did you want to spar? Field, forest, or indoors?"

Verdondi looked over the practice area, head bobbing. "I've never fought in a castle before. Let's try indoors, if you don't mind."

"Not at all." When Saviar had first arrived in Béarn, he had found himself intrigued by the castle facade training area as well. He headed toward it, Verdondi trailing.

"So what's an Erythanian doing in Béarn anyway?" the Northman asked as they walked. "You don't seem old enough for the army."

Saviar gritted his teeth. Though larger than most Renshai his age, he apparently still appeared somewhat younger. Calistin had already fought in a few battles on the shoreline, but Saviar could not join him until he passed his tests of manhood. "My grandfather's the captain of the Knights of Erythane, and my father's a knight, too."

"Really?" Verdondi sounded so excited, Saviar turned to face him. "Your father and grandfather are knights?"

"Yes." Saviar studied the young Northman. "Do you know of them?"

"The Knights of Erythane? Who doesn't know of the Knights of Erythane?"

Saviar had no answer, so he continued to the simulated castle interior.

"Competent and honorable warriors are appreciated everywhere."

Now in place, Saviar faced his new companion again. He gained a new appreciation for the paternal side of his family. He had become so accustomed to the Renshai belittling the knights' rigid code, to the normalcy of skilled swordwork. Until this trip, he had never realized just how much the populace adored and respected the knights or how far their influence extended. "That's good to know."

Verdondi studied the layout. "Are you in training, too, Saviar?"

"In . . . training?" A wave of ice washed through Saviar. He knew better than to mention his Renshai background to any Northman.

"Yes, in training." Verdondi looked at Saviar as if he had gone mad. "Are you going to be a Knight of Erythane, too?"

The question caught Saviar oddly off his guard. "Well, I . . . I'd like to."

"With a family like yours, how could you not?"

"I don't suppose I . . . couldn't."

Verdondi shook his head, clearly impressed. "Talk about honor. What father could resist pressing his son to follow in his footsteps?" He walked to the bottom of the spiral staircase and looked up it. "Your father sounds like a special man."

"He is," Saviar admitted, gaze following Verdondi's. "Isn't yours?"

Verdondi grinned. He stood straight and tall, and his chest seemed to expand with the motion. He was a well-built youngster with bulky muscles evident beneath his tunic. "My father is the captain of the *Sea Dragon*."

Saviar made an awed noise, mostly from politeness. He knew little about sailing or ships, but he suspected becoming a captain took knowledge, ability, and courage.

"He commands the ship, the crew, and is representing Nordmir at the Council meeting with the king of Béarn."

"Impressive."

"Captain Erik Leifsson. And I'm going to be a naval captain, too, someday." Verdondi added softly, "I hope."

"Sounds wonderful," Saviar said, now meaning it. "Traveling the world, commanding a squadron of men and a shipful of sailors, forging into battles." He shook his head in genuine awe. "I could live like that and never regret a moment."

A proud smile hung on Verdondi's face, and he drew himself up to his full height. "Defender or attacker?"

"Huh?" Once again, Saviar found himself driven into confusion and sounding silly.

This time, Verdondi accepted the blame. "I'm sorry. I changed the subject rather abruptly, didn't I?" He tipped his sword toward the spiral staircase. "Defender seems more suited to you, you being Erythanian and this being Béarn. My goal will be to reach the top, yours to keep me at the bottom."

Saviar hopped up the stairs, finally understanding. He sheathed the practice weapon. "Ready?"

Verdondi patted his hilt, still at the bottom of the staircase. "Ready." Suddenly, he drew his sword and charged.

Saviar met him more than halfway down, drew, and cut in one fluid motion. He caught Verdondi a blow to the head that jarred him backward. The Northman lost his footing and started to tumble.

Realizing he had badly overestimated his opponent, Saviar caught Verdondi's arms as he fell. The weight of the Northman nearly swept them both down the steps. Saviar jerked upward.

Verdondi struggled, staggered, then caught his balance. "Whoa, thanks. Can't believe I let that stroke get through." He clamped a hand to his head, then looked at his palm.

Saviar danced clear, sheathing his sword. He could not see where his blow had landed beneath the golden braids, but no blood stained Verdondi's pale hand. A solid bruising seemed more likely. "I'm sorry. Are you all right?" Stopping in the middle of a spar unnerved him. An amputation would have to have occurred before a Renshai would quit fighting, even in practice.

"Don't apologize for my incompetence." Verdondi rubbed at the sore spot, then looked at the railing. "I'm a bit thrown by the staircase. I've just realized why the craftsmen spiraled it rightward."

Saviar had not noticed. "Why's that?"

Verdondi again took up a position of attack. "Because my right arm's against the wall. See?" He tried to raise his sword, limited by the railing and the wall stones. "While yours is free, unhampered. Smart design. If it wasn't on purpose, it should have been."

Saviar touched the railing with his left hand, realizing Verdondi spoke the truth. Such details did not usually concern Renshai. In fact, he imagined his people demanding backward spirals just for the challenge. He considered the other staircases in the castle and realized they all twisted the same way. "I'm pretty sure it's by design."

"Clever."

"Want to defend for a bit?"

Verdondi looked up and down the stairs, clearly pondering.

"It doesn't matter to me," Saviar assured him.

"Well . . . if you're sure it doesn't matter . . ."

Saviar made a broad gesture to indicate Verdondi should pass him, then headed down the steps. He waited for Verdondi to reach the top, sword clutched in his right fist.

"Ready?"

"Whenever," Saviar called back. Then, realizing he, as the attacker, had to make the first move, he drew and charged upward with a battle scream.

They met nearer the top than the bottom this time, and their swords clashed together. Pain thrummed through Saviar's arm, the first time he faced an opponent with as much strength as himself. He parried deftly, then flicked his sword beneath Verdondi's. He could have disarmed the Northman but withdrew instead. It would have required a deft Renshai maneuver that would have made the other young man suspicious. Saviar had no intention of revealing his Renshai heritage to a visiting Northman of any age.

Instead, Saviar awaited an attack. It came high and sweeping. He riposted, then bore in with a gut shot that would have skewed his opponent had he not pulled it.

"I'm dead," Verdondi announced honestly. His arm drooped to his side. "No wonder you don't care if you're defender or attacker. You didn't tell me you were ambidextrous."

All Renshai were. If not born to use both hands equally, they learned to at such an early age it seemed as if they were. At any age, if one hand showed more promise than the other, they practiced only with the weaker one until they managed equal competence. It had not taken a thought for Saviar to draw left-handed. When the time came to attack, instinct had taken over. He smiled. "You didn't ask."

"You're full of surprises, Saviar Ra-khirsson." Verdondi headed down the staircase. "I'm considered one of the best warriors of my age, and you're making me look like a beginner."

Though grinning inwardly, Saviar allowed no sign of it to appear on his face. "I've just had more experience with the staircase. Why don't we spar on open ground?"

Verdondi gave a respectful bow. "How honorable of you to give up your advantage. You clearly are your forefathers' son." He headed toward the open practice area.

Following, Saviar bit his cheeks to keep from laughing. What Verdondi had attributed to knightly honor was actually a Renshai desire to make an easy battle more challenging and interesting. For the first time, Saviar truly appreciated his heritage: the obsessive focus on swordwork, the secret maneuvers, the endless practices. Even he, as yet incapable of passing his manhood tests, might actually be a match for three non-Renshai.

Verdondi braced himself, legs solidly beneath his body, knees bent, hand on hilt. "All right. I'm ready." His eyes followed Saviar's every movement.

Saviar took a position directly opposite Verdondi and beyond sword range. Though he kept his weight balanced, he strove for a more casual look and did not bother to clutch his hilt. "Begin."

Verdondi drew his sword. In the same space of time, Saviar freed his blade, lunged, and cut. Verdondi retreated, rescuing his legs but losing the opportunity for attack. Saviar saw an opening, but resisted, not wishing to humiliate his companion. Instead, he flipped his sword into position for a low cut that Verdondi successfully blocked with a quick parry.

Again, Saviar surrendered an opportunity, this time for a gut slash. Verdondi managed a hacking cut that Saviar easily dodged. He counted his openings, two this time, one nearly at his opponent's back. He resisted both to feign a high slash to the neck, followed by a swift slice to Verdondi's hip. Suddenly realizing the blow would fall, Saviar switched to a blunt side hit that slapped against Verdondi's hipbone.

"Damn it!" Verdondi halted the match again. "Your father is an outstanding teacher, and you have incredible natural talent."

"Th-thank you," Saviar stammered, cheeks flushing. No one had ever complimented his abilities with such strong words. Renshai used praise sparingly; excellence was simply expected. Saviar also did not bother to correct the misconception. Verdondi did not need to know it was his mother, not his father, who had trained him. He sheathed his sword.

"When I become a captain, I'm coming back to recruit you. That is, if you're not caught up with knightly duties." Verdondi jammed his practice sword into place as well.

Saviar grinned, "And I might accept . . ." The idea suited him until the reality of the details caught up to him. Eventually, a ship full of Northman would discover his heritage, and he would have no place to hide. He would have to either slaughter all his shipmates or die on their swords. He added his one out, as Verdondi had, ". . . if I'm not caught up in knightly duties."

Verdondi laughed. "It's all right if you are. Among knights, I'm sure your talents won't get wasted either."

Saviar finally found a response. "Thank you for your generous compliments."

Verdondi continued, "And being shipbound isn't all excitement and glory either. There's a lot of loneliness and tedium, too." He lowered his voice to a conspiratorial whisper, "Especially the girls. No women allowed on board."

Saviar's cheeks grew hotter. He had found himself staring at the female Renshai, enamored of their looks and grace, imagining situations of which no Knight of Erythane would approve. The girls had clearly noticed him as well. They giggled around him and found lame excuses to touch him, all of which excited him wildly. The idea of actually courting one, however, terrified him. "I . . . think I could handle that."

"And for every fascinating diplomatic mission, like this one, there are several hundred routine patrols."

Saviar wondered whether or not the spar had finished. He felt uncomfortable with a grubby practice weapon where his zealously tended sword should sit. He remembered what his grandfather had told him. "Did you come to barter iron ore with King Griff?"

Verdondi chuckled, then covered his mouth, clearly mortified by his reaction.

Confused, Saviar sought clarification. He shook back red-blond hair damp with sweat. "What?"

"I'm sorry." Verdondi glanced around the empty practice area, as if concerned someone might overhear. "It's just such a simple name for a man of such might and power."

Now, Saviar laughed. He had grown accustomed to the unpretentious name of Béarn's great king. It fit the childlike, bearish man
whose rulings seemed guileless and easy when he spoke them. Yet,
when examined, those same proclamations held a complexity belied
by the man's unpretentious wording and relaxed manner. Few could
remain so consistently fair and proper. He never seemed to make a
single mistake.

A common feature of all the greatest kings of Béarn, that effortless shrewdness soothed the populace, who treasured it and the man
who displayed it. They would not have loved him any less had he
borne the name Dirt, and they spoke his common moniker with a
sweet reverence that made it seem as worthy as any knight's title.
For centuries, a test designed by gods chose the proper heir to the
throne, and Griff had passed with ease.

"It *is* a simple name for such a great and wonderful man. But it
suits him."

Verdondi nodded, though he had no experience on which to base
his own judgment. "Any merchant could deliver a load of ore, normally. But with the pirates off Béarn's coast, it seemed prudent to
bring warriors."

"Like you and your father."

"Yes." Verdondi raised his head. Sunlight sparked highlights
through the pale mane of hair, sweat plastered into an array of spikes.
Wispy brows seemed to disappear against skin as white as skimmed
milk. "Also, we came to offer assistance against the pirate scourge
and the Renshai."

Saviar shook his head, trying to clear his ears. He had to have
imagined the last word. "And the . . . what?"

"The Renshai," Verdondi repeated clearly. "You must have heard of
the Renshai. Everyone has. You know, 'the golden-haired devils.' "

"Devils . . ." Saviar ran his fingers through the tangles of his hair.
A lump formed in his throat. "We don't call them that."

Verdondi finally headed for the racks where he had left their true
weapons. "That's because a Knight of Erythane would never deliberately offend anyone, no matter how evil or creepy. You're too
polite."

Evil? Creepy! The words hit Saviar like tongues of flame. He
wanted to spit back an angry retort, but he held his tongue. Not only
would his father and grandfather not approve, but it might start a
very real battle in the practice court. Killing the son of a visiting dignitary would result in a dangerous, international incident.

Verdondi looked away from Saviar to retrieve his sword.

At the moment, that casual gesture came across as a grave insult. No one dared turn his back on a Renshai.

"Everyone else calls them demons or devils, and rightly so."

Saviar's heart pounded. He had reached a point of no return. In his place, his mother would announce her heritage and wind up killing the brash young Northman. His father would sanction neither a lie nor a battle. Ra-khir would see an opportunity to educate, but he would also find the right words to do so. *I'm not a Knight of Erythane, and I'm not Kevral.* Saviar chose his own course, though it involved a lie of omission. "I appreciate warriors no matter their origins. The Renshai are superior swordsmen. They have protected the heirs of Béarn for decades, and our enemies are their enemies."

Verdondi exchanged his own sword with the mangled practice weapon, then grasped Saviar's from the rack.

The lump in Saviar's throat became a boulder. Instinctively, he sought the best way to reclaim his sword and dodge any attack the Northman might initiate. No matter who held it, any sword in any room with a Renshai could belong to him in an instant. If the Renshai wanted it, it was his.

Apparently oblivious to his companion's upheaval, Verdondi carefully turned the sword around and offered the hilt. "Here you go."

Relief washed through Saviar. "Thank you." He accepted the offering, swiftly exchanging the practice sword for his own in his sheath. Its presence calmed him.

The entire procedure came across as boring routine. Verdondi clearly had no idea he was talking to a Renshai, and Saviar had no intention of telling him. "I'm not going to argue the sins of the Renshai with you, Saviar. Knights clearly know how to find the best in everyone and everything. That's a virtue."

"I'm not a knight," Saviar reminded.

"Not yet." Verdondi smiled. "But you were raised in a family of them, and that's going to reflect strongly on your character." He raised a hand, as if to forestall an argument. "Don't get me wrong; I think that's wonderful. I can't imagine what it would be like to grow up that way, but I'd consider it a high honor, indeed."

The irony might have sent Saviar into spasms of laughter if not for the seriousness of the situation. The upbringing that so awed Verdondi was based on a misconception. Despite his parentage, for all intents and purposes, Saviar was raised the same way as any other Renshai. He answered the only way he could, "Thank you."

"But," Verdondi continued. "But you have to understand that your neighbors are not so tolerant and high in their ideals. They have not forgotten the rampage of the Renshai that left so many innocent Westerners dead."

"Rampage . . . ?" Saviar could scarcely believe they were having this discussion. "People are holding a grudge for things that happened *centuries* ago?" As he understood it, the Northlands banished the Renshai for their ferocity, a quality normally prized in the warrior Northlands. Well over three hundred years ago, the other Northmen drove the Renshai out, mostly for their tactic of dismembering those dead enemies they wished to dishonor and demoralize. Then, all Northmen believed that only an intact body could ever reach Valhalla.

Angered, the Renshai had swept across the Westlands and Eastlands in a blaze of war that had left entire cities in ruins. They battled anyone who would fight them and took the offerings of those who refused. Then, as now, the Renshai knew nothing but swordcraft. They had obtained their necessities through slaughter as well as barter.

"Centuries, indeed." Verdondi's hand went to his hilt, his eyes distant. "Centuries during which the Renshai have pretended to grow more civilized. Yet, they still practice secret warcraft and witchcraft. They still fight like demons."

"What?"

"They drink the blood of innocents to maintain their youth and vigor, living vast lifetimes of which others only dream."

"No, that's not—"

"They make unholy alliances with creatures of the icy darkness to grant them sword skills beyond anything a normal man could accomplish."

Saviar could scarcely believe what he was hearing. "Verdondi, that's just insane! They're great swordsmen because they practice. Pretty much every moment of every day."

"Maybe." Verdondi did not argue. "But most Erythanians think otherwise. Béarnides, too. In fact, groups of Erythanians have come to us to try to reclaim Paradise Plains."

Saviar's brows furrowed. He had lived in Erythane his entire life and never heard of the place. "Where are these Paradise Plains?"

"You would know them as the Fields of Wrath."

The lump in Saviar's throat had grown large enough to interfere with swallowing. "But that's . . . where the Renshai live."

"Now." Verdondi studied Saviar. "The Erythanians who lived there before the Renshai drove them from their homes, the Paradisians . . ." He pronounced it Paa-rah-*dee*-shins. "They feel their homeland was taken unfairly. That the Renshai should be killed or driven out so they can return to the land rightfully theirs."

Saviar laughed. No other reaction seemed appropriate. Verdondi looked personally affronted. "What's so funny?"

"Well, first. Historically, the Fields of Wrath were just barren, worthless land when the Renshai settled on them, with the permission of the Erythanian and Béarnian kings of the time. So infertile, in fact, that no crops grow on them to this very day."

"History written by the conquerors, no doubt."

Saviar conceded the point. Normally, the victors did write the accounts, usually by default; but that did not necessarily make them inaccurate. "Second, even if it were true, how can we right a wrong that took place several centuries ago? It would set an unbearable precedent. Every border in the Northlands would have to get redrawn, and many Western towns would simply not exist."

"But no one else is complaining."

No one else is complaining about Renshai, you mean. Saviar knew this so-called repatriation had little to do with logic and everything to do with prejudice. In those situations, it made little sense to argue. Whatever solution he and Verdondi agreed upon, if it were even possible to concur on the matter, meant nothing. The important conversation was currently taking place in the Council Room in Béarn. Suddenly, Saviar wished with all his heart that he had insisted on accompanying Kedrin there rather than allowing Ra-khir to talk him out of it. "But what if someone else does complain? What if this sets a standard so widespread that everyone wants the right to return to land claimed as ancestral? To what year, decade, century, or millennium do we set the map?"

To his credit, Verdondi gave the question due consideration. "I don't know," he finally admitted. "But is concern for precedent ever a reason not to do what's right?"

"I think," Saviar replied slowly, realizing he had entered the most earnest discussion of his life, and it was with another youngster. Had it not struck so personally, he might have enjoyed philosophizing. ". . . it depends on whose idea of right."

CHAPTER 10

Violence cannot solve every problem.
—Arak'bar Tulamii Dhor (aka Captain)

A CHEERY FIRE FLICKERED through the gathering dusk of the Dancing Dog, sending orange-and-yellow highlights leaping through the press of people. Alone at a wine-stained table, Subikahn sat with his back to the corner, trying to focus on the many patrons in the bar. But the images swirled into a gray wash of movement, and their conversations became a hum as indecipherable as night insects. Never in his life had he been among so many people at once; never in his life had he felt so unutterably, unconscionably lonely.

The darkness of Subikahn's corner washed over him. The same thoughts had paraded through his mind so many times, he had nowhere else to take them. They left him numb, uncertain, and incapable of understanding. In one horrible moment, he had lost everything: his beloved, his perfect father, his royal life. All the things that had ever made him happy had vanished with a single proclamation. His slumped shoulders held a burden heavier than anything he had ever before imagined. Even breathing took a massive effort. His food grew cold, his ale warm, and he still found himself incapable of mustering the will or strength to consume them.

The proprietor appeared to hover over Subikahn, a short, heavyset man with greasy hair. "Is the food not to your liking, Sire?"

Subikahn finally looked at his meal. Clearly, someone had gone to great lengths to make it presentable as well as tasty. Fresh pork took up most of the plate's center, surrounded by a wall of mashed, orange roots garnished with salt and herbs. The periphery contained a mixture of vegetables, cut into intricate designs. A second plate held a chunk of unusually light bread baked to a delicate gold and sprinkled with seeds. The rich, amber ale was clearly the best the inn had to offer. "The food is fine, sir. Wonderful even. I'm just not . . . hungry." He wondered idly if his appetite would ever return.

Subikahn pulled his purse from his pocket. It seemed woefully empty. Tae had severely limited his traveling funds, just enough to get him started. *Enough for now.* Subikahn realized he would have to ration what little the king had granted him or swiftly wind up sleeping in unsavory or vulnerable places. He dumped the entire contents into his hand. "How much do I owe you?"

The proprietor stared at the coins. His nostrils flared, then he looked at Subikahn with a sincere expression. "Your money's no good here, Sire."

A wave of heat passed through Subikahn. He felt suddenly chastened and guilty. "I—I didn't know. I—" He jerked his attention from the proprietor to his own palm, worried his father had given him dummies. *Why would he torment me?* Though not a large amount, the two silvers and seven coppers did appear properly minted. "But it's good coin of the realm."

The proprietor grinned. "I just meant I won't take money from you, Sire. You may have whatever you want, and it's on the house."

"On the house?" Subikahn knew what that phrase meant from his travels to and from Stalmize and Erythane. "But I have to—"

The proprietor did not allow Subikahn to finish. "Just tell your friends and father what a grand place we have here. The Dancing Dog is an inn worthy of nobility. True, Sire?"

Subikahn had chosen the inn at random, not for its appearance or decor. "Well, of course, but—"

"Enjoy yourself, Sire. I won't take payment from you." With that, the proprietor turned on a heel and headed back toward the kitchen.

Subikahn slumped into his seat, staring at the food. Now that he knew it would cost someone else money, he felt obligated to eat every bite. He took a spoonful of roots, whipped and soft but no longer steaming. They smelled spicy and inviting, but he still found himself incapable of hunger. He stuffed the spoon into his mouth before he could change his mind. It tasted like ashes; anything would, he guessed. The food slid down his throat and thudded into his stomach.

Memories descended on Subikahn like a flock of crows, pecking and poking at his sanity. He remembered romping on the floor with his father, mimicking dogs or snakes or monsters, whatever struck his fancy. No matter his workload, no matter the affairs of state, Tae had dropped everything, anytime, to play with his son. Subikahn's mind turned to his twin, Saviar, and their wild times in Erythane. When not engaged in the lightning exchange of swordplay, they shared their deepest fears, hopes, and dreams in quiet whispers that no one else could understand. He thought of Talamir, his Tally, the confidences they shared, the moments of tenderness that felt too flawless, too magnificent to be anything less than love. He longed for the gentle hand stroking his hair, for the firm grip of his lover's hand adjusting a sword maneuver, for the doting, almost violent passion of his kiss.

Subikahn realized he might miss the trappings of the castle in a vague sort of way, when the cold nights of winter set in, when his clothing became filthy and tattered, or when he slept on a bed of moldering leaves. But the people he loved mattered most. Without his brother, his lover, his father, he was not certain he could last another day.

A tear splashed onto the tabletop, followed by another. Only then, Subikahn realized he was crying. He lowered his head, afraid someone might see him. His mother disdained weakness, as all Renshai did. He had found little to snivel about in Stalmize Castle; and, when he did, his father had always presented a swift distraction. Now, in the depths of his despair, Subikahn was incapable of holding back the tears. He buried his face in his hands and wept.

For once, Subikahn's Renshai instincts failed him. He did not hear another claim the chair beside him until a light hand ran through the silky black strands of his hair. For the moment, he did not care if the other meant him well or ill. Whoever had come could have all the money in his purse, could stuff a knife through his ribs for all he cared. Grief stilled even the deeply embedded desire to live.

Nimble fingers unglued wisps of hair from Subikahn's forehead and brushed them into place. Then, gradually, warm arms enwrapped him, pulling him close. The softness of the clothing, of the chest, told him his quiet comforter was a young woman. She held him in an embrace that radiated warmth and caring, made him feel safe as he once had only with his father. Whether from pity or compassion, she knew how to hold a crying man.

For several moments, they sat this way, him weeping, her embracing. Then, soft lips touched his ear and a voice whispered comfortingly into it, "I'm taking you to your room. I'll have the rest of your meal sent there."

Subikahn did not protest. It seemed best to take him away from where others might see and judge him. Head down, feet shuffling, he allowed her to guide him up the stairs, through a short hallway and into one of the inn rooms. She steered him to the bed, where he sat numbly, uncertain what to do next.

The woman did not suffer from the same uncertainty. She caught him into her arms again, crushing him against her, stroking his hair, muttering words that sounded more like doves cooing than speech. To Subikahn's surprise, he appreciated her efforts. His mother had had her tender moments, and he knew she loved him. Yet, he could not remember her ever clutching him with such sweetness, ever radiating as much caring for his pain. He knew he should feel embarrassed for acting so helpless, so childlike, but strength and words mostly failed him and he managed only, "I'm so sorry."

"Sorry? Sorry for what?" Her closeness muffled her speech.

"Sorry for humiliating myself. And you. Sorry for making a scene in a crowded barroom."

She finally pulled away far enough for Subikahn to look at her. She appeared to be about his age, but world wise, with soft, brown skin and dark eyes that radiated knowledge beyond her years. She had boyish features that Subikahn found more attractive than the classic ideal of feminine beauty: her face round, her blue-black hair cropped short, her brows prominent, and her lips bow-shaped and thin. Though dark in every way Kevral was light, she still reminded Subikahn of his mother. "You didn't make a scene. And you needn't apologize for feeling sad."

Sad barely grazed the scope of what he felt. "My name is Subikahn."

She smiled. "I know that, of course, Your Highness. My name is Saydee."

"Nice to meet you, Saydee." To Subikahn's surprise, he did not want her to leave. She seemed capable of distracting him from his wretched contemplation as no one else had. "And just call me Subikahn, please."

"All right, Your—" Saydee flushed, the redness barely tinting her dark features. "—Subikahn." The name fell hesitantly from her tongue, and the color of her cheeks deepened. She released him completely and sat nervously beside him.

Subikahn looked around the room, noticing his surroundings for the first time in days. He sat on a straw pallet covered with a blanket woven with fancy designs. Though old and worn, poked through with bits of straw, it was skillfully plaited and patterned. A plain, but solidly built, chest sat at the foot. Balanced on it, he found a pitcher and bowl, a chamber pot, and a crock of tallow. A torch burned in a bracket on the wall, and the only exit was the door through which they had entered. He looked at Saydee again. She wore a clean, patched dress with an ale-stained apron. Solid legs peeked out from beneath it, and woven sandals hugged clean feet.

Saydee quailed beneath Subikahn's scrutiny. "Well, I guess I'd better be going now."

"Wait." Subikahn placed a hand over hers on the pallet. "Please stay a bit longer."

At his touch, Saydee's face seemed to glow. She glanced demurely at her hem.

Not wishing to give her the wrong idea, Subikahn added, "I'd like to talk a bit, if you can spare the time."

"I can. As much as you wish." Saydee gazed into his eyes and smiled.

Subikahn could not help smiling back, his first in what seemed like a very long time. "I . . ." His grin wilted. "I . . . lost someone special . . . to me." That was the most he felt comfortable confiding in a stranger, but it felt good to get even that little bit in the open.

Saydee nodded knowingly. "Do you want to talk about her?"

It intrigued Subikahn that she knew at once he meant a lover, even though she made the obvious mistake assigning gender. "No," he found himself saying before he could think. He had lost too many days to pining. He could not remember much of those but aimless wandering and self-inflicted starvation. Already, he had had to tighten his sword belt and tie up his britches. "No, for the time being, I just want to forget."

"I can help you," Saydee said softly, looking at him with passion as well as uncertainty. She shifted closer.

Nothing. Subikahn felt no attraction to her; no woman had ever excited him, not even the ones who gyrated around him or feigned accident to reveal a breast, a belly button, a thigh. Tae's words came back to haunt him now: "Subikahn, this will give you a chance to experience . . . other things." *Other things.* He knew exactly what his father meant by that. *He wants me to try loving women the way I do Tally. He wants me to try . . . to be . . . normal.*

Without thinking, Subikahn dropped his head in shame. His love was deviant, evil to the lawmakers of the Eastlands, yet it seemed so right and real. His father had given him so much through the years, had always done right by him. He owed it to Tae to try. Steeling himself, Subikahn leaned toward Saydee, caught her into an embrace, and closed his eyes.

Her lips touched his, then locked into a kiss. For a moment, it was a dry, dispassionate coupling. Then, Subikahn imagined her mouth as Talamir's, brought his lover's face fully to life in his mind's eye. The kiss grew moister, hungry. She sucked his tongue into her mouth and, to his joy, he finally responded. They fell together onto the bed, his hands exploring but avoiding those most womanly places, the ones that might break the fantasy Subikahn constructed in his mind.

Though desperately inexperienced, Subikahn found the proper places, made the appropriate motions, did what was expected. He dared not prolong the experience for fear of losing his nerve or his enthusiasm, so it ended quickly in an explosion of guilty pleasure that left him feeling dirty and embarrassed.

Neither his speed nor discomfort seemed to bother Saydee. She readjusted her clothing, which he had not bothered to fully remove, and snuggled into the crook of his shoulder with a satisfied sigh. He left an arm around her, staring at the ceiling, wondering how he ought to feel. He supposed the second time would come easier, and the third. Eventually, perhaps, he could even learn to enjoy coupling with females. Maybe Tae would accept Talamir if Subikahn also married a woman and created royal heirs. Many kings kept concubines, and Béarnian royalty married many times to assure a strong and continuing line.

Perhaps Talamir could live with that arrangement. Perhaps Tae could, too. At the moment, it seemed like a simple compromise; and Subikahn forced himself not to delve too deeply into this solution. If he did, he might discover its many flaws, might shatter the only dream that currently gave him hope.

Though engrossed in a complicated *svergelse*, Calistin Rakhirsson never lost track of his surroundings or the goings-on around him. He found the scarlet cocoon of violence, the perfect world that all Renshai knew when their every movement reached the ultimate level of competence. Nevertheless, he could count and identify every member of the small crowd that invariably gathered to watch him. His swords became an invisible blur, rarely appearing to the mortal eye as streaks of dancing silver. His hands merged with the hilts, and his arms traced seamless arcs, lines, and circles through the air. At the moment, no one challenged him, a fact that both relieved and disappointed him. He enjoyed his *svergelse*. Few had the skill to seriously oppose him, and he remained his own most formidable opponent.

Finally, one man broke from the crowd to leap between the deadly, steel slices. Kwavirse met one of Calistin's strokes with a solid block, then parried it into a low cut. Instead of the anticipated retreat, Calistin launched a blazing neck cut with his second blade, one his opponent scarcely dodged. In total control, Calistin bore in. Kwavirse retreated, spun leftward, then lunged into a perfect, and unexpected, *latense* maneuver.

Calistin whirled gracefully to meet it as a small blur of movement entered his peripheral vision. A second opponent joined the first, a small redhead who seemed awkward as a plow horse. Forced to pull a solid, committed stroke, Calistin found himself off-balanced by his own momentum. He turned a stagger-step into a graceful, spinning retreat, his swords forming a flying web of steel to protect him from either opponent's next strike. Only then, he recognized his second "opponent" as the unarmed, untrained Erythanian he had rescued from bullies.

"Kid, get out of here!" Calistin bellowed, prepared to defend against Kwavirse's next move.

Grinning, Kwavirse bore in. Calistin raised a sword for an easy parry, just as Treysind threw himself between the two blades. Fear touched Kwavirse's expression, and the grin became a grimace. Both combatants pulled their strokes, Kwavirse's tearing a piece of the boy's sleeve and Calistin's missing cleanly.

Calistin swore, driving around the boy to attack Kwavirse at his weakest. "Treysind, you moron." Calistin neatly flipped his sword to the flat to score a slap on the older man's left shoulder. He had to pull the second blade to keep it from skewering Treysind on its way to Kwavirse's hip. "Get out of the damned way!"

Kwavirse withdrew and gestured an end to the battle. "You win, Calistin."

He always did. It had reached the point where only three types of Renshai dared to challenge him: the youngsters full of themselves and their progress, the most competent who could find few other opponents at their level or hoped they had reached his, and the sickest and oldest of the Renshai who would throw themselves upon Calistin, wishing to die in furious combat rather than of illness, to find their places in Valhalla.

Attention focused on Treysind, Calistin barely nodded. He spoke in hopeful Renshai, "Another spar, another time, perhaps?" He could fight every moment of every day and never get tired of it. Each new opponent, every motion, taught him something new to expect in combat.

Kwavirse rolled his eyes toward Treysind, who stood quietly in front of Calistin, examining the new hole in his sleeve. "Only if you lose the shadow. I almost killed the little guy."

Calistin gritted his teeth, already angry at the boy. "Killing him might teach him a lesson."

Kwavirse chuckled. "True, but not one he could use in the future."

Calistin seized Treysind's arm with a violence so sudden the boy cringed. He looked up at his savior with stoic blue eyes that carried only a trace of fear. Others who had grabbed him in the past had clearly beaten him. "Come on," Calistin growled in Common, half-walking, half-dragging the Erythanian toward a patch of withered briars. "We need to talk."

Once there, Calistin practically threw Treysind to the ground. "What in coldest Hel is wrong with you?"

The boy gathered his feet under him to crouch at Calistin's feet. He sniffled, wiping his nose with the back of his hand. "Well," he started very slowly, his pace quickening with every word. "Fo' starters, I's a orphan what's growed up on tha streets. I's small an' weakish. Kinda ugly. Not smart at all. I don't talk so good. I looks kinda like a Renshai wit' dis orange . . . red hair, an' a lotta folks don't like that so's they beat me 'round, but I don't know how ta 'fend mesself wit' a sword an'—"

"No, no, no!" Calistin dropped to a crouch in front of Treysind. "I don't mean 'what's wrong with you' in general. I mean, why do you feel the suicidal need to interfere with everything I do?"

Treysind lifted his head. Hair fell in wild strands in every direction, including into his face. "I's jus' pratectin' ya, Hero. I owes ya my life."

Calistin heaved an exasperated sigh. They had already debated this point several times. Treysind would not leave him, and nothing he said would convince the boy not to die for his hero. "Fine, then. You owe me your life; I get it. But what good does it do me for you to skewer yourself during a simple spar? If you just want to die for no reason, why don't you go throw yourself in the well?"

"Well, I . . ." Treysind rearranged his legs under him in a pattern Calistin had never seen before. ". . . can't do that. I's gotta die savin' ya, Hero."

The Renshai thought he knew every wary position, but this one allowed the boy to look casually relaxed while still able to move in any direction in an instant. Calistin marveled at the simple logistics of the position. He adjusted his own crouch, modeling it, and found it as comfortable as his usual cautious squat, without looking so guarded and alert. "So jump between me and an arrow sometime, would you? If you insist on spending your life for me, that would be an actual useful way."

To his credit, Treysind gave the idea due consideration before speaking. "That would be fine, if I's could. But it don't do us no good if ya's daid 'fore tha' arrow comes."

Calistin sighed. He was wasting time with this silly discussion, time he could be spending sparring or practicing. "Kid, the best thing you can do for me is go away and leave me alone."

Treysind shrugged. "Can' do that."

The poor speech threw Calistin, and he dared to hope. "Did you just say you *can* do that?"

Treysind shook his head vigorously, sending his inhumanly orange hair flying. "Can *not* be doin' that. Can *not*. I owes ya m'life, Hero."

Calistin hesitated, torn between two actions. It seemed a simple matter, an act of mercy, just to run a blade through the boy and be done with it. No one would miss Treysind. Yet, though Calistin had killed a few pirates and several mortally sick or injured Renshai, he found himself incapable of slaughtering an unarmed, pitiful child. Explaining anything to Treysind seemed equally abhorrent. The Erythanian appeared incapable of grasping the concept that Calistin could defend himself better than anyone else in the world. He finally settled on something quick and easy. "Look, kid. Renshai sparring may look dangerous, but it's not."

"It's not?" Treysind's skepticism was tangible

"Not to other Renshai, no."

"But ya's usin' real sa-wards. An' so . . . so angry-like, deadly-like."

"It's how we train. But no other Renshai would ever hurt me."

"No?"

A thrill trickled across Calistin. He actually seemed to be getting through the boy's bricklike skull. "Never. I'm more likely to die tripping over you and . . . and falling into that well."

"I'd be fishin' ya's out, Hero. Right 'way, I's would."

Calistin was not so sure he would return the favor. "Of course you would."

Treysind nodded vigorously and somberly.

"So, we're agreed, then? No protecting me from other Renshai?"

Treysind considered for a very long time, gaze distant, features screwed up tightly. "I . . . s'pose . . . I . . . most times . . . I . . ."

It was hardly the sterling promise Calistin wanted; but, for the moment, it worked.

CHAPTER 11

The genius of one man can surpass the superior forces of another.
                                            —*General Santagithi*

SAVIAR OPENED THE GUEST ROOM door to a heated discussion that ceased instantly. The Knights of Erythane would never inflict their personal problems on anyone, not even a family member. Father and grandfather gave Saviar welcoming smiles despite his sweat-soaked, filthy clothing and the hair dangling into his eyes. Though they remained perfectly meticulous, as always, they never expected the same of others.

Saviar dropped to his bed, delicately removed his sword, and pulled his cleaning kit from his pocket. A Renshai always tended his swords before his person. "So, how did things go with the Northmen?" He unraveled a spotless white rag and a vial of sword oil.

The ensuing silence piqued Saviar's curiosity. He looked up in time to see the knights just breaking a serious, nonverbal exchange.

Ra-khir cleared his throat. "Not bad, Saviar; but not as I might have wished either."

Saviar set to cleaning his weapon, concentrating on the blade but still allowing himself to glance up often enough to read expressions. "Let me guess, it wasn't all about ore."

"It wasn't," Ra-khir admitted.

"They brought up Renshai."

"Yes."

"And the 'right' of Paradisians to return to their homeland."

A stunned silence followed. Saviar feigned total engrossment in his weapon but could not suppress a grin. It was rare that he could startle his father speechless.

When the hush continued long past surprise, Saviar finally looked directly at his father. The moment he met those green eyes, Ra-khir spoke, "How could you possibly know that?"

Saviar considered leaving the knights in suspense, but swiftly discarded it. They would worry about a leak in the Council Room, which could turn into a grave political incident. "I sparred with Verdondi Eriksson, the captain's son. We also talked." He did not have to add the last sentence, usually. Most warriors would not think twice about chatting during practice. For Renshai, it was a dangerous offense. Like turning one's back, it implied that one's opponent was so poorly skilled that concentration and wariness were unnecessary in his presence. It was regarded as grave insult.

Kedrin's eyes widened. "Does Verdondi know you're Renshai?"

Saviar returned his attention to his sword. "It didn't come up."

Ra-khir asked in a cautious voice pitched to sound matter-of-fact but not quite succeeding, "Did your relationship to the Knights of Erythane 'come up'?"

"Yes."

Kedrin added, "Probably just as well."

"Yes," Ra-khir agreed. "Probably."

Though Saviar continued to work directly on his sword, he could feel his father's gaze upon him. He set aside his project for a moment. "Papa, I'm not a fool."

"What?" Ra-khir sounded offended. "Of course you're not, Saviar. I've never suggested otherwise."

"I didn't lie, and I won't if directly questioned. But it wouldn't hurt to have Verdondi see me as a friend before he knows what I am. It might give him a reason to rethink the prejudice his people have drummed into him since birth."

"Timing is everything," Kedrin said softly.

Father and son looked at him simultaneously.

He wore his formal knight garb: the tabard with Béarn's rearing golden grizzly on a blue background on the front and Erythane's black sword against orange on the back. Though matured, his features remained strikingly handsome, and the red-blond hair he once shared with son and grandson had turned a distinguished silver. His appearance, his stance, commanded attention and obedience; and Saviar understood how the knights were known and respected even as far away as the Northlands. "In battle, in life, in diplomacy. Everything is timing."

Ra-khir smiled. "Don't tell me . . ." He closed his eyes and held his fingers to his temples, as if concentrating very hard and receiving an answer whispered by the gods: "General Santagithi."

Finding the origin of Kedrin's quotations had become an easy matter. As Kedrin studied the writings and history of the ancient

Western leader/general, he had become more enamored of his wisdom and methods. Considered the best strategist of his era, Santagithi had essentially single-handedly won the Westlands biggest war, the Great War, against a then-hostile Eastlands. He also had a connection to the Renshai. His daughter, Mitrian, was the mother of the half-breed tribe of Tannin and the grandmother of the non-blooded tribe of Rache.

Kedrin shrugged. "Scoff if you must, my son. Great men deserve their due, even long after death."

"Or, in Colbey's case, without the need to die at all." Ra-khir threw up his hands, as if in surrender. "And between my father and my wife, I'm starved for original thought."

"That," Kedrin returned playfully, "is what adolescent sons are for. After all, they know *everything.*"

Ra-khir returned his attention to his son. "In Saviar's case, I'm starting to believe that's true. Do you understand what your grandfather is saying, albeit secondhand, about timing?"

"I do." Saviar did not want to miss a detail. He had to find a way to prove to his father that he was as much a man as Calistin, despite not yet having passed his Renshai testing. "He's saying that I need to reveal the truth at the right time and in the best way. I can't wait until someone else tells Verdondi I'm Renshai or leave him feeling as if I'm deliberately misleading him and using him for information."

Ra-khir nodded sagely. "You do understand."

"Of course, I do." Secretly thrilled by his father's approval, Saviar returned to his oiling. Neither of his parents could be impressed easily. "Like I said, I'm not a fool."

"Ra-khir?" Kedrin said.

Ra-khir apparently caught the reference. "Yes, all right. I suppose you do know better."

Finished with his task, Saviar returned the sword to his belt. He started stripping off his training clothing. As the wet cloth peeled away, it left him damp, cold, and covered in gooseflesh.

Kedrin politely averted his eyes. "Saviar, the Northmen asked King Griff to exile all Renshai."

Saviar stiffened but refused to otherwise react. He knew the king of Béarn would never do such a thing. "How did the Northmen react when he said 'no'?"

"His Majesty," Ra-khir explained, "did not have to say 'no.' The Fields of Wrath are in Erythane, not Béarn proper."

Saviar pulled on a clean tunic. It smelled freshly laundered, a welcome relief after the tainted stiffness his garments had attained during travel. He dragged off his britches next. "So, he simply pushed the decision off onto King Humfreet? He didn't defend us at all?"

"This is diplomacy," Kedrin said. "Things are handled differently than in . . . real life. Wars and alliances are decided by a word or a pen stroke."

"All right."

"And," Ra-khir added, "the king did say that Renshai were courageous, competent, invaluable guardians and warriors. That he has always supported them, and they have never let him down."

"All right," Saviar said again, not wholly happy or comforted but still willing to listen. King Humfreet was a reasonable man but without the historical loyalty and wisdom of Béarn's royalty. Saviar suspected the knights had not yet come to the contentious part of the discussion, and that troubled him greatly.

Kedrin raised his head and heaved a sigh so small Saviar saw more than heard it. "Saviar, the Northmen have agreed to assist Béarn with the pirates."

"That's good." Saviar pulled on his clean britches. "No one knows more about pirates or pirating than Northmen."

"Saviar," Kedrin warned. "Your own prejudice is showing."

Saviar had never considered himself biased, but it seemed impossible to remain fair to people who had just suggested banishing his own family. "Sorry." He did not mean it, nor did it sound as if he did.

"They offered large numbers of soldiers." Ra-khir seemed torn between studying his son's reaction and giving him the appropriate privacy to finish dressing. "And asked only that they not have to serve with Renshai."

"You mean in the same unit?"

"I mean, in the same army."

"Oh." Saviar did not know what to say. One Renshai equaled three of any other warriors; yet, even counting in Renshai soldiers, the Northmen would still clearly outnumber them by thousands. "The king accepted that offer?"

"Not yet."

"But he'll have to," Saviar guessed. "How did Thialnir take it?"

"Not well," Ra-khir admitted. "Though, to his credit, he refrained from violence. A group of us are going to try to explain the situation to him."

"We'd like you to come along," Kedrin said.

Saviar glanced at his father, who did not contradict. At one time, they had clearly disagreed on this matter. "You would do better taking Calistin."

"Calistin?" Ra-khir shook his head. "I don't think Calistin would see the situation any differently than Thialnir."

Saviar had to concur. "Well, then. How many of the people who are going to talk to Thialnir can best him in a battle?"

"None," Kedrin said. "But we're planning to talk to him, not kill him."

Saviar adjusted his britches. "Diplomacy means something different to Renshai. He won't respect a man who couldn't kill him. That's why I suggested Calistin."

Kedrin heaved a more obvious sigh. "And who do you know who can best Calistin?"

"No one. Why?"

"Because . . ." Kedrin sat on the neatly stretched blankets of his own pallet. ". . . I imagine we will find it just as hard to convince Calistin as Thialnir. No, Saviar, you're the only Renshai we have. And the only one we need."

Saviar could not fathom his grandfather's endorsement. "I haven't even passed my manhood testing. Thialnir's a proven warrior, blooded and tested. They chose him to represent us."

"He won't listen unless you best him?" Ra-khir took a step toward Saviar.

"I'd have to give him a reasonably good fight at the very least. That will take years. I might never gain the ability to take on—"

Ra-khir seized his son's arm. "We have two days, Saviar. Let's get started."

Before the boy could protest, he was led to the door, Ra-khir in the lead and Kedrin following. Together, they headed back toward the practice courtyard.

With a quick apology and a spectacular bow, Ra-khir excused himself from the company of his father and his son before they entered the courtyard. To Saviar's chagrin, his father disappeared down a side corridor, but Kedrin did not seem put off by the abrupt departure. Instead he flicked the latch, and opened the door onto the familiar practice courtyard.

Saviar stepped inside. A haze hung over the courtyard, no longer illuminated by morning sunlight, and the obstacles seemed awash in silver. Kedrin glanced at the racks of practice swords. It suited him better not to train with live steel; yet he also knew that the Renshai always did. In the end, he did not exchange his blade but guided Saviar to the most uncluttered part of the grounds, free from debris and deliberate constructions.

"Now," Kedrin began, facing Saviar squarely, "I know you're not a beginner, so we'll skip right to the advanced training."

Saviar kept his expression sober. His *torke* claimed that any sword-work taught by *ganim* would be a lesson Renshai had learned so early in life they could not even recall not knowing it. Saviar kept his mind open, however. If anyone might know a useful, different technique it would be the captain of the Knights of Erythane.

"Show me your stance," Kedrin said, assuming a classic posture, knees bent, weight evenly distributed, right foot leading slightly.

"Which one?"

"Of course. You probably know a thousand." Kedrin laughed, relaxing. "This is rather like pouring a bucket of water in the ocean, isn't it?"

"Well . . ." Saviar stalled, not knowing what to say. "Perhaps . . . you could teach me some power moves."

"Power moves?"

Saviar made a few graceful motions to work the kinks from his legs. "Calistin keeps reminding me that Renshai maneuvers rely on quickness, not strength; but I naturally try to outmuscle everyone because I'm bigger."

Kedrin blinked, as if noticing Saviar for the first time. "You are my biggest grandson, but you're not exactly enormous."

"I'm bigger than any other Renshai my age."

Kedrin nodded thoughtfully. "I suppose you are. You favor your father and me. You'll fill out a lot over the next few years."

Saviar hung his head. "Don't remind me."

"*Don't* remind you?" Kedrin's pale brows rose in increments. "Savi, that's a *good* thing."

"Not for Renshai."

Kedrin disagreed and made it clear. "*Even* for Renshai. Quick maneuvers work great for Renshai, but size and strength don't harm them either. Look at Thialnir."

"He's huge," Saviar admitted.

"And one of the Renshai's most skilled fighters."

Saviar nodded. Until the realization that he might have to face the Renshai's leader in combat, he had never considered Thialnir's size before. The man was intimidating for reasons beyond his massive frame.

"Believing a large man must be slow has cost many warriors their lives, Saviar." Kedrin's blue-white eyes held a sincerity that went beyond truth. Not only did he speak honestly, he did so from the heart, from a need for his grandson to understand. "Handled well, size can become speed's greatest asset."

Saviar's heartbeat quickened. It seemed possible that Kedrin knew a lesson the Renshai would never teach him. "Can you . . . can you show me?"

"I can." Kedrin drew his sword with a fluency Saviar normally attributed only to Renshai. "Please stand back," he said, then laughed. "Sorry, I keep forgetting who I'm talking to."

Saviar could dodge any move his grandfather could make so quickly it might seem as if he anticipated the strike before Kedrin decided on it. He made a motion of encouragement. He had never before seen his grandfather draw steel. The Knight-Captain mostly instructed his charges verbally or demonstrated by repositioning the other man's arms, legs, or weapon.

Kedrin executed a series of deft warm-up strikes, then looked directly at Saviar. "Ready?"

Saviar nodded. Renshai were always ready for anything to do with swords.

Kedrin launched into the *ganim* version of a *svergelse*, his strokes powerful, committed, and yet still nimble and precise. His movements seemed a study in paradox: broad and strong, lithe and agile. Saviar saw nothing slow or clumsy in the captain's actions, and they lacked the ponderous ungainliness the Renshai ascribed to muscled outsiders. Kedrin could not match the speed and fiery grace of a Renshai, but that had to do with practice and dedication, not technique. Saviar watched, awed. He could adapt some of those power strokes into new and deadly Renshai maneuvers.

Diving into the flying cuts of steel, Saviar stayed his grandfather's hand with a careful parry and grab. Close in, swords bound, hand gripping Kedrin's wrist, he looked excitedly at the knight. "Teach me."

For an instant, Kedrin looked shocked. He studied the boy in front of him, making absolutely certain his blade had never touched Saviar. Once sure, he relaxed. "I will."

And Kedrin did. As the sun inched toward the horizon, Saviar learned techniques the Renshai would dismiss as foolish, adapting them to the deadly quickness of Renshai. Saviar knew it did him little good, and a lot of ill, to simply learn the ways of *ganim* swordcraft. With each new movement, with every suggestion, Saviar sought a way to incorporate it into the repertoire he already knew, to advance the maneuver into something as powerful as it was swift and unstoppable.

In the past, Saviar's bulk had always seemed an insurmountable hindrance. Constant swordwork kept him as lean as any Renshai, yet deliberate starvation only made him weak and slower. He could never shed the musculature of his paternal ancestors; the solid definition of his abdominal muscles never allowed his ribs to show. Now, he had found a way to use his build as an advantage, and the idea of pausing to rest after such a staggering discovery never occurred to him. He would continue to revise, to invent, until his grandfather passed out from exhaustion.

Not that Kedrin showed any sign of doing so. He reveled quietly in Saviar's every triumph. Though Kedrin had never stated so, it became clear from his actions and words that he had always wished for the opportunity to educate his grandsons. The time dedicated to Renshai training left little for other things. Though Kedrin had sneaked in lessons on beauty, relaxation, philosophy, and morality, he could never before compete when it came to weapons. Now, his day had come, and he seemed as unlikely to quit as Saviar himself, as relentless and infinite as the Renshai maneuvers.

It seemed like only moments before the door to the courtyard slammed open to reveal Ra-khir in all his knightly splendor, and a host of others behind him. For the first time Saviar could remember, he wished his father would disappear, to leave him in the world of inventiveness and joy that he currently shared with Kedrin.

Though equally engrossed, Kedrin could not have had a more different reaction. He sheathed his sword and executed a bow of great formality. Only then, Saviar recognized the group who had accompanied his father: the heirs to Béarn's throne. Shocked, he froze in position, sword still gripped in his hand.

Kedrin cleared his throat softly, pointedly.

Swiftly, Saviar jabbed his sword back into its sheath and dropped to one knee, head bowed.

Princess Marisole led the group. Only a few months younger than Saviar, she was the oldest heir, Queen Matrinka's first child. She favored her mother: her dark brown hair thick and lustrous, her figure full and curvy, her eyes a dark hazel that barely showed its green. Her large nose betrayed the bard's lineage; and, of course, the delicate lute she carried slung across her shoulder.

She ran to Saviar. "Get up, get up." She cuffed him playfully until he rose, then caught him into an embrace. She felt soft and warm against him, and he could not help noticing that she had developed breasts and hips since he had last seen her. He wrapped his arms around her, forcing his thoughts to his swordwork, to the weather, anything but her magnificent closeness. At his age, any touch from a pretty young thing excited him wildly. If his father or grandfather caught him reacting to a princess of the realm like a common tavern wench, he would suffer greatly for his body's betrayal.

"You moron," Marisole whispered, and Saviar noticed only her warm breath in his ear. "You're a friend, not a servant."

"I'm both," Saviar said as softly. "And the son of a Knight of Erythane. If I don't show proper respect, I'll get a spanking."

"Bow to me again, and *I'll* spank you."

Saviar could not resist pulling free and bowing broadly. "Promises, promises."

Marisole glared. Had they been alone, Saviar felt certain, she would have slapped him. And he definitely deserved it.

Prince Barrindar approached Saviar next. Sixteen, shy, and the spitting image of King Griff, he slouched toward Saviar as if embarrassed by his height. Though tall for his age, Saviar looked the younger boy squarely in the nose. The oldest child of Griff's third wife, Xoraida, and the only remaining male heir, Barrindar did not stand out the way Arturo had. Artistic, quiet, and blithely unworried about his future, he seemed almost a study in contrast to his more outgoing half brother. Arturo had chased life with an ardor Saviar shared: hoping to become a general in the charge of whichever sibling took the throne. Barrindar seemed content to let life take him where it would.

Saviar gave the prince a small bow that demonstrated respect without drawing attention, and Barrindar returned the gesture with a friendly smile and a tip of his shaggy, bearlike head. He withdrew to the far wall, and Marisole joined him.

The three youngest princesses came next, in a whispering, jostling group. Barrindar's full-blooded sister, Calitha looked Saviar up and down as if she had never seen him before. Essentially, Saviar realized, she had not. Their paths had not crossed for years, and she was a child then. Now, fourteen, she seemed to suddenly realize he was male. Her deep brown eyes sparkled, and she lowered her lids coquettishly. Then, her eleven-year-old sister, Eldorin, jabbed her with an elbow and whispered loudly, "Quit staring at him." Turning a brilliant shade of red from her chin to the roots of her hair, Calitha ran to her older siblings without voicing a greeting.

Saviar bowed anyway.

Eldorin waved, clearly not understanding her sister's reaction, nor that she had done anything wrong. Saviar gave her another bow, and she skittered behind her brother.

The third of the trio, thirteen-year-old Halika, ran up to Saviar and hugged him. She was the third and last of Matrinka's brood, and she barely resembled the rest of her family. Shorter and thinner, she sported Darris' mouse-brown curls, broad lips, and generous nose.

Saviar held her like a treasured sister, glad she did not excite him as Marisole had. He would have felt filthy and low. Instead, he whispered, "I'm so sorry about Arturo."

Tears glazed Halika's eyes, and her grip grew fierce. "Be careful, Savi. I don't want to lose another brother."

Suffused with warmth at the compliment, Saviar brushed a curl from her forehead. He knew most of the girl's affection for him had to come from Marisole's attitude and stories. As a child, he had spent much more of his time at Béarn castle playing with Marisole and Subikahn. In those days, two years had made a huge difference; he had thought of Barrindar and Arturo as babies. As he grew older, and the Renshai training commanded all of his time, his visits had grown less frequent and shorter. He barely knew the other princesses, including Princess Ivana Shorith'na Cha'tella Tir Hya'sellirian Albar, despite the fact that she was only a half year younger than him, only a few months younger than Marisole.

As Halika reluctantly withdrew and headed for her other siblings, Ivana ran toward Saviar. Her gait seemed simultaneously agile and awkward, as if she might become a dancer should she only first learn to walk. She looked almost animal in her homeliness: her small mouth and nose nearly disappearing behind remarkably chubby cheeks, her eyes canted and reddish-yellow in color, her hair thick and straight, without a hint of wave or curl. Its color was a strange blackish-blond, with highlights that looked red in places, nearly green in others. Her blocky body seemed slightly twisted and hunched. Her arms and legs were short and stout, but her fingers were contrastingly long and slender. She had tiny feet, swathed in toddler's slippers, that barely seemed capable of balancing her bulk. A bit of white froth perched at the corners of her lips.

Ivana loosed a sound that seemed more like a braying mule than human language and lunged into Saviar's arms as Halika had done. Saviar barely had time to brace himself before she slammed into him. He wrapped his arms around her with difficulty and tried to appear comfortable. Only propriety and politeness held him in place. He would have preferred to run from her in terror.

Saviar pressed his mouth to Ivana's shoulders, hiding the revulsion for which he felt desperately ashamed. Not only was Ivana a full princess of the realm, she had once symbolized a great union and the only hope for humans and elves alike. Elves could procreate only when an elder passed on, his or her soul repackaged into the fetus. Violent death meant a soul lost forever, and most of the elves had died in a great explosion. At the time, humans also suffered, from an inflicted sterility plague. When Tem'aree'ay became pregnant with Griff's child, it had seemed the perfect solution to both dilemmas.

Then, Ra-khir, Kevral, Darris, and a few companions obtained the item necessary for the elves to lift the sterility plague. Ivana was born. And everything changed. Repulsed by the princess, nearly all of the elves abandoned the company of humans to live quiet, unseen lives in the forests scattered throughout Midgard. As far as Saviar knew, only Tem'aree'ay herself remained, bonded to husband and daughter by a love that surpassed tribes, species, even near-immortality.

Saviar hoped that one day, he, too, would find a woman who loved him with such consummate and awesome passion, willing to give up everything just to be with him. He knew Griff would do the same for Tem'aree'ay as well, and Saviar craved the kind of love that would drive him to such madness. For, though Griff had married Queen Matrinka to appease the populace, and Xoraida to legitimately father human heirs, his enormous and tender heart belonged wholly to his elfin wife.

To have this creature, Ivana, be the result of a love so obsessive and fierce seemed the cruelest trick. And many considered it a warning: Leave creation to the gods. Only sorrow could come of meddling with it, of starting new species by mingling unlike beings. The gods had revealed their displeasure by punishing Béarn's king with this monstrosity, and all humans and elves should take heed. It was so easy to forget that her conception had once been considered the ultimate miracle, the answer to two of the greatest problems of the universe.

Finally, Ivana released Saviar and joined her siblings at the periphery. Only then, it occurred to Saviar to wonder why his father had gathered the heirs of Béarn to watch him practice, why Halika had cautioned him and worried for his safety. Saviar had greeted all the heirs, yet still an equal host stood, calmly watchful, at Ra-khir's side. A sinewy horde of brunets and blonds, male and female, some of them braided and all of them armed with swords studied his every movement from the sidelines. He knew them all, at least in passing;

and he also knew why they took such an interest in him. They were learning him: from the set of his build to the shape, origin, and insertion of every muscle. They were the guardians of Béarn's heirs, the only Renshai currently residing in Béarn.

And they were about to attack him. En masse.

CHAPTER 12

Renshai violence is swift and merciless, but never without cause.
—Arak'bar Tulamii Dhor (aka Captain)

TERROR SEIZED SAVIAR in an all-consuming instant that drove everything into slow motion. The mass of Renshai drew and attacked with a speed that would ordinarily have astounded, yet Saviar felt as if he had all the time in the world to die. Instinct took over, and his own sword rasped from its sheath. Then, fear retreated behind the courage trained into him since birth: to die in glorious valorous combat, to find his place in Valhalla, to fight until he drew his last gasping breath. He would do nothing in cowardice, but neither did Renshai training force him to act a fool.

Eyes on his foe, Saviar made a wild leap for the staircase. The forest of swords followed him, clutched in the hands of eager Renshai. Saviar bounded up, three steps at a time, then whirled to face his opponents on the landing. The other Renshai were on him in an instant, but the closed confines forced them to face him one warrior at a time, the others clamoring and howling on the steps like wolves.

And I'm the bone, Saviar realized, catching the first attack, by Asmiri, on his sword and parrying it harmlessly aside. Asmiri clutched a hilt in each hand, cursing the banister and wall that limited his right arm. Nevertheless, his left-hand strokes came blisteringly quickly, and he even managed a few surprises with the right. Hard-pressed to his defense, Saviar parried, blocked, and dodged without bothering to return an attack. He knew all of his attackers, and it chilled him. Every one had fought in the Pirate Wars, every one had already passed the tests to which he still only aspired; not one would go easy on a young Renshai they still considered a child.

Yet, when an opening came, Saviar seized it. He lunged into a miniscule space between Asmiri's weaving blades, jabbing hard enough to disembowel his opponent. Asmiri managed to dodge, barely, hampered by the Renshai behind him. Saviar's blade stabbed through cloth and grazed skin. Real blood followed its withdrawal, and Saviar paused for an instant, startled.

Saviar's *torke* always told him to keep his strokes real. Any adult Renshai who could not avoid the most deadly strike of a student deserved to die. It happened occasionally, though never to Saviar, who had not even drawn blood on a *torke*. "Asmiri, are you all right?"

Asmiri gave him a pale-faced, sour look. "I'm dead, all right?" Unable to properly retreat from the battle, he wilted to the ground in a feigned and awkward swoon. "Keep fighting."

I won! Saviar realized. *I actually won.* He had no time to revel in his triumph. The horde pressed forward, and Elbirine replaced Asmiri. Lost beneath the swiftly shifting feet, Asmiri worked his way cautiously down the stairs while his companions did their best not to step on him. Lithe, small, and fierce, Elbirine had trained with Kevral. Though approaching middle age, she moved with the quickness of a stooping hawk. "Overconfident, like your mother?"

Forced to leap backward to avoid a stunning strike, Saviar dashed his spine against the stonework. Because of her youth and attitude, Kevral had not been well liked by her classmates. Saviar had to wonder whether she annoyed them as much as Calistin did him. Head ringing, he surged into a slashing over-under combination. "No." He dodged a powerful slice from the small woman. "Just . . ." He parried. ". . . confident . . ." He lunged. ". . . enough."

A twirling maneuver saved him from a deadly jab, but opened his side momentarily. Steel tore his britches and the covering flesh and bruised his hipbone with enough force to bring unbidden tears to his eyes.

"Not fatal," Elbirine shouted, without giving Saviar any time to recover. She sliced and cut, surging in and out with fine movements so fast they seemed invisible. He managed to dodge or parry every one, at the same time collecting tiny rents and bruises that reminded him how close he had come to losing the battle.

"Come on, knight's son," Elbirine growled, meaning both the talking while fighting, and the words, as insult. By referring to his father, she meant to remind him that he was not all Renshai, but something less. "Get angry."

Saviar wished he could, but his training remained too strong within him. He knew that rage made men careless, the commonest cause for a fall. He did not like Elbirine. The Renshai guardians of Béarn's heirs had come to help him, at Ra-khir's request. Any Renshai would assist one of their own, and no Renshai could resist a battle. Yet, it soon became clear Elbirine wanted him to pay for all the humiliation she had suffered at the hands of his mother, from Kevral's superior skill and her patronizing manner. Saviar knew only that he could not allow Elbirine to best him.

And then, it happened. Saviar rose to a level he had heard about but never before reached. His mind remained free to study his opponent, to scan her every motion; yet his body reacted without the need for thought. All of his training came together in that moment. He did not need to consider a move before he made it. His body instinctively found the perfect maneuver and used it. Every attack had a defense and a counter, and his arms and legs performed them from years of brutal practice.

Elbirine stopped talking; she could no longer afford the distraction or the energy. Engrossed in his task, Saviar could not have formed coherent words had he wished to do so. He found a euphoria he never knew existed. His world became his sword, his excitement a giddy joy that knew no boundaries, his arms and legs carried out flawless Renshai maneuvers without hesitation. *This is it!* Saviar realized. *This is what Valhalla is like.* He never wanted the battle to end.

Then, suddenly, Saviar remembered Kedrin's teachings. As he executed a deft maneuver, he added a powerful end stroke that defied Elbirine's parry. She caught the blow hard on her blade, and the force of it stole breath and balance. She tumbled down the stairs. Renshai cleared the way, but not quickly enough. She took three of them with her, landing in a heap on the cobbles, tangled with Asmiri as well.

Wildly excited, Saviar prepared for his next assailant as Kedrin called over the fray. "Stop! Enough!" He pointed a warning finger at the remaining Renshai. "This battle is over."

Halting Renshai in combat was more difficult than reining a galloping horse pursued by wolves. The Renshai on the stairs paused. The ones on the ground sorted themselves in an instant and sprang to their feet. Saviar read attack in many eyes. Any word or quick movement would set them back on him. Slowly, cautiously, he sheathed his sword.

To Saviar's relief the others followed suit.

Kedrin explained, "Saviar has had enough for one day."

Saviar raised his brows to display disagreement. In truth, he wanted to finish the spar. His hip throbbed, his head ached, and he could feel the sweat-sting of several small tears. He could not, however, reveal weakness to other Renshai.

"He needs a good meal and a warm bath before his confrontation tomorrow."

Only then, Saviar realized how much time must have passed. The sun was gone, the courtyard dark.

Acknowledging each Renshai with a nod, so as not to appear to be turning his back on them, Saviar descended the stairs. Elbirine glared, but the others merely gave him a tip of their own heads. Kedrin fixed an angry stare on Ra-khir with an intensity that questioned the younger knight's sanity.

Marisole strummed her lute, then launched into a song of such beauty that the last of the hostility disappeared even from Elbirine's stance. The bard's heir sang of brotherhood, of the lethal grace of Renshai, of the virtues of knowing when a battle has truly ended. Her voice had grown stronger since Saviar had heard it last and her range massive. Each note carried a power that reminded Saviar of Renshai sword strokes and a finesse that defied understanding. If her notes wavered a semitone, he never noticed. She not only heard with perfect pitch, she sang it, every tone falling into its rightful place. And she ended with an invitation for Saviar to join the heirs for dinner.

As the last notes faded, Saviar approached Marisole and took her hands. "I'd love to," he said.

Kedrin interceded. "After he's washed up, of course, Your Grace." He gave the bow Saviar had neglected.

Reclaiming her hands, Marisole answered with a proper curtsy. "Please don't take too long, Savi."

This time, Saviar bowed. His grandfather would have it no other way. Despite his growling gut, he would rather have dropped off to sleep without bothering to eat. Though he looked forward to his too-long postponed meeting with Béarn's heirs, he worried about the necessary conversation regarding Arturo when he felt so battered and exhausted.

Kedrin placed his hands on Saviar's shoulders while the heirs trooped out, accompanied by their guardians. Only after the last one left the courtyard did he speak, "Saviar, you did fine in a difficult situation." He turned a dagger glance at Ra-khir.

Saviar had no wish to be present when his father and grandfather discussed what Ra-khir had done.

"And," Kedrin added, "I believe you'll do fine tomorrow as well."

Saviar was not so certain. He could not best Thialnir; he could only hope to earn his respect. Even then, the Renshai leader might not take well to the news about the Pirate Wars; and, this time, the battle might not end on the command of a Knight of Erythane. In the hierarchy of Béarn, Kedrin and Thialnir were considered equals.

"I'll do my best," Saviar promised. "I'll do you proud." He added only to himself: *Or die trying.* At the moment, the unspoken part of the promise seemed the most significant.

A bath and clean clothes worked wonders on Saviar, who felt refreshed despite the throbbing nicks and bruises that seemed to cover every part of him. Apparently, the heirs chose to wait for him because, as he approached the private dining hall, they were filing inside beneath the watchful eyes of their guardian Renshai.

Dodging his peers, who glared but made no move to intervene, Saviar scurried to assist Marisole. Barrindar arrived first, scooting back the seat of the eldest heir of Béarn with a gracious flourish. Saviar glanced around; but, as Halika, Calitha, and Eldorin already had servants assisting them to their seats, he simply chose the place at Marisole's left hand. He pulled out the chair to sit just as Barrindar started to settle into the same one.

Too late, Saviar realized his mistake. The only remaining male heir to Béarn's throne crashed clumsily to the floor, huge arms flailing.

Oh, gods. Before Saviar could move, Marisole and Barrindar's guardian stood between them, the Béarnide helping her cousin and the Renshai glaring daggers at Saviar. "I'm sorry, Your Grace." Saviar bowed repeatedly, finding himself unable to stop. "I am so sorry." *I can't believe I did that.* After what seemed like a hundred million bows, Saviar finally managed to scurry around the table to the only empty seat, across from Marisole at Halika's side. *I can't believe I dumped a prince of Béarn on the floor.* Unable to look at anyone, he buried his face in his arms. He could hear Marisole's soothing voice, soft and directed at Barrindar, her words obliterated by the stifled giggles of the other three princesses.

Only then, Saviar realized how swiftly Marisole had moved and remembered that the bard of Béarn also served as the king's personal bodyguard. He marveled at the thought of all she would have to face. Although Renshai women fought alongside their men, equally fierce, no other group of people supported the idea of women as warriors. Only Béarn expected it, and only in this one instance. Throughout history, the firstborn child of the bard was more often male than female; but Darris' own mother had also served in this position until her death had granted the job to him. Someday, Marisole would take his place, watching over whichever of the heirs passed the test that granted him or her rulership of Béarn.

An odd idea occurred to Saviar. *What if Marisole is the heir?* Such a possibility had never arisen before, given the cautious laws regarding who the heirs to Béarn could marry. Saviar wondered how such a thing might work: would the queen have to serve as her own personal bodyguard? The idea practically banished itself. As the bard, Marisole was also constrained to presenting new ideas only through song. The gods did not seem whimsical enough to force such a queen on the high kingdom of the Westlands. Court proceedings and strategy sessions would turn into an endless concert.

Halika stroked Saviar's damp hair. "It's all right, Savi." She snorted in another laugh. "It was an accident. Barri's not mad." She lowered her voice to a conspiratorial whisper. "He's sweet on her, you know."

Saviar looked at Marisole's blood sister. "Who?"

"Barrindar, of course." Halika's brows furrowed as she considered the undirected question. "He really likes Marisole." She rolled her eyes, as if she could never imagine anyone finding her sister attractive. "Only gods know why."

Barrindar and Marisole? The idea seemed madness. "But they're—" Saviar stopped himself before saying anything stupid. They were half siblings by birth yet did not actually share much blood. Matrinka and Griff were first cousins, an allowable royal marriage by Béarnian convention. When it came to bloodlines, Barrindar and Marisole were actually farther apart than their parents.

"—brother and sister," Halika finished. "Yeah, I know. Isn't it sickening?"

Saviar found himself more jealous than appalled. He had always known he did not fit the criteria necessary to marry a princess of Béarn. Nevertheless, perhaps because she was "safe" or the first girl with whom he had established a friendship, Marisole had occasionally figured in his dreams of the future. The realization surprised and embarrassed him. "Sickening? No. I think it's . . . it's . . . nice."

"You would." Halika stuck her tongue out at Saviar.

Servants circulated, bringing soup to every member of the group, including the guardian Renshai, who sat together at the opposite end of the table. A thick, cream smell filled Saviar's nostrils, along with a tempting array of unfamiliar spices. His gut growled loudly. Ignoring the food, Saviar finally looked directly at Barrindar. "I'm so sorry about what happened."

Barrindar waved away the apology good-naturedly. "Think nothing more of it, good friend." His spoon seemed to disappear into his massive hand, and he tended to his soup.

Saviar let out a pent-up breath, then took up his own spoon and ladled a hefty scoop into his mouth. Hotter than he expected, it burned his tongue, yet the magnificent flavor of spiced potatoes still came through. He gulped down half a mug of mulled cider, then several more spoonfuls of soup.

"So," said eleven-year-old Eldorin around a mouthful of food, "are you a knight or a Renshai?"

Saviar swallowed, the hot soup drawing a fiery line all the way to his stomach. "Renshai."

"Then why're you wearing knight's colors?"

It was the first time anyone had noticed. Even off-duty, the Knights of Erythane wore clothing in blue, gold, black, and orange, in a tasteful array that never clashed. Saviar had taken to emulating his father's colors in childhood, and the habit stuck. "My papa and grandpapa are knights," he explained. "That's what tends to fill our wardrobe."

"Oh." Apparently satisfied, Eldorin returned to her soup.

Saviar wanted to turn the conversation onto anything but himself, but bringing up Arturo's death too quickly seemed heartless at best. He tried to ease into the topic. "Um . . . how are . . . all of you?"

Replies of "good," "fine," and "well enough" came from every corner of the table. Then, Ivana let out a bray that startled Saviar. He barely managed to divert his spilling spoonful of soup into the bowl instead of his lap.

"I was aggrieved to hear about Arturo." Saviar addressed Marisole directly. "How . . . are you? In that regard?"

Halika interrupted before her sister could reply. "Don't ask *her!*" She tugged on Saviar's arm, and he released his spoon to avoid another near spill. "Her song about that is beautiful, but totally depressing."

Nods swept the group, even one from Marisole.

"They're all totally sad," Halika continued, "but getting past it little by little, day by day."

Again, the others nodded, more vigorously now.

Halika finished with something unexpected, "But I'm not sad at all."

Saviar blinked, then stared. "You're not sad about your brother dying?"

Calitha rolled her eyes, Eldorin shook her head, and Marisole and Barrindar gave each other knowing glances. Apparently oblivious, Ivana continued to eat her soup with noisy slurping that everyone politely ignored.

"He isn't dead," Halika said firmly.

Barrindar explained what Marisole could not, except in song. "Halika didn't see the body. Ergo, as far as she's concerned, he's not really dead."

Eldorin added, "She doesn't get the part about the sharks."

"I get it," Halika defended. "I just don't believe it. I think he sneaked onto a pirate ship. Or got rescued by a friendly one. He's just waiting for his chance to come back."

Marisole gave Saviar a look that told a story. She had clearly tried to explain the facts to her sister, but Halika would have none of it.

Directly beside Saviar, Halika read the glance as well. "What? It's not so far-fetched. No one thought Papa was alive either; and he became king."

Barrindar corrected, "No one knew Papa existed. He didn't come back from the dead."

"King Sterrane did. And he was probably the greatest king ever."

Barrindar clearly knew his history, "Sterrane wasn't dead either. He got spirited away by a wizard because he was the true heir. With magic. There aren't any wizards anymore, and not even Arturo believed himself the one the test would choose."

Halika refused to accept Barrindar's point. "There are elves. They have magic."

Eldorin snorted.

Calitha finished her soup and leaped into the conversation. "The pirates are not elves. And elves didn't spirit Arturo away. Sharks did."

"My brother's not dead." Halika folded her arms across her chest, mouth clamped. It did not matter what anyone else said on the subject; she was no longer listening.

Saviar was no stranger to denial. "If Halika wants to believe Arturo is alive, who is it hurting? No one really knows." He added softly, for Halika, "Perhaps she's even right."

Halika's arms sagged slightly, and she managed a smile.

One thing seemed certain to Saviar: the heirs did not need his comforting. They had a castle full of parents, nursemaids, courtiers, and servants as well as one another with whom to discuss the matter and any deep feelings of grief. He helped them best as a simple distraction.

"So," Barrindar said. "How about that Renshai battle?"

"Incredible!" Eldorin jockeyed around Halika to meet Saviar's gaze. "The way you handled them all . . . it was . . . awesome."

Saviar felt his cheeks flame. "I didn't . . . I mean I can't really . . ." Though he would have preferred the conversation go anywhere else, he put up with the subject to keep their minds off Arturo for a while. "It was all strategic positioning. If they'd caught me before I made the stairs, I would have gotten clobbered . . ." The last thing Saviar needed was for the other Renshai to get wind that he had boasted about his achievements in the practice courtyard. He would find himself attacked at every opportunity, assaulted by Renshai wishing to show him a true, one-on-one comeuppance.

"But they didn't," Halika finished. "And I thought you looked amazing."

Eldorin added, "Saviar *always* looks amazing. He's gorgeous."

The flush spread to Saviar's entire face. Unable to look at anyone, he developed a sudden, inordinate interest in his soup.

Apparently responding to something unspoken, Eldorin said, "What? Well, it's true. All the men in his family are. Everyone says so."

Saviar wished he could disappear.

"But not right in front of him," Calitha hissed.

The youngest of the group, Eldorin seemed incapable of understanding the problem. "But Mama says it's rude to talk about people behind their backs. And I'm not saying anything bad or untrue. And I like when people call me pretty."

With the patience of a big sister accustomed to being embarrassed, Calitha said, "I'll explain later." She gave Saviar's leg a sympathetic squeeze beneath the table.

The sudden, female contact on his thigh startled Saviar, and it took great effort to suppress the urge to leap to his feet. His soup finished, he placed the spoon beside his bowl. Looking up proved nearly as difficult, but he finally met Marisole's gaze. She was smiling. "I appreciate all your hospitality, but I really do need to get some sleep."

Disappointment flickered through Marisole's dark eyes. "Can't you at least stay for the main course?"

Saviar would have loved that. The soup helped, but he had worked up a tremendous appetite. "I . . . I have a big day ahead of me tomorrow."

"Saviar . . ." Marisole started, then stopped in evident frustration. She clearly wanted to tell him something, but the bardic curse restricted her to song.

Saviar dropped all pretenses. She deserved the truth. "I threw a prince on the floor. I charged into a delicate topic and reignited a family argument—"

Barrindar interrupted. "—and my little sister mortified you. So what? She does that all the time. And I've spent more than my share of time on my butt, thank you. Once more doesn't bother me. That's what family does."

"Family?" Saviar did not quite understand. His relationship with his brothers seemed alien in comparison.

"I consider you a brother," Barrindar said matter-of-factly. "Don't you?"

"Well, I think I already have my share of irritating brothers—"

"Oh, so now I'm *irritating?*" Barrindar said in mock indignation.

"What?" Saviar abruptly realized what he had said, and the other ways his words could be interpreted. "No, Your Majesty. I'm sorry. I didn't mean you. I meant—"

Barrindar waved Saviar off, while the girls snickered again and Marisole simply cringed. "Would you calm down, Savi. I knew what you meant. I was teasing."

Though embarrassed in six different ways, Saviar tried to banter. "Teasing, huh? Now you definitely feel like a brother."

They all laughed.

Saviar looked around at the faces of the heirs. Despite their daily responsibilities, despite having recently lost a brother, they seemed happy and comfortable with life. It was a feature of the proper heirs to Béarn's throne. They took adversity in stride and handled it with grace and dignity. "I guess I do consider you all my sisters and brothers." He looked longest at Marisole, the one with whom he truly felt a kinship. "I just never thought about it in those exact words."

"So." Barrindar gestured at Saviar's vacated seat. "Now will you join us for the main course?"

Saviar hesitated. "I'm likely to humiliate myself again."

Marisole smiled. "Great. We could use some entertainment."

And Barrindar added with a wink, "We wouldn't have it any other way."

CHAPTER 13

A great leader must inspire his men to self-sacrificing achievements.
Luckily, with Renshai followers, this is not hard.
—*Thialnir Thrudazisson*

THE LONG WALK DOWN the castle hallway felt like a death march to Saviar, the tension heightened by the somberly formal dress and demeanor of the Knights of Erythane who accompanied him. Though usually proud of both sides of his heritage, at times like this, Saviar would have preferred to have a normal father. He could use a strong pat on the back, verbal encouragements, and paternal suggestions that might even include shortcuts and cheats gleaned from Ra-khir's own childhood.

Kedrin and Ra-khir wore their knight's garb, with the proper countries' colors. Saviar dressed himself in tight-fitting gray and red, free from flowing fabrics that might hinder him in battle, from adornments that could inadvertently block a sword stroke, and selecting hues that demonstrated no allegiance or meaning. For the day, he would appear solely and purely Renshai.

Kedrin stopped in front of a door on the ground floor of Béarn Castle, then turned to face his son and grandson. "Ready?"

Saviar nodded.

Ra-khir lowered his head. "Yes, sir."

Kedrin knocked on the door, the sound echoing boldly down the great hall. Servants at the end looked toward the sound, then scurried around the corner and back to work.

A deep voice came from within, muffled by the door. "Enter."

Kedrin tripped the latch and pushed open the door to reveal a large, windowless room, sparsely furnished. A scarred, stained table filled the center, with half a dozen chairs placed patternlessly around it. Lit by lanterns in wide-spaced sconces, the room remained shadowed in splotches and bright in others. Thialnir sat near the far end beside tiny Minister Chaveeshia.

The contrast was almost laughably startling. Massive as any Béarnide, Thialnir was broad-boned and featured, his golden hair wound through with silver and hanging in multiple war braids. Age had creased his cheeks and neck, but his eyes and nose remained strong, predatory. His hands on the table looked huge to Saviar, who could not miss the enormous sword strapped across the Renshai's back. Though he felt a sudden desire to run, Saviar gave no sign of it. A lifetime of training would not allow him to show a hint of cowardice.

Chaveeshia should have disappeared into the shadow of the huge warrior, yet she did not. As Minister of Local Affairs, she regularly handled the representatives of Béarn's closest neighbors, specifically Thialnir for the Renshai and Kedrin for Erythane. If she felt uncomfortable pitted as the go-between in a confrontation between her charges, she did not show it. She wore her brown hair swept up in a no-nonsense style, and her hazel eyes held a clear air of courage and command.

The knights took the seats directly opposite Chaveeshia and Thialnir, leaving Saviar with a difficult, split-second decision. Hesitation would be seen as weakness. He could find a chair either at or away from the table at an aloof distance. Instead, he claimed the head seat and kept his features squared in interest. Whether or not he belonged there, he needed to look as if he did.

Only Thialnir bothered to glance in Saviar's direction, and the older Renshai appeared amused. He clearly felt he could best every man in the room at once, if necessary; and he was probably right. Saviar suddenly wished he had not agreed to come, though he didn't let his trepidations show. Vulnerability only goaded predators to attack.

Knight-Captain Kedrin cleared his throat. "Good morning, Thialnir Thrudazisson." He nodded at the Renshai. "Minister Chaveeshia."

"Good morning, Captain," Chaveeshia replied woodenly. Thialnir only grunted.

"I suppose you're both wondering why I've called you here."

Thialnir spoke first. "Not really. I'm sure it has something to do with that . . ." He fairly spat the word, ". . . Northman."

Formalities were wasted on Thialnir, and delay would only enrage him, so Kedrin went straight to the point. "As you know, they've asked King Griff to discharge the Renshai from serving in the Pirate Wars."

"Yes," Thialnir said. He kept his gaze trained on Kedrin; though, like all Renshai, he would see any threatening movement no matter from what direction it came.

"In exchange, they have offered their own armies to assist Béarn at no cost."

"Yes," Thialnir said again. "In war, I would rather have a single Renshai at my side than any army."

Kedrin blinked, and a slight smile played across his lips. "I believe he actually said, 'In war, I would rather have Rache at my side than any army.' But, as Rache was a single Renshai, the sentiment is the same."

Now, Thialnir blinked, frowning. "Who said that?"

Saviar tried to remain absolutely still. He knew to whom his grandfather referred.

Kedrin's brows rose. "The world's greatest general: Santagithi. The one who masterminded the defeat of the Eastlands in the Great War." He pursed his lips, then added, "Weren't you quoting?"

Thialnir barely moved. "I was simply stating a fact. One Renshai is more valuable than an entire Northern army."

To Saviar's relief, Kedrin did not argue the point. "Value is not the issue here."

Thialnir nodded his agreement. "The issue is whether or not King Griff chooses numbers over quality. Whether he spurns an ally or an enemy."

Chaveeshia stepped in. "That's not fair, Thialnir. Northmen are not the enemy; and no one will get spurned."

Thialnir did not bother to look at the minister, his attention still centered on Kedrin. "Northmen consider us the enemy. Those who appease our enemies cannot remain our friends."

Kedrin regained the upper hand. "Politics are not so simple, Thialnir. For His Majesty, the decision is not whether he prefers Northmen or Renshai. He has trusted only Renshai to guard his children, as many kings before him."

"So it's money?" Thialnir suggested. "Is that why you mentioned that the Northmen have offered armies at no cost? Would you begrudge the Renshai sustenance?"

"Money is not the issue."

Saviar knew the kingdom paid the Renshai to guard their heirs and for their assistance in the wars. It was a necessity. Since Renshai knew no other trade than warfare, they had no other goods or services to barter, no way to create their own economy. Instead, they sold their sword arms to Béarn in order to afford their food, clothing, swords, housing, and other necessities. The arrangement had suited both for a very long time.

Kedrin continued, "The king cannot risk offending all the countries of the Northlands en masse. We would no longer have a source for steel, no way to craft swords."

Iron ore had other uses, but Saviar realized his grandfather had chosen the only one that would matter to a Renshai.

"We might also spur war."

A light flashed through Thialnir's green eyes. "War," he said, almost reverently. "Béarn, Renshai, and their allies against the North." He smiled. "Why not? The West would no longer have to worry about ore once they owned all the mines."

Kedrin glanced at Saviar, as if for help. Saviar could think of nothing to say, so Kedrin continued speaking, "Two wars at once? Thousands would die."

"In glorious battle!" Thialnir half-rose from his seat in excitement.

Kedrin sighed, closed his eyes, shook his head. He started over. "The noblest aspiration for Renshai."

"Yes."

"But not for Béarnides."

"Pity."

Kedrin added, "And you must understand that the King of Béarn's job is to do what's right for Béarn. Not necessarily what's right for Renshai."

"And, surely, you must realize that I must do what's best for Renshai."

"Yes." Kedrin continued cautiously. "I'm just not sure you are."

That stopped Thialnir cold. His mouth became a stony line. His stare went icy, piercing.

Kedrin seized on the moment. "We spoke earlier of General Santagithi. According to history, he once faced a similar decision to King Griff's. Except, in his case, the Northmen demanded Rache Kallmirsson, the young Renshai who had been like a son to Santagithi and was now the captain of his army."

It was a part of the story Saviar had never heard.

Thialnir's scowl deepened. "I am not altogether unfamiliar with tales of Santagithi. Remember, his daughter and grandson became the parents of two of our three tribes."

Kedrin demonstrated his own knowledge of Renshai history. "The tribe of Rache stemmed from his grandson, Rache Garnsson, named for Rache Kallmirsson. And his daughter, Mitrian, was the mother of the tribe of Tannin."

Thialnir nodded gruffly. "And I don't recall any tales of Rache being surrendered to Northmen in the name of peace."

"Because he wasn't surrendered," Kedrin admitted. "Santagithi held off the Northern armies with carefully worded responses for as long as possible. Eventually, war became unavoidable."

Thialnir's full attention went back to Kedrin. "So, you're telling me that the greatest general of all time chose war over giving up his only Renshai." His eyes narrowed. "Aren't you making *my* point?"

"Maybe," Kedrin said. "Except that when Rache found out the underlying cause of the war, he rode North, intending to sacrifice himself for Santagithi and the others. In that case, the Renshai himself made the decision to allow his allies to live in the peace he knew they preferred rather than die for him. Now, I doubt he surrendered himself per se—"

Any Renshai would understand Rache's intention: to die in glorious combat taking as many Northmen as possible with him. Saviar got the point, but he wondered if Thialnir could. The Renshai had a duty, not only to their own people, but to their allies as well.

Thialnir sat in silence, head cocked to one side, clearly considering. He had come a long way in his many years on the Council. Initially, every situation was black or white, right or wrong. The Renshai solution was the only solution. Age had mellowed the old warrior to the point where he could consider nuances and politics, and he seemed more troubled than appreciative of his newfound diplomacy. His entire head turned suddenly to Saviar, and his gaze remained there.

Saviar forced himself to meet the intense green stare without flinching. He dared not show any fear.

When Thialnir finally spoke, he used the Renshai tongue, "Young Renshai, send the others away."

Though Thialnir spoke fluent Common Trading, Saviar acted as translator. "He wants to speak with me alone."

Kedrin and Chaveeshia rose immediately. Only Ra-khir hesitated, clearly worried for his son's welfare. Nevertheless, he did as Thialnir had bade and followed the others from the room.

While the others filed out, Saviar seized the opportunity to assure no sleeve or legging hampered his movements, that no furniture could impede the sudden draw of his sword.

As the door clicked shut, Thialnir's attention snapped directly onto Saviar.

Saviar's hand went instinctively to his hilt.

"So, you're the one supposed to beat sense into me, eh?" Thialnir ran his hands across the smooth surface of the table. "I'd have thought they'd use your brother."

Saviar told the truth. "It was my idea, sir." He met Thialnir's gaze levelly.

"Are you challenging me?"

"I'm prepared to, sir. If it becomes necessary."

The two stared at one another for several moments, neither giving ground. Thialnir's brows rose in slight increments until they nearly reached his hairline. "Saviar, what do you think of this whole situation?"

The last thing Saviar expected was for the violent, no-nonsense leader of the Renshai to ask his opinion. He stalled. "I think, sir . . ."

"Yes."

". . . the whole situation . . ."

"Yes?"

". . . is damned."

Thialnir chuckled. "Damned indeed, Saviar. What do you propose we do about it?"

Emboldened by his recent successes, Saviar spoke his mind. "I believe, sir, that the Renshai deserve consideration. We've remained loyal to Béarn for centuries, we've earned the right to respect, and we're an invaluable part of Western society with which no one should trifle."

Thialnir made a thoughtful noise that invited Saviar to continue.

"But our own gods chose King Griff as ruler on high of the Westlands, and I trust their judgment implicitly. Have you ever known the man to make an unfair or unreasonable decision?"

"I don't agree with everything he decides, Saviar, if that's what you mean."

Saviar leaned forward, still maintaining eye contact. "Unfair or unreasonable?"

Thialnir narrowed his green eyes nearly to slits. "So you think the Renshai should just stand by and accept whatever the king of Béarn decides."

"Oh, no."

"No?" Thialnir seemed taken aback. "So, what do you think?"

"I think," Saviar said, uncertain exactly what was about to come out of his mouth. "I think the Renshai have a right to demand certain things. For example, since Béarn breached the agreement, not us, we should continue to get paid. They should be able to afford it given that the Northmen aren't asking for any compensation, and Béarn should be able to barter losing Renshai assistance in the war against the price of iron ore."

Thialnir rolled his eyes, head shaking. "But it's not the money, Savi. It's the battle Renshai want." He waxed eloquent, light gleaming like emeralds in his eyes. "The exhilaration of the sword, the brilliant splash of blood, the chance to earn a place in Valhalla."

"I know that." Saviar tried to rein in growing impatience. "But that's not the negotiable part, unfortunately. So long as we're paid, concern for necessities need not distract us from our swordwork. And I think we also need to assure that the heirs of Béarn remain in our protection."

Thialnir was clearly listening.

"Removing us from that job would be the ultimate insult," Saviar realized as he spoke it. "To put lesser swordsmen in charge of protecting Béarn's most precious treasures." He shook his head angrily at the mere thought. "We cannot allow that."

"On that," Thialnir agreed. "We cannot compromise." He smiled. "You're a wise man, Saviar Ra-khirsson."

Saviar winced at the realization of what he had just done. "I'm not sure my father and grandfather would agree." He shrugged. "But they represent Béarn and Erythane, while we are always Renshai."

"Now, about that battle . . ." Thialnir rose. He was even more massive than Saviar remembered, a brick wall of a Renshai also endowed with lightning speed.

Nevertheless, Saviar leaped from his seat simultaneously. *Show no fear.*

"Are you actually challenging me?"

Saviar would have preferred to face a pack of starved dogs, but he gave no hint of his hesitation to Thialnir. "If necessary. I'm always up for a good row, sir. I just don't fancy the need to slay a great Renshai."

Thialnir grinned. It began with a chuckle that gained volume and timbre until it sprouted into a full-throated laugh.

Saviar saw nothing funny in the situation. "Are you laughing at me, Thialnir? Because, if you are, you leave me no choice."

Thialnir waved him off. "No, Savi, I'm not laughing at you. But the day a Renshai child defeats me is the day I commit *tåphresëlmordat*." The word literally translated to "brave suicide," the Renshai phrase for leaping into an unwinnable battle for the sole purpose of dying in glory for Valhalla rather than of illness or weakness.

Still gravely insulted, Saviar stood his ground. "I can defeat you, old man. My adulthood is assured next testing, and I am your worthy equal." He had spoken fighting words, and he expected an instant assault that did not come.

Instead, Thialnir considered the words, giving them a surprising amount of contemplation. Thialnir was better known for his swift and unstoppable attacks. "I am an old man, Saviar. I'm fifty-five, older than any Renshai need get, even in these accursed times of politics and peace."

Saviar felt a sudden pressure in his chest. He had triggered something unexpected. "Sir? With all due respect, you would not set any records for oldest living Renshai."

"Perhaps not." Thialnir retook his seat. "But age and too much 'affairs of state' have softened me. I want out. I'm tired of representing Renshai as a group. I want to go back to worrying about nothing but my sword arm."

Saviar stared. It seemed impossible that any Renshai adult would confide in him, especially about something so personal.

"Would you consider taking my place?"

Stunned, Saviar dropped back into his own seat. He had heard clearly but could only utter, "What?"

"Saviar Ra-khirsson, would you consider succeeding me as speaker for the Renshai?"

"But . . . but I'm not even a man yet."

"You just informed me you would definitely pass your next testing."

"Yes, but . . . I'm not even a . . . a full-blooded—"

Thialnir interrupted, anger tingeing his tone. "There is no such thing as half a Renshai. One either is or isn't, and you are."

Saviar knew the deal. Most offspring of Renshai and *ganim* were not considered Renshai at all. They had no right to any of the training. "Well, yes, but . . ."

"Do you know why we accepted you into the tribe, Saviar?"

Ra-khir never talked about it, but Tae had proven easier for the twins to crack. "You found my father worthy."

"Not exactly." Thialnir settled into his seat. Clearly, the battle Saviar had anticipated was not going to happen, and the young Renshai did not know whether to feel relieved or cheated. He did not relish the thought of more cuts and bruises or humiliation, yet he did want to test his sword arm against the great Thialnir.

"For a *ganim,* your father does have some competence with a sword. He is also courageous to a degree some would describe as insanity, a feature well appreciated by Renshai and one you demonstrate aptly. He's devoted, willing to commit to an ideal so strongly he will throw away his own life defending it. More importantly, to me at least, he could give the Renshai size without sacrificing quickness. If you managed to inherit your mother's agility and your father's strength, you would make a great asset indeed."

Saviar lowered his head. "Except I seem to have inherited my mother's strength and my father's quickness, as Calistin often says."

"Calistin," Thialnir said, "cannot see the buds for the roses."

It was the first negative word Saviar had ever heard uttered by a Renshai about Calistin.

Thialnir made another, wholly unexpected, pronouncement. "I was nearly twenty before I passed my tests of manhood."

"Really?" The word was startled from Saviar, one he never would have spoken had he time to think first.

"Men like us, Saviar. Men of speed and muscle, develop bulk first, then learn to work with and around it." Thialnir captured Saviar's gaze again. "In time, you will become like me. In time, Saviar, you will be one of the most formidable Renshai in history. And, I hope, you will lead the tribe."

It was the ultimate compliment. Saviar could do nothing but bask in it for several moments. *Me? A formidable Renshai?* Every young man believed himself destined for greatness, but few expected others to see it in them, especially others so respected. "Thank you, sir. Thank you so much."

Now, Thialnir frowned. "There is nothing to thank me for, young Renshai. I am simply stating what I see, what I saw in you even as an infant. I examined the set of your sinews, their attachments and arrangements. I knew then what you would become today, at least in physicality. You are very much like myself as a young man; and, since I have no offspring, it will be up to you to pass your strengths through the tribe."

Saviar flushed from the roots of his hair to his lantern chin. "Are you asking me to . . . to . . . ?" He found himself too embarrassed to speak the words.

"I'm asking you to marry within the tribe. And to pick someone fertile, please."

For Renshai, this was not such an odd request. Their women worked as hard as their men and hurled themselves into the same dangers. Many never cycled at all. Those who did still often had difficulties conceiving, carrying, or delivering. "I'll try, sir," Saviar said, eager to abandon the topic. His father had become a young parent, but Saviar did not feel nearly ready for such an enormous responsibility. He deliberately changed the subject. "Don't you worry that if I succeed you, I might be influenced by the Knights of Erythane rather than strictly representing the best interests of the Renshai?"

It was a complicated question that deserved a complicated answer but got only, "Nope."

Saviar found himself, once again, speechless.

Luckily, Thialnir filled the void. "You've proved yourself a smart and honest young Renshai. I don't believe you would accept the position if you couldn't do it properly."

"But I—" Not knowing where he was going next, Saviar was relieved when Thialnir broke in.

"And I've worked with your grandfather long enough to know that his strict and damnable honor would never allow him to take advantage of his relationship with you. He might advise, but he would never push you in the wrong direction."

Abruptly, Saviar gained a new respect for Thialnir, not only as a warrior but as a diplomat. Renshai disdained strategy, yet Thialnir clearly had developed a talent for it. As rash in his youth as any Renshai, Thialnir would clearly not leave the Council unscathed. Time and exposure had added sophistication to his speech as well as his actions. Thialnir was not the same Renshai that he'd been when he had agreed to represent the Renshai on the High King's Council. *How much will it change me?* Yet, Saviar realized something important. He was different from the other Renshai. He loved his swordwork as much as any, but he also wanted something more, the knighthood, for example. Or, perhaps, a chance to help steer the course of Renshai history. *Could this be the plan the gods have always had for me?*

"So." Thialnir propped his enormous elbows on the table. "Will you become my apprentice?"

It was exactly like a Renshai to expect immediate results, an impulsive answer to a lead-heavy question. "Please, Thialnir, sir. I need some time to think about it."

"Very well." Thialnir took the nonresponse in stride. "Will you, at least, accompany me to the Council meeting tomorrow?"

For the second time in two days, Saviar found himself invited to a meeting his father would prefer he not attend. *Clearly, it's fated.* "Of course," he promised. "I would be delighted."

Thialnir snorted with just a hint of smile. "Saviar, you're the only Renshai who would be."

CHAPTER 14

*The future is decided by battles, and it is not finished except by
them.*

—*General Santagithi*

SAVIAR PERCHED ON a familiar rocky outcropping south of the
Fields of Wrath, watching the sun crawl toward the western horizon,
trailing streaks of silver. Gradually, the sky diffused into its sunset
hues: bands of pink blossoming into orange and saffron, then melting into greens and exploding, farther out, into a vast spectrum of
blues and purples. Saviar managed a smile at the display, his first in
at least a week.

Focused fully on nature's artistry, Saviar allowed the annoyances
of the last six months, since the Northmen's arrival, to disappear into
the recesses of his memory. Nothing existed except this grand tab-
leau; everything human seemed insignificant in comparison.

"I thought I'd find you here."

The voice startled Saviar, and he found himself on his feet with
sword drawn in an instant. The darkness gathered around a small
man: swarthy, black-haired, and familiar. "Subikahn?" he whispered,
barely daring to hope.

"Do you always greet your long-gone brother with bared steel?"

Saviar sheathed his sword and caught his twin into an exuberant
embrace. "Subikahn! You're back." He laughed loudly, his troubles
fully forgotten. "I missed you."

"And I you," Subikahn replied in a muffled voice. "But I'd still
rather you didn't suffocate me."

Saviar released his twin, subsumed by excitement. "Sorry. Sorry."

Subikahn smoothed his tattered tunic, speckled with mold and
bits of leaf. He looked thinner than Saviar remembered. Twigs tangled into his long, soft locks. Darkness bagged beneath his eyes, and
scratches marred his cheeks. He reeked of sweat and filth.

Finally, Saviar responded to his brother's greeting words. "How'd you know you'd find me here?"

Subikahn studied the horizon, dropping into a crouch on the rocks. "Because we used to come here when we felt troubled and needed a distraction or some time alone."

Saviar looked back at the parade of colors radiating from the horizon as the last edge of sun sank beneath it. "What made you so sure I'd feel troubled?" It was an apt description, but Saviar doubted word of Erythane's unrest would have reached all the way to the Eastlands.

"Well." Subikahn did not bother to look at his brother. "First, testing day is approaching. If you want to become a man half as much as I do, you're brooding about that. And second, I'm distressed; and you're my twin. So you have to suffer whenever I do."

"I do?" Saviar had heard people claim that twins had an unholy, emotional bond but had never believed it.

"Sure." Subikahn made a gesture but still kept his gaze on the sunset. "We match in every other way, don't we? Why not in mood?"

Saviar laughed, and it felt good. No two brothers, let alone twins, had ever seemed more different. "Whatever's bothering you will seem less significant over a good meal with family."

"No."

The response caught Saviar off his guard. "No, what?"

"I can't go with you. I was given explicit instructions. I'm not allowed to 'run to Mother.'"

"Explicit instructions? Run to . . . ?" The words made little sense to Saviar. He seized Subikahn's shoulders and forced the smaller man to face him. "All right, Brother. Start explaining."

Finally, Subikahn met Saviar's gaze. Then, he lowered his head and stared at his shoes instead. "I don't want to talk about it."

"Why not?"

"Because I don't. I don't ever want to talk about it. With anyone."

"Subikahn, we shared a womb."

"Yes."

"And nearly everything else."

"Yes."

"So why not this?"

Subikahn remained silent for several moments, then finally managed. "I don't know."

"Oh." Torn between hurt and rage, Saviar debated his next course of action. "Did you come to . . . to test?"

"To test . . . yes." Subikahn struggled to raise his head again. "And to see you. I wanted to talk to you. I did. I really thought I could, but I can't. Not yet."

"Oh," Saviar said again, not certain where to go with the conversation. Pressing too hard seemed counterproductive. If Subikahn gave up his secrets under pressure, he might resent doing so, which could lead to permanent discomfort between them. Better to wait and give Subikahn the time he needed.

Subikahn steered the discussion in another direction. "What's bothering *you*, Savi?"

"Bothering?" Saviar tried to hide his own anxieties, not wishing to further burden Subikahn. "It's just . . . just the testing. I'm just worried about the testing. Don't know what I'll do if I fail again."

"Yes, you do."

Saviar had expected commiseration, not bravado. "I do?"

"Same thing you did last year. Practice harder, and try again next time."

Saviar rolled his eyes. "Well, yes. I suppose so. But isn't there a point where one just . . . when it's time to realize you're just not . . . ever going to be competent enough . . . to . . ."

Subikahn nodded. "Yes, but it's not at eighteen, Savi. That's just the average age of passing. Many don't succeed until well into their twenties."

"Well, yes, but Mama—"

"Mama is aberrant."

Taken aback by Subikahn's word choice, Saviar could not help laughing again. "And Calistin?"

"Weirder still. Need you ask?"

That reminded Saviar of the only fun news he had to share. "You're not going to believe this. Calistin . . ." He could not keep himself from chortling, unable to finish. "Calistin . . ."

"Yes?"

Saviar forced out the news, ". . . has a . . . a . . . a . . ."

"Yes?" A touch of impatience entered Subikahn's tone.

". . . a bodyguard." Saviar collapsed into a frenzy of mirth.

Though surely utterly confused, Subikahn could not help laughing along with his brother. "What?" he finally managed.

"This Erythanian kid latched on to Calistin. Calls him Hero and tries to protect him from everything. And I do mean everything."

"Erythanian? Is he competent?"

"He's a competent pain in Calistin's rear end. He's like all of ten years old, skinny as a stick, and probably never saw a sword before he met Calistin. Constantly under his feet, fetching him things, cheering him on. It's hilarious." Saviar could not help laughing again.

Subikahn snorted, still smiling. The dirt on his cheekbones cracked, as if he had not worn any kind of happy expression for a very long time. "I'm surprised he hasn't killed the little bug."

"I think Calistin sees him as one more challenge." Saviar ran with the insect analogy. "If he can remain the best swordsmen in the world with this blackfly buzzing and biting him, that makes him even better."

"What else is new since I left?" Subikahn seemed genuinely interested for the first time since his arrival.

Saviar saw that as a positive step, a way to drag Subikahn from his funk, perhaps far enough to share his own troubles. "Thialnir has chosen a successor."

"Really? Who?"

"Me."

Subikahn laughed harder. "Funny."

"Extremely," Saviar admitted. "But nonetheless true."

"You? Representing the Renshai?" Subikahn shook his head, teasing. "What a terrible thought."

Saviar winced, his heart suddenly as heavy as the growing darkness. He knew his brother meant the words as a joke, but he could not see the humor in it. "I wish I'd said 'no.' "

Subikahn caught Saviar's hand. "I was only kidding, Savi. You'll do great. I can't think of anyone I'd rather have representing us at Béarn's council." He nodded suddenly. "No wonder you're so worried about the testing."

"Yes, that's why mostly," Saviar admitted, giving Subikahn's hand a brotherly squeeze. "Subikahn, don't tell anyone this: I might deliberately fail."

"What! You can't do that! No one—" Subikahn sputtered wordlessly.

Saviar shrugged. "I already made my first leaderly decision, and it was a bad one. A very bad one."

Subikahn freed his hand to loop the arm across Saviar's shoulders and pull him down to a sitting position. The gesture was more suggestion than purposeful. A head shorter than his brother, Subikahn had to stand on the tips of his toes just to reach, and he did not have nearly the strength to force Saviar anywhere.

Saviar willingly dropped to a crouch with his brother. "I talked Thialnir into pulling us out of the Pirate Wars so that Béarn could use Northmen."

"Northmen? Why?"

"At the time, it seemed like the right thing to do. For many reasons, all of which are still valid. But I didn't figure on what happened next."

Subikahn nodded encouragingly.

Saviar waffled. He did not want to talk about the thing that troubled him, dreaded the details that haunted him; yet, he knew he could hardly expect Subikahn to talk about his problems if he would not return the favor. "Renshai prejudice is growing."

Subikahn shrugged. "We've always had enemies. We always will."

Saviar could not deny it. "But this is different. It's grown from insidious to blatant. All the old clichés come back to life: we murder children and drink their blood for immortality, we descend from real demons, we slaughter humans of every age and gender for fun and sport, then carve up their bodies for our stews."

Subikahn screwed up his features, looking even more Eastern than usual. No stranger would see a trace of his Renshai origins, and Saviar only could because of great familiarity. "Those myths were debunked in Colbey's time. We seemed immortal to enemies because looking young is in our bloodline, and we name newborns after fallen warriors."

"You don't have to tell *me* that."

Subikahn flushed. "Sorry. Of course not."

"King Griff refused a demand from the North that we be driven from the Westlands as monsters by deflecting the decision to Erythane."

"What?"

Saviar had to defend the king of Béarn. "He's right, you know. The Fields of Wrath are part of Erythane."

Subikahn glanced at the moon. Nothing but it, and the stars, interrupted the skyward stretch of darkness any longer. "Griff should have told them to cram it up their—"

"He did," Saviar interrupted. "In his polite fashion."

"My papa would have . . ."

This time, Saviar would have let Subikahn finish; but, to his surprise, Subikahn did not. Instead, his hands balled to fists, and he lowered his face again. "King Tae would have done that, I know. And there would be a war."

"Probably."

"Which, for Béarn, would mean fighting two wars on two fronts. Made worse by the fact that the North would have far superior weapons, given the iron ore crisis."

"Iron ore cri . . ." Subikahn started, then waved off his own question. "Now I see why Thialnir picked you."

"So now," Saviar continued, "much of Béarn is grumbling about the king's decision. Renshai hatred has become rampant. There's talk of replacing him; and I think Griff would agree to it, except none of his heirs could pass the stone test yet. Failing that is known to drive most men to insanity. And—"

Subikahn's dark eyes widened. "There's more?"

"Can you handle it?"

Subikahn nodded vigorously.

"A group of Erythanians claims to hold original title to the Fields of Wrath. They now call it 'Paradise Plains' and are demanding money and/or right of return from King Humfreet."

Subikahn continued to stare.

Saviar added, "The king refused. According to documented history, the Fields of Wrath were barren until the Renshai settled them."

"Good." Subikahn emphasized his word with a strong gesture.

"Driving the Paradisian movement underground, where it has swelled into prejudice and assassination."

"Assassination?" Still at a crouch, Subikahn withdrew. "The king's?"

"No. But several Renshai have disappeared under suspicious circumstances."

"Which explains why you're out here by yourself."

Saviar nodded. "Upsetting, isn't it?"

Subikahn put his face practically into Saviar's. "I was being sarcastic. I meant, with so many Renshai murders, you should not go pining alone in secluded places after sundown."

Saviar's fists balled. "I should become a coward instead?"

"Of course not." Subikahn sounded suitably offended by the suggestion. "But that doesn't mean you should commit suicide either." He nudged Saviar to his feet. "No Renshai would shrink from a real battle, but getting slaughtered by a stealthy assassin or stoned by a riled mob won't get you to Valhalla."

Saviar stood at Subikahn's urging. "All right, then. We'd best be getting home then."

"Not 'we.' You, Brother."

Saviar sighed. "Oh, so I have to avoid garroting and stoning, but those are perfectly all right for you."

"I've already told you. I'm barred from 'running to Mama.'"

"Barred by whom?"

"By King Tae Kahn of Stalmize."

Saviar could not imagine Tae doing anything that might discomfort Subikahn, or even Saviar. "Why?"

Subikahn turned away. "I've already told you. I'm not ready to talk about it."

Frustration gripped Saviar, and he winched his hand onto his hilt. Usually, a Renshai vented irritation or anger in a wild volley of swordplay.

The gesture was not lost on Subikahn. "You're not going to batter it out of me, if that's what you're thinking."

Saviar let go of his hilt. "A spar would be nice."

"Tomorrow," Subikahn promised. "In the light of day."

Unsatisfied, Saviar remained in position. "At least give me enough information to understand what you can and cannot do."

"Well . . ." Subikahn stroked his chin, though nothing had yet started growing on it. "If I tell you, do you promise to go home for the night?"

Saviar wanted to qualify the amount of information that would satisfy him. Weighing that need against the concern that Subikahn might just go completely silent on the subject again, he reluctantly agreed. "Yes."

"Do you remember that my granpapa sent my papa away to survive on his own?"

Saviar studied his twin. "You mean that horrible gap in Tae's life story that he refuses to talk about and swore he would never inflict on anyone?"

"That's the one."

"Yes."

"He inflicted it on me."

Saviar could only stare. His mind went utterly blank. He knew Tae, knew how much he adored his son, knew the lingering bitterness toward his own father for the exile. "No." He shook his head. "I don't believe it. Tae would never—"

"He would, and he did."

Saviar still could not grasp what Subikahn had told him. He opened his mouth, then closed it. He tried again but still managed nothing.

"It's no help you doing a fish imitation. It's true. And what's more, I deserved it."

Saviar finally forced out words. "Who did you brutally murder?"

Subikahn loosed an amused snort. "I didn't kill anyone, Saviar."

"Did you raze Stalmize Castle stone by stone?"

"Of course not."

Saviar continued guessing, "Act like such an incredibly spoiled little prince that Tae thought you needed—?"

"That would be closest," Subikahn admitted. "But I'm done with this game. I already told you I'm not ready to talk about it."

Taken aback again, Saviar fell silent. He had only been kidding with his last guess, but could not think of anything suitably catastrophic to make Tae banish his son. "So what are you supposed to do?"

"Travel all over. Not run to Mama. Return 'worldly.' "

"That doesn't seem so bad."

"You didn't hear Papa. He made it sound like a death sentence."

Though Subikahn had closed the topic, Saviar could not help saying, "You must have done something awful."

"Yeah."

"You did?"

"Yeah."

"Really?"

"Yeah."

Clearly Subikahn would not continue, so Saviar came at it from another angle, "What does Talamir think of all this?"

Subikahn stiffened.

Clued, Saviar persisted. "Where is your *torke?*"

"Still in Stalmize," Subikahn said, a little too casually. "I have to do this alone. If we both headed for the Fields of Wrath at the same time, I would have strong company. That would defeat the purpose of the exile."

Still believing he had found a clue, but not knowing what it meant, Saviar continued along the same lines. "So Talamir is coming home soon."

"That's my understanding."

A dead end. Saviar knew Subikahn would not put up with much more questioning and hoped the night might bring the situation into better perspective. "So, has your journey been the hardship your papa said it would be?"

Subikahn lifted one shoulder, then dropped it. "That's the thing, Savi. I've just gone from inn to inn, getting treated like a prince. It's the easiest thing I've ever done, and I'm not exactly sure what the point of the whole thing is. It's not like the criminal underground is intent on slaughtering me like they were my papa."

It did seem odd. "Well, you haven't stayed in any inns recently." Saviar gestured toward the distant Southern Mountain range. Once beyond the boundaries of the Eastlands, Subikahn had had to slog across the harsh and desolate desert known as the Western Plains, plow through one of the few mountain passes, and negotiate the maze of Westland forests east of Erythane. There, at least, he could have bought some supplies in one of several tiny Western towns and villages.

"I'm used to that route." Subikahn dismissed any suggestion of hardship, though Saviar knew better. The stretch between the Eastland border and the Westland forests was brutal, even in the best of times and accompanied by family and *torke*. "The Eastern innkeepers practically forced food on me, and I spent my money on more rations along the way. I stocked up plenty for the desert and mountains. Thieves only approached me once, and I dispatched them quickly enough." He grinned. "The day I can't handle a few brigands is the day I commit *tåphresëlmordat*."

Saviar glanced at the stars, finding familiar patterns in their twinkling sameness. It brought back happy memories of sparring with his brother on the rocks, talking quietly about things no one but a twin could understand. "For now, perhaps, you could commit to a bath. I'll bring you food and fresh clothes."

Subikahn opened his mouth, but Saviar talked over him.

"If you can take those things from innkeepers, you can take them from your brother."

"I shouldn't—" Subikahn started. "I won't—"

Saviar assisted, "The words you're looking for are 'thank' and 'you.' And it wouldn't hurt to add, 'best brother of all time.' "

"Thank you, best brother of all time."

"You're welcome. See how easy that was?"

"Very easy," Subikahn admitted. "This whole thing has been too easy." His voice held a twinge of pain, one only Saviar could notice. Though Saviar did not believe his brother was lying, Subikahn was definitely hiding something excruciating.

"Well, you're out of the Eastlands now. No one will treat you like a prince. And the North . . ." Saviar examined his brother's small form, from his black mop of snarled hair, past the sword at his belt, to the battered Eastern-crafted sandals on his swarthy feet. "They'll notice you don't belong there, but, at least, they'd never guess you're Renshai."

"Yes," Subikahn said. "And you're stalling. You promised to go home."

"And you promised me a spar tomorrow."

"Yes."

"You'll be here, right?"

"Would I forget to wish you a happy birthday?" Subikahn shuffled backward, his dark form disappearing into the shadows. Some of the early Renshai maneuvers came from time spent with wild barbarians during their travels. Subikahn excelled at those moves, enhanced by his father's agility and training. "Now go."

Happy Birthday. As hard as he tried, Saviar could not forget. *Nineteen tomorrow and not yet a man.* Grudgingly, he went.

The morning dawned clear and crisp, warm for autumn yet with a breeze that kept Saviar's sweaty muscles comfortable. He faced off with his *torke*, Nirvina, who had already twice knocked him on his buttocks. Most days, he found her a close match. Now, distracted by concern for Subikahn, he launched into his third attack. His sword glittered in a deadly arc that she met and parried. Saviar bore in, attempting to use his strength against her. Nirvina dodged easily, ducked beneath his sword arm and came up behind him.

Saviar whirled to face her, but not quickly enough. She slammed the flat of her blade against his chest. For the third time, he found himself sitting in the grass.

Nirvina glared, her features sharper than usual. Her thick, sandy hair lay stick straight nearly to her shoulders. Bangs dangled over her broad forehead, shadowing harsh blue-green eyes and a pinched nose. "Saviar, what in darkest, coldest Hel is wrong with you?"

"I'm sorry, *torke*." Saviar sprang to his feet. "My mind is elsewhere."

"Your mind is elsewhere than battle? What good is worrying about the future when you're dead?" Nirvina rushed him with drawn sword.

Saviar ducked under the strike, then spun and cut with proper dexterity. His sword wove over hers, and the tip found her hilt. He prepared to flick it from her hand, but she withdrew too swiftly. Her blade drove under his with lethal speed. He batted it down, recovered in a loop, then swept for her head. Nirvina ducked, opening her defenses for a split second that Saviar seized. He slammed his blade across her shoulders with enough force to send her staggering. This time, she toppled.

"That's better!" Nirvina rolled to her feet in an instant and clapped her hands. "Fight like that during your testing tomorrow, and you're a certainty. Fight like you did a moment ago, and you'll be nineteen before you reach manhood."

Saviar flinched. "I am nineteen. Today."

"Today?" Nirvina raised her brows. "Well, happy birthday, boy. Now that we've got your mind back, let's see what you can do."

She squared for another assault just as Erlse rode up, his brown mare frothy, her nostrils dilated. "We're gathering on the testing grounds," he announced, then pointed directly at Saviar. "Thialnir's asked for you especially." He spurred his mount into a gallop.

"What's this about?" Saviar wondered aloud.

"I don't know," Nirvina said, tone full of question and caution, "but I suggest we get there quickly."

They both hurried toward the enormous open field that served as the main square for celebrations and rare pronouncements, mock battles, and testing. They raced through stubble-strewn practice areas, around a cluster of cottages, and through a scraggly field of prairie grass. A mixed hubbub of voices, speaking at least two different languages wafted to them long before the main square hove into view. Ahead, Saviar noticed, a crowd of Renshai were already gathering. He also saw the black and orange banner of King Humfreet and several white chargers. *Knights*. The run itself scarcely winded Saviar, but his heart pounded as if he had raced for miles. He scarcely noticed he had lost Nirvina in his headlong rush.

Saviar slowed to a walk, weaving between the waiting Renshai. What he could pick out of their conversations seemed expectant and surmising; they did not yet know why the King of Erythane had come to call. Though he would have preferred to join his mother, who stood with Calistin in the midst of the crowd, Saviar dutifully headed toward the mounted king and his entourage. He would surely find Thialnir there.

As he drew closer, Saviar sorted out the visitors. About a dozen Northmen milled amidst the mounted king, his bodyguards, and six Knights of Erythane, including Ra-khir and Kedrin. Only one Renshai had joined them, the massive Thialnir, who scanned the crowd expectantly. As his gaze found Saviar, he called out, "There he is," and gestured broadly for the youngster to join them.

Saviar came, trying not to slouch. His every adolescent instinct pleaded for him to run and hide, yet he knew better than to delay, or even display poor posture, in the presence of the knights. Instead, he approached warily, his gaze scanning the most likely threat: the Northmen. All adult males, but one, they watched his every movement with clear suspicion. Saviar could not help meeting the familiar gaze of the last Northman, Verdondi Eriksson, the one he had sparred with in Béarn's practice room. The boy stared back at him, pale eyes wide and jaw gaping.

Ra-khir frowned, shook his head, and rolled his gaze to King Humfreet.

Catching the gist of his father's discomfort, Saviar swiftly performed a deep and gracious bow.

Thialnir chose that moment to thrust a scroll into Saviar's hands. "What do you think of this?" The political leader of the Renshai had always seemed so massive, solid and competent; yet his clammy fingers betrayed a nervousness his demeanor otherwise hid. His look seemed almost pleading. In the past, Thialnir had always seemed unflappable, terrifying, and rock-stable. Saviar wondered if the Renshai leader had softened in the past few months or only seemed to have because Saviar had seen his vulnerable side and learned the inner workings of the leader's job.

Attempting to appear nonchalant, Saviar rose, unrolled the top portion of the scroll, and silently read. The cause for Thialnir's discomfort became instantly clear. Written in a flowery hand, gratuitously verbose, it betrayed its author as a royal advocate. The entire first paragraph spoke of a binding agreement between the Northmen and the Renshai, discussing who represented each of these at the signing, how they would be referred to throughout the document, and the presence of the king of Erythane. Like most Renshai, Thialnir was a simple, proud man who cared little for anything other than swordwork, and the sheer mass of the contract might drive him to distraction.

Saviar looked up to find every eye upon him. He wished he could melt into the weeds like liquid, yet he also knew that Thialnir needed him. Desperately. He had little choice but to appear in charge. He bowed to King Humfreet again. "Your Majesty, if it pleases you, this is a long document. May I have some time to read it?"

The king smiled, his lips nearly disappearing into the thick, jowly creases of his moon face. "Of course, Saviar Ra-khir's son. Take all the time you need."

Relief flooded Saviar. His weeks in Béarn had given him courage when it came to addressing royalty, yet he had never spoken to the king of Erythane before. While formality ill-suited the commonly named Griff of Béarn, King Humfreet seemed to wear it as a mantle.

Saviar took a deep breath before continuing. He did not want to stretch his luck too far. "If it also pleases His Majesty, I would like to borrow one of your knights."

The grin broadened, revealing pearly teeth. "You may use the services of even my captain, if you need him, Saviar."

"Most generous, Your Majesty." Saviar would have settled for his father, but he dared not belittle such a charitable gift. He turned his attention to Knight-Captain Kedrin and bowed again. His mouth formed the words, "Come along, Grandpapa," but his mind knew better than to speak them as such. Instead, he kept up the necessary ritual, "If you would be willing, Sir Captain?"

Kedrin saluted Saviar, bowed to his king, then dismounted. Leaving the charger to his own devices, Kedrin came to Saviar's side, then followed him past the gathering, through a small field, and into the shade of the first row of cottages. There, Saviar loosed a pent-up breath but dared not drop all pretenses. Kedrin was on duty.

Upending an empty rain barrel, Saviar sat.

Kedrin settled onto a low wall of rock surrounding a small garden. "Would you like some help making sense of that document?"

"I would," Saviar said. "I'll get the gist of it, I think. I'd just like to be sure I don't lock us into something I don't understand." There was more to Saviar's concern. He wanted the chance to read the words in a hush that allowed him to absorb and make sense of them, but he also worried about misunderstanding. He could never forgive himself if he comprehended every word and still advised a course of action that endangered the tribe. Unable to continue in this manner, he finally dropped pretenses. "What's this all about?"

Kedrin studied Saviar without a hint of emotion. "Are you asking me as a representative of the Renshai? Or as my grandson?"

Saviar attempted to consider the question, but found himself too inexperienced to know which one he wanted. "Which will give me the most direct answers?"

"Grandson."

Saviar made a straight line gesture. "Speak frankly, Grandpapa."

Kedrin attempted a smile, though it came out tired and lopsided. "I've read the whole thing, Saviar, even helped draft portions of it to keep it fair."

Saviar unrolled the next paragraph, bobbing his head. It made sense that the king would employ the Knights of Erythane to keep the matter impartial and the contract binding. He read the next several paragraphs in silence. "The Northmen want to battle us? In single combat."

"One to one," Kedrin confirmed.

Saviar continued reading. Despite the excessive verbiage, he believed he teased out all the salient points. "If the Renshai win, we get back our ancient homeland in the North: Renshi." For once, the words on the document seemed too simplistic for what they described. Hundreds of years ago, Renshi had become divvied up among the neighboring tribes, and Saviar wondered how anyone could still recall the ancient borders. At the time of the Great Banishment, the North had consisted of seventeen tribes. Now, there were only nine. Even if they could redefine Renshi, it meant displacing the Gjar, Blathe, and Shamirins who currently resided there.

Kedrin anticipated the question, "Historians and mapmakers spent a long time defining the proper location. The Northern captain, Erik Leifsson, does have the dispensation of the high king in Nordmir to endorse the agreement."

Verdondi's father. Saviar could not help smiling. It had to have caught the young man by surprise to find his sparring partner, the son of a knight, was also a budding leader of Renshai.

Kedrin folded his arms across his chest. "Assuming they won, the Renshai would also keep the Fields of Wrath in Erythane. The Paradisians have agreed to fully surrender their claim to the land in that circumstance."

Saviar bobbed his head thoughtfully. Thialnir might see the gestures as immeasurably small. The Paradisians had no legitimate claim to the Fields of Wrath anyway, and the Renshai could take back Renshi by force if necessary. Still, Saviar could see the significance of these places to the Northmen. Sacrificing the land up North meant acknowledging the Renshai as one of them, a real tribe with an actual right to existence. Giving up the battle of the so-called Paradisians would force them to stop fueling the prejudice growing rampant in the Western world.

Saviar went back to the scroll to discover the penalty for a Renshai loss. Not surprisingly, it called for the Renshai to give up the Fields of Wrath and become exiles not only from the Northlands, but from the West as well. The rest involved assuring the compulsory nature of the contract, the conditions necessary to render it, and the proper signatories, with their endorsers described.

"Do you need me to explain anything more?" Kedrin prompted.

Only then, Saviar realized he had sat in silence for quite a long time. "No." He met the sea-foam eyes. "Grandpapa, what should I do?"

"You should discuss the details with Thialnir." Though true, the answer gave Saviar nothing. He tried to read the emotions hidden behind his grandfather's blank expression, without success.

Saviar sighed. "I mean, what should I do about the contract? Should we accept it? Decline it? Burn it at their feet?"

"That," Kedrin said, "is entirely up to the leaders of the Renshai."

Leaders? Plural? "Of which I am one?"

"Yes. You and Thialnir."

Suddenly, Saviar understood Ra-khir's lament about Kedrin and his riddles. "What would you do in my place?"

Kedrin rose and put an arm across his grandson's shoulders. "Saviar, I can't make this decision for you."

"Of course not." Saviar shook off Kedrin's touch, growing irritated. "But you can advise me. What would you do in my place?"

Now Kedrin sighed. He lowered his arm awkwardly, as if uncertain where to place it. "If I were you, Saviar, I'd be Renshai. I'm not. I can't take any responsibility for a group of people I can't possibly fully understand."

"You understand the politics. Things Thialnir can't . . . won't . . ."

"Give Thialnir some credit for experience," Kedrin said softly. "Do not underestimate his knowledge or his intelligence."

Thialnir was known for neither, rather for abruptness in everything, including decisions. "But—"

"And, I believe you understand the politics every bit as much as I do, Saviar. Perhaps more."

No longer confused, Saviar trembled with building anger. "Let me speak with Papa, instead."

"Sir Ra-khir will not make this decision for you, either."

Saviar spoke through gritted teeth. "Perhaps Sir Ra-khir would like to speak for himself."

"Not necessary." Kedrin tipped his head. "Sir Ra-khir is a Knight of Erythane, and I am his superior. In situations such as this, we're both sworn to objectivity."

Rage warmed Saviar's blood momentarily, then disappeared. He no longer wanted to punch his grandfather, only to cry and beg for his help. He did none of those things, though tears stung his eyes. "Please. I don't know what to do, what to say. Thialnir takes my suggestions very seriously."

"As he should." Kedrin remained maddeningly unhelpful. "I will send him over." He headed back toward the gathering.

As his grandfather walked away, Saviar found himself trembling, assaulted by uncertainty, by fear, by loathing at once. A tear slipped from his eye, and he wiped it away fiercely. He dared not let Thialnir catch him weeping. He concentrated on the details of the contract, rewording it as clearly as possible in his head, blocking out the emotions the issues raised. By the time Thialnir arrived, he knew exactly what he wished to say.

Saviar launched into the short version of the venture: the proposed one-on-one combat so like the one that had allowed the Renshai to claim Devil's Island in the North long after their initial banishment; the rewards in plain language without the attendant baggage; and the consequences of failure. He had only just taken a breath to explain the underlying politics when Thialnir raised his giant hand.

"The Renshai have been challenged, and we will fight."

To the great leader of the Renshai, it was all that obvious, that simple.

Saviar opened his mouth, even as he realized there was no sense in arguing the point. Thialnir saw the whole thing in black and white: fight equals courage, refusing meant cowardice. No long-winded explanation would change Thialnir's mind, so Saviar salvaged the situation the only way he could. "At least, sir, let's add some safeguards to the contract. Define the end point of the battle, for example. Death or first blood?"

"Death. One less scheming Northman."

"When and where should it occur? What constitutes a fair battle? How should we handle noncombatant interference?"

Thialnir approached each question, only to have Saviar cut him off with the next one. To the youth, they were merely examples for future discussion.

As Saviar paused for breath, Thialnir addressed the final question first, "The last one-on-one Northman Renshai battle I know of suffered from exactly that interference."

Saviar knew his Renshai history. "Colbey versus the Slayer."

"Valr Kirin," Thialnir filled in the name. "Valr" meant Slayer, a nickname for the North's greatest warrior at the time. "Kirin's son leaped to his father's defense and wound up getting him killed instead."

Saviar stuck with the salient point, "And some Northmen used that as an excuse not to honor the contract."

"Good point." Thialnir patted Saviar's shoulder, a touch he accepted as he had not his grandfather's. "We will have it entered that any interference in the battle voids the contract."

It sounded wise, until Saviar considered further. The clause, used wrongly, could just as easily become a means for the Northmen to cheat. "Except, let's say the Northman is losing—"

"A certainty." Thialnir bobbed his enormous, graying head. "If some cowardly Northman shot our Renshai in the back, the end result would not count."

Saviar did not allow himself to get distracted from his new point. "—so a noncombatant deliberately kills *the Northman* for the sole purpose of voiding the contract. That would give them leave to enter a fresh, new contestant against our tired one. They could keep doing that until they got the upper hand."

Thialnir snorted. "Except, they would never get the upper hand. The worst of our men could slaughter the best of theirs three times over."

"True." Saviar would not argue things that did not matter. "But four times over? Five? At some point, even a Renshai gets overwhelmed."

Thialnir grunted something incoherent but finally conceded. "What if we say it's only enemy interference that voids the contract? That way, if the Northmen shoot down our warrior, it's a disqualification. If they kill their own warrior, they simply lose."

Saviar could not see any flaws in Thialnir's new argument. He nodded. At least now they had an answer to the challenge. All that remained was hashing out the final details. Though glad to have the decision out of his hands, Saviar worried about the situation. Win or lose, the lives of the Renshai would change spectacularly. He only hoped it would prove for the better.

CHAPTER 15

Because Kevral is Renshai, she will do as she pleases and suffer the consequences gladly.

—King Griff of Béarn

THE DAY OF THE BATTLE dawned in dreary solemnity. Rope-wrapped stakes squared off the battlefield on the Fields of Wrath, and Knights of Erythane patrolled around them, keeping the crowd in check. Surprised by the sheer number of spectators, Saviar stood on the outskirts of the gathered nobility, Northmen, and Renshai, glad Thialnir seemed comfortable handling the final details without him.

Though he noticed someone approaching to his right, Saviar did not bother to acknowledge it. He hoped the other would realize he had no patience for idle conversation.

"Why didn't you tell me you were Renshai?"

Saviar stiffened, then turned slowly to face Verdondi. He flushed, dodging the quick blue eyes. "You . . . you didn't ask." It was a feeble argument, and he knew it. He had never expected the information to come out this way. *Timing is everything.* Kedrin had said, and Saviar knew he should have told the truth a long time ago.

"Who would think to ask a young man in the practice area of Béarn Castle such a question?"

Saviar bit his lip, too guilty to laugh. Anyone who knew King Griff hired Renshai to guard his heirs would expect them in the practice area as often as possible.

"You said you were the son of a Knight of Erythane."

"I am."

"A Knight and also a Renshai?"

"My mother . . ." Saviar finally met the young Northman's gaze. ". . . is Renshai."

Verdondi's nostrils flared. "Oh."

"Yes, 'oh.' " Saviar started to turn his attention back to the proceedings, but Verdondi was not yet ready.

"You still should have told me."

"You're right," Saviar admitted, "I should have. But my father and grandfather would not have tolerated bloodshed in Béarn Castle."

Verdondi's brows arched higher. "Bloodshed? I—" His lids abruptly fell from abnormally wide to squintingly narrow. "I get it. You think far too little of me." He grunted out an irritated sigh. "I deserve better."

"I'm sorry." Saviar made a little bow. "I should not have assumed." Believing the conversation finished, he glanced out over the crowd, sifting Renshai from the vast array of Erythanians. Even a few Béarnides had made the trip, their enormous physiques and shaggy dark heads towering over most of the others.

"Who's your champion?"

Saviar continued to study the crowd as he answered, "My baby brother, Calistin."

"Your *baby* brother?" Verdondi seemed shocked by the answer. "I know Renshai look younger, but just how old—"

Saviar did not bother to wait for the end of the question. "He's eighteen. I'm nineteen, as of today."

"Your champion is only eighteen?"

Saviar nodded.

"And you look reasonably close to your . . . real age."

"I do."

"So not all Renshai—?"

"I favor my father's side of the family," Saviar interrupted swiftly. He did not want to get into an argument over rumors; Verdondi might actually believe they slaughtered infants and performed foul rites with the blood to keep their youth. "But Calistin seems to carry more of our mother's bloodline. To me, he seems about . . . six."

Verdondi swallowed hard. "He . . . looks . . . that young?"

"Looks?" Saviar finally studied his companion. "No, he looks—I don't know—thirteen, fourteen. He just *acts* six."

Verdondi laughed, and even Saviar managed a smile. He had no fear for his brother. No swordsman in any part of the world could possibly best Calistin.

The young Northman sobered quickly. "Look, Saviar. I ought to warn you. Your baby brother may be in trouble."

Saviar made a throwaway gesture. "Don't worry about Calistin. He could handle three armies, if he had to; and he'd be the first to tell you he could."

Verdondi cleared his throat cautiously. "It will take more than confidence to kill Valr Magnus."

Though he had never heard it before, the name sent a chill through Saviar. Northmen did not idly bestow the nickname of their centuries-famous hero, Valr. Magnus implied magnificent, the best. Though not uncommon as a name or piece of a name, Magnus had never, to Saviar's knowledge, accompanied the word, "Slayer." To the Northmen, this warrior was special.

Verdondi explained, "He showed such great natural prowess as a child, he has never had to do anything other than swordwork. He's not expected to hunt, book-learn, or assist with any chore. He is the sword, and the sword is him. No one can beat him."

A dark sense of foreboding clutched Saviar's chest, quickly dispelled by reason. Calistin had a similar history in a culture that initiated swordplay in infancy, where every moment of every day allowed for a spar or lesson, and he had regular opponents who could challenge him. Calistin also knew the Renshai maneuvers, to which this Valr had no access. Saviar could not imagine any man quicker or more capable than his brother. "Calistin can. And will."

The conversation put Verdondi in a precarious position. If he stated the usual platitude, "I hope so," it meant standing against his own father and people. To state otherwise, however, meant wishing death and grief upon Saviar's family.

A sudden shout rescued Verdondi. Saviar's attention shifted suddenly to the battlegrounds, where Calistin, Thialnir, and two Northmen waved their arms around in obvious disagreement.

"Excuse me." Saviar rushed toward the ruckus without waiting to see if Verdondi had granted his pardon. He drew up just as King Humfreet, Knight-Captain Kedrin, and two other knights arrived on the scene.

"What seems to be the trouble?" the aging king demanded.

Saviar quietly took a position beside Thialnir, trying for discretion. If no one noticed him, concerns about his identity and status, whether or not he belonged in this exalted group, would not arise.

If anyone noticed Saviar, they gave no sign. The two Northmen bowed to the king before one responded to the question. "Your Majesty, we are only trying to keep the proceedings fair."

Thialnir snorted.

Kedrin's jaw tightened, but he did not reprimand the Renshai. Saviar knew his grandfather had grown accustomed to Thialnir's blatant disregard of royal convention from Béarn's Council. Still, the king of Erythane was more traditional in his requirements.

Ignoring Thialnir, the Northman who had spoken continued, while the other bowed repeatedly. "Your Majesty, we all agreed on a fair battle, yet it is well-known that Renshai do nothing other than train for murder."

"Combat," Thialnir corrected.

"Combat, then," the Northman accepted Thialnir's word politely, though the lines around his mouth tightened. "And even a mediocre Renshai can take on the best three warriors of any other people."

"So?" Thialnir interrupted gruffly again. "Of what purpose is this fact? They called the challenge."

The other Northman stopped bowing long enough to speak. "Your Majesty, please. We all agreed to *fair* combat."

Saviar tugged discretely at Thialnir's tunic, trying to get his attention. The Northmen played a crafty game, attempting to look all innocence when they knew their champion spent as much time honing his craft as any Renshai.

Intent on the Northmen, Thialnir seemed oblivious to Saviar.

"Well," King Humfreet said, fingering his graying beard with clear thoughtfulness. " 'Fair' does imply no obvious outcome, does it not, Knight-Captain?"

Directly addressed, Kedrin executed a grand gesture of respect. "Well, Sire, I suppose it could be interpreted in that—"

"This is insanity!" Calistin demonstrated none of his grandfather's pretty manners. "My *mother* could trounce the best warrior the Northmen have."

The group dropped into stunned silence, amplifying the familiar voice that followed, "I accept."

Every eye turned toward Kevral, who elbowed her way through the crowd. "Those cowards can't whine about fairness when their champion faces *me*."

"No," Saviar whispered, his hand falling from Thialnir's clothing. "No," he said louder, but his voice disappeared into the murmurs that followed. Even Calistin whirled to face Kevral; he had clearly intended his words only as a taunt.

"I accept," Kevral repeated. "Now where's my target?"

Saviar seized a huge handful of Thialnir's tunic and pulled so hard he all but disrobed the Renshai leader.

Finally, Thialnir glanced at his apprentice.

Saviar hissed, "You can't let her fight. The stakes are too high."

Thialnir shook his head, his voice just above a whisper. "She accepted the challenge, Savi. To deny her would be to dishonor her."

He smiled wickedly, "Besides, what better vengeance than to slaughter their best man with a *girl.*"

Saviar found it impossible to think of his mother as a girl. Though remarkably skilled in her day, still a better warrior than himself, she was well into her thirties. Age had to take some toll on her agility. "Thialnir, no. Their champion is . . . is . . . well . . . unusually competent."

"Your mother," Thialnir returned stiffly, "is Renshai." Without further explanation, he strode out of Saviar's reach.

Events seemed to progress in strangely slowed motion. Saviar could only watch as Calistin conferred with Kevral, as Thialnir, the Northmen, and the Erythanians explored the finer points of the upcoming conflict. His mind muddled, refusing to grasp details. Centuries ago, the Renshai had met a similar challenge by pitting a random member of the tribe against the Northmen's best. That had resulted in a humiliation that had blossomed into prejudice. How much stronger would the hatred flare if a female elder, a mother of three adults, slaughtered the Northmen's best? And, while Saviar had not worried for Calistin at all, anxiety twitched through him at the thought of Kevral in his brother's place. She could lose, she could die, and the Renshai would become double exiles.

Saviar had always known he would one day lose his mother violently. Like all Renshai, she craved death in combat to join the eternal war in Valhalla. But to risk her life for such a heinous matter, a contest born of bigotry and intolerance, seemed wrong. Perhaps the cause was not good enough. Perhaps the gods and their Valkyries, their Choosers of the Slain, would consider such a contest unworthy. Perhaps, the loser would not reach Valhalla. The thought sent a desperate shiver through him. For so many reasons, Kevral had to win.

A hand fell on Saviar's shoulder. *Father?* Ra-khir did not share the Renshai's desire to die in valiant combat. Saviar could only wonder how much anxious pain his father suffered now. He whirled to face Verdondi. Surprised, he only stared.

"I'm sorry," the young Northman said. "I know what it's like to be orphaned."

"Orphaned? What do you mean orphaned?" Sudden realization enraged Saviar. "You think my mother will be defeated."

Verdondi paled, if possible, his features nearly bloodless. "Well . . . I just meant . . . there *is* a . . . a chance . . ."

"No!" Saviar spoke through gritted teeth. "Ridiculous. My mother is Renshai." Fire seemed to course through his veins. It was all he could do to keep himself from attacking the young Northman, and that loss of self-control triggered the logical thoughts that had, thus far, evaded him. Saviar realized his anger stemmed not from insult, but because he feared the very possibility Verdondi had raised.

Unaware of Saviar's internal turmoil, Verdondi tried to extricate himself from the situation. "I didn't . . . didn't mean any offense. I . . . just . . . just wanted you to know that . . . I understand. You see, Captain Erik is actually my uncle by blood. My . . . my parents were . . . killed." He seemed on the verge of tears, which snapped Saviar fully out of his fury. He did not want to humiliate the only Northman who had acted as a friend.

Not trusting himself to speak of the matter at hand, Saviar asked in a flat tone, "What happened to your parents?" From the corner of his eye, he watched the preparations. Kevral crouched in the middle of the combat area, calmly cleaning her swords. Saviar searched for her opponent.

"A group of brigands assaulted my mother. She returned home clinging to life. My father took them all on in vengeance, but they overpowered him. She lived on for a few months, but she felt responsible for his death. Eventually, infection overwhelmed her."

"That's horrible."

Verdondi closed his eyes, gritted his teeth. "Yes." He forced himself to continue, "They, the ones who killed my parents, were Northmen of our own tribe. So I came to see there are good and bad in every group of people." He looked askance at Saviar, seeming almost to plead. "Among Renshai, too?"

The Northman had dared to share his most vulnerable moment, and Saviar found himself feeling strangely protective. He had never thought of his tribe in those specific terms. Renshai were simple to understand: life and death intertwined, based solely on a swordwork they considered the only pathway to eternal glory. Saviar thought of his younger brother and the many times he had wanted to throttle the pompous pest. "Among Renshai, too," he finally agreed.

Verdondi seemed about to say something more, but no words emerged.

Saviar rescued him from the trouble of speaking. "Excuse me, again. I'd like to visit with my mother before the battle."

"Of course," Verdondi gestured for Saviar to go.

Saviar studied the battlefield as he approached. Knights still patrolled the roped-off area, large enough to support three battles at once. Someone had cleaned the area of debris, leaving only a fine film of crushed weeds over the dirt. Clearly, the Northmen were taking no chances of giving the Renshai any advantages, including familiarity with the grounds or use of their vast experience waging war on hazardous terrain. Shadows of foliage and the nearest cottages marred the otherwise clean perfection of the field. Two large trees towered directly over the makeshift arena, though not a single shed stick lay beneath either of them. Saviar could see a fresh wound where someone had hacked down and filed a bit of root that might have caused a trip hazard. *Under the guise of fairness, they will see to it every advantage is theirs.*

As if to prove Saviar's point, Valr Magnus finally leaped over the ropes to enter the combat area. Kevral watched him, clearly judging every movement, and Saviar instinctively did the same. Though large, he was not muscle-bound, and moved with a quickness that spoke of remarkable agility despite the armor that encased his chest and abdomen. He kept his arms and legs bare, but clutched a helmet in one hand and a sizable shield in the other. The broadsword at his hip appeared well-made.

A thought occurred to Saviar, and he veered from Kevral to Thialnir where the Renshai leader stood with the Northern captain, the king, and Humfreet's knightly entourage. *Time to turn the tables.* "Sir." Saviar addressed Thialnir, though he spoke loudly enough for the knights and the king to hear. "Is it *fair* for the Northman to wear armor while our champion has none?"

Thialnir turned to face Saviar directly, his movements haughty but a smile playing across his lips that only Saviar could see. "We've discussed this, Savi. Their solution was to offer Kevral some as well, but she refused to hide behind hunks of metal like a coward."

Saviar had to bite his lip to keep from laughing. He dared not look at the Northmen lest he further aggravate the situation. Renshai shunned even jewelry because it might deflect a blow. Allowing anything but one's own quickness and skill to escape and answer an attack was perceived as the lowest form of weakness among Renshai. Saviar had known the answer before he asked the question and only brought up the subject in the hope that he could goad Valr Magnus into shedding his own protections.

But the Northmen's champion took no notice of the conversation. He stood in the arena, studying everything, including his opponent. Kevral seemed oblivious to his scrutiny, though Saviar knew she noticed every detail, every movement.

Feeling his grandfather's gaze boring through him, Saviar made a dutiful bow to the king, though he still addressed Thialnir. "Forgive me for raising a matter already addressed. I just could not imagine a true warrior seeing the inequity and choosing to wear his armor anyway." He stopped there. If he directly disparaged Valr Magnus as a cheater or a coward, he would attract his father's ire. As it stood, they all knew what he meant; and he had stated it surreptitiously enough to skirt rudeness.

King Humfreet clapped his hands suddenly. "Silence!"

Saviar cringed, at first believing the command directed at his insolence. Then, he realized the king of Erythane addressed the entire gathering.

The crowd quieted. Only then, Saviar truly noticed the vast numbers of people who had gathered. They stood in masses, the smaller ones attempting to see around the taller. Renshai children perched on parental shoulders to watch. Erythanians and Renshai sat in tree branches, on boulders, or on cottage porches. A few even squatted on the rooftops, a precarious position given the Renshai's lack of knowledge and experience when it came to construction. They might battle on any surface, but their ability to properly and safely erect buildings was limited.

Standing in the vicinity of the king, Saviar had an unobstructed view of the proceedings. No one dared block King Humfreet, not even the knights of Erythane, though mounted knights repeatedly shooed away anyone else who stepped too near the ropes.

Kevral rose, her movements casual. She seemed utterly composed, as if out for a stroll rather than facing a great challenge the outcome of which would determine the future of an entire tribe. She sheathed her first sword, a perfectly crafted blade she had received from Colbey. At the time, she had needed to battle a demon, and he knew her plain, steel weapons could not touch it. His had a hint of power simply because it had so long graced the hand of a god. She considered it her greatest treasure, and it never left her side.

Kevral sheathed her second sword as lovingly, a slender blade that once bore the name Tisis, *Vengeance*. Ironically, it had slain the first Valr, Valr Kirin, in a battle more than three centuries ago. The *Einherjar*, Rache, had gifted it to Kevral after she bested another of the Gloriously Slain in fair combat. In Valhalla, Rache had befriended Valr Kirin and gave Kevral the sword that she promised to rename. She now called it *Motfrabelonning*, Reward of Courage, and cherished it nearly as much as her unnamed weapon.

Valr Magnus stepped toward her. Sunlight sheened from his breastplate. He moved with a catlike lightness that belied the heavy armor and the shield he now wore strapped to his forearm. He had handsome features below boyishly tousled gold hair that fell in curls around his ears. His sinewy limbs hinted at speed and dexterity well beyond the norm. He stood more than a head taller than Kevral and was at least twice her weight. With a wave to someone in the crowd, he pulled a gleaming helmet over his head.

Saviar's heart pounded, and he found himself incapable of turning away.

"Ready?" King Humfreet called to the combatants.

In reply, Valr Magnus unsheathed his mighty sword. It seemed to draw the attention of the sun, flicking shafts of silver among the audience. Many turned away, apparently blinded by the reflection.

Kevral gave nothing. She simply stood just beyond the range of Valr's sword, her weapons in their sheaths, her expression carefree. As always, she kept her hair chopped functionally short, and she looked more boy than woman in her straight-cut tunic and breeks.

A figure stepped up beside Saviar. He stiffened, hoping it was not Verdondi again. He liked the young Northman, but his repeated attempts at conversation were becoming annoying. At the moment, he felt incapable of conversation, concerned solely with the battle. He was Renshai, first and foremost. For now, he just wanted to blend among his people, to hate Northmen and the situations they repeatedly thrust the Renshai into with their challenges and biases. The Renshai just wanted to be left alone and in peace. Why could the Northmen not honor that simple request?

Calistin's voice hissed in his ear. "She's got him."

Saviar looked at his brother. The young man rarely deigned to engage him in equal discussion. "What?"

"Mother's the better warrior. She's going to win."

Saviar responded the only way he could. "Of course she's going to win. She's Renshai."

Treysind shoved fiercely between them, his carroty mane bristling. Calistin frowned slightly but did not reprimand the boy. "No, I mean look at their builds. She's smaller, and he'll have more power; but Renshai maneuvers—"

"—don't rely on strength but on quickness and skill," Saviar finished impatiently. "Everyone knows that."

Calistin looked around his "bodyguard." "I—I know you know—I just mean—"

Saviar did not have patience for unnecessary chatter, whether from the young Northman or from his baby brother. "Yes, yes. She'll do fine." He needed the words to convince himself as well as Calistin. "She'll do just fine."

"I didn't mean to—I didn't expect her to say—"

Nothing could have driven Saviar's focus from the upcoming battle, except for his cocksure brother seeking reassurance from him. It was so wildly uncharacteristic, so staggeringly unexpected, that Saviar choked on his own saliva. At a time when he most wished to say something, he could do nothing but surrender to a fit of violent coughing.

The king made a sweeping gesture. "Let the battle begin!"

Before the sentence ended, Kevral struck like a snake, zipping through Valr Magnus' guard. Her sword cut across his shield, scratching a perfect line in the steel. She lunged again immediately, leaving no time for a return strike. Forced to defend again, Magnus sprang safely aside. This time, he managed a blazing riposte that Kevral dodged.

Saviar's throat finally handled speech. "It's not your fault, Calistin. No one blames you."

The Northmen shouted rhythmically, "Valr! Valr! Valr!" To Saviar's surprise, much of the Erythanian audience took up the chant. The Renshai remained silent.

Magnus' speed bothered Saviar. Whatever Calistin saw in their physiques that gave Kevral the advantage defied his not-quite-as-practiced eye. Magnus moved like a dancer, despite the heavy armor, and he clearly bided his time. He had learned to use the shield as a weapon rather than relying on it to fend every blow.

Kevral's next assault was a deadly blur of weaving steel. The sword in her left hand struck six times in less than a second, and the right bore in to inflict unrelated chaos. Magnus might have faced two separate foes for all the logic in their intertwining movements. He caught one attack on his sword, another on his shield, three more on various parts of his armor. Another, he parried, redirecting it fiercely and following up with a blazing attack that forced Kevral to withdraw and realign.

This time, Magnus attacked first, a furious feint followed by a blow full of strength and passion. Kevral caught it on a cross between her swords, needing both hands to slow the attack. Even then, it must have stung fiercely. She gave gradually with the force, slowing the momentum so as not to force an immediate, agonizing stop. An abrupt twist jerked the sword from his grip.

But Magnus moved with it, grabbing the hilt and yanking furiously. For an instant, his balance wavered. Seizing the opening, Kevral bore in with a blow toward the neck that dented his helmet but left the flesh intact.

Magnus loosed a howl of rage. His features went taut with driven anger, yet Saviar noticed something else in his expression, something out of place and unexpected. "Is that . . . a wicked, little smile?" he asked of no one in particular.

"He's testing her," Calistin guessed. Apparently appeased by Saviar's words, he sounded more like his usual confident self, "getting a feel for how she moves, her favorite actions."

Though troubled by Magnus' strategy and patience, Saviar doubted it would make a substantial difference. Renshai had no overriding tactics, no patterns; and Kevral would know better than to repeat a maneuver.

The two combatants attacked simultaneously, with a speed that defied Saviar's ability to follow. Steel flashed, arms and legs wove with terrifying speed, metal crashed against metal. Rents appeared in Kevral's clothing, scratches, dents and holes in Magnus' armor. And, on occasion, blood splashed, following a sword arc. Saviar did not know whose, but neither gave a bit of ground, so no one had sustained a serious wound. Yet.

Saviar's jaw ached. One clenched hand gripped his hilt so tightly it left impressions of the knurling on his palm. His fingernails chewed into the other. He tried to relax, tried to feel certain that Kevral would prevail, that all would go well for the Renshai; but he could not stop himself from worrying. She was a phenomenal warrior, more than a match for any Northman. *Any Northman!* he reassured himself. Yet, the war did not always go to the most competent. Renshai lost battles . . . occasionally. Renshai died . . . often. *Mother, why did you have to take that challenge?*

For an instant the two disengaged. Though neither panted obviously, their nostrils flared repeatedly. Sweat sheened them both, darkening the leather on their hilts. Both sported rips, tears, and gashes in clothing and flesh, mostly light limb wounds. Then, as suddenly as they had stopped, they charged again. Kevral sprang aside, her blades invisible as they carved lethal patterns through Magnus' defense. He charged right by her, missing, spinning to avoid the deadly steel. Blood splashed from Kevral's blade, and Saviar saw the welling scarlet stain on Magnus' thigh.

She got him! Joy welled up inside Saviar. *He's lost.*

Magnus tottered a step, then caught his balance. He glanced at the wound, then back to Kevral.

Kevral remained in position, swords readied; but she did not press. Apparently, she used his moment of weakness to catch her breath. If she had gashed the main artery, he would die before he took another step.

Valr Magnus remained standing, sword readied in his hand. With a bellowing battle scream, he rushed Kevral again.

"No!" Calistin shouted suddenly, bounding toward the ropes. "Above! Mama, look up!"

Only then, Saviar noticed a movement in the tree branch over Kevral's head. A man plummeted from it.

Kevral attempted to dodge both dangers simultaneously. She avoided Magnus' headlong rush with a deft spin, but the leaping figure caught her a glancing blow across the right shoulder. She staggered for balance, just as Valr Magnus turned and thrust. His blade pierced her left side, and their combined momentum drove it deeper.

No! Saviar chased his brother, heedless of the Knights of Erythane. *No! No! No!*

Kevral collapsed.

Magnus planted a foot on her abdomen and ripped his sword free. A rush of blood followed, bright red and pulsing.

Kidney strike, Saviar realized, suddenly wishing he knew less anatomy. *Fatal.*

Hands seized Saviar's arms, jarring him from the ropes. In a blind fury, he drew and cut, feeling momentary resistance and a mild, muttered oath.

"Let him go!" someone shouted authoritatively. "We don't need more bloodshed."

The grips disappeared from Saviar, and he vaulted over the ropes to Kevral's side. "Mama," he whispered, feeling like a lost child. "Mama."

Seemingly oblivious to Saviar's sudden presence, Valr Magnus was busy using the tip of his sword to find a gap in Kevral's ribs, to finish a job that was already done. The blood no longer spouted, but leaked; and the color had turned dark as wine. She was already dead.

Stunned grief blossomed suddenly to anger. Saviar tensed to launch himself at Valr Magnus, but Calistin's gasp froze him in position. He glanced at his brother instead.

Calistin stood in reverent awe, gaze locked on Kevral's body. "Do you . . . see it . . . ?"

Saviar had no idea what his brother meant, but the distraction did give him a moment to think. Valr Magnus had killed Kevral in fair combat. If Saviar killed the Northman in front of hundreds of witnesses, he would hang for murder. Feeling impotent, he sheathed his swords and went to his mother instead.

Kevral had died swiftly, a look of grim determination and pure battle joy still locked on her features. Her grip remained steady around the hilts of both swords, but the blades lay still in the dirt. There was nothing Saviar could do for her; he could only honor the weapons she had held so dear. He reached for the nearest one, the slender long sword, *Motfrabelonning* and took it into his hand. The leather was still warm and slightly damp. He could smell her scent, light beneath the suffocating reek of blood.

An image sprang to vivid life almost in Saviar's face. Startled, he jumped backward to find himself facing an enormous woman, a giant, bathed in golden light. She wore battle gear, including a helmet, that should have hidden every evidence of femininity; and, yet, he somehow knew that beneath the armor she was curvaceous and beautiful. Shrewd blue eyes peered out from hawkish features, and a cascade of yellow hair flowed around them. Beside her stood an exact, but insubstantial, duplicate of Kevral. Vital and happy.

"Ma—" was all Saviar managed.

Kevral smiled, her face glowing. "Keep it, Savi."

Saviar had no idea what she meant but found himself incapable of questions. He could only stare.

"The sword," Kevral explained. "Rache asked me to return it when I earned *Valhalla*, but the *Valkyrie* says I cannot bring anything with me." She gestured at the accompanying figure.

A tear dribbled down Saviar's cheek. Then another. Feeling paralyzed, he made no move to wipe them away.

"Don't cry, Savi. I'm so very happy. This is what I've always wanted, what I've worked for my entire life. I'm chosen for Valhalla."

Saviar knew she spoke truth, but the reality overwhelmed him. *I can see a Valkyrie. A Valkyrie! And Mama's spirit. How can that possibly be?*

"The other sword belongs to Calistin. I regret I have nothing equal for Subikahn, except for some advice: He will find happiness when he is true to what the gods have made him."

The *Valkyrie* said something to Kevral that Saviar could not hear, then took her arm.

"And tell your father I have always loved him."

A silent bolt of lightning opened the sky so suddenly it startled Saviar anew. A golden haze surrounded the *Valkyrie* and the new *Einherjar*, then disappeared as quickly, leaving nothing but the real world to intrude upon Saviar's fantasy. Unable to process what he had just seen, Saviar crumpled to his bottom, still clutching the sword.

A shadow fell over Saviar, and Calistin's voice yanked him from his trance. "Get up! Saviar, that's not a defensible position."

Saviar shook his head to clear it. The noises of the crowd flooded back into his consciousness, undecipherable and deafening. Valr Magnus had left the arena, and Ra-khir sobbed over Kevral's body. Without thinking, Saviar rose to a crouch.

"You saw them, didn't you?" Calistin's tone sounded almost accusatory, yet there was also a hint of worry.

Saviar could only nod. He looked at the sword in his hand. The blade needed a thorough cleaning before he could sheath it. Calistin held the sword Colbey had given their mother, and he clearly knew it belonged to him.

"How?" Calistin asked, now sounding more like a little brother turning to an older, wiser one. "How could we—?"

Saviar had never seen Calistin so vulnerable, and it brought out his protective instincts. He finally found his tongue. "I don't know." He continued to stare at his newly acquired weapon. "But it seemed to have something to do with this." He shook *Motfrabelonning.* "I couldn't see anything till I took it. I think it holds some sort of . . . of . . . magic."

Calistin looked at the weapon in his own hands, swallowed hard, then lowered his voice still further. "Saviar?"

"Hmmm?"

"I wasn't holding any weapon when I saw her. I just . . . I just . . ." Calistin dropped to Saviar's level. ". . . saw her. Then Hildr dropped from the sky—"

"Hildr?"

"Hildr, Warrior. The *Valkyrie.*"

Saviar blinked. "She told you her name?"

"I just knew it." Calistin's brow furrowed at the realization of what he had just said. "Not sure how, but I did."

Saviar glanced over the crowd. An argument had broken out, surely over the injustice of the battle. Apparently, no one else had seen the ghost and the *Valkyrie*; but he doubted anyone had missed the man leaping onto Kevral from an overhead branch. "Calistin?"

"Hmmm?"

"I don't think we should mention this to anyone."

Calistin nodded vigorously. "I'm not saying anything."

Saviar turned his gaze on Ra-khir, where he cradled Kevral's limp form, his grief etched across features smeared with tears. Saviar gritted his teeth, his heart aching. He had never seen his father in so much agony. His every instinct told him to console, but duty drew him elsewhere. "Calistin, you'll have to comfort Papa."

"Comfort?" Calistin rocked back on his heels. "Me?"

"Of course, you. He's your father, too."

"Yes, but, I don't know how to—"

Saviar glanced toward the king, where Erik Leifsson and Thialnir waved their arms around in clear argument. "You're going to have to do your best." Springing to his feet, Saviar ran toward the conflict. His brother's protestations chased him. *Incredible swordsman, hopeless human being.* For the first time in his life, Saviar actually felt sorry for Calistin, for what the Renshai had turned him into. *So competent, yet so ignorant about so many things.* He wove past the Knights of Erythane, still stationed to keep noncombatants off the field, though no longer as busy. Nearly all of the spectators had broken off into little groups to discuss the events, and a growing number watched the argument taking place before the king.

The Knights of Erythane allowed Saviar to pass unchallenged. He arrived just in time to hear Erik present his plea. "Your Majesty, it was the Renshai, themselves, who added the friendly interference clause."

Thialnir exploded, dispensing with formality. "I meant Renshai! Renshai would not interfere with—"

"Your Majesty," Erik kept his tone tightly modulated, a stark contrast to Thialnir's shouting. ". . . we all agree the interferer was Erythanian, is that not correct?"

King Humfreet appealed to Kedrin. "Knight-Captain? Do we have the man's identity yet?"

Kedrin stepped forward and executed a flourishing bow. "Sire, it was Frendon Harveki's son. An Erythanian as far back as history can determine."

The king cleared his throat, pulling at his beard. "And what does this Frendon Harveki's son say about his actions?"

"Nothing, Sire," Kedrin said carefully, attention fully on his liege. "We found him dead, his throat slit."

A slight smile played around Thialnir's lips, and Saviar prayed he did not laugh. It would make the Renshai look even coarser.

Erik's face drained of color. "Murder," he growled.

The king took the news in stride. "Under the circumstances, one could hardly expect otherwise."

It was a subtle insult to the Renshai way of life, but it did not bother Saviar or, apparently, Thialnir.

King Humfreet continued, "Are there family members or friends who wish to speak on his behalf?"

Kedrin performed another bow, not as grand as the first. "Sire, they refuse to come forward for fear of reprisal . . ."

Erik loosed an irritated snort but said nothing derogatory about the Renshai. Whether he did so in deference to royalty or so as not to antagonize Thialnir, Saviar could not guess.

Captain Kedrin glanced toward Erik in warning. ". . . but they told us he had nothing against the Renshai. They said he climbed the tree to get a better look at the combat. They think his fall was an accident."

Saviar frowned in disbelief.

Erik made a gesture, which the king acknowledged. "Your Majesty, King Griff in Béarn informed us that Renshai fall under Erythanian jurisdiction." Though he spoke innocently, his intentions seemed anything but to Saviar. "Is that not correct, Your Majesty?"

A shiver traversed Saviar's spine, but he refused to show it. He remembered his grandfather's description of that conversation. The Northern captain had asked King Griff to purge the Renshai from the West. Griff had coolly responded that the Fields of Wrath were a part of the sovereign city of Erythane and that he had no authority to banish anyone from King Humfreet's country. Though the high king of the entire Westlands by title, Griff rarely interfered with the dominion of other rulers, unless it involved a spat between them or if the highest authority in those lands requested his aid. The king of Béarn had also used that opportunity to essentially force the Northmen into agreeing to help against the pirates.

At the time, King Griff's strategy had seemed masterful. Perhaps, to a Béarnide, it might still appear that way. But, to Saviar Ra-khirsson, it created a serious problem they might not find a way to solve.

King Humfreet admitted, "The Fields of Wrath fall within my boundaries, yes."

Thialnir stood with his head tipped sideways, lips tight, obviously trying to read Erik's intentions. Saviar, however, knew exactly what was coming.

"Well, Sire," Erik addressed King Humfreet directly and seemed to take no notice of the nearby Renshai. "Since Renshai are Erythanian by admitted residence. And the man involved was also Erythanian, the 'friendly interference clause—'"

"No!" Thialnir boomed suddenly. "Renshai are Renshai. Erythanians are . . . not Renshai."

"I'm looking at the contract." Erik held the competition rules in his fist. "And I don't see the word "Renshai" anywhere in the 'friendly interference clause.'"

"That's hog manure!" Thialnir's debating style left a lot to be desired, but his point was valid enough to Saviar. "We didn't mean—"

"Meaning is implicit in the wording." Erik's calm demeanor made a sharp contrast to Thialnir's blustering. That did not bode well for the Renshai. Neither did Thialnir's lack of respectful titles.

Saviar jumped in. "Your Majesty, if I may please clarify." He waited for Humfreet's nodded acknowledgment before continuing, a detail not lost on Captain Kedrin. "What my colleague is trying to say is that when someone says 'Renshai,' they don't mean Erythanian. And when they say 'Erythanian,' they are deliberately excluding Renshai. Sire, when both are together, we say 'Erythanians and Renshai.' They are not interchangeable."

"And if I may, Your Majesty." Erik performed another bow, still trying to appear more formal and respectful than either spokesman for the Renshai. "When tribes of our people come together, we identify them separately, Sire. Nordmirians, Ascai, Skrytila, and so on. But we are still all Northmen." He bowed again. "Your Majesty, just because non-Renshai Erythanians use the simple form 'Erythanians' does not make the Renshai any less Erythanian."

King Humfreet said nothing in reply, only studying the three men in front of him. His lips remained sternly pursed, his chin cupped in both hands. Finally, he turned to Kedrin. "Knight-Captain, what opinion do you have in this matter?"

Once again, Kedrin performed a ceremonial motion that made the others look simple and common. "Sire, it is my opinion that both sides speak the truth. Captain Erik Leifsson is quite right when he says Renshai are Erythanians."

Saviar stiffened. He could hear his own heart pounding in his ears.

"But, Sire," Kedrin continued. "I also believe that when the Renshai spoke of friendly interference, they did not specifically intend to include all Erythanians."

Saviar did not need the clarification and wondered if Kedrin's words helped the king at all. It all seemed so obvious.

Erik ran a hand through his hair, then released it. Gold highlights flickered through the braids. "Your Majesty, had we known the Renshai would use their clause to play with wording and intention, we would never have agreed to it. Had one of our ilk fallen from a branch, would it have mattered to anyone whether he was Aeri, like Valr, or Nordmirian, like myself?"

The king's hands remained on his chin as he glanced from one speaker to the next. Finally, he rested his attention fully on Kedrin.

The Knight-Captain held a copy of the contract scroll in his hand, clearly reading and rereading the appropriate paragraph.

A long pause followed, during which no one spoke. Finally the king cleared his throat loudly. "Well, Kedrin?"

The Knight-Captain met the king's gaze with another flourish. "Well, Sire. As anyone entering a contract knows, it is the job of the signers to ascertain that any ideas or intentions are fully covered by the words."

Saviar went utterly still. This did not bode well; yet, surely, his grandfather would not condemn the Renshai to exile.

"Because, Sire, those left to interpret the contract, whether moments or centuries later, usually have nothing but the exact wording on which to base their decisions." Kedrin never faltered, showed no outward emotion as he dealt, in his professional capacity, with an issue that could tear his family apart.

Saviar's stomach roiled, then seized with the sudden urge to vomit. He fought it, not wanting to walk away and risk missing a single word.

The king remained absolutely and grimly focused on Kedrin. Clearly, he intended to take whatever advice the knight offered.

"Your Majesty," Kedrin concluded. "Unless we find evidence that Frendon Harveki's son had some connection to the North or to the Paradisians, we have no choice but to go with the letter of the agreement."

Saviar's stomach bucked against his control. Dizziness assaulted him, and he imagined his features looked positively green.

Thialnir glanced at Saviar. "Is he saying—?"

Worried for his control, Saviar did not answer, not even with a nod.

Captain Kedrin added, more directly. "Your Majesty, barring the aforementioned evidence, I believe we have no choice but to consider Frendon's fall as friendly interference. We have to side with the Northman."

Now, Saviar staggered off to vomit.

CHAPTER 16

Death is inevitable, but to live without glory is to die every day.
—Knight-Captain Kedrin Ramytan's son

TO QUEEN MATRINKA, IT SEEMED as if the world had ended. Though safe in Darris' arms, seated on their bed, she felt dark and cold, sobbing uncontrollably, wondering if she would ever feel joy again. "Mior, Arturo, then Kevral," she gasped out. "She is . . . she was . . . my best woman friend."

Darris shifted.

Knowing he was going for his lute, Matrinka said, "Darris, don't."

He paused in mid-movement.

"Don't sing." Matrinka's voice emerged clearly, no longer muffled by Darris' chest.

Darris' grip tightened, but he said nothing. The bardic curse severely hindered him. If he wished to speak significantly, Matrinka knew, he had to do it in song. To deny him that outlet meant leaving him utterly helpless.

At the moment, Matrinka did not care. The beautiful perfection of his voice, the unwavering notes of his instrument, had carried her through the most difficult times. It soothed the rawness in her soul, but its solace was temporary, a balm. To move beyond the tremendous burden of grief, she first had to face it.

"I love you," Matrinka said.

Darris moved back against her. "And I love you. Won't you let me—"

"No." Matrinka did not wait for him to finish. "I need to sort out my own emotions, without help. I'm still obsessing over a cat, and I can't believe we lost . . ." A fresh wave of misery washed over her, and she had to force the name around a sudden, enormous lump in her throat. ". . . our son."

Darris clutched her.

"Arturo is gone, Darris. He's not ever coming back."

"I know."

Matrinka read the same deep grief in his tone as she felt in her own. Despite the law, despite what the populace believed, Arturo was his son, too.

"Let me sing, Matrinka."

Matrinka could not. "No, Darris. No." Explaining it would take too much effort at a time when she felt empty. She appreciated his comforting, but he was far too good at it. For now, she needed to suffer the grief simply to feel human.

A loud knock bounced from the bedroom door. Darris stiffened and released Matrinka. Most of the servants knew of the king's arrangement with Darris, but he still made an effort to hide his inappropriate relationship with the queen. Releasing Matrinka, he rose and smoothed his damp tunic. She did not bother to try to look presentable in the privacy of her own chamber. "Come in."

The door swung open to reveal Rantire crouched fiercely, peering through the opening to assure no danger faced King Griff in Matrinka's room. The Renshai bodyguard glared at Darris. By law, the bard was the king's most personal bodyguard; but, in his absence, Rantire performed his job with savage and tactless seriousness. Granted the position by Colbey's son, Ravn, Rantire believed herself sanctioned by gods; and Griff had promised she could guard him in Darris' absences. Often, Matrinka knew, he regretted that decision, but he would never go back on his word. Behind Rantire, the king waited patiently, his black hair disheveled but his beard neatly combed.

Two cats wound around Griff's feet, mewing plaintively for attention.

"Darris is here," Griff announced.

Rantire snorted. "He's always here." She meant it as insult, not judgment. The triangular relationship did not matter to the Renshai; Darris' inadequacy as a proper bodyguard did.

"Nevertheless," Griff said, "you're dismissed."

Rantire grumbled something unintelligible, her bronze braids swaying around sharp features. "I'll be right outside if you need me, Sire."

"Duly noted." Griff looked pleadingly at Matrinka. "May I please come in?"

The cats did not wait for an invitation but slithered through the opening and leaped onto the bed, butting their heads against Matrinka's hands to demand a proper petting.

"Of course." Matrinka did not bother to dry her eyes as more tears joined the puddle on her dress and coverlet. "Please join us." She did not have the energy to attend to the cats.

Griff stepped inside the bedroom, shutting the door behind him, much to Rantire's obvious chagrin. Seeing Matrinka's mental state, he went right to her, gathering her into his arms.

The differences immediately became apparent. The huge bear of a man enveloped Matrinka where Darris had merely embraced her. His beard tickled her cheek, soaking up the moisture clinging there. "I'm so sorry," he said, and he clearly meant it.

Matrinka could hear Darris gathering the cats and shoving them back out into the hallway.

"It's been a year for tragedy, Matrinka. Our son, your friend, and so many good men lost."

"And now, we're without guards for the rest of our heirs. All the Renshai will have to leave."

"Not Béarn."

The words shocked Matrinka. She turned her face up to look at Griff, but he held her too closely.

The king explained, "I'm not bound by any agreement made by the king of Erythane."

Matrinka had never considered that. A glimmer of hope rose where none had existed before. "So the Renshai can stay? They can move here?"

Griff relinquished his grip, allowing them to see one another's faces. His looked tired. Lines had developed along his mouth and eyes, and a hint of gray touched his temples. "They can, but I doubt they will."

The suggestion upset Matrinka. She saw her last chance slipping away. "Why not?"

"Because, while I am not bound by the agreement, the Renshai are. I wouldn't banish or punish any Renshai who didn't obey it, but I think most of them, maybe all, will leave with their people."

"Even . . . Rantire?" Matrinka could think of no one more likely to stay, though she would not miss Griff's overeager guardian.

"Rantire will have to make her own choices." Griff shrugged. "It won't be easy."

"No," Matrinka admitted, her thoughts already far beyond the conversation. "But couldn't we . . ." She turned Griff a desperate look. "Couldn't we just . . . tell the *Northmen* to leave. Banish them and let the Renshai . . . just stay."

Darris paced wildly. Clearly, he wished he could be the one doing the comforting, the one providing explanations that might help her mood; but Matrinka's demand had robbed him of the opportunity.

Griff's gaze followed Darris' frantic path, but he did not tell him to stop. "Matrinka, you know it's not that simple. The Renshai made a contract. Whether or not most believe it, they are a people of great honor. And the Northmen . . . I'm afraid we need them. Without their ore, without their sword arms, we will lose this war."

The word struck Matrinka hard. "War?"

Griff's massive shoulders rose and fell. "I don't know what else to call it. Over the years, the pirates have been coming at us in ever greater numbers, and they've begun to fight with a coordination and ferocity that doesn't make sense for simple bands of looters. They've been testing our defenses far longer than we've acknowledged or realized. This is . . . well, it's a war, Matrinka."

"What are we going to do?" she whispered.

"What can we do? We're going to fight it, however we can. And, right now, that means with Northmen."

Darris glided to the edge of the bed. "Who are these pirates, Sire? Do we know yet?"

Griff shook his head, lips pursed. "You're well-studied, Darris. Perhaps you can tell me."

"I'll . . . try."

"Redheads," Griff started. "Nearly to a man, and their hair tends toward the thick and curly." He ran a hand through his own bushy mane. "Their skin is medium in tone, their features run the full gamut, except for the eyes which are always dark." He paused for input from Darris, who gave him nothing but an interested and curious stare. "They use short, curved swords, serrated and balanced well. Some of our men have reused their armor. It's well-crafted leather including helms and gloves. Sound familiar?"

Not to Matrinka. An entire battalion of redheads seemed unthinkable, even in the North, where blonds predominated anyway. Excluding Renshai, every Northman she had ever met had pale eyes and skin. Even Darris stood in stark confusion, brows deeply furrowed.

"But we did finally manage to capture one."

Darris came alive. The other piece of his curse sent him on an eternal quest for knowledge. "What does he say, Sire? Who are these brutes? Why are they attacking us?"

Griff managed a slight smile at the anticipated barrage. For all his inability to teach without song, Darris had no problem seeking answers. "Whatever he's saying, no one can understand it. The language isn't anything recognizable to any of our translators. It's as if he came from—"

"—another world?" Matrinka tried. It no longer seemed far-fetched to her since Darris, Kevral, and Ra-khir had traveled to such places by elfin magic.

"Well, yes." Griff cleared his throat. "As if. But we're not at the point where we think that's so. The elves deny having opened any portals, and they have no reason to lie about it. No other creature on our world has the power to—"

Darris fairly trembled with need. "What about the gods? They could—"

"I don't have any direct connection to the gods, Darris." It was not completely true. As a child, Griff had enjoyed the company of what he thought was a make-believe playmate. In fact, Ravn Colbeysson had watched over him, knowing he would one day become the king of Béarn. They had not, however, made contact for many years, not since Ravn had charged Rantire with the responsibility. "But I hardly think the gods would bombard us with an otherworldly army without announcing a reason."

Matrinka nodded thoughtfully. The gods rarely worked in subtle ways. Everything they did, they did with pomp and grandeur. "Maybe the magic originated in the other world. We did not open a way for them; they opened a way to us."

Griff's shoulders heaved again. It was an unanswerable question. "We might know *if* we could find a way to communicate with our prisoner."

Darris took his lute in hand; though, true to Matrinka's request, he did not play. "Music has a language all its own, Sire. One anyone can understand."

Griff studied the instrument in his bard's hands, releasing Matrinka and rising. "Your music certainly does. It's worth a try."

Matrinka considered. Darris' songs could charm anything: animal, human, even god. He could transform his listeners through emotion, evoking calm or agitation, grief or wonder, anger or joy in an instant. If the prisoner knew any of the common languages, Darris could surely coax him to use it. But the more she heard about these invaders, the more Matrinka believed they came from another world, where an overlapping language seemed unlikely. Darris' gift allowed him to provoke emotions; but, unless his listener was also under a bardic curse, he had no way to respond to whatever Darris invoked. "There is another possibility."

Both men looked at her.

"There is a man in this world, I know, with an uncanny penchant for languages."

Darris blurted, "You mean Tae?"

Griff carefully restored the title, though he still, after nearly twenty years on the throne, seemed uncomfortable with his own. "High ruler of the Eastlands, King Tae Kahn of Stalmize?" His eyes narrowed, and he shook his head, dislodging his black mane of hair. "Surely, we have men here able to work closely with our prisoner and, eventually, find a way to talk with him and get answers."

"Surely," Matrinka agreed. "But none nearly as quickly as Tae. He learned Renshai from the babbling of his infant son, and even knows some barbarian. He can fluently read and write Béarnese, for example, and many other obscure languages as well."

Darris nodded briskly, clearly remembering their first encounter with Tae, who was then a desperate street urchin. They had needed information about the existence of a possible missing heir to Béarn's throne, and Tae had sneaked into the Sage's twelve-story tower to read the scrolls. His information had led them to Griff.

Matrinka continued to work on the king. "Tae's father started him on multiple languages at birth, for spying purposes. And Tae seems to have developed some special area in his mind that lets him—"

Griff held up a hand. "I believe you. I just don't know how we can ask a king to travel so far to help us without any benefit to his own kingdom. I can pay him, but I imagine he has plenty of riches of his own."

Matrinka had to agree. *More than he can imagine using in a lifetime.* "Tae will come." She felt certain of it. "For the chance to see old friends and for the challenge." She lowered her head, grief assailing her again. "And he should hear about . . . Kevral from . . . mutual friends."

Darris headed toward Matrinka instinctively, then stopped and looked at Griff.

The king did not seem to notice, lost in thought. "What do you think, Darris?"

"I think . . ." Darris said softly, his attention still fully on Matrinka. Her sorrow clearly pained him. ". . . Matrinka's suggestion is sound." He fluttered his hands just over the lute strings, walking the boundaries of teaching without singing. He had the right to voice an opinion, but he had to make sure he stated only known information. "As you said, we will need to win over our prisoner; so, when it comes to watching him, we should use only those guards capable of maintaining neutrality. It would be too easy, and utterly understandable, for the prisoner to suffer abuses."

Griff appeared shocked at the mere suggestion, though he did not argue.

"Meanwhile, I'll try to make friends and establish some communication with music. By the time the king of Stalmize arrives, we should have a firm foundation for him to work from."

Griff still did not look convinced. He spoke slowly, "Fine, then. I'll start working on a letter for the messengers to run to Stalmize." He headed for the door, then turned, "Darris?"

Darris froze in position, obviously torn between his obligation to his king and to soothing Matrinka.

Matrinka knew Griff had two reasons for wanting the bard's company. Griff had become much more assured in his speech, though he still dropped into simplicity at inopportune times. He needed the bard to oversee the letter, possibly even to write it. His other need was less obvious. Without Darris at his side, he would be forced to suffer Rantire again.

"Go," Matrinka instructed Darris in a whisper. "He needs you more."

Darris sighed softly, nodded stiffly, and followed his liege from the room.

King Tae Kahn of Stalmize wove, full-speed, through the banister railing, gliding through openings that seemed too small to accommodate a cat. Most of the servants ignored his antics, accustomed to them. Only the maid, Alneezah, stood by with a block of ice, prepared to nurse the bruises he occasionally stamped on his skull. So far, he had not let her tend him, believing he deserved whatever pain his mistakes earned him.

Imorelda sat on the bottom step, twitching her tail. *I miss him,* she whined for the twentieth time that day. It had become a mantra, her first thought in the morning and her last at night. She slipped it into every mental conversation.

Long past tired of the game, Tae responded without sympathy. *You're a cat, by all gods. You have the memory of a soupspoon.*

Imorelda turned a circle on the stairs, ending with her back toward Tae and her tail twining enormous S's of agitation. *I have a fine memory. Better than yours. And I miss him.*

Tae snorted, stopping his practice to stare at the tabby's back. *You don't even remember his name.*

Subikahn, the cat snapped back immediately. *His name's Subikahn. And you made him go away.*

The echo of his son's name in his head irritated Tae more than he expected. He missed Subikahn far more than Imorelda could. *Leave me alone.*

The cat said nothing more, but her tail continued to lash.

They had argued this point too many times to do so again. As the days and weeks, then months, went by, Tae had tried to fool himself into thinking of this as just another normal separation. If he did not dwell on the memory, he could convince himself that Subikahn was in Erythane, basking in the love of his mother and the grueling lessons of his *torke.* But things always happened to remind him of the truth. When Imorelda was not moaning about Subikahn, his spies brought information about the escaped Renshai traitor. They had caught up to Talamir twice. Both times, the Renshai had defeated them, leaving a spray of corpses in his wake. Tae no longer wanted Talamir killed, but retrieved alive. The Renshai did not deserve a quick, painless death. He had caused too much suffering not to endure some himself.

Alneezah approached. "Sire, have you hurt your head?" She removed a chunk of melting ice from her bucket with tongs.

"Many times," Tae admitted. "But I'm fine, Alneezah. Thank you." As if to demonstrate, he dove through the railing again.

Alneezah watched, expressionless, the ice still clutched in her tongs. Tae rolled to his feet. "Why do you do this, Alneezah?"

Alneezah tipped her head. "With all due respect, Your Majesty, it seems to me that you're the one doing something odd."

"Indeed." Tae could hardly deny it. "But I meant hover over me. Keep me safe. Nurse my wounds."

Alneezah shrugged, as if Tae had asked the most obvious question in the world. "If I didn't, who would, Sire? You have no mother, no sisters." She added, blushing as she did so, "No wife." She glanced at Imorelda. "And the love of your life has no hands."

Tae followed her gaze. "She's also mightily selfish."

Hey!

"She's not selfish, Sire." Alneezah defended Imorelda against her liege. "She's a cat. She's only doing as cats do."

She's right, you know.

The maid continued, "You love them, and they love them." She winked toward Imorelda. "It works out perfectly for everyone."

Funny and smart. Imorelda lifted a long, silver-striped leg and licked it from hip to knee. *Marry her.*

I'm not going to marry anyone.
I know. Imorelda continued cleaning herself nonchalantly. *And that's half your problem.*
Half?
The other half is too complicated for a mere human to understand.
Is it?
Yes. Imorelda started on the other leg, clearly with no intention of elaborating.

It occurred to Tae he had best not press. He was in no mood to listen to a litany of complaints. However, he could not help teasing, *Well, I haven't exactly seen you with any toms.*

You certainly haven't seen me mooning over my best friend's tom for the last eighteen years. A tom I can't ever have.

Tae got the message, and it fueled his irritation. *I'm not mooning over . . . her.*

Her name is Kevral, and you are. You've been using her as an excuse not to get close to other human beings.
I'm close to you.
I'm not a human being.
You sure think you are, but you're far more irritating. Tae did not send that message to the cat. *I'm close to my father.*
On and off. Love and hate.
I'm very close to my son.
Not anymore.

Battling a sudden urge to kick Imorelda down the stairs, Tae turned his attention to Alneezah. More to prove the cat wrong than from any personal reason, he asked, "Are you free for lunch?"

Alneezah froze in position. Her nostrils flared. Unobtrusively, she glanced over her shoulder, apparently looking for the recipient of the king's invitation.

Amused by her antics, Tae leaned against the banister. "I mean you, Alneezah. Are you free for lunch?"

"Am I free, Sire? Me?"

Tae had never seen Alneezah so flustered before. Usually, she seemed utterly unflappable, meeting even the most bizarre accidents with humor and commonsense. His brows inched upward in question.

"I suppose so, Sire. I mean, I guess that depends on you. I work for you. Am I free?"

Tae rubbed sweat from behind his neck with a hand. "I don't need any ice right now, so it would appear so. Will you join me?"

"For lunch?"

"Yes." The conversation amused Tae, took his mind off his troubles for the moment.

"In the kitchen?"

Tae never worried about where he dined. Often he skipped meals completely. "If you prefer. Or, we could take our meal in the courtyard."

Alneezah finally smiled, an attractive gesture for its open genuineness. "The courtyard will work fine, Sire. Would it be all right if I prepare the food myself?"

The request caught Tae off guard. For an instant, he succumbed to dark instincts he could never quite shake. Could she have chosen to spend so much time around him in order to gain his confidence? It would prove simple enough to poison his food when she already had her hands in it. Tae belittled his own paranoia. *That's right, stupid. An assassin spends years winning me over, then warns me before killing me.* He trusted his judgment when it came to people, more so than anyone else's. Alneezah was exactly what she appeared to be.

"That depends, Alneezah. Are you a good cook?"

She laughed. "The best."

"The best, huh?" Tae headed up the stairs to change. "Then how can I possibly refuse?"

Imorelda yawned, stretched, and followed Tae. He expected her to gloat; but, instead, she brought back the thread of their previous conversation. *★You know why I haven't taken a tom?★*

Though Tae had never thought much about it in the past, he now discovered he had many theories. They included her tight bond to him and the realization that any other cat might seem too stupid in comparison for her to waste her time with them.

★Because if I filled this castle with kittens, as my mother did in Béarn, you would throw me out on my gorgeous, pointy, little ears.★ Imorelda shook her head. *★That place is overrun with scores of moronic purrers.★*

Tae turned, brows arched. *★You should be careful what you call them. They are your brothers and sisters, after all.★*

★Grandnieces and grandnephews. Great great great grandnieces and grandnephews.★ Imorelda made a snorting sneeze. *★Basically, strangers.★*

It amused Tae to see how his own personality seemed to have shaped Imorelda's. Mior had had a much sweeter mistress and a temperament to match. *★Well, Matrinka can hardly kick out Mior's descendants, can she?★* He continued up the stairs.

Imorelda ran up beside him. *★I would. Cavorting amongst themselves and acting like plain old cats. They're an embarrassment to the lineage.★*

What are you saying, Imorelda? That if you had kittens, I could just give them away?

After a couple of months, of course. We could hardly keep them all running around the castle marrying their brothers. They need to make their own lives.

Tae could scarcely believe what he was hearing. *And, yet, you're still chiding me for sending my full-grown son out into the world.*

Imorelda had no problem with the incongruity. Apparently, she did not even see it. *I miss him,* she said.

Tae sighed and finally admitted. *Imorelda, I miss him, too.*

CHAPTER 17

No matter how honorable, the death of a loved one is tragic.
—Sir Ra-khir Kedrin's son

SAVIAR WATCHED RA-KHIR glide forward and backward in the swing seat he had built for his occasional quiet nights with Kevral when duty called neither of them away. The movement had become repetitive to the point of insanity, the squeak of the leftmost spring a dull, chanting song that was giving Saviar a headache. "Papa?" he tried for the fifth time in a row.

Ra-khir seemed not to notice his son, his eyes glassy and distant. He kept his hands by his sides on the wooden seat, his legs dangling still, his body heaving just enough to keep the swing in motion.

Saviar waited for the swing to complete one of its forward arcs, then sprang on board. The contraption swayed rhythmically, but the young man kept his balance with ease. Crouching beside his father, he seized Ra-khir's hand. "Papa!"

Ra-khir finally turned his head toward his eldest son. "Oh, Saviar. Do you need something?"

"Of course I need something." Saviar had grown impatient. Three days of catatonic mourning was enough. "I've already lost my mother. I don't want to lose my father, too."

"That's not going to happen." Ra-khir's tone remained flat, haunted, gently remote. "I'll always be here for you, Saviar."

Will you? You're not even here right now. Saviar clenched his jaw. "And your mother will . . ."

". . . look down on me from Valhalla. I know. At least until someone names a child for her, and she becomes forever bound to them, like all Renshai *Einherjar.*" *If someone names a child for her.* It occurred to Saviar that doing so might not suit anyone. *Who wants to be associated with the Renshai who got us banished?*

Ra-khir jerked, shook his head, and stopped the eternal swinging. His eyes filled up with tears. "Saviar, she's gone. Kevral is . . . gone."

Saviar gathered his father into his arms. It felt weird, utterly unnatural. His father was a large, strong man who never crumbled under pressure. This was the same hero who had faced off with Colbey Calistinsson without flinching, who had single-handedly challenged the city of Pudar to war. "Papa, you're upsetting us all. You married a Renshai; you knew you would outlive her."

"She's always been too skilled to die. And I thought I could—"

"You couldn't." Saviar did not want his father to finish that sentence. It might dishonor his mother's courage. "No one can protect a Renshai. No one should try."

Ra-khir casually reached out a toe to restart the swinging.

Saviar planted his own feet to prevent it. He would not risk losing Ra-khir's attention again. "Papa, I don't understand . . ."

"And I'm not sure I can explain." Ra-khir loosed an enormous sigh. A tear trickled from each eye, but they did not fill up again. "No matter how much I knew that Kevral's antics would get her killed sooner or later, my heart never did. I just can't believe—"

"That's not what I wanted." Saviar kept his face directly in front of Ra-khir's, their noses nearly touching, forcing his father to look. "When I said I didn't understand, I didn't mean your devotion to Mama. That, I understand perfectly; you both loved one another ardently. I get it. What I don't understand is why Grandpapa ruled the way he did. Clearly, Mama was winning that battle. And, clearly, the Erythanian's interference was the only reason the Northman won."

Ra-khir made a noncommittal noise.

"So how could any sane man rule against us?" Saviar found moisture filling his own eyes, and brushed it away with angry fists. The thought had smoldered for the last few days. He felt terribly betrayed by one of the few people he had once wholly trusted. "Does Grandpapa want us to go away forever?"

"Of course not." Ra-khir finally took the initiative, returning his son's embrace fiercely. "Kedrin loves you. You know that, Savi."

"Do I?" Saviar's soft question was lost in the folds of Ra-khir's tunic, full of his unique scent, unusually strong. He had not moved from the swing in days. "Then how could he make such a horrible mistake?"

"Saviar." Ra-khir held the young man away so he could peer into his face again. "I have no right to second-guess a man who is not only my father, but my commanding officer."

Saviar snorted and dodged his father's gaze.

"What does that mean, Saviar?"

Now, Saviar met his father's green eyes savagely. "It means you've never shied away from a challenge before. Why would you pick now to become meek over an issue of clear injustice?"

Ra-khir sucked in a deep breath, held it a moment, then let it out slowly. He repeated the process before speaking. "Savi, your grandfather is a man of the greatest honor. I do not know exactly how he came to the conclusion he did; but I do know that, if he made such a decision, it is the fairest one possible."

Saviar did not appreciate the answer. He turned his head to look out over the Renshai village, with its randomly spaced cottages and cluttered battlegrounds. "You know what I think?"

Ra-khir did not bother to answer the obviously rhetorical question.

So, Saviar continued even without direct encouragement. "I think Captain Kedrin didn't want to get accused of bias because his grandsons are Renshai. I think he deliberately ruled against us to avoid appearing influenced. That's what I think."

"You do your grandfather an enormous disservice."

Saviar gave no quarter. "Perhaps he deserves it."

Ra-khir took another drawn-out breath. "If you truly believe that—"

"I do."

"—then you should take it up with Kedrin."

Saviar jerked his attention back to his father. "Can't you?"

"I'm not the one questioning his decision."

The response floored Saviar. He spoke through gritted teeth. "Are you saying . . . you think he was right?"

"I'm saying only that it's not like him to be wrong. On anything. And when it comes to honor . . ."

Saviar ground his jaw, afraid what might emerge from his own mouth if he spoke again.

". . . no one can better him. Did you know he did not defend himself against a false charge of treason because doing so would have harmed the honor of Béarn?"

Saviar could not stop himself from speaking in anger. "So he's not so much biased as stupid."

"Saviar!"

Saviar looked away, determined not to apologize.

"You're not too old for a switching."

Saviar did not care. "Beat me, if you wish. It won't change the fact that Kedrin is wrong."

"Right or wrong, he is your grandfather and the Knight-Captain. He deserves your respect."

Suddenly overwhelmed with emotion, Saviar understood the need to become lost in the routine of the rocking swing for days at a time. "Of what use to him, my respect or the lack of it? Soon enough, he'll never see me again."

"Never see you?" Ra-khir's grip tightened. "Of course, he'll see you. He'll see you every day."

Saviar could only stare. In the depths of his grief, Ra-khir had apparently become delusional. "Papa, I'm banished. I have to leave the Westlands. Forever."

Ra-khir stood up, still clutching Saviar's shoulders where he crouched on the swing seat. "Son, no. You don't have to go anywhere."

It made no sense. "I don't?"

"Your mother is dead. You're mine now, mine alone. And I'm not Renshai."

Stunned silent, Saviar could only stare.

"I thought you knew, Saviar. We cleared it. You and your brothers are staying."

"We are?"

"Calistin can keep your Renshai maneuvers fresh. And you can start your knight training, Saviar. That is, if you're still interested."

"I can?" Saviar shook free of his stunned trance, needing to communicate more than two syllable questions. "You've discussed this with Calistin and Subikahn?" He could not believe his brothers had not even mentioned it.

"Well, Subikahn's still in the East, but I'm sure he'll choose to stay with you. And Calistin . . ." Ra-khir paused thoughtfully. "I guess I haven't talked with him about it yet, either. I just assumed—"

Assumed he'd choose blood family over Renshai. Calistin? Saviar shook his head. His father was dreaming.

"Well, Calistin's been a man a long time now. He doesn't need the tribe to do as he wishes. I doubt anyone could make him go anywhere if he doesn't want to."

Ra-khir's choice of words hurt. "I'd be a man, too, if the duel hadn't postponed my testing."

"Of course you would." Ra-khir's voice did not hold a hint of patronage, yet Saviar's insecurity added it. "But this works out better in one way. Since you're still considered a child, you belong with your only living parent. Here, in Erythane."

In Erythane. Saviar could scarcely believe it. What would the Fields of Wrath become without Renshai? How could he live from day to day in a home filled with strangers stepping on the ghosts of his past? The same father who had so heroically won Saviar the right to become Renshai was taking it all away in an instant. "But . . . I'm Renshai."

"And you always will be." Ra-khir's hands dropped away. "But you're also my son, a child without a living Renshai parent. The king himself has decided you can stay."

Saviar kicked at the ground, restarting the rocking he had denied his father only moments earlier. Ideas swirled through his mind, unable to form a coherent pattern. In the blink of an eye, an Erythanian had leaped or fallen from a tree, and the entire world had changed forever. For the first time in as long as he could remember, Saviar felt like a lost child, as vulnerable as a newborn kitten. "Papa, please. Please talk to Grandpapa." He did not know what else to say. "Please."

The swing sang out its familiar, rhythmical squeak. Ra-khir slowly shook his head. "That," he said in a voice barely above a whisper, "is something you must do for yourself."

The front door to the cottage banged open, awakening Saviar from a deep sleep he did not remember entering. Before he could think, he found himself on his feet, sword in hand. The instant the hilt settled against his callused palm, he no longer felt naked, though he still wore no clothing. He ran into the main room to find Calistin already there, dressed in his sleeping gown and clutching the weapon their mother had left him.

Thialnir stood in the doorway, framed by moonlight. "We're leaving now."

Saviar stared. "Now?" Cold night air washed across his naked flesh, deeply chilling.

Calistin added, "But they gave us a fortnight to prepare."

A frown scored Thialnir's massive features. "The merchants are refusing to sell to Renshai. The sooner we leave, the farther we can travel before our stocks run out."

Saviar shook the last vestiges of sleep from his brain, trying to comprehend what Thialnir had told them. "The Erythanian merchants won't—"

Thialnir interrupted. "Our money's not silver enough for them anymore."

Calistin narrowed his eyes. "Are our swords sharp enough? Renshai don't need money."

"No." Saviar saw the danger. "There's enough Renshai prejudice. We don't want our last impression on Erythane to be of slaughter and theft. Better we do as Thialnir suggests and leave quietly in the night."

Thialnir looked between the boys. Clearly, he preferred Calistin's idea, had probably considered it long before the youth had mentioned it, but had already chosen the wiser, more frustrating course. "Colbey committed us to a new way: swords for hire. He wanted us to win over, not skewer, the hearts and minds of the West."

Calistin snorted. "See where that strategy has brought us? Three hundred years later, we still suffer from the same misplaced hatred. The same gods-damned bigotry. The early Renshai had the right idea: Kill for the joy of battle; take what we need from the corpses."

Saviar rounded on his younger brother. "How can we disabuse others of the notion that we're savages when some of our own still believe it? Still *endorse* it?"

Thialnir raised his hands to forestall the budding argument. "Enough! I have many more Renshai to rouse, and I hope you'll do the same." He gave Calistin a glare that spoke volumes. An underlying gleam made it clear Thialnir wished they could do exactly as the young man suggested, yet it also held a warning. No matter how tempting, Calistin must not act upon his desires.

Treysind wandered sleepily from Calistin's room. Despite Calistin's threats, the boy had taken to sleeping in a spare corner there. Apparently spying no danger to his hero, Treysind yawned and quietly observed the exchange. The only one in the house still sleeping, apparently, was Ra-khir. For reasons Saviar could not explain, his father's incaution irked him.

"We're gathering on the south border," Thialnir said. "If you're coming, get your things and meet us there." He turned on his heel and strode out the door.

"*If* we're coming . . . ?" Calistin's brows rose in slow increments, and he turned toward his brother.

Saviar's ire rose further as he realized Ra-khir had not yet discussed staying with Calistin, had left the difficult explanation to his older son. "I'm not sure anyone could make you leave if you didn't want to go."

Calistin grunted. It was simple truth.

"And Papa says we have permission to stay."

"We?"

"You, me, and Subikahn."

Calistin's brows remained arched. "Because we're the sons of a knight?"

"No." Saviar thought it best to avoid discussion of manhood and childhood. "Because our only living relatives are Erythanian, not Renshai." He tried not to look too eager for Calistin's response, hating to admit how much he valued his little brother's opinion.

To Saviar's chagrin, Calistin went right for the argument he had dodged. "I'm a man and a Renshai. The details of living relatives do not matter. I would never forsake my tribe."

"Nor I," Saviar added hastily; though, at the time he had fallen asleep, he had still grappled with the decision. "I'm just explaining why Thialnir used the phrase 'if you're coming.' "

"Fine." Calistin strode toward his room, looking for all the world like a man despite his boyish size and features. "Let's pack, then, and tell Papa good-bye."

The idea of involving Ra-khir rankled Saviar. Partly, he did not want a scene, did not want to explain to his honorable father why they had to leave, did not want Ra-khir trying to talk him out of the decision. He needed to become a man before he could return to Erythane, even if it meant he could never return at all. "I'll pack. But let's not wake Papa. He's still distraught over Mama. He doesn't need to grapple with another loss." It was a weak explanation. Obviously, Ra-khir would have to deal with their leaving whether or not they told him first.

But Calistin accepted it without comment. He trusted Saviar implicitly when it came to matters of emotion and heart.

"You'll need clothes, Hero's brother." Treysind stated the obvious. "You start swinging sharp things around dressed like that, you might lose something important."

Saviar could not help smiling. "You're coming with us, Treysind?"

"Of course."

Calistin groaned as he returned to his bedroom. "But you're Erythanian, kid. You're not banished."

"My place," Treysind declared emphatically as he followed Calistin, "is at your side."

Dead at his feet's more like it. Saviar headed for his own room to pack. He felt bad for the little Erythanian doomed to die by his own crazed decision, yet Saviar fully intended to enjoy his brother's discomfort while it lasted.

Ra-khir paced the edges of the Bellenet Fields for what felt like the thousandth time that day. Silver Warrior grazed, seemingly oblivious to his rider's consternation, his bridle dangling properly from his saddle, the packet of knightly garb lying neatly wrapped on top. In the distance, Ra-khir could see his father working the men on the fields, talking, gesturing, and demonstrating techniques. It seemed like an eternity before the captain finally left his troops to their own devices to address his son.

Ra-khir's heart rate quickened at his father's approach. He had rehearsed what he wished to say seventy times, yet memory disappeared as the tall, well-muscled man approached him.

"Sir Ra-khir." Kedrin acknowledged him with a nod. "Surely, you're not ready to assume your duties."

"No, Captain." Ra-khir felt his gaze straying to his boots and forced himself to look at his father. "I've come to . . . to tender my resignation from the Knights of Erythane."

Kedrin stiffened ever so slightly, the only indication that the words surprised him. "Tender your resignation, Sir Ra-khir?"

"Yes, sir."

Kedrin continued to stare at Ra-khir, still betraying no clear emotion or reaction. "Are you aware, Sir Ra-khir, that such a decision would have to be permanent? That you could never return to my service or to that of any Knight-Captain who succeeded me?"

Ra-khir swallowed hard. The knighthood was all he had ever wanted as a boy. He had worked so hard to attain his position, and it meant nearly everything to him. Yet, his family, he realized, meant more. "Yes, Captain. I do understand."

"You no longer believe in our purpose, our honor? Sir Ra-khir, is being a Knight of Erythane no longer fulfilling to you?"

"It's not that." Ra-khir felt a lump growing in his throat. Tears stung his eyes. "It's not that at all, Captain. It's just . . ." He found himself incapable of finishing, unable to speak words he could scarcely believe himself.

"Yes?" Kedrin encouraged.

"The Renshai left last night, sir." The voice did not sound like his own.

"I'm aware of that." Kedrin looked back at his charges, who were working diligently in his absence. "I've heard."

"My sons . . . my boys . . . went with them." Ra-khir fought a losing battle to withhold tears. Despite his best efforts, they dripped down his cheeks. He put a hand over his face to hide them. "I'm sorry, Captain. I . . . I just can't . . ."

"No apologies necessary, Sir Ra-khir. You're on deferment because of grief. I could hardly fault you for . . . grieving."

Ra-khir could only nod.

Kedrin removed his hat and put an arm across Ra-khir's shoulders. "Ra-khir." He dropped the "sir" to indicate they now spoke as relatives, not leader and subordinate. "We found a way for them to stay, but, ultimately, Calistin and Saviar are grown. They're allowed to make their own decisions."

Ra-khir understood Kedrin's point. He forced himself to speak. "I'm not sure they did."

Lines creased Kedrin's brow. "What do you mean?"

Ra-khir swallowed hard. He had to force out the next few words. "I haven't been a very good father."

"Ra-khir—" Kedrin started, giving him a stern look; but Ra-khir raised a hand to stop him.

"I don't mean over the years, I mean since Kevral . . ." It surprised Ra-khir that he still found it nearly impossible to say. His throat seemed to close off completely, and the tears quickened; but he forced himself to say it, ". . . died. I-I got so caught up in my own sadness I didn't . . . didn't even try to allay theirs."

"You loved her." It was not an excuse, just a simple statement of fact.

"More than I knew anyone could. She fills my dreams with happiness, with hope. Then I wake up, and she's not there. Nothing is there but this huge, dark, empty hole." Ra-khir could no longer see for the tears, and his eyes already ached and burned. "I don't think I can go on without her."

"You can," Kedrin said sternly. "And you will."

Ra-khir nodded, unable to speak. He would never stoop to the dishonor of suicide. A long silence followed before Ra-khir found his tongue. Even then, his voice emerged thick and slurred. "Papa, I have to go after them. Whether or not they choose to return, they must know they aren't . . . orphans."

"I understand."

Ra-khir forced one last nod. "So you accept my resignation, then?"

"No."

It was the last thing Ra-khir expected, an immediate denial without explanation. He steeled his resolve. "Whether or not you accept it, I will go after my sons."

"I know."

Ra-khir scarcely dared to believe he had to explain, "And if I am still a part of the Order, everything I do or say in the course of finding them will reflect back on the Knights of Erythane."

Kedrin's manner stiffened, and it became instantly clear that they no longer spoke as father and son. "Sir Ra-khir, when you go where you need to go, you will have no choice but to ride your charger and wear the colors of the Order. Remember this: anything you say or do reflects back on the Knights of Erythane, on King Humfreet and on King Griff, who you represent." With that, he turned on his heel and headed back to the Bellenet Fields and his charges.

Ra-khir could only stare at Kedrin's retreating back. *He just said what I said,* he realized. And yet, the exact same words held so much more significance from Kedrin's mouth. "I won't disappoint you," Ra-khir promised, too late for Kedrin's ear.

CHAPTER 18

So long as I'm moving, I'm alive.
—King Tae Kahn of Stalmize

EXHAUSTION HOUNDED TALAMIR as he dragged through the Eastern forests, avoiding the prominent pathways that seemed to breed enemies. He could not recall the last time he had slept; the days and weeks blended into a constant battle. Whenever he stopped to eat or rest, he could hear the footsteps and rustlings surrounding him. Sometimes, they manifested as groups of fearless attackers that he dispatched in droves. Other times, they fought amongst themselves and disappeared, leaving only memories of harried, Eastern whispering or the meatier sounds of fists or boots striking flesh. More than once, he had awakened scarcely in time to thwart a silent assassin standing over him with dagger readied.

Talamir had long since broken his promise to Weile Kahn not to kill the king's followers. The sheer numbers of the attacks had forced his hand, and fatigue had drained any ability to finesse. An arrowhead remained lodged in his left thigh, draining pus, blood, and greenish fluid; he needed a healer to safely remove it. He carried a bloody slice across the side of his neck where he had startled the would-be assassin barely in time. Bruises in rainbow colors stamped his arms, legs, and back, as much from sleeping on branches and rocks as from battle. His clothing hung in tatters on a frame thin from hunger. Aside from the sword, which he kept in perfect repair and cleanliness, he might have looked the worst sort of scrofulous beggar.

Only two things kept Talamir going: his instincts for survival and battle pounded into him by the Renshai since birth and his love for Subikahn. He wondered if his lover suffered the same fate, if Tae had become insane enough to send murderers after his son as well. What Talamir had learned so far suggested otherwise, but he trusted few of the rumors: a girl who claimed to be carrying the prince's baby, a sign on an inn in the tiny town of Yborach proclaiming that the Prince of Stalmize had slept there, and an aging whore who proclaimed Subikahn the gentlest, most considerate lover she had ever experienced.

Talamir paused to pick his way through a tangle of undergrowth. Water sprinkled him, dislodged by higher leaves, and mosquitoes assaulted him in a sudden drove. He did not bother to slap at them. It would require more energy than he could spare; and, oddly, he appreciated the itch of their welts. It reminded him he was still alive as well as took some attention from the throbbing in his injured thigh and the sting of the gash near his throat. That one he hated most of all. It enraged him that he had let an enemy draw close enough to inflict it.

It frustrated Talamir as much that the only information he had managed was clearly false. No woman would ever carry Subikahn's baby. And, while Talamir agreed with the whore's assessment, a kind and considerate lover, the prince would never grow so desperate as to pay a woman for sexual favors. Subikahn was a man's man, through and through, without mistake or reservation. Women were friends, mothers, sisters, and cousins, but never, *never*, lovers.

Talamir ground onward without intention. His mind waded through a nest of cotton, and his mouth filled with a saliva so thick and flaky he barely recognized it as liquid. His legs kept moving long after his will to walk departed. He barely noticed the bits of brush that snagged in his eyes and hair; he could not have described anything he saw. He moved on mindlessly, soullessly, because it never occurred to him to stop.

"Hold it right there, Renshai!"

Talamir heard the words, but they were meaningless. He tried to focus on each individual sound, assigning sense to each syllable in turn. *"Hold." Hold, hold, hold. What am I holding. "It." Hold . . . it. What is "it"? What does "it" want. "Hold it." Hold it. Stay still, Talamir.*

Talamir froze.

Clicking sounds echoed all around him. Talamir saw the circle of crossbowmen, but the significance of their presences refused to register. *"Right." Right is not left. Right is right. "There." Here? I am here, aren't I? "Renshai." Ren . . . shai. That's what I am. That's a reference to me.* Then it all finally came together. *Hold it right there, Renshai! I'm in trouble.* Operating solely on instinct, his hand already clutched his hilt.

"What do you want?" Talamir said, his voice a bleak croak he did not recognize.

"Drop the sword, and we won't hurt you," one man said. "The king wants you alive."

Alive? Talamir did not have the strength to wonder whether that boded well or ill for him. For the moment, though, alive seemed better than the alternative. All of his training drove him to attack, but he had enough presence of mind to realize that his first movement would be met by a hail of quarrels. Dying a pincushion's death would not get him to Valhalla. "Alive suits me just fine," Talamir said. "But no Renshai can drop a sword."

"Throw it, then," the man suggested. "Or lay it down."

Talamir would have rolled his eyes, but the movement might prove enough to strain his consciousness to its limit. "The problem is the blade touching ground, not the manner in which it gets there."

A pause followed. At least, they seemed reasonable enough to entertain Talamir's request, which was more than he expected. They still worried about him, even though he doubted he had the power for more than a sword stroke or two. Feverish, dehydrated, and fatigued, he might manage to kill one or two before they took him down, assuming they chose to fight him directly rather than just outnumber him with bows.

"If we send someone to take it from you, will you kill him?"

Talamir had to consider the possibility. It would not help his situation if he did, yet he did not know if he could control his deeply ingrained impulses. He did, however, know the correct answer. "No."

"You'll come peacefully?"

Talamir found himself slipping in and out of consciousness. He could not find the strength to answer, even had he understood the question. "I . . . I—" Ringing filled his ears, and a blanket of flickering stars stole all vision. His voice sounded inordinately distant. "I . . . am . . ." He could not remember what he planned to say. Then the darkness claimed him.

※

Back pressed against a tree trunk, Saviar surveyed the sleeping Renshai all around him. He wanted to rest as well, knew he desperately needed it, but found himself awash in thoughts so intense they stabbed him fully awake the instant he started to drift. Every time he closed his eyes, thoughts paraded through his mind, keeping sleep at bay and raising emotions he would rather avoid. Irritation and anger mixed inseparably with grief and hatred. He felt abused and used, victimized and driven, hated and hating all in a mass he could ignore only while awake. When he had something to look at, he could set aside the confused tangle of thoughts that haunted him. But the instant his lids sagged shut, it all intruded upon him again. He could only hope that if he forced himself to remain up long enough, exhaustion would win out over all of his concerns.

The music of night insects rose and fell in a cyclical hum pierced by the occasional owl hoot, fox call, or snore. Wind rustled the leaves overhead and bowed the weeds all around Saviar. He shivered, chilled by the night wind.

Then something touched his right shoulder.

Startled, Saviar leaped to his feet, sword freed and cutting stems before he could think. A shadow reared up in front of him. He charged it.

"Brother, stop!" Subikahn hissed, springing aside.

Saviar barely managed to redirect his blade, slamming the tree trunk instead of his twin. The impact thrummed through his fingers. "What in coldest Hel—!"

"Quiet," Subikahn demanded. "What's wrong with you?"

"What's wrong with me?" Saviar whispered back as forcefully, jamming his sword into its sheath. "You know better than to sneak up on another Renshai!"

"I thought you heard me. I said your name."

The lapse only fueled Saviar's rage. "Well, unless my name was changed to . . ." He imitated the whirring noise of calling foxes. ". . . I didn't hear you. You're getting more like your sneaky little father every day, and it's going to get you killed."

"Not today." Subikahn dropped to a crouch, easing his back against the same tree Saviar had vacated.

By my graces. "Where've you been?" Saviar demanded.

Subikahn stared. "I didn't expect a party, but you could at least act glad to see me." He added as emphatically as possible at a whisper, "Brother."

Saviar heaved an enormous sigh, then dropped to a crouch beside Subikahn. He did love his twin, but at the moment, he did not feel charitable toward anyone.

"I've never been far, Saviar. Not since we talked. I saw what happened. With . . . Mama, I mean."

"Who didn't?"

Subikahn's voice fell lower still, and Saviar had to lean in to hear, which only irked him further. "Who do you think killed that Erythanian bastard?"

Saviar jerked to attention, staring at his brother. "The one who fell . . . on . . . Mama?"

"He didn't fall. He jumped, the bastard."

"No one knew who killed h—"

"Now you do."

Awe crushed aside Saviar's other emotions, for the moment. "How did you manage it in front of everyone? Without anyone knowing?"

"How did I just sneak up on a Renshai without getting killed?"

Saviar rolled his eyes. "Because I controlled my impulses. I seriously doubt Frendon Harveki's son graciously impaled himself on your sword."

"Not exactly," Subikahn admitted. He examined his fingernails. "But someone had to do it."

"No." Saviar could scarcely believe that the last remaining bastion of sanity in his family had just confessed to doing something so stupid. "No one had to do it. At least not before we pulled a confession from him." He rounded on his brother. "You kept us from proving—"

Subikahn snorted. "Proving nothing. He wasn't going to admit to anything but an accident, not without torture. And then, no one would believe him."

"Whatever you say." Saviar would not let go. "At least we had a chance."

"He needed to die."

"Eventually. After we got some information." The entire world seemed to have gone daft at once, and Saviar found himself even more agitated than before his brother's arrival. He rose and turned away. "You're a moron, Subikahn."

"What?" Subikahn's voice finally rose above a whisper. "I thought you'd appreciate—"

"That my brothers are morons? What's to appreciate?"

"Oh, so I'm in the same category as Calistin now?"

"You put yourself there. You took away our only chance of proving deception on the part of the Northmen." Saviar waved his hand, scarcely daring to believe he had to explain. "Even if we got the information by torture, even if no one believed his confession, it would at least give us a starting point for investigation."

"Investigation?" Subikahn blinked several times in succession, as if trying to ascertain he spoke to his own brother and not a stranger. "You really think an investigation would make any difference? The Erythanians are rid of us. Do you actually believe it matters to them whether that happened fairly?"

"We don't have to convince the populace, you idiot." Saviar found whispering too constraining, though it saved his brother from a tongue-lashing. He moved farther from the sleeping Renshai, clambering around trees, debris, and deadfalls. "We only have to convince the king."

Subikahn followed silently; at least his movements made no sound. "I'm not sure he'll be any more sympathetic."

"The king of Béarn understands our usefulness."

"But it's the king of Erythane we have to convince."

Saviar muttered, "The king of Erythane is a moron."

Subikahn continued to follow until they had gone far enough to assure no one could hear them, even speaking at normal volume. "So he's a moron, too? Is everyone in your little world a moron?"

Saviar beetled his brows. "So far, *I've* managed to escape that fate."

Subikahn quoted someone or something Eastern: "When you feel you are the last bastion of sanity in a world gone mad, should you question the mind-set of the many . . . or the one?"

Saviar dismissed the suggestion, never doubting his own worldview. It made too much sense. "If the Renshai believed 'right' was defined by numbers, they would no longer exist. No, Subikahn, it's not all in my head."

Subikahn nudged the discussion in a new direction. "Fine, then, genius. Banned from the North *and* the West. Do the Renshai plan to live on the moon?"

Saviar still felt like the only human in the area endowed with a brain. "You, of all people, ought to know about a part of the world called the Eastlands, what with your father being king of it and all." Doubt seized him suddenly. "You're not saying Tae wouldn't let the Renshai live there, are you? Because he's never seemed like the type to—"

Subikahn held up a hand. "There's only one Renshai he'll stop."

Saviar stared. "You?"

"I'm banished, remember?"

"Under the circumstances . . ."

Subikahn shook his head. "I'd rather face the entire North than my father. He has more eyes than a budding fat-root, and the men who work for him show no mercy."

Saviar threw up his hands, now without a modicum of doubt that the entire world had fallen into a vast vat of foolish idiocy. "Subikahn, your father loves you. He wouldn't let his men kill you."

"A man who can't keep himself alive is not worthy of that life." Now Subikahn cited Colbey. "My father believes it, and the Renshai would not disagree."

It was easier to avoid the subject. "Stop quoting people," Saviar demanded irritably. "I got enough of that from Mama, Calistin, and Grandpapa."

The distraction worked. Subikahn asked incredulously, "Kedrin's quoting Colbey now, too?"

"Not Colbey." Saviar wished he had not raised the point. It did not matter. "Ever since the Sage let him read those old history scrolls, the ones about the Great War, he's taken to quoting that . . . that famous Western general with the long, weird name."

"General Santagithi?"

"Yes, that's the one." Saviar studied the brother he had called a moron. "How in coldest, darkest Hel did you know that?"

Subikahn smiled. "My papa makes me read everything. In just about every language." He sighed. "At least the ones I've managed to master. I don't know how he does it. I'm surprised he doesn't talk to animals, too."

"He does, Subikahn. To Imorelda. I've heard him."

"Well, yes; but she's different. People often talk to their pets. It's not like he's out in the stable braying or wallowing in the sty." Subikahn's eyes narrowed suddenly. "And you can distract me until horses neigh in the Common tongue, but I'm still not setting foot in the Eastlands."

"But—!"

"No."

"Subi—"

"No. Nothing you can say will change my mind."

"Not even that I have no choice but to go. That we might never see one another again if—"

Subikahn snapped to sudden attention, hand falling to his hilt.

Alarmed, Saviar grasped his own sword and tipped his head, listening. Hearing nothing, he started, "What's—?" Before he could complete the sentence, a half dozen men wearing scales of armor or links of chain charged toward them.

Saviar's sword whipped out in plenty of time to meet the rush. His blade opened a gash in one man's neck before he thought to tend defense. Blood splattered, and the man collapsed soundlessly. Immediately, Saviar faced another opponent wielding an ax. The blade chopped for him as he spun aside, missing cleanly. Saviar riposted, but not quickly enough. His enemy jerked aside, his weapon not yet in position for another strike. Saviar lunged under his guard, jabbing as he moved. His blade buried deep into the man's gut, striking bone. He toppled, wrenching Saviar's sword from his grip.

"Hey!" Saviar sprang for the hilt. The odor of bowel contents soured the air. Blood slicked his fingers and slathered his hair, but he worried more about lack of respect for his lost weapon. Subikahn fought the other four valiantly, but he clearly needed assistance. Saviar planted a foot on the enemy's flopping body, seized his hilt in both fists, and yanked. The sword eased slightly, then whipped suddenly free, sending him staggering. He regained his balance in an instant, sword raised, howling toward the warriors who menaced his twin.

The men had surrounded Subikahn, who mostly executed broad defensive sweeps to keep all of them at bay. Saviar fell on one from behind, tearing open a chunk of flesh and ripping through a kidney. Knowing no one could survive that injury, Saviar moved on without hesitation. The second man met him sword to sword. Blue eyes, clearly of Northern origin, bored into Saviar's.

"Die, blood-sucking Renshai!"

Saviar did not reply. He only swept in for a chest stroke the other man easily parried. Sword thrown clear, Saviar drew it back swiftly to block an adept attack, followed by a clumsy one. *Couldn't wait.* Impatience proved his opponent's downfall. The attempt to make two quick attacks opened his defenses, and Saviar's blade sliced through his thigh. An instant later, Subikahn's sword severed his spine.

Saviar whirled to face the next enemy, only to find them all dead. "What in Hel? Northmen?"

"Some," Subikahn said. "Not all." He crinkled his nose at his brother. "You're a sight. Is any of that blood yours?"

Saviar examined his limbs and clothing, stained with blood and speckled with torn flesh. Nothing stung, and he could not remember a single stroke coming close to hitting him. "I'm fine. I just opened a lot of large vessels."

A war cry echoed over the woodlands, "Mooodi!" It was the call of an injured Renshai charging bravely into what might be her last battle. The familiar crash of steel on steel exploded through the forest.

The others. As one, the twins raced toward the main part of the Renshai encampment, the sounds of battle growing louder with every step. Saviar's attention riveted on a blur of activity at the edge of the camp. There a small bundle of energy swirled like a tornado, mowing down everything in its path. Yet, despite the superhuman speed and grace of the combatant, he fell into awkward lapses that seemed stunningly out of place. *Calistin,* Saviar realized in an instant. *And he's hurt.*

Without thought, Saviar redirected his advance toward his brother. So many times, he had wanted to kill Calistin, but the world would end in fire before he would allow anyone else to do it. "Modi!" he screamed, not because of wounds, but simply as a battle cry. He wanted to divert as many enemies as possible from Calistin to himself.

As Saviar charged down upon Calistin and his foes, he realized what he had, at first, mistaken for weakness was something altogether different. Calistin fought with his usual ungodly dexterity, holding four enemies at bay while his blade glided toward a fifth. Suddenly, Treysind ran in, shouting, an overlarge sword swinging chaotically in his fist. Forced to redirect or kill his would-be savior, Calistin pulled the stroke with a curse, then buried his blade in another attacker before Saviar even saw him spin. In the same movement, Calistin riposted a killing blow meant for Treysind, then sprang around the boy's wild, unpredictable stabs and weavings.

Two of Calistin's opponents disengaged to attack the new threat bearing down on them. Pressed to his own defense, Saviar lost sight of brother and living annoyance. He met a brutal attack with a parry that opened his opponent's defenses for an instant. Too late, he extracted his weapon. The opportunity was gone, and he found himself defending against the other enemy.

These two proved more difficult than Saviar's previous opponents, survivors of Calistin's rabid attacks. He found himself meeting blades in every direction, hard-pressed to tend defense. One slashed his sleeve and another drew a fine line of blood from his calf. Still, Saviar pressed in, driving one aside with his shoulder, to focus on the other. A wicked stop-thrust ended that one's assault, as he skewered himself on *Motfrabelonning.* Saviar stepped back to face his last opponent, only to see Calistin sitting calmly on a log cleaning his swords.

Saviar vented his irritation against his enemy, his sword whipping in every direction. Forced to defense, his opponent retreated with every step, the crash of blade against blade herding him backward. Then his foot came down on a fallen branch. It snapped beneath his weight, throwing his balance backward and opening his vitals to Saviar's blade. A throat slash ended the battle, and the Northman collapsed onto the limb that had proven his downfall.

Panting, Saviar glanced around the camp. Bodies littered the ground, Renshai and enemy alike. Some Renshai finished final skirmishes while others sorted through the dead, finishing off enemies, dividing out Renshai who had a chance for survival from those who did not. The latter would be given the opportunity to die engaged rather than slowly succumb to fatal wounds.

Saviar waited until he could speak without long pauses to breathe before rounding on his little brother. "Calistin, you know I came to help you."

Calistin glanced up from his polishing; and, beside him, Treysind mimicked the action. "I didn't ask you to."

The response maddened Saviar. A frown scored his features as he lowered his weapon. "You didn't have to ask. I came to your aid because I . . . love you."

Calistin stared. He was clearly guessing at the proper response, "Thank you?" he tried.

"You're welcome." Saviar responded with all the heartfelt sincerity Calistin lacked. "When you saw me still struggling with your enemies after you had finished, why didn't you do the same for me?"

Calistin indicated the dead men with a foot. "You didn't need me."

"I could have."

"You didn't. You killed them all on your own. You're a man now, Saviar."

Anticipating an argument, Saviar felt as if his brother had just punched him in the gut. "What?"

"You killed a man in combat. More than one, in fact. You're blooded. You're a man whether or not you've passed your tests of manhood."

Saviar continued to stand in stunned silence. His sword remained in his grip. Every instinct screamed for him to honor the weapon his mother had given him, to scrub the blade gleaming before he even considered tending his own wounds. Yet, he found himself unable to speak, unable to think. *Calistin's right. I am a man.* "I just meant . . . I just thought you should have . . ." Knowing he could never win a war of words in his current state, Saviar walked away to tend his sword. The confrontation, the teaching of basic kindness and humanity, would once again have to wait.

CHAPTER 19

Loyalty cannot be commanded, nor respect impelled by force.
—General Santagithi

AS USUAL, CALISTIN HAD NO idea what was bothering his brother, nor did he waste much thought on wondering. Instead, he wandered out over the camp turned battlefield, glad that Treysind chose not to follow him. Apparently, the Erythanian no longer saw any danger to his hero in the situation and needed some time alone to process all that had happened. The truth never occurred to Calistin: Treysind remained seated on the deadfall, nostrils filled with the reek of blood and open bowel, mind saturated with death, and vomiting every scrap in his gut.

As Calistin wound his way between the corpses, his anger grew. He recognized colleagues and teachers amongst them; and even children had not been spared. They lay in gruesome poses, features locked into determined grimaces and, sometimes, even battle-mad smiles. Swords lay, dishonored, upon the ground, steeped in the entrails of enemies. Blood still oozed from the freshest wounds. At last, he found the one he sought, a young woman of sixteen named Sitari. She sprawled across two other bodies, both Northmen, the portion of scalp over her right ear torn open, trailing a gleaming white hunk of sinew and skull and exposing brain tissue purple with clots and dirt.

Calistin had heard her death cry as he tussled with seven opponents, too far away and too late to come to her aid. She had continued fighting surprisingly long after a wound that could have taken down a mountain lion. He had listened to her high-pitched battle calls in the distance, strange and determined. Now, he stared at her body, so lifelike in death, still shockingly desirable. He had never told her how he felt about her, though he hoped she had known. She had treated him with the same starry-eyed reverence as the others. Yet, there had been so much more to their relationship, at least in his mind. She was the one in most of his adolescent fantasies, though he did not yet have the development, or the social skills, to act on them.

"Good-bye Sitari," Calistin whispered, then looked up toward the heavens. In the morning, she would awaken in *Valhalla* to the first of an eternity of battles. All day, she would fight the other souls of the bravest and most worthy of the dead. In the evenings, the "survivors" feasted, and they all came back to life in the morning to battle again. It was the fate every Renshai desired. Someday, he knew, he would see her there.

Calistin glanced around for Sitari's sword, planning to honor it, only to find it partially jutting from the abdomen of a Northman. The man still had enough energy to paw at it aimlessly, like a turtle turned on its back so long its feet continue to paddle long after it already believes itself dead. With a single step, Calistin came to his side and jerked the blade free.

A rush of filthy-looking blood followed. The Northman hissed in agony.

Calistin pointed at Sitari with the blade. "Did you kill this woman?"

The Northman took a ragged breath, and scarlet trickled through his teeth. "I killed . . . her." He sucked in more air. "And the bitch . . . killed me. It would seem . . . we're even."

Calistin kicked him. Blood dripped from the blade in his hand to mingle with the stream leaking from the dying man. "You're not going to Valhalla."

"I believe . . ." A glaze covered the blue eyes, and he did not meet Calistin's gaze. ". . . I am."

"Not after I dismember you." It was a forbidden act, Calistin knew, the one that had first gotten the Renshai banished from the North. At the time, all Northmen believed only the soul of an intact corpse could ever reach Valhalla. The Renshai had cut apart enemies as a means to dishonor them as well as to demoralize their fellows. In the last century, however, it had become common knowledge that missing a body part did not bar a brave warrior from Valhalla.

"Do it, Renshai," the Northman gurgled. "End this."

Calistin hated the Northman's defiance. He wanted a show of cowardice, anything to prove the man unworthy of a warrior's greatest reward. "You'll scream like the craven you are. And, missing pieces, you won't find Valhalla."

The Northman gasped for his last breaths. "Not . . . true."

"Are you sure?" Calistin dropped to a crouch beside him. "Are you quite sure? Because you're risking your eternal soul." He preyed upon that last shred of doubt that exists in every mind. No matter how fervent a man's certainty about magic, about the supernatural, he always carried a shred of doubt buried somewhere deep in his psyche. There, and only there, be monsters. "I'm a Renshai, remember? Demons, you call us."

Something sparked briefly through the dying man's eyes.

Was that a hint of fear? Calistin allowed himself a smile. "And demons know how to damn."

The Northman's lids slid closed, and he managed only four more words: "I am not afraid." As the last left his lips, his entire body suddenly relaxed, releasing a wash of blood.

Abruptly angrier than he could ever remember, Calistin hacked at the corpse's neck until bone cracked beneath the blows. He did not quit until every last tendon and shred of flesh separated, and the head rolled free of the body. Only then, he felt a presence behind him and whirled, still clutching Sitari's sword. A *Valkyrie* stood in front of him.

The figure towered over Calistin, enormous, swathed in armor, yet still oddly and desirably feminine. A shield lay strapped across her left arm, a sword swung at her hip, and a spear lay thrust through her belt. She stepped uncomfortably close, seeming not to notice Calistin at all.

"No!" Calistin shouted.

The *Valkyrie* stopped, glanced around them, then back at Calistin. Then, apparently believing he addressed someone else, she started toward the corpse again.

Calistin stepped solidly between them, stuffing Sitari's sword into his belt near the left sheath that held the weapon his mother had given him. The gesture smeared fresh Northman's blood across his tunic, but he would not allow Sitari's blade to touch the ground again, to further dishonor it. "You cannot have him."

The *Valkyrie* blinked. She stared at Calistin.

Calistin met her gaze directly and with level violence.

"Human child, you have no right to interfere with *Valkyries*. The battlefield souls are ours to take as we see fit."

"This one," Calistin said firmly, "you may not have."

The *Valkyrie* roared, "Get out of my way!" She tried to step around him, but Calistin moved with her. In a blink, he had freed both of his swords and held them at her throat.

Surprise flashed through her eyes, then disappeared. She seemed not to notice the bared steel at her neck. "Little man, you have pluck.

But you are braver than you are wise." She studied him over his swords, ignoring them as she might twigs in a child's grubby fists. She raised a hand to bat them away, but Calistin only tightened his attack and hoped she would not force him to draw blood. "What a pity and a waste you have no soul."

Calistin had no idea what she meant, but it sounded like an insult. "You cannot have him," the Renshai repeated.

Apparently, the blades finally bothered the *Valkyrie*, because she back stepped and drew her own enormous sword.

Excitement rushed through Calistin. Even tired from his recent battles, even enraged by her taunts, he relished the chance to fight a creature of such stature. He withdrew just enough to make the battle a fair one, to give her a chance to strike first.

The *Valkyrie* obliged, taking a sweep that showed remarkable speed for such an oversized blade. Calistin dodged it gracefully, then bore in for an attack of his own. To his surprise, size seemed not to hamper her at all. She moved with the dexterity of a Renshai, avoiding his attack and returning one of her own with lightning speed.

Calistin laughed, thrilled to finally find an opponent with skill rivaling his own. He caught the attack on one blade, only to find it stronger than he anticipated. Driven a step backward, he twisted to bring himself out of line with the corpse. Bad footing had turned many a battle tide.

Pressing her advantage, the *Valkyrie* struck again. This time Calistin parried, managing a crisp riposte with his mother's sword that the *Valkyrie* redirected. Again, she bore at him. Calistin dodged, lunged, and drove for another furious, two-bladed assault that the *Valkyrie* met with a flurry of defense.

Joy suffused Calistin as he fought the first real battle for his life. He could die; she might actually best him, and that realization brought an excitement he could barely fathom. The *Valkyrie* went on the offensive now, jabbing and sweeping with remarkable speed and skill. Calistin dodged and parried, avoiding blocks, with the memory of her strength still strong in his mind. He drove in relentlessly, with one sword, then the other, drawing the combat closer, trying to take advantage of his smaller size and shorter weapons. Clearly anticipating his intentions, the *Valkyrie* kept her steps always sideways and backward, mindful, like Calistin, of the many obstacles around them.

At last, Calistin managed a studied cut beneath the left sleeve of her byrnie that sliced undertunic and flesh. Blood trickled from the opening, winding down her wrist, between her fingers. The *Valkyrie* stiffened, clearly startled by the wound, opening herself to another attack that she barely remembered to defend.

"Who are you?" she demanded, batting aside both of his weaving blades. "Who in darkest, dampest, coldest Hel *are* you?"

Calistin wove a bold web of attack. "Calistin Ra-khirsson of the tribe of Renshai."

The *Valkyrie* blocked the sword in his right hand, Kevral's, the one with which he had injured her. She seemed less concerned with the other, which scratched harmlessly across the links of her byrnie. "Renshai," she said, without the hatred that seemed to drip from the word when others spoke it. "Your death will be a pity."

"Yours more so," Calistin returned as he fought. Renshai training taught him never to converse in battle; it interfered with concentration. That small lapse had also turned the tides of battles. "I do not intend to lose." He dove for an opening, more interested in bringing the fight in close than in actually scoring a hit. He became suddenly aware of another presence, but his instincts told him the second bore him no threat. Yet.

A female voice cut over the din of combat, obsessively compelling. "Calistin Raskasson, stop immediately!"

Calistin nearly had a seizure in an effort to fight the compulsion. If he went still, he died.

The *Valkyrie* lowered her sword.

Only then, Calistin ceased his own assault, retreated to a safe distance, and turned to face the speaker. Habit drove him to correct her mispronunciation of his father's name, but the sight of her struck him dumb. Long, honey-blonde hair fell to her shoulders in thick, burnished waves, outlining a perfect face. Every feature seemed chiseled by an artist so loving he spent years on every cut. Usually, art sought the beauty no reality could ever capture. Here, it seemed certain, no man could improve upon her, no mere craft of mortal making could ever capture such breathtaking exquisiteness. Lashes, dark despite her pallor, curled from large eyes the color of brilliant sky. Her nose was perfectly straight and of just the right size. Her lips were full, moist, and red as berries. Her neck was delicate, white, and lineless, and enhanced by a choker of fluid gold incised with twisting, weaving patterns. She had strangely powerful shoulders that suited her. Generous, vivacious breasts began a series of curves that precisely defined proper female proportions. Long, shapely legs completed the picture. The simple dress she wore seemed unworthy of her, and the sword at her hip only made him desire her more.

Calistin found himself sinking to the ground in front of her, as if he faced royalty. He caught himself, turning the movement into a wary crouch.

"You will not interfere with *Valkyries*," she commanded.

"But she was about to take . . ." Calistin found himself gesturing dully. "He's not worthy of—"

Her voice was like music; he could listen to it forever. "It's not your job to decide who's worthy. That job belongs to Shrieking and her sisters." She made a movement toward the *Valkyrie*. Bracelets glimmered on her wrist, until they became lost beneath her sleeve.

When it came to words, Calistin knew he fought a losing battle. He sheathed his swords; they alone could help him, but he refused to attack the vision in front of him. "But he's . . . racist. A hater of Renshai, without just cause."

The woman smiled, as did the *Valkyrie*. At least, she made no further move toward the Northman. "Calistin, if the *Valkyries* limited themselves to those who like Renshai, Valhalla would contain only . . . well, probably only Renshai."

That sounded delightful to Calistin, exactly how a place like Valhalla ought to work, but he knew better than to say so. That would make him seem equally bigoted.

"I believe you know, Calistin, that the quality the *Valkyries* seek is courage. Valhalla is the reward for *any* warrior who dies bravely in battle."

"Yes, but . . ." Calistin pursed his lips. He was not used to mincing words. "Doesn't a man's character count at all?" Even as the question left his lips, it seemed wrong. It was the sort of thing one of his brothers might ask. Nevertheless, he continued, his own voice sounding odd in his ears, "His causes mean nothing?"

"Nothing," the woman confirmed. "Many a friendship has been formed in Valhalla. Some over days, others only over millennia. Your brother's sword is a testament to that."

Motfrabelonning. Calistin knew the story. "I . . ." He glanced at the Northman's headless corpse. ". . . won't . . ." He paused, knowing he now fought only a war of stubborn will that he could not win. ". . . don't think . . ."

"Calistin," she said firmly. "If you insist on interfering with *Valkyries,* the gods will have no choice but to smite you down."

Calistin's heart rate quickened, not from fear but from excitement. For a moment, he imagined himself surrounded by Frey, Heimdall, and Vidar, exchanging lightning sword strokes until their superior might destroyed him. He could think of no better, no more worthy, way to die. That would surely earn him a place in Valhalla.

"And that would be a terrible shame. It would wound your father deeply."

"My father knows I'm Renshai." Calistin still felt odd about the way he and Saviar had left Ra-khir, desperately grieving for, of all things, a Renshai. "He knows it's my mission, my destiny, to die in combat. What could please him more than me falling to the might of the gods themselves? Surely, the *Valkyries* would choose me, and I would have my fiercest wish, the only thing that really matters."

The *Valkyrie* called Hlökk, or Shrieking, finally spoke, "We never took men felled by Thor's thunderbolts nor shot down by Ullr's distant bow. And you, Soulless One, can never find Valhalla no matter how bravely you die."

It was the second time Hlökk had called him soulless. A sword thrust through his heart could not have shocked, or hurt, Calistin more. He glared at the *Valkyrie,* hands balled on his hilts, uncertain whether to scream, attack, or cry. Never before in his life had he felt helpless. "What do you mean?" he said, not trusting his voice above a whisper.

Hlökk did not answer, only stepped around Calistin and reached toward the fallen Northman.

Calistin rounded on the other woman, whose identity suddenly became desperately important. "What does she mean? And who are you?"

But the beauty had silently vanished in the moment he had looked away, leaving no sign she had ever existed. Calistin whirled back toward the *Valkyrie,* only to find her gone, too. "No!" he screamed. "No! No! No!" His blades cut the air where the women had stood, meeting no resistance. "Why would you—How can this be?" He launched into a crazed flurry of *svergelse,* his blades cutting the air all around him. "What did you mean? *What did you mean?*"

Brush crunched, and Treysind appeared suddenly at Calistin's side, taking no apparent notice of the flying steel for the moment. "Hero! Hero! What's wrong, Hero?" His distress was tangible. "Is ya hurt?"

Calistin howled in frustration and anger. His insides felt like liquid fire. He swung wildly, sending Treysind into panicked retreat. He wanted to shriek at the heavens until his throat turned raw, to fight enemies until one finally claimed him, to die hacked beneath the blows of a million swords. "I do have a soul, you foolish wench. I . . . have . . . a . . . soul!"

"A course ya gots a soul, Hero." Treysind soothed from a distance, hand over his mouth and nose to filter out the odors of death. "Ya's got more spirit than any four other mans tagether."

Calistin froze, then turned to stare at his unwanted sidekick who now watched from behind a tree trunk.

"Ev'ry human gots a soul," Treysind continued. "Ya is human, ain't ya, Hero?"

The question seemed utter nonsense. "Do I look like a horse to you? Of course I'm human."

Treysind shrugged, hand still clamped to his face. "Then, ya was born wit' a soul. Did ya sell it ta demons?"

"No!" The very suggestion enraged Calistin. It was exactly the accusation he expected to hear from some lazy fool who would rather attribute skill to nefarious magic than to credit long hours of practice and hard work.

"Is ya gived it 'way ta some magic creature?"

"Gived it . . . ?" Calistin shook his head. "What nonsense is this? Certainly not."

"Then," Treysind announced simply, "ya still gots it. Which means ya *do* gots a soul."

"Of course I have a soul!" Calistin turned his back on Treysind, as if the boy had initiated his doubts. Then, realizing how stupid that sounded, he shrugged and laughed. "Everyone has a soul." But his attempts to shrug off the *Valkyrie*'s insult, even shouted out in anger, fell short. Restlessness assailed him, overcoming the fatigue of his many battles. Calistin did not know how, but he had to prove it. "I need some time alone."

"I's keepin' m'distance, Hero," Treysind promised. "We's all needs some sleep." He started to glance around the woodlands, then stopped. His gut heaved.

Calistin ran a hand through his sweat-damp hair, allowing it to fall in a random array of boyish spikes. It was just long enough to annoy him; he looked a bit older with it closely cropped. Treysind misunderstood. Calistin was not talking about a short break to rest and regroup. What he needed was time, and a lot of it. His last thousand attempts to rid himself of the boy had failed, and he expected no better results now. Nevertheless, he felt the need to try. "Treysind, don't you think your debt to me is paid?"

Treysind looked at his own feet, seeming more uncomfortable than confused. "What ya meanin'?"

"I mean, you saved my life many times over today." It was not true, but Treysind had to believe it to justify his intrusions during combat. "We're even now, right?"

Treysind released his hold long enough to shake his head vigorously. "It ain't a matter a 'even.' Ya saved m'life. Now I's obil'gated ta keep ya from dyin'. Fo'ever."

"Forever! Your mission is doomed." Calistin laughed, the humor a strangely welcome relief. "No one lives forever. Even with the Great Treysind as his bodyguard."

"Tha's my intentshin," Treysind replied, with all seriousness. "Pa'haps yas'll be tha first."

"Second," Calistin replied. "Because to protect me forever, you'll have to live forever, too."

"Whither or not I's succeed's in tha hands a tha gods." Treysind finally smiled at a realization. "What, by tha way, live . . . fo'ever."

"Yes, but I am not a god." Calistin's own words sparked a revelation. *But I think I recently spoke to one.* He suddenly thought he knew the identity of the woman, and it made him decidedly uncomfortable. *Golden necklace, unbelievable beauty. Could that have been Freya?* The urge to drop to his knees became unbearable. He was seized with the undeniable need to pray. "Treysind, could you check and make sure my brother came through the battle?" It was a ruse to rid himself of the boy. Calistin had spoken to Saviar since the bulk of the hostilities had ended, and Treysind knew it.

Nevertheless, nodding vigorously, Treysind rushed to obey his Hero's request. Calistin dropped to the ground. And prayed.

Treysind hurried through the brush, avoiding bodies, nose pinched against the horrific odors that defined the death and destruction around him: feces and blood, metal, sword oil, urine, and rancid fat. It all blended into a hideous, overpowering stench that threatened to overwhelm him. Before long, he could taste it, and plugging his nose seemed more folly than sense.

The forest around had gone quiet. Many small pyres burned, surrounded by Renshai with bowed heads, praying for the souls of their dead, for their own survival, for courage and skill in future battles that would likely see them in their burning companions' places. Treysind knew his own fate was not much different. He had bound himself to Renshai, and their enemies would not differentiate him from them. They would assume him a Renshai, with his red hair and pale eyes, and they would slaughter him with the same exuberance. And yet, Treysind could not leave. Despite the constant threat of murder, despite their many battles, the Renshai had become his people, the only ones he had ever considered his own. Treysind had never felt so safe, so happy and secure, as he did in Calistin's presence.

As the stench became a part of him, Treysind noticed it less. Even the sight of openmouthed bodies with wide, glazed eyes ceased to bother him anymore. He finally found the courage to rummage through the enemy's belongings. He took a short sword from the hand of a dead Northman, then slipped the belt and sheath from the corpse's bloating body. From another, he took a pack, tossing out spare clothing, washing supplies, and other unnecessary gear to stuff it to the brim with foodstuffs from every nearby pack. He also kept two utility knives he uncovered and a purse into which he threw every coin he found. Burdened by his booty, Treysind headed out to find Saviar.

Not far from the spot where they had assisted Calistin, Saviar and Subikahn continued the argument the recent battle had interrupted. Saviar found himself, once again, in a war of words that seemed unnecessary and blatantly foolish. "Subikahn, you're too bright to act this thickheaded. Now, of all times, the Renshai need to stay together."

"Agreed." Subikahn ran a finger along the knurling of his hilt. They had already cleaned and tended the blades in an irritated silence. "And, as long as they stay out of the East—"

"Which is the only place they can go." Saviar had bound the superficial wound on his calf and tied up his flapping sleeve.

"—lands, I will remain with them," Subikahn finished as if his twin had never interrupted.

"It's the only way they *can* go."

"And the only way I can't."

Saviar sprang for the loophole, "Except that, as a Renshai, you're also banished from the North and Westlands."

Subikahn's brows wormed upward. "Which means the only places I can legally go are the Faery Worlds and Asgard. And, since I'm not a contingent of elves who can open portals to other worlds, and the gods aren't rushing to invite me around to tea, I'm limited to those places humanly reachable."

"So," Saviar pressed, "since every part of the world is equally off-limits, it makes the most sense to remain with your brothers and your tribe."

"Yes."

Saviar's hopes soared. He finally seemed to have gotten through to Subikahn.

"Unless they choose to go eastward."

Saviar closed his eyes tightly, feeling his head begin to throb. "Subikahn."

"Yes?"

"Didn't we just establish that all directions are equally off-limits to you?"

"No."

Saviar opened his eyes. Nothing had changed. The gray light of evening still poured over a forest dark with bodies. Subikahn remained standing in front of him, looking more curious than alarmed. "A moment ago, you said 'yes.' Now it's no?"

"Yes," Subikahn said, the reply utterly ambiguous. "All off-limits, but not equally so. Because, if it comes to disdaining the laws of my enemies or of my father, I'd rather face the enemies. I respect King Tae Kahn far more than all of the Northmen combined; and I fear him more, too."

Saviar had to know. "What in deepest, darkest, coldest Hel did you do?"

Subikahn opened his mouth, then closed it in a deep sigh. "I can't tell you, Savi. I can't tell anyone."

"We shared a womb," Saviar reminded, not for the first time.

Subikahn returned a wan smile. "As I remember it, you hogged most of the space."

Stopped short by the comment, Saviar stared. Though neither of them could possibly remember, it had to have been true. He had been a much larger infant than his twin, and the disparity remained to this day. He probably currently outweighed his darker brother by nearly double. A smile wriggled across his lips before he could stop it, but he did manage to suppress laughter. "This is serious."

"Extremely." Subikahn sucked in another deep breath and released it slowly. "I thought my bond with my father was as solid as the mountains. I thought nothing I could say or do would harm it. And yet, look what happened." He met Saviar's gaze, eyes moist.

Saviar's blood seemed to turn to ice water. He could not imagine anything so terrible that it could damage the bond between twin brothers. Yet, a week ago, he would never have believed anything could sever a doting father like Tae from Subikahn either. *Maybe he's right. Maybe it's better if I don't know.* And yet, the idea irritated as much as troubled him. The entire world seemed to have gone crazy, and his family led the charge. His mother had made a foolish decision out of pride and derision, one that had ultimately taken her from her family and doomed the entire tribe. The infallible Knight-Captain had made a horrendous decision. Their once-brave father had allowed grief to turn him into puddled goo. And Subikahn had done something so unspeakably evil he could not share it even with his twin. Battered, nearly broken, abandoned by everyone he ever trusted, Saviar felt like crawling into a deep hole and remaining there forever.

Suddenly seized with the desire to hurt his twin, Saviar turned away and noticed a small figure moving toward them.

Always wary, Subikahn melted into the shadows, whispering. "Is that . . . ?"

Saviar knew exactly what Subikahn intended to ask. "Yes, that's Treysind." He waited for the boy to approach before asking, "What can we do for you?"

The "we" apparently caught Treysind off guard because he looked around briskly until his gaze finally landed on Subikahn, still and silent against the bushes. "Hero sended me." He studied the half-Easterner cautiously. "He wanted me ta makes sure ya's was alrigh'."

"Really?" In no mood for family games, Saviar took the announcement with a grain of salt. "The Great Golden Idol of Renshai deigns to wonder if I'm alive or dead?"

Treysind glowered, the look odd on his young features. "A course he cares. Ya's his brother. He loves ya."

Saviar snorted. "The only person Calistin loves is Calistin."

"Hey!" Treysind grasped the hilt of his new sword awkwardly. "Tha's . . . tha's mean. It's insultin' ta . . . ta Hero."

"Yes, it is." Saviar forced himself to speak civilly, though it took an enormous effort of will. He was rapidly beginning to hate his entire family. When it came to human emotion, Calistin deserved every affront he could hurl; but Treysind was blameless. "I'm sorry I said that to you." It was the closest he could come to an apology, meager but apparently enough for Treysind, who nodded and uncurled his fist from the hilt.

"Hero really sended me ta make sure yas was well. He rilly do love yas." Treysind clearly believed it important that he make Saviar understand. "Honest. He's jus' . . . not rilly good at showin' it."

"He's not doing any worse than the rest of my stupid family," Saviar mumbled, quietly hoping Subikahn heard him.

"What?" Treysind apparently did not.

Saviar refused to repeat it. "Nothing. Why don't you take me to him? Right now, I'd like to be with someone who . . . loves me . . . who wants to be with me." He deliberately turned his back on Subikahn, but still managed to hear his twin muttering.

"Oh, stop acting like a baby."

"Go to Hel," Saviar whispered back savagely.

Apparently oblivious to the exchange, Treysind brightened noticeably. "I's sure Hero'd enjoy his brothers' comp'ny." He turned his attention to Subikahn. "Is yas coming, too, Hero's other brother?"

Subikahn stiffened. "I . . . no. How did you . . . ? No. I have to go. Alone, apparently. The fewer people who know I'm here, the better." He glided silently into the brush.

Alone, apparently. Those words stuck with Saviar while the others faded. *He can't be suggesting I accompany him. Can he?*

Treysind narrowed in on a different phrase. "How's I knowin' . . . who yas is? Hero loves ya both. He talks 'bout ya, so's I knowed who yas was even wit'out meetin'." He grinned, clearly thrilled by his analysis. "I's bein' sure ta tell him ya's well, too."

"No!" Subikahn reappeared. "Didn't you hear me say I don't want people knowing where I am?"

"I tells Hero ever'thin'."

"Of course you do." Saviar could not help reveling in his twin's discomfort, though he knew it was wrong. His father would never approve of such wicked pleasure, nor his grandfather. Yet, at the moment, Saviar did not feel kindly disposed toward any of them. "And you should. It's not fair of Subikahn to expect otherwise."

Subikahn hissed just loudly enough for Saviar to hear, "You obnoxious, lumbering bastard." Then disappeared.

Exhausted, grouchy, mad at the entire world, Saviar followed Treysind in silence.

CHAPTER 20

Sometimes hatred is just hatred.
—Kevralyn Tainharsdatter

THE HORSE PLUNGED to a rattling stop, and Imorelda dug her claws into Tae's leg for balance. The king looked out from their tiny cart to see the familiar, massive mountains that cradled Béarn Castle. Excitement flooded through him, tinged with relief. A light sleeper from necessity, he had awakened to every bump, clatter, and neigh as they traversed the messenger route behind an endless stream of galloping horses. By far the fastest way from Stalmize to the West, it employed a long line of men and horses standing always at the ready to travel at top speed any time of day or night, in all types of weather, usually to deliver decrees, notes, and occasional important packages. Interference with the messenger lines spelled instant death, but it was never meant for hauling humans and cats. Battered and bruised by the trip, exhausted from lack of sleep, at least they had finally arrived: a journey of several months condensed to less than one.

Apparently assuming Tae asleep, the rider did not disturb his passenger. Tae watched the young man dismount and head toward the palace guards, his movements slow, deliberate, and weighted with fatigue.

We're here? Imorelda yawned and stretched across Tae's lap.

We're here. Tae had no interest in the customary formalities that had to follow. The guards would inform the proper dignitaries, who would have to leave their comfortable beds to tend to a royal guest. Procedures would require following, servants would be roused to handle him, and all of it demanded a politeness his tired mind could barely muster. All Tae really wished to do was sleep. *I'm going in the hard way.* He chose the words for Imorelda's sake. To him, suffering through the official procedure was the most difficult and tedious way of all. *You coming with me?*

Imorelda leaped lightly from the cart. *No, thank you. I'd rather not get shot off the castle walls.* She gave her left leg a thorough lick. *If you survive, I'll meet you inside.* She trotted toward the main gate, one more cat amidst hundreds.

Thanks. Creeping alone into the night shadows, Tae approached the outer wall of the castle and listened for the footsteps of the booted guards on top. At length, one approached, heels clicking against stone. Tae waited until the man had fully passed, then clambered up the stones like a spider, flung himself over, and clung to the other side. Already accustomed to the darkness, his eyes adjusted easily to the courtyard. He had not visited Béarn in years, yet it had changed little. The flower beds and vegetable gardens had shifted a bit, and a new guardhouse had joined the old near the north tower. Otherwise, it looked as he remembered it. The only movement he saw was cats slinking through the vines and pathways; the only voices came from the front gates, where the rider announced his imminent arrival to the waiting sentries. The overpowering, distinctive odor of feline assailed his nostrils.

Cautiously, Tae lowered himself to the ground, then headed briskly for the proper wall. He had not climbed it in nearly twenty years, and then he had used self-made bracers fitted with steel claws. Now, he relied on his years of practicing on his own tower walls to scale without need of anything but his own dexterity and strength. Fingers wedged into miniscule cracks, toes gripping through his soft, thin soles, he headed for the familiar fifth-story window, with its gauzy curtains rippling in the breeze.

Once there, Tae paused at the sill to get his bearings. The room appeared much as he remembered, the canopied bed holding a large figure he knew well. Matrinka had never lost the weight from the first of her three children, and she had added more through the years. Three cats shared her bed, one on the pillow curled against her head, one tucked at her feet, and the last stretched to its full length along her back. Furniture stood like towering shadows, and the rectangular shapes of two doors broke the fine line of the walls. All of these things passed Tae's inspection in an instant as he searched for danger. Likely, a Renshai guard shared this room with the queen, a quick, deadly master of the sword who would kill Tae first and wonder about his identity later. He would have to dodge the lightning sword strokes until Matrinka recognized and rescued him.

Yet, to Tae's surprise, he saw no other human figure, no movement other than the irregular sweep of the curtains. He lowered himself to the floor, still tensed for a wild attack that did not come. Finally, he crept cautiously toward Matrinka and swept aside the canopy.

The ginger-colored cat at the foot of the bed rose and started toward him, purring.

Ignoring it, Tae studied Béarn's queen. Her thick curls swept across the pillow and surrounded her gentle features like a mane. Her face held more lines than he remembered, and long strands of white hair lay knitted among the black. *Age has touched us all,* Tae realized, but he also knew Matrinka's appearance had never been what won her so many admirers. She was sweet and gentle, loving and kind, with the sort of nature that attracts long after youthful vigor fades.

"Matrinka," Tae whispered loudly.

The ginger cat caught up to Tae and rubbed its entire body against his arm. Turning to repeat the process, the cat raised its tail as high as possible to tickle Tae's face.

Absently, Tae stroked the animal, gaze still fixed on Matrinka, who had not moved.

"Matrinka," he repeated, this time nudging her shoulder gently.

The queen's soft, brown eyes popped open. She rolled toward Tae, dislodging the other two cats, a massive black and white and a plump little calico. They both yowled a complaint. Another cat scratched insistently at the bedroom door.

Matrinka jerked to a sitting position, pulling the blankets over her sleeping gown. "Tae? What in the gods' names are you doing here?"

Tae forced a smile through his exhaustion. "Always great to see you, too." He glanced around the room, still wary. "Where's the crazed Renshai?"

Matrinka placed a hand over her mouth and yawned daintily. "Does anyone know you're here?"

"Do you think I'd be in the queen's bedchamber if they did?"

Matrinka rolled her eyes and gave Tae a searching look. "You didn't."

"Didn't what?"

"Didn't climb in that window." Matrinka turned her gaze toward the curtains.

"Didn't I?" Tae continued to search for a bodyguard. By now, any Renshai worth her weight in salt would have sliced him into jerky. "And here I thought I did."

"And I thought you gave up sneaking around like a common thug when you became king."

"I've never been common or a thug." Tae shrugged. "And if a king can't sneak around, who can?"

"Come here." Matrinka held out her arms.

Tae embraced the queen, feeling tiny in her arms and enveloped by the sisterly warmth of her. To a man, Béarnides were a massive, mountain people, large-boned with coarse features. They shared the dark eyes and hair of Easterners, but all resemblance ended there. Eastern hair was fine and soft compared to the dense, bristly locks of Béarnides that tended to curl; and the Easterners bore a swarthy hue that made these people of the mountains look pale as Northmen in comparison.

The moment they released one another, Matrinka lashed out a hand that caught Tae squarely across the cheek.

He jerked backward, shocked. "Ow, damn it! Why did you do that?"

"Because you did something extremely foolish, and your mother isn't here to slap you."

Tae rubbed his aching face. He had never handled violence well. "My mother never hit me in her life."

"She should have. A lot. Maybe you wouldn't be so stupid if she did."

Tae had to admit that Matrinka had a point, though he did not like the way she made it. "I thought we were friends. You're making me sorry I came to see you."

"Good."

The scratching at the door became more animated, accompanied by vigorous meowing.

"The last five people who struck me are all horribly dead."

Matrinka refused to relent. "So kill me. You'd put me out of my misery."

It was the last thing Tae ever expected to hear from easygoing, sweet-tempered Matrinka. All anger vanished immediately. "Matrinka, what . . . ?"

Paws flicked beneath the door, and the noises turned to heart-rending yowls.

"Can I let that cat in, or will a horde of guards descend on me?"

Matrinka wrapped the blankets around herself, dislodging the cats, then walked to the door. She opened it a crack to admit a silver tabby angrily fluffed, tail twitching. The cats already in the room rushed to the opening, squeezing into the hallway. No cat, it seemed, could resist an open door. Matrinka shut the panel before guards could look in or any more cats could enter.

What took you so long? Imorelda plopped down on the floor, smoothing her coat back to normal with her tongue, her tail still lashing.

From long experience, Tae knew their mind-communication had limits. Outside, on open ground, he could generally "hear" her about as far as he could see her. Indoors, they nearly always required a presence in the same room. Walls, floors, ceilings, and doors cut them off completely.

I'm sorry, Tae sent back. *I only just got here myself.*

The cat made a loud noise, halfway between a growl and a purr.

Tae ignored her to focus on Matrinka, who walked slowly back toward him from the door. "Matrinka, what's going on?"

I was about to go look for your broken, bloody carcass under the window.

Matrinka sank back to the bed and closed her eyes. "It's been a monstrous year, Tae. I don't know how much more I can take."

Tae recalled Matrinka's strength through the many and varied adventures they had survived together. They had weathered deaths and injuries, wars and poisonings, wrongful imprisonments and miraculous escapes. It seemed so long ago, when they were young and inexperienced, irresponsible and youthfully immortal. Nothing had seemed impossible. "Is it the pirates?"

Imorelda leaped onto the bed and crawled into Matrinka's lap.

Matrinka stroked the cat, at first absently, then with focused attention. "It's Imorelda, isn't it?"

"Yes."

A true queen. She recognizes my exquisite and exceptional beauty.

Tae could not help teasing, *What she recognizes is your putrid smell.*

"You're talking to her, aren't you?" Matrinka clearly attempted a happy tone, but she could not hide the deep sorrow that tinged it.

If I stink, it's only because I've been forced into close quarters with an unwashed human for so long." Imorelda turned her back on Tae, kneading Matrinka's lap as she moved. *I've bathed. Have you?*

"Yes," Tae admitted. "We're conversing, but it's not very nice."

Matrinka's question was wistful, "What's she saying?"

Tae flushed, smiling. "She says I reek."

Matrinka gave the cat a stern look, "Imorelda! That's not ladylike."

Perhaps not, but it is true.

"Is she still talking to you?"

"To you, actually." Tae tried to think of a tactful way to steer the conversation back to Matrinka. "You miss Mior, don't you?"

"Terribly," Matrinka admitted, but refused to be sidetracked. "Imorelda was talking to me?"

"I think so. She responded to your comment."

"I didn't 'hear' her."

"I'm sorry."

"Why?" Though simple, the question held angst Tae dearly wished he could assuage. More than anything, he knew, Matrinka wanted back the relationship she had shared with Mior.

"I don't know," Tae admitted. "I don't know why you could converse with Mior but not Imorelda. I don't know why none of these other cats shares their special talent. I'm sorry, Matrinka. I don't understand it any better than you. I have no answers."

Matrinka cleared her throat. "Darris thinks Mior's line might be similar to his. The bardic curse passes always to the firstborn."

Oh, so I'm a "curse" now?

Sometimes. Tae sent back. "I've always wondered why the bards choose to have children. No children, no more curse."

Having children is curse enough. Imorelda snuggled into Matrinka's lap. *Nasty things.*

"Do you ever wish you didn't have Subikahn?"

The question struck too close to home. Anger boiled in the pit of Tae's stomach. "Of course not. But I didn't inflict him with a curse either." *No, a Renshai* torke *did that for me.*

Leaping on your head when you're trying to sleep. Sucking you raw. The blood, the vomit. And I can't stand the taste of placenta.

Matrinka continued to defend her decision. "Well, we love Marisole. And she sees her musical talent as a gods-given gift, not a curse."

Glad to forget his own offspring for a while, Tae focused in on Marisole. "The musical part isn't really the curse, though, is it? It's the infernal quest for knowledge and the inability to speak except in arias."

"They can speak; they just can't teach."

Tae waved dismissively. "Spare me the details. I find Darris tedious, but you love him and that's all that matters." He still did not understand Matrinka's discomfort. "You're very lucky, you know. You're a queen, with a wonderful husband who asks nothing of you. How many men would let their wives sleep with lovers and happily claim the children as their own? How many would allow hundreds of cats to roam the palace? A king shouldn't have to entertain visitors in a great hall stinking of urine and vinegar."

Matrinka stared, clearly stunned. "It . . . stinks?"

"Of course, it stinks. It's full of cats. Don't you notice it?"
Hey!

"No." Matrinka's voice went small. "I'm . . . being selfish, aren't I?"

"Not selfish, just determined." Tae sat next to Matrinka on the bed. "I think you gave it your best try; but the next Mior, if there is one, isn't coming from this horde." He made a vague gesture toward the door.

"Maybe Darris' idea?" Matrinka scratched behind Imorelda's ears, to much delighted purring.

"Was Imorelda firstborn?"

"Second, but the only female in the litter."

Imorelda stiffened. *Are you talking about me having babies? Because I'm not having any babies.*

Light flashed through Matrinka's eyes. "I've been thinking Mior's ability was stronger than Imorelda's. Because she learned to communicate with both of us. If we could breed back into the line—"

Are you listening to me? No babies!

"Careful." Tae's mind went to another line breeding. "Remember why dear King Griff allowed Darris to sire his children with you. You're his first cousin, and he worried that the closeness of your blood would create morons and cretins."

Matrinka rose, still clutching Imorelda, and the blankets fell away to reveal her sleeping gown. Attention distant, she seemed not to notice that only a thin layer of fabric separated her from the man in her bedchamber. Though stout, she still sported pleasantly proportioned curves, and her breasts had grown enormous. "I'm not talking about a brother. I'm thinking more of a great great nephew. If we can concentrate the bloodline, just a little, maybe—"

Reminded of Matrinka's womanhood, Tae looked away. She was the closest thing he had to a sister, and he did not want to start seeing her as a sexual being.

Tell her no! I'm not having any babies. I don't want any babies.

Finally, Tae addressed the cat, *Why not?*

Because I'll get fat. Like her.

That's not nice.

And my nipples will turn all pink and hangy forever.

Not forever. Just for a couple of—

Forever. I've seen it. And I don't want to lick any rear end but my own.

That one baffled Tae. *You'd have to lick someone's—*

That's how you get kittens to make—

Matrinka whirled suddenly. "I'm sorry, Tae. I'm wasting your time worrying about cats and kittens. You must be exhausted."

Tae wished she had not mentioned it. Fatigue crushed down on him like a lead weight, and it suddenly became difficult to hold his eyes open. The urge to sink into the covers became nearly overwhelming. "I am . . ." He yawned. ". . . a bit."

"And I never did tell you why I'm so upset."

Tae gave in, allowing his lids to slide down, though he continued speaking in the dark. "I thought it was Mior . . ."

"Arturo is dead."

Tae's eyes shot open. "What?"

"Murdered by pirates. Then, I lost my best friend—"

"Lost your . . ." Tae refused to concentrate on the words and what they might mean. "I thought *I* was your best friend." The joke was feeble, at best.

"Tae."

Matrinka had his attention.

"Kevral . . ."

No.

". . . is . . ."

No, no, no! Tae filled in every word he could think of but the right one: happy, different, Renshai, troubled, sick, hurt. He concentrated on an Eastern song, cycling it through his head, anything to blot out that last word.

". . . dead."

"No, she's not."

Matrinka set Imorelda on the bed beside Tae. "She's . . . not?"

"She can't be." Tae heard his own words from a distance. He could not recall forming them, nor deliberately speaking. "It's not possible."

"Tae." Matrinka took his hands. Her palms enveloped his smaller, finer fingers, soft against his calluses. "I saw her body placed on her pyre."

"No."

"She's dead, Tae. Kevral is dead."

Imorelda wove between their arms to climb into Tae's lap, purring comfortingly. He did not ask any questions. He did not want to know.

But Matrinka told him what he needed. "In battle, of course. Against a Northman. The way she always wanted to go."

Tae said nothing. His hands became dead weight in Matrinka's grip. He lowered his head, lids gliding closed again. He wanted to sleep, did not care if he ever awakened.

Matrinka leaned in close. "And her death exiled the Renshai from the West, which is why I have no bodyguards but the men outside my door."

Ordinarily, Tae would have a witty comment about how well the Béarnides had protected their queen from a prowler. He could have killed or kidnapped her by now. But words failed Tae utterly. Even coherent thought eluded him. Only the merciless exhaustion bearing down on him seemed real.

Imorelda stood on her hind legs and patted his cheek with a paw. She yowled. *Are you all right?*

I will be, Tae managed to send. *After I get some sleep.*

Matrinka got the message, too. "Lie down, Tae. You're deadly tired." She lowered him to the mattress, released his hands, then rearranged her blankets over him. "I'm so sorry I burdened you before you . . ."

Tae was asleep before she finished.

Treysind whirled, sword banging against his leg. "Hero's goned."

Saviar only nodded. That had become apparent quite some time ago, but the little Erythanian had insisted on checking the entire battlefield.

"He cain't be goned. He wouldn't—" Treysind looked to Saviar for help, eyes glazed with building tears, but the Renshai could supply nothing.

Saviar could only imagine the boil of emotion: sorrow and anger, worry and uncertainty. He shared only one, a welling sense of betrayal that did not originate with Calistin's disappearance. The decision of his youngest brother to leave in silence only fueled his certainty that the gods had struck his entire family mad. *You, too, Calistin?*

"He sayed he talked ta . . . ta a god." Treysind's voice caught in sobs. "She tole him . . . he . . . dint got a . . . a soul."

Cut by Treysind's anguish, Saviar drew the boy close. "I've often thought he didn't have a heart. Sometimes I've wondered if he has a brain. But a soul . . ." Saviar rubbed Treysind's back instinctively as the boy sobbed into his tunic. "Everyone has a soul."

Treysind sniffled, voice muffled. "Tha's what I's tole him."

Abruptly, a memory popped into Saviar's head. He recalled a day from his early childhood when he overheard his parents talking about Calistin, spiders, and someone who lacked a soul. They seemed serious and intent, but they stopped talking as soon as they noticed him. At the time, he had discarded the discussion as boring parent-talk. Now, he tried to remember exactly what he had heard in detail, without success. *Is it actually possible Calistin lacks a soul?* It would explain so much. Then, the deeper realization struck Saviar. *No soul, no Valhalla.*

Treysind yanked himself free of Saviar's hold. "I's gotta find him." He threw his pack back onto his shoulder. It made him look smaller, more insignificant, if possible. "I's gotta." Without another word, he ran deeper into the woods.

Saviar did not attempt to stop Treysind. Wherever the boy went, whether or not he found Calistin, would be safer than remaining with the Renshai. Alone, he had a chance. With Renshai in a strange land hunted by enemies and without Calistin's protection, his life was measured in days. For several moments, Saviar stood in uncertainty. His loyalties had always lain with the Renshai and with his family, but those two things no longer went together. Every member of his family had chosen a different allegiance that had little or nothing to do with the ties that had always bound them.

Saviar stared at the dark heavens, the crescent of moon, and the spattering of stars, dim behind a curtain of clouds. "What do I do?" he asked the gods but received no answer. That came from within. For, as irritated as he felt toward his father and grandfather, the lessons he had learned from them in better, wiser times prevailed. Whatever paths the men of his family chose, he would continue to walk the line of responsibility.

Head low, feet shuffling through leaves and mold, Saviar headed toward the odor of smoke, where he knew he would find freshly kindled pyres and the rest of his tribe. There was no good way to deliver the news he carried, so he dawdled, concentrating on how the leaves parted in front of him, on the Northmen's bodies lying in grotesque poses, on the actual possibility that Calistin had spoken with a goddess. Under ordinary circumstances, he would consider such a thing insane. Yet, he still vividly remembered the *Valkyrie* at Kevral's death. Calistin had seen it, too, and it did not seem that far a stretch that he might have interacted with a goddess, too. Especially on a battlefield, where so many of the fallen Renshai had called upon Sif. The Northmen, too, he supposed shouted out for the strength, wrath, and favor of their most beloved deities.

All too soon, Saviar located the main clot of Renshai, tending pyres, and found Thialnir in the mix. Each living Renshai he found filled him with relief. They might have lost fifty, but they remained two hundred and fifty strong and would never be caught off guard. Those who had died were mostly the weakest: the elderly, children, the ill, the lesser fighters. With each consecutive battle, the Northmen would take more casualties for every one they inflicted.

Thialnir greeted Saviar with a tip of his head.

Saviar walked over, dreading what he needed to say. Nevertheless, he blurted it directly; Thialnir had no patience for sugarcoating or pussyfooting. "Calistin has left us." Even as he spoke, Saviar realized his words could be taken as a euphemism for death.

But, Thialnir knew exactly what he meant. He nodded thoughtfully. "I thought this might happen."

Startled, Saviar shut his mouth with a click of teeth.

"And it is how it should be."

"It . . . is?"

Thialnir watched sparks shoot up from a pyre in a line, the smoke winding toward the heavens. "He has unfinished business with the Northmen. That was his fight, not Kevral's."

Saviar had never thought of it quite that way. "Yes, but it violates our word, our honor."

Thialnir smiled but did not turn his head. "Our word, maybe. Honor . . . is a subjective thing."

No, it's not! Strong as it came to him, Saviar did not speak the thought aloud. At the moment he had no intention of causing more strife. Also, he thought it wise to consider Thialnir's words. For all of his apparent impetuousness, the leader of the Renshai often displayed a simple, underlying wisdom that most did not take the time to understand. It occurred to Saviar that honor might seem rigid to him because of his upbringing by a Knight of Erythane. Despite living among Renshai, he had picked up more than a few lessons from Ra-khir. "I should also tell you, sir, that Subikahn will not be able to help us negotiate a haven in the Eastlands."

"Oh?" Thialnir's single syllable begged answers that Saviar did not have.

"All I know is that father and son are estranged."

Thialnir made a thoughtful noise, finally looking at Saviar.

"I don't know if that will affect the Renshai's dealings with the kingdom."

"It may." Thialnir's massive hand massaged the hilt of his sword. "It depends on whether the king attributes the problem to Subikahn's Renshai training."

Saviar grimaced. He should have made Subikahn tell him at least that much, but he had become too concerned about knowing it all to think of that possibility.

"But King Tae Kahn is a fair ruler. No matter the reason, he will give us the opportunity to talk, to convince him of our value to the Eastlands."

Thialnir's calm approach to the matter soothed Saviar's tortured soul. If Thialnir could handle the loss of a sixth of their numbers, of their most skilled warrior, and of their only connection to the Eastlands with such grace; Saviar could weather the storm of his family as well.

"And you have my blessing to join either or both of your brothers, if you so choose."

Saviar could only stare. "How did you know Subikahn . . . ?" Eager for the answer, he did not even bother to complete the question.

A smile cut Thialnir's grim, weathered features. He ran a hand through sweat-darkened silver-and-gold locks. "I didn't know. You just told me. How else could you have known about his problems with King Tae?"

"Well, yes, but . . ." Saviar hated revealing his twin, but he had had to let Thialnir know the danger. "You won't tell anyone, will you?"

"No. But it sounds like he might need you."

Alone, apparently. Subikahn's words returned to haunt Saviar. *He expected me to join him, and I teased him instead.* "I thought *you* needed me."

Thialnir yawned, looking around the pyres. "I did, and I will in the future. You're obviously responsible enough to return when your brothers' need for you is no longer so urgent. Of course, we can use every sword arm, Savi. But, when it comes to talking to Tae, I can handle that alone. No procedure, no flowery words, no fuss. He's as earthy as they come. We'll get a yes or a no, without contracts full of twists, verbal or written."

"And the Renshai?"

"Thialnir shrugged one massive shoulder. "Will do just fine. We always do. Not because we're the chosen people of the gods, though we are. And not because we're descended from demons, which we're not." He placed a fatherly arm across Saviar's shoulders. "It's because we're talented, hardworking, and resourceful. And that's the Renshai secret." He ruffled Saviar's hair with his other hand.

Saviar suffered a sudden and unexpected pang of homesickness. He not only missed the Fields of Wrath, but the loving father he had cursed daily since his mother's death.

"Whether we land on harsh islands or barren deserts, we will thrive, as we always have. There will always be hordes of jealous people who resent our abilities and attribute our successes to dark magic, trickery, or deceit. But the truth of the matter, Saviar, is that we are willing to put in an effort most are not. Instead of complaining about our misfortunes, or blaming others, we work to turn them around. We do not wallow in self-pity, we fix the problem. In the last three hundred years, Renshai have never started a war, yet we finish all of them—and win, even vastly outnumbered. And, while people claim to love honor, to revere heroism; in actuality, they despise it because it reminds them of their own shortcomings, makes them feel inferior. And so, Renshai will always survive and always be hated."

Saviar did not know what to say. He had never heard Thialnir speak so long, nor so eloquently. Obviously, and understandably, he had given the matter enormous thought.

"When people want to hate, they will find a way. It may require distortion of facts. They may have to rewrite history. But they will justify their hatred and still believe themselves to be good people. Unlike honor, truth is not subjective; yet even those who believe themselves most virtuous will find ways to rationalize their own prejudices, even while condemning others. Loathing Renshai has become so natural, so ingrained, that people don't even consider it an immoral thought anymore. The more successful we become, the more times we survive, the deeper that rage grows. Otherwise decent people would side with Northmen who slaughter *them* simply because those Northmen are *our* enemies. 'The enemy of my enemy is my friend' only applies when it doesn't mean siding with Renshai."

Saviar studied Thialnir's craggy face. *Who are you?* "That's . . . a very negative way to look at the world."

Thialnir patted Saviar's shoulder. "Trust me, Saviar. I've lived a long time, listened to a lot of morons in nobles' clothing."

"Why are you telling me this?" Saviar had enough problems without his leader heaping on more.

Thialnir removed his heavy arm, turned gracefully to fully face Saviar, and put a hand on each of the younger man's shoulders. "Because you're about to go among real strangers for the first time, and you need the tools to stay alive. Be proud of who you are, but there may be times when you want to hide it, even if it means lying."

Saviar scowled, bothered on three counts. First, Thialnir simply assumed he had already chosen to chase his brothers. Second, his father had taught him to embrace honesty at all times. And third, the words sounded suspiciously like a slight to his swordsmanship. "I can handle myself."

"You can defend yourself," Thialnir corrected. "That is not the same as 'handling.' "

"I understand diplomacy. You've seen me use it."

"You're fluid enough," Thialnir admitted. "Friendly interference clause aside." He rolled an eye in Saviar's direction, then smoothly looked away. Clearly, he did not intend to blame, only to explore Saviar's own emotions on the matter.

Thialnir's last words hit Saviar like rocks, and that surprised him. He had gone over the wording of that clause in his head a million times, wrapping his thoughts around it, amending it in his dreams. He thought he had left the guilt behind, but it clearly remained only shallowly buried. He could not stop himself from answering defensively, "My clause wasn't the problem. It was the ridiculous interpretation of it that lost the battle." Saviar realized he had to convince himself more than he did Thialnir. He could never fully escape the worry that he had permitted the treachery against his mother and ultimately doomed the Renshai. "And don't go telling me how fair and perfect my grandfather is."

Still clutching Saviar's shoulders, Thialnir fully met his gaze, brows rising. "I frequently disagree with Kedrin, including his interpretation of this clause. I didn't bring it up to blame you for what happened, Saviar. It's no more your fault than it was Calistan's. I'm simply trying to make a point."

"Which is?" Saviar prompted carefully.

"You're still young and a bit naïve, though not nearly as much as either of your brothers. Just realize this: as a Westerner, you will be judged on the basis of your actions and character. As a Renshai, you will be judged on the basis of others' prejudices. If a Northman dismembers you, those who know you as Renshai will find excuses to rationalize his behavior."

Saviar rolled his eyes, tired of the speech. "But if I dismember him, they'll punish me. Except, I wouldn't dismember anyone, not even my worst enemy."

"No, Saviar. You don't understand." Thialnir's pale eyes seemed to bore through Saviar's. "If you do nothing but defend yourself, you will be punished and despised. If you dismember him, they will not only slaughter you, they will use it as an excuse to condemn the entire tribe of Renshai."

It seemed like rampant paranoia. "Really?"

"Really." Thialnir released Saviar's shoulders, but not his gaze. "The kings of Béarn are chosen by a fail-safe test. A ruler like Tae comes along once in a millennium or two, if the world is lucky. You will find the rest of the West's leaders, and those of the North, as fallible, fragile, and opinionated as any of their followers.

Saviar nodded. He believed he understood Thialnir's point and would take it to heart.

"Your brothers . . ." Suddenly, the words stopped coming so easily to Thialnir.

But Saviar appreciated the point. Despite his inhuman skill, though he had fought in the Pirate Wars, Calistin knew very little of societies and strangers. Subikahn had split his time between the Fields of Wrath, with its sole focus on swordplay, and his indulgent, royal father.

Thialnir finished lamely. "They need you, Saviar. More than I do."

"I'll do my best," Saviar promised, wondering how he would find either of his brothers. The cares of the last few days, once overwhelming, now seemed petty in comparison. His mother had done what any Renshai would have. His father's collapse spoke volumes for the love he held for Kevral; Saviar could only pray he found a woman worthy of such intense affection in his own life. Banished from the face of the universe, Subikahn had a right to choose which law he violated. And Calistin . . . was Calistin. Saviar saw no sense in trying to analyze someone, it seemed, he could never understand. *Subikahn was right. It's me, not the world, that went insane.* "But I'm not a very good liar."

Thialnir managed a single barking laugh. "That," he said, "is not a flaw." He headed back to help tend the pyres, without bothering to watch Saviar go.

Though it seemed futile, Saviar rushed back to the spot where he had left Subikahn. His twin had learned the art of concealment and silent movement, not only from the Renshai, but also from his father. By now, he was probably halfway to Pudar, flitting through shadows and cursing his brother with every step. Saviar had about as much chance of finding him as the most timid squirrel in the forest.

But as Saviar dashed into the clearing, he found Subikahn leaning casually against a tree. "What took you so long?"

Saviar laughed, catching Subikahn into an embrace and practically dancing with joy. "How'd you know I'd come looking for you?" He added quickly, "And don't remind me we shared a womb. That didn't give *me* any mind-reading powers."

"I didn't know. I hoped."

"And it paid off." Saviar released his twin, spreading his arms wide. "Here I am."

"Lucky me." Subikahn slung a light pack over his shoulder and headed into the brush. "My reward: I get to travel with a man who refers to me as 'idiot.' "

Saviar followed his brother. "Not anymore. I reserve that name for our idiot brother."

"I take it his interest in your health was . . . less than sincere?"

"Just a ruse to allow him to escape without his . . . um . . . shadow." Saviar could not understand how the same brush that glided soundlessly around Subikahn crunched and rattled beneath his own feet.

"Poor Treysind."

"Lucky Treysind, if you ask me. At least now he has a chance to join some normal family in the West. To survive longer than Calistin's next battle."

Subikahn wove through a ring of trees. "Where do you think he went?"

Although they had been talking about Treysind, Saviar knew Subikahn meant Calistin. "Straight North, I'm sure. To even the score."

Subikahn made a thoughtful noise. "And us? Where are we going?"

Saviar snorted. "I'm following you. Please don't tell me you're following me. I'm not fond of circles." He clambered over a deadfall. Whatever else Subikahn decided, he hoped it included dinner and sleep.

"I'm going to investigate. I believe I can find enough evidence to prove the Northmen cheated, get the decision reversed, and win back our homeland." Subikahn corrected, "Homelands. Both of them."

Saviar heaved a sigh, but listened. Right or wrong, foolish dream or possibility, it was not a bad idea. "There's one thing I forgot to tell you while I was calling you an idiot and you were calling me an obnoxious, lumbering bastard—for which only one of us has apologized, by the way."

"Which one?"

"Me. I promised not to call you an idiot anymore."

"And yet, you've managed to sneak it into the conversation three times. And that's not actually an apology."

"Fine. I'm sorry I called you an idiot."

"And I'm sorry I called you 'lumbering.' "

The implication did not escape Saviar. "Hey!"

Subikahn laughed. The sound seemed strange; yet, somehow, it shattered the suffocating mantle of grief, outrage, and irritation that had hung over Saviar since the Northmen had challenged the Renshai. Nothing had changed; and yet he had.

"What did you forget to tell me?" Subikahn stopped pushing through brush to regard his brother. "Before we got sidetracked by name-calling?"

Saviar flushed, feeling foolish. At the time, it had seemed inappropriate, his father's desperate attempt to use his status to save his sons from the fate of their comrades. Now, it might well save their lives. "We're not actually banished."

Subikahn's eyes seemed to bulge from his face. "What?"

"Papa negotiated some sort of deal because we're only half-Renshai and our only living relatives, our fathers, are not . . ."

". . . Renshai." Subikahn finished. "So, I'm only really exiled from the East."

"Yes."

"And you called me an idiot for not going with you there."

"I apologized."

Subikahn whirled back the way he had been going, though he did not take another step. "So we don't need to blither around in secret."

Thialnir's words remained strong in Saviar's mind. "Well, I'm not sure it's wise to investigate openly. I really don't feel like explaining our situation to every passerby who wants to report us, and I'm sure the agreement at least implied a certain amount of discretion on the part of us and my father."

"So, we shouldn't go around slaughtering in the name of the Renshai."

"That's really not funny." An idea wound its way into Saviar's mind, and he spoke it aloud before he could consider it fully, "While we're investigating, maybe we could do . . . good deeds?"

Subikahn cocked his head. "Good deeds? You mean, like Knights of Erythane."

It was not exactly what Saviar had in mind. "All right. Like knights."

"Help people with broken equipment or injured animals?"

"Yes."

"Fight off brigands and bandits?"

"Sure."

"Rescue damsels in distress?"

Saviar smiled. "My personal favorite."

"Just out of the kindness of our big, fluffy hearts."

"Well," Saviar admitted. "I do actually have a motive." He looked directly at his twin, hoping Subikahn would understand and not think him crazy. "We wait until the populace loves us. Only then, we reveal that we're Renshai."

"Why?"

"Because." Finally forced to consider, Saviar hesitated. "Because it will make us feel good, *and* it will force people to reevaluate their knee-jerk hatred for all things Renshai."

Apparently, Subikahn actually considered the proposal, and his answer became more important to Saviar than he ever would have guessed.

Please think it through. Please don't be facetious. The silence that followed was the longest of Saviar's life.

"That's actually not a bad idea . . ." Subikahn could not help adding, ". . . for an obnoxious, but not lumbering, bastard."

He said it with such a broad grin, with such obvious love, that Saviar found it impossible to take offense. For the first time in months, Saviar felt happy, complete, and also tired and hungry. "I need to eat," he announced. "And sleep."

Subikahn dropped to the ground. "I thought you'd never ask."

CHAPTER 21

If everyone knew how others would react to what they do, things
might go smoother. But they'd be really REALLY boring.

—*Mior*

THE DUNGEON CORRIDORS STANK of mold, urine, and long
unwashed flesh so rank it became physically painful to Tae's nose.
Keyed to the location of every prisoner, he slunk through the confines unseen, except for the guards, who followed orders to ignore
him. Finally, he came to the proper wall that would allow him to
listen without being seen and waited for the group of guards and
interpreters to step into place.

Soon, they arrived, a motley contingent of massive, uniformed
Béarnides with weapons, accompanied by a thin, sandy-haired
Erythanian, a portly balding Westerner, and an elderly woman who
walked with a cane. As they stepped into place in front of the cell of
the captured pirate, Tae gestured to them to proceed.

"We brought some visitors," one of the guards explained in a
booming voice. He spoke slowly and distinctly. "We're just trying to
find out if you need anything." He waved at the woman, who stepped
forward next.

Leaning on the cane, she spoke in careful Northern, the singsong syllables emerging graveled by age. "Can you understand me?
Please acknowledge if you can. We only want to make your stay more
pleasant."

Tae could not see the prisoner's reaction, but he heard a shuffle
of movement and no reply.

The thin man spoke next, his voice as reedy as his figure. "Can
you understand me?" He used one of the many Western tongues; all
so similar to Tae that he thought of them as simple dialects of the
same language. "Can you understand me?" he said in another.

When he reached his fifth, the prisoner finally responded with a few words of his own. Tae focused firmly on the sounds, tone, and timbre. It had to contain frustration, perhaps contempt; it would help to see the gestures that accompanied the words. Despite most beliefs otherwise, there were no unfailingly universal gestures; but emotion was still readable in the force and boldness of them. Tae found facial cues far more reliable and cursed his need to remain hidden, even though he had insisted upon it.

Everyone in the translation party turned to look at Tae as if to ask if he had heard enough.

Tae would have liked more, but their obvious concentration on him jeopardized any future plans. Once the pirate knew of his presence and talent, getting information would move from difficult to impossible. He shook his head, waved dismissively, and headed back out of the prison, without waiting to see what the others did.

Several guards and a snarl of cats met him at the exit. The men clearly wanted to ask him what he had learned, but they remained silent. They knew better than to upstage the king.

Tae did not say anything. He needed to consider his strategy and his words carefully before they rushed him to his meeting with King Griff, Queen Matrinka, and whichever trusted guards and advisers they chose.

Plaintive mewing accompanied them as they hurried down flights of spiral stairs and through long hallways. Then, something hooked the hem of Tae's tunic. Still moving amid the clot of guards, he looked down as a cat clawed its way up his side, gouging fabric and flesh alike.

Tae reached down, snagged Imorelda, and placed her on his shoulders. She stretched out around the back of his neck.

A guard reached for her. "Sorry, Sire. Usually, they're not that bold."

Imorelda slashed a pawful of nails at the man's hand.

Anticipating the attack, Tae lurched, forcing Imorelda to tend to her own balance instead. The unsheathed claws pierced his shoulder like needles. "Leave her," he gasped. "This one's mine."

"Yes, Sire." The man retreated.

Ease up!

Imorelda obeyed, though not without protest. *Walk more carefully, and I won't have to do that.*

Tae knew better than to argue with a female or a cat. *Of course. It's all my fault.*

The guards paused, while the leader knocked briskly on a door.

It opened almost immediately to reveal a small room that contained only four people and a table surrounded by chairs. Tae knew everyone inside: the king and queen of Béarn, Darris the bard, and Rantire, Griff's fierce Renshai bodyguard. Matrinka and Griff gave Tae acknowledging nods, while Darris bowed decorously and Rantire only stared with aggression.

Tae waited until his escort left, closing the door, before speaking. "Ah, so one Renshai remains in the West."

Clearly addressed, Rantire did not seek permission from her liege before speaking. "Vows to gods take precedent over any human decree."

Tae could not argue. Colbey's son, Ravn, had bestowed the job of Griff's guardian on the Renshai, and her loyalty was total and unwavering. It was also obsessive and annoying.

Matrinka asked the question on every mind, "So, were you able to understand him?"

Clearly mortified by his guardian and his wife, Griff offered their guest a seat. "Please, make yourself comfortable."

Tae did not worry about politeness or formality, but he did appreciate the delay. Choosing the nearest chair, he sat, and the others did the same. "I didn't," he admitted.

Matrinka sagged. "It's hopeless, then?"

Tae explained, "He's not speaking any known language of our world." Imorelda clambered gingerly from his shoulders into his brand-new lap.

Griff leaned forward, "Are you sure?"

Tae nodded, stroking the animal absently.

"Because," the king continued carefully, "there are several languages. And maybe you've just never heard . . ."

Tae remained silent, allowing the king to finish his thought; but, as Griff trailed off and clearly awaited an answer, Tae explained. "I speak all ten of the major languages, Griff. Even ancient barbarian. Even elfin, though not necessarily with great fluency. Anything else is simply a dialect, and I can figure it out quickly. Now, I only heard a few words, but this . . . this was . . . different."

They all went silent, waiting for him to explain.

Tae had nothing more to say. Five or six words, spoken by one individual, was not enough to make pronouncements.

"So," Matrinka broke the silence. "You're saying these pirates come from another world?"

Tae shrugged. He did not feel competent to make a statement of such significance, but it seemed like the only logical answer.

They do, don't they?

★If I knew, Imorelda, I would tell my friends.★
Darris opened his mouth, then closed it with a sigh. He rose and started pacing, the Renshai watching him through slitted eyes.

Tae understood his discomfort. The bard wished to speak but remained constrained by the curse.

Griff clearly also noticed his bard's distress. "If you need to sing something, Darris, feel free. We would all love to hear it."

Darris nodded. He did not carry an instrument with him, nor did he need one. Tae had long ago noticed he mostly resorted to it when performing or when trying to evoke emotions. In a pinch, Darris had no trouble performing a cappella, his songs fashioned on the spot, though his rhyme scheme lacked the richness and beauty of the songs he inherited or deliberately wrote. The bard cleared his throat and cringed apologetically:

> *To bring Outworld enemies would require*
> *An angry god all wreathed in fire,*
> *Or strong* jovinay arythanik*:*
> *Combined magic of elves, none of whom could panic.*
>
> *For magic is needed to open the portals,*
> *A deed that could never be done by mere mortals.*
> *Yet neither gods nor elves have suggested*
> *That humankind must be divested.*
>
> *But in the Sage's tower high,*
> *I found the tale of an armory by*
> *The enormous city we know as Pudar,*
> *Three centuries past, or about that far.*
>
> *As he prepared for the Great War,*
> *King Sterrane's friend, Garn, he took a tour,*
> *And tried a weapon bigger than he*
> *From a warrior 'cross the Western Sea.*
>
> *Who came, they said, when the world was young,*
> *A giant of a man who left no crumb*
> *But that massive sword too heavy for man.*
> *Perhaps his descendants have come to our land?*

As Darris finished the last note, he looked askance at his companions. Clearly, he sought answers to his question, not praise for his song; which, despite his phenomenal voice and perfect pitch, was notably clumsy.

Tae considered the information in thoughtful silence. He had known that bringing in humans or creatures of parallel worlds required the magic inherent in a portal. He and his companions had traveled through several as they pieced together the ancient, broken Pica Stone that now tested the heirs to Béarn's throne. Each opening had required a massive number of elves working their magic together. It could never occur by accident. Tae had to concede and broke the silence, "Surely, if gods or elves intended to destroy us, they would open a portal to a world with man-eating monsters rather than simply subject us to an endless sea battle."

Imorelda batted Tae's hand but said nothing.

"Well," Matrinka added. "Griff, Darris, and I discussed this before; and I've given it some thought. If I had to choose between gods and elves, I'd have to guess the latter. If the gods wanted us gone, they could simply . . . um . . . unmake us, right? Slam us with fire or floods, famine or lightning, and they wouldn't need to open a portal." She glanced around the group. "Right?"

Darris turned his gaze directly on Tae. Clearly, he wanted to say something but hoped his Eastern friend would obviate the need for more singing.

Imorelda stood up in Tae's lap, planting her paws on the edge of the table. *The gods do things that don't make sense sometimes.*

Tae softened the words, "The gods aren't always predictable. Still, Matrinka makes a good argument. It doesn't do them any good to punish us if we don't know we're being punished or why."

Darris' head bobbed sideways. Apparently, he felt Tae had made an interesting point, but not the one he was hoping for.

Tae tried again. "I don't think it's elves either. They chose to go off on their own, to leave Béarn. They know they're welcome to return at any time. If they had a grievance, they would bring it to you." He jerked his head toward King Griff. "Wouldn't they?"

Griff bobbed his shaggy head. "Tem'aree'ay visits them regularly. She tells me they're happy." He laced his fingers through his beard. "As I recall, when the first pirating incidents happened, the elves were still here. We would have known."

"Unless it happened accidentally." Tae scratched behind Imorelda's ears, and she raised her head high to expose her throat, practically driving her head against his moving fingers. "While they were opening portals for us to gather the Pica shards."

Murmurs swept the room. It seemed the most logical answer.

"Or," Matrinka added, "they come from across the ocean, like Darris surmised."

"A giant of a man," Tae quoted. "With a sword so big most men couldn't lift it. Are these pirates enormous?"

Again, Darris tipped his head from side to side, indicating "yes" and "no" simultaneously.

Griff explained. "Well, no. Not most of them. But my men report more than the normal number of impressively-sized warriors, and we have captured a few weapons that befuddle our strongest."

"Big?" Tae tried to clarify.

"Huge," Griff confirmed. "A few. But most are normal-sized. Impressively well-tempered and forged, too. Early on, many Renshai were happily taking enemy swords in lieu of payment."

Matrinka's eyes widened at a fact she clearly had not heard before. "And you know how picky Renshai are."

Imorelda made a noise distinctly like a sneeze. *Not too picky, apparently. One made a baby with the likes of you.*

Tae ignored the insult. *She means about their swords.*

So they're more careful with their swords than their children?

Renshai? Yes.

Sounds about right. Imorelda curled back into Tae's lap. *Nasty things.*

Renshai? Or swords?

Children.

Tae disengaged to ask Béarn's king, "I presume you still have some of these weapons? Their make—?"

"Our best experts couldn't identify the workmanship, though they were most impressed by it. We reused as many as we could. The ones too damaged or large, we melted down and recast." Griff sighed. "Iron ore shortage, you know."

"I know." Tae did not wish to discuss trade issues now. The East still had a reasonable amount, but its price had tripled because of the West's shortage. Only the North still had a strong, steady supply. "It's common, though, for armies to see the other side as having a greater percentage of larger men."

When no one said anything, Tae continued.

"Just as it's customary for enemies to multiply during battle. You know, a few dozen men seems like a hundred when you're fighting for your life. And a hundred men seems more like ten thousand."

"Yes," Darris finally spoke again. "But these are Béarnides."

Tae glanced at the king and queen, and he got the point. Matrinka had sported a whale-boned frame even before she carried the extra childbirth weight, and Griff had always looked more like a bear than a human. Tae chuckled. "Yes, I suppose when Béarnides start reporting an unusually large number of huge warriors, it's probably not exaggeration." Though he enjoyed the conversation with his old friends, it seemed pointless to continue in this vein. "So, we seem to have established that the enemy comes from beyond our known boundaries, likely from beyond the Western Sea. What next?"

"I don't know," Griff hung his leonine head. "I thought if only we could communicate, we might parley. Or, at least, learn what to expect. Right now, we're fighting this war blind. We don't even know what they're after." He shook his head. "But if *you* can't talk to them . . ."

Tae allowed his brows to creep steadily upward. "Who said I can't talk to them?"

All eyes jerked instantly to the Eastern king, who remained utterly composed, more from habit than intention.

"Eventually," Tae added, the plan he had considered on his walk taking a more solid form in his mind. "Given the right circumstances."

"Go on." Darris leaned far forward in his chair, excitement lighting up his hazel eyes.

Tae kept his attention on Griff. "Didn't you tell me you managed to capture a second man?"

"Two days ago. Yes."

"Can you put the two together? In the same cell?"

Griff's head started to shake, slowly at first, then with more force. "Tae, the reason it took us so long to take prisoners is because these enemies fight to their last breath. When things look hopeless for any one of them, they choose death over capture. In fact, several took the lives of companions and their own rather than surrender."

Though not directly spoken, Griff's issue became clear to Tae. "It's hard to kill yourself alone without sharp or heavy objects."

"It is impossible," Griff finished, "to strangle yourself with your bare hands."

That made conjoining cells unworkable as well, since one could reach through the bars, and the other, presumably, would allow it. "So," Tae continued, "you could put them in the same area, so long as there was one entire cell between them."

Griff nodded, clearly waiting for Tae to explain.

"They could talk freely. And, if some ratty little thief got put in the cell between them . . ."

"No!" Matrinka leaped to her feet. "I'm not letting you lock yourself in that filthy, disgusting place."

Rantire started laughing, the sound startlingly loud and out of place given the intensity of the discussion. "Your Majesty," she managed between guffaws. "You just called—the king of the Eastlands—a ratty little—"

Matrinka would have none of it. "I didn't call him that. He called himself that."

"I know." Rantire could scarcely get the words out. "You only concurred." She lapsed into another fit of laughter.

Imorelda patted Tae's ear. *A more fitting queen would have her beheaded.*

Matrinka is the best queen in the world and totally fit for her job. "Actually," Tae continued aloud, "I didn't say who the ratty little thief was, but thanks for clarifying it, Matrinka."

Matrinka flushed. Rantire could not stop grinning, but at least her laughter ceased.

"I only meant I would pretend to be a ratty little thief who happened to get imprisoned between them. In the past, I've learned languages just by listening to conversations." Tae added for Rantire's sake, "It's how I picked up Renshai, for example."

Rantire's jollity disappeared completely.

"And I still say 'no.' " Matrinka placed her hands firmly on her ample hips. "We are not going to lock Tae in that horrible place, wedged between two killers."

Griff cleared his throat softly. "I'm not sure we have a choice."

Matrinka whirled to face her husband, clearly speechless.

"We can see to his comfort there. Warm, soft blankets, good food."

Though the idea pleased him, Tae knew it could not happen that way. "No. If they see me getting special treatment, the captives will guard their tongues."

Matrinka opened her mouth, but Tae spoke over her.

"Believe me, the eyes of inmates miss nothing. In fact, it would be best if we could do this without the guards knowing."

"But that's just stupid, Tae!" Matrinka had to get her words out. "Someone might hurt you. Even the guards themselves. And the food. It's . . . it's unsanitary."

"I'm sure I've eaten worse."

"You have?" the words were clearly startled from Griff. His features screwed into a knot. "Ewww."

Tae barely stopped himself from laughing. Despite nearly two decades on the throne, Griff still fell back into his naïve farmboy ways at times. In fact, childlike simplicity seemed to be a prerequisite for passing the tests that chose the king of Béarn.

Matrinka looked positively pained. "How will we talk to you? What if you find out something important? Or you're hurt? Or in trouble?"

★I always take care of you.★ Imorelda yowled. *★Is she insulting me?★*

★Not deliberately. You know she loves you.★ Aloud, Tae spoke for the cat. "Imorelda can let you know if I'm in trouble."

"How?" Matrinka demanded, apparently forgetting Rantire and Griff did not know about her bond with Mior nor Tae's with Imorelda. "You're the only one—"

Tae interrupted before she could say more. "She can be very persistent and persuasive when she needs something."

Imorelda stalked across the table toward Matrinka, tail lashing.

Rantire snorted. "You mean like a fish head? What good does it do you to have your cat badgering the cook?"

Mid-movement, Imorelda lowered her head and advanced on Rantire.

"She's extremely intelligent for a cat," Tae explained. "She understands more than most people give her credit for."

Rantire eyeballed Imorelda, hand falling to her hilt. "Yeah? Well if you don't want the furball in tonight's stewpot, you'll call her off me."

"Rantire!" Darris grumbled warningly. "Show some respect. Tae is a king."

Imorelda sat on the table and calmly licked her paws, as if she had merely intended to do so from her first movement. *★I hate her.★*

★I'm not fond of her either,★ Tae admitted. *★But she does take good care of King Griff.★*

Rantire glared at Darris but forced a curtsy. "Forgive me, Your Majesties. I was out of line."

Griff nodded his acceptance despite the obvious insincerity of the Renshai's apology.

Tae simply ignored it. "All right. So schedule me for weekly torture sessions or something. Just make sure whichever guard is supposed to administer them knows I'm actually meeting with you, and he has some acting experience so that he doesn't give it away."

Matrinka pounced on a single word. "Weekly?"

"You want me to suffer beatings every day?"

Matrinka's mouth fell open. She looked positively horrified. "You're not really going to get tortured, and we could get you out for at least one good meal a day."

Tae heaved a sigh, wishing he could have met with Griff alone.

The wise, innocent king would not harry him with speculation. "Matrinka, this is learning, not magic. You can't expect me to glean anything useful day by day. I have to fully immerse myself in this language, and that's hard enough when I only have two speakers and they're constrained by locks, guards, and distance."

Tae avoided mentioning that he would have to suffer at least a small amount of violence during the briefings. Cosmetics would not fool his new neighbors, especially if they started rubbing or flaking off. He had a high tolerance for pain but hated it as much as anyone. "Like it or not, this will take time." Knowing Matrinka would have a new question for every answer, Tae rose. "Now, if it's all right with everyone, I'd like to prepare. I need to totally undo my bath and combing, dress down into some rags . . . you know, enjoy myself."

Griff pulled at his beard. "How will you make yourself unrecognizable to the guards?"

"Very few prison guards have seen me up close more than once or twice. Even most of those should be fooled by grime, location, and clothing." Imorelda returned to Tae's arms. "They won't expect me in a cell, so they won't recognize me there. If one does, you can let him in on the secret so long as he can keep it."

Tae rose, hoping that would forestall more questions. They could not anticipate everything; the details would fall into place.

Imorelda clambered up Tae's chest and draped herself across his shoulders. *You're not fooling me. You don't want to do this.*

Of course, I do. It's an adventure.

Liar! Imorelda patted his face with a plushy paw. *Admit it. You can't stand closed-up places you can't get out of. When you have a choice, you don't eat garbage, and you don't wear dirty rags. Although you do turn everything nice into dirty rags.*

Tae walked toward the door, still engaged in this internal dialogue. *Are you saying anything I wear should be considered tainted just because I'm wearing it?*

Imorelda slapped him again, this time with just a hint of claw. *I mean you shred the seamstresses' handiwork by crawling around and climbing like a child. Only you can't do that here, because it might alert the guards to what you're doing. So you're going to have to consort with pigs and cows, aren't you?* Imorelda crinkled her kitty nose. *Disgusting.*

Tae had not yet given any thought to the "how." Imorelda was right, though. He did secretly dread the job he had demanded. It had taken him years of hard work to overcome the panic that used to assail him in enclosed places in the wake of his imprisonment in Pudar. Accustomed to doing whatever he wanted, whenever he wanted, and at no one's say-so, he did not look forward to being manhandled by strange guards who believed him a thief or an Eastern spy. *It's not a matter of what I want, or what makes me comfortable.* He reached for the door latch. *I'm the only person who can crack this language, and I'm doing it for the security, not just of my friends in Béarn, but for the entire world.*

The entire world? Imorelda sneezed. *Aren't you being just a bit . . . melodramatic?*

Maybe. Tae tripped the latch and opened the door. *But I don't think so. I don't know what these pirates want, but it's obviously not to negotiate. Not if they're taking and leaving no prisoners.* He stepped out into the hallway, inhaling the familiar smells of Béarn castle: mustiness, cat dander, and baking bread. Though enticed by the food, he deliberately turned away from the kitchen. Nothing would draw suspicions more than a captive gaining weight in prison. *I think we're only seeing the first wave. They're testing us before sending in a larger force to take our land or our ore or, simply, our lives.*

I still think you're overthinking this.

Maybe, Tae conceded. *But we can't afford to assume it. Because, if I'm right, we're all in dire trouble.*

CHAPTER 22

Ninety percent of an effective trap is surprise.
—King Tae Kahn of Stalmize

TALAMIR AWAKENED TO a sense of alarm and imminent death, surprised to find himself more comfortable than he had felt in weeks. Healers had removed the arrowhead from his thigh, pumping him full of herbs. The cold floor of the cell eased his many wounds and bruises, and his belly felt full for the first time in many days. He could scarcely remember his meal the previous night; he had eaten it with such gusto he could not recall tasting it. It had existed only to fill the void in his gut, and it had satisfied its purpose admirably.

Renshai training kicked in swiftly, revealing the presence of two guards outside his cell. Though Talamir had an overall feeling of unease, they were not the cause of it. Their demeanors seemed relaxed, nonthreatening and, oddly, weaponless. They clearly posed no immediate threat, and he saw no reason not to let them know he had awakened.

Sitting up, Talamir looked around him. He sat in the middle of a small cell containing nothing but a chamber pot and the bedraggled blanket he had ignored the previous night. He rose and used the pot, taking comfort from the normalcy of the sound of urine splashing into clay. From the smells around him, he knew several prisoners had missed their targets, but he took pride in aiming every drop into its rightful place. Missing would only make his cell more disgusting, and targeting the guards would assure food mixed with filth and spit, manhandling, and a more painful death.

The guards spoke softly to one another before approaching his cell. Talamir did not recognize them specifically, though he had probably seen them around the castle. Both sported the fine black hair, swarthy skin, and dark eyes of Easterners; but, there, all resemblance ended. One had fine, almost chiseled features. Tall, young, and willowy, he seemed almost delicate. The other was average height, middle-aged and well-muscled, with scarred features. Much to Talamir's surprise, neither carried any obvious weaponry, not even a sword; and that annoyed him. It suggested they did not see him as enough of a threat to need weapons to contain him.

"Are you ready for your audience?" the younger one asked politely. "Or do you need more time?"

Sarcastic replies about finishing perfumed baths and changing into suitable silks came to mind, but Talamir discarded them. So far, the guards seemed kind enough, and it would be foolish to antagonize them. "I'm not sure I'll ever be ready to face King Tae Kahn."

"Then you're in luck," the older man said. "The king is away on business. You're meeting with his regent, Lord Weile Kahn."

Talamir relaxed a bit. So far, the king's father had shown him significantly more leniency. Whether it would hold up given that he had not fulfilled his promises remained to be seen. "Oh. I . . . suppose . . . I'm ready, then. Thanks for asking."

The middle-aged guard jiggled a ring of keys until he separated out the one he wanted. He jabbed it into the lock, studying Talamir as he did so. "You are going to come peacefully, right? Because that would definitely be in your best interests."

Talamir gave no answer. Currently, he had no reason to fight. But, if circumstances changed, he would not hesitate to do so, at the expense of almost anyone's life. Their lack of swords further irked him because it meant he could not arm himself from their lapses.

Apparently, they did not require an answer. The one guard opened the lock with a deft twist, then pocketed the keys in a motion so swift Talamir did not see exactly where he put them. The other watched him, hawklike. Whatever their reasons for remaining weaponless, it clearly had nothing to do with a lack of agility or competence.

Talamir glided cautiously from his cell, uncertain what to expect. The taller, thinner Easterner led the way, while the other fell into step behind Talamir.

They led him past other prisoners, who watched them curiously but remained silent in the gloom. They also walked past other guards who gave the procession acknowledging nods. To Talamir's surprise, his escort did not lead him toward the stairs that opened onto the castle proper. Instead, they took him to a small room that he suspected they used for interrogation. Talamir's heart pounded, and his mind raced. He had no specific information they needed, and he expected any brutal death they chose to inflict upon him to wait for Tae's return. Surely, the king would not want to miss it.

The leading guard opened the door to reveal a small room, its bare walls speckled with dark brown stains that could represent blood as easily as dirt. The only furnishings were four rickety chairs, though all three of the men inside remained standing. Two were swathed in elite guard black with silver veils, no weapons evident. Weile Kahn stood in the back, a strangely looming and unreadable presence.

It seemed odd to Talamir that a man so average in height, build, and coloring could radiate so much power. He seemed strangely massive, stunningly handsome, the very definition of charisma even standing perfectly still. Talamir was a Renshai *torke,* trained to face the biggest dangers of the universe without a moment's hesitation. Nevertheless, he felt intimidated, barely able to meet the older man's gaze as his escort departed, closing the door behind them.

Weile spoke first, "How is my grandson, Talamir?"

Talamir swallowed hard. He could lie, but he felt certain it would backfire. A man like Weile did not ask a question to which he did not already know the answer. "I hear he's doing very well. The innkeepers treat him like a star, and the women . . ." He swallowed hard. "The women seem to find him irresistible."

"Yes, well. He is the prince of Stalmize."

"Unfortunately," Talamir mumbled before he could think.

Weile studied the Renshai. "You'd best get used to that, Talamir. Because the populace tends to consider itself prime owners of the king's offspring. *Our* prince. *Our* princess. And as Subikahn is Tae's only child, it's presumed he will become the king someday."

Talamir went on the defensive. "That's not why I love him, if that's what you mean." He turned his gaze toward the other men in the room, assuming Weile trusted them with any words that might pass between them. "I have no designs on any throne. I would love Subikahn were he the meanest beggar in Erythane."

Weile Kahn grinned indulgently. "Talamir, I'm not concerned about any designs you might have on the throne. I gained it, stole it most would say, from its previous owner who proved incapable of protecting it against me. If we can't keep the kingship in our family, then we don't deserve to have it either."

Talamir cocked his head, trying to anticipate the Easterner's point.

Weile did not wait for his guest to puzzle out the answer. "I'm just saying even rough-edged kings have responsibilities. Despite what most people believe, they cannot simply do as they please. Those royal duties did not suit me, so I passed them to my son. Tae handles the position far better than I did, but even he is beginning to realize that his subjects want a queen." His dark eyes, so like Subikahn's at first glance, held a stony edge his grandson did not share. "They will have it from Tae or from Subikahn. More likely, from both. You, Talamir, can never be queen."

The words startled the Renshai, who had never considered such a thing. "Queen?! Of course I can't be queen. Who said I wanted to be queen? I'm a man."

"And men aren't known for sharing the things that matter most to them."

Now, Talamir understood. Subikahn would likely have a wife in addition to his lover, and the populace would demand children as well. Talamir had not yet considered the future in such detail. "I will deal with whatever it takes to keep Subikahn. He is my love, my life, my very happiness." Anger suffused him at the unfairness of it all. He had finally found a kindred soul mate, and he had no choice but to picture his beloved cradling a beautiful, young bride. There was no positive way to view the situation, but he would not allow it to stop him.

"Ah, in the heat of young passion, you could give no other answer. But love matures, Talamir, and you need to think not about what you can suffer now, but how you will suffer in the future."

This was not the conversation Talamir had expected. "Future, Sire? I have no future. I'm sentenced to die by slow torture for high treason and rape."

Weile Kahn made a thoughtful noise, as if he had fully forgotten those details. "Yes. So, what should I do with you, Talamir?"

The question caught Talamir even more off guard, if possible. "Let me go?" he suggested.

"I tried that." Weile glanced at his veiled companions. "I even gave you my sword. By the way, it's never looked better. Thanks for taking such good care of it."

As a Renshai, Talamir could have done nothing else, but it seemed distantly possible Weile might not know that. "You're welcome, Sire."

"You made me a lot of promises when you left, Talamir."

The reminder further irritated Talamir. His fists curled around empty air. He was hiltless, naked, before his accuser. "You made promises, too," he reminded with cautious venom. "You said you would hold your men back, but they hounded me relentlessly. I agreed not to kill them, but they made it impossible."

"Those," Weile said crisply, "were the king's men, not mine." A smile haunted his lips but did not quite show through.

Talamir got the idea that something other than his own decisions and prowess impressed Weile Kahn. It took him several moments of silent thought to realize Weile had underestimated, and now appreciated, Tae's resourcefulness. "Whosoever they were, I had to kill them to survive. And I had to survive to keep my promise to protect Subikahn."

"Which you didn't."

"I didn't fail," Talamir pointed out. "He's alive and well, thank the gods."

"Is he?"

The simple question cut like a knife. Talamir's heart skipped a beat. "What—what do you mean?" He studied the veiled figures for some outline of weapons. If Subikahn was in danger, he would do whatever it took to rescue him.

Weile remained composed, his every movement controlled. He seemed less oblivious to the fact that he faced a troubled Renshai with only two apparently unarmed guards, than unconcerned about it. "My grandson has passed the boundaries of the Eastlands."

"He's a competent warrior." Talamir still did not understand why Weile worried so much about Subikahn's safety.

"But naïve," the regent said. "For all his sword training, he's young and inexperienced in the ways of the world."

It all seemed to come back to the same answer. "Then let me go again. I'll find him, keep him well."

Weile shook his head. "No, Talamir. That will not end well for you."

The pronouncement, though somber, seemed utterly nonsensical. "Well," said the Renshai. "*Not* letting me go will *definitely* end badly for me."

"You can't run from Tae forever."

"I can try."

"Not if you really love Subikahn."

Talamir's attention jerked fully to Weile Kahn. "What do you mean?"

"I mean that it's impossible to have a strong relationship with someone whose parents hate you."

"Why?" The word emerged as more of a demand than a question.

"Because it's not a sustainable situation; it's highly uncomfortable for the one caught in the middle. Sooner or later, your beloved will have to make a choice between lover and family. And that choice, however it is made, never results in long-lasting happiness for anyone involved." Weile's dark brows edged upward. He waited for Talamir's reply, clearly expecting something significant.

Talamir considered, knowing whatever came out of his mouth needed to be intelligent. So far, he had not managed to impress Subikahn's father. He could not risk alienating the grandfather as well. When nothing of great usefulness came to him after several moments, he tried to elicit a hint without sounding stupid. "I know I need to win over the king. I just don't know how to do that from a cell."

Weile waited expectantly, in silence, so Talamir glanced past him toward the guards. The squatter one bobbed his head slightly, encouraging.

Talamir cleared his throat. "I could guard Subikahn . . ."

The guard's head shook hastily, in slight motions.

Cued, Talamir added, "But we've already tried that unsuccessfully. I could go . . ."

The guard cringed, head still shaking.

"I could stay . . ." Talamir amended. "I could stay here and . . ."

The guard raised and lowered his head once. Talamir wished he could see the man's expression.

". . . and do something that might make a good impression on King Tae."

The guard pantomimed drawing a sword and thrusting.

"I could . . . kill . . ."

The guard's head shook faster.

Weile Kahn said, "He's suggesting you offer to train the regular guards." He twisted his head to look at the elite guardsmen behind him. "Right?"

Both men stood utterly still, their expressions hidden behind silver veils.

Weile did not wait for a response but returned his attention to Talamir almost immediately.

More surprised by the suggestion than by Weile's apparent ability to see behind him, Talamir stammered, "Me? Train Eastern guardsmen?" It made no sense. "Tae would never allow that."

"But I would. Right now, and for the foreseeable future, I'm in charge."

Talamir wanted to say more, but words failed him.

Weile did not suffer a similar fate. "You're a teacher, right? A sword instructor."

"Well, yes." Talamir wondered why his brain seemed to refuse to fully function. "A *torke*. I train *Renshai*."

"Regular guardsmen would be . . . easier?"

"Easier," Talamir repeated. "Yes, surely easier. But—" *What's wrong with my damned tongue.* "I can't teach them Renshai maneuvers."

Weile shrugged. "So don't. Teach them basic things. Things that make them better, more confident warriors. Things that make you . . . indispensable."

"I . . ." Talamir started, uncertain where he was going. ". . . can do that." As the words left his mouth, he realized they were true. "I *can* do that. But, if you let me out, how do you know I won't just run."

"I don't," Weile admitted, but he did not seem the least perturbed. "But if you do, I will have learned something important about you."

Talamir knew better than to ask what that lesson might be. "Thank you." The words seemed woefully inadequate. Despite having surrendered the throne to his son, Weile Kahn still held more power than most kings; and Talamir understood that the leader of the underground had no obligation to him. "You've shown me mercy and many kindnesses I don't deserve."

"You will earn them." It was not a show of trust but a clear warning. "If you hurt my grandson, if you break his heart, you will face agony beyond the sensibilities of Tae Kahn to inflict."

Talamir had no idea what Weile meant but felt certain he preferred ignorance. As much as he loved Subikahn, as right as their relationship seemed, he could not help believing his life might have been better had he never traveled to Stalmize, never became a *torke*, never met Subikahn at all.

Howling curses at his captors, Tae stumbled through the hallways to his cell, his arms pinched and pinioned by a pair of Béarnian guards, each twice his size. His hair hung in a lank filthy snarl, his clothing torn and frayed, his skin already bruised by the roughness of their handling. One released him to unlock the cell door. Still playing, Tae lurched to free himself. The other guard tightened his grip, squeezing until Tae's arm throbbed and the pain nearly incapacitated him. The instant the door jarred open, he felt himself thrown angrily inside. He tumbled, heels over head, slamming his skull against the stone wall that comprised the back of the cell. Pain exploded through his head, scrambling his thoughts. Then, the door slammed shut, and the lock clicked with ominous finality.

Suddenly, Tae wished the Béarnian royals had let a few more people in on the truth. His head hurt so badly he nearly vomited, and returning blood flow made his arms throb. He forced himself to rise, though it severely tested his balance, and tried to look tough and unruffled by their treatment.

Instantly, Tae's mind retreated to his days in Pudar's prison, under sentence of death. Then, he had shared his cell with other prisoners, ones happy to kill or maim a newcomer for his share of the food. Panic assailed him in a sudden rush, scattering his thoughts. He wanted out, he needed out, and no tactic seemed too farfetched to earn his freedom. He ran to the bars and pulled at them, only to find them so solid he could not move them in the slightest. He lowered his head and focused his view, aware he needed his wits wholly about him. The terror receded, replaced by familiar, cold rationality. He was not a prisoner; he was only on a mission.

Assailed by pain but with his heart rate slowing back to normal, Tae slumped against the bars. Next, he did what any prisoner would, surveying the area around him with a feigned composure that suggested he could handle anything that dared to threaten him. The prisoner to his right studied him through harsh, dark eyes beneath a prominent knitted brow. Though no larger than an average Béarnide, he still towered over Tae. Wide shoulders and broad hips spoke of a stoutness he had lost in the Béarnian dungeon, and his nondescript clothing hung from his slowly thinning frame.

Tae locked eyes for only a moment, and the cold of the contact seeped through him. There was hatred in those predatory orbs and also a hint of despair that might make him as dangerous to himself as to Tae.

A smaller and leaner, but no less desperate, man occupied the cell to Tae's left. He wore similar bland clothing, more filthy, with old bloodstains on the sleeves. Though softer, his brown eyes also revealed a deadly loathing, either for Tae or, more generally, for his surroundings. To Tae's surprise, he read fear in this man's expression, unmatched by his fellow, yet strong and clear. Hand gestures, words, tone could vary from culture to culture, but expressions remained the one constant on which he could rely. His left neighbor was terrified of something, and Tae sincerely doubted it had anything to do with himself.

Across the walkway, a Béarnide peeked out from the bars to give Tae the same scrutiny. He seemed harmless despite his size, probably a petty criminal. Yet, Tae had no other choice but to use him as an example. "Yah, ya ugly Béarnide!" he jeered with a hiss. "What're ya lookin' at?"

The Béarnide stiffened but did not return the challenge. He backed away from the bars to disappear into the shadows of his cage.

Tae dismissed him with a wave and a glob of spit that struck the bars of the other man's cell. "Ya're all a buncha cowards, y'are."

A few rumbled challenges followed Tae's proclamation, but as none of those prisoners was clearly visible, he ignored them. Instead he turned his attention to the pirates to either side. He had no way of knowing how to gain their goodwill; their upbringings would likely prove too alien to guess. Tae could only count on his own experience, that to win over tough men, one had to prove himself at least as equally brave and tough.

Without warning, Tae lunged at the larger of the pirates.

Clearly startled, the man retreated with a hiss; then, to Tae's surprise, immediately lurched forward. A swift grab managed to capture a piece of Tae's shirt.

Tae attempted to free himself without appearing to retreat. Trying to maintain composure, rather than following his survival instincts, proved Tae's downfall. With a jerk, the man yanked him closer. The other beefy hand closed over more fabric, and Tae found himself in an abrupt and inescapable chokehold.

Still in control of his faculties, Tae hammered the man's arms from below, once, twice, three times, trying to dislodge them. But he might as well have slammed against solid iron for all the good it did him. The pirate's grip only tightened expertly.

Breath refused to leave or enter Tae's lungs. He gasped spasmodically, suddenly realizing his life was measured in moments. He tried to roll backward, without success. The iron grip held him in place. He threw himself forward, grabbing for any part of his attacker's anatomy and hoping he caught something exquisitely sensitive. His throat locked open, desperately sucking, and his lungs felt as if they would burst through his chest. Stars whirled around his eyes. In a moment, he would lose consciousness and any chance for escape.

Then, something dark hurtled through the air, spitting and yowling, to land on the stranger's head. The man screamed, dropping back and releasing Tae so quickly the Easterner sank to his knees. Before he could think or wonder, Tae scrambled beyond further reach of his attacker, not caring how clumsy or desperate he appeared. Air rushed back into his lungs in an agonizing contraction, and he breathed in and out so quickly it worsened his dizziness. It took him a moment to recognize the furry, silver dervish tearing, clawing, and biting at the stranger's face.

Imorelda!

Tae got no acknowledgment as the cat remained singularly focused on mangling her target.

Tae rose carefully. He knew better than to give direct orders to a cat. *Imorelda, please, get away! He might hurt you.*

Still fluffed to twice her normal size, Imorelda bounced to the cell floor and growled menacingly at the stranger.

He's quicker than he looks, Tae warned. *Please. Get out while you can.*

Imorelda remained facing the stranger, back firmly arched, though she did take several rearward steps toward Tae.

Slip out the front, if you can, Tae suggested. *If they know we're a team, they'll get more cautious.*

Imorelda whirled suddenly and ran through the front bars, galloping into the darkness. *Maybe if they know we're a team, they won't be so quick to murder you.* An angry howl escaped from the shadows. *Isn't saving your foolish life worth a thank you?*

Thank you, Imorelda, Tae sent dutifully. He resisted the urge to rub at his neck, instead glaring at the pirate. The other man did not return the look, more concerned with his own lacerated scalp and face. He rubbed blood from his cheeks and nose with the back of his sleeve, blinking several times to adjust his vision, then uttered a string of savage words Tae took to be the equivalent of swearing. *Just my luck. The first words I learn in their language, and I can't use any of them.*

From behind Tae, the other pirate spoke.

This earned him a reply laced with similar words. From it all, Tae took away the term for cat, *yonha*, and a few other words he tucked away for later comparison. The syntax seemed a bit sideways, with adjectives and nouns switched in their places. He thought he sifted out a descriptor for Imorelda as "savage" and for himself, "stupid." They referred to him as "takudan," which he supposed more likely meant "little rat" or "idiot" than "brave neighbor." It was not the impression he had intended to make, but at least he had them talking.

Suddenly, Tae realized Imorelda was still addressing him. * . . . not even listening!*

Sorry, Imorelda. I'm working.

Tae imagined her tail twitching in angry bursts. *If it weren't for me, you wouldn't be alive to work.*

Tae did feel grateful, but he could not waste any time in idle conversation. *You're right. You saved my life, and I am eternally grateful. I owe you the finest fish and hours of rubbing. But right now, Imorelda, I need to listen.*

The cat mumbled something incoherent, but the moment was lost. The pirates returned to their own problems, the larger one nursing his wounds and the smaller moving to the darkest corner to use his chamber pot.

Damn. Tae remained on the floor of his cell, enjoying the simple act of breathing. His gambit had failed miserably, but he was not without further tricks. He just needed to keep the pirate's deadliness and quickness firmly in mind.

Misery found Tae in the dark, dank depths of Béarn's dungeon, dragging out thoughts better left buried. He refused to further contemplate the son he had alienated, the Renshai who had ruined his life, nor the woman he had loved and lost. Those topics could paralyze him, make him careless and dim-witted at a time when his life and the world depended on his wile and agility, so he banished those concerns.

And suddenly Tae found himself thinking about the maid, Alneezah, which caught him utterly off his guard. He had not realized she meant anything special to him, but he clung to the image of her with a great fondness he had never before recognized. He pictured her demure expression: gentle brown eyes that simultaneously managed to show concern and amusement for his antics, the pink circles of her high-set cheeks, the pert nose and heart-shaped lips. He found himself smiling at the image. As common as she seemed, as unfathomable as most found him, she understood him in a way few others could.

⋆Marry her.⋆ The words brushed Tae's mind.

Startled, Tae nearly answered aloud. *⋆What?⋆*

⋆You should marry that woman. She's good for you.⋆

Tae felt his cheeks grow warm. He had not intended to project his thoughts. *⋆How did you know . . . ?⋆*

⋆How could I not know. You're splashing her image all over the place.⋆

⋆I am?⋆ Tae truly had no idea. He had not even realized that Imorelda still remained silently hidden in the dungeon. *⋆And stop telling me that. I can't marry her.⋆*

⋆Why not?⋆

Why not, indeed? Nothing legal or physical stopped him from marrying anyone he wanted. He could hardly claim that his blood was too royal to mix with commoners. *⋆I don't love her, Imorelda.⋆* Tae sighed inwardly, wondering how much time the cat might occupy grilling him about human emotion. *⋆People aren't like cats. Despite the apparent contradiction of my son, we don't just mate and move on to better things.⋆* He added to forestall insult, *⋆Not that there's anything wrong with that, if you're a cat.⋆*

Imorelda let the species differences lie. *Are you sure you're not in love with her?*

That being the last reply Tae expected, he tried not to let surprise show on his face. No one knew he was having a conversation besides Imorelda. To onlookers, he would appear insane by reacting to absolutely nothing. *I know what love feels like. I loved Kevral.* A pang of regret touched him, and he had to banish a tear forming in his eye. He would miss the little time they had managed to spend together since her marriage.

And you love me, and you love Subikahn.

Tae's chest tightened. He did not want to think about his son right now, could not afford the emotions it would raise. *Of course. But differently.*

Exactly!

As Tae had no idea what she meant, he waited for her to explain.

Love is felt in different ways. Just because something is fast and intense doesn't make it better. In fact, sometimes that kind of knock-you-on-your-ass love wanes as quickly as it formed.

Tae could not help contemplating the cat's words. Like Mior, Imorelda had moments of blinding insight. *You mean—?*

Imorelda did not wait to have her intentions explained to her. *I mean, when you fell for Kevral you were nineteen. Mature love, adult love, doesn't usually come in a rush of naïve passion. It's cautious, slow-growing, steady. Full of thought and wonder.*

Tae wondered why he had never thought of such a thing. It certainly explained why he had never married. He was searching for that overwhelming, gut-wrenching fervor he had felt for Kevral. Yet nothing else in his life ever seemed that extreme, no decision so obvious and easy as when he had asked Kevral for her hand. He shook his head to clear it. He had no time for philosophical discussions or idle speculation. *Thank you for the insight, Imorelda, as well as for saving my life. If you would, please, go to Matrinka now. She needs someone to ease her soul over my decision. She needs to know I'm all right here.*

Imorelda made a sneezing sound from the darkness that displayed her displeasure. *Are you all right? I'd hate to lie to a queen.*

Since her only positive form of communication with others was rubbing and purring, Imorelda could hardly be considered a liar. *I'm fine. I promise not to get within reach of either of them again.*

Or do anything to provoke the guards?

Tae did not currently intend such a deed, though he could not rule it out if circumstances demanded it. *Or that either,* he promised, not nearly as concerned about telling the truth as putting the cat at ease. She distracted him from a job he wanted finished as swiftly as possible, for his own good as well as Béarn's.

Tae did not hear Imorelda leave, but he felt certain she had done so. With a sigh, he curled up on the cold, hard floor of his cell and pretended to sleep.

CHAPTER 23

It's the horrific things in life that make a man careful, wiser.
—*King Tae Kahn of Stalmize*

ON HIS SIXTH DAY in the Béarnian dungeon, Tae found himself trundled roughly into a thick-walled interrogation room no larger than his cell. Shoved inside, he stumbled. He could have caught his balance but did not bother, instead easing his tumble onto the solid stone floor. The guards did not need to know the full range of his dexterity, nor did he need to risk tearing muscles or ligaments. A few more bruises added to the mass seemed a much smaller price to pay.

The door slammed shut, leaving Tae in utter darkness. He lowered his head, reveling in the sudden peace and quiet, the chance to drop his guard and fully assess his person. He stank. Bruises stamped his body, the worst at his throat where the pirate had attempted to strangle him. His hair hung in tangles, and filth covered every part of him. Though once his natural state, it bothered him now. He had not felt so disgustingly vile for the latter half of his life. *I'm getting too old for this.*

The door winched open, admitting a beam of light. Tae remained in place, taking his cues from whoever opened the door.

Several moments passed in silence until Tae finally raised his head to see who had joined him. A tall, broad figure in a blue cloak played lantern light across him, then closed the door. "Oh, Tae," she said.

Recognizing the voice, Tae leaped to his feet and tried to look happily animated. "Matrinka. What in the name of all gods are you doing here?"

Carefully setting down the lantern, Matrinka caught Tae into a fierce embrace. "Oh, Tae," she repeated. "Are you all right?"

"I'm fine, but you don't want to touch me." Tae added with a smile, "I reek."

Tae's words did not put Matrinka off, though she did finally release him. "A good bath will take care of that." She ran her fingers into his hair, though they barely penetrated. "Then a combing—"

"No, Matrinka. No." Tae untwined her from the no-longer-silky black strands. "I can't come back from a torture session groomed and perfumed."

She hugged him again, speaking wistfully and with clear personal pain. "Must you go back?"

"Yes." Tae's answer left no room for argument. He had not accomplished nearly as much as he had hoped. "One thing I wouldn't mind, though, is getting out of small, enclosed places."

"Of course." Matrinka let go. She swished off her cloak and placed it lovingly over Tae. While he adjusted the sleeves and hood to hide his features, Matrinka scooped up the lantern and opened the door.

Swiftly, they walked down a corridor that did not take them past any prisoners, out of the dungeon proper, and into the torchlight of the main castle passages. Something brushed against Tae's leg, then twisted to twine along the other one, stealing his equilibrium. Tae hopped, stumbled, and barely caught his balance.

Matrinka steadied him. "Are you all right?"

Tae looked down to see Imorelda purring up at him. *Watch your feet, you oaf. You nearly crushed me,* she accused.

Tae responded to both of them, "Imorelda tried to break my legs."

I did not!

"She can talk," Tae added conspiratorially to the only person who knew it. "You'd think she'd warn me before doing something stupid."

I shouldn't have to warn you. And claiming you is my right, not 'something stupid.'

"Mior used to do that, too," Matrinka said wistfully. "I miss that."

"You miss having your legs broken?" Tae shook a head lost beneath the folds and hood of his cloak. "The day I miss that, you have permission to kill me."

Matrinka snorted. "Killing you would be easy. It's keeping you alive that drives us near to madness." She ushered him into one of the first-floor meeting rooms.

Tae stepped around her and into an enormous room filled with plush chairs and a single large table with smaller, harder seats around it. King Griff rose to face the door, his bodyguards, Rantire and Bard Darris, at attention beside him. The room's only other occupants were the ubiquitous silent page in one corner and a couple of cats lounging in the most comfortable chairs.

What caught Tae's attention, though, was a steaming plate of food on the table. The aromas of real meat, baked bread, and freshly cooked vegetables twined across the room, overwhelming even his own stench; and Tae found himself walking toward it before he could think to practice the decorum a king's presence demanded.

Luckily for Tae, he was also a king and among friends who did not require formality. Darris bowed low; Rantire afforded him a respectful, though grudging, nod. King Griff merely smiled in happy welcome. Either from her usual concern, or to cover his rudeness, Matrinka ushered Tae swiftly to the table. "Eat, eat!"

Tae took his place at the head of the table, seizing a fork and shoving the first piece into his mouth without bothering to identify it. It was a tuber, buttered and seasoned, and the taste seemed to explode as he bit into it. Flavor washed through his mouth, so intense it overwhelmed his other senses. He chewed happily as the rest of the world faded in comparison.

Griff sat at the opposite end of the table, while his guards took the chairs on either side of him. Matrinka placed herself beside Darris, at Tae's right hand. Only the seat across from her remained vacant, at least until Imorelda claimed it as a stepping stone to the table and Tae's feast.

Gimme, gimme, gimme!

Lost in his personal heaven, Tae could not have stopped Imorelda from taking whatever she wished. The cat hooked a piece of meat, pulled it toward her, and grabbed it with her teeth.

Tae finally swallowed. "Wow, this is good." He watched Imorelda worry her piece of meat, growling softly. "Sorry about the animal on the table."

Griff waved off the apology. "Believe me, we're used to it." He turned Matrinka a loving smile, and her cheeks gained a pinkish hue.

Tae savored a few more bites of tuber, lamb, and greens before putting down his fork. As good as it tasted, he knew better than to eat too much. Gaining weight on prison food would look mighty suspicious, and he knew the others waited eagerly for any news he might have. "They're definitely from far elsewhere. Not only is their language completely foreign, but their gestures as well."

"Outworlders?" Griff suggested. "Or from across the sea?"

"Yes." Tae suspected Griff wanted to know which, but the Easterner had no certain answers. "The Outworlders we've faced or heard of always have some sort of magical abilities. Gods, elves, dwarves. Spirit spiders and other creatures. These pirates seem human. At least, I would have used magic, if I had it, in their situation."

Griff nodded guardedly.

Tae suspected the King of Béarn was hiding disappointment. Tae had promised miracles and, so far, delivered very little. "They don't talk to one another nearly as much as I'd like or expect, and the ways I have to goad them usually don't work out well for me." His hand went instinctively to the bruises at his throat. "But I have managed to learn the basic rules of their language and enough individual words to make crude conversation, if I had to."

Griff's next nod held out more hope.

"All I really know so far is that they hold us in complete contempt. They look at us . . ." Tae paused to regroup and make the proper point. ". . . all of us, not just the other prisoners, as animals to slaughter at their whim. They don't seem to differentiate at all: soldiers, guards, men, women, children."

Matrinka shivered. Griff's expression turned sour. Darris leaned in to listen, but Rantire seemed more interested in watching the door. The page simply recorded everything, as custom dictated. He could not share one word of what he witnessed with anyone except the Sage who guarded Béarn's history and secrets with the spirit and ferocity of an eagle.

Tae wished he had divined more, though he had not intended to tell everything. It all needed refinement that could only come with time. "As far as I can tell, the two you captured are foot soldiers. They refer to their commanders as the *Kjempemagiska*." Tae assumed the accent of the pirates as he spoke the word. "And they seem to hold them in great awe."

Tae looked down at his plate. He had to take just a couple more mouthfuls before he went back to the hell of Béarn's dungeon. He stuffed a piece of bread into his mouth, chewed, savored, and swallowed.

Griff clamped his lips shut and waited for Tae to finish. Only after the bread completely disappeared did he speak. "Tae, do you really think you can learn more from these . . . pirates?"

"I'm sure I can." Tae harbored no doubts. "I just need more time."

"Don't go back." Matrinka spoke so softly, Tae could barely hear her. "Please don't."

Tae understood her point. He did not relish returning to living like a beast in a cage, antagonizing deadly neighbors and earning the ire of the guards. Age seemed to compound everything he despised as a youth. The pain hurt worse and lasted longer, his reflexes seemed slower, his demeanor less useful, and his accuracy less lethal. On the other hand, he had gained in wisdom and patience. Those things would see him through the necessary hardships. "Matrinka, pardon me if I sound like I'm using you as a common servant; but, could you get me another piece of that wonderful bread?"

Matrinka grinned and rushed to do so. She had obviously put together the feast to soothe and please him. "I'd love to." She hurried to the door.

Tae waited only until it clicked closed behind her to climb out of his chair and walk toward Rantire. "Hit me," he said.

"What?" the word startled from Griff, and he half-rose from his seat.

Tae had eyes only for Rantire. "Hit me, Renshai. I can't come back looking better than when I left. The guards, and my cell mates, believe I'm getting—"

Rantire moved like a shadow. Tae barely had time to blink before the Renshai's fist filled his face and agony blasted through his nose. Driven backward, Tae became tangled in the empty chair and toppled to the floor. It scraped his ear and left arm, barked his right shin. Tae scrambled free, only to find his hands, cloak, and tattered shirt covered with blood.

"Damn it!" Tae shouted, catching the flow in his cupped hands. He tried to staunch the bleeding with a fold of the cloak, but it hurt too much to add pressure. "I didn't mean for you to break my stupid nose!"

Rantire looked at Tae, arms folded across her chest, her lips pursed in a self-satisfied smile. "If you don't want something done right, don't ask a Renshai."

Tae knew he had taken his chances going to Rantire, but he also knew Darris and Griff would not have had the nerve to harm him at all. They might even have stopped Rantire had they known what he planned to do. But he had thought she might show some restraint. At least, as a woman, she might not prove so strong.

The door opened, and Matrinka slipped inside, displaying a fresh piece of bread and a mug of something steaming. Her eyes widened, she let out an outraged scream, and dropped food and drink. The mug bounced, splashing hot liquid across the floor, furniture, and Tae's ankles. Still focused on the pain in his face, Tae barely noticed the burn.

Matrinka slammed the door and rounded on her husband. "I leave for one moment, and you attack him?"

Gingerly, Tae clamped hold of his aching nose.

"We didn't attack him," Griff explained. "He asked Rantire to hit him."

Matrinka's head swiveled toward the Renshai and her cocksure expression. The queen's hands balled to fists. For an instant, Tae thought the peaceful Béarnide might actually start a fight; but Matrinka's hands loosened, and she tended to Tae instead. "You're an idiot," she said in exasperation. "You're both stark raving idiots."

Under the circumstances, Tae could hardly disagree.

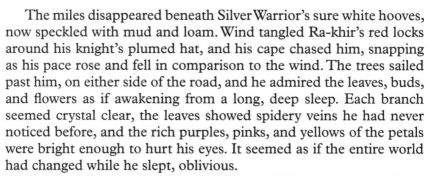

The miles disappeared beneath Silver Warrior's sure white hooves, now speckled with mud and loam. Wind tangled Ra-khir's red locks around his knight's plumed hat, and his cape chased him, snapping as his pace rose and fell in comparison to the wind. The trees sailed past him, on either side of the road, and he admired the leaves, buds, and flowers as if awakening from a long, deep sleep. Each branch seemed crystal clear, the leaves showed spidery veins he had never noticed before, and the rich purples, pinks, and yellows of the petals were bright enough to hurt his eyes. It seemed as if the entire world had changed while he slept, oblivious.

Oblivious. The word seemed to suit him. *What am I missing? What did I say? What did I do?* The last week had passed in an empty blur. Ra-khir had performed his duties in a blind, deaf trance. He knew he had groomed Silver Warrior, because the horse still whickered at the sight of him, and white hairs clung to every set of clothing. He knew he must have taken in food and water; he was still alive, still breathing. His body had taken over the dull routine without need for mind or spirit.

The agony of his loss had not left him. It still twinged at the slightest memory of his beloved Kevral. Yet she no longer wholly occupied his thoughts. Saviar and Calistin, his sons, had left him in the dark of night, without so much as an explanation or even a "farewell." He knew his words and wishes had no power to keep them safe; yet he could not help feeling as if the crazy superstitious notion could somehow manage what he had physically failed to do.

Did I insult them? Ra-khir hoped his suggestion that they remain in Erythane had not violated some deeply ingrained Renshai tenet. *Did I drive them away?* He believed he understood the Renshai as few *ganim* ever could. Most thought them lawless and unstructured, the very definition of chaos. Nearly all of the Renshai disparaged the Knights of Erythane for their rigid adherence to a code of honor.

Yet few understood that the Renshai, themselves, had conventions equally unyielding and strict.

Renshai did fight without pattern or strategy, but were consistent in this observance. They all shunned armor or adornment that might deflect a blow, believing that depending upon anything but one's own skill in battle was tantamount to cowardice. They insisted on making every member of the tribe ambidextrous, they refused any weapon not a sword, and they forced sword-training even onto their infants. Complete and utter attention to the sword was their only way: they demanded the most enduring iron, the finest temper, and their devotion became like that between priest and deity. A sword touching ground was a sword gravely dishonored. And every single Renshai sought Valhalla as his final reward.

Ra-khir had done his best to understand and support every detail of the Renshai way, yet he had clearly failed. His wife was dead. His sons hated him for reasons he could not fathom. Saviar and Calistin had done worse than abandon him; they had not found him worthy of a simple "good-bye."

Or did they? Ra-khir wondered if he had mislaid the conversation. He had lost track of time so often since Kevral's death. Things happened in a floating fog, done but not remembered. Reality and dream mingled inseparably, but neither brought him the knowledge he needed. His sons had not said a word before departing. They were good young men, raised right, which meant the fault fell on their father. And that left Ra-khir with the glaring question that had troubled him since before he had left Erythane. *What did I say? What did I do to make them hate me?*

Ra-khir could not recall ever feeling so alone, so very lost. He had faced demons and armies, treachery and betrayal, even stood on the perfect fields of Asgard, spoken to gods, and looked upon Valhalla. All of these things he had done with trepidation, yet with courage. Kevral's death had shaken him as nothing else ever had, and it seemed so very senseless. She had courted death even before he had first met her, when he believed her a boy, taunting him on the knights' practice grounds. Like all Renshai, she had rushed recklessly into every battle, desperately seeking the glorious death that would earn her eternity in Valhalla.

Yet, Kevral had never died. And, as the years passed, it had seemed as if she never would. Like Colbey Calistinsson himself, the more she hurled herself at danger, the more skilled she became until it seemed inevitable that the death she sought would always evade her. It was a paradox that perplexed the most competent Renshai, but it had secretly pleased Ra-khir. Despite being a consummate Renshai, Kevral had seemed destined to live to a ripe, old age. So destined, in fact, that Ra-khir had unconsciously come to count upon it. But she had not even lived long enough to meet her own grandchildren.

She's in Valhalla, Ra-khir reminded himself for the thousandth time. *The boys will name a grandchild for her, and she will look down upon her young namesake and guide her every sword stroke.* Yet doubts descended upon Ra-khir, as they always did. Kevral had battled demons, kings, and immortals. Though it had occurred in battle, her death fighting a mortal Northman had seemed so unnecessary, so ordinary. He worried the *Valkyries* might find it too inglorious to warrant Valhalla.

And there was still the item of the spirit spiders. Ra-khir had been present when Kevral got bitten by one, had heard the elves proclaim that the creatures fed upon their victims' souls. Later, Kevral had told Ra-khir that the Fates had proclaimed her intact. She had a soul, and she could still find Valhalla. Those words had never fully reassured him, however. He worried she had spoken a lie only to assuage his fears. What if Kevral had no soul? What if she never found Valhalla? The thought was too terrible for him to contemplate.

Enough! Angrily, Ra-khir chased doubt from his mind. He had dwelt too long upon his anxieties, upon his losses. The time had come to find himself again, to display the honor and courage that had, heretofore, defined his life. Right or wrong, Kevral had made her choice. Overconfident Kevral, her peers had called her; and, if that audaciousness had led to her ultimate demise, it was also the quality that had drawn him to marry her. Kevral had died the way she had lived, battling foolishness and injustice without a hint of fear.

Finding himself withdrawing into his thoughts again, Ra-khir forced himself to focus on his surroundings. Again, he marveled at the decorative patterns of the leaves and flowers, found familiarity in the pocked roadway, where the tracks of boots, hooves, and cartwheels marked the way. The few passersby waved cheerily at Ra-khir, and he tipped his hat in silent greeting to each and every one. Birds twittered in the treetops, flitting between branches and sending showers of berries down upon the trail. Ra-khir heard a few tap down on his hat and wondered how disheveled he must look. It never failed to astound him how the older knights, especially his father, managed to look pristine and proper in every circumstance. Ra-khir always felt gritty and sweat-slicked, and his clothing seemed to require cleaning and pressing from the instant he decided to wear it. Though as long as Ra-khir's, Kedrin's hair never knew a knot, while Ra-khir's seemed to snarl in a mere whisper of breeze.

As dusk fell over the road, forest gradually gave way to tended fields and scattered buildings. Silver Warrior slowed to a walk to avoid the ankle-turning stones until they became packed into cobbles. His hooves clopped against the solid stonework, and he lowered his long, white neck to study every footfall.

Ra-khir found his own attention trained on the upcoming village. At first, he thought a herd of animals ran loose inside it; but, as he drew closer, he realized the movement came from gathered people. They stood at the border, clearly awaiting something momentous. The children ran in giggling circles, trailing long strings of knotted rags. The adults stood, attentively facing the roadway and Ra-khir. His heart quickened, and he wondered if he should skirt the town. He hated to think he might have interrupted an important celebration: perhaps a significant marriage or a local holiday.

As they drew closer, Silver Warrior's gait grew increasingly slower until each hoof fall landed with a singular, unrhythmical thump. The crowd stood in silent contemplation. Even the children went still, some to stare and others to hide behind parental legs. Finally, Ra-khir drew his steed to a halt in front of the line of waiting people.

A long silence followed. No one seemed to know what to say or do. Finally, Ra-khir executed the most formal bow he could from atop his charger, flourishing his hat in a genteel motion.

Applause followed Ra-khir's bow, gracious and loud. One man stepped forward and also bowed, his head nearly touching the roadway. "Welcome Knight of Erythane. Thank you for gracing our town with your presence."

A cheer went up. Rags of various colors fluttered through the air, and the bolder children screeched excitedly. Others peeked out from behind their parents.

This is for me? Shocked, Ra-khir could think of nothing to do but introduce himself, "I am Sir Ra-khir Kedrin's son, Knight to the Erythanian and Béarnian kings: His Grace, King Humfreet, and His Majesty, King Griff."

Cheers and more applause followed his pronouncement, as if he had performed some spectacular feat. Embarrassed by their attention, Ra-khir found himself staring at the blue-and-gold ribbons braided into Silver Warrior's snowy mane. Knightly honor decreed he remain properly dignified and in control at all times. He had not done that over the last week; but he had, apparently, managed to maintain the image.

The spokesman smiled. "Welcome to Dunford, Sir Ra-khir. Have you time to join us for a meal? Our inn is not fancy, but the food is better than tolerable."

The entire group seemed to hold their breaths collectively, awaiting his answer.

Though desperately hungry, and even a bit tired, Ra-khir wanted nothing more than to find a few answers and move onward. However, his honor as a knight would not allow him to insult good people who, he now realized, had gathered solely for him. "I would love to join you all for a better than tolerable meal."

Another cheer went up from the crowd. They stepped aside to allow Ra-khir to pass.

Ra-khir dismounted in a single, fluid motion. Flicking back his cape, he seized Silver Warrior's wide leather bridle by the cheek strap spanning between decorative conches. He flipped the reins free and gathered them into his gloved left hand. The horse regarded its master through one dark eye, its delicately arched neck sheened with foam and sweat. "Hey, old boy," Ra-khir whispered, and an ear twitched sideways to listen.

With his hands full of bridle and reins, Ra-khir could spare nothing for his clothing. His tabard hung askew, his black silk shirt lay wrinkled and sweat-plastered to his chest, and the angle of his broadsword was completely wrong. Knight-Captain Kedrin would verbally flay him, but the citizens of Dunford did not even seem to notice.

The speaker and two others led the way. Everyone else walked alongside Ra-khir in a great band, chattering amongst themselves. Ra-khir tried not to listen, but he could not help overhearing parents telling their children the significance of a knightly visit. They spoke of ancient legends and how the word of a knight should be trusted implicitly. To hear them tell it, the Knights of Erythane were the human incarnations of honesty and honor, and their word was absolute law. They pointed out his colors: the blue and gold of Béarn and the black and orange or Erythane, worn at all times by every knight. The children ogled the broadsword at his hip, and some reached out to touch him or his horse as though such a thing might heal them of afflictions.

For the first time since leaving Erythane, Ra-khir secretly wished his father had let him quit the knights. The attention, though kind, unnerved him. He would rather ride off immediately with a handful of jerky and a few answers. Though accustomed to dreary, long-winded formality, he found himself saddled with all-too-human impatience. Yet, he had no choice but to display the honor of his kind, to weather the hospitality of his hosts, and to hope the Renshai did not get too far ahead of him meanwhile.

Though large for a village inn, the building could hold only half the residents at one time. The women and children veered away from the mud-and-stone building, pausing only to well-wish, curtsy, or touch their guest. Obliged to respond to each and every one, Ra-khir bowed what seemed like a million times, spoke several hundred thanks, and granted all verbalized requests for light contact. Some simply touched a sleeve or a glove, others kissed the hem of his cape or tabard, while the children seemed to favor a stroke of Silver Warrior's lathered chest or flank.

At length, only the men remained, streaming into the inn or talking in small groups. A stable boy approached Ra-khir and lowered his head.

Ra-khir granted him a grand bow, which brought a smile to the young man's lips.

"Beggin' youse pardons, sir. May I tends to youse horse?"

Ra-khir pursed his lips. The vast majority of the knight's chargers got their care from grooms, but Ra-khir had always insisted on tending Silver Warrior himself. In this circumstance, however, it seemed insulting to put the horse before his many eager hosts. Reluctantly releasing the bridle, he nodded. Worried they might not allow him to pay for anything, Ra-khir slipped the boy a couple of silvers. "He's very special." A whole litany of needs sprang to his tongue, but he knew better than to speak them. This youngster knew exactly how to treat a fine animal, and the payoff would see to it that Silver Warrior received the best of care. "But getting a bit long in the tooth."

The stable boy pocketed the silver and nodded. "I'll sees ta it the ol' boy gits plenty o' lovin' cares."

"Thank you."

Several men gestured for Ra-khir to enter the building, and he did so at their urging. Afraid to cause a pile-up at the entrance, he walked the length of the common room to a large, round table in the farthest corner. The instant he chose a seat, the men of Dunford rushed to fill the nearest ones like children playing one-chair-less. Soon, men filled every position, scooting chairs and tables, while others found the best places to stand.

Though uncomfortably closed-in, Ra-khir suffered in silence. His honor prevented him from demanding breathing room or, even, from shedding a cape or tabard from his oppressive amount of clothing. He did, however, remove his hat and gloves, as was proper inside any establishment. "Hello," he said.

A hundred hellos answered him, like a loud, uncoordinated echo.

Ra-khir cleared his throat, feeling it impolite to rush right into business. The gesture resulted in a painful cough, his throat dry and dusty from travel.

In an instant, a barmaid appeared at Ra-khir's shoulder, clutching a mug of light-colored ale. He had no idea how she had negotiated the crowd so quickly. "Here, sirra," she said, placing the mug in front of him on the table. "This is for you, courtesy of Lenn." She gestured toward the bar. "He said to tell you the house special is on the way."

Ra-khir followed the movement of her arm to a portly, middle-aged man wearing an apron over his linens. He threw a friendly salute toward the knight.

Ra-khir returned the salute more grandly and briskly; he knew no other way. "Tell him, thank you. And to keep track of my tab."

"He said to tell you . . ." The girl took a deep breath, clearly trying to quote her boss exactly right, ". . . if you try to pay, he'll break your arms."

"Ah!" Ra-khir could not help smiling. "How can I refuse such a gracious invitation?" He sifted a few coppers from his purse and pressed them into her hand. "Did he say anything about not tipping the staff?"

Her fingers closed over the coins, and she threw a surreptitious glance toward Lenn.

"Don't tell him, eh? I like my arms the way they are." Ra-khir distracted Lenn by rising and making a formal bow of appreciation in his direction.

Lenn bowed back, then turned and disappeared into the kitchen. Other serving girls pressed through the crowd, amid a sudden flurry of drink and food orders throughout the common room. Apparently, serving the knight cued the others. Had Ra-khir known that bit of etiquette, he would have ordered before entering; his throat felt parched, and his stomach rumbled.

"Thank you, sirra," the girl whispered before diving into the crowd to take her share of orders.

Ra-khir remained stiffly formal, as his title dictated. He glanced at the faces around his table: sunburned, dust-etched, wrinkled, nodding to each in turn before asking, "I wondered if a group of warriors preceded me to Dunford, about three hundred strong and in need of supplies."

Murmurs ran through the crowd, denying such a sighting. Only after the noise died did one man speak alone, "Sir Knight, I did not see such an army. But, only two days ago, I sold my wares to the beams to a group of five men who packed out my cured and fresh meats in a horse-drawn cart. Every one of them wore a sword at his hip. They could be feeding a multitude like you describe."

"Aye," said another. "And they bought out my cheeses, didn't care the type."

"And my vegetables," piped in a third.

Suddenly, every memory was jogged, and several started talking at once about the clothing, foodstuffs, and other necessities they, a wife, or a friend had sold to this apparently enormous group.

Ra-khir had no doubt they spoke of the Renshai, glad the tribe had shown the sense to mostly remain in hiding. Even smaller villages did not take well to the sudden appearance of a militia.

A man swaggered up to Ra-khir's table, ignoring the elbows jabbed at him by his peers. "Sir Knight," he slurred, huffing fetid breath on all of those around him. Clearly, he had started his drinking hours earlier. "There were Renshai in the woods. A friend of mine barely escaped with his life."

"Ignore him," those nearby suggested. "He's always—"

But Ra-khir could not afford to dismiss him. "Renshai, you say?"

"Renshai," the man repeated. In some parts of the world, it was considered a swear word too vile to speak. "They all carried swords, even the women and the tykes, he said."

"That sounds like Renshai." Ra-khir had no choice but to encourage him. "Are you certain they attacked him, though?"

"They're Renshai," the man reminded, as if this was enough to guarantee violence. "He barely escaped with his life."

"So . . ." Ra-khir tried carefully, ". . . they wounded him."

"Cor, no!" The man made a wild gesture that sent others ducking and scurrying to avoid getting hit. "Renshai don't wound. They get holt of a man, they kill him . . . brutally."

Ra-khir heaved a large sigh. It seemed unnecessary to point out the ludicrous flaws in the drunkard's statement. If three hundred Renshai wished to catch a man, he would be caught. And, if they intended him harm, he would be harmed. "I do not believe your friend was ever in any danger."

The drunkard froze in his strange and awkward position, arms akimbo. Whispers spread through the common room, then died to silence. The group hung on Ra-khir's next pronouncement.

"It is true that Renshai are skilled warriors and that their women learn warfare alongside their men."

The crowd did not discuss Ra-khir's words, clearly awaiting the "but" that had to follow.

Ra-khir did not disappoint. "*But* . . . in all other ways, they are like every Westerner."

"Westerner." The word swept the room. One man finally addressed Ra-khir directly. "You consider them Westerners, Sir Knight? Like us? Our allies?"

Ra-khir could scarcely believe they did not. "Of course, the Renshai are Westerners. They have lived in the West for centuries and have wielded their swords in defense of Béarn's heirs. They are more than our allies. They are . . . *us!*"

Now conversations flared like fires throughout the common room. The drunkard toddled off, shaking his head. The serving girl seized the sudden lull to slip through the crowd and deposit a plate of food in front of Ra-khir. The tantalizing aroma of roast pork and roots, boiled greens and brown bread tickled his nostrils. Dirt-specked saliva filled his mouth, lubricating his throat.

Cautiously picking up a steaming root, Ra-khir took a small bite, closed his mouth, and savored the sweetly starchy flavor. Luckily, it was not hot enough to burn his tongue, and he followed it with a swig of what turned out to be excellent ale.

By the time Ra-khir swallowed, the first question reached him. "Knights of Erythane cannot lie, can they?"

Though more interested in his food, Ra-khir knew the conversation had to take precedence. He had an obligation to help a society overcome ignorant bigotry, especially against his family. "It is against our code of honor to do so. The Order would never maintain a knight who had knowingly spoken falsehoods." The explanation seemed unnecessary. Even if knights spent their entire existence spewing lies, anyone answering such a query would say nothing different than Ra-khir had. "A knight would willingly die rather than forsake his honor in such a way."

Again, the common room buzzed with conversation, this time accompanied by nods. Ra-khir pounced on the opportunity to eat and drink, cursing the deeply ingrained manners that forced him to do so slowly and with decorum. He wanted nothing more than to tear into that food, without having to worry what dripped down his chin, what soiled his uniform, or what noises accompanied his feast. But, ever the proper knight, Ra-khir attended to every manner as the men in the common room came to a consensus. His father's words, an echo of his own, haunted him. *Remember this: anything you say or do reflects back on the Knights of Erythane, on King Humfreet and on King Griff, who you represent.*

At last, the largest man at his table, who now also nursed food and ale, spoke. "Sir Ra-khir, we have been taught since infancy to dread Renshai. They are the demons who steal away naughty children in the night, the cause of every inexplicable death because they need to drink our blood to keep their youth and vitality. But none of us has encountered a Renshai, at least not that we recognized as anything but another man. If a Knight of Erythane swears that these self-same Renshai are our fellows and our allies, we have no choice but to believe and trust you."

Ra-khir nodded with respect though his thoughts raced. He could scarcely believe he had solved a centuries-old problem with a single proclamation. *Is it really this easy?* He knew the truth, had witnessed it in Béarn and in Erythane, where they knew firsthand that the Renshai served as faithful bodyguards to the princes and princesses, where Renshai assisted them in every skirmish. It did not take much to scrape off the veneer of tolerance and find a teeming mass of festering hatred beneath it. Still, a surface layer of forbearance was a start. "Leave them in peace, and the Renshai will not bother you. Ask them for assistance in wars and battles, and they will happily provide it."

After that, the male citizenry of Dunford dug into their repasts, and Ra-khir finally got a chance to eat—unhurriedly and with proper etiquette.

CHAPTER 24

Hundreds of years have not bred the ferocity out of wolves, nor Renshai either.
                                                    —*Councillor Zaysharn of Béarn*

RA-KHIR SHOVED HIS WISHES to the back corner of his mind, choosing instead to spend the night at the inn in Dunford. His heart told him he could survive days without sleep, that need would keep him moving long after his limbs collapsed and his eyes refused to remain open. But Ra-khir knew better. Whatever he might find himself capable of tolerating, he could not inflict that nightmare on Silver Warrior. He needed information as well as speed, to spread the true word about the Renshai, and to get enough rest to handle all situations properly. Whatever else he wanted or needed, he was a Knight of Erythane first. Sleepless men did not make the best or most rational decisions.

The familiar work of readying Silver Warrior soothed Ra-khir. He tended every hair with curry and brush, though the young groom had already done an impressive job for him. He rewove the blue-and-gold ribbons through mane and tail, his thoughts directed and certain. He knew which route the Renshai must have taken. Banned from the West and North, they could only go eastward. Reins in hand, Ra-khir cinched the saddle into place, gave Silver Warrior a solid affectionate pat with his gloved hand, and prepared to mount.

A man standing nearby sidled closer, just enough to violate Ra-khir's personal space. Without a hint of discomfort, Ra-khir turned.

As the knight's gaze swept him, the man's face turned from pale pink to blushing scarlet. "Sir Knight," he blurted out. "I . . . I don't know if this is significant . . ."

Ra-khir smiled and nodded encouragingly. "Please tell me."

"Well, the night before the . . . the Renshai visited, a man came all the way from Erythane."

"Another knight?" Ra-khir puzzled over the news, seeking its significance. He knew of no one who had made the journey.

"Not a knight, a plain middle-aged man. He carried a pocket load of Northern coins." The Dunforder shook his head, "Several gold pieces, more silver and copper. He bought a round for the regulars in the name of a nephew who he said had been murdered."

Ra-khir's brows beetled. Killings happened in a city as large as Erythane, and sometimes relatives attributed foul motives to even the most accidental of deaths. "What name was this?"

The man's shoulders rose and fell, accompanied by a small huff of breath. "I don't recall. But he spent quite a bit of money on gewgaws and trinkets, women and luxury clothing, including a pair of silk shoes and a pointed cap with an enormous tassel. When he left, though, he was still a wealthy man."

"Hmmm." Ra-khir had no idea who this man might be, nor if the information held any importance, but he appreciated knowing anything out of the ordinary. "Thank you for letting me know, kind sir."

"You're quite welcome."

Ra-khir flipped the reins over Silver Warrior's head and prepared to mount again, only to be interrupted by another man.

"Excuse me, sir."

Though impatient to chase down his children, Ra-khir obligingly gave the stranger his attention. The Dunforder wore gray linens with long, tattered sleeves. A bow and quiver lay slung over his shoulder. A mop of brown hair flopped over his head and half his face.

"I thought you should know that those Renshai aren't the only army in the area."

That gained Ra-khir's full interest. "Odd that. Who else is out there?"

"Northmen, by the look of them, maybe some Erythanians, too. Lots of blonds, talking in some odd language. I'd have thought those your Renshai, except they had spears and axes and everyone knows Renshai only use swords. Armor, too. And there weren't any women."

Ra-khir's heart seemed to stop beating, and his hand raised to his suddenly tight chest. "How . . . how many did you see?"

"Hundreds. They didn't come to town, but I'm a hunter. I saw them on the road."

"Thank you." Bad as it sounded, Ra-khir appreciated having the news. There could be only one reason the Northmen had chosen to travel south and east. They were following the Renshai. It only remained to be seen whether they did so to ascertain the Renshai kept their vow to leave the Westlands, or to brutally slaughter them all before they reached the East. "Thank you for the information and the hospitality." He swung up into the saddle, taking the reins.

"Knights of Erythane are always welcome here," the hunter assured him, stepping away from Ra-khir and Silver Warrior.

Tipping his hat to the crowd gathered to see him off, Ra-khir trotted toward the packed dirt roadway.

East of Dunford and north of the Southern Weathered Mountains, Calistin dragged into his first Western city, his tattered, filthy cloak rain-plastered to skin and jerkin and his hair in wild spikes. The sky had barely lost the sun beyond its western horizon, leaving a cloud-swollen haze that guided him through the muddy streets. He slogged between rows of simple cottages, their thatched roofs swollen with water, their inhabitants locked in against the weather. Bedraggled chickens huddled beneath the overhangs.

Calistin followed the sound of a creaking sign through the gloom, to a sagging wooden tavern. The sign itself had cracked and peeled from wear. Once, it had clearly borne a design, but only bits of paint remained, including the Common letters "T", "V", and "N". Smoke curled from the chimney. Glad for a chance to rest and eat, Calistin tripped the latch.

The door swung open to reveal a cozy interior filled with nine round tables, a rickety wooden bar with stools, and an assortment of men. Two young barmaids wove through the crowd, and a barkeep stood behind the counter tapping the contents of various barrels into bowls and mugs. When he found no open tables, Calistin flopped onto a stool in front of the bar and studied the other customers.

The men ranged in age from older teens to gray-bearded elders. Most had leathered faces and callused hands, and their hair colors ranged from Béarnian dark to sandy blond or grizzled white. Many ate from coarsely hammered plates and drank from lopsided bowls. The odors of roasted meat, bread, and tubers perfumed the air.

The barkeep, a fat, bearded man with freckled arms, approached Calistin and swiped a dirty rag across the place the Renshai had chosen. It looked no cleaner when he finished, and the rag left a sticky film. Leaning forward, he smiled patronizingly. "So, boy. What can I do for you today?"

Calistin took an immediate dislike to the barkeep who spoke the Western tongue in the weird, high-pitched singsong people usually reserved for animals and infants. "You can get me some food and a mug of ale."

"Ale?" The barkeep's lids rose over eyes recessed like a pig's. He laughed wildly, as if responding to some unspoken joke.

Deadly serious, Calistin watched the barkeep's antics with waning patience.

Finally, the barkeep explained. "Aren't you a bit young for ale, son?"

Calistin gritted his teeth, fighting a rising wash of temper. "First, I'm not your son. Second, I'm a man and perfectly capable of determining when I'm hungry and thirsty. And, third, I wasn't aware ale had an age requirement."

The barkeep stopped laughing. His massive elbows dropped to the counter in front of Calistin, and he leaned in. His breath reeked of alcohol and rotting teeth. "I find that children don't handle their liquor well, and they often don't have money to pay for what they're asking for."

Enraged by the insult, Calistin did not even consider the fact that the man had a point. He carried no coinage. He never had to worry about paying; no matter where he went, no matter what he wanted, someone always jumped in to cover him. In a blink, the barkeep lay on the floor, a sword at his throat in the hands of an angry Renshai. "Just get me a plate of food and a gods-be-damned mug of ale." In the same tight-lipped, lethal tone, Calistin added, "Please."

The barkeep lay in stunned silence, his eyes round as coins.

It all happened so quickly, so quietly, that the conversations continued unabated. Calistin withdrew and sheathed his sword in a single motion, utterly unruffled. In contrast, the barkeep scuttled from the floor and ran to his casks, shaking uncontrollably.

Calistin surveyed the crowd again, studying the men with an expert eye. Within moments, one of the barmaids sidled over to him, placing down a plate containing a greasy chicken leg, a pile of whipped tubers, and a handful of crusty brown bread. She placed a mug beside him, turning her back to the barkeep. "Listen, honey," she purred. "The food's all right, 'cause I served up that; but I ain't vouching for the ale. Oscore's been known to spit in the bowl of anyone he don't like, and I'm bettin' he might've pissed in your'n."

"Thanks for the warning." Calistin looked past her to the other men in the tavern. "Do you happen to know if any of them is considered a decent swordsman?" He selected the one most suitable, a well-muscled tall man with a long oval, clean-shaven face. "Maybe him in the reddish cloak?"

The barmaid followed Calistin's gaze, then laughed. "That's Burnold, the blacksmith. A wizard with a hammer, but he wouldn't hit a mule if it kicked over his forge and set his house on fire. He can make a decent weapon, but he'd never use one."

Calistin grunted. "Too bad. He's built for war."

The barmaid giggled, looked at Calistin's somber expression, and stopped immediately. "Sorry 'bout that. I thought you was joking."

Calistin shoveled a handful of tubers into his mouth. They tasted bland but filling, and he found himself gulping down another before he could consider his manners. For the moment, his gut ruled his head. "I don't joke," Calistin announced around the mouthful.

"Oh, I'm so sorry." The barmaid reacted as if he said he had lost a body part. "I love laughing. It just feels . . . good."

Calistin shrugged. His brothers exchanged silly comments all the time, but he never found the humor in them. "So," he reminded. "Your best warrior?"

"Oh." The barmaid swept a glance over the patrons. "You're in luck. He's still here." She inclined her head to a table in the farthest corner near the fireplace. "Karruno's the big one in black."

Calistin followed her motion to a bulky man swathed in a well-laundered black cloak. Nearly middle-aged, he had a rugged face that might have looked handsome if not for a jagged scar running the length of his left cheek. Unlike the blacksmith, he wore a sword in his waistband and a dagger thrust through as well. He sat back in his chair, only a mug in front of him, and his two companions cradled their own drinks as well.

Knowing how swiftly a challenge can become a brawl, Calistin examined all three of the men while he bolted the bread. The one she called Karruno had the mannerisms and dress of a fighting man, though his subtler movements and the draw of his muscles told Calistin otherwise. His abilities, whatever they might be, came solely of practice. He lacked the proper depth of sinew, the perfect placement of muscular origins and insertions that would make him a natural-born warrior. Calistin knew that a good teacher and experience could make a world of difference, but a man without the inherent advantages of build could never truly become the best.

Finished with the tubers and bread, Calistin looked at his ale. "This is no good?"

She wrinkled her nose. "I wouldn't drink it."

Calistin rose, mug in one hand, chicken leg in the other. "Can you get me one that is?"

The barmaid shook her head slightly. "Oscore handles all the drinks." She considered. "I could get you some water, if you're just thirsty."

Calistin remained standing. "None of that reused bathwater. As clean as you can find, please."

"I'll see what I can do, honey," she said as she headed around the bar.

Calistin tore through the chicken leg with his teeth, dropped the bone on his plate, then headed across the room toward Karruno. As he walked, he licked grease and mashed tubers from his fingers, then wiped them on britches only just beginning to dry from the rain.

Ignoring the curious stares that followed him across the barroom, Calistin approached Karruno. Without waiting for a break in the conversation, he announced, "Karruno, I challenge you to a fight."

Karruno stopped speaking and looked up. "Are you talking to me, boy?"

"Man," Calistin corrected.

"What?"

"I'm a man."

The three Westerners glanced at one another, condescending smiles pasted on their faces.

"Very well," Karruno said through his wicked grin. "Are you talking to me, young *man?*"

"Yes," Calistin confirmed, still clutching his ale. "You are Karruno, the best swordsman in these parts?"

The companion to Karruno's left, a tall, heavyset man with a short, graying beard spoke next. "That's him. Expert soldier when he's not slopping pigs or slaughtering chickens."

Karruno punched his companion in the arm before turning his attention back to Calistin. "What do you want, little stranger? Can't you see we're busy talking?"

Accustomed to immediate and absolute consideration, Calistin found these men irritatingly dense. "I told you. I want to fight you."

Karruno tossed back the last of his drink. "You mean a duel?"

"Yes."

"Why? Does my mere existence offend you, little man?"

Karruno's companions laughed.

As usual, Calistin found the comment more grating than amusing. "A true warrior needs no reason for combat but accepts every challenge for the sheer joy of battle."

Karruno's brows rose. "Is that right?"

Calistin had never had to defend a Renshai proverb. "Of course it's right."

"Then," Karruno said, looking around the table, "I guess I'm not a 'true warrior,' at least not by your cute little definition."

Calistin knew an insult when he heard one. "I'm challenging all the best swordsmen of the world." He intended to enter the Northlands with a powerful reputation behind him. When he found Valr Magnus, he would not just best the Northman, but destroy him utterly. From swordmaster to buffoon, from warrior to coward, the North's great master of the sword would fall from history, from memory, from Valhalla.

"Why?"

Calistin had no intention of revealing his life story to strangers. He simply wanted to battle, to diffuse his anger in a wild flurry of combat, to learn the tricks of the best *ganim* swordmasters before he met the challenge of Valr Magnus. "Because it suits me."

Karruno clearly did not appreciate that explanation. "Suits you, eh?" He tossed knowing glances around the table. "It suits him to challenge all the best swordsmen in the world."

"Of course it does." The last of the trio finally spoke. Short, broad-faced and coarse-featured, he sported a dark mustache speckled with foam. "If he wins, he looks like a great hero. If he loses, it doesn't matter. He's only a boy, after all."

"I'm a man," Calistin corrected for the third time. "And my name is Calistin."

"What's in it for me, Calistin?" Karruno leaned forward, lacing his fingers on the table in front of his empty mug. "If I lose, I look the fool. If I win, it's simply foregone." He made a dismissive gesture. "Now, go home, boy. You've wasted enough of our time."

Karruno's companions made similar motions, and all three turned away from Calistin. They leaned forward, as if thoroughly engrossed in the conversation they had long ago lost.

Fire lashed through Calistin's veins. His nostrils flared. He understood that these men did not know him or his abilities, but their willingness to turn their backs to him meant they considered him no threat. And that was the gravest insult of all. Without another thought, Calistin dumped the contents of his mug over Karruno's head.

Ale cascaded in a foamy, golden wave, soaking Karruno's dark mop of hair, his no-longer-meticulous black cloak, and pooling in his lap. All three men were on their feet in an instant, rounding on Calistin. "You gods-damned little pissant!" Karruno yelled. "I'll wring your scrawny neck."

It was exactly the reaction Calistin wanted. His hand slid to his hilt, but he waited for his opponent to draw first.

The bar fell silent, except for the sound of ale dripping from Karruno's clothing. Every eye in the place went suddenly to their table.

Oscore shouted from across the room, "Take it outside!"

"Fine!" Karruno glared down at Calistin, a full head and shoulders taller than the Renshai. "You want to fight, we'll fight." He made a stiff motion toward the door.

The tavern emptied in a rush, as every man inside funneled to the streets to watch the battle. Soon, they formed an eager circle around the soggy farmer and Calistin. Karruno threw off his sodden cloak to reveal torn and soiled britches and a plain linen shirt. The sword and dagger still girded his waist. He shook ale from his hair.

"What's the end point?" Calistin asked calmly.

"First blood," Karruno growled, drawing his sword.

Faster than thought, Calistin drew, lunged, and retreated. "Done."

"What?" Karruno raised his sword arm to reveal a sticky trail of scarlet dribbling from the back of his hand. "Damn it. I wasn't ready yet."

Calistin shrugged. "Are you ready now?"

Sword drawn, Karruno crouched. "Yes."

Again, Calistin made a lightning draw-cut and resheathed the weapon in a single motion. "Done."

This time, a bright red line scratched across Karruno's forearm.

Karruno's face purpled. His fingers went white around his sword hilt. "Damn you to the pits, you smug little bastard! I'm going to kill you!" He sprang for Calistin in a wild fury.

Calistin easily dodged the assault. "So now the end point is death?" He did not wait for an acknowledgment. "Very well." His blade licked out only once through Karruno's furious assault and cut across the farmer's throat in a deep, fatal line.

Karruno's eyes went enormous with surprise. He dropped his sword and clutched at his throat, gasping in a single, bloody breath before collapsing to the ground.

"Done," Calistin said, wiping his blade on a soft cloth before returning it to its sheath.

For several moments, the crowd stood in stunned silence. Then some ran to Karruno, too late to help him but trying fruitlessly to do so. Others charged into the streets, swallowed by the shadows. A few remained in place, staring at Karruno's body or openmouthed and furious at Calistin. No one challenged him, however.

Finished with his task, Calistin headed out into another night of lonely sleep in the cold, wet Western forests.

CHAPTER 25

Cowardice is always wrong, but it is acceptable to abandon a battle if it can only result in killing friends.
—Colbey Calistinsson

THE SUN BEAMED OVER the western forests, promising a beautiful day of travel, and Saviar tried his best to savor it. He had discovered the purpose his life had lacked for weeks, he had found his twin brother, and the funk that had settled over him since his mother's death finally seemed to have lifted. No one was dying or mourning to excess. No one was stalking or harassing him to the point of violent confrontation. Even the denizens of the forest seemed oblivious to the two Renshai in their midst. Birds flitted between the trees, exchanging happy twitters. Squirrels scrounged unhurriedly for nuts, and tiny lizards sunned themselves on rocks still damp from the previous day's rain, moving only when a shadow fell directly across them.

Still, Saviar had to force himself to revel in the warm, clear comfort of balmy weather and the fresh aromas of evergreens and undergrowth. He and Subikahn would devote themselves to a conventional heroism his life had sorely lacked, and he anticipated so much exhilaration and worthiness in their future. It had taken immense tragedy to get them to this point, but those misfortunes were mostly behind them. He wished he could find the will to enjoy every glad moment his mind and heart could spare.

Yet, despite the weather, and Saviar's deliberate focus on positive thoughts, two days spent trudging silently through the western forests frayed at his mood. He had not given much thought to the journey, instead imaging himself and Subikahn performing heroic acts and earning grateful companionship, the finest drink, and plates heaped with fresh-cooked food. Between their feats of courage, the twins would discuss the time they had spent apart, learning great new insights about one another, and becoming ever closer.

Subikahn and circumstance, however, seemed absolutely determined to sabotage Saviar's glee. Whenever the redhead tried to engage his twin in conversation, his attempts resulted in gruff monosyllabic responses. No matter what he said, the topic veered to Subikahn's private dilemmas, which always resulted in an angry plea to let bitter secrets lie. Furthermore, Saviar had the feeling that his furtive brother was deliberately avoiding inhabited areas, forcing them to subsist on journey bread, weeds, and berries. Those seemed to satisfy the smaller, slighter Subikahn but left Saviar with a painful hole in his belly that further devastated his mood.

In a last desperate effort to revive his failing joy, Saviar whirled through a glittery sprinkle of sunlight. "So, Subi," he said, in the happiest tone he could muster. "Just tell me something good that's happened to you recently."

Subikahn jerked his head toward Saviar, clearly startled by the question. His black hair hung in stringy tangles, twined through with twigs and leaves. Though his lifelong brother, Subikahn looked strangely alien that day: his features so very Eastern, his skin darker than Saviar remembered. It seemed odd to Saviar how a months-long separation could make the most intimate friends and family appear so utterly foreign. "Something good?"

"Something good," Saviar insisted. "It can't be *that* hard."

"Talamir . . ." Subikahn fairly choked on the name, and Saviar thought he saw a welling tear. "He . . . he said I would definitely pass my tests of manhood."

Not wanting to ruin the moment, Saviar did not mention that it no longer mattered; they had both become men through warfare. Instead, he glommed onto the positive. It was the most words Subikahn had strung together since they had started on this journey. "Mama said the same to me."

"Mama did?" Subikahn's brow furrowed, and he shook his head dubiously. "Mama? Not a chance."

Saviar stopped walking to confront his brother directly. He felt the familiar ire rising, the one he thought he had finally fully shaken. The last remnants of his forced good mood drifted away like smoke. "What do you mean, 'not a chance'? You think I'm lying?"

"I just can't see Mama saying it. No maneuver in the history of Renshai was ever done well enough to please Kevralyn Tainharsdatter."

They both added simultaneously, "Unless Calistin did it."

Stilted laughter followed. Saviar could not remember the last time he had found anything funny; but, oddly, even sharing a joke with his twin did little to lift his slumping spirits. The anger he had kept suppressed for two days seeped out, no longer containable.

Subikahn added soberly, "Well, he really is pretty amazing."

"And he's the first to admit it," Saviar could not help growling. "Damn it, now you've wrecked my mood."

"Sorry," Subikahn said, not sounding it at all. "But it seems to me you started this conversation."

"Yeah," Saviar said, not bothering to track the thread all the way back to its beginning. "I told you what Mama said, and you called me a liar."

"I didn't," Subikahn protested. "I merely stated that Mama was never, shall we say, 'free' with her praise."

"But she did believe I'd pass my tests."

"All right."

"She did!"

Subikahn snapped, "I'm not arguing with you."

"No, but you don't believe me."

"If you say it happened, it happened. Saviar, I've never known you to lie."

At the moment, no words would have soothed Saviar. He fumed, for reasons he could not wholly explain. "You think you're a better swordsman than me. Don't you?"

Subikahn stopped walking to study his brother. "I'd be a poor excuse for a Renshai if I didn't believe I was a better swordsman than *everyone.*"

"You don't think you're better than Calistin."

Subikahn smiled. "Well, that would just be stupid."

Saviar could not understand why this conversation bothered him so much. He thought he had overcome his rage against his family, his belief that all of them had gone insane. Yet, he still found Subikahn's words an irresistible challenge. "Oh, but it's not stupid to think you're better than me?"

Subikahn heaved a deep sigh. "Look, Savi. We're both blooded, pretty much at the exact same moment. We're men now, tests or no. What does it matter who's better than who?"

"I don't know!" Saviar admitted, still shouting. "I don't know why it matters, but it does. It matters."

"Not to me."

Saviar turned away. His own irrationality frightened him, but it refused to go away. "So Talamir said you'd pass?"

"Virtually assured it."

Saviar grunted. "Well, if he's such a great *torke*, where is he? Why isn't he helping the Renshai when they need every sword arm?"

Subikahn's jaw set. "Leave Talamir out of this."

"Why?"

"Because I said to." Subikahn's tone went dangerously flat.

Saviar knew he had gained the upper hand, and he found himself incapable of not exploiting it. "Why? Was he detained by a phalanx of Eastern *girls?* Is he too much of a coward to face real Northmen?"

"That's it!" Subikahn threw up his hands. "Draw your weapon, Savi."

"Did he get waylaid by a terrifying band of roving *squirrels?*"

"Draw!" Subikahn hollered.

Saviar turned away, that gesture alone an implicit declaration of war. "If you'd just tell me what's going on instead of leaving me—"

"Draw, you obnoxious lumbering bastard, or I'll cut you down where you stand."

Saviar whirled back to face an angry Renshai with sword in hand. Subikahn's face had gone red as brick clay, his knuckles white around his hilt.

They had sparred before, of course; but always under the watchful eye of a *torke*, who could step in if a wayward stroke began to fall. Realizing he had gone too far, Saviar relented. "I'm sorry, Subi. I didn't mean any of it. It's just I'm so sick of—"

Subikahn was not so forgiving. "Draw, you sniveling coward. Or are you afraid to face a man half your size?"

"Fine." Saviar could no longer back down without appearing craven. "But, if I win, you have to tell me *everything*."

"All right!" There was acid in Subikahn's tone. "But, if I win, you have to shut up about Talamir. And about my having secrets."

"Fine!"

"Forever!"

"Forever?" Jarred completely from his rage, Saviar stared. "You mean, you'll *never* tell me *anything?*"

"Maybe never. If you lose." Subikahn added in that same searing tone, "You're just worried because you know you're going to lose, aren't you?"

"Not a chance!" Saviar drew his swords and lunged at his brother.

Subikahn met the attack with a deft in-and-out dodge and parry maneuver that put Saviar instantly on the defensive. Saviar freed his left sword and threw up the right to catch Subikahn's blade. Steel rang against steel, driving the birds into sudden silence and sending the squirrels scampering.

Saviar threw off Subikahn and stepped back to realign. Suddenly realizing they had never chosen an end point, Saviar announced, "It's first would-be fatal touch that wins it."

"Agreed." Subikahn dove in with a vicious offensive that left Saviar scrambling to defend. He met each blow with a block, dodge, or parry but did not manage a single riposte. Finally, an opening presented itself, and Saviar thrust for Subikahn's gut. He met empty air as the smaller man skipped aside, then disappeared into the brush.

Surprised by his brother's odd, hiding tactic, Saviar spun to prevent an attack on his flank. "You're running away, you coward? Come out and face me like half a man."

No reply followed, and Saviar abruptly realized he had absolutely no idea where his brother had gone. He lowered his body weight, moving constantly, graceful but erratic. He did not want to leave any openings for Subikahn to catch him unaware or from behind. Though rarely invoked, the Renshai maneuvers did include stealth and forest movement, lessons Subikahn had nearly single-handedly revived. *Where in Hel is he?*

The answer came as a blazing kidney stroke that Saviar barely dodged. For an instant, he lost his balance. A flurry of sword strokes followed as he sought to regain it, wedded only to defense until he was back in control. The strategy paid off. Soon, Saviar found himself not only stable and ready for attack, but in the superior position. Now sword to sword, he used a deadly combination of quickness, agility, and strength to batter at Subikahn, herding him steadily backward toward a waiting clump of nettles.

Now, Subikahn found himself wholly on the defense, only dodging the lethally accurate hammer blows of his twin because blocking sapped his strength. Pounded, his expression turned from cocky to concerned. Only his lithe movements spared him from two well-aimed blows, one to the side of the head and another to the throat.

Only then, as Saviar bore in one more time, did Subikahn blaze in a thrust for Saviar's gut. He moved like lightning, but his foot mired in detritus, slipping. His stroke went low, opening his upper defenses. Saviar slapped a triumphant, side of the sword "killing stroke" against Subikahn's ribs with bruising force.

Then, agony seared Saviar's left thigh as flesh parted before a line of exquisitely sharp steel. Against his will, his leg folded under him. He rolled from instinct, stopped short by pain so achingly intense it stole all focus. He found his swords raised in his defense without any conscious memory of hefting them, and Subikahn stood over him with an expression of helpless terror.

"Modi!" Trained to wall up pain and keep fighting, Saviar struggled to a stand. Subikahn's left-hand sword skewered the outer part of his thigh, resting solidly against the bone. "Mooodi!"

"I'm sorry," Subikahn said. "I'm so sorry. I didn't mean to—"

They had both seen many wounds before, as well as death itself. Yet, the image of his own leg encasing a sword, knowing his brother had inflicted the injury, left Saviar stunned for several silent moments. "Get it out," he finally said.

"But—" Subikahn started. Renshai training included only enough herbal lore to help prevent infection. They battled to the death, and survivors' scars were considered badges of honor. Nevertheless, they both knew to leave a penetrating object in place. Its removal would start bleeding they might not be able to staunch, the usual cause of death in combat.

Saviar did not care. The pain encompassed his entire being, and the area where steel wedged against bone was so excruciating it made coherent thought impossible. "Pull it out, damn it! Pull the damn thing out! Pull it out!"

"Savi, I'm so sorry. Please forgive me. I swear I didn't mean to—"

Saviar found himself incapable of concentrating on words. "Pull . . . it . . . out!" He braced his hands on the protruding hilt, his breathing turning to ragged gasps of anguish, "Subikahn, pull it out, or I'm killing . . . both of us."

"All right. Lie down." Subikahn gave his brother a light push.

It proved too much for Saviar's delicate balance. He collapsed, and the impact sent another shock of pain through his thigh. He tried to shift position, but his injured limb would not obey. "Gods! I can't move my leg."

Subikahn dropped to the ground beside Saviar. "Of course, you can't move your leg. It's pinned to the ground."

Pinned . . . Realization struck Saviar in a jolt. The blade had not just penetrated his thigh, it had run him through completely. His fall had buried the point in the dirt, fixing it in place.

Subikahn knelt over his fallen brother. "Savi, you know we're not supposed to remove—"

Saviar had taken all he could stand. He lunged toward his brother, seizing the fabric of his tunic, near the throat, in both hands. "Pull it out, Subikahn; or I'll pulverize you!"

Apparently wise enough to shut his mouth, Subikahn did not

mention that, affixed to the ground, Saviar could not pulverize a butterfly. "All right. Just let me prepare some bandages to stop the bleeding."

"Hurry," Saviar growled, releasing his brother. *Torke*'s lessons had often left him with a myriad of bruises and contusions; but, all of those together did not equal the pain he suffered now. He closed his eyes, listening to the sound of cloth tearing and rustling, invoking the Renshai mind techniques that usually allowed them to fight past the agony of even a fatal wound. "Hurry," he whispered.

"Ready," Subikahn announced. Something cold and sticky flooded the wound, its sting a welcome contrast to the blaring, biting agony. Then, the pain intensified, and Saviar felt steel slide backward through his thigh. The sword clanged against rock or wood, freed from his leg, and the sound shocked Saviar into opening his eyes.

Subikahn took no notice of this new distress. Instead, he stuffed wet rags into the hole in Saviar's leg, then wrapped it around with bandages so suffocatingly tight they rivaled the pain already in his thigh.

Saviar glanced to where he had heard the noise. Sure enough, Subikahn's sword lay in the dirt. The sight scandalized Saviar, even through his pain. "Your sword is . . . it's on the . . . ground."

"Yes." Subikahn acknowledged the most terrible crime in Renshai law. "I thrust it through my own brother. Nothing could dishonor it worse."

Subikahn had a point. He already needed to atone to the weapon, yet he made no move to do so. It was a process that would take weeks or months. Hoping to speed it along, Saviar sat up and said softly, "If it helps, I forgive you."

"You forgive me?" Subikahn's eyes were hollow, empty.

"I forgive you."

Tears glazed Subikahn's eyes into black marbles of self-loathing. "Well, I don't forgive me. I can't ever forgive me, and I doubt the gods or my sword can either." He caught Saviar into a frantic embrace. "I'm sorry, Saviar. I'm so so very sorry."

"I know you are." Saviar wrapped his arms around his brother. "But it's just as much my fault as yours. We knew better than to spar in anger, without *torke* present."

"But what if . . ." Subikahn could no longer hide the tears; they came out in his voice, even muffled against Saviar's tunic. ". . . what if I've . . . killed you?"

"Killed me?" Saviar remained in position, knowing Subikahn needed the contact. "Do I look dead to you?" He answered more from bravado than truth. They both knew what happened to badly wounded warriors, in spar as well as battle.

"What if I can't stop the bleeding?"

Saviar examined the bandages. "It's not soaking through. I don't see any red at all." Only then, he noticed scarlet splashes across the fallen leaves and a small puddle where he had lain. "Except what's already on the ground, and that's not a lot."

"What if it gets . . . tainted?"

Saviar knew the only possible reply and spoke it without need for consideration, "Then, I attack you, and you finish me off so I can die in battle and find Valhalla." He tried not to dwell too long on that point. Punctures, it seemed, nearly always infected; and the deeper the wound, the worse the outcome. He had never seen one all the way through a limb before. Those Renshai dying of disease or illness nearly always came to Calistin, trusting him to end their suffering in a way acceptable to the *Valkyries.*

"What if," Subikahn started in a voice so small Saviar had to strain to hear it, "I can't do it."

The suggestion was sacrilege. "Then," Saviar said firmly, disengaging from his brother, "you doom me to Hel." Not liking the turn of the conversation, he staggered to his feet. His left leg ached with the slightest pressure, and the muscles felt lax as winter weeds. He limped toward a sturdy mirack trunk, seeking a branch that could serve as a crutch.

Subikahn remained on the ground, looking as pitifully wronged as his sword. And sobbed.

CHAPTER 26

It is heroic and glorious to die for one's country. But, whoever has
seen the horrors of a battlefield knows it is far sweeter to live for it.
—General Santagithi

AS THE MILES DISAPPEARED beneath Silver Warrior's hooves, Ra-khir's thoughts gave way to a new cycle of worry. Now that he had received the warning, he could see the myriad boot and hoofprints stamped into the road. A large group of people had recently passed. He doubted the prints belonged to the Renshai, who had more likely forsaken the easy roadway for the deeper cover of the woods.

The sun stood high in the sky when Ra-khir discovered an enormous break in the foliage where a regiment of men and horses had broken through it. Leaves and twigs splashed across the roadway, and broken branches clung to shattered new growth trees and vines. Notches in the trees revealed where wild sword or ax slashes had injured them as men hacked through the undergrowth. Hoofprints packed down the brush to make a new and obvious opening into the forest.

Ra-khir followed, with trepidation. He heard no horn blasts or screams, no chiming of weapons slamming against one another. If a war had occurred, it was finished now, leaving the woods eerily silent. Still, he could not help wondering if he was about to enter combat. He did not fear it; he could hold his own in battle. The Knights of Erythane trained daily and to a superiority that any but a Renshai would envy.

A battle of this sort would also place Ra-khir in a precarious position. Assuming the situation was exactly as it appeared, if the Northmen had tracked down the fleeing Renshai and attacked them, Ra-khir had every right to join the cause of his sons. However, it seemed unlikely he would have such clear-cut answers before the situation forced him to take a side. He would not fight against Calistin and Saviar, of course; but killing Northmen while in the direct and on-duty service of the kings of Erythane and Béarn could have serious diplomatic consequences as well.

A more religious man might have prayed, but Ra-khir put his faith in himself and the rigid moral code he had vowed to follow. When he encountered the situation, his honor would tell him what to do.

All too soon, Silver Warrior whinnied a warning as they walked through a shattered copse of thistles to reveal the remains of a war. Crow wings thundered as they abandoned their feast, cawing angrily at the interruption. More patient, a buzzard looked up and studied him, beak trailing a string of bowel. Blood striped the weeds and trunks, and sword cuts gouged the bark. Bodies lay motionless, flopped across the ground in various positions. Some looked as natural as sleep, while others lay with eyes wide open, staring in rage, determination, or stark terror.

For an instant, nothing registered. Ra-khir slid from his horse's saddle and examined the dead without a hint of understanding or emotion. The buzzard finally conceded, its enormous wings slapping the air, sending an icy chill through Ra-khir's suddenly clammy skin. Then, details filtered into his consciousness. Most of the dead were Northmen: hair yellow as butterflowers or as red as his own. Others had the blander look of Erythanians or central Westerners. Many had lost their eyes to the birds, but the ones remaining looked nearly as pale as their bloodless skin. No one could mistake the scene for a mass poisoning. Sword wounds marred every body, a few missing limbs or heads, many still wearing bits or hunks of armor, even helmets.

"Oh." The word slipped past Ra-khir's mouth unbidden. "Oh, gods." His gaze became frantic as he studied the corpses, looking for anything familiar. Though he did not discover a single Renshai corpse, there could be no doubt who had fought this battle. Few swords remained, those inferiorly crafted weapons thrown haphazardly around the battlefield; but other types of weapons, valuable armor, and jewelry remained with their previous owners. Only the Renshai would overlook the inherent worth of such items while the Western world suffered from a shortage of iron ore. These were, to Renshai, items of cowardice and beneath their dignity even to touch.

A movement caught the edge of Ra-khir's vision. He whirled, still clutching Silver Warrior's reins. A small, thin donkey the size of a large dog looked back at him, its muzzle grizzled and its back bowed from age. Behind it stood a wooden cart currently holding an assortment of bric-a-brac from the battlefield. Glancing a bit further, Ra-khir discovered a boy cowering behind one of the corpses.

"Hello," Ra-khir called out, his voice a mixture of question and welcome.

Pinned by Ra-khir's gaze, the boy did not try to hide further. Instead, he stood up to reveal an unexpectedly lanky frame covered in ill-fitting, patched linen. Dirt smeared his cheeks and limbs, and his hair was a brown snarl that dangled into his face. "Hello," he returned in the Western tongue, the same one Ra-khir had used.

Uncertain where to take the awkward conversation, Ra-khir chose to introduce himself. The formality this entailed seemed ludicrous, under the circumstances. "I am Sir Ra-khir Kedrin's son, Knight to the Erythanian and Béarnian kings: His Grace, King Humfreet and His Majesty, King Griff."

The boy shuffled his bare feet in the dirt. "I'm Darby, sir."

"Darby," Ra-khir repeated, for lack of anything better to say.

"Yes, sir."

Ra-khir glanced around at the carnage before asking the obvious question. "What exactly is a boy doing on a battlefield, Darby?"

Darby cleared his throat and shifted from foot to foot, stalling. "Well, sir, I wouldn't lie to a Knight of Erythane."

Ra-khir nodded encouragingly. The basest hypocrite would give no different answer. "That's good to know."

"I . . . thought . . ." Darby paused to stare at his feet. "Well, I just figured . . ."

Ra-khir waited patiently.

"The battle was over, and . . . and . . ." Darby sighed. So far, he had said essentially nothing in a whole lot of words. ". . . and the victors left so much they clearly didn't want or need. So, I thought . . ."

"You would take it?" Ra-khir supplied.

"Well, yes, actually, sir. My ma and I and my sister could use it." Darby finally met Ra-khir's gaze. "Is that bad, sir? It's not a crime," he added hastily, "least not in these parts. Abandoned stuff belongs to the one who found it."

Ra-khir considered. "I don't believe it's bad, no. But can your ma and sister really use these weapons? And armor?"

Darby flushed. "I thought I'd sell it, sir." He added quickly, "Is *that* bad?"

"No," Ra-khir admitted. "Once the combatants have moved on, and the owners of the property are dead by other hands, I see nothing inherently evil in making decent use of what's been left behind."

Darby heaved a loud sigh. "Thank you, sir."

"For what?"

"For putting my conscience at ease."

Ra-khir shrugged, surprised it mattered to the little urchin. "What's a fine boy like you, one that listens to his conscience, doing in a woodland battlefield?"

Darby stared. Then, apparently worried about the rudeness of doing so, he rubbed his eyes with a filthy fist. "No disrespect, sir. But haven't we already had this exact conversation?"

Ra-khir laughed. He had asked the same question, in a slightly different form. "I just mean, most urchins don't care much about the morality of their actions. You have some breeding, Darby. Why aren't you out apprenticing a trade, something more refined than battlefield robbery?"

Darby took a backward step, sucking air through his teeth. "Robbery, sir? Didn't you just say . . . ?"

"Poor choice of words." Ra-khir hurried to put the boy's mind at ease. For reasons he could not wholly explain, he liked Darby. "If the owner is dead in deliberate combat, and the victor has no interest in the spoils, then they become fair game for seekers such as yourself."

Darby gave a heavy nod.

Realizing he had gotten sidetracked, Ra-khir tried again. "So how come you're legally scavenging a battlefield rather than apprenticing a regular trade?"

Darby shrugged. "I haven't any trade to apprentice." There was more to the story, they both knew.

Ra-khir continued to look at the boy, brow cocked.

Darby stared back, defiantly at first, than with less assurance. Finally, he cracked. "My pa died in an accident that involved a . . ." He considered his words carefully, ". . . popular leader. A lot of people blamed my pa for it, so hardly anyone wants to mix around with us."

"That's not fair."

Darby threw up his hands. "Fair or not, it's how it is." He rubbed his hands together, and dirt fell in peels from his palms. "My ma gets work now and then, when they can't find no one else. Same with me, when there just aren't enough other men to do the job. My sister . . . well, the only things men want her for, they can't have."

Ra-khir's expression became as deadly serious as Darby's.

"I'm trying to gather up as much of value as I can before bigger men find this treasure and take it."

Ra-khir sighed. He knew what he had to do, even if it meant further delays on his hunt. These corpses were fresh. He had nearly caught up with the Renshai, but duty bound him, as always. *A Knight of Erythane is honorable in every situation, not just when it suits him.* "Darby, you gather what you want on that wagon and your person. When you're finished, Silver Warrior and I will help you get it safely home." He patted the horse affectionately, earning a dry-nosed snuffle for his loving gesture.

"Really?" Darby stared, his obvious joy tempered with awe. "You'd do that for me?"

"What sort of knight would I be if I didn't help someone in need?"

"But I'm not really—" Darby started. Then, apparently realizing he was talking himself out of a princely escort, he let the argument drop. "Thank you. Thank you so much, sir." He hurried off to finish loading the cart.

Ra-khir removed Silver Warrior's bridle to allow his loyal white stallion to graze. He continued to study the battlefield until he spotted a string of haze floating toward the sky. He followed it to the smoldering remains of a massive pyre. Wet ash filled a hole apparently hacked into the ground using the discarded helmets of Northmen, which now lay, filthy and abandoned, near the hole. A slurry of charcoal and charred bones filled the pit, leaving nothing identifiable in the way of clothing, soft tissues, or features. Renshai had built it, Ra-khir felt certain. Clearly, they had won the battle, cremated their dead, then moved on, leaving the Northmen's broken bodies for the crows, dogs, and buzzards to devour.

And the Northmen either had no survivors or those had retreated too far away to tend their own dead. Yet. If they existed, Ra-khir hoped they did not return before Darby collected his spoils. He did not want to oversee disputes over whether or not the boy had taken something of value or desecrated their dead. Darby clearly meant no disrespect and had obeyed the laws of property abandonment.

Tears welled in Ra-khir's eyes as he stared into the pit, watching gray ash curl in the wind. The smoke had withered to a trickle, and no clear fire remained. That meant at least a few hours, more likely a few days, had passed since the pyre was lit. He wondered whose scorched bones still occupied that pit, whose organs formed the ash, whose teeth still clung to their smoldering jaws. A scavenger might find some lumps of melted coins in the heap, but not a single sword. Those required loving restoration, if necessary, and the honor of use. In the best circumstances, they would go to a relative or to a child named after the deceased in tribute.

Saviar might lie in there, Ra-khir realized. *Or Calistin.* That seemed far less likely. He found it impossible to consider his youngest's death, not only because of his preternatural sword talent, but because people of Calistin's temperament never seemed to die young.

Saviar seemed a far more likely victim of the Northmen's attack, not quite yet a man by Renshai standards, never having experienced a real battle. Ra-khir felt the familiar cold touch of despair, but this time he did not succumb to it. He had no way of knowing the fate of his sons, and it did no good to mourn in ignorance. Until he received word of their deaths, from a reliable source, he had no choice but to believe he could still find them alive.

Ra-khir stepped back from the pit. The quiet stillness of the forest, the gentle breeze caressing the leaves all seemed to belie the grotesqueness of the scene in front of him. Once again, he glanced over the corpses: the sightless eyes, the bloodless faces, the bits of gore splattering the ground and tree trunks. One, in particular caught his attention, a Northman's headless torso, the neck hacked to pieces, clearly after death. Here, someone had vented his anger in a burst of violence so bloody it brought to mind the ancient accusations against the Renshai tribe that had led to their initial banishment.

Ra-khir turned away. There was nothing more he could glean from the carnage. He headed back to find Darby with a well-loaded cart, still stuffing coppers into his pocket.

The boy looked up at Ra-khir's approach. "I'm ready when you are, sir."

Ra-khir nodded. Though relatively small, the cartload dwarfed the even tinier donkey. He whistled for Silver Warrior, who came to him at a brisk trot.

It seemed like sacrilege to hitch up the magnificent steed like a common cart horse, and it would take an inordinate amount of time to jury-rig a harness and larger traces. "I'll follow," Ra-khir said, replacing the bridle. Silver Warrior held perfectly still as the tack fell into its accustomed place. The knight flicked the reins over Silver Warrior's ears, seized the saddle, and mounted. "If you would please tell me where we're going."

Darby watched the interaction between knight and steed with obvious interest before taking his own place at the donkey's head. "Keatoville." Grabbing the cheekpiece of a crude rope halter, he urged the donkey forward. It strained at the harness. "It's just a short walk east and south."

Ra-khir coaxed Silver Warrior forward until his chest bumped the wagon, providing enough momentum to get the donkey moving. The cart groaned, threatening to shatter, and the wheels creaked in protest.

Soon, they settled into a pattern, the donkey trotting easily, the horse pushing from behind, the wheels squealing in a steady rhythm. The boy marched at the head, whistling. He looked back frequently to meet Ra-khir's gaze, apparently to reassure himself that the knight remained with them and was having no difficulties. Ra-khir appreciated the boy's misplaced concern. Darby was clearly accustomed to responsibility, presumably from serving as the man of his family.

SilverWarrior occasionally snorted at the slow pace of the wagon, and Ra-khir quelled his own impatience. Darby moved at a reasonably brisk pace, paying close attention to the donkey's comfort. The little animal lathered quickly, turning its hide a dark brown, but its head never sagged and its hooves drummed a steady pace on the packed dirt roadway.

Worried for Darby, Ra-khir had just thought to suggest a stop for lunch when the not-too-distant sound of a cocking crossbow captured his full attention. He scanned the roadway and forest, finding nothing.

Darby stopped moving and pointed toward a rocky outcropping ahead and to their left. "There."

Ra-khir squinted. Bright sunlight blurred two figures, but the crossbows looked clear enough. The sound of another cocking came from a copse of bushes to Ra-khir's right.

Releasing the donkey, Darby edged toward Ra-khir. "What should we do?" he whispered.

Ra-khir cleared his throat. As a Knight of Erythane, he had the kingdoms of Erythane and Béarn at his back. *What would Kedrin do?* Ra-khir knew exactly how his Knight-Captain father would handle the situation, yet it seemed foolish with lives at stake. *A Knight of Erythane always chooses the right way, not the easy way.* He hissed back at Darby, "Do what you think best. I'll follow your lead as I can."

Darby stared in stunned amazement, mouth gaping. Then, his jaw snapped closed, and he nodded his head decisively. "What do you bandits want from honest men in broad daylight?"

Two men stepped from the forest on the right side of the pathway. These did not carry bows, both large and burly, armed with swords and axes. Their clothes were filthy, their hair snarled with burrs, their faces scratched and scarred. "Honest men, eh? I see a junk boy with a cartload of goodies that don't look like his'n."

"They're my . . . 'n," Darby affected the dialect of the highwayman. "If you doubt it, you need only ask the Knight of Erythane riding behind me."

Every bandit eye went to Ra-khir.

Ra-khir saw the utter futility in introducing himself in this situation. "They're his . . ." he could not help adding, " 'n." In his cultured tone, the colloquialism sounded positively ludicrous.

No one laughed.

"That ain't no knight," one bandit growled.

The other nudged him with an elbow. "I think it is, Nat. Look at 'im."

"Ain't no knight gonna be travelin' with this young punk."

Seeing no way to avoid it now, Ra-khir swept off his hat. "Sir Ra-khir Kedrin's son, Knight to the Erythanian and Béarnian kings: His Grace, King Humfreet and His Majesty, King Griff." He replaced his hat, studying the men in front of him. He could take them, he realized, both of them. The crossbowmen, however, were another matter.

Nat spat on the ground.

The other man nudged him again. "Look at what he's wearin' and ridin'. If he ain't no knight, he's doin' a damned good inidation. Else, he tooked that stuff off'n a knight, in which case I don' think we wants to cross 'im, eh?"

"We're willing to fight," Darby said, snatching an ax from the cart pile with a quick, dexterous motion that impressed Ra-khir. He held it in battle position. Clearly, someone had at least started him in weapons training.

Nat snorted. He glanced from the bowmen on the pinnacle to the one on the opposite side of the trail. "I says we jus' shoot 'em and be done with it."

Ra-khir hesitated. He knew the bowmen would have doubts, if not because of murder, because this particular one could leave them hunted by two mighty kingdoms. It would be easy for him to remind them of their folly. A life-or-death situation, like this one, virtually obligated him to take control. Yet Ra-khir pictured his father: always resplendent in his knight's garb, the perfect picture of a Knight of Erythane, his commitment to every principle unyielding. Knight-Captain Kedrin would finish what he had started. He would let Darby parley, despite the mortal danger. To do the same, Ra-khir had to bite his tongue. Hard.

"Shoot us, then." Darby's voice held nothing but calm bravado. Only Ra-khir stood near enough to see the boy's hands shaking on his weapon. "Earn a cartload of trinkets and the wrath of the high king. The penalty for interfering with the duties of a knight is a traitor's death. What do you suppose they would do if you killed one in cold blood?"

Darby's words were not strictly true, but there was no law that compelled Ra-khir to correct such misunderstandings or to argue minutiae. Under certain circumstances, the penalty could become that high.

Silence settled around them, broken only by the donkey. It snorted restively, pawing at the dirt. The bowmen shifted in obvious discomfort. Nat might command the strike, but they would be held at least equally accountable for the killing.

"Or . . ." Darby continued, his voice unexpectedly loud in the hush. ". . . you can let us go, and I can tell you where I found this . . . junk." He used their terminology, making a gesture toward the loaded cart. "I took only a small portion. There's enough left to make all of you wealthy."

Ra-khir caught himself nodding. He had not meant to become a truth detector for thieves.

The other swordsman looked hopefully at Nat. "That sounds all right, don' it, Nat?"

Nat scratched his stubbly chin. "Sounds pert' good." His eyes narrowed. "If'n it's true. An' he don' lie 'bout the location."

"How we gonna know that?" The highwayman looked at Darby as he asked the question.

Darby shrugged. "It's not far. You'll have time to go there, see if I'm lying, and still get back to catch us before we make town."

Nat grunted. It was hard to argue with such logic.

Ra-khir supposed the men might find the battle site, mark the location, and come after them anyway; but he doubted it. Once they saw the battlefield and the potential it held, they would want to stay and plunder before someone else found it. "You're giving up a lot," Ra-khir whispered.

Darby did not bother to turn to face the knight. "I have more than enough."

Nat and the other man talked softly together while the bowmen remained in place, their weapons still cocked but no longer directly aimed at knight and boy.

"All righ'," Nat finally said. "Start talkin', boy."

Darby cleared his throat then explained, in reasonably clear terms, how to find the battle clearing.

When he finished, Nat made a broad, arching gesture. "Come on, men."

The click of disarming crossbows followed the command, then the highwaymen disappeared into the forest.

Only then, Darby collapsed onto the dirt. The ax slipped from visibly shaking hands. "Why . . . why did you do that?"

"Do what?" Ra-khir asked innocently, listening for the sounds of the departing men to assure himself no one had remained behind to watch them. He did not think they would. No thief would want to risk losing a share of treasure.

"Let me . . . me . . . handle that?"

"Why wouldn't I?" Ra-khir rubbed Silver Warrior's neck. The well-trained steed had remained still and silent throughout the ordeal. "I knew you could do it." He showed no trace of his own trepidation. He wanted Darby to believe he had trusted the boy implicitly. He would have done nothing different for his own sons.

"But you scarcely know me. And both our lives were at stake."

Ra-khir doubted the highwaymen would actually have slaughtered a Knight of Erythane, though Nat had seemed just stupid enough to do it. "I'm a good judge of character. You have courage, Darby, intelligence and moral fiber. I knew you could handle it, and you did."

Darby climbed to shaky legs. He hefted the ax and tossed it back onto the pile. "Coming from you, Sir Knight, that is high praise indeed. And I thank you."

Ra-khir nodded. "And thank you for not proving me wrong and getting us killed."

Darby laughed.

"Did you ever consider becoming a knight yourself?"

Darby drew himself up to his full height. "Only my whole life! Isn't that the dream of every Western boy?"

Ra-khir had to admit it had been his. At least, from the day he discovered his actual father was one. "Apparently not. Not one of my sons has followed in my footsteps, though one did consider it." He tried not to think too hard about Saviar. The young man who had spoken with him so earnestly months earlier had disappeared without a word.

"Oh," Darby said with clear surprise. "I wish I—" he started, then apparently changed his mind. "A knight wouldn't allow himself to feel envy, would he?"

Ra-khir shook his head. The message had come through despite the lack of words. Darby wished he had had the same opportunities as the knight's boys. Of course, he had no way to know about the Renshai half of their heritage.

Darby smiled crookedly and returned to the donkey's head.

CHAPTER 27

Death in combat is not the end of the fight, merely its pinnacle.
—Renshai proverb

SAVIAR INSISTED ON FINISHING a full day's walk, though his leg ached so unmercifully he could concentrate on nothing else. That, in itself, bothered him. Renshai were trained from infancy to fight not just through pain, but because of it. Fatally wounded, they called upon Modi, the god of wrath, to give them the strength to take their enemies with them. Now, the single, simple act of walking demanded Saviar's full attention, and he felt like a failure and a craven. He appreciated that Subikahn remained silent, disappearing at frequent intervals to scout the way. If his twin had hovered over him, treating him like an invalid, Saviar might have felt driven to carry out his threat to kill them both.

For once, Subikahn made no complaint when Saviar ate heartily from their dwindling stores. "I've filled all the waterskins," he explained. "And I can get plenty more, so drink as much as you want."

The amount he needed to satisfy his thirst surprised Saviar, but he took his brother at his word. As he finished, he could feel the cold of the liquid seeping into his blood, chilling him deeply. He shivered. "Do we have any more wine?" They had confiscated it from a dead Northman at the beginning of their journey, savoring a few mouthfuls at a time. Now, Saviar hoped, it would warm him and take the edge from pain that seemed to multiply exponentially as the day wore onward.

Subikahn winced. "I used it all on the wound. It's supposed to help keep it from getting tainted."

"Which? The wound? Or the wine?"

Subikahn managed a lopsided smile at the flimsy joke. "It's been longer than a day. I need to redo those bandages before we go to sleep."

Saviar looked at the rags wrapped around his thigh, now sweat-stained and filthy. The flesh of his fingers looked oddly pale near his leg, and they trembled beyond his control. "Where are you going to get more?"

"Wherever I have to."

"Hmmm, well, I'd rather not have to travel naked, especially now that it's getting so cold." Saviar expected an evening breeze, usually cherished its touch against his sweat-bathed limbs; but he suddenly felt awash in ice. "In fact, if there's an extra cloak you don't need to tear up, I'd like to wear it."

Immediately, Subikahn removed his own overwear and offered it to his brother. "Here."

"I can't take—"

"I'm comfortable, actually." Subikahn dropped the cloak at Saviar's feet, then turned to dig through their packs. "If I get cold, I'll take it back. Or I'll find something clean."

"Thanks." Saviar wrapped the extra cloak around him, no longer in the mood to joke. Still warm from Subikahn's body, the fabric seemed to embrace him, yet he still felt icy to the bone. His limbs began to shake.

"Lie down," Subikahn suggested. "I'll start a fire, then get to work on that wound."

"Not yet." Saviar reluctantly staggered toward an open patch of ground. For the first time he could remember, he loathed the bare thought of swordplay. "I need to practice."

Subikahn set to digging out a fire pit. "Of course, we'll practice. But it can wait till you have clean bandages." He gestured at a spot near the freshly dug depression. "Lie down, Savi."

Saviar looked at the indicated place. Though nothing more than one open patch among many beneath the woven canopy of forest, it looked exquisitely comfortable. He wanted to stretch out in the fallen leaves and dirt, to stare quietly at the stars, to let a roaring fire drive its heat through his frigid body. Yet, lifelong lessons die hard. If he curled up now, he might fall asleep. "We have to practice."

"We will." Subikahn jabbed a finger at the ground. "As soon as I change those bandages."

Protesting took too much effort. "All right." Chills racked Saviar's body, his jaw chattered, and the urge to draw every scrap of cloth tightly around him became nearly impossible to ignore. He dropped awkwardly to the ground.

Subikahn hovered around him, tucking clothing, tearing bandages, gathering wood. Amidst the normal sounds of his brother's preparations, still fighting the chill that gripped him, Saviar fell into a restless sleep.

Keatoville turned out to be a tiny hamlet only steps off the beaten path. Had Ra-khir not discovered the battlefield and Darby, he would probably have ridden past without noticing it at all. Neat rows of cottages surrounded the few necessary businesses; and a communal meeting hall, that probably served as a tavern as often as a gathering place, stood directly in the center of town.

People stopped and stared as Darby rode in, accompanied by a Knight of Erythane, their jaws sagging, their chores forgotten. In silence, Darby led the donkey to a dilapidated cottage on the farthest edge of the village. He drew up alongside the wooden construct, its beams settling and its caulk repeatedly patched. The thatched roof had turned brown and moldy with age, and it surely leaked. "We're here," he announced.

Ra-khir dismounted. "You live here?" He tried to keep incredulity from his voice. Though it drooped, the cottage was clean. He could tell someone had jammed straw-filled mud into every budding crevice, smoothing it carefully. They obviously tried to keep their home in shape, but time had ravaged it and no able-bodied man had spared them the few hours it would take to assist with regular maintenance. Now, it would probably require a complete rebuilding.

Darby flushed. "I try my best, sir. Really I do."

Ra-khir glanced around at the crowd that had followed them to the ramshackle cottage, watching in a curious hush.

"If I was just a bit stronger, I could push those logs into the right places, and my sister could—"

Ra-khir interrupted in a strong voice pitched to carry. "I just can't believe that, in this entire village, there's not a single, decent man willing to help a widow and her children keep their dwelling habitable."

His words had the desired effect. A wave of scarlet suffused the villagers, especially the males, and they shifted with nervous whispers.

Darby stood, rooted, his mouth still open but no words emerging.

Ra-khir rubbed his gloved hands together. "I'm on a vital mission, but I'll simply have to delay it. The kings of Béarn and Erythane will surely understand why I have to stop to rebuild a cottage for a village that has forgotten how." His hands paused in mid-motion. "Well, perhaps they won't understand. I certainly don't."

A well-dressed, thin man stepped forward, "Well, you see, sir—" he started but was interrupted by a burly fellow in linen.

"You continue your mission, Sir Knight. I'll help this family re-build." He spoke into a shocked silence.

Murmurs swept the gathering group.

"And I," shouted another from the back.

A chorus of similar promises followed.

Darby lowered his head, but even the corner of his face still visible to Ra-khir revealed a smile.

Ra-khir nodded. "When I come back through here on my return, I expect to find a brand-new cottage. And I expect you all to charge exactly what good neighbors should, what I would have charged." He looked from volunteer to volunteer, needing to make certain guilt, not the full donkey cart, motivated the villagers.

The burly man shouted the proper answer. "Nothing, of course, sir."

Ra-khir favored the man with a bow and flourish of his hat.

Applause followed.

The door to the cottage swung open, and a woman stepped outside. Though tall and quite slender, she showed a hint of delicate curves through her worn and faded shift. She had the face of an angel: creamy white, blue-eyed, and high-cheeked, with a strong straight nose and ears that disappeared beneath a thick cascade of honey-brown hair. She had long legs that promised shapeliness with more regular meals. Her movements were gliding, robust and sure, with a dancer's agility.

Catching himself staring, Ra-khir forced himself to look at Darby. "Is that . . . your . . ."

"Mama," Darby said. "Yes."

The word ". . . sister" died on Ra-khir's tongue. "That's your mama?"

As the fact had already been established, Darby clearly felt no need to reply.

A girl peeked out from behind her, in that awkward stage between childhood and adolescence. She, too, would look beautiful if she had a bit more meat on her too-skinny frame. Ra-khir could understand why the men wanted her for acts about which Darby had refused to speak.

Ra-khir swallowed hard, then bowed to Darby's mama as if to royalty. "I am Sir Ra-khir Kedrin's son, Knight to the Erythanian and Béarnian kings: His Grace, King Humfreet and His Majesty, King Griff."

Clearly taken aback, the woman said nothing for several moments. Finally, she found her voice, though scratchier than Ra-khir expected. "Er . . . um, I am Tiega." She obviously felt the need to add more, as he had. ". . . um . . . Tiego's daughter . . . er . . . of Keato-ville, Westlands."

Ra-khir replaced his hat and smiled. "Pleased to meet you, Tiega. You have a fine son in Darby, ma'am."

Without a hint of modesty or hesitation, Tiega replied, "Yes, I do, sir." She looked over at the donkey cart and its load of goods. "But is he in some sort of . . . trouble, sir?"

"No, ma'am," Ra-khir said emphatically. "These items belong to Darby, fairly won and scavenged. I just thought I'd see such a moral and enterprising young man safely home."

Tiega smiled sweetly at Ra-khir. "Thank you, sir. Your kindness is appreciated."

Ra-khir thought he saw a spark of interest, but he had to ignore it. It was too soon. His grief remained too raw and painful.

Darby walked to his mother's side to hold a whispered conversation. He pulled a handful of coins from his pocket and dumped them into her palm. She stared at the money, clearly shocked.

The crowd began to disperse.

Ra-khir cleared his throat. "Well, I've fulfilled my promise, so I guess I'll be on my way." He reached for Silver Warrior.

"Wait," Tiega said. "Can't you stay for a meal, Sir Ra-khir? I can cook anything you like, so long as Darby can buy the ingredients here."

Ra-khir would have loved to stay. A home-cooked meal sounded wonderful, and the company of a handsome woman more so. "I'd like that, ma'am; but I've gotten behind on my mission already. I will return to see your new cottage." He emphasized the phrase to remind the village men of their promise. "And I'll have a warm stew, then, if you'll prepare it."

"I will," Tiega promised.

Ra-khir hauled himself into the saddle.

"Sir Ra-khir?"

Ra-khir reined his steed to face Tiega directly. "Yes, ma'am?"

"I wondered if you might take Darby with you."

"Ma'am?"

"As an apprentice, I mean. A squire."

Ra-khir hesitated. He had never considered himself an advanced enough knight to train an apprentice, though his rank and service time were sufficient. If Saviar had followed through on his interest, Ra-khir would have given him to someone else, worried about his objectivity and his relationship. He glanced at Darby.

The boy stood with hands clenched with desire, his eyes nearly blazing. Only then, Ra-khir noticed they were the same fiery blue as his mother's.

"Becoming a Knight of Erythane takes many years of grueling work. It's hard, it's often tediously boring, and it requires a dedication to morality, to the Order, and to the kings that transcends logic, life, and family. Only the best are chosen, and most of them don't finish the training."

Darby pursed his lips, nodding.

"If you fail, you've essentially wasted that many years of your life you could have spent learning a useful trade." Ra-khir saw no reason to mention that the time would not be wholly lost, as most of the dropouts had enough weapons training to become soldiers in the kings' employ. "Darby, would you like some time to think about it?"

Darby turned Ra-khir a look of seriousness so grave it transcended death. "I've thought about it all my life. I want to be a knight, sir. I'll do whatever it takes."

"It's a lifelong commitment."

"More's the better."

"To accompany me, you'll need a horse."

Darby motioned toward his haul. "I'll buy one."

Ra-khir had not bargained on a companion, yet the idea did not bother him. He gave Tiega a hard look. "My mission is dangerous."

Though he had addressed the mother, Darby answered for her. "I know how to fight, Sir Ra-khir. And I know how to dodge." He added with a conspiratorial smile, "If circumstances allow it, and there's no dishonor in it, I can also hide pretty good."

"Pretty *well*," Ra-khir corrected. Another feature of the knights was impeccable speech and diction, most of the time.

"I can hide pretty well," Darby dutifully fixed.

"And his training will have to take place in Erythane and Béarn, which means that even if he survives the mission, you may never see him again."

"Oh, I'll see him again, sir." Tiega met Ra-khir's gaze without a hint of fear. "I'll move. I'd be gone from here already if I had the money for travel." She smiled broadly. "And, now I do. By the time you come back through here, I intend to have all of this junk sold and have purchased more horses. If Darby has performed satisfactorily, we'll all accompany you back to Erythane." She added carefully, "Assuming you'd allow us to go with you, sir. Otherwise, Keva and I'll get there on our own."

Still partway behind her mother, Keva nodded forcefully.

The new cottage seemed moot now, but Ra-khir did not allow the village men off the hook. They should have assisted Tiega and her family from the moment she lost her husband. "What man in his right mind wouldn't agree to ride with two beautiful women?"

Keva giggled, and Tiega grinned. "Flatterer! And I thought Knights of Erythane weren't allowed to lie."

"We're not." Ra-khir wheeled Silver Warrior and let the significance of the comment hang. "I meant every word I said." He made a broad gesture at Darby. "Come on, apprentice knight. We've a horse to buy."

Darby charged to Ra-khir's side, and the two men headed toward the center of Keatoville.

⁜————

Subikahn studied his sleeping brother in the light of the blazing fire. Snuggled near it, beneath every article of clothing not shredded for the bandage or on Subikahn, he finally stopped shivering. Still, he moved restlessly, moaning frequently and occasionally crying out in his sleep.

With a sigh of painful resignation, Subikahn brushed away enough of the coverings to reveal the bandaged leg. Saviar twitched and muttered but did not awaken. His skin felt dry and remarkably hot. The lack of sweat told Subikahn his brother's temperature was still climbing, and his agitation probably stemmed from the wild sort of dreams and nightmares that only fever can induce. *What have I done?*

Terror seized Subikahn. He had lost his parents, his lover, and he had no idea where his younger brother had gone. He could not, would not, lose his beloved twin as well. The very thought threatened to plunge him into madness. *Hold on, Savi. Hold on.* Tears distorted the image of his suffering brother. It all seemed utter, impossible insanity, the whole scenario, itself, a torturous fever-dream. *My mood started the argument. I demanded the fight. I plunged that sword into his thigh, and I ripped it free, filthy from the ground.* Nearly paralyzed with guilt, Subikahn realized one thing more. *If not for my selfish desire for solitude, we would be nearer a town. I could get him a healer, some herbs, some help.*

Subikahn's gaze returned to the bandages. Blaming himself would not ease his brother's misery nor help him treat the wound. He had to remove them, to gaze upon it, and to use the few tools in his arsenal to attempt to heal it. Still he hesitated, fearing what he saw might rob him of the last vestiges of hope. *I'm a warrior. I'm a Renshai.* Steeling himself, Subikahn gently unwound the bandages.

Swollen red streaks appeared first, at the outer edges of the un-covered area. Subikahn sucked air through his teeth and forced him-self to continue. Another few loops dropped to the ground, revealing more inflammation, puffier and angry in its scarlet hue. Then, the last hunk of cloth came undone amid a wash of blood-streaked pus. Subikahn gasped sharply and glanced at his brother, only to find Saviar looking back at him.

Confusion and pain glazed the familiar blue-white eyes. Saviar's cheeks carried ruddy circles. "I'm dying."

"No!" Subikahn shielded the wound with his body. Realizing he had answered too quickly and loudly, he sought the right words to reassure. "Your body's just fighting to keep it from getting tainted. You're going to be fine."

Saviar seemed not to hear. "I saw my pyre, and the cold lonely hill where the wind scatters the ashes. A voice told me . . . I'm all alone. Forever . . ."

"Just a nightmare." Subikahn turned his back on his brother to fully block his view of the wound while he worked. "A stupid, ridicu-lous nightmare. You're going to be fine, Savi. Go back to sleep."

"No. Help me up. I have to die in combat."

"You're not going to die!" It was more than a statement, it was admonishment and self-reassurance. If Saviar died, Subikahn would die with him. He could not go on alone. "Now stop this death talk, and go back to sleep."

Saviar swallowed hard. His eyes drifted closed.

Subikahn sucked in a deep lungful of air; but, before he could release it, Saviar continued.

"I'm cold, Subi. So very very cold. Hel is dragging me into her frozen realm. Please." Just talking seemed a great effort. He licked his lips with a tongue that looked dry and swollen despite the copious amount of water he had drunk that evening. "You have to help me up. You have to help me commit tåphresëlmordat."

"Shut up!" Subikahn had heard all he could stand. "Shut up, Sav-iar! You are *not* going to die. Not yet. Not for a very long time."

"I . . . Hel—"

"If she comes, she'll have to get through me." Subikahn drew *Mot-frabelonning* from Saviar's sheath. "This is the sword that let you see the *Valkyrie* when Mama died, right?" He did not wait for an answer. "If Hel comes near, I'll see her. She'll have to battle through me to get you."

"Subi—"

Subikahn would not listen to protest. "That's it, Savi. Go to sleep. I *will* see you in the morning."

"I'm not dying?"

"You're not dying." Subikahn did not allow a hint of doubt to enter his tone.

"You're sure?"

"I'm sure," Subikahn said with all the certainty and finality in the world, though he experienced none of it. He knew only one thing. *Saviar cannot die.* His own heart could not afford the pain. When Saviar's stopped, his did as well. If Hel came to claim Saviar, she would face a battle like none other, and she would lose. Subikahn would not stop until he spent every iota of strength, skill, sanity, and breath.

Saviar drifted back into sleep while Subikahn carefully tended the wound, bathing it with water and, inadvertently, with tears.

CHAPTER 28

The warrior dedicated to death is all but unstoppable.
—General Santagithi

DARBY CHOSE A COMPACT chestnut gelding with an easy dis-position, a decision that pleased Ra-khir. The boy had a reasonable eye for conformation, movement, and soundness; the chestnut would manage long distances at a comfortably fast pace. Its more subdued color would blend into background field and forest, though that seemed a minor concern given that he rode alongside the snow-white, beribboned beacon that was Silver Warrior. And a gelding would not distract the knight's stallion with challenges or heat cycles.

Though high summer, the day remained cool as they rode in si-lence along the packed dirt roadway, traveling ever eastward along the Southern Mountain range. It would take weeks to reach the passes that would bring them to the Western Plains, the ancient site of the Great War; and, from there, into the Eastlands.

Hoofprints pocked the roadway, and the recent breakage of side-line foliage told Ra-khir they would not have to travel nearly that far. A large group had passed by recently, and he would have bet everything he carried that the sign was left by the Renshai. Like any crowd that included children and a limited number of horses, they traveled much more slowly than a pair of horsemen. And Ra-khir saw evidence that they'd stopped more than once to crash through the brush and, probably, practice sword maneuvers.

Little conversation passed between them. Ra-khir saw no rea-son to burden Darby with his family problems, and the boy kept his curiosity well-hidden. It seemed better to Ra-khir to demonstrate the ways of knighthood to his new charge rather than preach them. Words had little impact compared to actions, and Darby would suf-fer enough long-winded speeches in his future to make up for every moment of blessed silence. The Knights of Erythane participated in the formal events of both kingdoms and had to learn to remain in position through the most pompous, boring, and repetitive proceedings known to humankind.

Midday came and went, with Ra-khir choosing to remain in the saddle as they ate. With each hoof fall, they drew closer to their goal, and he would rather come upon the Renshai in twilight than darkness. Any one of them could make short work of the knight and his charge, and they would need little excuse to do so.

The strategy paid off. Shortly past sundown, Ra-khir found a huge hole in the roadside plant life where a multitude had broken through, clearly to find a campsite. Bits of fur clung to thistles and branches, scraped from the flanks of horses. Motioning Darby behind him, Ra-khir plunged through, winding Silver Warrior between the tree trunks and copses. Soon, he could hear the sounds of muffled conversation, sword blades slamming together, and whetstones rasping against steel.

Ra-khir found himself so focused on these welcome sounds that Darby's whisper startled him. "We're not going to fight this army, are we?"

Ra-khir smiled. *We wouldn't last long.* "No. These are friends."

Relief washed across Darby's face, displacing a greenish tinge. "I'm so glad to hear that, sir."

As they drew nearer, Ra-khir held his stallion to a slow pace, kept his hand from his hilt, and made no attempt to hide or move quietly. He would give the Renshai no reason to assume he meant them any harm.

Though he risked a kick, Darby kept his horse directly on Silver Warrior's tail.

Ra-khir brushed past a clump of thistles to get his first look at the camp. Renshai were scattered amidst trees and across a small field. Many were engaged in practice skirmishes with one another that looked deadlier than most wars. Others sat cleaning or sharpening blades.

Ra-khir rode up to a relaxed group tending their weapons. They all certainly noticed him, yet they made no move to challenge him. Their composure sent a shiver through Ra-khir. Darby might see it as a strange and cool disinterest, but Ra-khir knew better. These Renshai simply did not see the two newcomers as a threat. Any of them believed they could dispatch the two horsemen without bothering to prepare.

Ra-khir recognized all of them but remembered the names for only two of the five, a man and a woman of similar age to his sons. "Hello, Ashavir. Hello, Tarah. Hello, other Renshai."

Recollection flashed across their faces, and the two identified by name both smiled.

"Well, hello, Calistin's father," Ashavir said in greeting. The Renshai often referred to him in this manner, and almost always in regard to Calistin rather than Saviar. Though it seemed disrespectful, as though his name were not worth learning, Ra-khir knew the Renshai intended it as a compliment, linking him with the Renshai's greatest warrior. "What are you doing all the way out here?"

"I've come to visit my sons." Ra-khir also grinned, trying to make the request sound casual. He expected them to laugh. He had implied traveling an inordinate distance for conversation over tea.

But the smiles faded from all of the Renshai's faces. The ones not addressed returned to their business. Tarah glanced toward the center of camp, and Ashavir cleared his throat.

Ra-khir's heart seized in his chest. Their evasiveness suggested he would not find his boys here, and Ra-khir could think of only one reason why. *Killed by Northmen? Both of them?* He closed his eyes. *Gods, no. Don't let that be true.* He had already considered the possibility, but he now realized he had never actually believed it.

"You'll need to talk to Thialnir about that," Ashavir said carefully. "He's center camp, working on a fire."

Ra-khir knew better than to question further. It would only waste time. His chest felt as if someone had filled it with boulders, and it took longer than it ever should to get Silver Warrior headed in the indicated direction. His thoughts narrowed to a single channel. *Saviar, dead. Calistin, dead. Didn't say "good-bye."* His heart already accepted the inevitable, its beat unsteady; but his brain would not allow him to believe until he heard those precise words.

The fire was already blazing when Ra-khir arrived. Massive Thialnir stood among many other Renshai, surrounding the corpse of a deer. Several had knives in hand as they debated how and whether to take the fur off the beast before searing it. Under other circumstances, the conversation might have amused Ra-khir. The consummate swordmasters were hopeless when it came to such simple tasks as hunting and cooking. He wondered how they had even caught and felled the beast. *Probably surprised it and fell upon it with swords.*

At Ra-khir's approach, the Renshai turned toward him, en masse. Ra-khir dismounted and addressed Darby. "Show them how to skin a deer, would you please?"

With a nod, Darby dismounted and headed toward the corpse. Ra-khir turned his attention to the Renshai. "I need to speak with Thialnir. In private."

The enormous leader of the Renshai seemed relieved to let a boy stranger take over his task. He rubbed his hands together, dislodging chunks of dirt, and walked toward Ra-khir.

Swiftly, Ra-khir whipped the bridle from Silver Warrior to allow the hungry stallion to graze. He did the same for Darby's chestnut before heading off to a secluded spot with Thialnir. "My sons . . ." he started, before they had even finished walking beyond earshot. ". . . are they here?"

Thialnir did not make Ra-khir wait. "No, Ra-khir, they're gone."

"Gone?" Ra-khir needed more. The Renshai rarely used euphemisms, especially for death.

"Calistin rode north to demand the battle that should have been his to fight."

Ra-khir inhaled sharply in sudden understanding. "He's riding into thousands of enemies to challenge Valr Magnus?"

Thialnir smiled, which seemed inappropriate to Ra-khir. "Did you expect otherwise, Sir Knight? *Pen-fruit* doesn't grow on *hadongo* trees, and *aristiri* hawks don't hatch from lizard eggs."

Ra-khir managed only a slight upward twitch of the corners of his mouth. It was more of a tolerant smile than an amused one. "I get it. You're saying Kevral was a maniac, so I should expect the same from my boys."

"Kevral?" Thialnir reared his head backward in exaggerated surprise. "Kevral was simply one of many brave and talented Renshai. The maniac, as you so eloquently put it, is Calistin's father."

Me? Ra-khir did not know what to say.

"As I understand it, you single-handedly declared war on the Westlands' largest city."

"Well, yes, but—"

"And engineered a prison break through the high kingdom's impossible maze."

"That was—"

"Looked upon Valhalla while alive, volunteered to face unknown physical and magical dangers on multiple worlds, and even took Colbey Calistinsson's prized stallion."

"Now wait a second! I didn't *take* Colbey's horse. He gave it to me." Ra-khir realized how ridiculous that sounded even as the words left his lips.

But Thialnir only smiled more broadly. "I rest my case."

It was not worth arguing, even if it weren't all true. Ra-khir sighed. "You couldn't stop Calistin?"

"I could more easily have stopped the *Ragnarok*, I think." Thialnir's grin turned lopsided. "Besides, he disappeared immediately after the battle. There was no chance for talking."

Ra-khir knew he had no choice but to go after Calistin, to keep him from committing suicide out of a sense of obligation or, worse, retaliation. "And Saviar?"

Thialnir looked around Ra-khir toward the fire. "Saviar, I could have stopped. But I didn't."

Ra-khir blinked. It sounded like a foolish answer, but Thialnir was no fool. For the moment, he reveled in the knowledge that both boys had survived the battle and let Thialnir explain.

"His brothers needed him more than we did."

"Brothers?" Ra-khir felt certain he had heard the plural. "You mean Subikahn was here, too?"

As always, Thialnir got right to the point. "Yes, though not officially. He remained hidden."

Ra-khir's brow furrowed, and he fell silent as he pondered the significance of that information.

As if in direct response to the thought, Thialnir explained. "Calistin's too impulsive and would benefit from Saviar's common sense. And Subikahn returned without his *torke,* which means he's in some kind of trouble in the East. Given that he's a prince, it's likely serious; and his refusal to actually join us, his own people, suggests he may have murdered Talamir and can't face us. Saviar claims he got himself banished from the Eastlands."

"Subikahn banished from the *East?*" It seemed utterly impossible.

Thialnir's huge shoulders rose and fell again. "I don't know if it's true, but Subikahn and Calistin needed Saviar more than I did. So, I told him to go. It didn't take much encouragement."

Ra-khir loosed a pent-up breath, thrilled to learn all three of Kevral's boys still lived, at least until their own stupid, adolescent bravado got them killed. *At any rate, they're together. United, it would take an army to bring them down.*

"By the way," Thialnir added, not quite conversationally. "I promised not to tell anyone about Subikahn."

Ra-khir froze. He raised his head ever so slowly to meet Thialnir's gaze. "Then . . . why did you tell me?"

Thialnir loosed a chuckle. "Because you needed to know. If I'd mentioned in advance it was something I wasn't supposed to pass along, you wouldn't have let me tell you."

"Of course not."

"But now that you know, you'll have no choice but to keep the secret, too. So, no harm done."

Though glad he knew, Ra-khir wished Thialnir had not deceived him. No Knight of Erythane would willingly become complicit in the breaking of confidences. But now that he had the information, Thialnir was right. He had to keep it confidential. "Not very nice, Thialnir."

Thialnir rolled his eyes. "Renshai aren't known for their sweet dispositions." He extended a hand in friendship. "Can I make it up to you with a good meal and a protected place to spend the night?"

Ra-khir knew he had a lot of work ahead of him. Tracking hundreds of people moving together to a known destination had proven easy. Following three youngsters randomly northward across the enormous Westlands would prove a much more formidable task. "I accept your hospitality with gratitude, though I question your honesty about that meal."

Thialnir's brows rose in question.

"Any group of men about to hurl an unskinned, unbutchered deer onto a blazing fire knows absolutely nothing about cooking. The stink of burning hair itself might kill us all, and it will take a week to cook through whole."

"Ah, but I didn't lie, Ra-khir. You and your . . ." he paused.

"Apprentice," Ra-khir filled in. "Darby."

"You and your apprentice are here to oversee the cooking; so, if you stay, you will get the good meal I promised."

Ra-khir could not deny the reasoning. "Thank you, Thialnir. We accept your kind, and honest, invitation. I consider it an honor to dine among Renshai."

Thialnir smiled but said nothing. The words were diluted by the realization that, not long ago, Ra-khir ate with Renshai every day. *I consider it an honor to dine among Renshai.* Likely, Thialnir had never heard such a thing before. And it pleased him.

Subikahn awakened with a start to find himself flopped over a deadfall, his brother's sword still clenched in his fist. He had no memory of falling asleep nor of what might have awakened him. The fire had burned down to ash and glowing cinders. Beside it, Saviar sprawled beneath piles of clothing, breathing in uneven snores and moans.

Breathing. That one realization reassured Subikahn. He sprang to his feet, shaking the last vestiges of slumber from his thoughts and movements. Only then, he realized it was a misplaced sound that had awakened him. He cocked his head, trying to rediscover it: the shuffle of a human footstep, a ladylike sneeze. Poking his head through the brush, he glanced along a path so lightly traveled he had assumed only deer walked it toward the pond from which he had filled their waterskins. Now, he saw a young woman striding along it, carrying an earthen jug.

Hel? Dressed in a light, swirling fabric, auburn hair billowing in the breeze, she little resembled the half-rotting, centuries-old depictions of the Underworld goddess Subikahn had seen. Yet, he also knew the gods had magic to shapechange. They also had plenty of minions.

Subikahn leaped onto the pathway, sword raised. "You cannot have him!"

The girl screamed, dropping the jug, which shattered in the dirt.

Torn between attacking and apologizing, Subikahn lowered his sword.

The girl ignored the broken crockery to focus fully on Subikahn. She turned sideways, raised her hands, and took a cautious backward step. "Stay away from me! I'm warning you!" A breathy quality stole all threat from her tone. Terror leached through her bravado. A misty outline, like heat haze, grew around her.

"Are you a minion of Hel?" Subikahn demanded, afraid to immediately discount the possibility. If he guessed wrong, he might doom his brother's soul.

"Am I . . . what?"

"A minion of Hel," Subikahn repeated impatiently. "Are you a minion of Hel?"

"A minion?"

"Yes!"

"Of . . . Hel?"

"Yes!"

The young woman paused. Even from a distance, Subikahn could see her eyes narrow. "Are you entirely moonstruck?"

Subikahn knew he had to sound insane, yet he dared not take a chance. He stuffed the sword into his belt. If she was a supernatural creature, she ought to disappear. Yet, she remained, although he could no longer see the shimmering vapor that had encompassed her. Not all was normal about this stranger. "I'm not crazy. I'm just protecting my brother."

"From minions of Hel?"

"Yes."

"And you're sure you're not—"

"I'm not crazy." Subikahn continued to watch her every movement. "And you know I have reason to be wary of you. You're not entirely . . . human."

The girl jerked up her head. "I'm not?"

Subikahn touched the hilt of Saviar's sword and again saw the haze he had previously noticed. When he released the weapon, the glow disappeared. "There's an unnatural fog around you. Is it magic hiding your true appearance?"

"A fog . . ." The girl's hands went to her mouth. Her demeanor tightened, seeming more excited than distressed. "You can see it?"

That being self-evident, Subikahn saw no reason to answer.

"My name is Chymmerlee." She pronounced it *Kim*-er-lee, with a faint trace of an accent Subikahn could not identify. "Look again. Can you still see the aura?"

Discreetly, Subikahn touched the sword and studied the figure in front of him. She had the lean, lanky appearance of a teen, perhaps a year or two younger than himself. Straight, red-brown hair fell just past her shoulders, cut short in layers around an oval face with large eyes and a pert nose. The shimmering haze had disappeared. "No," he admitted. "It's gone. And you look otherwise the same."

Chymmerlee took a few cautious steps toward Subikahn. "You're a mage."

For reasons he could not wholly comprehend, Subikahn took the pronouncement as an insult. "I am not."

She stopped again, this time near enough he could see that a few freckles dotted her nose and cheeks. Her eyes were a pale blue-gray. "You know nothing of magic?"

Subikahn tightened his grip on the hilt, warningly. "I know enough not to let someone who hides behind it near my injured brother." He crouched, prepared for battle. "I also know nothing human can cast spells, only gods and elves."

Chymmerlee made a clicking noise with her tongue, and her hand went to her mouth again. "Your brother's injured? And we're stand-ing here bandying words?"

Subikahn remained in stance.

Chymmerlee closed her eyes, seemingly oblivious to the threat. Either she had powerful magic that she believed could get her safely past a readied Renshai or she was wholly ignorant of combat. "You thought I was . . . and your brother . . ." Her features opened in sud-den understanding. "Your brother's not just injured, he's dying. And you thought I came to—"

"You cannot have him," Subikahn repeated.

"I don't want him!" Chymmerlee rushed toward Subikahn. "At least, not in the way you think I do."

The sword whipped up.

Chymmerlee stopped abruptly, loosing a frightened squeak. Finally, she recognized the danger. "Don't hurt me. Please. I'm trying to help."

Subikahn wanted to believe her. "How?"

"I have some healing skill. Not a lot, but if I can get him stabilized, we can transport him to my people. They might be able to save him."

Subikahn hesitated. It had to be a trick, yet hope gripped him with such suddenness he found himself shaking. "How do I know you're not going to kill him? That you're not a minion of—"

"—Hel?" she filled in. "Is he well enough I have time to convince you?"

No, Subikahn realized. His father had an uncanny ability to read people's intentions, one he at least partially shared. But he saw a vast difference between guessing the intent of a human stranger and an Outworlder. *If she's sent by Hel, and I let her touch him, I've doomed him. But if she is what she says, and I don't, I've killed him.* His intuition told him to trust Chymmerlee, but his mind warned otherwise. The only elf he had ever seen was the second wife of King Griff. It seemed a coincidence beyond believing that a friendly Outworlder would happen to show up at the same moment he expected a hostile one.

Chymmerlee said nothing. She no longer had the aura, and she looked inarguably human.

In the end, Subikahn trusted his heart. "Come on," he said gruffly. "But if you harm him, you will not live to gloat about it." With trepidation, he led her to the camp, focused on her every movement.

Chymmerlee moved with the grace of an acrobat, but not the awesome glide of an elf or goddess. Dutifully, she watched him for cues, attentive to the sword that he kept locked in his hand. If magic flared, Subikahn wanted to make certain he saw it at its earliest incantation.

Saviar still lay where Subikahn had left him, buried in a pile of laundry beside the failing embers. Attention on Chymmerlee, Subikahn cautiously removed each fire-warmed cloak, tunic, or undergarment and dropped it into a heap beside the sleeping figure. The last layer was damp, soaked through with sweat, and pulled free to reveal the pallid figure beneath it. Saviar's wet clothing clung to his finely-chiseled muscles. His hair hung in limp, red strands.

Chymmerlee spoke for the first time since the pathway, in the awed whisper usually reserved for religious ceremonies. "He's beautiful."

It was a common reaction, and true, yet it seemed remarkably out of place. To Subikahn, his twin looked hideous: his breaths rattling, his skin sallow, his lids fluttering strangely over glazing eyes.

Chymmerlee sank to her knees beside Saviar, Subikahn hovering like an anxious father. She raised a hand, and a faint glowing outline appeared around it.

In a flash, Subikahn threw himself between them, sword at Chymmerlee's throat.

She staggered backward with a desperate whimper, her features twisted in a mask of terror, her arms drawn tightly against her.

"What are you doing?" Subikahn demanded. "That was magic."

Frozen in position, clearly afraid to move, Chymmerlee stared wide-eyed at Subikahn. "Of-of course it was magic. How-how else did you expect me to help someone this far gone?"

How else, indeed? Subikahn had not thought that far ahead. Every healer he had ever known used herbs to treat their patients. He lowered the sword but remained between the sorceress and his brother. "How will I know if it's healing magic . . . or murder?"

Chymmerlee's arms fell back to her sides. The fear drained from her face, replaced by a grim determination that made every freckle stand out. "We haven't time for a dissertation on types of magic, and I didn't come here to be assaulted. I'm trying to save your brother's life. Are you going to stand aside or not?"

She had a point Subikahn could not deny. Either he trusted her and let her work, or he dispatched her. No one could succeed at anything under the conditions he had created. Subikahn stepped aside, jamming the sword back into his belt. "Just don't hurt him. Please." He knew he sounded pathetic, but he found it impossible to do otherwise. "Please. My twin means everything to me."

Chymmerlee stiffened, clearly startled, but she moved back toward Saviar and knelt beside him. Once again, the glow surrounded her palms. She glanced warily at Subikahn, who deliberately raised his hands in a peaceful gesture. Apparently satisfied, she drew circles over Saviar's still form before stopping directly over the bandages encircling his leg. She looked up. "May I take these off?"

Subikahn nodded stiffly, reassured by the question. If she had intended to steal his soul, she would not need to worry about such details.

Chymmerlee unwound the bandages. As each layer fell away, the stains became larger and darker, until the last pieces came free, releasing a torrent of red-brown pus. The edges of the wound had blackened, and snakelike bands of scarlet wound under his tunic and down to his toes. Saviar stiffened slightly and loosed a coarse grunt, but he did not otherwise move. His eyes remained closed.

"This wound has festered badly."

"I know," Subikahn said softly. "I know. Is there anything you can do?"

Chymmerlee's expression revealed nothing, and a year seemed to tick past before she answered, "I'll try." Her hands hovered over Saviar's leg, shining brightly, and every movement left a sharp trail of light. "I'll need some quiet time. Why don't you fashion a litter? My work will be for naught if we can't move him to a more capable healer."

Subikahn appreciated having something to do other than study her every movement and worry. Hel could not come for Saviar as long as Chymmerlee moved him always a few moments farther from death. He saw no real purpose to her request. He was not strong enough to carry Saviar alone, and it seemed unlikely she could do much to help. They might manage to drag him short distances, with great effort, but it would take a month to reach even the nearest town.

When Subikahn returned with an armload of sturdy wood, Saviar did not appear much different. The flow of pus had stopped, though whether because Chymmerlee had staunched it or the amount trapped in the bandages had run its course, he did not know. The edges of the wound did seem more purple than black, and the red streaks looked, perhaps, a trifle less angry. Saviar continued to sleep. He no longer grunted, and his chest rose and fell in regular breaths. Though he had hoped for more, Subikahn would take whatever help he could get. Without Chymmerlee, Saviar would not have lasted the day.

Subikahn crouched at his brother's head, peeling away copper-colored hairs sweat-plastered to a forehead that still felt dangerously fevered. He stared at Chymmerlee, suddenly feeling desperately indebted and ashamed. He wanted to apologize but worried that talking might interrupt her concentration. He had so many things he wished to say, so many questions to ask. But, for now, he concentrated only on his project.

CHAPTER 29

The hardest task in war is to lie in support of those engulfed in the fight.

—*General Santagithi*

WHEN SUBIKAHN FINISHED CRAFTING a litter large enough to support his broad-boned, powerful brother, he found Chymmerlee pawing through their packs. *A thief, too?* Irritation flared, swiftly suppressed. She could have everything he owned in payment for bringing Saviar back from the brink of death. "Looking for something?" he asked, trying to hold judgment from his tone.

Chymmerlee dropped the pack, cheeks flushing in raw circles. "I'm sorry. When I expend that much energy, I get desperately hungry. Your packs are practically empty. Don't you men carry anything to eat?"

Subikahn dropped down beside her, feeling foolish. "I've got all our clothing piled on Saviar, and I'm afraid we're better warriors than hunters."

"Saviar," Chymmerlee repeated, looking toward the sleeping figure. "Is that your brother's name?"

"Yes." Subikahn suddenly realized his major breach in etiquette. "And I'm Subikahn. I'm sorry I didn't tell you sooner."

"Well, you were too busy . . . um . . . threatening me." Chymmerlee's smile made it clear she meant no malice.

Nevertheless, Subikahn lowered his head. "I'm sorry about that, too. I was just—"

"—worried about your brother. Who wouldn't be?"

"Yes." Subikahn rose. "I'll get you something to eat. I've got a good idea, now, what's not going to make us sick."

Chymmerlee laughed, though Subikahn had not intended his words as a joke. "Why don't you let me do the gathering. My tastes run a bit grander than just not getting sick."

Subikahn smiled sheepishly. "All right. I'll restart the fire." He headed toward Saviar while Chymmerlee disappeared into the woods, his waterskin in her hand.

Subikahn stirred the ashes, finding an occasional enduring ember. He tossed on a handful of kindling, watching one tenacious cinder blacken a threadlike fork of a larger branch. Gradually, a thin line of smoke emerged, then a spark rose into a tremulous fire. Subikahn rearranged the kindling to take advantage of the flames before turning his attention to his brother.

Saviar's face looked more familiar than it had in days, his sturdy jaw and classically handsome features restored from the pall of pain and concern that had enwrapped them for the last several days. He placed his fingers against Saviar's neck, rewarded by a strong, steady beat. Chymmerlee had not disturbed the plastered layer of clothing, but had simply laid a single cloak over him. The leg was rebandaged. The red lines dragging out from the wound had not wholly disappeared, but they looked less swollen, less prominent, and extended only to his upper thigh and mid-calf.

"Saviar," Subikahn said in a loud whisper. When he got no response, he spoke louder and added a sturdy shake. "Saviar!"

Saviar responded only with a grunt. The tip of his tongue appeared briefly between his lips, then disappeared back into his mouth.

"Saviar, wake up!"

Saviar only snuggled deeper into the cloak. His lids did not even flutter.

"Wake up! Wake up!" Subikahn screamed into Saviar's face. He shook his brother so hard he worried to further injure him.

Again, Saviar grunted and moved a bit, but he did not open his eyes or attempt speech.

Subikahn threw himself to the ground beside his brother. What good did it do to drag Saviar from Hel's grip, only to leave him alive but senseless? The gratitude he had felt only moments earlier turned to resentment. He knew he should not judge until he had all the facts from Chymmerlee, but he suddenly worried that she would never return. The possibility that she did work for Hel, that she had saddled the brothers with the worst possible fate for all eternity crept into his mind and refused banishment. Terror merged with rage and hatred, a sense of utter failure, and it boiled into a mixture nearly beyond his control. It was all Subikahn could do to keep himself from chasing after Chymmerlee. Perhaps, that too, was what she wanted. While he ran after the messenger, Hel could safely swoop in and claim her prize.

By the time Chymmerlee returned, skirt loaded with strange roots, stems, and a single coney, Subikahn was pacing angrily. The waterskin slung over her arm left a wet patch on the side of her shift.

Subikahn had promised himself to prod gingerly but found himself rounding on the woman, helpless to stop himself from shouting. "What have you done to him! What have you done!"

Chymmerlee's features knotted in concern. She dumped her load unceremoniously and ran to Saviar. "What's happened?"

"He won't wake up!" A teary jerk in Subikahn's voice slaughtered the righteous anger. "I can't wake him." He choked, no longer able to hide behind rage. "What's wrong with him?"

Kneeling at Saviar's side, Chymmerlee rocked backward. "Subikahn, I told you I was only going to stabilize him. I can stop more poison from getting to his organs, but he needs to handle what's already there himself."

Subikahn did not understand. "Poison? I didn't—" He broke off, ashamed to tell Chymmerlee where Saviar's wound had come from.

"The kind of poison I'm talking about comes from festering wounds. If it gets bad enough, it travels through the body and damages organs: heart, brain, kidneys, everything."

Subikahn did not know what to say.

"That's why people with infected wounds die."

Subikahn had never thought of it that way. He understood how a festered limb might require amputation, but he never quite appreciated how it led otherwise strong warriors to fade away. "How can he 'handle' it if he's unconscious?"

Apparently satisfied with Saviar's condition, Chymmerlee returned to sort the foodstuffs. "That's the best way to handle it. If you take the strain of regular work off the body, you give it time to heal itself."

Subikahn shook his head. "But how can he heal without food and water?"

"He can't," Chymmerlee admitted, looking up from her sorting. "We'll have to get those things into him without him having to . . . ingest them."

Subikahn stared. The words made no sense to him. "How can you take food and water without . . . ingesting?"

"We'll manage." Chymmerlee offered three lumpy, brown tubers. "Bury those in the ashes."

Subikahn accepted the tubers, though they looked more like rocks than food. "Are these any good?"

"A delicacy," Chymmerlee assured. "Any chance you can skin the coney?" Though she had carried it over, she clearly did not wish to touch it again.

Subikahn felt certain he could figure it out. "Sure. Don't you want to?"

Chymmerlee made a noise of revulsion, and her features matched it perfectly. "This may sound stupid after I just cleaned a festering wound, but I don't like seeing blood."

It did sound stupid, but Subikahn was too polite to say so. He had spent enough time in the Eastlands to know most women were nothing like those of the Renshai. They suffered a squeamishness that would have left Renshai women rolling their eyes and snorting. He took the coney, and his utility knife, and set to work removing fur and skin from the meat.

While he worked, Chymmerlee piled round black berries in front of him, along with an assortment of weeds in red and light green. She set aside a couple of fat, semirigid stems, then went right to eating her berries, shoving them into her mouth in unladylike handfuls.

Subikahn pretended not to notice, even when Chymmerlee questioned him with a partially chewed mouthful still in place. "So, Subikahn, did I rightly hear you call Saviar your twin?"

Accustomed to disbelief, Subikahn nodded, braced for the inevitable questions. He continued his work on the coney, the skin yielding easily to the sharpness of the blade. A line of blood twined across his hands, and he checked to make certain it came from the carcass. A blade that well-honed sometimes cut without pain. "We're actual twins, yes. Born to the same woman, the same pregnancy."

"Would it be correct to guess that one of you resembles your parents while the other doesn't?" Chymmerlee seemed about to make a stunning revelation, so Subikahn's response had to catch her off guard.

"Actually . . ." Subikahn paused, scraping cautiously around the rabbit's legs. ". . . we both look very much like our fathers."

That comment elicited the usual blank stare.

Subikahn studied the food in front of him. He pinched a berry with his least filthy hand. It felt mostly firm, slightly yielding, the type of berries that might crunch before they gave up a sweet load of juice. He tossed it into his mouth. It broke open with a bit of noise, less a crunch than a squeak, releasing a spicy, nutty flavor he could not place. "Yes, it's possible, and it happened. Thrust into life-or-death situations, Mama slept with two good friends in close proximity. We were the results."

"Oh." The word emerged thoughtfully.

Subikahn got the idea her consideration had less to do with the oddity of two-fathered twins and more to do with the pronouncement she had intended to make. "What were you thinking? Before I told you about the two fathers, I mean."

"Well," Chymmerlee said softly. "I've been thinking about your ability to see magic. It requires Outworld or mage blood to do that."

Subikahn only nodded as he finished the skinning. He worried that admitting a sword had done the seeing for him would lose him Chymmerlee's assistance. Right now, with Saviar comatose, he needed her desperately. "Me? I have Outworld or mage blood?"

"Apparently. I thought you, or, more likely, your brother, was a *placeling.*"

That was a term Subikahn had never heard. "*Placeling?*"

"A creature with fey blood 'placed' magically into a human womb. Sharing a gestation with a *placeling* might have given the other twin simple abilities as well, such as seeing magic."

Now it was Subikahn's turn to just stare. "Does that . . . happen . . . often?"

"Extremely rarely."

Subikahn stabbed the skinned coney with a stick and held it in the fire. The pelt at his feet lay bloody and shredded, useless for anything; but at least the meat did not seem to contain any hair.

"It's one of those things that are more legend than truth, but I know of at least one case where a god hid his indiscretion with a mortal from his wife by placing the infant produced into the womb of a different mortal." Chymmerlee shivered, face pinched in revulsion. "That nearly ended in disaster."

The story sounded too similar to Colbey Calistinsson's history to believe it otherwise, yet Subikahn said nothing. Her last comment suggested she might not approve of Renshai. Right now, he needed her goodwill more than her trust. "And you thought my brother might be . . . a similar case?"

Chymmerlee grabbed the last handful of berries in front of her. "It would make sense why you can see magic but have no knowledge of it. And, let's face it . . ." She gestured at Saviar. ". . . isn't he just a bit too perfect to be wholly mortal?"

For reasons Subikahn could not explain, he felt a twinge of jealousy at the remark. He had no sexual interest in Chymmerlee, nor in any woman, but the frequent comments about his twin's remarkable appearance wore on him. "He looks just like his *mortal* father. Even more like his *mortal* grandfather."

Chymmerlee shoved the berries into her mouth and chewed thoughtfully. This time, she swallowed before continuing. "Have you ever seen your brother do anything that seemed miraculous?"

"You mean other than attract every female on the continent?" Chymmerlee giggled.

Subikahn thought it best to stick as close to the truth as possible when it came to Saviar. The knight's son had great difficulty lying, a weakness his twin did not entirely share. "He said he saw a *Valkyrie* once."

"Gosh." Chymmerlee absorbed that information.

Subikahn did not mention it had appeared at their mother's death. Valkyries chose only warriors, and only Renshai regularly allowed females to fight. "But that's the only 'miraculous' thing I can think of. He's a nice, scrupulously honest, irritatingly polite young man with some decent sword skills; but I consider him as normal as any brother." *More normal, in fact, than Calistin.*

"You mean, he's sweet, too? And kind?"

Subikahn sighed, feeling like a go-between in a cruel game of puppy lust. "Well, he is, after all, my twin brother whom I love and who, up until a moment ago, was just about dead." *I almost killed him.* Guilt flared anew. "I could hardly say he was an evil bastard, now, could I?"

Chymmerlee laughed. "No, I don't suppose so." Her expression turned thoughtful, and she cocked a brow. ". . . but is he . . . ?"

". . . sweet and kind? Yes." Subikahn responded honestly. "A young lady's dream. The perfect man."

Chymmerlee studied Saviar in the firelight, speaking softly, almost to herself. "It's a shame one like that came so close to death . . . might still . . ." She trailed off, but Subikahn got the message.

As opposed to an ugly, worthless oaf like me. Under ordinary circumstances, Subikahn might have made a sarcastic comment about how the beautiful naturally deserved longer, fuller lives than the plain, how their deaths were so much more undeserved, so much more poignant. But, at the moment, he suffered too much guilt for his role in his brother's predicament to belittle it. Instead, he only nodded. And suffered in silence.

Rain pounded the Western forests, turning the ground into a leafy, muddy soup. Silver Warrior and Darby's chestnut gelding, now named Clydin, stumbled through the muck at a pace resembling that of a mired turtle.

His silks soaked through to the skin, his hair hanging in wet red strings, Ra-khir did not bother to complain. He had known more than weather would keep him from following the three boys' trail directly. He had minimal tracking skills, and the young Renshai would surely stick to the deep woodlands now that they no longer traveled in a large group. Without horses, they had no need to follow roadways instead of picking their way through forests, and the latter probably seemed safer. Ra-khir had never intended to track them by sign but rather by information gleaned in nearby Western towns.

Darby, who had remained silent prior to meeting the Renshai, now had a million questions. "Those were real Renshai, weren't they, sir?"

"Yes, Darby, those were Renshai." From habit, Ra-khir rubbed at a dirt spot on Silver Warrior's neck but only managed to spread it further. "Your first encounter, I presume?"

"They didn't have horns or tails or anything! And they didn't even try to kill us."

Ra-khir smiled. In some ways, Darby seemed so mature for his age, but this had clearly rattled him. "Renshai aren't demons, Darby. They're human, just like you and me, except for their thorough devotion to the sword."

"And their Northern origins," Darby added.

Ra-khir nodded. "And their Northern bloodlines, though those have become diluted since they've lived in Erythane for *centuries.*" He wondered how long it would take before the Renshai simply became a known staple of the West, without the need for clarification. *Millennia, maybe? Certainly, not within Darby's lifetime.*

"Centuries? Really?"

"Really." Ra-khir appreciated the opportunity to teach. Though he preferred doing so through deeds, right now he cherished the distraction from the cold discomfort of the rain and the knowledge that he currently looked very un-knightlike. His father would have given him a dressing-down if he saw the disheveled face he presented. Luckily, he had no intention of entering any inhabited places until he got his appearance back under control. "Renshai denounced the attacking of innocents for sport at least three hundred years ago, long before the birth of any of those now alive." *Except Colbey.* Ra-khir did not add the thought aloud. He did not want to get bogged down in a discussion of ancient Renshai history but rather in the more recent facts that no one seemed to know or teach.

As Darby looked interested and curious, Ra-khir continued. "To my knowledge, they have never broken that vow. Since then, they have served as the bodyguards to all of the Béarnian princes, queens, and princesses. Even the current king has a Renshai bodyguard, in addition to the traditional bard who has always held that position. When wars blossom, the Renshai stand with the West, because it is their homeland as well. Or was."

"Was?"

Ra-khir wound between copses of thistles. "Until recently, when the Renshai lost a challenge to Northmen and were banished from the North and the West."

Darby nodded his understanding, and dislodged rainwater rolled down his forehead. "So that's why they're here. Headed eastward."

"Right." Ra-khir looked ahead, trying to anticipate an easier route through the brambles that would not get them trapped in impassable foliage and deadfalls. He hoped they'd find a manufactured roadway soon. Once the rain stopped, the moisture would draw the blackflies and mosquitoes in droves. "And they have harmed no villages or towns. Their only battle was the one where you and I came upon the results."

"Northmen attacked them." Darby had obviously listened to the Renshai over dinner the previous night, though he had spoken very little.

"Right."

"Why?"

Ra-khir hesitated. He could not get inside the heads of Northmen, but the answer seemed obvious nonetheless. "Their hatred is strong, Darby. When generation after generation has distorted history far beyond truth and made it seem as if aggressors were victims, it can spawn a hatred so intense that it defies any logic. As a group, Northmen have intended to exterminate each and every Renshai for so long it has become a part of their national psyche, their day-to-day obsession. They spew this vitriol to their innocent children, telling them a special place in Valhalla exists for slayers of Renshai, no matter the means. To die killing Renshai is their ultimate honor."

"Because they also believe Renshai are demons?"

Ra-khir shook his head. "I don't think so, Darby. Deep down, they know Renshai are humans. They bleed like humans; they die like humans. But it suits the Northmen to spread the stories because superstitious Westerners believe them. And, the more support they garner for their hatred, the more they justify and spread it. Someday, they hope, the entire world will hate Renshai as much as they do."

Darby nodded ever so slightly, surely contemplating what he had learned about Renshai in his own upbringing. At least, he seemed fully willing to discard the stories on the word of a Knight of Erythane. That boded well for the West and the Renshai.

If Darby is representative, then we knights have a duty we have neglected for far too long.

"So why do the Northmen want the Renshai in the Eastlands?"

Again, Ra-khir had to speculate. "I don't think they necessarily do. First, the Northmen simply drove the Renshai from the North; but that didn't work. The Renshai returned. Next, they confined all the Renshai to one island in the North. That might have worked, except the Northmen reasoned that while they had all the Renshai in one place, it would prove easy enough to annihilate the entire tribe in one enormous battle."

"It didn't work."

"It nearly did. As history tells the story, only two Renshai survived. And they were both males."

Darby stared. "Two males cannot reestablish anything."

"Especially," Ra-khir continued, "when one died young and the other was infertile. But it turned out that a few Renshai had not actually returned to the North. And, though the Renshai who did originally deemed them traitors, it was through them that the current line was established. Less purely, of course, but the sword training mattered as much as the bloodline. However, because the Renshai tried to maintain both, it has taken them centuries to get their numbers back into the hundreds. Because, for a half-blood Renshai to receive any training, his non-Renshai parent has to be deemed worthy at the time of his birth. Renshai standards are near-impossibly high, so that happens only rarely."

A light appeared in Darby's eyes. He had made the connection. "And you were deemed worthy, so your half-blood sons are Renshai."

"Yes," Ra-khir admitted. "Though I'm still not entirely sure how. Renshai do not have the same opinion of knights that the remainder of the Westlands does."

Darby studied Ra-khir with an expression akin to worship.

Suddenly, Ra-khir wished he had not broached the subject. He had not meant to brag. He dropped the tangent to finish his point. "The Renshai's numbers have apparently gotten large enough to bother some Northmen. As near as I can figure it, they intend to get the Renshai banished from every part of the world. That would put every world leader in the position of having to execute any Renshai they found. One by one, the Renshai would get killed or go into hiding, which would make it unlikely they could find one another. The ultimate hope would be that Renshai parents would not train their children for their own safety, and the race would die out entirely."

"That's . . ." Darby sputtered. "That's . . . just . . . evil."

"It is."

"We should help them. We should attack the Northmen and—"

"No." Ra-khir knew lack of experience, not morality or intelligence, sent Darby toward thoughts of war. "Hatred cannot be combated with more hatred, and not every Northman is to blame. While a large majority do hate Renshai only because of lies their parents taught them, there are still some who see no problem with peaceful coexistence or have even managed to overcome their learned prejudice. What good would come of slaughtering the good with the bad?"

"But—"

Ra-khir had not yet finished. "Also, the Northmen have done such a thorough job spreading their lies and prejudice, that most Westerners have lost their objectivity. Even when the Renshai do nothing more than defend themselves, they are seen as the aggressors and condemned. Even when they do nothing whatsoever, it is said that they stole the land they occupy and they should be driven from it."

Darby's mouth remained open, but no words emerged. His expression mingled rage with bewilderment.

"It's a tricky problem, one Renshai and logicians have struggled with for centuries. You and I are not likely to solve it in a fortnight, let alone a single discussion."

Darby closed his mouth. "So what can we do?"

"We do," Ra-khir said calmly, "exactly what I've just done. We change the minds of people slowly, one by one, if necessary. We do it morally and honestly, for a single lie would betray us. And we hope that, eventually, right prevails."

CHAPTER 30

*One man cannot be skilled at everything; each has his own special
excellence.*

—*General Santagithi*

THOUGH IT MEANT FALLING farther behind, Ra-khir took the
time to dry out and neaten himself, his steed, and his gear before riding
into the first Western city he and Darby came upon. He had no way of
knowing exactly what route his boys had taken, but it seemed logical to
ride straight northward and ask about them as he traveled. They would
stand out in the small villages and towns, not only for being strangers
but for the oddness of their trio: one enormous redhead, one wiry and
dark, and the last childlike and as golden-pale as any Northman; and
yet all brothers. Their obvious weaponry would also draw attention,
and Ra-khir knew no Renshai would ever hide his swords.

As promised, Ra-khir never forgot that he represented the Knights
of Erythane. By the time they found the first small village, he had
combed his hair, washed out every stain, straightened each bit of his
clothing, groomed his steed to gleaming white, and properly worked
the ribbons back into Silver Warrior's mane and tail. Darby watched
each chore with fanatical interest, as if to memorize not just the actions but Ra-khir's individual movements and even his breathing.
That Darby's intentions were sincere, Ra-khir never doubted, and
he promised himself not to let circumstances drive him to irritability.
Darby meant only well, and his intensity would make him not only a
bother, but an excellent knight candidate.

Forest gave way to farmland, which opened onto a quaint little village. Though it was broad daylight, few people walked the streets, still
muddy from the rain. Water dripped from the thatched roofs of myriad
cottages, and the people Ra-khir passed seemed not to notice them at all.
They kept their eyes downcast and conversed only in ragged whispers.

For the first time since leaving Erythane, Ra-khir made it all the way to the central tavern seemingly unnoticed. Intending only a short stay for information, he hitched Silver Warrior to a nearby railing, tended briefly to the animal's comfort, then waited while Darby did the same for his mount. Almost immediately, the stallion dropped his head, eyes closed, to nap.

Ra-khir held the door open for Darby but entered first, as good sense warranted. More trouble lurked in unfamiliar drinking places than on quiet village streets, and he had a duty to protect his smaller, younger charge.

The door opened on a warm tavern with only nine tables, all but one unoccupied. A few more stools stood empty around a rickety, wooden bar. A dying fire flickered in its grate. Though stale, the odors of last night's dinner and spilled ale piqued Ra-khir's hunger. Travel rations could not compare with a home cooked meal, even if it only consisted of cold leftovers.

Since he needed information, Ra-khir chose the barstool nearest the occupied table. Four men sat around it, talking softly in a huddled mass. A stout barkeep approached, his beard outlining a face filled with a combination of discomfort and outrage. He leaned on the counter, which groaned under his weight, and displayed flabby, freckled arms. "Good day. What can I get for you men?"

Darby grinned as he took the stool beside Ra-khir, clearly pleased at being addressed as a man.

Ra-khir hated to spoil Darby's thrill, but it needed doing. "We'll have two plates of whatever you have, please. Some ale for me, and a bowl of goat milk for the boy."

The barkeep turned, muttering something under his breath, of which Ra-khir caught only the word "boy."

Believing he would get more information from the gathered men than the prickly barkeep, Ra-khir turned toward them and waited to catch one's eye.

It took longer than he expected, but a burly, coarse-featured man finally looked his way.

Ra-khir smiled. "I apologize for interrupting, but I wondered if any of you gentlemen might have seen three young strangers pass through here recently?"

Heads shook, a few mumbled words passed between them, then the one who Ra-khir had addressed finally answered. "No groups of strangers, sir. Only one."

A younger man covered in dirt added, "Aye, one we wish had never come." He squinted, studying Ra-khir. "Pardon me, sir; but are you a knight?"

Ra-khir rose from his seat as courtesy demanded and gave his familiar introduction with a bow and a flourish. At the conclusion, he had the full attention of all four of the men.

"Pleased to meet you, Sir Ra-khir," the burly man said. "Pardon us if we wish you could have gotten here a few nights earlier."

Ra-khir could only give the men an empathetic gesture and his attention. He had had no way of knowing they had need for a Knight of Erythane. "Oh? What happened then?"

"Stranger came in here." This time the eldest at the table spoke, a squat man with sagging, weather-beaten skin in faded leathers. "Not much more'n a boy, really. Challenged one of our best farmers to a duel, which he naturally refused."

As the speaker paused for breath, the first man took over the narrative. "But the stranger wouldn't stop badgering him until they had that duel. And the boy butchered ol' Karruno right out there in the street, then walked away like it weren't nothing."

Ra-khir's throat squeezed. He had to know. "Was this stranger a childlike blond with absolutely no sense of humor and two swords at his hips?"

All four men stared. At length, one spoke. "Sure was. Is Erythane looking for him?"

"No," Ra-khir said honestly. "But I am. Personally. He didn't happen to leave his name, did he?"

"I heard he did, sir," the younger man said, putting his ale aside. "But no one remembers exactly what it was. They say it started with Cal, sir."

Ra-khir only nodded as thoughts raced through his mind. Calistin had come here alone, causing trouble. Thialnir was right, Calistin did need the wisdom of his older brothers; but, apparently, they had not caught up with him. At least not as of that previous evening.

Darby watched the exchange in total silence. Ra-khir appreciated that he did not blurt out anything regarding Renshai or Ra-khir's direct relationship to Calistin. He already felt responsible.

"Does Karruno have a widow? Children?" Ra-khir knew money would not make up for such a loss, and it would seem crass to offer; yet the man's family would need something to tide them over until they found relatives to assist them. If he gave his coinage directly to them, no one would know.

A few of them chuckled. The first man replied. "No, sir. A lot of women was interested, but he wasn't ready to settle down."

The news relieved Ra-khir of some of his burden, but he still felt responsible for the tragedy. Relatives or other farmers would take over Karruno's property and deal with his crops and livestock, but no one could ever truly replace the man himself. He looked at Darby, making no effort to hide his pain.

Darby made a noncommittal gesture but remained silent. It was not his place to speak.

The barkeep swept back in to toss down two plates of meat, tubers, and vegetables along with the requested drinks. He paused suddenly, studying his patrons more carefully. "Hello. You wouldn't happen to be Sir Ra-khir, a Knight of Erythane, would you?"

Ra-khir's heart skipped a beat. *They know.* Nevertheless, he would not lie, even if it meant taking the punishment for his son's indiscretion. "I am."

The barkeep nodded smugly. "Thought I recognized a man of character."

Ra-khir felt grimly undeserving of the compliment.

"Messenger rode through this morning. If we saw you, we were to tell you to go back to Erythane."

"Back to—" Ra-khir could scarcely believe it. His father knew he had no intention of returning without finding his missing sons. Clearly, Calistin needed someone with common sense to guide him.

"Apparently, Béarn's under attack, and they need every able sword arm."

No! Ra-khir knew as much about the Pirate Wars as anyone, yet no one had ever before considered it frank warfare. Apparently, something had changed for the worse. If Béarn needed him, he had no choice but to abandon everything and return. He looked at Darby. "As soon as we finish eating, I need to take you home."

Darby took a long gulp, then turned Ra-khir a stern look that brooked no argument. "My 'home' is now Erythane. I have as much right to protect the high king's city as anyone." His brave words would have landed more forcefully had he not sported a mustache of goat's milk.

Ra-khir graced the sentiment with the dignity it deserved. "Very well, Darby. As soon as we're finished eating, we'll head for Béarn." He had no real intention of allowing the boy to fight, but Darby could remain reasonably safe with the other knights' apprentices in Erythane. He wondered in how many towns and cities the messengers had left word for him and how many additional swordsmen would heed the call as well.

Ra-khir dropped three gold coins on the countertop. "Whatever is left from our payment needs to go to Karruno's funeral and family. A man that beloved deserves the best."

The barkeep's nostrils flared as he swept up the coins. "That's very generous, Sir Ra-khir. Please return anytime. Anytime!"

"Most gracious of you." Ra-khir gave back the polite reply, though he did not believe his family would prove as welcome as himself. He worried for Subikahn and Saviar, for Calistin most of all; but he knew where his loyalties had to lie. His father knew how important this mission was to Ra-khir. Knight-Captain Kedrin would only have called him back from necessity. He had no choice but to heed the call. *When Béarn is in trouble, the Knights of Erythane will always be there.* Ra-khir realized something else. *Right now, Béarn needs the bodyguards to its heirs, and the Renshai's swords, more than ever.*

⚔———

Calistin awakened in a wet and shivering fog. A week had passed since his adventure in the Western tavern, a week spent slogging through a forest that seemed inexhaustible. Using the sun as a guide, he tried to keep his movements as northward as the towering trunks and tangled undergrowth allowed. After twice catching himself wandering in circles, he learned to stop walking at sunset, devoting himself to swordcraft and sleep until the morning. It not only honed his skill but also served as distraction from the hunger gnawing always at his belly.

Desperately thirsty, he sucked at leaves on the nearest tree, singling out the curled ones that had best collected the rain. Each sip was frustratingly small, insect portions that barely touched the fire in his mouth, the parching of his throat, and still dropped like lead into his empty stomach. He had tried eating the plants around him, but the nettles stung his gums and the others tasted more like dirt than food. Tough and stringy, he found them tasteless and impossible to satisfactorily chew. He tried cooking roots, but they charred into ash rather than plumping into the fragrant tubers he knew. In the past, food and water came to him. The Renshai saw to it that their great champion never wanted for anything.

Now, the effects of slow starvation frustrated Calistin into fits of rage. His lightning-fast reflexes slowed, and he found himself struggling to remember the intricacies of the more difficult maneuvers. When engaged in *svergelse,* nothing else mattered; but, the instant he stopped, the hunger bore down on him again, insistent and impossible to ignore. As of yet, he had not found plant matter he could stand. No bird or bunny stayed long enough to accept a physical challenge, and Calistin had never trained to chase down cowards who could fly.

Uncertain when he would find his next collection of water, Calistin lapped moisture off every leaf within his reach. Surely, his travels would soon bring him to civilization or, at least, a stream. He dreamed of stumbling onto a farm field. A pig or sheep would not think to run from a lone human, and he could swiftly make up for a week of hunger.

Torn between finding every drop of water and the need to move onward in the hope of locating more, Calistin finally continued walking. Every muscle in his body ached, and his kidneys felt like boulders. He could not remember the last time he had needed to relieve himself. His clothing reeked, touching his skin in icy patches, then peeling away. Wind cut through myriad holes, and enemy blood had stiffened to prickly wrinkles.

As Calistin walked, he imagined a feast of roasted pheasant and spiced cider, laid on a bed of fancy greens and succulent roots, dressed with vinegar. He could almost smell the odor of roasting meat, then he believed he did. He knew it had to be his nose playing tricks, but his mind told him otherwise. A light breeze from the east definitely carried the irresistible scent of cooking.

Calistin's mouth went thick with something not quite saliva. He no longer cared whether or not the odor was real; he could not tear his concentration from it. He had little choice but to follow it. He ran a few scenarios through his thoughts as he half-ran, half-stumbled toward the food. They were traveling merchants, or bandits, or royals on an outing. It did not matter. They would share, or they would die. If he had to kill someone to get it, he would relish the opportunity to fight. In the end, he felt hungry enough to roast and eat his opponent as well.

As Calistin drew nearer, all doubt vanished. The smell grew stronger, and smoke curled through the bushes. He sprang into a small clearing to find a rabbit skin laid out on a log and the meat hissing and spitting in the fire. No nearby human tended it. Calistin found himself shaking. Even in his desperation, he knew better than to reach into open flames with hands he relied on so completely. He also refused to dishonor a sword, instead casting about to find a large enough stick. Abruptly, he found himself face-to-face with Treysind.

A grin split the boy's dirty face, and he flung himself into Calistin's arms. "Hero, I's finded ya! I's so glad I's finded ya!"

Startled beyond words, Calistin allowed the boy to fully embrace him. "Treysind? Is that *your* dinner?"

Calistin's damp and filthy tunic muffled Treysind's reply. "It's ya's if ya's wants it, Hero. Ya hungry?"

The question was gross understatement. Finding a stick, Calistin poked the meat from the fire, not caring about the dirt he dragged across it. He ripped off a chunk. Feeling the first stirrings of pain that indicated he would burn flesh if he didn't let go, he popped the morsel into his mouth instead. Logically, he knew it was stupid. The grease burned his tongue much quicker than it would callused fingers, but Calistin did not care. He barely chewed before swallowing, then tore off another hunk. Before he knew it, he had the carcass stripped to the bones.

Treysind watched him, beaming.

Only then, as the warmth spread through his gut, Calistin realized two things. First, his tongue and throat stung from the too-hot meat. And, second, he had not left a scrap for his companion. "I'm sorry, Treysind. I guess I was too hungry to think about you."

"Don't worry 'bout me." Treysind gestured at the fire, where a second coney already roasted. "Ya's kin have that one, too, if ya's want. I kin git plenty more."

Calistin looked from the boy to the fire and back. Then he repeated the motion. "You can?" He did not understand how a child who could not fight his way through an empty field could succeed at something at which a Renshai had so miserably failed.

"Sure."

"How?"

Treysind held up a long bow. "Wit' dis."

Calistin could not help recoiling in distaste. Renshai shunned bows as cowards' weapons. *Yet*, he realized, *Treysind isn't using it for battle.* "Where'd you get . . . that?"

"I taked it off a dead Nort'man."

"A dead . . . ?"

"When's they 'tacked yas. 'Member?"

Calistin could not forget. "You stole it?"

Treysind shrugged. "He weren't usin' it no more. I thinked I could put it ta better use."

Calistin had to admit Treysind had. He looked eagerly at the cooking rabbit. It would take a lot of food to make up for several days without. "You're a marvel, Treysind."

Treysind threw out his chest, grin enormous. He seemed to glow with pride.

Only then it occurred to Calistin how important his praise was to the boy. And how rarely he gave it.

"I's gots more food, too, if ya's want it. An' some water."

"Water?" Calistin grew even more excited at the prospect of a full swallow of liquid. "You have water?"

Treysind dragged a pack from a cluster of brush into the clearing. He rummaged through it, then tossed a skin to Calistin. "Here. Have as much as ya wants ta. There's more."

Calistin uncorked the skin and poured water into his mouth. Though silty, it soothed the pain of his tongue and throat. To him, it tasted like a wave of golden honey: sweet, silken, and utterly welcome. He chugged it down, unable to stop until he had drained the contents. Only then, he lowered it. "Thanks."

"Ya's welcome," Treysind said, with far more enthusiasm than the phrase warranted. "Ya's verry *verry* welcome."

An awkward silence ensued. Calistin looked skyward, through the tapestry of branches, like brown knitting against the blue expanse of sky. "Ready to move on?"

"Wit' ya?" Treysind's smile grew broader, if possible. "Ready." He slung the pack across one skinny shoulder. "Where's we goin'?"

"North." Calistin started walking, then stopped. "Ultimately. For now, the nearest town." He turned to face the boy. "I don't suppose you happen to know where that is?"

Treysind's head bobbed, and he pointed westward. " 'bout a day thataway."

"Thataway it is." Calistin switched direction. "Perhaps you should lead."

"Wit' plesher, Hero." Head held high, Treysind marched in the indicated direction.

Calistin followed, silently running sword maneuvers through a brain already much clearer for nourishment. A sensation kept intruding on his thoughts, a feeling of foreboding that had nothing to do with enemies. His mind told him he had left something important undone, something of as great a significance as missing a daily practice. As much as he tried to put the feeling aside, it gnawed at him, grinding, almost unbearable. He believed it involved Treysind in some fashion, but that did not make sense. He had, after all, remembered to thank the boy.

As the two travelers moved lightly and easily through the brush, Calistin remained silent, lost in his own thoughts. Treysind stayed quiet also, apparently in deference. He frequently paused to study the Renshai, opened his mouth as if to speak, but nothing ever emerged. Their walk continued, clambering over deadfalls, shoving through overgrowth, dodging briars. Treysind occasionally paused to pluck flowers, leaves, and stems, and stuff them into his pack.

By midday, the pack seemed to have grown much heavier; Treysind fairly dragged it. And Calistin found himself assailed by hunger again.

"Time for a break," the Renshai announced, crouching against a wall of foliage that consisted of a massive fallen branch, wound through with vines and caught by bushes. "Are you tired, Treysind?"

Treysind nodded, dropping the pack. "An' hungry, too. Ya wants me ta shoot more food?"

Calistin nodded. He could think of nothing he desired more. "I'll make the fire."

Treysind removed bow and arrows from the pack. "There's more water in here, too, if ya's wants some. He'p yasself." Without waiting for a response, Treysind rushed into the woods with his weapon.

Calistin gathered twigs and branches, mouth watering with real saliva now, at the prospect of another roasted rabbit. By the time he had the fire blazing and the initial kindling charred, Treysind returned with three birds dangling from his hand: a quail, a dove, and a larger, colorful species Calistin could not identify.

Calistin had no idea what constituted a successful hunt, nor whether Treysind had real talent compared to others who made their livings catching food. He saw only a quick, satisfying meal brought by the boy he had, for so long, considered utterly incompetent.

Treysind raised his hand to display his catch.

Calistin grunted his appreciation. And smiled.

Treysind dumped the birds on the ground at his own feet, sat on a stump, and started plucking.

Leaving the fire and meal preparation to the boy, Calistin launched into life-affirming *svergelse*. A sword in each hand, he felt free from earthly worries, unfettered from the normal forces that bound him to the world. With movement came ultimate power. His swords sliced, jabbed, and glided through air, never in one position longer than an instant. Faster than sight, they skipped away, powered only by his arms and his imagination. For the first time in days, he felt good, his mind cleared to fully follow the lethal dance of his blades.

"Hero!" Treysind shouted, clearly not for the first time. "Hero!"

Irritated by the interruption, Calistin shoved aside the instinct to slaughter the boy. It would be so easy, barely a dip in motion; yet that thought bothered him enough to stop the practice instantly. "What is it?" He could not so easily keep the gruffness from his tone.

"Sorry if I's botherin' ya, Hero. Food's gettin' cold, though."

Calistin looked at the fire, still burning brightly, to the seared, unidentifiable meat laying nearby on beds of leaves. Tiny onions, cooked brown, surrounded the feast. He sheathed his swords. "Looks delicious. Where'd you get the onions?"

"Picked 'em while we's walkin'."

Calistin crouched in front of the food.

"Gots some sweet canes, too."

"Canes?"

Treysind handed Calistin a warm, thick stem, then dropped to the ground with one of his own. He took a huge bite off the top.

Calistin did the same. The piece was woody and tasteless. He chewed for several moments while Treysind watched in fascination.

Finally, the boy spoke. "Ain't ya gonna spit it out?"

By this time, Calistin had it ground into enough pieces he had to sweep it from his mouth with his fingers. It took more than a few tries to dig and spit out all the little bits.

"Ya don't eat canes, Hero. Ya sucks 'em." To demonstrate, Treysind put the tube up to his mouth.

Again, Calistin copied the motion. Warm, sweet sap flowed into his mouth, an unfamiliar taste for which he had no comparison. Startled, he jerked the stem away to study it.

Treysind tipped his own stalk farther and farther back, then lowered it and wiped his mouth on the back of a grimy sleeve. "Good, ain't it?"

"Very," Calistin admitted. "I've never had anything like it." He took another experimental taste. "How'd you figure it out? How to eat it, I mean. I'd have tossed it as a tasteless hunk of wood."

"When ya's hungry, ya figures out lotsa stuff."

Calistin disagreed, still staring at the cane. "I was starving. I never figured it out."

"It he'ps if ya's hungry alla time."

"Yeah." Calistin found himself staring at Treysind now, considering him in a whole new light. The boy was a survivor in a way he could barely comprehend. His *torke* always taught that a brave and competent man needs nothing but sword skill, and it always seemed right. Yet Calistin had learned in the past few days that the best swordsman in the world could not bully his dinner from trees. "Treysind," he started.

"Yeah?"

Calistin paused, not at all certain what he had planned to say. It seemed important, the type of thing a preoccupied father says to a son to make up for all the time he did not give the boy when it really mattered. But no further words came to him, and he managed only, "Could you pass me some meat?"

Treysind cupped his hands around the largest portion and shoved it, and its protective leaves, toward Calistin. "Try this. I don't know 'zactly what it is, but I's haded one bafore an' it tasted real good."

Calistin accepted the portion and tore off a piece of dark meat. More patient this time, he made certain it was not too hot before popping it into his mouth. It had a richer, moister flavor than most fowl, and the well-crisped skin made a pleasant contrast. He also thought he tasted some spice. "Wonderful," Calistin agreed. "Thanks."

Treysind dug into the quail, making appreciative smacking noises as he ate.

The more he ate, the more certain Calistin became that Treysind had added something savory to the meat. Yet that seemed nonsensical. Finally, curiosity got the better of him, and he lowered the bone he was stripping to ask. "Treysind, how is it that a boy who thinks moldy cheese is a prize knows how to fix food like a palace gourmet?"

Treysind dropped his own food to bounce excitedly. "Rilly? Ya thinks I's that good?"

Calistin had some actual experience to use as a comparison. Unlike Saviar, he had never dined at Béarn Castle, but he had eaten with King Tae as a child. "I think so. How?"

The words came out in such a rush, Treysind seemed to trip over them. "Well, I dint know. I mean, I's never had ac'shul meat ta work wit'. Least never more'n a scrap a somethin' I cou'n't figure out what it's used ta be. Just taked whatever I could from trash or streets or whatever. So's I never knowed how good . . ." Treysind paused, clearly trying to focus. "So's once't I's figgered out how ta use this thing." He gestured at the bow. "I's tryed ta figger out how ta make—"

"Whoa!" Calistin had to stop the flow of words. "You just figured out how to use it? You mean, just since you took that particular bow?"

Treysind bobbed his head repeatedly. "Never gots one bafore. So's I's started workin' on how ta make 'em smell good cookin', ya know, see if I's kin 'tract ya. I's tryin' lotsa flowers, plants . . ."

Still a sentence behind, Calistin stopped Treysind again. "You were trying to attract . . . me?"

"Course. I'd losted ya. An' I knowed Renshai ain't great food makers, so's I thought—"

Shocked silent, Calistin let Treysind continue without interruption while he considered the meaning of what he had just heard. The boy was clearly resourceful, and a lot more clever than Calistin would ever have given him credit for.

"—if I's could learn, I could bring ya ta me, since I weren't havin' much luck findin' ya, least not since that town where ya killed that man . . ."

"So, basically . . ." Calistin spoke slowly. ". . . you taught yourself to accurately shoot game with a bow, cook it, and spice it, as a way to find . . . me?"

Treysind cocked his head, clearly not understanding the point of the question. "Worked, dint it?"

"It did," Calistin had to admit. "And what a clever, simple little plan. Teach yourself to become a first-rate hunter and a topnotch epicure just to find someone who . . ." Originally intending to insert "didn't want you to find him," Calistin decided it might sound too offensive. He had ditched Treysind on purpose, and not for the first time; but speaking the words might gravely affront at a time when he preferred to understand. ". . . just to find someone."

"Ya's wort' findin', Hero. Whatever it tooked."

Calistin understood his appeal to Renshai and other adults who might envy or hope to benefit from his prowess. The boy's motives, however, confounded him. "You mean, because I can protect you?"

The look Treysind gave Calistin was fierce, and he took a snapping bite at his food. "Not 'cause a that." He chewed as he spoke. " 'Cause ya needs me ta 'tect ya."

Calistin laughed before he could stop himself, great humiliating belly guffaws that left Treysind looking vexed and angry. The boy returned to eating, shoulders hunched over his meal.

Calistin turned his attention back to his own food. Usually, long pauses never bothered him, but this one did. The conversation was clearly over, at least until the next stop. And, though he could not explain it, he felt as if he had lost something important.

CHAPTER 31

You can search forever in an empty well, but you will never find diamonds.

—*Mior*

THEY CALLED THEMSELVES THE Mages of Myrcidë, and they descended upon Saviar like a tidal wave. At first, Subikahn hovered over them, clinging to *Motfrabelonning*'s hilt. Soon, however, the flashes and flares of their auras became a distraction that sapped, rather than increased, his alertness. He had no choice but to trust Chymmerlee's tribe. Without her aid, he knew, Saviar would already be dead.

Chymmerlee took Subikahn's arm and led him from the chaos, and he found himself following in silent gratitude. For three days, they had traveled together, her magic buoying her end of Saviar's litter. Subikahn had exhausted himself with worry as well as effort. Yet, somehow, Saviar clung always to a life that seemed more like a lingering death.

Chymmerlee had finally brought them to a series of hidden caves at the edge of the Weathered Mountains. So well-hidden, in fact, that magic had to play a part in their concealment. The Myrcidians lived simply, it seemed, without frippery or finery to mar the homey simplicity of their interconnected lodgings. However, they looked reasonably fed, their clothing free from holes and patches. Windows opened onto the mountains, revealing their grandeur and beauty, yet, somehow, invisible from outside the caves. The mages did not suffer from a darkness that should plague any society so secreted.

Though he doubted he could escape through it, Subikahn still felt more comfortable next to a window overlooking the forests of the Westlands. Clouds partially swathed the sun, keeping the temperature comfortably cool, and a breeze blasted occasionally through the opening, carrying the aroma of flowers and summer greenery. For a concealed cave, it wholly lacked the stifling dusty, moldy odors he expected.

Chymmerlee delicately lowered herself into a wooden chair nearby. For the first time, Subikahn noticed she had a grace suitable for swordsmanship. "You should sit, too."

Subikahn shook his head and started staring through the window at the bobbing branches. "I prefer to stand, if you don't mind."

"As you wish." Apparently intrigued by Subikahn's attention to the outdoors, Chymmerlee leaned in her chair to look through the window also. "If anyone can save Saviar, they can."

Subikahn made a noncommittal noise. He had already trusted his brother to these strangers, these Mages of Myrcidë. "And if they can't?"

It was a foolish question, with only one answer. "Then he will die. But at least we will have given him a chance no one else could."

Subikahn made another wordless noise. He had no right or reason to complain, only the knowledge that the Myrcidians could not fail. His own life ended the moment they did. Suicide would condemn him to Hel; at least, he would join his brother there. He could never enjoy the perfect rewards of Valhalla knowing he had damned Saviar never to experience them.

Chymmerlee took Subikahn's hand. Hers felt soft, comforting, so unlike Talamir's callused fingers. Her touch alone eased some of the pain. "How did Saviar get that wound?"

It was not the first time Chymmerlee had asked, not the first time Subikahn had dodged the question. "First," Subikahn said, "tell me about your people. They clearly aren't elves. So where does their magic come from, and why do they hide from the world?"

Chymmerlee hesitated, avoiding Subikahn's searching gaze, becoming sharply focused on the scene outside the window that even Subikahn, in his short time there, had memorized. Finally, she sighed. "You've trusted us with the most precious thing in your life. I suppose it's only fair we trust you as well."

Subikahn nodded encouragingly. He truly was interested, and he felt certain the long story would also distract her from wondering about Saviar's injury, perhaps for a few more days.

"The Mages of Myrcidë did not always seek the shadows," Chymmerlee began. "Once, we were a powerful people. Some of the world loved and revered us, others feared our magic; but all knew us as a necessary part of society." She smiled sheepishly. "At least that's what I'm told. It was centuries past, long before my grandparents' births, that Myrcidians walked freely among the peoples of the West."

"And yet," Subikahn said softly, "you're not in the legends, not in the annals of history. I've never heard tell of the Mages of Myrcidë."

"Though we went by that very name, even then. And if we've been scrubbed from history, it is only because of one group of people, the most savage to ever slaughter their way across our world."

The Fenris Wolf came to Subikahn's mind. *The evil god, Loki. The hordes of Hel's dead who rose up for the* Ragnarok *that nearly ended the world.* Yet, he was not surprised by her next words.

"The Renshai." Chymmerlee fairly spat the name. "The Renshai's spree of murder saw the end of every mage. They branded the Myrcidians their greatest challenge, and they refused to end the battle until every mage was dead. Every mage, that is, but one. And that one mage, though he never fathered a child, did make it into the historical writings."

Subikahn forced his thoughts past her hatred of Renshai, knowing it too well to show any giveaway expression or gesture. He worried not for himself, but for Saviar. What if his ill brother said something in ignorance, something revealing? Could Subikahn convince the Myrcidians to discard the crazed ramblings of a dying man? Instead, he forced himself to focus on the one surviving mage. He knew he had heard of at least one Wizard. "Was it . . . the Eastern Wizard? The one credited with returning the great King Sterrane to his throne?"

"Shadimar," Chymmerlee supplied the name, and Subikahn recognized it. "That was him. The most powerful of the last four Cardinal Wizards, and the only one born to Myrcidë. Nearly immortal, he was forced to see his people destroyed, their utmost treasure plundered."

Chymmerlee's words brought back stories from the opposite viewpoint. Subikahn guessed which item the Eastern Wizard had prized, but every Renshai knew that the greatest of the Cardinal Wizards had been Colbey Calistinsson himself, the Western Wizard forced to stand against the other three—in triumph. "The Pica Stone."

Now, Chymmerlee stiffened, revealing the discomfort Subikahn had so well hidden. "You know of the Pica Stone?"

"Everyone knows the Pica. It was shattered, its pieces scattered throughout the many worlds. When its magic was needed, mankind and elves worked together to find its shards and re-create it. Now, it's Béarn's treasure, the testing item used to select the future high kings and queens."

Chymmerlee stared. "The Pica Stone was mended?" Her eyes widened with innocent awe. "It still exists? Our elders will want to know this. Will *need* to know this."

Subikahn wondered how they could not *already* know this. It had happened eighteen years ago. Shortly after his birth, his own parents had led the expedition. He had believed the recovery of the Pica common knowledge, but he supposed the secrecy of the mages might keep them ignorant of the goings-on in the rest of the world. "You said *all* of the mages were killed but one, and that one never fathered a child. So . . . where do you come from?"

The question jarred Chymmerlee back to the story, though she clearly needed to further mull his revelation. "The mages . . . were never allowed to marry commoners; it was thought to dilute the line, our power. Yet, apparently, a few did sneak off and create mixed offspring. Either these were unknown or deliberately ignored. But, centuries later, Jeremilan was born to common parents. Apparently, he carried the blood of two of those secretive unions, enough to grant him the power to discover and open the secret store of our ancestors."

"Secret . . . store?"

"A trove of lore and information, hidden for centuries and magicked so that only one of sufficient mage potential could happen upon it or open it."

"So," Subikahn put the details together. "This Jeremilan, born of common parents, had enough mage blood to become the new father of Myrcidë."

"Exactly."

"And the mothers of Myrcidë?"

"Well—it helps that mages can see auras."

The answer seemed to bear no relation to the question, and Subikahn stared questioningly at Chymmerlee. "Auras?"

"That glowy thing you saw around me that made you all crazy. That's an aura."

Subikahn remembered. "In all fairness, I thought you were a minion of Hel, and you were going to use that 'glowy thing' to kill my—" Abruptly realizing he once again sounded crazy, he laughed. "What's the purpose of that 'glowy thing,' that 'aura,' anyway?"

Chymmerlee also laughed. "I'm not sure auras have a purpose, other than helping magical beings recognize each other. It's just a byproduct of magic." The explanation made sense to Subikahn, but the words that followed did not. "You have one, you know."

"I have one?" Understanding seeped through. "You mean a glowy, aura thing?"

"Yes. You have an aura. A 'glowy, aura thing,' if you prefer."

"But I don't have any mag—" *I do,* Subikahn realized suddenly. *I have the sword.*

"You do." Chymmerlee echoed Subikahn's thought, then took a different tack. "Apparently, you have enough mage blood in you to grant you one. I haven't seen an aura on your brother yet, but he's been unconscious."

And I have his sword. Things came together in that instant. *Chymmerlee only helped Saviar because of my aura, because she believed we're of mage lineage.* Subikahn shivered at a terrible realization. He had no idea how long he could hide the truth from wielders of magic, no way to understand in how much danger it placed them. Clearly, the Myrcidians had the potential to wield great power, and they did not like Renshai. Saviar had demonstrated a bit more caution and craftiness than his famously guileless father and grandfather, but he would not know to hide his origins. They had, after all, intended to create a new, friendlier face for the Renshai.

If Chymmerlee had any inkling of the desperate boil of thought consuming Subikahn, she gave no notice. "Jeremilan searched for auraed people. When he found them, he got to know them. And, if they showed proper interest, he inducted them. At length, we had a small band with which to repopulate the mages."

"A small band?" Subikahn forced himself to keep his attention on the story, though more concerned for what Saviar might say upon awakening. He remembered the problems the Renshai had when they had been forced to re-create their tribe. Inbreeding remained a Renshai concern, which he assumed was why they agreed to accept him and his brothers despite their half-blood status. "Doesn't repopulating take a rather *large* band? Otherwise, you wind up marrying brothers and sisters, fathers and daughters."

Chymmerlee blushed. "It helps that mages outlive other humans, so we had time to pick, find, and choose. But, yes, we do have trouble finding new and unrelated blood. That's one of the reasons we're so eager to help you and Saviar. It's been many decades since we've added anyone not already in the clan."

Subikahn chewed his lower lip.

"You have the aura; and, unless your mage blood comes wholly through your father, your twin should have some, too."

Needing at least as much goodwill for Saviar as himself, Subikahn said quickly, "Oh, it's definitely not from my father."

Chymmerlee's brow beetled. "How do you know that?"

"Because my father can trace his wholly *Eastern* lineage to kings." It was at least partially true. Tae Kahn's bloodline was as pure and regal as mud, but it was almost certainly solely Eastern. And he was the king, though it had nothing to do with bloodline. "Mama's the

Westerner." *Also true, though not by blood.* It was all Subikahn could do to suppress a chuckle at the irony. His life depended on fooling mages into believing he descended from their pure line, when, in fact, he did not carry a single drop of even the meanest Western blood.

Chymmerlee clasped her hands, and her face lit up. "That's wonderful!"

Her exuberance surprised him. Subikahn could not recall the last time he had seen such obvious joy. "Wonderful?"

Chymmerlee brought her hands in front of her face, clearly trying to suppress her excitement. "It means Saviar has mage blood, too." Her efforts at hiding her mood failed. Her happiness came out in a light tapping of her toes that resembled pent-up dancing.

Subikahn rolled his eyes. He had seen that expression before. "You're in love with him, aren't you?"

"In love?" Chymmerlee narrowed her eyes, simulating horror; but the flush growing across her cheeks gave her away. "Why, I hardly know him. I've never even spoken to him. He's in a coma, by the gods." She pursed her lips sternly. "Besides, I'm sure a handsome man like Saviar already has too many girlfriends."

Subikahn returned his gaze to the window. The scene outside had not changed, the only movement the bowing of branches in a light breeze. He wanted to lie, to tell her Saviar's heart was taken; but he could not bring himself to do it. Right now, he needed the mages to like them, and Chymmerlee had done enough for Saviar to deserve better.

"Oh, they notice him, all right. But Saviar's always too caught up in swordwork to pay them any attention. I suppose some young woman will turn his head someday, but it hasn't happened yet." Subikahn smiled kindly. "You're free to try."

Chymmerlee lowered her head demurely, but Subikahn could tell just by her forehead that she wore an enormous grin.

Gradually, a morose feeling stole over Subikahn, for reasons he could not explain. Jealousy seemed impossible; he felt no attraction to Chymmerlee. For a moment, he wondered if he worried over losing Saviar's attention, but his heart told him otherwise. It was Talamir he missed, the courting dance, the heady days when a young man feels those first stirrings of affection but does not yet know where to take them and worries that the object of his interest will not return his love.

Chymmerlee's voice disrupted Subikahn's thoughts. "I'm eighteen."

The words seemed so out of place, Subikahn had to wonder. *Did I ask her? I don't remember asking her.*

"Well, I said we outlive other humans, which is true. I didn't want you to think that I only look young because I'm magical. And I'm really thirty or something."

Subikahn had never considered the possibility. "We're nineteen." Suspicions aroused, he asked, "And just how long do mages live?"

"True mages, the original mages, they went five hundred or so years."

Subikahn jerked his gaze from the window to stare at Chymmerlee. "Five hundred?"

"Sometimes seven or eight hundred. But we mixes may not live so long. Jeremilan is over two hundred, I believe—"

"Jeremilan is still alive—"

"—but we've had others who lived normal mortal spans or only slightly longer. In general, it seems like the more mage blood, the longer the life; but a lot of the purer bloods actually die in infancy or childhood."

Inbreeding. Subikahn nodded. The mages had a definite problem.

"I'm sorry. I'm boring you with all this information."

It should have been tiresome, yet Subikahn found himself intrigued. In the back of his mind, he realized he held a serious stake in knowing these details. *The Myrcidians helped us because they think we're mages. They need new blood.* A sharp lump filled his throat. *Could it be they want us for breeding stock?* The idea sent a shiver of dread through Subikahn. He had already suffered all the loveless sex he could stand, and he had no intention of attaching himself to these mages for the remainder of his life. For now, however, he had no choice but to play along. "Boring me? No, I'm fascinated." Subikahn finally sat. Placing his hands on his chin, and his elbows on his left thigh, he leaned toward Chymmerlee. "Please, tell me more."

As Treysind had predicted, they reached a town the following day. Surrounded by farm fields lush with summer crops, the buildings clustered at the center. Treysind stopped to fill the waterskins at a well, while Calistin glanced around the streets seeking some logical gathering point, such as a tavern. Finding none, he turned his attention to the people, all of whom stared at the strangers as they passed but none of whom paused to talk.

Treysind seemed to take forever. Besides carrying at least six waterskins by Calistin's count, he also kept careful track of his companion's location at all times. Apparently, he worried that Calistin would take advantage of an inattentive moment to disappear again. It was not an unreasonable fear.

As Calistin waited for Treysind to finish, he noticed a placard posted atop the well:

Sheaton Laws:
1. No killing
2. No stealing
3. No brawling
4. Do not display weapons of any kind
5. Only the bucket may enter this well

Calistin smiled, rearranging his sword belt to assure his swords showed prominently. Only a competent warrior would dare confront a man violating any of the first four rules, especially one so obviously well-equipped. While Treysind continued filling waterskins, Calistin leaned casually against the well, in flagrant violation of the law, and waited for the repercussions.

Now, Calistin noticed that the citizens whispered to one another as they passed, and a small crowd began to gather along the closest buildings, a safe distance from where he stood.

As they did so, Treysind grew visibly nervous. He paused frequently to glance at the growing chaos of spectators.

Finally, a man approached. Tall, broad-shouldered, and clean-shaven, he appeared to be about thirty. He wore a clean pair of brown britches, a tan woolen shirt, and a tunic belted at the waist. A cloak covered his outfit, but Calistin could make out a hilt buried beneath it. Though not openly, the man clearly carried a sword.

Calistin's opinion of the stranger plummeted. No Renshai would hamper his sword arm by pinning his weapon beneath fabric. He turned the newcomer a look of bored nonchalance.

Treysind stopped his task, set aside the last of his waterskins, and drew up beside Calistin.

The man extended a hand in greeting. "Welcome to Sheaton." He used the Common Trading tongue.

Calistin only nodded.

"Thank ya's!" Treysind said exuberantly.

Calistin frowned but said nothing, leaving the next move to the stranger.

The man let his hand drop to his side. "My name's Howall. I keep the peace here in Sheaton."

Calistin met his gaze.

Treysind looked at Calistin. Taking his cues from his hero, he also went silent.

The crowd seemed to lean forward collectively, listening for an answer that never came.

Locked into a one-sided conversation, Howall continued, "Just wondering if you read, young man."

Not wanting Treysind to answer and make them both look stupid, Calistin finally spoke, "I read."

Howall's brows inched upward. Clearly, he had assumed illiteracy accounted for Calistin's flagrant violation. "Did you happen to notice the laws of our town?" He tipped his head toward the placard.

Calistin did not bother to turn. "I noticed."

Treysind whirled, staring at the sign, though it seemed unlikely he could make anything out of it.

"Then, you know we don't allow the open display of weapons here."

Having already decided to answer only direct questions, Calistin said nothing.

Treysind looked from Calistin to Howall and back. "We ain't meanin' ta vi'late no laws . . ."

Calistin frowned, wishing the boy would just shut up, and not for the first time. "Yes I am. I'm meaning to violate the law."

Treysind's jaw clamped suddenly closed.

Howall's nostrils flared. "You mean to . . ."

"Yes."

"Why?"

Calistin also meant to irritate. "Why not?"

Treysind reached for Calistin's hand, but he jerked it away. The boy whispered, "What's ya doin', Hero?"

Howall kept his attention on Calistin. He peeled aside his cloak just far enough to grant access to his own weapon. "Then I'll have to ask you to leave."

Calistin never moved from his cavalier position against the well. "Ask, then."

Howall's brow furrowed. "What?"

"You said you would have to ask me to leave."

"Yes."

"So ask."

Howall's hands balled to fists. He had clearly lost patience, which pleased Calistin. "Young man, you're not funny. Will you either put away your weapons or leave Sheaton forever?"

"No."

"No, you will not pack up your weapons? Or, no, you will not leave?"

The conversation had grown tedious to Calistin, who was ready for his battle. "No, I will not 'either put away my weapons or leave Sheaton.'"

Again, Treysind reached for Calistin's hand, this time managing to brush it before Calistin knocked Treysind away.

"Neither?"

Treysind hissed, "Let's jus' go, Hero."

Now, Calistin recalled why he wanted to ditch his devoted companion. "I believe I made myself clear."

The crowd had shuffled closer. Howall seemed to take no notice. "Then you leave me no choice, stranger. I'll have to remove you from Sheaton."

"All right." Calistin finally stood up straight. "You may try."

Howall's brows shot up. He seemed more curious and uncertain than angry. "Very well." He reached for his hilt and started to draw.

Faster, Calistin whipped his blade out and slammed it against Howall's hilt, pinning it. A foot sweep sent Howall toppling, with Calistin's sword at his throat.

The crowd gasped, shrinking from the violence.

Calistin sheathed his sword in one fluid motion, exasperated by the ease of his victory.

Howall clambered to his feet. The light had gone out of his eyes, replaced by a flicker of fear.

"Would you like to try again?" Calistin suggested.

Howall set his jaw, then grabbed for his hilt. This time, he got it free before Calistin's blade licked through, chopping it from his grip.

Calistin could have caught it but did not respect his opponent enough to do so. Howall's sword crashed to the cobbles as Calistin sheathed his own weapon. He looked askance at the self-proclaimed peacekeeper. "Is that the best you can do?"

Howall's gaze went to his weapon on the ground. He started to reach for it, watching Calistin as he did so. Clearly, he did not wish to make himself any more vulnerable.

Calistin stepped away, less in a show of good faith than to denigrate. He did not need any advantage to destroy this pitiful excuse for a town guardian.

Howall picked up his sword but made no move toward Calistin. Nor did he look at the crowd behind him.

It was all too easy, and that bothered Calistin more than anything. This man, this best Sheaton had to offer, was not worth the time it had taken to talk to him. He addressed the crowd. "You deserve better." With that, he lunged in again.

Howall attempted to parry. Once more Calistin cut the sword from his hand, and then bore in for a power stroke that would claim the man's head.

"No!" Treysind leaped between them, forcing Calistin to harmlessly redirect his attack or skewer a friend.

Calistin chose the former, reluctantly. At the moment, it seemed more satisfying to cut through boy and man alike.

Howall tumbled to the dirt, Treysind flopped on top of him. "Don't kill 'im!" the boy shouted, scrambling for a better position. "He's jus' doin' his job."

"Fine." Though he would have preferred a clean beheading, Calistin sheathed his weapon. "Not worth cleaning his coward's blood off my sword." He stomped on the grounded weapon, the ultimate Renshai insult, then turned toward the farm fields. "Let's go."

Treysind sprang to his feet with a muttered apology. Grabbing his pack and waterskins, he scrambled after Calistin.

Not a word passed between the two until they had left the farm fields of Sheaton far behind and settled into a clearing beneath a thick overhang of trees. Though they prematurely darkened the area, the interwoven roof of branches also kept the ground free of underbrush. Calistin crouched, glancing around for kindling.

Treysind walked to the opposite side of the clearing, his back to the Renshai.

For several moments they remained in this awkward position. Calistin finally broke the silence. "I'll build the fire again, if you'll catch the food."

Treysind muttered an answer Calistin could not hear.

Calistin rose and walked to Treysind. "I said—"

"I heared ya," Treysind said, his words muffled by the hands he placed over his mouth and chin. "An' I sayed 'no.'"

"No?" Calistin repeated, puzzled. "You want to make the fire and brave eating what I find?"

"I's leavin', Cali . . . Cali-Stan. Ya ain't my hero no more."

"I . . . ain't?" Calistin did not know whether to question further or celebrate. He found himself laughing.

Treysind's arms slammed against his own chest. "Shouldn't figger ya'd care."

Calistin considered, surprised to find he did care. After trying so hard, so long, to lose the boy, he had finally come to grips with the realization that it would never happen. In the last day, he had even come to appreciate Treysind's wit and company. It seemed impossible he would lose it now. "I do care."

Treysind turned, as shocked by the sentiment as Calistin. "Ya cares?"

Now that he had spoken the words, Calistin realized they were true. "Of course, I care. If I didn't, I'd have killed you a long time ago."

"Then why's ya always laughin' at me?"

"I don't—" Calistin started, but Treysind interrupted.

"Ya do. Ya never laughs at nothin' funny. Only . . . only *mean* stuff."

"Mean?" Taken aback, Calistin did not know what to say. No one had ever spoken to him in this manner. His first instinct, to dismember the boy, passed swiftly. Calistin had spoken honestly; if he was going to kill Treysind, he would have done it long ago. "What do you mean by . . . mean?"

"Mean! Mean!" Treysind unfolded his arms. "Ya know, not nice."

Calistin shook his head. He did not need the word defined. He simply did not understand the concept. "You're saying I laugh at mean things?"

Treysind cocked his head, and his brilliant orange hair slid across one ear. "When someones trips an' looks silly, tha's funny. If they breaks they leg, it ain't funny."

Calistin shook his head. "I wouldn't find either of those things funny." Still, he considered Treysind's point beyond the poorly worded explanation. He did tend to find himself silent when others laughed with great amusement. He also frequently laughed alone, like just moments earlier when he belittled Treysind about his decision to leave. Clearly, denouncing his hero had meant a lot more to the boy than to Calistin.

Treysind turned away. "Ya's right. It prob'ly wouldn't be funny ta ya till ya breaks they's other leg, then kills 'em."

"What?" That went way beyond the explanation, and it seemed utterly unfair. "Treysind, what's actually bothering you? I'm not good at riddles."

Treysind's eyes became blurry puddles of white and blue. "When they's telled me ya killed that guy in the streets fo' no reason, I dint belief 'em. Then I seed what ya nearly done in Sheaton . . . y'ain't my hero no more."

Calistin rolled his eyes but did not dare to laugh. "Treysind, you've seen me kill before. You know it's what I do."

"I seed ya kill men what attacked ya, men what woulda kilt ya if they could. But I ain't seed ya torture no ones bafore. I ain't likin' bullies what kills fo' no reason."

Suddenly, the whole situation gained clarity. Calistin remembered how he had rescued Treysind from street toughs and understood how the boy might liken what had happened in Sheaton to the day they met in Erythane. *Only now I'm the one hurting a helpless innocent; and he's the one who swooped in, at great risk to himself, to save the victim.*

Calistin found himself desperately uncomfortable. He had never bothered to consider the world from another's viewpoint before. Many times, in conflicts with his brothers, his father had asked him to consider how Saviar or Subikahn might feel. Always, he had dismissed the idea, focused on his own innocence, his own needs and desires. He would say whatever it took to extract himself from the situation.

Nothing mattered but his swords, his practices, and becoming the consummate Renshai. Other people were merely props to use in his quest to become quicker, faster, more deadly. Anyone who could not significantly exercise his sword arm was unworthy of his attention, or even of life itself. They deserved nothing but derision and ridicule. *Laughter.* A band seemed to abruptly circle Calistin's heart, tightening and squeezing painfully. *"Ya never laughs at nothin' funny. Only . . . only mean stuff." The little* ganim *is right.*

Treysind was still talking. ". . . prob'ly gots a wife an' chillen. They dint do nothin' ta deserve losin' they's Papa. An' all's he did was try ta keep tha law—'s not like he was tryin' ta hurt ya . . ."

"You're right," Calistin said softly, expecting his concession to please his companion.

But it merely sent Treysind off on another track. "Ya's a killer, Cali-Stan, but I's never belief thems what sayed ya's jus' a killin' device without a—"

"—soul," Calistin finished. It explained so much.

Treysind blinked away tears. "I's gonna say a cons'ience. I knows ya gots a soul. Ever'one's gots a soul."

"I don't," Calistin said. "The gods say I don't. And if I don't have a soul, how can I be expected to think of anyone but myself?"

Treysind stared. The tears he had been fighting to keep back jarred loose, rolling down his cheeks. " 'Cause doin' what's nice and what's right don't gots nothin' ta do wit' havin' a soul. It's choosin' ta be a good person. An' havin' a cons'ience. That ain't something ya's borned wit' or the gods gived ta ya. Tha's somethin' ya decides ta have fo' yaself."

That put the onus back on Calistin, and he did not like it. "But I wasn't raised to—"

"I wasn't raised atall," Treysind interrupted. "But I still knows it ain't good ta hurt people what ain't hurtin' ya."

Calistin sighed. He found all the talk about morality irritating, and he always vented his strongest emotions on battlegrounds and practice fields. He had skimmed into a deep part of his psyche he had never tapped before, and it seemed dark, terrifying, and completely unnecessary. "Treysind, you can't catch a rabbit with a sword. Believe me, I've tried. I haven't got any money either. So, if you leave, I'll have no choice but to kill other travelers for their food."

Treysind wiped away his tears swiftly, and none followed. "So's, if I stays wit' ya, ya ain't gonna kill no ones?"

Calistin could not promise that. "Treysind, I'm challenging these warriors for a reason. I'm preparing to face my mother's killer. When I find him, I'll have practiced in real battles with many different *ganim* and will have built a reputation."

"Does that repoo . . . repyute . . ." Treysind started again. "Does ya gots ta be knowed fo' bein' a rut'less killer?"

"It helps."

"Rilly?"

"Yes."

Treysind sighed and tried again. "Can't ya be a rut'less killer a . . . a rut'less killers insteada nice folks?"

"That," Calistin had to admit, "would be even better. But—"

"Ya'd git knowed fo' bein' a killer, but pee'ple could still like yas. Ya could be ever'one's hero."

Once again, Calistin forced himself not to laugh at an idea that Treysind clearly found important. "It's not that simple, Treysind. The best fighters in town aren't always going to be demons. Even if they are, finding them would take time I don't have."

Treysind finally smiled. "Tha bestest villains often is tha bestest fighters 'cause no one kin catch 'em ta punish 'em wit'out gettin' kilt. If I kin finds 'em for ya, will ya practice on 'ems 'stead a guards an' good men?"

It seemed the perfect compromise, though Calistin worried that he might tie himself to something irritatingly hampering. "So long as you can locate these men quickly, and they give me at least a good challenge."

"I kin," Treysind promised.

"And, when I'm fighting, you stay out of it. Completely. You can't be diving in to 'protect' me."

Treysind's lip quivered, and he stood in silence several moments before finally forcing out, "All righ'."

"Then I will," Calistin agreed. "And now, will you please handle the meal?"

Treysind rushed to his pack for his bow.

CHAPTER 32

*Success never happens by luck; it is a matter of careful planning
that, sometimes, closely resembles happenstance.*
                                          —*General Santagithi*

MATRINKA REPOSED ON THE tall, canopied bed in the center
of her bedroom, the curtains drawn back to reveal the bureaus, ward-
robes, and the shelves that lined her room. Back propped against the
headboard and knees drawn up to support the large, silver tabby in
her lap, she petted Imorelda with the wistfulness that seemed to assail her whenever she found herself alone with her thoughts.

Three weeks had passed since Rantire had smashed Tae's nose.
Gradually, the blue-black bruises had faded from around his eyes;
and a bump had formed in the center where the bones knitted together without her ministrations. He looked more gaunt and haggard
at every meeting, and he imparted less and less useful information.
Meanwhile, the pirate attacks grew more frequent, more deadly,
and the news coming from the front more harsh and horrible. She
guessed it was worse even than she knew; Griff tended to protect her
from the worst of it.

"I'm worried about him," Matrinka told the cat as she ran her
hands over fur slick from her repetitive stroking. Few hairs came free,
most already swirling through the air of her room. "Your master is
courageous, but he's also a fool."

Imorelda purred heartily. Matrinka suspected she agreed. The
queen could almost hear the cat's response in her head, as she had
heard Mior for so many years. It seemed petty and self-indulgent
to pine over an animal when so many humans were dying for her
kingdom. Yet Mior had been so much more than just a cat: a confi-
dante, a physician, a sister, and her closest friend. "I hope he knows
how lucky he is to have you." Matrinka smiled as she spoke. She
knew how precious their bond was and took pleasure in the realiza-

tion that Tae had such an extraordinary relationship that no one but Matrinka knew about or understood. "You're a beautiful cat and a special friend."

Imorelda rolled over, still purring.

Matrinka rubbed her belly with appropriate gentleness. Few cats enjoyed the enthusiastic scratches that dogs preferred in this area. As she worked over the cat's favorite places, she studied her room. Once, the shelves had held an assortment of wooden and ceramic knickknacks, most of which closely resembled Mior. Now, they lay empty. The myriad cats that filled the castle had shattered enough for Matrinka to pack the rest away.

Can anyone hear me? Matrinka sent her plaintive call into the emptiness. She used to test every newborn kitten, every cat she passed; but months had gone by without even a single attempt. *If you can, please answer, even if only to say you don't wish to talk.*

I can hear you. The response touched Matrinka so faintly, she thought she had imagined it.

Matrinka froze, her hands stilling on the cat.

Imorelda caught Matrinka's hand, clawing lightly.

Did . . . did someone . . . answer? Matrinka held her breath, scarcely daring to believe. Failing the Pica test had driven her cousins and siblings mad, those not slaughtered by elves before the truce. She, too, had failed. Perhaps she had finally succumbed to insanity as well.

I answered. The voice came to Matrinka's head, louder now, more sure.

Matrinka's heart pounded. Still afraid to trust what she had heard, she hesitated before asking, *Where are you?*

I'm right here. Imorelda grabbed Matrinka's stilled hands. *Right here in your lap.*

Matrinka looked down to find Imorelda staring at her through intent green eyes. *You, Imorelda?*

Yes.

It should not have wholly surprised Matrinka. Mior had eventually managed to communicate with Tae as well as her. Yet she and Imorelda had never managed to directly converse before. *How?*

Imorelda righted herself and shook out the remaining dislodged hairs. *I don't know. I was listening to you talk about how stupid my stupid master is and agreeing with every word. Then, I realized I could coordinate your words with your thoughts. Finally, I found your voice. It's different than Tae's, like on a different . . . pitch. Like how meows vary in deepness from cat to cat.*

Matrinka suspected it translated better as the range of human

voices, but she veered from the technical. It did not matter. *So . . .*
She scarcely dared to hope. *Can we talk now? Or is it a temporary
thing?*

I've locked on your pitch, Imorelda reassured. *We should be able
to talk same as me and Tae.*

Matrinka sat up and released a whoop of joy.

Imorelda rolled out of her lap onto the bedspread with an angry
hiss. *Unless you insist on throwing me. Then, I just won't talk to you at
all.*

Matrinka gathered the cat and hugged her. *I'm sorry, Imorelda.
I'm just so happy.* It did not matter that she and Tae lived so far away.
At least, when he visited, she would have the opportunity she had
awaited for so long.

Me, too. Imorelda began to purr again. *Now I can tell you all the
best places to pet.*

Matrinka laughed. Imorelda reminded her so much of Mior. *Of
course, you can. But, also, you can take messages between me and Tae, if
you don't mind. And I'll have someone to talk to whenever you visit.*

You mean besides my stupid master?

*Besides your master, yes. He's like a brother to me, you know. I love
him dearly.*

I know. But loving him doesn't make him any less stupid.

Matrinka could not help worrying that she would lose the future
opportunities, that Imorelda would forget how to communicate
with her, or something might happen to the cat in the Eastlands.
*Imorelda, why do you suppose I could talk to your mother, and now to
you?*

Imorelda settled back into Matrinka's lap, still purring. *I suppose
it's because you're one of the rare humans with a gift for speaking with
your mind. And you're good-hearted, and—*

Matrinka waited breathlessly for the cat to finish. When she did
not, Matrinka continued to stroke the striped fur casually and questioned. *And—*

And, you have a closeness, a bond for— Imorelda was clearly having difficulty putting the concept into coherent words. *—certain
cats.* She stopped purring to concentrate. *I'm not sure exactly, but it
seems to require a certain type of closeness in the early relationship.*

Matrinka considered. She had first met Mior when her grandfather, King Kohleran, handed the calico to her as a grimy ball of fur
rescued from a sewage pit. Imorelda had come to Tae as a gift of love
from Mior herself. *I think I understand. The cat has to come into our
possession by the kindness of a loved one.*

Imorelda's purring resumed. She rubbed a shoulder against Matrinka's hand. *You have too many cats.*

"What?" It was the last thing Matrinka expected to hear from a feline.

You have too many cats. They interfere with talking and bonding. Even if you had one you could communicate with, how would either of you know it?

The proclamation left Matrinka speechless. Many people had told her, in ways ranging from tactful, to careful, to irritated, that her cats had overrun Béarn Castle. The servants griped about it all the time, though never to her face. Most put up with it because they loved the soft-spoken and gentle queen of Béarn and accepted her one eccentricity. But it had never occurred to Matrinka that the very thing she had done to try to breed another Mior might be keeping her from accomplishing that exact goal. *Oh, Imorelda. What should I do?*

Imorelda looked up at Matrinka as if she found the queen particularly dense. *Get rid of all these cats.*

Though simply spoken, the words were madness. *How can I possibly do that?*

Imorelda continued to stare. *Surely you don't have a deep attachment to all of them. Why, I doubt you know how many you have or that you can even tell a lot of them apart.*

Matrinka had to admit that Imorelda spoke the truth. *But I'll never find homes for all of them. There must be hundreds.*

Thousands, if you don't do something soon. Imorelda butted Matrinka's hands, twining between them to get the attention back to its previous level. *Put them out; they can fend for themselves.*

Matrinka doubted it. *Not all of them.*

Then build sheltered cages and pile them inside with food and other things they need. There are herbs and surgeries that can render them sterile, and we know elfin magic can do that as well.

Matrinka redoubled the petting. *I suppose that would not be inhumane.*

In fact, I wouldn't mind a few of those herbs myself.

That surprised Matrinka who adored her own children and could scarcely imagine life without them. Losing just one had nearly destroyed her. *Oh, Imorelda. Don't you want a family?*

Tae and Subikahn are my family. And you.

But kittens—

Kittens are disgusting.

—are charming, Matrinka finished.

What? they sent simultaneously, as each realized what the other had said.

Kittens are wonderful, Matrinka explained. *Darling little furballs who love everyone and play all day.*

Imorelda disagreed, *They're churlish little varmints with the dexterity of turtles and the manners of rats.*

Matrinka could not help chuckling. *Are we talking about the same thing?*

Kittens. Imorelda's lower lip curled. *Yuck.*

This did not bode well for Matrinka's future. *Imorelda, maybe just one litter. For me?*

Yuck. Imorelda turned her back, tail lashing.

You see, I think it's just possible that this mind ability is passed from mother cat to first daughter or some such. Like the bardic gift. Matrinka put a hand back on Imorelda, only to have the cat shrug free.

I'll make you a deal. I'll have a litter, if you eat the placentas, lick the babies clean, and feed them from your nipples.

Matrinka rolled her eyes. Obviously, she could not handle those duties as stated, but she did not quibble. At least, the cat had left the way open, if only a crack. She could throw away the placentas, wipe the kittens clean with towels, and craft a bottle small enough to feed them, if necessary. Perhaps, though, Imorelda's maternal instincts might take over during pregnancy or after the kittens were actually born. *You have a deal,* Matrinka said.

Compared to the tiny towns and hamlets Calistin and Treysind had thus far encountered, New Lovén seemed like a metropolis, big enough to merit an actual dot on the world map. Cart traffic rumbled through cobbled streets, threatening unwary pedestrians, and shopkeepers hawked their wares from sheltered doorways or covered stands. Like most of the Westlands, the people ran the gamut when it came to appearances: their hair colors ranging from a dark brown nearly indistinguishable from Béarnian black to a tousled sandy, and several children sported locks nearly as golden as Calistin's. Face shapes, nose sizes, body types ran a vast spectrum that seemed to come from a myriad sources all meshed into one. Even their skin tones displayed more variability than most: the vast majority cooked a healthy brown by the sun but none as olive as Easterners nor as sallow as Northmen.

Treysind fidgeted as they neared the town proper, nervous about leaving his hero. Calistin had promised to stay clear of trouble, but he never seemed to feel bound by promises, at least not to his young companion. "Ya'll wait fo' me?"

Calistin studied the town, appearing perfectly calm and in control. But, the hand sliding near his left hilt betrayed a discomfort only Treysind could recognize. A hint of annoyance entered his tone, and he did not look at the boy. "I said I would."

"An' ya ain't gonna go gettin' into no trouble?"

Calistin turned his companion a withering look.

Accepting that, and knowing better than to push any harder, Treysind darted across the road and around the back of the shops. There, in the alleyway, he knew he would have the best chance for a private conversation with one of the owners.

Sure enough, within three blocks Treysind discovered a middle-aged, heavyset grocer with a stained apron dumping a bucket of scraps. Scrawny dogs surrounded him, their tails waving merrily, snatching the bits of food before they could hit the ground. One growled, snapping at his neighbor, and the grocer immediately stopped to give the offending dog a nudge with his foot. "No, Rawly. Wait your turn, or you don't get nothing."

Though not the least bit hungry, Treysind could not help suffering a pang of regret at the idea of so much food wasted on animals. This man might not consider the peelings, moldy bits, and cores fit for human consumption, but Treysind had eaten worse and savored every mouthful. Still, he waited until the man had finished and turned before approaching. "Sir?"

The grocer stiffened. The bucket crashed to the ground, splashing slime that drew the dogs closer. His gaze jerked to Treysind.

Treysind stepped fully into the sunshine, hands out to indicate he held no weapons. "Sorry if I's startled ya, sir."

The grocer snatched up the bucket and wiped his brow with the back of his other hand. "Scared me half-dead, child. What are you doing skulking in the alley?"

"Ain't skulkin'." Treysind tried to reassure. "I never skulks, sir. Jus' wonderin' if ya's got any trouble wit' . . . wit' *brawlies*." He used the slang term for street gangs that hassled businessmen for money. The usual scam was to promise that no harm would come to the store if they were well-paid to guard it. Of course, the only danger to the store was from the *brawlies*, themselves, if the shopkeeper refused their offer.

The man's eyes narrowed, but a hint of hope flashed through them briefly and disappeared. "Who's asking?"

"Name's Treysind." He tried to look as composed as Calistin always did. "Gots a compan'on what hates *brawlies*. Kills 'em, even. Fights 'em one at a time, all at once't, in big ol' packs. Don't matter. Bigger the challenge, better he likes 'em."

Clearly intrigued, the grocer lowered the bucket. Dark bangs hung over green eyes that displayed interest and caution simultaneously. "He any good, this friend of yours?"

"Never loses. Not never."

"How many times has he fought? Like . . . once?"

Treysind could not count the number of times he had personally witnessed Calistin in battle or spar. "Hunnerds. Fighted fo' Béarn 'gainst them pirates. Even's bested Renshai."

"Renshai?" The man's brows furrowed, and he loosed a harsh laugh. "Now I know you're lying."

"Renshai," Treysind repeated, trying to look as dead serious as he could. "I's seed it. Seed it more'n once't."

The grocer scratched his head, still clearly unconvinced; yet he could not discard such a significant possibility without fully exploring it. "And, I suppose, this friend of your'n wants money to take care of my . . . problem."

"Nope. Ain't wantin' no money."

That clearly took the man aback. "So what's he doing it for?"

Now that he had the grocer's full attention, Treysind considered his words. He could not afford to squander the grocer's interest now without risking losing his hero, too. "I telled ya. He hates *brawlies*. An' he loves ta fight. Wants ta work he's sa'ward an' earn some glory fo' he's name."

The grocer grunted into a silence that stretched uncomfortably long.

Treysind tried to imagine the thoughts spinning through the grocer's head, wondering what kept him from plunging into what seemed like a perfect situation. He supposed the grocer needed to exercise a certain amount of caution. If Calistin lost, and the *brawlies* found out the grocer had given up their location, they might harm him or his store.

"I ain't fightin'," Treysind reassured the man. "An' m'hero ain't knowin' wheres I learnt how ta find them *brawlies*." He hoped that addressed the grocer's concerns without adding to them.

"Well," the grocer finally said. "You didn't hear it from me, but them *brawlies* come out as soon as it gets dark and the shops close down, looking for their share of the profits." He glanced around to ascertain they were alone, then moved nearer to Treysind and lowered his voice further. "They normally use the alley, too."

Treysind nodded encouragingly. He hated *brawlies* even more than the shopkeepers did. They practiced their bullying on street kids, took what little of value they could find, and thought nothing of raping, maiming, or killing boys like Treysind.

"Your best position's three doors down." The grocer made a gesture westward. "Khalen, the fabric-seller bought a load of expensive Eastern material last fortnight and hasn't found a buyer yet. He's short on cash since, and the *brawlies* been tapping him for every copper. I'm the only reason his family's eating, and he's hinted about doing something desperate."

"Thanks." Treysind wrestled down a smile. It would not do to appear gleeful, even though he felt like dancing. Calistin had become his hero by mowing down *brawlies*. It seemed only fitting to satisfy that endless Renshai bloodlust, that eerie godlike skill, by pitting it against the worst miscreants society had to offer. No compromise had ever seemed more appropriate. And he, Treysind, had given birth to the idea and brokered its commission. He, Treysind, had done something totally and unarguably right. For the first time in his life, he felt empowered, capable, and smart. He turned, preparing to leave.

The grocer muttered under his breath. "In for a copper, in for a gold." He called to the boy, "Treysind?"

Treysind stopped, whirled.

"They usually come in a group of five. Sometimes six. Their leader, they call him Savage, he's enormous. I'm a tall man, but he's got a head on me. And strong . . ."

Treysind nodded, waiting for the grocer to continue.

The man pursed his lips and shook his head. "Just tell your friend these ain't your regular small-town *brawlies.*"

"Don't worry. He likes 'em big."

"I just don't like to see young heroes killed by their own bravado. Such a waste."

Treysind refused to worry. When it came to warfare Calistin never made mistakes. "Gonna take more'n a mess a *brawlies* ta take down Cali-Stan." With that, he turned again and retreated.

Treysind could barely hear the grocer's soft reply, "I hope you're right, boy. I just hope you're right."

CHAPTER 33

There is always an escape, even from a hopeless situation. Unfortunately, sometimes it requires you to grovel.
                                          —*King Tae Kahn of Stalmize*

TAE AWAKENED TO THE SOUND of yowling, Imorelda in clear distress. Immediately, the smells and sounds of prison night assaulted him: urine and vomit, sweat and feces, whimpers, moans, and sonorous snoring. Worried to awaken the other prisoners, Tae reached out to Imorelda with his mind. *Quiet, please. Imorelda, what's wrong?*

She tricked me, Imorelda moaned. *The queen of Béarn tricked me.*

Tae sat up. *Matrinka? She's the least cunning person in the entire world.*

I told her I'd have those nasty kittens if she ate the placentas, licked the babies clean, and fed them herself.

Tae knew Matrinka was desperate enough to do any or all of those things for a new companion. *And she agreed?*

Yes, can you believe it?

Tae blinked. As the drowsiness of having just awakened receded, he realized the ludicrousness of Imorelda's statement. *Wait. You can only talk to me. How did you manage to get across the specifics of that deal?*

Imorelda shrugged off the most important part of her story. *Oh, I can talk with her now.* She added immediately, *Isn't it awful? Horrible, mewling brats clawing at my insides. Maybe I should have said she had to carry them, too.*

Imorelda, focus! Tae tried to follow his own advice. He had done nothing more threatening than take a seated position, but he could tell by the change in his neighbors' breathing that both of them had awakened. Deliberately, he lay back down, curling onto his side, facing the bars. *You can talk to Matrinka now? How?*

Imorelda remained silent a moment, then showed Tae a thought more concept than words, a comparison to the variety of pitches spanned by human voices. Apparently, Imorelda "spoke" to Matrinka on a different thinking level. Once Tae wrapped his mind around that concept, it opened whole new possibilities.

Imorelda, you know how you sometimes catch a thought I'm not actually trying to send to you? Like when I was picturing Alneezah.

Yes. Self-satisfaction accompanied the sending. *And you don't even know it.*

Can you do that with Matrinka, too?

Another pause. *I . . . don't know. It didn't happen.*

Tae tried carefully, *Could you . . . do that . . . to other people, do you think? Maybe all people can—* He could not continue. The thought was too grandiose and shocking. *What if Matrinka and I are not the only ones with this ability? What if all humans can learn to communicate with their minds?* He knew elves had a mental form of communication, called *khohlar,* which they could direct at exactly one elf or at everyone in the room, including humans. Gods had also addressed people using only projected thought. *What if we have this talent, too; but we just never realized it before?* It seemed impossible. Humankind had existed too long not to have stumbled upon such a thing in its history. *Especially in the days when they had more direct interactions with Outworlders and deities.*

Imorelda stepped from the shadows to sit in front of Tae's cell. She licked cobwebs from her paws. *I don't think so. I've tried to send thoughts to others, but they never act like they heard.*

Tae felt certain if they had heard, they would have shown some reaction. *But you couldn't communicate with Matrinka before, either. Now you can.* Tae had to know. *Try saying something to that drunkard across the way. Try on every level you can.*

Imorelda turned her back on Tae in an obvious gesture of disdain. Since it was all done through the mind, she did not have to face the person she addressed. Her tail lashed irritatedly.

For several moments, she remained in this position, while Tae feigned sleep.

Nothing. He's dense as a rock.

Tae closed his eyes in disappointment. Clearly, not all cats could use their minds this way. Imorelda disdained normal cats as "morons who can barely communicate their basic desires." Why should he expect humans to come in fewer varieties than felines?

But your neighbors are chatting.

Tae had to restrain himself from leaping to his feet. *The pirates *are talking? With their minds?** That changed everything. **What are they saying?**

How should I know? I don't speak gibberish.

Dense as a cat-shaped rock! Tae intentionally stifled the thought. **Imorelda, can you get me to their . . . their voice level?**

Get you there? Imorelda considered an instant. **You mean carry your mind to the pitch of their conversation?**

Tae bit back his impatience and forced himself to remain polite. **Please.**

I'll try. But I've never done anything like that before.

Me either, Imorelda. But it's desperately important.

Tae could feel the touch of Imorelda's mind, like a wordless whisper, seeping around his thoughts. Then a dizzy sensation gripped him. He seemed to float, mind and body, rising upward as swiftly and easily as a bird in flight. He sensed great effort trickling through Imorelda's thoughts. Sounds reached him, at first as subtle and unfathomable as the creak of trunks and the rattle of leaves in wind. Then, gradually, the noise took form as distinct words punctuated by concept and emotion that made them easier to follow than if someone had spoken them in one of the languages he knew.

—stop feeling guilty. They're animals, Jaxon, with no more understanding than a cow or a dog or a pig. This came from the larger of the two, the one who had attempted to throttle Tae.

I'm not so sure anymore, Dillion. They make noises at one another. They have expressions. They certainly seem to be communicating. Sometimes.

Dillion brushed off the observation with a hefty dose of skepticism. **Cows and dogs and pigs make noises at one another, too. They're not words; and they're not talking.**

I can hear they're not words. The unspoken implication came through as concept. Clearly, wherever the pirates originated, all manner of intelligent creatures used a single language. The possibility of multiple tongues never occurred to them because it went so far beyond the logic of their experience. Communication, whether spoken or mind-sent, came in only one form; and they seemed incapable of considering anything else true speech. **But they look so much like . . . like us.**

*Of course they look like us. Don't you remember what the Kjempemagiska *said?** The awe that always accompanied this word came through much more savagely in mental communication, accompanied by a fear bordering on terror. Tae caught a vague image of giants wielding terrible magic. **It's not their true form. They take it, instinctively, from sight of us. They use it to disarm us.**

Jaxon heaved a sigh, clearly unconvinced. *But they use it so well. So naturally. And I've never seen them take other forms.*

Oh, no? Dillion asserted. *Did you miss that striped beast that tried to take my head off? He fairly shredded my face.*

Of course, I saw it. But I think that might have been an actual . . . animal. If the takudan *between us could shapechange, don't you think he'd take a form that would let him out of that cage?* With the addition of direct emotion and perception, Tae discovered the term they used for him meant "sewer rat." *An actual* takudan *could fit between those bars and escape.*

We know they're of animal intelligence, that the ships and weapons they use were things left by our Kjempemagiska *when they visited centuries earlier and attempted to civilize these savages.*

Jaxon said nothing, clearly unconvinced.

Dillion continued, undaunted, *So, if the* Kjempemagiska *built these cages, which they must have, they may have placed magical constraints upon them. Perhaps it's impossible to shapechange from the inside.*

Jaxon extended the thought. *So, you're saying the one who ripped up your face changed form outside, came in as a creature that fit between the bars, and was able to go out the same way?*

Exactly.

Tae concentrated on the conversation, afraid to have any thoughts of his own. He had no idea how much effort Imorelda expended to keep him listening to the exchange, but he did notice that she remained silent, even as the pirates discussed her in an unflattering way.

All right. Jaxon accepted the premise, though doubt still showed through. *But, Dillion, can you name any other animals that can sail ships, whether or not they can build them? What kind of animals use tools, like axes and shields and swords? And how do animals work together well enough to . . . to manage a place like this?* Jaxon made a gesture that encompassed the prison. *And even we're not capable of shapechanging; that's magic, the realm of our Masters. Are you saying mere animals have powers we don't?*

Discomfort ground through Dillion's reply. He glanced around, as if worried a *Kjempemagiska* might overhear. *Fish breathe underwater, deer outrun us, birds actually fly, and, last I checked,* jarfr *can rip the snot out of most anyone. Aside from that last, all things we can't do and the* Kjempemagiska *need magic to perform.* The uneasiness grew to the level of clear distress. *So what if these beasts we're fighting have some very rudimentary communication skills and have learned to use left-behind tools in a primitive way, for war. They're still not* alsona, *Jaxon. At best, they're something in between animal and* alsona. *Call them creatures, instead of animals, if the word suits you better. The* Kjempemagiska ... * Real fear entered the sending now. * ... *refer to them as animals, so animals they are to me. *

Jaxon accepted the explanation. *So what do we do, Dillion?*

Do you want to suffer ernontris?* The word had no translation, but an image came to Tae's mind unbidden. He saw a circle of giants kicking a living, human torso. Limbless and blind, bleeding, the man screamed in agony as they tortured him in some sort of gleeful game. An enormous basket filled with similarly disfigured people lay nearby.

Though he had seen more than his share of horror, Tae found acid in his mouth and drooled it onto the stone floor. Had he swallowed, he would have retched, emptying the contents of his gut on the dungeon floor. He could not risk the pirates knowing he was awake nor the possibility that some of the meal Matrinka had secured for him might come out with the rest.

Jaxon visibly trembled. The fear Tae had noticed in his features when they first met colored his thoughts now. *Of course not.*

Then we finish our mission. We kill as many of these animals ... these creatures as possible. And, when the first chance arises, we kill ourselves or one another.

No reply followed, other than the residual terror. Jaxon rose and paced to the opposite side of his cell, and lay back down.

Tae found his thoughts snapped back so suddenly, he had to fight nausea again. Pain rang through his head, and it took inordinately long to realize Imorelda was speaking.

Did it work?

Yes, thank you. You're the absolute best.

At everything, Imorelda added immodestly.

Tae's head hurt too much to nod. *I heard ... it all.*

Me, too, Imorelda stated. *But I didn't understand a word of it.*

That surprised Tae. He had found it so easy to catch every single nuance, he had simply assumed Imorelda did, too. *Is that why you didn't say anything? Or did taking me to their level just require too much focus to speak?*

I could have talked. I didn't have anything to say. I couldn't even understand them.

That explained a lot to Tae and opened some interesting possibilities. At first, he considered having Imorelda speak for him, but that seemed foolish at best. Even if he could coach her through the language, her catty sensibilities would overrule any control. *Do you think it's possible you could take me to their "voice level" securely enough I could speak to them?★*

★*Why?*★

Now that the men had broken off contact, the situation had become less urgent. Imorelda had done a great service and deserved an explanation. ★*They have some serious misconceptions about us I'd like to fix.*★ Although not the most important to him or the rest of the world, their impressions about Imorelda would make better examples for the cat. ★*They think you're a male human, for example.*★

★*What?*★ Imorelda's reply mixed startlement with offense. ★*So, they're morons?*★

★*Not necessarily morons. Just . . . differently experienced. Their world is, apparently—*★

★*Incredibly weird?*★

★*I was going to say more magical, but your words work as well.*★ Still lying on his side, Tae grinned at the cat. ★*So, can you help me?*★

★*I don't know? Why don't you just talk to them the regular way?*★

It was a good question, and Tae had no great answer. It might impress the pirates more to come at them with what they clearly considered a higher form of communication. On the other hand, the unnaturalness of it, and the need to use a mediator, might steal some of Tae's concentration and the method's power. ★*A very good point, Imorelda. I'll try that first.*★

Tae remained in position a bit longer, considering his approach. The last time he had attempted communication nearly resulted in his death. Finally, he sat up again, yawned, stretched, and glanced at his neighbors.

Dillion crouched, staring out the front of his cell. Jaxon remained on the floor, as far from Tae as the bars allowed.

Previous experience, and the overheard conversation, told Tae the smaller pirate was, by far, the more approachable. Tae cleared his throat, organizing the words he had managed to learn. He had added vastly to his vocabulary just in the last few moments. Mental speech defined as it presented. "Greetings, Jaxon."

The pirate stiffened so suddenly, Tae worried he might have torn some muscles. He rolled over to look up at Tae. "Did you just . . . talk?" His gaze shifted past the little Easterner to his own companion in the next cell.

"I did," Tae admitted. "We *are* intelligent. We are not animals."

Jaxon only stared. His hands began to tremble. "Did you hear that, Dillion? Or am I—?"

"You're not going crazy, Jaxon," Tae said, slowly and distinctly. "I am talking to you."

"I hear him, too," Dillion admitted.

Tae looked over his shoulder as Dillion moved to the set of bars directly between them, the ones through which he had strangled Tae. The Easterner knew better than to approach, and he wanted to know the location of the larger pirate at all times.

They both fell silent. Certain he must be missing something, Tae sent his next message to Imorelda. *Are they talking in their minds?*

Imorelda hesitated only an instant. *No. They're completely silent.* Another moment passed. *I think they're both dead.*

Tae fought back a smile. *Not dead. Just very, very surprised.* He looked from Dillion to Jaxon and back. *Imorelda, would you please let me know immediately if they start talking by mind?*

All right.

The background noise continued: prisoners shifting, coughing, snoring. In the distance, urine splashing into older urine. But, near Tae, silence reigned; and he broke it with a gentle caution that revealed no emotion. "I think," he started carefully, "it's time for us to talk."

Refusing to loiter in alleyways like a common thief, Calistin hunkered down outside the New Lovén fabric-seller's doorway, polishing and oiling his blades. At first, the passersby gave him a wide berth. But, as he squatted calmly and paid them no obvious heed, they whisked about their business, pausing only to stare at the boyish stranger who had nothing better to do than tend to swords that clearly needed no further attention.

Sensing nothing more dangerous than suspicion, Calistin did not even bother to return their stares, simply waited for Treysind to let him know when the ruffians arrived. The sun touched the horizon, trailing hazy bands of colors muted by cloud cover that barely hinted at rain. Darkness followed quicker than usual, aided by the overcast. The citizens scurried about their final business, while merchants folded shutters over their stands or closed and latched their doors.

Calistin finally sheathed his weapons, rose, and stretched. He found himself eager to battle, hoping that a group of five or six toughs might actually prove a worthy challenge. At the least, it brought him one step closer to Valr Magnus. His jaw clenched at the thought. The best warrior the Northmen had to offer would die at the hand of a

Renshai, this time in the fair fight that should have happened on the Fields of Wrath.

Treysind ran out from behind the fabric shop. "Hero, they's comin'."

Calistin glanced at the fabric-seller's still-open door. Clearly, the merchant hoped to coax in the last straggling customers.

Calistin and Treysind walked inside. The untidy little shop held bolts of fabric on every level surface: tables, chairs, and shelves. The odors of fresh wool and billy goats hovered in the air, partially smothered by a sweet spice Calistin did not recognize. A door behind stacks of material apparently opened onto upstairs living quarters while another, sturdily fastened with broad bolts and two large locks, led to the alleyway.

A small, balding man who looked as if a strong breeze might carry him away spun toward them. Fear etched his features, then melted to relief. "Can I help you, boys?" Then his gaze dropped to the swords at Calistin's belt, and his expression again turned grim.

Calistin opened his mouth to explain that killing the shopkeeper was not worth dirtying his swords over, but Treysind spoke first.

"Don't worry, sir. Hero ain't gonna hurt ya none. He's gonna he'p ya wit' ya's problim."

"Problem?" the man, apparently Khalen, repeated. "I don't have—"

As if to prove him wrong, something heavy slammed repeatedly against the fastened back door.

The fabric-seller swallowed hard and raced to secure the front door. "You boys better get out now, or you might get hurt."

Calistin started to laugh, silenced by a glare from Treysind.

Khalen's face turned greenish and lapsed into terrified creases. "You're with . . . them?"

"No!" Treysind said quickly. "I's tole ya. We's here ta he'p ya 'gainst 'em." He turned toward Calistin. "Tell 'im, Hero."

There did not seem much to tell. "We're here to help you," Calistin repeated. "We're here to kill the *brawlies*."

"Kill?" Khalen repeated uncertainly.

Three young men burst into the shop, slamming open the panel and knocking Khalen sprawling. One shouted into the street, "Front's open! He's here." They wore dark leather and black cloth, each with a sword at his hip. Their hands appeared callused, their faces weather-beaten and scarred. The youngest looked about sixteen, the oldest well into his twenties. Dark bangs fringed killer eyes, and bright red circles defined their cheeks. They seemed not to notice Calistin and Treysind as they moved menacingly toward Khalen.

The fabric-seller scrambled to his feet, only to take several mincing, backward steps. He swallowed hard.

Two more toughs appeared in the doorway. The last, an enormous figure in his early twenties, sported a frosty gaze without a hint of mercy. He calmly shut and latched the door behind them. Clearly the leader, he took in details the others had skipped over, including the presence of the two young strangers. "What's this, Khalen?" He gestured at Calistin and Treysind. "Your children?"

Before Khalen could answer, Calistin announced, "I'm a man."

Every eye went to him.

"I passed my tests at thirteen."

"Thirteen?" the one who must be called Savage repeated derisively. "You mean . . . yesterday?"

The *brawlies* laughed.

"I'm eighteen," Calistin informed them.

The Savage snorted. "If you're eighteen, I'm a hundred and six."

"Then," Calistin informed him, "you'll be the oldest man I've ever killed."

Treysind cringed. Calistin suddenly realized the boy did that a lot when he spoke.

Silence descended over the room as everyone waited for Savage's retort.

Finally, the enormous man laughed, waving dismissively. "I like your audacity, boy. That's why I'm going to give you and your little friend there a chance to leave now. Alive." He gestured to one of his cronies to open the front door.

The youth obeyed without hesitation. The latch clicked back open, and the panel eased inward.

Calistin watched the door but made no movements of his own. He measured Savage: well-muscled yet agile, probably quicker than one might expect for a man of his size. The others would prove no obstacle, only interesting distractions.

Treysind retreated a few steps in the wrong direction. Clearly, he intended to keep his promise to allow Calistin to handle the fighting alone. The Renshai remained firmly in place.

Savage frowned. "You're trying my patience, boy. I'm not usually this generous."

Calistin refused to be baited with words. "I'm not the one delaying this battle, old man." He glanced around at the other *brawlies*. "Your friends may leave, if they wish. They're hardly worth a sword stroke."

None of the toughs took a step. Swords rasped from sheaths.

"My men are loyal." Savage made a sharp gesture, and his nearest companion hurriedly shut and relatched the door.

"If they're so loyal," Calistin taunted. "Why do you feel the need to lock them in?"

Savage drew a wicked-looking, curve-bladed sword with a serrated edge that reminded Calistin of the ones the pirates used in Béarn. A dagger appeared in his left hand as well. He cut the air with them. "Put the bugger in carry position!"

As one, the toughs moved in on Calistin, and Khalen retreated to the farthest corner.

Calistin faked a yawn as the first man made a clumsy cut. The Renshai leaped onto one of the tables, stepped on the *brawly's* shoulders, then vaulted over them to face the leader directly. Only then, his swords cleared their sheaths, cutting for Savage.

Savage managed a hurried block that caught one of Calistin's blades. He dodged the other, inadvertently slamming a hip into one of the many tables. Bolts of cloth tumbled to the floor. "Get him!"

Already in motion, the *brawlies* charged Calistin from behind. He spun full circle, parrying one strike, slicing a deep gouge through one's jerkin, and knocking a third to the ground. He completed the move with a strike to Savage's face that nearly claimed his nose. Blood exploded from the wound, gushing down his face.

Savage howled with pain and anger. He attacked in a brutish frenzy that left no room for defense. Calistin danced around the wild strokes, excited as a toddler in his first spar.

"Behind you!" Treysind screamed.

Calistin had not forgotten his other opponents. In fact, he had already numbered them in the order he intended to kill them; it added an extra dimension of difficulty. He skipped through a weaving web of steel, feeling more than seeing it. His backstroke laid a man out, unconscious but alive—it was not yet his turn. Then Calistin bore in, stabbing straight through Savage's abdomen to skewer the kidney behind.

Shock paralyzed Savage's face. Forced to step on the man's toes to liberate his sword, Calistin ripped the blade free, flinging gore across the folded silks and cottons, to meet the expected rush from behind him.

Savage collapsed, taking down three tables with him. Calistin faced the other four *brawlies,* no longer at his back. None charged him. They all stood, staring at the crumpled body of their leader, except for the one lying on the floor, knocked cold.

Calistin realized he had miscalculated. By taking out the leader first, he had staunched the others' will to fight. "Have at me!" he howled, advancing. "Don't just stand there, you whimpering cowards! Have . . . at . . . me!"

The three young *brawlies* glanced at one another, then lunged toward Calistin. But the bloodlust had disappeared, replaced by an uncertainty that stole the surety and power of their strokes. Calistin did not even bother to parry. The challenge had to come from within, and he placed conditions on his success that hampered him. Staying with his assigned order, he used a single stroke to tear one *brawly* from stomach to shoulder and slash open the neck of another.

Calistin dodged under the fountain of blood, avoided the organs spilling out of the first, and turned to face the last tough standing. This one retreated, which suited Calistin. *Let the coward hide. He's not next.*

"Mercy," the last conscious *brawly* begged. "Mercy, please, master. I won't cause no more trouble. I promise. I promise!"

Calistin kicked the youth he had knocked out. He stirred, groaning.

"Get up," Calistin demanded. "Get up and defend yourself, or die a blithering coward like your friend there." Calistin tipped his head toward the remaining man.

The indicated *brawly* sank to his knees, his gaze going to Khalen and Treysind.

The downed tough turned Calistin a groggy look that earned him another kick. "Get up!"

Instead of rising, the *brawly* closed his eyes and sank back to the floor.

Disgusted, Calistin inserted his blade through the rib cage and into the heart, watching his victim stiffen and then go utterly still. Freeing his sword, he looked toward the last of the *brawlies* who now cowered behind several tables.

As the Renshai met his gaze, the man lowered his head. "Please, sir. Spare me. Whatever you want, I'll do it." Slowly and deliberately, he laid his sword on one of the tables and raised his hands to show them empty.

Calistin scoffed. Light as a cat, he moved toward the man. "You would rather die disarmed then fighting? The very definition of a coward."

"Yes," the man agreed. "I'm a coward. Not worth the effort of killing me, sir." He gave Khalen a wild, pleading look, eyes welling with tears. "But I can be useful in other ways. I can, sir. I can . . . I can . . . clean up." He made a cautious gesture, as if worried anything more might be misinterpreted as an attack. "I can undo the bad we've done."

Calistin took another step closer. "Shall I show you the same mercy you would have shown this merchant?"

"We were just after money. We wouldn't have hurt him."

Calistin took another step.

"Honest."

Khalen finally spoke, softly, as if to an overwhelmed child, "Spare him. I'll put him to work."

"He'll put me to work." The *brawly* seized on this opening. "And I'll do it, too. Happily and well."

Calistin glided around the last table, and the *brawly* cringed toward Khalen.

Treysind spoke from the shadows. "Hero, I thinks ya should let 'im go."

Calistin did not care what his little companion thought. He had been promised five to six fighting men and got the equivalent of three.

Treysind added, "He ain't worth bloodyin' yas sword."

Calistin shook the blade, dislodging a clot of gore. "It's already bloody. And what's it to you if he lives or dies?"

"It's not nothin' ta me," Treysind had to admit. "But I feels sorry fo' 'im."

Now, Khalen intentionally stepped in front of the *brawly,* though he did so nervously. The top of his head barely reached the young man's chin. "Hero," he said, using Treysind's name for Calistin. "I appreciate what you've done for me, but it's over. Someone has to clean this mess, and it's certainly not going to be you."

"I'll do it," the *brawly* chimed in. "I'll handle the bodies. I'll fix every table and wash every scrap of fabric. You can kill me if I don't."

Calistin weighed the promises against the satisfaction of cracking open the young man's skull.

Treysind did not wait for Calistin to reply. "Settled, then. Yas fix up Khalen's shop perfec', an' he don't kill ya." He indicated the merchant, then the Renshai, in turn. "Ya's not workin' or tries ta run off, he kills ya."

Calistin ground his teeth but did not speak. Once again, Treysind had dared to barter for him, and he did not like it. Griping about it, however, would only diminish him in his opponent's eyes. He could easily lunge around tables, Treysind, and Khalen to kill the *brawly* in an instant. He would be done before anyone figured out his intention.

"I'll work hard, you'll see. You'll never have seen a man work so hard."

Khalen turned his attention fully to the young man. "You do as good a job as you're saying, you'll have a job and a place to live when you're finished."

Calistin sighed, knowing the situation had gone way beyond him. Suddenly gripped with the need to honor his sword, he pulled a cloth from his pocket and set to work.

Someone pounded on the door, and a muffled voice penetrated the panel. "Khalen, are you all right?"

Treysind unhooked the door and opened it to reveal several merchants, the grocer at the front. Most were unarmed, though a few carried notched swords, cudgels, or pointed sticks. They all cast glances, wild-eyed and speechless, around the fabric shop.

"He's dead," one said hopefully, then added exuberantly. "Savage is dead."

Several whooped or cheered, but most simply stared.

The grocer stepped inside. "Thank you, Treysind." He turned toward Calistin. "Thank you, Cali-Stan."

The Renshai restored the inflection. "Ka-LEES-tin. My name is Calistin."

"Thank you, Calistin," several muttered, stepping inside. They seemed more stunned by the carnage than appreciative, but Calistin did not mind. He had done it for his own reasons, not to earn their adulation. Without looking up, without replying, he continued tending his swords.

Once again, Treysind chose to answer for him. "Ya's welcome. He's glad ta do't, he is."

The rest of the conversation flowed past Calistin, unheard, as the need to put his swords right became the sole focus of his universe. Should anyone or anything threaten, it would draw his full attention in an instant; but anything less did not deserve his notice. Treysind could and would handle it better.

CHAPTER 34

Skill is enough.
—*Kevralyn Tainharsdatter*

TAE LUXURIATED IN THE plush chair set especially for him in Matrinka's personal quarters, Imorelda snuggled and purring in his lap. King Griff perched on a similarly comfortable seat, while Rantire, the Renshai, hovered over him. Darris stood near the window, and Matrinka sat cross-legged on her canopied bed, surrounded by sleeping cats.

Tae had known the moment his message, through Imorelda, had reached Matrinka. The guards had released him, bowing and scraping in apology for the way they had treated him. He had been allowed free access to every room of the castle, and his escort to the queen's very bedroom remained reverential and gracious.

"I think," Tae said with utmost caution, "we need to consider releasing our two prisoners."

Griff's brow knitted. Darris' eyes closed in consideration, while Matrinka nodded broadly. She replied first. "They can tell the other pirates we're actually intelligent beings. Then they'll leave us alone. Right?" She glanced around the room, eyes shining.

Tae heaved a deep sigh. *If only it were that simple.* "Matrinka, deep down, I think most of them know we're human. By now, those who have directly fought us have to realize it, even if they won't admit it, even to themselves. In war, one always demonizes or belittles the enemy to ease the guilt of what otherwise feels like unmitigated murder. They're not really killing us because they think we're animals; otherwise, they'd slaughter our cats, rats, and fish with equal enthusiasm."

No one could get a question out faster than Darris. If knowledge existed, he had to possess it. "So why *are* they killing us, Tae? Did they tell you that?"

"They did." Tae leaned forward. "They want—I should say, they feel they need—our land."

"Land?" Griff blinked several times in succession. "How much do they need?"

Tae smiled, certain the king of Béarn was generous enough to bestow a barony on the pirates, if they only asked politely. "It's not a matter of need, Griff. They want it all."

"That's unreasonable!"

Tae would not allow himself to laugh. He loved the simple generosity of the royal Béarnides, especially Matrinka's sweet naïveté. "Of course, it's unreasonable. War is always unreasonable."

Matrinka tried again. "But if they *all* knew they were trying to steal that land away from other humans. Wouldn't that make a difference?"

Darris patted Matrinka's arm in sympathy and also as a warning. Even the gentle king knew the answer to her question.

Tae explained anyway. He had not yet told them everything he had learned. "The pirates aren't doing this for themselves, Matrinka. They're doing it for their *Kjempemagiska.*" He used the pirate's own word, then explained, "For their masters."

Curiosity piqued again, Darris abandoned Matrinka to shift nearer to Tae. "Their *Kjempa* . . . their masters?"

Tae knew Darris would need to get the word right, so he pronounced each syllable distinctly. "Kee-*yemp*-eh-ma-*jee*-ska. Giant beings, maybe twice the size of humans, with powerful magic. The nearest thing we have are—"

"—gods," Darris filled in, with obvious awe.

"Yes. But our gods don't normally walk among us. Or meddle daily in our affairs."

"Theirs do?" Griff asked the obvious question.

Tae tried to explain what he knew from the information the captured pirates had given him and from the mental communication that had occurred during their conversation. "From what I understand, the *Kjempemagiska* could easily massacre or enslave the pirates, who call themselves *alsona*. Which, as far as I can tell, just means 'people' or 'humans.' Instead, the *Kjempemagiska* live mostly in peace with the *alsona*. The trade-off is when the *Kjempemagiska* want something, such as new territory for their expanding population, the *alsona* do exactly as they are told or suffer torture and death of themselves and loved ones."

Tae fell silent, allowing the information to sink in all around him.

Matrinka broke the hush first, with a suggestion clearly phrased so as not to make her sound foolish. "So, if we offered our extra land to the *alsona*, that would open more room for the giants. And everyone would be happy."

★She's so cute,★ Imorelda sent. *★I'd love her, if she hadn't just tricked me into doing something hateful.★*

"A clever idea." Tae knew Matrinka meant well. "Unfortunately, the giants don't want a piece of our world. They want all of it. They don't wish to live without their soldiers and servants. The soldiers don't wish to leave their homes, for the most part. And, if the *alsona* fail, the *Kjempemagiska* will become our next opponents. When they don't get what they want, they've been known to rip humans in half or kill dozens with a single spell."

As Tae expected, the news did not go over well. Matrinka gasped. Darris seemed to be desperately searching for alternatives. Worried creases marred Griff's face, and Rantire paced furiously back and forth, as if already protecting Griff from the gods themselves.

No one asked what to do next; they had no choice but to gather every ally in the known world to repel the invaders. Because everyone, from the farthest corner of the Northlands to the deepest part of the Eastlands, had a dire and personal stake in winning this war.

Griff's soft voice punctuated the silence. "We'll need the elves, too."

Elves, immortals, the gods themselves.

Rantire made a point even Tae had not considered. "If these magical giants are anything like demons or gods, only certain weapons can harm them. And, as far as I know, our world's only bewitched items are all in the hands of Renshai."

"Renshai." Griff managed a crooked smile. He had never wanted to banish his allies, and the idea of calling them home clearly pleased him as nothing else spoken in this room had done. "Call them," he ordered. "Call everyone in every part of the world. I'm declaring this an all-out war."

———————

Though many of the merchants of New Lovén offered a comfortable bed, Calistin and Treysind spent the night in the forest. Calistin preferred the solitude and worried about growing too soft. The concern about highwaymen and Northmen kept him sharp and might give him the opportunity to hone his sword arm again.

Treysind laid out a veritable feast, complete with fresh vegetables, soft brown bread, and even a bit of butter. "I knows why ya wants us here 'stead a nice, warm beds."

Calistin walked over and crouched in front of the food. A cyclical hum of crickets hung in the night air, occasionally pierced by the whirring call of a fox. Since Calistin already knew why he had made his decision, he did not press for an answer.

Treysind continued anyway, "Ya don't like talkin' ta pee'ple. Ya ain't no good at it, an' ya don't wanna take tha time ta learn."

Calistin reached for the bread, topped with a smear of butter. He tore off a hunk. "Most people aren't worth talking to."

Treysind ripped off a smaller piece of bread and popped it into his mouth. He spoke around chews. "All pee'ple's wort' talkin' ta, if ya knows how ta do't. It jus' takes pra'tice gettin' good at it."

Calistin took a bite off his piece of bread. It tasted freshly baked, with just a hint of some sweet spice, and the butter made a perfect contrast. He savored it, swallowing before speaking. "Why should I waste my time talking to people who don't matter? What possible good could come of that?"

"Ya might find out where all tha bestest West fighters is at."

Calistin rolled a bright orange root from the pile. "I'm finding that out just by asking. I'll talk long enough to learn what I need to know."

Treysind fished out his own root, shook off the dirt, and took a bite. It crunched loudly between his teeth. "But if theys don't trust ya, theys don't tell ya nothin' useful."

Calistin snorted. "And if they do trust you, they yammer at you ceaselessly. Nothing more boring than that."

"Ain't there?"

"No."

Treysind grinned broadly and kept the expression on his face even as he ate.

Calistin ate, too, savoring the silence for several moments before curiosity got the better of him. "What are you so happy about?"

Treysind swallowed a mouthful of root. "Tha way things turnt out. I's happy."

Still irritated by the end result, Calistin could not help saying, "You're happy I left a dangerous punk alive."

"Yup."

"Even though he'll probably regather the gang and start harassing merchants again."

Treysind grabbed another root and another piece of bread. "That ain't gonna happin." He sat back, his grin broadening. "He's gonna do's a great job cleanin', which is gonna make Khalen verry verry happy. Then Khalen's gonna hire 'im. They's gonna work tagether till they gets ta bein' bes' frien's. Evensh'ly, they's gonna be like father an' son."

Calistin stared, scarcely believing what he had just heard. "For a street punk, you sure are sunny."

Treysind shrugged. "Hain't nothin' sunny ta it, Hero. I's kin tell jus' by talkin' ta 'em. Yas could tell, too, if yas tried."

Now it was Calistin's turn to shrug. "Why should I try? I don't care what happens to them."

"An' 'stead a makin' mo' en'mies fo' yaself, ya maked some frien's this time." The smile seemed to take over Treysind's face completely. "Tha merchants was grateful 'nough ta give us lotsa stuff." He patted the fat backpack, then opened it. " 'cludin' these, which ya def'nit'ly needs." Treysind tossed a set of clean britches and tunic toward Calistin, who caught them from habit. "Plus, a man what's needin' he'p in his shop gotted some, an' a boy what's needin' parents and direcshuns gotted 'em. An' ya learnt ya don't gotta kill ever'one ta make a diff'rince."

Calistin snorted, twirling a root between his fingers. "I didn't learn anything like that."

Treysind studied his food. "Well, ya shoulda. 'Cause it's true."

Calistin felt the heat of rising ire; but, before he could vent it, Treysind spoke words that caught his attention completely.

"An', by talkin' ta pee'ples, I's finded out where all tha bestest West fighters is at."

Calistin straightened. The root stilled in his hand. "You mean you weren't just talking hypothetically about that?"

"Hypo what?"

"Hypo—" Calistin knew Treysind would never get the word, just as he would never properly manage the Renshai's name. "There really is a place where the best Western fighters go?"

"There's a school," Treysind explained, still eating. "Kings an' gen'rals sends they's men there fo' trainin', an' others go jus' ta learn. It ain't far from here."

Calistin's heart rate quickened. He found himself smiling as fully as his companion.

"See, talkin's good fo' somethin' "

Though grudgingly, Calistin had to admit it was. "Anyone could have found that out by asking the right question."

"No, Hero." Treysind's grin vanished and he leaned in, as if discussing something of utmost importance. "Ya can't ask tha question if ya don't know what question ta ask. This comed out talkin' 'bout other thin's that we wouldn't a been discussin' if we dint start discussin' nothin'." He threw his hands up as if making a brilliant point.

Despite the strange delivery that did not make much sense, Calistin took home the point. "So, tell me about this school."

"I's gonna do better'n that," Treysind declared. "I's gonna take ya there."

Taking Calistin to the warrior's school proved more difficult than expected. Treysind disappeared repeatedly to cast about and regain his bearings; and the Renshai took advantage of the wasted time, venting his frustrations in wild flurries of *svergelse*.

Finally, Treysind plopped down on his backpack in a thready roadway and stared sullenly into the distance.

Calistin studied his companion. He had never seen such a sour expression on the boy's face. "Any luck?"

"No, I ain't gotted no luck!" Treysind snapped. "If I'd a got luck, wouldn't I been takin' ya there?"

Calistin's eyes widened. The Erythanian had never used that tone of voice on him before, and he did not know how to react to it. "Treysind?" he said in a flat tone full of warning.

The boy looked up, his expression going from sullen to horrified. "I's sorry, Hero. I's rilly sorry. I shouldn't never talk ta ya like that."

Calistin had not really minded. It felt oddly good for the boy to treat him like a person rather than an idol for a moment. Yet, he did not feel comfortable encouraging disrespectful behavior in a companion either. "I understand. I'm frustrated, too."

"There's supposed ta be a big ol' twisted *herbont* tree nears a westway path, but I ain't seein' it. I's thinkin' maybe we's did go tha wrong way at tha las' crossroad."

Irritation flashed through Calistin, then disappeared as quickly. It seemed impossible for him to be upset at the same time as his companion. Someone had to keep a calm head. "It's not that far back. Let's take the other fork."

Calistin's reasonability seemed to have a positive effect on Treysind, who sprang to his feet, shouldered his overstuffed pack, and waddled back the way they had come.

Calistin followed, a nasty thought occurring to him. "Treysind, you don't suppose those merchants were having a bit of fun with us."

Treysind did not look backward. "Whatcha mean?" he called over his shoulder.

"Maybe there is no school. Maybe they just told you that to get us . . ."

". . . losted?" Treysind finished. "No, sir, Hero. They's wouldn't a done that. They's too grateful, Hero."

Calistin was not so sure. "Maybe they were having fun at our expense. Or telling you what they thought you wanted to hear."

Treysind turned to face Calistin but continued walking . . . backward. "No, *sir*. They wouldn't a done that, Hero. I kin usual tell when pee'ple's lyin'. They wasn't. Jus' like I knowed that *brawly* wasn't lyin'. He's gonna turn hisself aroun' an' work honest."

Calistin never doubted the sincerity of the young street tough, only how long that attitude would last after his companions' killer left New Lovén. Once the danger was gone, the fear would lessen, and he might well revert to his old, vicious tactics. Treysind was right about the merchants, however. They had no reason to mistreat their saviors, other than the destruction of the fabric-seller's shop.

After a short stop for a midday meal from the backpack, Calistin and Treysind found the fork in the road, this time choosing the direction they had not yet taken. Calistin did remember that Treysind had paused in this same place a long time before selecting the pathway they now believed was incorrect. The route back to New Lovén was clearly marked and well-traveled. The other two much less so.

They had taken only a few steps when Treysind stopped suddenly. "Someone's here."

Calistin squinted through the forest. A figure perched casually amidst the trees, working with something in his hands. Calistin prided himself on reading a man by build and movement. Simply by the way the gods put him together, how they arranged each muscle and sinew, he could calculate whether he faced a real opponent. Movement provided additional clues: fluid or choppy, confident or hesitant, graceful or awkward or anything between. But this man or woman was too far away to assess and had not yet made a significant motion. *Perhaps it's a soldier come to train, a warrior who fancies himself competent.*

Treysind finished the thought unconsciously. "Maybe he's knowin' where this school's at."

Calistin did not reply but strode toward the stranger, muttering to Treysind. "Now remember. You are not to interfere in any battle."

"But, Hero, I's gotta protec'—"

"You don't, and you know it. You played stupid for a long time, but you're not at all. You know I fight better without you, and you're . . ." Calistin did not have the time or energy to attempt diplomacy, ". . . worse than useless at it. So stay out of my way, even if I get attacked by an entire army."

"No," Treysind said petulantly, trotting at his side. "I ain't lettin' no ones kill m'hero."

"The only way someone's going to kill me is if *you* trip me up." Calistin did not wish to return to that stale argument. Once he had talked Treysind into letting him handle the *brawlies* alone, he had expected the boy to realize that the Renshai worked best without him, at least when it came to battle.

As they drew nearer, Calistin got a better look at the stranger. He sat on the tangle of branches formed by two leaning trees, a lean, grizzled man of average size and spectacular age. His hair remained full, but it had turned a pure, snowy white. His skin seemed pallid, papery, and showing every vein. Wrinkles shrouded blue-gray eyes that had probably once been steely. Nevertheless, he carried two swords, one at each hip, and their split-leather grips looked as well-worn as their owner. He glanced up quizzically as they approached but did not move from his natural seat.

Calistin stopped in front of the stranger and studied him. Treysind pulled up beside the Renshai. The stranger regarded them back but also said nothing.

At length, Treysind broke the silence, speaking the words Calistin should have said as soon as he approached. "Good day, sir."

The man leaped from his seat, more gracefully than Calistin thought possible for his age, and bowed to Treysind. "Good day, young man. I'm pleased one of you knows some manners."

Calistin scowled at the insult, though deserved. He saw no reason to waste time with amenities, especially now that the other two had handled them. "Can you point us to the warrior's school, old man?"

"That depends."

Calistin narrowed his eyes, taking a dislike to the elderly man who stood in the way of his goal. "You either know where it is, or you don't. On what can that depend?"

The stranger did not seem the least put out by Calistin's demeanor, which did not yet rise to the level of threat. "On who you are and what your purpose is there."

Calistin considered refusing to answer, but it seemed pointless. He had nothing to hide, and the old man would not guide them on their way if he refused. "I'm Calistin, and I plan to challenge their best fighters."

"Do you?" The elderly stranger walked a slow circle around Calistin, as if examining livestock for sale. "That seems a waste, Calistin. Why would you wish to humiliate yourself like that?"

"Humiliate?" It took Calistin a moment to realize what the stranger meant. "Old man, I don't intend to lose."

"No one ever does." He made a clicking noise with his tongue, as if finding something wanting in Calistin's appearance. "And yet, no matter how competent the man, there is always someone better: faster, stronger, more clever."

Calistin screwed up his features into the meanest look he could muster. "Look, old man. I don't need a lecture. I just need directions."

"No, no." The stranger continued to circle Calistin. "You don't need to challenge the school. Why, you couldn't even best an old man."

Calistin gritted his teeth. It was getting progressively harder to hold his temper. "You mean . . . you?"

"I suppose, for example."

Calistin laughed. When neither of the others joined him, Calistin only laughed harder. "Are you challenging me?"

The old man shrugged, as if the Renshai had just invited him for a stroll. "Why not? Aren't you up for it?"

Calistin could scarcely believe what he had heard. "But you're . . . you're an . . . old man."

"I'm an old *warrior,* Calistin. Surely, you realize only the best fighters live long enough to become old."

"Well I . . ." Calistin had never considered it. The Renshai dove into battle with such gusto, they rarely got old. At the first hint of frailty, most attacked a better warrior, usually himself, as a form of suicide. ". . . I imagine it's either competence . . . or cowardice."

The stranger's hand twitched but did not reach for a sword. "Every man who dared call me coward has gone to his grave learning otherwise."

Calistin shook back his hair and limbered his arms. A grin snaked across his lips. A battle was a battle, even against an addled old coot. "So the end point is death, then?"

"Death?" The old man spoke with an odd tone that expressed neither surprise nor concern. "Death seems a waste. Either the school loses a teacher, or an arrogant student of the sword dies way too young." He gave the matter further consideration, scratching at the white stubble on his chin. "Perhaps we can end it when one of our butts touches the ground? The one with the muddy rump loses."

It seemed like a weird and humiliating choice, but Calistin appreciated a challenge. "All . . . right."

"We can always fight to the death later, if you're still insistent."

Calistin frowned. Though the stranger had said nothing obviously offensive, he could not help feeling patronized. He did his best talking with his sword, however, so he gave no reply. Instead, he stepped out onto the road and gestured for the old man to make the first move.

The stranger obliged with a lightning swiftness that took even Calistin's breath away. He drew, but not fast enough, forced to dodge the first blow and barely parrying the second. He took the third stroke on his blade, only then realizing that the stranger fought with both weapons, one in each hand. He scarcely managed to draw his own second sword in time to weave a web of defense that kept the other man half an instant at bay.

The stranger stepped back. "Had enough?"

"I'm not on my ass yet!" Calistin bore in with the frenzy he usually reserved for Renshai. A lunge and a sweep met air, then a third strike became a parry as he found himself on the defensive again. He riposted with a wicked Renshai maneuver intended to carve muscle from his opponent's leg. Instead, he found his own knee hooked out from under him. He spun for balance and dropped to a crouch, saving his backside and his dignity, then launched himself at the old man again.

The assault became a whirlwind of deadly motion and fury. Swords danced, men leaped, dodged, spun. Silver glimmers flashed through the forest. Then, abruptly and without understanding exactly how, Calistin found himself on the ground, the tip of the old man's blade at his throat. Stunned silent, he froze, glancing up the line of steel to an expert, aging hand, then along the arm to an unsmiling face.

Looking as dazed as if he had taken several blows to the head, Treysind huddled behind a tree. If he had interfered with the combat in any way, Calistin had not noticed him.

The sword withdrew, replaced by a proffered hand.

Ignoring it, Calistin bounded to his feet. "Again," he growled.

The old man complied. Like quicksilver, he threaded around and through Calistin's attacks, toying with his defenses. For several moments, they waged a battle that seemed perfect and endless before Calistin found himself, once more, on the ground. He scuttled up instantly, but the damage was done. He had lost.

Without a word, the old man sheathed his swords and returned to his seat on the intertwined tree limbs.

Calistin also put his swords away, and brushed leaf mold off his posterior. He could not help staring. "Who *are* you?"

"I told you," the stranger seemed no more winded than Calistin. "I'm a teacher at the school."

"But you must have a name; it should be known far and wide."

The stranger shrugged. "I'm simply called Teacher or Amazir, *swordmaster,* because the blade is my weapon of choice. You may call me what you wish, Calistin, though I prefer you drop the address you've used so far."

Calistin had to think back to remember. "Old man." A grin stretched his lips.

"Not that it's false. It's just that, when you get to be my age, you don't need the constant reminders."

Calistin shook his head and studied the stranger again, but nothing stood out as extraordinary. His build seemed average in most ways, though Calistin could make out the well-apportioned, if not particularly large, sinews. He had keen eyes for one so old; the steeliness had returned. Yet nothing else about him could explain his exquisite mastery of the sword.

"Why are you staring at me?"

Calistin ceased his inspection, blushing that it had become so obvious. "It's just that . . . well . . . no one's *ever* bested me before. Not since I've become a man."

"As I said, no matter how competent you are, there is always someone better."

"Really." The old man had no way to know that Calistin had battled every Renshai, had fought in the Pirate Wars, and had even faced a *Valkyrie.* He could not fully comprehend his latest victories; but Calistin did and had to ask, "Have you met anyone who can defeat you?"

The man sometimes called Amazir smiled. "Not yet. But the day I do, I'll either go to my pyre happily or find my sword instructor, depending on how I handle the situation."

Calistin was not stupid. He believed he knew exactly what this man meant. "Are you offering to teach me?" He had long outstripped his many *torke* and had spent the last several years creating new maneuvers to keep him improving and occupied. The idea of learning new techniques from the old warrior left him desperate with yearning. Worried he might lose the opportunity, that the old man might think he meant the question sarcastically, he added quickly, "Because I'd like that. I'd really like that. More than anything else in the world, truly."

"Well." Amazir seemed unsurprised by Calistin's enthusiasm. "I'll have to ask your current teacher if there's room in the group for me as well."

"My current . . ." Calistin watched in surprise as Amazir turned to address Treysind, who had stepped out from the trees once the battles ended. "But he's not . . ." Assuming the old man meant to humor the boy, Calistin went silent and watched their exchange.

The old man made a serious bow. "Would you allow me to assist you in training this talented, but brash and unsophisticated, young man?"

Treysind pursed his lips thoughtfully. "Ain't tha school gonna miss ya?"

Amazir shrugged. "They have other instructors." He jerked a thumb toward Calistin. "And it appears this young Renshai needs me more."

Calistin began to wonder if he would ever fully reunite his top and bottom lips. Every word this aged warrior spoke took him completely off his guard. "How . . . how did you know I'm . . . ?"

Amazir laughed. "First, you have a classic Northern appearance, but you're in the Westlands."

That did not impress Calistin. Currently, it seemed, many Northmen had come this far south; and Westerners, themselves, were the most diverse people in the world.

"Second," Amazir continued, "your accent is Western, not Northern."

"I can do Northern," Calistin explained. "When I'm speaking Northern."

"Third," Amazir continued undaunted, "you're overconfident, aggressively impetuous, and socially irritating."

Treysind piped in. "Them's jus' his *good* traits, sir."

Calistin focused his glare on the boy.

"And fourth, you look about the same age as this fellow . . ." He indicated Treysind with a tip of his head, ". . . but you're more like his father."

"Hey!" Calistin could not let that one go. "I'm eighteen; he's like about ten."

"I's eleven," Treysind said.

Calistin threw up his hands, his point made. "So I'd have had to have had him when I was seven." Realizing he had left open a teasing point, he amended. "My *wife* would have to have had him when I was seven." That also needed fixing, "If I had a wife, which I don't." Even as the comment emerged, Calistin realized that put him into a potentially worse situation. "Not that I don't plan to have one eventually. I mean, I do love Treysind, but not like a *lover* or anything. I'm not a pervert. I love him like a . . ." Now, Calistin stopped completely.

No matter what he said, it seemed to make perfectly innocent things sound ever more sleazy.

". . . son?" Amazir inserted.

Calistin groaned. "Let's just say a brother."

Treysind wriggled like a happy puppy. "Ya loves me like . . . like fam'ly? Ya rilly does?" He clenched his hands and trembled, as if forcing himself not to dance with glee.

Calistin could only stare. "Well, of course. Why else would I let you travel with me? Haven't you noticed that the only people who annoy me as much as you do, and live, are my stupid, irritating brothers? If I didn't think of you as one of them, I'd have killed you a long time ago."

Treysind let out a muffled squeal of excitement.

Calistin looked at Amazir for guidance. "How could he not know that?"

"Apparently," the old man replied softly, "this is the first time you ever told him."

Though he had taken the tirade with a grain of salt, Calistin could not forget that the old man had referred to him as "socially irritating." "You mean I have to *tell* him?"

Amazir laughed. "Well, if you're otherwise relying on signs like 'you didn't kill him yet,' then yes. You definitely have to tell him things like that. In fact, you could start just saying a few positive things in general to him."

Treysind looked at Calistin expectantly.

Placed on the spot, Calistin flushed. He did not know what to say, and nothing upset a Renshai more than an utter disarming. "I *do* say positive things to him," he mumbled.

Treysind's brows slid upward.

"You do?" said Amazir.

"Sure, I . . . I thank him when he brings food."

"He do do that," Treysind defended.

Amazir snorted. "Nothing any man with a hint of manners wouldn't say to a total stranger who brought him an ale in some tavern."

That reminded Calistin of something else. "And I called him clever when he figured out how to find me after I ditched him."

Amazir stood on the balls of his feet, perfectly balanced. "And which part was the compliment? The 'ditching'?"

"The 'clever' part, of course. He's a smart little boy and surprisingly good with people, especially for an orphan."

Treysind beamed.

Amazir also smiled. "That wasn't so hard, was it?"

Actually, it was; but Calistin had no intention of admitting it. He simply grunted. "I thought you were going to train me in swordwork, not in how to humor my tagalong."

Amazir's grin widened, and he winked at Treysind. "I can't train you in anything until I've gotten permission from your other teacher." He bowed grandly to the boy. "Again, young sir, I ask you. Would you allow me to assist you in training this Renshai?"

To Calistin's surprise, Treysind did not answer right away but seriously considered the proposal and asked a studied question when he finished. "Is I gonna hafta feed ya, too?"

The boldness of the question, though reasonable, took Calistin aback. The only people in his life he had ever learned to treat with respect were those who had the talent to kill him.

Amazir nodded, "I'm afraid so."

Treysind rubbed his chin, still thoughtful. "Well, I s'pose I kin handle it. If Hero wants ya, I wants ya."

Calistin looked between his two companions, surprised to find both so serious. Obviously, they truly considered Treysind the decision-maker, no matter how ridiculous the assertion. Nevertheless, Calistin did not argue. He had what he wanted, the greatest teacher who ever lived, and he could think of nothing that mattered more.

CHAPTER 35

Courage is its own reward. Dying with honor matters more than Valhalla.

—General Peusen Raskogsson

DARKNESS DESCENDED OVER the western forest by the time Calistin finished his first session with Amazir. Bruised, scratched, and aching, he sat on a deadfall to clean, oil, and honor his swords, feeling better than he could recall in many years. The session brought back sweet memories of his youth, when his mother had drilled him beyond exhaustion and he felt like he had accomplished more than the gods themselves. New maneuvers, exciting details, a level of understanding that superseded the entirety of his life to that moment. Every day felt fresh, every new moment a chance to become more competent. Sleep, meals, conversation became nothing but distractions from what he might learn.

Those giddy days had disappeared during the years without real challenge, when he had to solicit his opponents in groups to achieve the modicum of danger that made him feel alive. He had become the only teacher who could truly challenge himself, bringing movements ever more complex, ever more deadly. Amazir knew many things he did not. Amazir had opened a whole new world. *By the grace of the gods, Amazir is me in sixty years.*

Finished, Calistin sheathed his swords and limped toward the campfire and the aroma of roasting meat. During the lesson, he had not thought about his stomach. Now, it growled wildly, and saliva bubbled into his mouth. Suddenly, his appreciation for both of his companions grew. *Today, I might just be the luckiest man alive.*

As he drew near the camp, Calistin could hear Treysind speaking, ". . . ain't so bad, once't ya gits passed tha mean stuff."

Amazir laughed, clear and healthy, without the graveliness that usually accompanies age. "Isn't the 'mean stuff' exactly what makes someone bad?"

"No." Treysind was clearly having trouble making his point. "Tha mean stuff's jus' on tha outside. Inside, in his spirit, he's rilly good."

"You're quite sure."

"Well, I knows it, but he don't belief it. Tha's why he acts tha way he do."

"What do you mean?"

"He thinks he ain't got no soul."

Calistin stiffened, more curious about Amazir's answer than angry Treysind had revealed his secret. The boy did seem to have common sense enough when it came to dealing with outsiders.

"Why does he think that?"

"'Cause he beliefs some magic critter tol' him. Some angel or god or somethin'. But I seed him, an' he weren't talkin' ta no ones at tha time. Jus' yellin' at em'ty air that he *do* gots a soul an' . . ." Treysind trailed off.

A moment passed, while Calistin leaned closer, trying to make out a conversation that had drifted too low just when he most wanted to hear it.

Then, abruptly, an arm circled Calistin's waist and a sword poised expertly at his throat. He went still, and a voice hissed into his ear. "It's not nice to eavesdrop."

Trusting his new teacher not to kill him, Calistin spun free of his grip. As expected, the sword withdrew to allow the maneuver without opening his neck. "I'm sorry. I didn't mean to listen in—"

Amazir glared at his student. "Yes, you did. You stood there quite long enough to announce your presence, yet you didn't. When friends talk, you join them."

Irritated by the whole affair, Calistin turned sullenly. "You're not my father."

Amazir pounced. Calistin barely managed to whirl in time to face an angry swordmaster with two blades crossed at Calistin's throat. "Don't you ever turn your back on me!"

It was the supreme gesture of disrespect, and Calistin knew it; but he had not expected any *ganim,* even one so skilled, to catch the subtlety. "I'm sorry," he said, holding adolescent angst at bay. For once, his life depended on it. "I won't do it again. I promise."

Amazir sheathed his weapons in an eye blink. "A capable *torke* teaches more than swordsmanship."

"*Torke?*" Calistin stared in sudden accusation. "You're Renshai, too, aren't you?"

"Yes."

Though it had seemed certain a moment before, Calistin still had not expected that answer. "Yes?"

"Yes."

"Why didn't you tell me earlier?"

"You didn't ask."

Calistin started to splutter, then inquisitiveness, once again, overcame his temper. "How can that be? I've never seen you or heard of you. There aren't so many Renshai one could go unnoticed, at least not one of such age and skill. So who are you?" Recalling the Renshai tendency to appear younger, Calistin sucked air through his teeth in a hiss. "And just how old are you anyway?"

"Do you actually want answers, Calistin? Or are you just going to keep firing questions at me?"

Calistin fell sheepishly silent.

"Because I think Treysind deserves to be a part of this discussion, and we should return to the camp to talk."

Calistin did not see how any of this involved a street boy from Erythane, but he would not argue with a *torke* he respected. Silently, barraged with thoughts and questions, he trailed his new teacher back to the campsite.

Treysind had laid out three meals on piles of stacked leaves, an assortment of fresh fowl, roasted roots, and dried fruit.

Hungry as he felt, Calistin was more interested in information than eating. He sat in front of his meal but waited only until Amazir took his seat before turning to confront the elder. "And now, *torke*, my answers, please."

Amazir laughed, then sobered an instant later. "I imagine the first thing you wish to know is . . ."

Calistin expected the old Renshai to start with his name, so the elder's next words caught him by surprise.

". . . about your soul."

The enticing aroma of the meal seemed to utterly disappear. Calistin could only stare in shock and anticipation. "You . . . you know . . . ? I . . . do I have . . . one?"

All humor left the old man's face. "I'm afraid not."

Calistin's original source had seemed infallible, yet he had still hoped he had misunderstood. "I really don't? How can that be?" He glanced at Treysind, who took a sudden, inordinate interest in eating. He wondered if the boy should be privy to the conversation at all.

Amazir was not the type to dismiss Treysind's presence and speak openly by accident. He had, thus far, been overly solicitous of the boy. If he believed Treysind should hear this, then Calistin would not argue. "I presume you know that your parents saved the world from a sterility plague."

Calistin nodded. He knew the general story. Dark elves had inflicted the plague upon humankind, and the light elves had assisted in its lifting. The task had taken Kevral, Ra-khir, and some friends to multiple worlds, including that of the gods. "I was there," he said cryptically, testing Amazir.

The old Renshai smiled. "In utero, yes." He studied Calistin's face as he continued, "It soon became clear that the plague only took effect when a woman cycled. In an attempt to maintain humankind that some considered cruel and others heroic, pregnant women were expected to carry another child as soon as possible after delivery. Others attempted to fertilize young women shortly before they officially became . . . young women."

Calistin cringed at the thought. He doubted those young innocents had much choice in the matter.

"I'm not condoning what they did, Calistin; but desperation can force otherwise good people into making decisions that might seem appalling in normal circumstances. And it also opens the way for evil to do what comes naturally." Amazir cleared his throat but did not touch his food. "Kevral had just given birth to the twins when that truth became apparent."

Treysind continued to eat, but he did so randomly, his attention locked on the men.

"So she and Papa did their duty and had me right afterward." Calistin tried to move the story along. Though interested in his past, the soul issue currently intrigued him more. That, he had to know. "What happened to my soul, and how do I get it back?"

"Very well." Amazir shook his head with a hint of displeasure but skipped to the part Calistin had requested. "On one of those 'other worlds,' your parents discovered spirit spiders."

Treysind swallowed and finally spoke. "*Spirit* spiders?"

"They're a type of demon," Amazir explained. "Clothed in magic, they appear as they wish; but their natural form is giant, highly intelligent spiders. They feed on spirits, not blood. One bite robs a man not only of his life, but of his very soul."

Calistin shivered. It seemed the worst of all possible creatures. Even a glorious death in battle meant no place in Valhalla for their victims.

"And Kevral," Amazir finished, "was bitten."

It took a moment for those words to sink in. "My mother was bitten?"

"Yes."

"But . . . she lived."

"A miracle, it seemed at the time."

A sense of dread crept into Calistin, chilling through his marrow. "And she went to Valhalla." He felt certain of it; no one could convince him otherwise. He had seen her soul rise and speak, had seen the Valkyrie who took it.

To his surprise, Amazir did not dispute the assertion. "She did."

Treysind gasped, and with the sound understanding came to Calistin as well. "Because . . . it was . . . *my* soul that was eaten."

Amazir pursed his lips but did not need to speak. They all knew Calistin had spoken the truth.

"So . . ." Calistin suddenly found himself air-starved and realized he had forgotten to breathe. He gulped in a lungful of air. ". . . I . . . have no . . . soul."

"No soul," Amazir echoed, with only a hint of Calistin's angst.

"So . . . it's true. I'll never find . . ." Calistin had to force out the word that still filled his every ambition. ". . . Valhalla."

Amazir shook his head, though whether in agreement with the negative contention or in opposition to it, Calistin could not guess. "Longer ago than you want to know, a god once told me I would never reach Valhalla."

Calistin jerked his head up hopefully. "Was he right?"

Amazir stared. A smile edged across his lips. "I know I've slowed down a mite with age, but surely you don't think I'm dead."

"Of course." Calistin felt foolish in addition to devastated. "But . . . I mean . . . is he going to be right? Have you lost your soul, too?"

Amazir rose, his food still untouched. "Actually, he didn't give me a reason, simply told me I'd never make it there."

Assailed by a fog of desperation, utterly demoralized, Calistin could only ask, "So what . . . did you do?"

Amazir turned away to look out over the vast forest. "I chose not to believe him. To do otherwise meant abandoning the only thing that gave my life meaning. Intimidating enemies by stealing the promise of Valhalla is a trick invented by Renshai, you know, back in the days when we deliberately dismembered our foes."

Calistin's studies made him defensive. "But that was centuries ago."

"Yes."

"And also untrue." Calistin remembered when he had tried to prey on the dying Northman's superstitions, to no avail, right before a Valkyrie took him. Whether it occurs before, after, or during battle, loss of a limb or part does *not* bar a brave warrior from Valhalla."

"Yes." Amazir turned back to face Calistin. "And yet, the practice demoralized our enemies and, also, nearly resulted in our extinction. And haunts us to this day."

Now Calistin found himself equally monosyllabic. "Yes."

"My point is that I chose not to believe the god."

"The god was lying?"

"I did not say that." Amazir dropped to a crouch in front of Calistin. "I said I chose not to believe him. Because, no matter the truth of his assertion, I had no choice but to prove him wrong. Otherwise, I had lost all reason to fight, and fighting was all I knew. Besides, I had based much of life on doing what others pronounced impossible."

Warmth filled Calistin despite his distress. He had finally discovered a kindred soul, the only man in existence who shared the very features no one else seemed capable of understanding. And, yet, this man had appeared out of nowhere, unknown, when he should have been famous throughout every land, most especially to every Renshai. The thought stopped Calistin cold. "You're not real, are you? You're a figment of my imagination, how I picture myself in sixty or seventy years."

Treysind laughed, which startled Calistin. He had nearly forgotten the boy's presence. "He ain't no figment. Or if he is, I sees and hears it, too."

Calistin clung to the idea. Now that it occurred to him, he believed he saw a definite resemblance between this aged man and the one he saw in the mirror. "Then he's a lifelike projection sent by the gods to show me my future."

Amazir's expression turned cold. "I go where I wish; no one 'sends' me anywhere. I am not, and never will be, you. And I am brutally, unreservedly real as you will discover at your next practice."

Calistin could not help wincing. He'd already suffered more than enough pain from their last session. The sharper discomfort of bruises and lacerations were rapidly giving way to the ache and scream of overtaxed muscles. Years had passed since anyone, even himself, had driven him hard enough to leave him aching. He had come to believe that, no matter how hard or long he worked, he had moved beyond any ability to cause this kind of soreness. Amazir had proved him wrong. "Forgive the assumption, *torke*. It's just that we're in such great parallel."

"And not all of our similarities are coincidence," Amazir explained.

"Because the Renshai leaders know potential and talent when they see it, and they train it accordingly. You and I are neither the first nor last Renshai to hold such promise."

"And the gods' pronouncing us both unable to attain Valhalla? How does that fit in with our training?"

"It doesn't," Amazir admitted. "But it's not coincidence either."

Where once despair threatened to overtake all, a glimmer of hope arose. "Is there a solution to my problem?"

"There is."

Calistin had to know. He would do absolutely anything to win back a chance at Valhalla. "What is it?"

But Amazir only rose and waved at Calistin's dinner. "Eat. You need the nourishment."

Calistin did not even glance at the meal. "You know I would give up food altogether for that answer."

"And you will get it," Amazir said, returning to his own piled meal. "In due time. When you've earned it by giving your all to your lessons." He sat, snagging a cold, roasted wing.

Calistin thought he might burst, yet he knew nagging his *torke* was as dangerous as it was foolish. Instead, he turned his attention to his meal and did as he was told.

Calistin had always drawn the hardest, most vigorous teachers. Even after he surpassed them, he had always driven himself to the point of exhaustion. Yet none of that compared to the technique, finesse, and plain bone-wearying detail he suffered with every lesson from his new *torke*. He bolted food without tasting it, too hungry to chew. He slept so deeply he could not remember lying down; and, always, his every moment filled with movement or memory of movement, and how to make it better.

What should have taken a day of travel took a week; and, at the end of it, Calistin finally took the time to insist, over another hastily devoured meal put together by Treysind, that Amazir tell him how a soulless man might reach Valhalla.

"Ironically, the answer lies," Amazir explained, "in the part of your story that you most believe you already know, the piece you skipped right over when we discussed how you lost your soul."

That particular conversation remained engraved, in vivid detail, in Calistin's memory. Nevertheless, he had to consider what his *torke* meant.

Amazir did not wait for Calistin's recollection, "You know you were conceived during the sterility plague, as near as possible to your brothers' births, to maintain your mother's fertility."

"Yes." It all seemed so foolish now. His mother had never borne another child, perhaps because she had birthed three children in the space of a year or, like many Renshai, she simply lived too violent and harsh a life to conceive or carry another baby. Infertility, miscarriages, and stillbirths were all a natural and common part of Renshai life. More miraculous, the actual births.

"And I told you that the plague had made many men desperate, stooping to acts of cruelty they would never have considered in ordinary circumstances to assure the continuation of humankind."

Calistin recalled all that, and nodded.

"And, as you can imagine, the kings were most distressed, and their loyal followers. For, if their line perished, they reasoned, who could possibly rule in their place?"

"Nearly anyone?" Calistin ventured. He did not hold the awe for bloodline that many did. His parents did not raise him to believe ancestry mattered much.

Amazir laughed. "As I agree, but others gain silly attachments to things of little import. To equate shared blood with love is to doom all of us to marrying our mothers and sisters. Yet, to the king of Pudar, blood meant a great deal. He had recently lost his beloved older son to murder, leaving no heir. He branded his younger son a fop and a fool, but no one else could sire the line. So, he imprisoned Kevral and forced her to lie with his younger son until she either cycled or was proved to be with child."

Amazir's words lit a fire in Calistin's veins. Rage filled him, so hot it caused him pain; and the urge to slaughter the entire Pudarian royal line seized him. "He raped my mother? My mother?" That led to another scorching realization. "I'm a child of rape? And my blood . . . my blood . . ." Suddenly, he wanted to slice open every artery, to drain himself of the tainted, now boiling, life-fluid of his enemy. It explained so much, not the least of which why he looked as different from his brothers as they did from one another.

Treysind moved toward Calistin, as if to drag him into an embrace, but stopped short of actually completing the action. He knew better.

"No," Amazir said softly. "The prince no more wanted a part of it then Kevral, but he had little choice."

Calistin refused to believe it. "A man always has a choice."

"He would have been killed."

Calistin folded his arms across his chest, still seething. "I doubt that. Then the king would have no heirs at all."

"As I said, King Cymion thought little of his younger child. He would have executed him without much provocation."

Calistin gave no quarter. "The threat of death doesn't matter. A good man would choose to die rather than commit such a vile crime."

"But Prince Leondis surmised, rightly, that if he was executed, the king would have taken his place in Kevral's bed."

Calistin made a noise of outrage and revulsion. "She would have sliced his manhood from him and fed it to his dogs. Then she would have killed him."

Now Treysind cringed and made a sound similar to Calistin's.

Amazir only smiled. "I'm quite certain she would have, had she not been jailed and fully shackled, with her newborn twins as hostages."

"So I'm an heir to the throne of Pudar." Calistin tried to muster some interest in the idea but failed miserably. At the moment, he would rather carry Treysind's blood than King Cymion's.

"No."

Treysind and Calistin jerked their heads to Amazir simultaneously and in just as shocked a silence.

"No?" It made no sense. Calistin knew only nine months had elapsed between the birth of his brothers and his own, and he had carried full term. "How could . . . ?" He recalled heroic tales from his grandfather about how his father had single-handedly challenged the army of Pudar to rescue Kevral from their prison. Knight-Captain Kedrin had never mentioned the details Amazir elaborated now, but Calistin knew the stories had to intertwine. "Papa?"

"Acted with courage befitting the bravest Renshai, but he did not arrive in time."

Treysind did not give Calistin a chance to gather his thoughts for a full question. "So who's Hero's real father?"

Amazir gave Treysind the first stern look ever aimed, by him, at the boy. "Ra-khir is not fake or false. He *is* Calistin's real father."

Treysind looked even more confused, staring at his feet to avoid the harshness of Amazir's gaze. "But yas sayed he didn't 'rrive in time."

Calistin rescued the boy. "He means Ra-khir is my real father because he claimed and raised me. Bloodline doesn't matter, and a man's seed alone doesn't make him a father." He gave Amazir a pleading look. "Nevertheless, I would like to know whose ancestral line I carry." He could not help adding, "And it's my right to know. My parents should have told me."

Amazir nodded sagely. "In their defense, they were sworn to secrecy. A Knight of Erythane would die before he broke an oath, and Kevral loved him too much to risk losing him by violating her own promise."

"She loved *me*, too," Calistin found himself saying defensively. "Or so she said."

"Poor Kevral," Treysind murmured, apparently catching a detail Calistin's outrage forced him to miss.

No longer irritated with the boy, Amazir nodded. "Imagine having to live with such a secret. To keep it meant violating her son's trust, but to reveal it meant betraying her husband and her own honor."

Calistin fell silent. He had not yet looked at it from Kevral's viewpoint, might not ever have done so if not for his two companions. He suspected most of the details of his life might look different from others' perspectives, yet he refused to analyze them. He might not like what he found.

"And one last event helped tip the balance. Your blood grandfather gave his blessing to Ra-khir as your father. He promised that his family would not interfere."

"An' yet," Treysind said with uncharacteristic thoughtfulness and an intensity of expression that focused squarely on Amazir, "ya has now, hasn't ya?"

Amazir smiled.

Calistin gawked. "Are you saying . . . ?" He turned from Treysind to Amazir. "Are you confirming . . . ?" He shook his head to clear it, wishing his mouth would work. "You? *You* are my blood grandfather?"

"I am," Amazir admitted simply. "But I wasn't planning to tell you just yet. Your astute companion has a tendency to help you when you least deserve it, usually at my expense."

Calistin expected his mind to fill with questions, but he found only one and that he aimed at Treysind. "How did you know? How could you possibly know?"

Treysind only shrugged his skinny shoulders. "Who else's gonna know so much 'bout ya? Or care 'nough ta cram it through ya's big, fat head?" He added the simplest detail as if in afterthought, "An' yas looks 'ike some, too."

Calistin studied the wrinkled old man in front of him and wondered how anyone could notice anything similar about them. Only then, he remembered he had once considered the possibility that Amazir was a vision of his own future.

Amazir laughed. "You should not see any resemblance, regardless. I've altered my appearance."

"It's tha eyes," Treysind explained. "Ya can't das'guise '*em.*"

It seemed a family trait of Kevral's children, that, when it came to appearances, each tended to most favor his paternal grandfather. Subikahn looked more like Weile Kahn than anyone else; and Saviar had inherited all of Kedrin's splendor, including his natural, damnable charisma. Suddenly, Calistin had to know what the future held in store for him. "So what do you really look like? Can I see? Please?"

Amazir rose with a quickness that belied his age, though Calistin had become accustomed to it. Only as the swordmaster disappeared into the brush to change did some of the more important queries rise to Calistin's mind. It seemed petty to worry about appearances when so much of his origins still remained obscure. Amazir could answer so much, if Calistin only thought to ask the right questions.

Treysind moved closer. "Yas all righ', Hero?"

Treysind's worry seemed nonsensical. "Of course I'm all right," Calistin snapped. Why wouldn't I be all right?"

"He gived ya big news. Don't it matter ta ya?" Treysind threw himself into Calistin's arms, embracing him.

Uncertain how to handle the situation, Calistin remained still, allowing the warmth of the boy to reach him. It was a hug that radiated brotherhood and understanding, and it did make him feel a bit better. He would die before he would admit it, however. "Get off me, Treysind." He gave the boy a light shove. "What's wrong with you?"

"Nothin'." Treysind backed away. "Jus' tryin' ta make ya feel better." A glimmer of disappointment flashed through his pale eyes. "Ain't I doin' it right? 'cause I ain't got much practice."

Once again, Calistin found himself looking at the world through Treysind's eyes, an orphan scarcely old enough to remember a mother's love, if he had ever known it. "No, I'm sure you're doing it right . . . if I was a great big *girl.* I can handle my own problems, no matter how overwhelming they might seem to you."

Clearly hurt, Treysind turned away.

Calistin closed his eyes and sighed. "Look, Treysind. Don't think I don't appreciate your trying to help me. I do, but—"

To Calistin's relief, Amazir returned before he had to come up with the words to finish. Previously, his *torke* had appeared ancient; now, he seemed merely aging. His hair was Northern golden, with a liberal sprinkling of silver. His features looked solid, chiseled, with blunt cheekbones and a gently-arched chin. Four straight scars marred one cheek, in lines, just in front of his ear. The body remained lithe, lean, and sinewy; but the skin now looked healthy and well-veined instead of paper thin. The eyes remained the same timeless and intense blue-gray. It was not, Calistin realized, a particularly handsome or homely visage, but one that might easily disappear into a crowd. And he believed he did see some resemblance in the oval of his *torke's* face, the fine straight nose, pointed chin, and the average-sized lips; but, most of all, in those damnable, piercing eyes.

The questions remained, but Calistin found himself nearly incapable of asking. Hating one's *torke* was a time-honored occurrence among Renshai; he doubted a single one of his students could stand him. He demanded only respect and obedience, never love. Yet to discover that this man's son had raped his mother would drive him past outrage to murder. Amazir's words still rang in his ears: "Your blood grandfather gave his blessing to Ra-khir as your father. He promised that his family would not interfere." What cold and terrible arrogance would cause a man to believe he had a right to any child conceived to his family through rape.

But Calistin did not ask. He could not. For to do so meant losing the one truly good thing that had happened since the Northmen had come to Béarn. If he never learned the answer to that obvious question, the truth became solely what he made it out to be, nothing more and nothing less. He might never learn to love or trust this man who had taught him so much; but, at least in ignorance, he could continue to learn from Amazir's spectacular talent.

CHAPTER 36

The urge to humiliate another is too often at the root of valor.
—Knight-Captain Kedrin Ramytan's son

SOMETHING BRUSHED SAVIAR'S forehead. His fingers inched instinctively for his sword, but his hand closed around nothing. Someone had apparently managed to disarm him. He turned the motion into a sleep movement, judging his surroundings in eye-closed darkness. He felt the heat of a nearby body, and a hand touched his face again. Quick as a snake, he grabbed the stranger's wrist, only to find his own movement unbearably clumsy. As he opened his eyes, a high-pitched scream rang through his ears.

Saviar stared into a terrified, young female face. Intelligent eyes, gray-blue in color, were wide open. The nose was straight above large lips in a longish oval face, and her ears were invisible beneath thick waves of mahogany hair. A spray of freckles decorated her cheeks.

An instant later, Subikahn also stood over him. "Savi! Saviar, you're awake."

That being self-evident, Saviar saw no reason to reply. He lay in an unfamiliar, stone-walled room with no memory of how he had gotten there. "Where are we?" His voice emerged as an unrecognizable croak, and his throat felt on fire.

"You tell him." The girl pulled her hand from his grip, and Saviar made no attempt to stop her. His twin did not look entirely at ease, but they clearly were not in any imminent danger. He also noticed, at once, that Subikahn wore *Motfrabelonning*. "I'll go let the others know."

Saviar struggled to sit up, surprised at how difficult he found that simple motion. He felt strangely weak, thinner than he remembered, but he still managed to demand the necessary. "Give me back my sword." Now seated on a blanket-covered pallet, he looked at Subikahn's wildly uncombed hair and lines impressed onto his cheeks by whatever folded cloth he had used as a pillow. "And you look awful!"

A smile touched Subikahn's lips, but he did not respond to the insult, even with friendly banter. He passed over the sword, and Saviar drew it protectively into his lap. "I'll explain everything soon. For now, just promise me you won't tell *anyone* we're . . ." He lowered his voice to the barest whisper. ". . . Renshai."

"Why not?" Saviar managed hoarsely. He tried to fasten the sheathed weapon to his belt, his fingers responding with a sluggish, frustrating awkwardness.

Subikahn glanced over his shoulder. "I'll explain later. Just promise me."

"But I—" It took him twice as long as it should have, but Saviar managed to reattach his sword. An immediate sense of relief fell over him.

"Promise!" Subikahn's voice remained low but gained force. "Just do it."

"All right." Saviar knew he would learn nothing more until he did as his twin asked. "I promise; I promise." He dropped his own voice to a whisper that kept the pain to a bare minimum. "Now tell me where we are."

Subikahn sighed and back stepped. Before he could answer, however, a group of strange men and women burst into the room, all talking simultaneously. They used the Western tongue with an accent Saviar did not recognize, and he found it impossible to follow any particular conversation.

An elder at the front of the pack raised a hand, and the group gradually fell silent. Though feeling dizzy and sick, Saviar studied his every movement. He had a slow deliberateness about him that would make him an inferior swordsman, and his muscles had clearly withered with age. However, his limbs did not tremble and his light brown eyes remained clear as he returned Saviar's scrutiny. "Tell us your name, young man."

Saviar opened his mouth, but Subikahn answered first. "I told you. That's my—"

Frowning deeply, the elder cut Subikahn off with a gesture. "I need to hear it from him."

The young woman Saviar had caught earlier threaded her way through the pack to stand at Subikahn's side. She spoke softly to him, and Subikahn nodded reluctantly.

Saviar cleared his throat, then wished he had not. It felt as if tiny shards of metal had become embedded in it. "My name is Saviar Ra-khirsson." True to his word, he said nothing more, leaving off the details of his tribal affiliation.

The elder smiled. "And mine is Jeremilan Ham's son."

Subikahn stiffened, and his gaze whipped to the speaker. He stared, which cued Saviar to be on his guard. He noticed nothing special about the man. White hair fell to narrow shoulders, and his wrinkled face told little about his mood. He wore a robe that, though not inordinately tight, fit well enough to reveal weapons, if he had carried any.

Apparently oblivious to the Renshai's interest in him, Jeremilan made a casual gesture toward Subikahn. "Do you know this young man?"

Saviar rolled his gaze to Subikahn, more from politeness to the elder's request than from necessity. Subikahn had not instructed him to avoid any topic but their status as Renshai; and he felt certain his brother would have warned him if any other information was dangerous. "That's my twin brother, Subikahn."

Murmurs traversed the group. Either Subikahn had not told them the relationship; or, more likely, they had thought him a liar.

Jeremilan's next question gave Saviar no insight. "Saviar, do you know where you are?"

Saviar shook his head carefully, so the movement did not intensify his vertigo. "I have absolutely no idea. Can you please tell me?"

The girl turned Subikahn a dirty look, and he shrugged. She had specifically instructed him to explain their location while she gathered the crowd now filling the room, but Subikahn had spent that time extracting a promise instead.

"You're with the Mages of Myrcidë, Saviar." Jeremilan studied him for some reaction to the news, but Saviar gave him nothing but honest bewilderment. The word "mage" had magical connotations, but he had never heard of this Myrcidë.

"Mare-see-DAY?" Saviar tried.

Jeremilan restored an inflection that sounded more Western than foreign, "Myrcidë. Long before either of our births, it was a village. Now, it's simply a title."

Either of our births? The comparison seemed ridiculous. Jeremilan appeared older than dirt. "I see." Saviar could think of nothing better to say.

Murmurs and nods ran through the crowd. Clearly the words struck them far more profoundly.

"Saviar, at the risk of alarming you, I'm going to perform a little spell over you." Jeremilan continued quickly, "It won't hurt, and it won't harm you in any way."

Saviar touched his hilt but did not seize it. He wanted the reassurance, without appearing to threaten. He looked to Subikahn for guidance. His brother had clearly taken the measure of these mages while Saviar was sleeping.

Subikahn's lids swept unhurriedly down and upward, and he nodded encouragingly.

Jeremilan lowered his head and muttered a few guttural syllables that sounded more elfish than human. A glow blossomed from his fingertips.

Saviar's hand tightened on the hilt.

The mages did not move, though Saviar got the impression of them all pressing closer. Only Subikahn noticed his brother's defensiveness, and he spoke in reassuring tones, "Easy, Saviar. It's all right."

A fuzzy light sprang to life around Saviar, and the crowd retreated slightly with whispered comments and measured smiles.

Then, as suddenly as it had all come, it disappeared. Jeremilan stepped back.

"What was that all about?" Saviar demanded, gaze fixed on Subikahn.

This time, the girl answered. "We just needed to know if you had an aura. If the blood of Myrcidians runs through your veins."

Saviar could not imagine that to be true. "And . . . does it?"

"It does!" Jeremilan called triumphantly, to scattered applause. "In both of you. Which must mean it comes from your mother."

Our mother, the Renshai. Saviar could not wait to get Subikahn alone. The last thing he wanted now was questions about their mother, especially on the heels of Subikahn's warning. As the vertigo dissipated, the nausea resolved into an intense and angry hunger. He felt as if someone had stabbed him deep in the gut; yet, somehow knew that food would help quench the fire. "I'm famished," he announced, mostly to change the subject but also as an abrupt and overriding realization. Strangely, he felt as if he had not eaten in days.

Jeremilan's expression looked stricken, and several members of the audience lowered their heads. A pair nearest the door rushed from the room. "Of course, you're famished. We'll get you something to eat and drink."

"Thank you." A sense of relief washed over Saviar, but it did not last long.

"Do you suppose it's possible to bring your mother here?"

Subikahn pushed his way to Saviar's side. "I'm afraid that's impossible."

Saviar was struck by a fresh wave of grief. He thought he had moved well past this stage, but tears formed in his eyes and leaked before he could stop them. He felt weak and ill, and very much in need of his mother.

"She's dead." Subikahn announced flatly. "Accidental. She got caught in a feud not of her making."

"Accidental" pushed the boundaries, but it was otherwise strictly true. Saviar lowered his head and let his brother speak for him.

But Subikahn let his words disappear into a dense silence, finally broken by Jeremilan.

"Well, this is sad news for all of us. Would it be too much to hope for uncles? Aunts?"

Subikahn shook his head.

"Well. At least we have the two of you."

Have? Saviar did not like the phraseology. *Are we prisoners?* Subikahn's quiet demeanor, as usual, gave him no clue.

The next two weeks progressed in a blur of activity and exhaustion so complete that Calistin never remembered sleeping, eating, or attending to hygiene. The weather came and went without notice; if he got soaked or cold, he did not recall. Every new maneuver, every nuance of swordplay, however, remained indelibly engraved on his mind, muscles, and psyche. He became the eager student every *torke* prayed for, the one who pushes himself past pain and human endurance, the one who can never learn enough.

The questions went unconsidered, unasked, so it caught Calistin by surprise when his *torke* demanded an answer of his own. "Calistin, what is it you're preparing to do? Why are you heading North, and how does it serve you to slaughter the best warriors of the Westlands?"

Calistin shook his head to settle the new contents. Buried beneath techniques and details, he had to dig for the answers to actions that no longer drove him inexorably northward. "I . . . have a battle to fight. One that my mother fought for me . . . and lost."

Amazir summed up the explanation in a single word, "Vengeance."

Calistin saw it differently, "In a manner of speaking, I suppose; but it's not blind anger. As I said, it should have been my battle."

"Calistin." Amazir sheathed his swords and motioned for his student to do the same. "No one blames you for suggesting your mother take your place. No one believed you seriously meant those words, not even Kevral when she accepted."

Calistin's brows rose. They felt heavy, difficult to move even that far. The exhaustion he cast aside hours earlier now threatened to overwhelm him. He sheathed his blades gingerly, worried more for their security, their needs, than his own. "So you were there, too?" This *torke* drove him to madness. "Do you have a trove of disguises? How can it be that you've lived among my own people, but I've never noticed you before?"

"Calistin, it's time."

"Time?" Calistin had no idea what his *torke* meant. "Time for what?"

"Time for you to learn how to win back Valhalla." Amazir headed toward the clearing and cook fire where Treysind prepared another meal.

It was the moment Calistin had waited for ever since he discovered Amazir might have a solution, yet he found excitement impossible to ignite. He was just too achy, too tired, too full of ideas to grasp more. Nevertheless, he trailed his *torke* in expectant silence. Clearly, he intended, as always, to include Treysind in the discussion.

As the two men approached, the boy went into a flurry of activity, shuffling food from ground to warming fire to the piled leaves they used for plates.

"Thank you," Calistin said to Treysind, meaning it. Without the boy, they surely would have starved by now. He wondered how many meals had passed that he had devoured in silent fatigue, without a single word of gratitude to the hardworking cook.

"Ya's so verry welcome, Hero," Treysind replied with bubbly eagerness. "Hopes ya likes it."

I'm so hungry, Calistin realized, *I could eat bark and appreciate every bite.* He did not speak the words aloud. He was not sure exactly how, but they might insult Treysind. "Oh, I'll like it," Calistin managed. "I always do."

Amazir smiled and crouched in front of his own pile of food. He, too, seemed starved, shoveling food into his mouth without bothering to breathe between bites.

Treysind must have already eaten, because he stood between them, replacing any food they finished, whisking away bones and stems, and attending the two Renshai like royalty.

"When your mother was trapped in Pudar, she asked me to help her out of her predicament," Amazir explained. "And sending my son was the only solution I had at the time."

Calistin braced himself, bite of roasted meat half-chewed.

"He was young, Calistin, a virgin. And he left the decision entirely to her." Amazir stopped eating in order to directly meet Calistin's gaze, to speak plainly and clearly. "She wanted Ra-khir to father any child she had; we all know that. But, at the time, that was not one of her choices. She could carry a prince or a Renshai, and she chose Ravn."

Ravn? The name brought it all together in a rush. Abruptly, Calistin found himself sitting on the ground, his usual wary crouch forgotten. Flat on his buttocks, he paused in stunned silence, dizzy with fatigue and understanding. Everything came together in that moment: the aged, unknown Renshai who seemed to know everything, who could best him in a battle and teach him concepts beyond anything he had ever considered. "You're . . . you're . . . Colbey. My blood grandfather is . . . is . . . Colbey Calistinsson?" How apt his own name finally seemed, shared with the great grandfather who now watched over him from Valhalla.

Colbey laughed at a situation that seemed anything but humorous to Calistin. "Only a Renshai would find more awe in a Renshai's bloodline than a goddess'."

Calistin's bones seemed to turn to water. He could scarcely maintain his position, even with his rear firmly planted on the ground. "My blood grandmother is . . . is . . ." It seemed like sacrilege merely to think it, to suggest it aloud might bring the gods' wrath down upon him.

"Freya, yes. Can you imagine anything grander?"

Calistin found himself incapable of imagining anything. Nothing in the world seemed more fantastical, more impossible, than the truth. "So I'm a . . . a . . ." He did not know how to finish. He carried the blood of gods, yet also of mortals. "What the hell am I?"

"You're Calistin Ra-khirsson. The son of Kevral Tainharsdatter and Sir Ra-khir, and a Renshai of great potential skill."

Though Calistin already knew the answer, he could not help feeling disappointed. "I'm not immortal?"

Amazir Colbey Calistinsson shook his head sadly.

Calistin scrambled to a crouch, besieged by emotions that baffled and enraged him. "If none of this matters, if nothing has changed, why are you telling me this? I could have gone to my grave blithely believing myself the fruit of my father's loins. Now, I'll find myself reexamining every moment of my childhood, suspecting every word my parents told me." He rose, pacing, though every movement hurt and his limbs felt lead-weighted. "Everything I've done and been is a lie. What other deceptions have my loved ones hidden from me?"

Treysind's gaze followed Calistin's every step, and the expression on his face looked painfully pinched. Clearly, he wanted to help but did not know how.

Colbey twirled a finger through a mound of mashed roots, then licked it from his fingers slowly, savoring.

For reasons he could not explain, the immortal's nonchalance fueled Calistin's irritation nearly as much as his own inability to determine his next course of action. He wanted to distance himself from everyone related to him, whether by blood or family ties. He had already lost Kevral. He had run from Ra-khir, from his brothers, even from his people. It seemed only natural to rid himself of Colbey as well, yet he needed one more answer. "You said . . ." he started, bothered by the sulky surliness in his own voice, "that I might find a solution to my problem in this story you dumped on me."

Colbey's brows edged upward. For an instant, Calistin thought his impudence might lose him his soulless existence, but then the immortal Renshai laughed. "You're lucky I have an adolescent son of my own, Calistin. I'm accustomed to being spoken to in that manner, though not often. Ravn pays dearly for it. Next time, you will, too."

Ravn? It sounded ridiculous to compare the man who had sired him to himself for age. Yet, Calistin realized, if gods and immortals grew older at the same pace as humans, they would all look like wizened piles of ash and bone. At the moment, he did not care what Colbey did to him. He doubted the practices could get any harder, any more brutal. He believed his *torke* knew his every limit and deliberately took him just beyond them. He worried more for never getting the information he so desperately needed, and for that reason alone he softened his tone. "How do I save my soul, *torke?*"

"You can't."

The simple negative response made Calistin's temper boil again. "Then why are we having these discussions? Why don't you go away and leave me to my misery?"

"Because I remember my own all too well. I was in my eighth decade before I discovered my blood parentage, wondering why I remained spry while others withered around me. No one dared claim a lack of courage kept me from my destiny with Valhalla, but Odin taunted me, swore I would never find that one place that matters most to Northmen of every tribe but, especially, to Renshai."

Calistin gritted his teeth. He had his own problems to worry about without listening to those of another man, even one dubbed the greatest Renshai of all time. Calistin's mother had spent most of her life emulating Colbey, his sword skill, his wisdom, even the feathered cut of his hair. "Odin lied, didn't he?" Even as the words emerged, Calistin wished he had not spoken them. The gods could do far worse to a man than kill him.

Apparently Calistin's concern showed on his features, because Colbey reassured him. "Odin died at the *Ragnarok*. He cannot hurt you."

It was a serious point of religion; knowing the truth might end much of the world's bickering. Renshai, most Béarnides, elves, and a few others believed the *Ragnarok*, the Great War prophesied to end the reign of the gods had occurred. In their version, Colbey had intervened, changing the projected tide of the battle and rescuing some of those slated to die. Most Northmen believed the *Ragnarok* had yet to come. Those two main beliefs, and myriad related ideas, accounted for most of the current religions of the world. Only a few still worshiped the old gods of the West or the East's single unnamed deity.

Calistin knew no one would change his or her beliefs based on a truth pronounced by him, but curiosity forced him to ask, "Exactly which gods did the *Ragnarok* claim?" He did not expect an answer.

Yet Colbey gave a straightforward one, "Odin, Aegir, Heimdall, Thor, Loki, Bragi, Tyr, and the goddess Hel. The monsters Fenrir, the Midgard Serpent, and King Surtr of the Fire Giants went with them."

Calistin could only stare, blinking occasionally. "You . . . told . . . me?" he finally sputtered out.

Colbey shrugged. "You asked. And a man needs to know who he can freely curse and blaspheme." He added conspiratorially, "But don't go overboard. Vidar leads the pantheon now, and he is still Odin's son. Some of the others left behind loyal wives, and there's nothing more dangerous than a woman insulted."

Calistin laughed awkwardly, taken aback by the whole situation. It seemed impossible that he was sharing a guilty grandson moment with an immortal from Asgard.

Colbey's expression turned serious again in an instant. "I felt caught in the ultimate unwinnable situation. The more I tried to die in battle, the more I honed my craft. And the more skilled I got, the less likely anyone could kill me in battle. I seemed destined to die of age or illness, a coward's death, yet even those things seemed in no hurry to take me."

Now the parallel came together for Calistin. "The god blood you carried aged you slower."

"So far, Odin's decree has proved correct. My soul has not entered Valhalla, because I haven't died. Odin did not expect me to get this far. He intended to kill me centuries ago." Colbey glanced at the sky, and those predatory eyes gained a glint of pure evil. Clearly, he delved into memories so intense he would not share them. "Things did not work out that way. And I have been to Valhalla, many times, though only as a visitor."

"My mother visited Valhalla, too." Realizing how obvious that sounded, Calistin amended. "Before she died, I mean." He looked intently at Colbey, needing confirmation of the story. He had never doubted it until now, when nothing about his family seemed real anymore.

"Twice," Colbey confirmed. "She remains the only mortal to do so while alive. What you don't know is that the *Einherjar* invited her to remain with them, a situation the *Valkyries* abhorred but could do absolutely nothing about. At the time, Kevral believed her soul lost, not yours."

Under any circumstance, it was the greatest thing that could ever happen to a Renshai. Given the chance, Calistin would accept the opportunity in an instant, without a single thought. His heart pounded as he imagined battling the bravest warriors throughout history, day in and day out for eternity. Lacking a soul became meaningless so long as he remained alive. And, if someone managed to kill him, it would be worth the time he had had, even if only a morning.

Colbey clearly knew exactly where Calistin's mind had gone. He added softly, "They even promised to pull any lethal blows they might manage to land, to keep her alive and soulless there forever."

Calistin sighed at the perfection of it. "No chance on Asgard, Midgard, or any other world could match it. What could be more perfect?"

"An' yet . . ." Treysind spoke his first words in so long Calistin had forgotten the boy remained with them. ". . . she dint stay."

It made no sense to Calistin, "Why?"

"Why do you think?" Colbey made a gesture at Treysind, urging silence. He wanted Calistin to answer the question.

Calistin considered several moments but could find no answer. Nothing could top the *Einherjar's* offer. No sane Renshai would refuse it, especially one who had no other means to get there. He shook his head, pondered the situation a bit longer, then shook his head again. "I don't know." He thought about the time line: after the bite of the spirit spider but before . . . before what? He sought an important clue. "Was I born yet?"

"Still inside."

Calistin gasped at the vast magnificence of his next thought. If Kevral had accepted the *Einherjar's* gift, he would have been born in Valhalla. Raised and trained by the best swordsmen in the world, he would have known no other world but the heaven to which every Renshai, every truly great warrior, aspires. Were he not already sitting, he might have collapsed. "There could be no greater reward, no better life, than one from birth to afterlife in Valhalla."

"Perhaps," Colbey said, the word a Renshai sacrilege, at best. "But then, what would a hopeful young warrior have to strive for? History has shown that children raised with every whim indulged learn to appreciate . . . nothing."

Calistin supposed Colbey spoke truth. His mother quoted him so often, so enthusiastically, that the boys learned to accept his every word as profound scripture. Yet it seemed utterly impossible that anyone could tire of Valhalla. After all, the *Einherjar* spent eternity there, and they were the most content beings in any world. "Why?" he sputtered out, more in anger than curiosity. "Why did she refuse? Why?"

Colbey frowned, then turned his attention to Treysind. The boy raised and lowered his skinny shoulders, an expression that begged tolerance on his face. Colbey shook his head, lips pursing in clear exasperation. "She had a set of infant twins who needed their mother and her guidance. She had a man who loved her enough to die for her. In fact, he would surrender his life today if he had any reason to believe it would bring her back."

Calistin did not think anything Colbey said could vex him further, but that managed. "That's stupid. He knows she's in Valhalla."

"Does he?"

"How could he not?"

"Because, like all pure mortals without swords imbued with magic, Ra-khir doesn't see Valkyries. He's not even entirely certain Kevral didn't lose her soul to the spirit spider. Not a day has passed since her death that he has not begged me for a sign, anything to reassure him that Kevral found Valhalla and is happy."

"You see my father every day?"

Treysind rolled his eyes. "He's meanin' through prayers, ya rock-dense moron."

Every eye jerked to the Erythanian, who turned a brilliant shade of red and feigned a sudden interest in cleaning up the meal.

Colbey smiled. "I mean through prayer, you rock-dense moron. He begs me through prayer."

Calistin felt as if he floated above the clearing, detached and confused. He had heard all he could handle for one day. Tact and logic, never his strong suits, fled entirely from his repertoire. "So why are you torturing him? Why don't you tell him?"

Colbey must have realized that his charge had reached his limit, because he accepted, without comment, the disrespectful question in addition to the tone of voice. "Because, Calistin, the denizens of Asgard have more important things to do than interact with mortals. It is the job of Ra-khir's sons to comfort their father, to put his mind at ease, to point out what they already know as indisputable fact."

"Saviar . . ." Calistin started, thinking back to when they left Erythane. Saviar had insisted they not awaken Ra-khir. At the time, Calistin had known it was the wrong thing to do, knew it would crush Ra-khir to find his sons missing; but Calistin had trusted his older, wiser brother. Only now, he realized Saviar's irritation and impatience with their father's grief had caused them both to mistreat him terribly. "Saviar said . . . and I thought . . ." Calistin could not remember the last time he found tears in his eyes. "We were cruel."

"Yes."

"To someone we profess to love."

"Yes."

Calistin could no longer control the exhaustion that pressed him to the ground. He believed the swirl of thought and emotion that battered him would keep him awake all night but found himself asleep so fast he remembered nothing more.

CHAPTER 37

If one chooses a course of action solely for the purpose of dying, it loses all glory, honor, and meaning. It diminishes a warrior to desperate self-destruction.

—*Colbey Calistinsson*

SAVIAR STROKED THROUGH an awkward parody of *yrtventrig*, holding the last pose hopefully while Subikahn paced in an angry circle around him.

"No! No! No!" Subikahn knew his own frustration had to mirror Saviar's. It pained him to see Saviar's discomfort so plainly displayed. Maneuvers he had once performed to near-perfection had become tight and graceless. "Where's the fluidity? Where's the power?"

"It's coming," Saviar promised.

Subikahn nodded stiffly. He could not deny that Saviar had improved to a great extent in one short week, regaining more than half of his strength, a hefty dose of stamina, and most of his agility. Still, it drove Subikahn near to madness to see his capable brother forced to regain lost ground rather than progressing toward ever more significant achievements. "Again!"

"Again," Saviar agreed, launching into the Renshai maneuver without a hint of the animosity he had sometimes shown their *torke*. They both knew that the more time he spent with his swords, the faster he would return to his former glory. His last performance would not have satisfied the least discerning Renshai.

Subikahn glanced up to the grassy hill, where Chymmerlee kept her vigil. She had interrupted them only once, to bring Saviar a ladle of water that Subikahn had slapped coldly from her hand. The look of shock and betrayal on her face had inspired a stab of guilt that Subikahn had kept hidden. He had never apologized, and Chymmerlee had learned to keep comforts, words, and self away until the sessions finished.

This time, Saviar performed a passable version of *yrtventrig,* his sword capering like a live thing, his feet skipping lightly over weeds and stone, his arm demonstrating the calm fusion of deadly quickness and power that belonged to Saviar alone. It was not his best performance; if he were fit, it might have seemed a bit lazy and notably slow. However, the creases on his sweat-streaked face made it clear to Subikahn that Saviar had done the best he could currently manage.

"Not bad," Subikahn admitted.

Saviar beamed, which caught Subikahn off guard. He was not trained as a *torke,* and he had only once considered his twin something other than an equal. That lapse still haunted him, and he had spent all of Saviar's recovery atoning to his sword.

"We're done until after supper."

Saviar dutifully sheathed his swords. "You're sure?" His gaze strayed toward Chymmerlee, as Subikahn's had moments earlier.

"I'm sure."

Saviar remained in place. He clearly had something to say.

Subikahn did not rush it. He checked over the perfect edge of his sword, delaying until his brother managed to work through his reluctance.

At length, Saviar said, "Do you . . . like her?"

"Her?" Subikahn followed Saviar's gaze. "Chymmerlee?"

"Yes. Do you like her?"

It seemed a nonsensical question. "Of course, I like her. She saved my brother's life."

"Yes." Saviar moved with restless dissymmetry. "But when I say 'like,' I mean—"

Subikahn finally got it. "—desire?" he suggested. "Lust? Do you mean do I want to thump her?"

Saviar's cheeks flamed. "Um . . . that's not exactly . . . I mean . . . I just . . ."

He's still a virgin, Subikahn realized suddenly. *Up until this year, so was I.* "I'm sorry, Saviar. I shouldn't have been that crude." He added reassuringly, "Don't worry. I'm not interested in her . . . that way." He could not help asking, "Are you?"

"I think . . ." Saviar did not look at his twin, still blushing. "I think . . . I might be. How . . . how do you tell?"

How do you tell? Subikahn had never considered his emotions in physical detail, but he tried for Saviar. "Do you want to be with her nearly all the time?"

Saviar nodded.

"Does her every look, every touch, every smile usurp the rest of the world for that one moment?"

Saviar's brow knitted in thought. "I—"

"Do you want to . . ." Not wishing to further embarrass his brother, Subikahn softened his question, ". . . kiss her?"

"I already did," Saviar admitted, the flush still clear on his face. "Her lips tasted so good, so . . . familiar."

Subikahn placed a hand on his hip in mock sternness. "Don't you think you should have asked me about my feelings for her *before* you kissed her?"

"I . . . I . . . suppose. I'm . . . I'm sorry . . . I . . ." Saviar's eyes narrowed. "I thought you said you weren't interested."

"Not interested in *her.*" Subikahn smiled. "I'm still perfectly interested in teasing you."

"Funny."

"And it's no wonder she tasted familiar. You know, while you were 'out,' we shoved a reed down your throat and she chewed up your food so you wouldn't starve to death." Subikahn waited for a look of utter disgust that never came.

Saviar's cheeks finally found their normal pale color. "She did that for me? That's so . . ."

". . . disgusting?" Subikahn inserted.

". . . sweet. So caring."

Subikahn rolled his eyes. "You like her 'that way,' all right. Have at her."

"Have at?" Saviar gave his twin another irritated look. "You're talking vulgarities again."

"No. Practicalities. Sex is the only real relationship you two can ever have."

Saviar shook his head, one side of his upper lip drawn upward. He clearly found the turn of the discussion distasteful. "How so?"

"Because bringing our bloodline into theirs is all the Myrcidians really want from us." Subikahn turned away, not wanting to see the disappointment on his brother's face when he pointed out the only viable truth. "They know we can't throw spells, so we're useless to them in that regard. We can help strengthen and vary their line, I suppose; but we'll also further dilute it. Only you and I know we don't actually have a trace of the magical blood they're expecting from us."

"I've been thinking about that—" Saviar started, but Subikahn broke in.

"No, Saviar, it's not us giving off that aura. It's just the sword they're detecting."

"Is it?"

"Yes." Subikahn did not want Saviar deluding himself for love. "I haven't seen a 'glow' since I gave it to you. I could see them plainly while I held it, whenever they used magic."

"But Renshai have interbred with other peoples they conquered. Maybe—"

"Maybe some Renshai carry the blood of Myrcidë. Maybe. But it's not likely to be us. Mama descended from the line of Modrey, the most pure-blooded Renshai." Subikahn shook his head. "I'm sorry, Savi, but Kevral Tainharsdatter was Renshai through and through. And, if the mages of Myrcidë ever find that out, they'll run *us* through and through." He mimicked a sword thrust into each of their guts.

Saviar did not argue, though they both knew death by Myrcidians would not come in the form of a sharpened weapon.

Subikahn sighed loudly. He knew the time had come. "Savi, there's something I need to tell you."

Saviar looked at him brightly, all interest. The seriousness in Subikahn's voice had clearly not escaped him.

Saviar had no memory of the events preceding his coma. Subikahn had told his twin that an attack by Northmen had resulted in the wound in his thigh. The lie had slipped past his lips without forethought or intention. When it came time to admit his own hand in the wounding, the words would not come, his mouth would not allow him to speak the truth. "You still remember nothing of the day you got hurt?"

"Nothing," Saviar said.

"So you don't remember . . . our duel?"

"Duel? We dueled?" The skin around Saviar's eyes crinkled. "You mean spar, don't you?"

Subikahn did not wish to argue semantics. "Spar, then. What made it a duel to me was that we had a wager riding on it. If I won, you would stop bothering me about my 'secret.' If you won, I would reveal it."

Saviar nodded sagely. "Ah! So we were sparring, dueling if you wish. So that's how the Northmen caught us off guard."

Subikahn did not disabuse his brother of that notion, nor did he confirm the lie. He preferred Saviar go to the grave believing a stranger had inflicted the wound that nearly killed him, not for his own sake but for Saviar's. His twin had already talked about his disappointment in their younger brother, in their mother, in his grandfather, and, most especially, in his father. Saviar had one family member left to believe in, and Subikahn would not betray that trust, no matter how wrongly given. They had both acted with childish bravado, foolishly. The guilt for that mistake was Subikahn's alone to bear.

However, Subikahn refused to prey upon his brother's memory loss for his own gain. Though it might shatter their bond as fully as admitting the stabbing, Subikahn had to fulfill his promise. "Saviar, you won that duel."

"I did?"

"And you earned the right to know what happened in Stalmize, if you still want to know." Though he did not expect it, Subikahn hoped Saviar would play gallant and allow the mystery to remain hidden.

"Of course I want to know."

Subikahn glanced up the hill to ascertain that Chymmerlee remained in place, that she had not slipped within earshot as their practice finished. "Remember, it sundered the bond between my father and myself. You know how close we were. Don't you worry that it might do the same to us?"

"No," Saviar said with a matter-of-factness ill-suited to the significance of the moment. "Because you said it didn't involve murder, and nothing less than the deliberate slaughter of family members could pull us apart."

Subikahn huffed out a breath he did not realized he was holding. "All right. Here it is." He paused, not for dramatic purposes but because once he spoke the words, he could not retract them. "My lover . . ." He glanced at Saviar.

His twin waited patiently, a blank expression on his face.

". . . is . . ." It came out in a rush. ". . . Talamir."

Saviar blinked. He gave no other reaction. "Talamir?" he finally said. "Your *torke?*"

Subikahn nodded, still waiting for understanding to sink in to Saviar's mind.

"I don't think there're any rules against loving your *torke*. Are there?"

Clearly, Saviar did not understand. "I didn't say I loved him, Savi, though I do. I said he was my lover."

"All right."

Saviar still did not seem to understand the significant point, so Subikahn went right to the heart. "Don't you get it, Savi. I thumped another man."

Saviar's brows knitted, not in disgust but in consideration. "What was that like?"

Astounding. Subikahn did not speak the word aloud. Though true, it did not address the actual intent of the question. "It was like . . .

like having sex with another man." It clearly needed saying, outright and clear as finest crystal. "Saviar, I've made love with women, too; and I didn't enjoy it. I greatly prefer men, and Talamir is the only one I want. Forever."

"I get it." The rephrasings and repetition seemed to have done their job. "So, why is this a problem for King Tae?"

Or not. "Why is this a problem . . . ?" Subikahn could not believe his brother's deliberate denseness. "Saviar, aren't you hearing me. I slept with a man. And when I say slept—"

"You mean sex," Saviar finished. "You've explained that. I admit it's a bit unusual, but you're not the first male lovers in history."

"It doesn't bother you?"

Saviar's broad shoulders rose and fell. "Why should it? It means you and I won't compete over the same . . . um . . . lovers. Right?"

Subikahn laughed, as much from relief as the idea that he could ever contend with handsome, honest Saviar when it came to attracting a mate.

"Like our fathers did."

Saviar had an undeniable point. Tae had had little to offer Kevral compared to Ra-khir, yet she had slept with both of them. Of course, she had chosen Ra-khir in the end.

"So you're not repulsed by me?"

"Often," Saviar joked. "But not because of who you love."

Subikahn smiled, openly, genuinely. Never in all his imaginings had he expected his brother to take the news so well. He had pictured himself justifying, pleading, crying, shouting. This was too easy. *Does he really, truly understand what I'm saying?* He wanted to gush, to fawn all over his twin, to tell Saviar that no better brother existed in the world. Yet, only the barest portion of his appreciation emerged, "Thanks, Savi."

Saviar dismissed the less-than-effusive praise with a wave. "Thanks for what? Loving my brother the way he is? It's only as it should be."

Saviar made it all sound so simple. "My father didn't see it that way. It's a capital crime in the East, and he's convinced Talamir raped me."

"Did he?"

Subikahn could not make sense of the question. "Did who what?"

"Did Talamir rape you?"

Rage and sadness stirred within Subikahn. He had not allowed himself to dwell on the situation for a long time, focusing all his worry and attention on Saviar. "Of course not."

"Tell that to your father."

"I did. He won't listen. He wants to believe that Talamir took advantage of me, that I'm completely innocent. He thinks if I experience the world, I'll realize Talamir actually did coerce me. That I'm not really a . . . a *bonta*."

"A what?"

"A *bonta*," Subikahn repeated. "It's a vulgar, Eastern term for a man who sleeps with men." The need to explain took some of the sting from the word.

"*Bonta*," Saviar repeated, to Subikahn's surprise. "*Bonta, bonta.* Hmmm." He looked directly at Subikahn. "I like it. If I ever have a daughter, I think I'll name her Bonta. Bonta Saviarsdatter."

Subikahn could not help laughing. The term could never hurt him again. "Saviar, you're an idiot."

"Yes," Saviar agreed. "And don't you ever forget it." His smile suddenly wilted; then, as quickly reappeared, broader than before.

"What?" Subikahn demanded.

"I just remembered something. What Mama told me to tell you when she gave me the sword." He patted the hilt of *Motfrabelonning.* "It didn't make sense to me at the time, and I was so focused on having seen a *Valkyrie,* on having Mama speak to me after death."

Subikahn held his breath. He had never worried about not getting one of Kevral's swords. She had exactly two; it only made sense for her to gift them to the sons who had attended her death.

"She said . . ." Saviar paused just long enough for Subikahn to worry that the proper portion of memory had disappeared along with the recollections surrounding their duel. "She said," Saviar started again, " 'Tell Subikahn he will find true happiness when he is true to what the gods made him.' "

Subikahn considered the words for several moments, not wanting to misinterpret his mother's dying message. He thought he knew, but he needed confirmation that he was not just putting the spin on them that he preferred. "What do you suppose she meant by that?"

Saviar tapped his foot, giving his brother a sidelong look. "I think she was trying to say . . ."

The pause made Subikahn impatient, "Yes?"

"She was trying to say that . . ."

Subikahn's next utterance held suspicion. He had a feeling Saviar was baiting him. "Ye-es?"

"Get used to being a *bonta,* because it's what the gods made you."

Subikahn finally let out his held breath in a ragged sigh. "I was hoping you'd say that."

The weather grew cold much more quickly than a change of seasons could explain. Calistin had lost track of time but doubted entire months had passed without his knowledge. The forest gave way to twisted, struggling trees and brush burned by frost. Evergreens predominated, dull-spined and prickly, and the ground lay frozen into hard craters that hampered the footwork of his new sword maneuvers.

Children scurried through the brush, gathering stray bits of wool that clung to brambles and limbs. They stared at the trio as they passed, sometimes gawking at the blazing sword practices, but they did not run frightened nor approach with questions. Soon, Calistin noticed sheep droppings near the bits of wool, then the animals themselves placidly grazing on tough shoots and scraggly nettles.

Treysind dashed up to announce, "There's a town ahead." Ordinarily, interrupting a Renshai's practice meant death or, at least, the threat of it. But Colbey and Calistin went at it so much, it seemed impossible not to catch them during a session or spar. Treysind had taken to shouting from a distance when he wanted or needed their attention. By the time they reached him, he apparently reasoned, they would not impulsively disembowel him in a frenzy of misplaced battle rage.

This time, Colbey took the disruption totally in stride. He ended a complicated demonstration with an abrupt sheathing of both swords. "Ah, yes. That would be Aerin." He gave it a crisp Northern pronunciation: Ah-REEN.

"Aerin," Calistin repeated, breathless from practice. He tried to remember why that name sounded so familiar. His eyes widened in sudden recognition. "As in the tribe of Aeri?" Realization struck like lightning. "We're in the Northlands?"

Treysind and Colbey both laughed, and the elder continued, "We sort of thought you'd realized that when we passed through the Weathered Mountains."

Calistin could only stare. *How could I miss a range of mountains?* He recalled traveling amidst green hillocks and deep valleys, but he had expected rugged, snow-capped peaks and naked stone. Béarn lay nestled among the mountains, the castle carved directly from the granite slopes, so he supposed the terrain had not seemed strikingly different from normal.

Treysind sprang immediately to Calistin's defense. "When ya cuts through passes covered in green stuff, it ain't that diff'rinter than normal forests is. An' it ain't like ya gived 'im much time ta look 'round an' enjoy tha view."

None of that mattered to Calistin. He found himself staring at the barren landscape with new eyes. Ultimately, the Renshai belonged here; or, at least, they once did. The tribe sprang from this hostile land at a time when their infants spent their first nights alone outside, to assure only the strongest received benefit of scarce resources. Here, the ancient Renshai lived and died in bloody battles fought against their neighbors. It had become a mantra to the Renshai that they would one day return to the homeland they had not occupied for centuries. "Next year," went a common celebratory prayer, "may we dance in Renshi."

"Where?" Calistin said softly, somehow knowing Colbey would properly interpret the question.

Colbey went right to the heart of the mostly unspoken query. "Renshi used to sit just east of Aerin. Now, some of it belongs to the Aeri but most to Shamir. You will travel right across it to get to Nordmir, which sits even farther eastward."

Calistin could not imagine a better tour guide. "You can show me where my people . . ." He amended, "Where *our* people originated. So much history—"

"No, Calistin." Colbey looked out over the Northlands with a clear wistfulness that defied his words. "I can't go with you any farther."

Calistin's heart felt as if it froze in his chest, no longer beating. "But . . . I . . . need you. Now most of all."

"No," Colbey repeated. "You never needed me. I just satisfied my urge to assess and interfere."

Calistin supposed the immortal Renshai spoke truth, yet he knew his life would have taken an entirely different turn without their meeting. "How will I ever know if I mastered those maneuvers you taught me?"

"You'll know. And you'll invent the rest and more. You have the drive, Calistin. And you're lucky enough to have the build and natural talent, too."

"But it will take me *years.*"

Colbey laughed so hard, several children looked up curiously from their wool gathering, and Treysind smiled broadly.

Even Calistin could not stop the corners of his mouth from twitching upward. "Am I that funny?"

"Apparently, you inherited at least one thing from me. My damnable impatience. And that, Calistin, is no fair gift." Colbey glanced into the sky with an almost apologetic look. "I suppose it goes hand in hand with practicing oneself into oblivion in a quest for perfection. We cannot wait for anything and find fools nearly impossible to suffer. And it is that very curse that makes it impossible for me to accompany you any longer."

Calistin knew Colbey had been born in Renshi, had lived there for some time prior to the tribe's banishment. He had participated in the long and ancient exodus which had resulted in the Renshai leaving a trail of destruction and devilry through the West and East, earning the hatred of all the peoples of the world. "You're saying you don't want to look upon the world of your childhood?"

"I'm saying," Colbey said slowly, "that I can't. Everything an immortal does on Midgard leaves a mark well beyond his intentions. If I enter a city of Northmen, there will be a battle, and it will not end well for Aerin. I no longer have a right to participate in mortal combat, no matter how much I might crave it."

Calistin supposed he understood, but he yearned for Colbey's knowledge more than anything in the world. Like a drug, it had entered his system and become all-consuming. Nothing mattered but his next practice; it gripped him with all the raw, basic desire of an addiction. "Then I'll give up my battle. We can go back West, and you can train me."

Aside from a pained wince, Colbey ignored the suggestion. He had made his point. He had come merely to talk, and that decision had had consequences far beyond his intentions. "Calistin, I came to tell you something that I never actually said. Every time I broached the subject, we wound up burdened by explanations, in a different place."

Calistin studied his *torke*, trying to focus on his words rather than his own urge for just one more spar. Colbey's leaving bothered him beyond this one need. Once the elder left, Calistin would find himself with too much time on his hands to ponder all the information dumped upon him. He would have to decide how he felt about his past, his family, his blood. He would have to consider emotions he would rather pack away forever. His very platform, his understanding of reality, would collapse beneath him. "It's about my soul, isn't it?"

Colbey nodded, his expression unreservedly sober. "Your only hope to enter Valhalla comes through the bloodline you otherwise would never have needed to know. Had it not been for the spirit spiders, I would have left your situation as it was, your family foundation solid, and your mind unfettered with concerns for heredity."

Calistin lowered his head, uncertain. He waffled between wishing he had never found out and rage that no one had told him as a child. Once, he had demanded to know why his parents had kept this secret from him; another time, he had berated Colbey for telling him at all. He had a right to know where he came from, yet that knowledge came with pain and burdens for all involved. He realized now that he struggled with the same ambivalence about knowing what to do for his lost soul. "Without a soul, what hope do I ever have of reaching Valhalla? The purpose to which I dedicated myself since infancy, to which *all Renshai* dedicate themselves from infancy, no longer exists."

"The *Valkyrie* should never have told you."

Calistin might have agreed, had Colbey not since offered him hope. "But then I would have died worthy and never found Valhalla."

"Yes," Colbey agreed, "and her mistake opened the way for me to help you. Because now, instead of interfering with mortals, I'm only making up for another immortal's lapse. Calistin, I believe your only hope of finding Valhalla is the same way I did it."

"Immortality?" The suggestion confused Calistin. "But you said I'm not immortal."

"You're not," Colbey explained. "Yet."

Guarded hope arose, mingled with confusion. "Yet? Isn't immortality something you're born with?"

"Usually." Colbey glanced at the wool gatherers to assure none of the children came near enough to overhear their conversation. Though Northern, they also likely understood the Western tongue. "Because it's extremely rare, even since the beginning of the world, for immortals and mortals to interbreed. And, of course, you realize even immortals can be killed, they simply don't die of disease or age."

Calistin had never paid much attention to such details, or anything that did not pertain directly to Renshai and swordcraft. "I've heard elves have an end age. That they're not true immortals."

"Semantics." Colbey seemed resigned to the necessary tangents that allowed him to make his point. "Elves live centuries at least, millennia at best. When an elf's time comes, his soul gets recycled into the body of a newborn. Without a passing, there can be no new elfin life. Cyclical immortality some call it, but immortality nonetheless. The Cardinal Wizards, when they existed, had a similar system. They chose their time of passing, and their souls joined that of their chosen successor, which allowed each to become subsequently more powerful." He winced at some distant memory. "Unfortunately, in my opinion, it also made them more and more crazy. Whether or not the previous Wizards became spiritual guides and assisted with magic, it could drive a man beyond insanity to have the thoughts and voices of others in his head."

Treysind finally spoke, "Sounds like ya gots firsthand 'perience."

Colbey made a noncommittal gesture. If he did, he would not discuss it. "The point being that there's not much history to go on when it comes to mortal/immortal crosses. There are no known examples of Wizards or elves interbreeding with mortals until Princess Ivana."

Calistin grimaced. The grotesqueness of that child had driven every elf but her mother into hiding.

"But, as near as I can figure it, the few of us with a significant amount of divine blood can earn our immortality."

Calistin asked the only question he could. "How?"

Colbey met Calistin's gaze levelly, like a man speaking truth, not stalling or playing. "I don't know."

Nevertheless, Calistin huffed out a loud sigh. He hated social games and nearly always lost them. "You don't know? Or you don't want to tell me?" He added angrily, "Let me guess: you want me to figure it out for myself because that's part of the whole damned process."

Colbey only stared, as did Treysind.

Calistin tried to explain his overreaction, but it only came out sounding more bitter. "Look. When it comes to battle, I'm the . . ." He bit off the word that usually came next: "best." He could not speak it in front of Colbey, who had already shown himself to be the superior warrior. ". . . one you want," he finished lamely instead. "But I'm ignorant about a lot of other stuff. Even simple things. I just never . . ."

"Had the chance to learn it?" Colbey suggested. "Never had the need?"

"Yes," Calistin snapped defensively. "It's the only way to become the best at something. To live it from sunup to sundown and into your dreams. Because every moment you're eating, sleeping, or engaging in unnecessary conversation or entertainment, you're missing a chance to improve your skills. And time is one thing you can never get back."

Colbey bobbed his head thoughtfully. "Thank you, Calistin. I can't say I haven't lived those very words at certain times of my life. But I do hope you spared some time to learn the Northern tongue, because you're going to need it for the next few weeks or months." He pursed his lips, "Unless, of course, you intend to walk into the first tavern you see and announce your tribe. Then, I can virtually guarantee you won't need to know any other words."

Calistin snorted. "I can handle myself against dozens of Northmen."

"But eventually, the hundreds that follow will overcome even you. Is that how you want to die?"

"It's how every Renshai wants to die."

Colbey did not say another word, but his brows slid upward.

Treysind's face revealed all the emotion the others did not. His features creased in agonized worry, and he wrung his hands in frantic circles. "If ever' Renshai wants it, how's come they don't jus' all do it?"

"Yeah," Colbey said taking up a position directly beside Treysind. "How's come they don't?" Although he mimicked the boy's speech, he did not do so in an insulting manner, and Treysind clearly took no offense.

"Because," Calistin started heatedly, then paused to consider. As he did so, his mood went from heated to less so, and finally to embarrassment. He felt the warmth move from deep within him to only the surface of his skin. "Because deliberate suicide is only courage if there is no other way."

"Go on."

"If one chooses a course of action solely for the purpose of dying, it . . . it . . ." Though Calistin had heard it from his mother and other Renshai, he could not remember the rest of the quotation.

Treysind gave it his own twist. "It's jus' stupid."

"Couldn't have said it better myself." Colbey smiled and winked conspiratorially at Calistin. It was one of his own famous sayings his charges had mangled.

Calistin could not help grinning. It was the first time he and Colbey shared a joke at Treysind's expense rather than his own.

Colbey turned serious almost immediately afterward. "I'll leave you with this: First, don't hurry. With or without true immortality, your divine blood will cause you to age far slower than even the average Renshai. The gods do nothing quickly. Immortality can never be won overnight or with a singular action. It will require you to think, to emote, and to behave in a manner that makes you worthy of Asgard at all times. Competent swordsmanship, Calistin, will not be enough. Until now, your ignorance may have helped you, but—from this point on—it can only hurt."

Calistin licked his lips and closed his eyes, suddenly terrified for reasons he could not wholly understand. His life, once so simple, had become complicated beyond all reason. No longer could he hide behind his strict dedication to his sword. Other matters demanded his attention, and the Renshai no longer tended to his every other desire, obviating his need to think, to consider, to grow. He raised his head to beg reassurance, to ask one more question, then another, to prevent Colbey from leaving him when he most needed guidance. But, when he opened his eyes, the old Renshai was gone.

CHAPTER 38

*Never despise your enemy, or you may lose the chance to research
his strengths and weaknesses. Too many wars are undertaken with
faith in one's own genius and the belief that the enemy has none.*
          —General Santagithi

THE STREAM BUBBLED MERRILY through the mountains, a
silver sliver reflecting sunlight into Saviar's eyes. He perched on a
deadfall that bridged the water, his legs dangling, right hand clasped
around Chymmerlee's, the left clutching a flat stone. He drew his
arm back, flicked his wrist, and sent the stone skipping.

Chymmerlee counted aloud, "One, two three, four, five . . . six.
You beat me."

Saviar watched the rings widening from each touch, then his stone
sank, leaving a wake of tiny bubbles.

"And with your left hand." Chymmerlee gave their entwined
hands a shake. "And I thought I was so good at this."

Saviar did not bother to mention that which hand he used did not
matter. Renshai trained to use both equally; any tendency to favor
one got fixed in childhood drills. He pulled her hand toward him,
drawing her along, and pushed forward for a kiss.

"Saviar!" Subikahn appeared out of nowhere.

Startled, Saviar dropped Chymmerlee's hand, reaching for a
sword hilt, leaping in front of her to guard her. Instead, his quick
movement sent her careening from the log. She tumbled gracelessly
into the muddy stream with more thud than splash.

Subikahn's tone changed from one of excitement to horror. "Sav-
ee-ar!" He charged into the water.

Aghast, Saviar stared at Chymmerlee in the stream. Sitting, the
water came up to her waist, her clothing soaked, face and hair a
mucky mess. "Chymmer, I'm sorry. I'm so sorry." Helplessly, he ran
first one way, then the other, trying to divine the fastest way to her.

Jump, you idiot. He sprang into the stream, the weight of his landing spraying Chymmerlee and Subikahn, who had grabbed her elbow to help her out of the water.

An instant later, Saviar found himself standing in brown water up to his shins, staring at his brother and his friend splattered head to toe in wet filth. Subikahn graciously held Chymmerlee's arm, his hair dripping plant matter and mud.

Realizing he had only managed to make things worse, Saviar flushed. "I'm sorry," was all he could think to say. "I was trying to help."

"Yes," Subikahn noted, shaking the mess from his hair. "How thoughtful. Thank you."

Saviar looked at Chymmerlee, waiting for her to slap him, to cry, to call him something worthy of the idiocy he had just displayed. She started shaking, gently at first, then harder. Laughter emerged from her, sweet and bell-like. She stooped, scooped up a handful of mud, and threw it at Saviar.

Saviar could have dodged it, but surprise held him rooted in place. The mudball hit him in the stomach, slapping against his tunic, then running in a wet line back into the water. He remained in place until the second handful of mud sped toward him. Then, he attempted to duck. Mud splattered into his hair as it whizzed by, the bulk of it missing. "You . . . wench," he sputtered.

Subikahn joined the action, dredging up handfuls of muck and hurling them at his brother.

"Hey," Saviar yelled. "Hey!" Opening his mouth turned out to be a bad idea. The mud tasted of fish and greenery, and he spat out bits of rock and filth. "All right, then! If that's how you want it." He grabbed his own muck, feeling a ball smack against the top of his head as he dropped into a crouch.

It devolved swiftly. Water splashed in mighty, man-made waves, mud flew in all directions, shattering into watery bits as it hit a target. It became a three-way war, as Chymmerlee's aim betrayed her and she hit Subikahn one too many times.

Saviar laughed, careful to keep his lips clamped tight as he did so. Mud weighted his feet and gushed over his boots to leave him wading through mush. His filthy, sodden clothes clung to every part of him, and his hair dripped large clumps of grime. He had to squint to keep the mud from his eyes, though he could see it clinging to his lashes. Whenever he tried to wipe it away with the back of a hand, he only wound up adding more. He could not remember the last time he had had so much fun.

Shielding her face, Chymmerlee giggled, finally wading to shore.

Saviar stopped, an unthrown mudball dissolving through his fingers. He sneaked a glance at Subikahn, who looked like a man-shaped swamp monster. "Truce?" he suggested.

Subikahn lowered his arm.

"Do I look as bad as you two?" Chymmerlee asked, stripping mud from her hair.

"Worse," Subikahn exclaimed before Saviar could say something more comforting. "But, then again, Saviar was smart enough to anticipate the battle by shoving you in first."

Saviar cringed, wishing Subikahn had not mentioned the initiating event, even in jest. He liked Chymmerlee's reaction to his foolish and clumsy mistake. So many women would have gotten angry and flayed him, at least verbally, for it. "I really am sorry about that. I didn't mean to—"

"—cheat?" Chymmerlee supplied; and, now, Subikahn laughed.

"No." Saviar thought back to how the mud war had started. "I didn't expect to get startled by my brother running up sounding like he had news of great import, then accidentally sweeping a beautiful girl off her balance." The smile disappeared from his face. "Did you shout out my name for an actual reason?"

Chymmerlee smiled at the compliment, the movement barely cracking the mud on her face.

Subikahn brushed futilely at his clothes, his demeanor growing more serious. "Actually, I did." He glanced at Chymmerlee, then apparently decided she had paid enough to hear the news as well. "Remember how I told you I saw a small army pass through the lower woodlands last week?"

Saviar nodded. He had not believed it, thinking Subikahn had misinterpreted what he saw. "And another one, a smaller one, yesterday."

"Yes," Subikahn confirmed. "And a bigger one today. And, this time, I talked to some of the soldiers."

Saviar froze. "You did?"

"They were Northmen." Subikahn shook like a dog, dislodging large chunks of drying muck. "I think they liked meeting an obvious foreigner who could speak their language."

Apparently more surprised by Subikahn's revelation than concerned for passing armies, Chymmerlee chimed in. "You speak Northern?"

Saviar held his breath, wondering if his brother was about to reveal their secret.

But Subikahn waved off the question. "I speak a lot of languages. My father, I think, could communicate with creatures from distant stars if he had to."

Saviar made a gesture to hurry Subikahn to the important issues. "Why are armies moving through the mountain passes?"

"Apparently, Béarn is under siege."

"What?" The word was startled from Saviar.

Dutifully, Subikahn repeated, "Béarn is under siege. The pirates are massing just offshore."

Saviar flipped his arms to dislodge more mud, wishing Subikahn had stopped the game in light of this information. "We have to go. We have to do whatever we can."

The reactions to this statement could not have been more different. Subikahn's "Of course" made strange contrast to Chymmerlee's shouted, "No!"

Saviar waded to shore, keeping his step as light as possible so the water could wash out his boots. "Chymmerlee, there's no decision to make here. Subikahn and I have to defend Béarn."

"No!" Chymmerlee ran toward Saviar as he emerged. "I just found you. I can't lose you."

Saviar embraced Chymmerlee, suddenly uncomfortable with the wet and dirt that had seemed so entertaining moments earlier. "I'm not going to forget you. We'll come back."

"Better yet," Subikahn said softly. "Your people should come with us."

"What?" Saviar found himself shocked again.

"You've heard the stories coming out of Béarn. These attackers, they seem to have access to magic. Why shouldn't we?"

Chymmerlee answered before Saviar could. "Because my people can't afford to lose even one mage. We're in hiding, for hundreds of years now, for a reason."

Subikahn shook his head. "Well, it seems your time has come. This enemy isn't logical or decent. They don't parley, and they don't take prisoners. If Béarn falls, the rest of the West will go with it, and the North and East will find themselves in a far worse position when the pirates come to them."

"Really?" Chymmerlee said, very softly. The hand she brought to her mouth trembled.

"Really," Subikahn said.

Saviar released her. "We'd better wash and change, then. I'm not sure anyone could take us seriously the way we look right now." Chymmerlee seemed willing to consider the possibility, but he doubted the others would be so easily convinced. He would need the bathing time to think, to pick out the words necessary to convince. He alone had leadership and speaking training. The job, he knew, would fall to him.

$$\dagger\!\!-\!\!-\!\!-$$

Traveling through the Westlands, Calistin had become accustomed to pristine farmland that gave way abruptly to bunched and solid cities, so the scattered layout of Aerin caught him unprepared. Here, the ragged farmland consisted mostly of gaunt animals grazing on stunted grasses and fowl scavenging dung for insects and undigested seeds. The dwellings were communal longhouses as much as cottages, and smoke twined from every chimney.

People scurried about in the twilight, carrying groceries and water, conversing in their musical language. Hammers rang on forges, sheep bleated plaintively, and the swishing and banging of woodworking filled the evening air. Odors mingled: cook fires, smoke, and the syrupy scent of lumber. As usual, Calistin found himself hungry and not for the usual travel fare, as good as Treysind made it. More than anything, he wanted a platter of freshly roasted mutton and a frosty mug of ale.

It took Calistin's ears time to adjust to the language delivered in its native singsong. But, after catching enough snatches of passing conversation, he realized, with relief, that his training had been adequate. He could understand Northern and, he hoped, speak it well enough to be understood. He also recognized the letters that spelled out "inn" on a nearby building. Relieved, he hurried toward it, Treysind directly on his heels.

As he walked, Calistin noticed other details. Towheads and redheads predominated to the point where the rare man with even a hint of brown seemed out of place. In Béarn and Erythane, they called a person with lighter brown hair a blond. Here, Calistin imagined, they might consider that same person dark. Many of the men openly carried weapons, and some of the boys play-sparred with twigs when they thought their parents were not looking. No one seemed aware of the newcomers who looked enough like the Aeri to pass for neighbors.

Calistin opened the door to the inn. Smoke billowed out the opening, funneled by the wind. Coughing, Treysind scampered inside, leaving just enough room for Calistin to quickly shut the door. The smoke returned to wrap the patrons in a warm, comfortable haze. Calistin supposed his eyes would adjust quickly enough and chose the nearest table so as not to stumble around awkwardly in the mist. Treysind flopped into the chair across from him. "Ain't unnerstandin' a word what they says."

Calistin nodded, starting to look around until a barmaid distracted him. She placed herself directly at his right elbow and leaned onto the table. Dressed in a tight uniform of black with white lace, her plump body bulged at the cleavage. Not yet caught up in his adolescence, Calistin scarcely noticed.

"Hallo," she said with a well-practiced cheerfulness. "What can I get you, boys?"

"I'm a man." The words came out as easily in Northern as they did in Common. "I've earned my manhood."

The barmaid's brows rose, but she did not question. She stood up straight and turned her attention to Treysind. "Does that go for you, too, young sir?"

Calistin started to look over the other patrons again, only to realize that Treysind would not answer. He had enough trouble with the Common and Western tongues. "No, he's still a boy; but you can call him Treysind."

"Treysind," she repeated. "What an exotic name." She brushed back long, yellow hair, tacking it behind one ear. "I like it."

Calistin did not bother to tell her it meant "offspring of the ashes" in the Erythanian dialect.

"Ya's talkin' 'bout me." Treysind recognized his name. "What's ya sayin' 'bout me?"

Calistin forestalled his companion with a raised hand. "We'll have two plates of mutton and two mugs of ale."

"Ale?" she repeated.

"Ale," Calistin confirmed. "Don't you have any?"

"Of course we have ale. But don't you . . . boys . . ." She amended quickly, ". . . boy and man. Don't you think you're a bit young for full-fledged ale?"

Not again. Calistin stared at the barmaid. She was pretty in the way all young women are but had large, broad features that appeared somewhat asymmetrical. "Do you question the choices of all your patrons? Or only mine?"

The barmaid's face turned a brilliant shade of pink. "I'm not . . . I mean I don't . . . It's just that the younglings . . .who drink ale . . . don't grow as well or as clever as . . ." The color faded from her cheeks, and her expression turned stern and motherly. "Is Treysind your little brother?" She did not await an answer before continuing. "Because I don't think your mother would approve—"

Calistin caught his own hand slipping toward his sword, the only outward sign of building rage. "My mother is dead, you nosy wench. And it's none of your damned business how I raise my little brother! Now, get me the damned ale and the damned mutton before I go back there and get it my damned self!"

The barmaid retreated without another word and disappeared into the mist.

The door opened, and another group of Northmen came inside, stirring up the smoky interior just as it had started to settle.

"Why's ya yellin' at her, Hero?"

Calistin sighed and turned his attention back to Treysind. "Nothing important, Trey."

The boy sat up straighter. "Ya called me 'Trey.' "

"Yeah. So?"

"So's, no one's ever called me 'Trey' bafore." Treysind mulled the situation. "I likes it. Sounds like somethin' a brother would call me."

Calistin shrugged, bobbing his head. "I guess that fits, then. She called you my little brother."

"She did?" Treysind bounced in his chair. He looked positively giddy. "That why ya getted mad?"

"No. I just don't like a stranger asking me personal questions and judging me when her job is just to fetch me food when I ask for it." Calistin smiled at the realization. "In fact, that irritated me so much, *I* even called you my little brother."

Treysind's eyes widened so they seemed enormous. "Rilly?"

It obviously meant a lot to Treysind, and it did not hurt Calistin in any way. "Sure, why not? You practically are. I mean, we're both basically orphans, you irritate me as much as Saviar or Subikahn, and we're together all the time." *All the* damned *time; I can't get rid of you.* "And you look about as much like me as either of my actual brothers."

"Ya thinks ya's papa would . . . 'dopt me?"

Calistin had never considered it. "Ra-khir?" He frowned in consideration. "I . . . don't know. I really don't know him as well as I should." The emotions that followed caught Calistin by surprise. He had always realized his father was a good man, but he had dismissed all the Knights of Erythane as deluded, untalented do-gooders. Since he had outgrown horsy rides and kiddy games when he was very young, he had given his father little attention or thought. Nothing mattered but the Renshai way: the sword, the arm, and the craft that bound them. "It wouldn't surprise me if he did, but it's not really necessary. I'm a man, and I can choose my brothers with or without my parent's blessing."

Treysind's smile seemed to loop around his face. It sparkled in his eyes and displaced his cheeks upward. It even seemed to show upon his brow. "I gots a brother. A *hero* brother. Someone what . . . what . . ." Treysind bit back his next exuberant word, then allowed it to slip out as a question, ". . . loves me?" The smile wilted. "Tha's too much ta ask, ain't it?"

Calistin felt the usual cold barrier slide into place, the one that kept him at arm's length from the world. He did not like the realm of emotion; it distracted him from the one truly significant concept in life. Yet, when Calistin looked upon the boy's desperately hopeful features, he knew he could not ignore the question. The cruelty such action would inflict would be too great. "Of course, I love you, Trey. Families love each other, even when we can't stand each other. Even when we want to cut one another's guts out, we don't do it. Because, no matter how obnoxious, inane, and annoying we find one another at times, deep down, the love is always there."

Treysind stiffened. For an instant, he seemed poised to leap into dance, to shout or whoop, to display his joy in a whirlwind of uncontainable action. Somehow, he managed to control his glee, but it still showed in the ecstatic glimmer in his eyes, the glow of his cheeks, and the quiver of excitement that seemed to take over his body.

The words came. Much to Calistin's surprise, he found Treysind's joy contagious. He could not help grinning, could not help feeling pleased with himself and the effect he had had on his companion. It had taken some effort; yet, for the first time in his life, it seemed entirely worth the bother. His own words, as untried and crude as they were, had brought untold happiness to a boy who had had little enough of it in his short lifetime. All it had taken was a few words more carefully chosen than usual.

The barmaid returned shortly. Calistin noticed at once that she carried nothing in her hands. "Avard wants to know if you got money to pay for what you ordered."

Money again. Calistin did not know how to react. The last time someone had demanded it from him, in the tavern in Ainsville, he had killed Karruno and skipped town in the chaos that followed, without paying. Back home, he had never had to worry about money, had barely even bothered to learn the value of the various coinage. He had no idea if the North used a system in any way similar to the West's. In all of his experience, he had never seen anyone pay for something before receiving it, and he had noticed other patrons tossing down coins only as they left. Calistin recognized an insult when he received one. "Why should I pay for food and drink you haven't brought me yet?"

The barmaid fidgeted, clearly nervous. "Avard says you're young, and he's never seen you in here before. He just wants to make sure you have enough money to pay for what you eat."

The barkeep in Ainsville had made the same request and not nearly so politely. Calistin looked at Treysind, but the boy only stared back at him, still smiling. He did not speak a word of Northern. "My brother handles all the money."

The barmaid's brows narrowed in suspicion, but she turned her attention directly on Treysind. The boy squirmed in his seat.

"What's goin' on?" Treysind asked softly in Western. Usually, they conversed in the Common Trading tongue, but that was the most used language in the world. Likely, the barmaid spoke it, and Treysind wanted to keep this private.

"Money," Calistin said. "She wants it in advance."

"Why are you whispering?" the barmaid said loudly. "And what language are you speaking anyway?"

Calistin did not wish to draw attention that might give away his heritage, not after Colbey had cautioned him against it. Only one tribe of Northmen lived in the West. "It's our tribal tongue," Calistin lied. "My little brother had an accident as a baby and has trouble learning languages. He's only mastered tribal, and he's not particularly good at that, either."

"Tribal, huh?" The explanation did not satisfy the barmaid. "I've never heard anything like it. What tribe are you from?"

Calistin picked the farthest tribe, the one with which she would probably have the least experience. "We're Gelshni, if you must know. But it's not—"

A voice boomed out from behind them. "Ah, boys. There you are. I've been looking all over for you."

Calistin whirled to see a huge form emerge from the haze. A massive hand touched his shoulder.

The newcomer spun a chair from a nearby table, then thrust it between his legs to sit between Calistin and Treysind. He looked askance at the barmaid. "I'm sorry, Griselda. Have my boys been giving you trouble?"

The woman curtsied hurriedly. "I'm so sorry, Valr. I didn't know they were with you." She turned toward the kitchen, then stopped abruptly. "Is it all right for me to bring them mutton? And *ale*, sir?"

Valr. The name rang through Calistin's ears. Ignoring the conversation, he studied the man who claimed to know them, who had joined them, uninvited, at the table. He wore heavy leathers stained by sweat and travel grime; but the large, lithe figure was unmistakable. Calistin might forget a face but never a warrior figure. *Valr Magnus.* He had not only run into the very enemy he sought, for reasons currently beyond comprehension, the man had come to him.

"Aye, fine. Whatever they want. I'm paying."

The barmaid scurried to obey with newfound deference.

Only then, Calistin met the other man's gaze with a coldness that could have frozen a summer pond. The familiar, handsome features completed the picture. He looked the part of the hero, his cheeks rugged and high-formed, his nose not too prominent and perfectly straight, his chin chiseled. Fine blue eyes studied Calistin from beneath a tousled mane of golden hair. "Valr Magnus." Calistin fairly spat the name.

That caught Treysind's attention. He already stared unabashedly at the man who had joined them so unexpectedly. Now, his expression revealed revulsion and fear.

Magnus nodded as if Calistin had merely spoken a polite greeting. "Calistin Kevralsson. I thought you would find me."

"Calistin *Ra-khirsson,*" Calistin corrected, though he took no insult. He was at least as proud of his maternal heritage. "And it would appear *you* found *me.*"

The large man belted out a laugh. "Well, I suppose so, seeing as how I recognized you from a whole two tables away. That's clearly more significant than you trailing me across the entire Westlands, through the Weathered Mountains, and into Northern tribal lands."

Calistin did not allow himself to see the humor in it. He refused to share a joke with his bitterest enemy. "Don't flatter yourself. I didn't follow you."

Valr Magnus' brows rose, and he tipped his head. "So you're not here to face me in fair combat?"

Calistin saw no reason to lie now. "Of course, I am. But I didn't follow you. I expected to find you in Nordmir."

"Why Nordmir?"

"Because . . . you're Nordmirian."

Valr Magnus' expression did not change. "That will come as a great surprise to my Aeri parents."

"Aeri . . ." Calistin realized he had no real reason to assume the tribe of the proclaimed best Northern swordsman was Nordmirian, other than knowing it was the site of the North's high kingdom and the source of the most vicious Renshai hatred. Valr Kirin had come from there, and the legend must have stuck in Calistin's mind. "Fine. Aeri, then. What's the difference? All Northmen are the same."

"Including Renshai?"

"Of course not."

"Ah." Valr did not bother to delve deeper.

The barmaid appeared swiftly, balancing two heaping plates of mutton and two mugs of foamy ale. She placed them in front of Calistin and Treysind, then curtsied. Light seemed to dance in her eyes as she addressed Valr Magnus. "And you, Valr? Would you be having more, sir?"

The Northman turned her a smile, and her knees buckled. For a moment, Calistin thought she would melt onto the floor in front of him. "Just a bit more of that ale, please."

Regaining her equilibrium instantly, the barmaid rushed away.

Valr looked at Calistin's drink. "It's good. Not like that horse piss that passes for ale in the West."

Calistin felt no obligation to defend the Western taverns, but it irked him that Valr Magnus seemed determined to turn the ugliest of feuds into normal conversation. "Maybe it's just you they're serving horse piss. Maybe they think it's all you deserve."

"Maybe," Valr added conspiratorially, "it isn't even horse!"

It took Calistin a moment to realize what Valr meant, that the barmen and maids might be the source of the urine. His face wrinkled in revulsion reflexively. "That's disgusting."

"But all I deserve," Valr reminded Calistin in the Renshai's own words.

Treysind finally cut in, using the Common Trading tongue. "Can't yas two speak Common? I wants ta know what ya's sayin'."

Valr responded before Calistin had a chance. "I speak a few languages. Perhaps we can use the one that you know most fluently."

"That's it," Calistin explained. "Trading. I'm afraid that's as articulate as he gets."

"So's I don't talk so good," Treysind said around a mouthful of shredded mutton. "Least now I kin unnerstan's yas." He looked directly at Calistin. "So ya's finded him."

Calistin nodded.

"Ya's gonna fight?"

"Yes," Calistin said, not caring what Valr Magnus answered. "We're going to fight. To the death."

Treysind turned his attention to Valr Magnus. "That righ'?"

The Aeri shrugged. "To the death, apparently. Assuming that was, in fact, a serious challenge."

"It was," Calistin confirmed.

Treysind shoveled in another mouthful of meat, speaking around it. "So what's yas waitin' for? Yas talkin' terms out?"

"Not really." Valr Magnus looked up as the barmaid wound her way toward him. "I just wanted to get to know the man who's going to send me to Valhalla. Assuming he wins, of course."

Calistin found his rage giving way to confusion. He had envisioned his meeting with Valr Magnus many times, and it never went anything like this. In his mind, the Northman immediately assaulted him as soon as he pronounced his name and tribe. "Oh, I'll win," he mumbled as the barmaid set down the mug by Magnus' right hand.

"Thank you," Magnus said, waving the barmaid away.

She hesitated a moment, as if to say something, then scurried off in silence.

"Very well, then," Magnus said, without a trace of fear. "Any messages you want me to take your mother?"

Calistin's eyes narrowed, and he studied the man in front of him, seeking offense in his question. The mere mention of the mother Magnus had killed suggested flippancy and intent to rattle. Yet, Calistin realized, in one question the Aeri had essentially decreed Kevral a courageous warrior and Calistin the better swordsman.

When Calistin gave no reply, Magnus turned his attention to Treysind, eating and drinking with gusto. "What's your name, young man?"

Treysind waved a hand. "Oh, ya kin call me 'boy.' It don't 'fend me like it do him." He swallowed a wad of food so huge, Calistin could see it go down his neck. "Name's Treysind."

A few moments passed in silence before Valr finally said. "Is that your whole name?"

"Yep." Even though he continued talking, Treysind stuffed more mutton into his mouth. "I's a orphan, so's I ain't got no Nobody's son ta tack on there. Don't know whose son I is, acshly. An' I ain't got no title or tribe or nothin' neither."

"You're not Renshai?"

"Hel, no." Treysind said it with an enthusiasm that surprised Calistin, given how much Treysind wanted to become his brother. "An' as Hero says it, I wiel' a saword 'bout as good as a cat do." He held up grimy hands with bits of mutton stuck to them. "Paws, appar'ntly."

Magnus took a sip of his ale. "I suppose it's reasonable for me to assure you that, if you lose the battle, I'll make sure no one harms your friend."

Calistin had not even considered Treysind's welfare; and, in light of Colbey's recent words, that bothered him. He tried to attribute the lapse to courage. "That's not necessary, since I'm not going to lose. Not to you."

"Probably not," Magnus did not lapse into false bravado, though he demonstrated no fear either. "But even the greatest of warriors makes a mistake sometime. And that mistake is usually his last."

Calistin appreciated the implication that he was, in fact, the greatest. "I don't make mistakes."

Magnus smiled. "Well, whatever your possible errors, you certainly don't suffer from a surfeit of humility."

Calistin was not entirely sure whether or not he faced an insult. "False modesty is not a virtue."

"Nor pride," Magnus added. "Be that as it may, aren't you going to eat your dinner?"

The plate beckoned but, thus far, Calistin had managed to resist. "You'd like that, wouldn't you? To face me slowed by a bellyful of meat."

Valr Magnus clamped his jaw, obviously biting back his own irritation. "Not at all. Nor slowed by starvation. I want to find Valhalla in the most magnificent battle of my life. I want to love every minute of my existence as *Einherjar*. I don't want to spend years or decades waiting for you to join me so I can finally face you at your best. And if I won? What joy or pride can come from defeating an opponent not at his best? Then, when I finally joined you in Valhalla, would it be to find you stewing in bitterness? I think not."

Calistin could barely believe what he was hearing. "It didn't seem to bother you any that your people cheated so you could murder my mother."

For the first time since he had joined them at the table, Valr Magnus lost his suave composure. He simply stared at Calistin, his features pinched, an artery throbbing at his temple. "What," he finally managed, "are you talking about?"

"The man who jumped on her. Surely you noticed."

Magnus moved nothing but his mouth. "You mean the Erythanian spectator who slipped and fell? He could just as easily have landed on me."

"But he didn't, did he?"

"Dumb luck." Magnus ran a finger through the condensation on his mug. "Many a misstep, many a falling branch, even the weather has turned the tide of battle."

"Yes," Calistin agreed. "But this wasn't a natural phenomenon, was it? This was the work of a man."

"I would say the 'misfortune' of a man."

"And I would say the deliberate action of a hired cheater."

"That's a strong accusation." Magnus' jaw remained clenched after speaking. "One that begs proof."

Calistin closed his eyes, trusting his other senses implicitly to warn him of danger. He could still vividly picture the scene on the Fields of Wrath. He opened his eyes before speaking, "I saw the man in the tree, the only one in the tree. That Erythanian did not fall; he leaped with intention and deliberate aim."

"Forgive me if I seem unreasonable. I just don't believe my own people would practice such trickery nor demonstrate such little faith in me." Magnus met Calistin's gaze directly, his pale eyes full of honest wonder. "It's not uncommon for the losing side of any battle to see fouls where they do not exist, to call them even when they don't see them."

Calistin leaned toward his rival, holding his gaze with as much intensity as he could muster. He tried to emulate Colbey's dire stare and hoped he had inherited the necessary color and power. The mountain-hard gray tinting the standard Northern blue eyes seemed to make all the difference. "I am trained to notice everything. I can see the potential in any warrior just by studying the layout of his muscles, can evaluate his training in a single move. That Erythanian was an arrow well-timed and trained. His fall was no accident."

Valr Magnus did not quail beneath Calistin's stare, but he did back down with a deep sigh. "Calistin, I can tell you're sincere. You believe every word you spoke—"

Calistin did not wait for a "but." It would enrage him, and he did not want to start their battle inside a tavern. It could never lead to the fair one-on-one fight he needed. "I believe because it's true." He leaned in further, straddling his food with his arms. The intoxicating aroma of the mutton filled his nose. "I'm not a deluded child rushing in to defend his mama. I'm a man, older than I look, a competent warrior who has won many battles, in and out of real warfare."

"Yes, but—"

Calistin continued over the Aeri. He needed to finish. "I'm considered not only the best of the best when it comes to combat but also when it comes to teaching the most capable warriors in all the world. These eyes . . ." He raised his brows and fully opened his lids, ". . . miss nothing."

"But that Erythanian, they explored his history. And there was nothing—"

"Of course not. That deceit was well-planned and executed. It had to be." Calistin saw the uncertainty on Valr Magnus' face and knew he had scored an important victory, one that, for once, had little to do with swords and combat. "And you had to know—"

Treysind placed a hand on Calistin's leg in clear warning.

Valr Magnus seemed to emerge from his trance, and his considered look turned angry. "If you're accusing me—I most certainly didn't—I bested a Renshai in single combat." He started to stand. "I did it with honor and integrity. Don't impugn my—"

Treysind jumped in to rescue his hero again. "He's jus' sayin' ya had ta know he's got good seein', not ya had ta know 'bout tha trick."

"Oh," The Aeri dropped back into his seat. "I thought you were going to accuse me of having a hand in deceit or of knowing about it in advance."

It was exactly what Calistin had been about to say, but he was smart enough to take the reprieve Treysind had won him. The truth was, he no longer believed his intended accusation was right. "Of course not. No warrior brave enough to face the best of the Renshai, twice now, would sully his courage by trickery. The gods would never have such a man in Valhalla."

Valr Magnus sat back with a guarded smile, arms crossed over his chest. They were a warrior's arms, strong and sinewy but not bound by muscle. He had that rare, near-perfect build that left his abilities nearly limitless. Calistin would pay money for a class of students exactly like Magnus, at least in figure. "Calistin, if you give me some time, I can find answers to your accusations. If I discover that we bested your people by trickery, I will do whatever is in my power to lift their exile or, at the very least, base the future of the Renshai on a truly fair fight. Or we can have that battle now and let the details fall where they may. I leave the choice, Calistin Kevralsson Ra-khirsson, entirely up to you and will abide by whatever decision you make."

Calistin knew what he wanted. He had not come so far, had not inflicted his rage on the best warriors of the West, to wait.

A hand fell to Calistin's shoulder. For an instant, he imagined it was Colbey's, reminding him of his need to act in ways that affected the history of the entire world, not just of himself. Killing Valr Magnus, while infinitely satisfying, would not save the Renshai from their plight. But the fingers belonged only to Treysind, the touch a silent gesture of warning and support. "I—," Calistin started, unable to finish, torn between right and need. "I want—" He knew exactly what he wanted and doubted he could suppress it. Other words would not flow from his tongue.

The door to the tavern banged open suddenly, sucking the smoke and warmth from the room. An army stood in the doorway, bristling with weaponry and dressed in matching colors: aqua and bronze.

Calistin's heart raced with excitement. Only one possibility occurred to him: they had discovered that a Renshai sat among them and had come to do battle, a hundred or more to one. And, he realized, he relished the challenge.

Valr Magnus sprang to his feet. "What's wrong, Olvirn?"

The leader of the mass blinked in the hazy light. "It's Béarn. Pirates are overtaking the coast en masse, and King Griff has asked for every army, every warrior the world can muster."

Calistin sprang to attention. His heart rate quickened still further, galloping like hoofbeats in his chest.

"I'm coming," Valr promised, then looked at Calistin. "If I can bring my . . . friend. He may not look like much, but he's the best swordsman I know."

Calistin had no choice but to nod, their feud forgotten for the moment. If the West's high kingdom fell, the rest of the world would surely follow. He had at least as big a stake in the outcome of that war as any of the gathered Northmen.

The army retreated from the doorway, and Valr Magnus looked at Calistin. "I'll insist they put you under my direct command."

Calistin glared. "I won't obey you."

"Nor anyone else, I don't imagine." Valr Magnus headed for the door. "You'll infuriate any Northern commander; but, at least I have the satisfaction of knowing that, when it's all over, we'll battle one-on-one to the death."

Choiceless, even in his own mind, Calistin followed in silence.

And Treysind dutifully trailed his hero.

CHAPTER 39

Béarn's kings have followed their hearts through eternity and are acclaimed for their wisdom.
    —Tem'aree'ay Donnev'ra Amal-yah Krish-anda Mal-satorian

IT SEEMED TO SAVIAR RA-KHIRSSON that they might just as well have met with the Mages of Myrcidë smeared in filth and reeking of creek water for all the good his arguments did them. Again and again, he presented his points, using different words, different tones, his most eloquent pleadings. Jeremilan and the others only shook their heads sadly. Saviar could have achieved the same results by shouting at the mountains.

Saviar sighed, rolling his gaze over the craggy walls, the strange, one-sided windows, and the twenty-six adult mages ranged on various pieces of furniture. He sought out and found Subikahn leaning casually against the wall. The twin only shook his dark head sadly. He had nothing to add. Chymmerlee crouched in front of the group, facing Saviar, her hands clenched and held to her lips.

Saviar tried again. "You're not understanding the gravity of this situation."

Jeremilan spoke politely, with only a hint of impatience. "I believe we are."

"If Béarn falls . . ."

"If," Jeremilan repeated. "Béarn is very strong and has many allies."

"Deservedly so." Saviar tried to make a new point where the others had failed. "Despite its position as high kingdom, Béarn grants great freedom of rulership, of worship, of usage to all the Western countries beneath her. Her king is fair, her decisions just, her taxes minimal."

Jeremilan did not argue. "Yes."

"If Béarn falls," Saviar started again, this time not pausing to allow interruption, "our lives are essentially, quite possibly literally, over."

"We don't know that," Jeremilan said.

Saviar would not succumb to such a weak argument. "It's true the future is unknown, but only a dolt blinds himself to its clear predictions. So far, we know that the enemy wishes only to kill us, that they make no other demands and slaughter those who even attempt to parley. To assume a bright future in the face of that knowledge is idiocy of the highest order."

A murmur swept the room. Young Saviar had not quite called their centuries-old leader a fool. Twice.

"Careful," Subikahn mouthed.

Jeremilan rose, clutching the arm of his plush chair with one withered hand. "Are you suggesting we're stupid if we don't follow your advice?"

"I'm only saying . . ." Though glad he had finally riled his audience, Saviar chose his words with care. He did not want their new enthusiasm to end in magic cast at himself. ". . . that Béarn needs us. And that you stand to lose your very lives if you don't assist her."

"And if we do assist?" Jeremilan's voice remained strong despite his age. "We will all survive?"

"I . . . can't promise that," Saviar admitted.

"In fact," Jeremilan pressed his advantage. "We are certain to lose at least a few lives in battle, especially when the enemy realizes we're the source of any magic."

"We can protect you." Now that Jeremilan had, at least, imagined the possibility of helping, Saviar could not afford to back down. "We will keep your casualties to a minimum."

"The two of you?"

"What? No. All of us. All of Béarn's allies would certainly—"

"Would they?"

Again, the question caught Saviar off guard. It seemed perfectly obvious to him.

"Because people tend to revile things they don't understand. In Shadimar's day, people shunned, despised, or pretended to be mages. The Renshai saw our strangeness as reason enough to annihilate us."

Saviar threw up his hands, wondering if the mages would benefit from younger leadership. "That was a long time ago. Things have changed."

"Have they?"

"Of course. Centuries cannot pass without progress. Swords have become sharper, stronger, cheaper. Food storage techniques have advanced to the point where a king can keep a shed of meat safely through the winter, preventing starvation anywhere in his kingdom. Horses are larger, sturdier. They can travel longer distances. Elves, *elves* live among us. So very, very much has changed."

"But not basic human nature."

Saviar rolled his eyes. "Even what you call basic human nature."

"Is that so?" Jeremilan started to pace, and the others respectfully gave him a path. "There are no wars?"

"Well . . ." Saviar could hardly deny them, given what he was asking the mages to do.

"Northern tribes no longer squabble over territory? Countries no longer need borders? Nationalities no longer exist because Easterners, Westerners, and Northmen breed freely together?"

Saviar did not see the purpose in this argument. "You can take anything to its extreme—"

"And where are these elves you spoke of? Why can't you use their magic?"

"Hopefully, someone close to the elves will convince them to come also."

"Why does someone have to convince them?" Jeremilan stopped to face Saviar directly. "Don't they walk freely among you?"

"Well, no," Saviar was forced to admit. "But they could if they wished to. Elves are . . . well, elves. They're capricious and unfocused, the very definition of chaos. They've lived reclusive lives for as long as the world has existed. That doesn't change in a decade."

"Are you certain humans didn't drive them to seclusion?"

"No!" Saviar did not have time to divulge the entire history of the elfin race coming to live on Midgard. At one time, the elves had tried to slaughter the humans, whom they believed responsible for the destruction of Alfheim. Later, they had seen elfin/human hybrids as the answer to their ever-shrinking population. "In fact, the king of Béarn married one, and one of the Bérnian princesses is half-elfin."

"True as that may be . . ."

It irked Saviar that Jeremilan left the possibility open that he was lying.

". . . the reasons elves gave for going underground may have been phrased self-protectively. If they stated they were hiding from humans, the humans might see them as enemies and actively hunt them down."

Saviar made a disgusted noise. "You have a wondrous knack for seeing the worst in everything, sir. No great civilization was ever built on pessimism."

"True." Jeremilan smiled. "But the man who sees the worst in everything rarely walks into danger."

"Only because he never walks into *anything*."

Jeremilan clearly did not see that as the insult Saviar intended. The old man merely smiled. "We have survived as long as we have because we remain secluded, like elves. No one knows we exist, and we wish to keep it that way. I have lived through the rise, fall, and destruction of many Northern tribes, including the one that tried to utterly destroy the mages."

Saviar hesitated, at first thinking that Myrcidë had survived two attempted massacres. Then it occurred to him that Jeremilan referred to the Renshai, that the elder did not realize the tribe had refashioned itself and returned, much the way the Myrcidians had. Saviar saw no reason to correct that misconception now. It might goad him to break his promise to his brother. "You've remained safe because humans who had no knowledge of magic and elves would have no reason to seek you. These invaders, however—"

"Are an unknown threat that reportedly might know some magic, according to you. We'd rather face that unknown than the known certainty of war."

Saviar pursed his lips. He had absolutely nothing more to say. "That's your final answer?"

"It is." Jeremilan's response held no hesitation.

Saviar glanced around the room at the silent adults. "Is no one brave enough to defend his home, his tribe, his family?"

A few murmurs swept the crowd, but no one came forward.

"Very well," Saviar said, walking toward his brother. "You have tonight to reconsider. Subikahn and I will be leaving in the morning."

"No!" Jeremilan's voice seemed to thunder through the confines. "You may not leave."

The demand blindsided Saviar. He whirled back to face the mages' leader, hand falling to his hilt. "You mean to hold us prisoners?"

Subikahn silently moved away from the wall.

The entire room seemed to shift backward, though no one seated actually arose. Jeremilan's tone softened, and his gaze followed Saviar's hand to his sword. "You have to understand. The mages must stay together; we cannot risk anyone finding us."

Saviar appreciated their point, but it did not matter. He would damn himself to Hel before abandoning Béarn to thugs and murderers. "The West needs us; we're going. The only way to stop us is to kill us; but, if you try, we will take many of you with us."

"No!" Chymmerlee popped to her feet. "No fighting." She ran to stand directly in front of the twins. "Pawpaw, can't you make an exception? I'm sure they won't tell anyone about us." She turned to face Saviar. "Would you?"

"I wouldn't," Saviar promised. Subikahn, he noted, said nothing. Several of the mages shifted.

Saviar clamped his hilt tighter. "At the first sign of a flaring aura, any sign whatsoever of magic, I'm going to attack."

The mages went deliberately still. Jeremilan's nostrils flared. "You can't kill all of us."

"Perhaps not." Saviar would not dub any battle impossible. "But how many mages can you spare, Jeremilan?"

They stood in silent stalemate for several moments. Saviar stared out over the group, watching for the slightest glow. Blind to any potential magic, Subikahn waited anxiously behind his brother. Any threatening movement Saviar made would translate into a lethal assault on the mages by his brother. Realizing that, Saviar made no overtly hostile motion. Yet.

Jeremilan spat. "We never should have saved your life. We should have let you die in the dirt like a wounded deer."

Chymmerlee sucked air through her teeth.

Mean as the statement was meant to be, Saviar could hardly argue. "I appreciate what you did for me, but it does not change the fact that the West needs us. Your mistake, Jeremilan, was not saving me. It is in choosing not to stand with the West—and fight."

Jeremilan turned away in a savage movement, but made no other motion Saviar might construe as magic. Beside him, Subikahn stiffened. Chymmerlee edged closer to both Renshai. "Grab me," she whispered.

The request caught Saviar off his guard. "What?"

Subikahn took over. Seizing Chymmerlee around the waist, he drew her closer. A knife appeared suddenly in his other hand, migrating to Chymmerlee's throat. "Let us go unimpeded, or we kill her."

Chymmerlee jerked her head to look sideways at him, and Subikahn had to readjust to keep from accidentally cutting her. Though Chymmerlee had made the suggestion, she had clearly expected Saviar's touch, not Subikahn's.

Jeremilan whirled back to face the young men. "No!" he screamed. Light flared momentarily.

"No!" Chymmerlee repeated. "Don't do it."

To Saviar's relief, the magic died as swiftly as it had arisen. He had no real intention of killing either of them.

Jeremilan sagged, wearing every one of his years. "Please." His tone lost all of its former belligerence and strength. "Go, then. Just don't hurt our Chymmerlee."

Saviar hated to leave things this way. "I promise, sir. So long as your mages do not attack or harass us, we will leave in peace. Chymmerlee will be released, unharmed, we will say nothing to anyone of the mages, and we will return here when we can."

Subikahn had to speak. "So long as you allow us to do so safely."

Jeremilan waved a hand feebly. Every mage's eye followed their leader, hung on his every word. "Thank you. Will you, at least, allow us to seal this deal with magic?"

Saviar hesitated.

Subikahn did not. Still clutching Chymmerlee, he explained in no uncertain terms, "We don't use magic, and we have no way of knowing exactly what spell you've placed upon us."

"Nor do we know if we can trust your word," Jeremilan countered.

Saviar knew he could remind the mages that he currently held the upper hand, but it seemed better to save that as a last resort.

Again, Subikahn took over the negotiations. "Saviar's father is a Knight of Erythane. His grandfather is the Knight-Captain who allowed himself to be executed rather than break a vow, even to one who deserved no loyalty."

"That sentence got commuted," Saviar explained, so as not to seem a liar in case Jeremilan ever discovered that Knight-Captain Kedrin still lived. "And lifted when the rightful king retook his throne, but not through any action of my grandfather's. I take the integrity of my line extremely seriously."

"A fact that never ceases to irritate me," Subikahn said softly, though at least a few of the mages probably heard him. "Saviar intends to follow his father into the knighthood."

Though startled by Subikahn's knowledge, Saviar made a effort not to demonstrate his surprise. No matter the source of the statement, it was truth nonetheless.

Jeremilan wrung his hands. Saviar could almost hear the insides of his skull spinning, considering his options from every angle. The situation clearly did not afford him the time he needed to think through every possibility. "You promise to release my great granddaughter . . ."

Great granddaughter? Saviar realized that explained why Jeremilan had given up so abruptly. It occurred to him that she appeared to be the youngest of the mages, which meant they had not had a healthy baby born in many years.

". . . unhurt, keep our existence and whereabouts a secret, return to us, and . . ." Jeremilan fixed his gaze on Subikahn, ". . . assure that your brother does the same."

"I so vow, but only with the reassurance that we are free to come and go as we please from this time onward." Saviar could hear the hissing of exchanged whispers behind him, between Subikahn and Chymmerlee, but could not make out what they said.

"Agreed." Jeremilan heaved a great sigh. "Now, release my great granddaughter."

"Not yet," Subikahn said, before Saviar could answer. "Not until we're safely beyond reach of your magic."

"You don't trust me?" Jeremilan's face purpled. "We've saved your brother's life. I've promised. What more could you possibly need?"

"My—my brother's just being overly cautious." Saviar cast a warning glance at Subikahn, who still held Chymmerlee against himself. He seemed to be enjoying it a bit too much for Saviar's liking. "Of course we trust—"

"I don't," Subikahn broke in rudely. "I'm sorry, but I can't leave fully armed enemies directly at my back. I will know if anyone follows, and Chymmerlee will remain with us until I'm absolutely convinced of our safety. If you pursue us, you will have broken your vow, and we will no longer be bound by any of it."

Again, they seemed to have reached a stalemate, one that seemed utterly unnecessary to Saviar. He wondered if it had something to do with the conversation between his brother and Chymmerlee.

"It's all right," Chymmerlee said, without a trace of the fear she should be feeling in a hostage situation. "I know my way and how to stay safe. Saviar won't let any harm come to me, will you?"

Saviar wished he could control the blush taking over his cheeks. He did not want to look like an awkward teen in this life-or-death situation. "Of course not."

Jeremilan stepped aside and gestured toward the door, a formality to his otherwise casual movements betraying the discomfort he tried to hide. He surely did not like the arrangement, but he seemed reluctantly committed. "Be careful with her, Saviar."

"I promise," he said, letting Subikahn and Chymmerlee precede him through the exit. All of his promises seemed ultimately moot. Even if Béarn won the war, he would probably die in the battles. If their enemy won, there would be no survivors at all.

Saviar allowed Subikahn to lead the way, knowing his more stealthy brother would find the quickest route to Béarn that would also befuddle anyone who dared try to pursue them. He had no idea how Subikahn managed it. The woodlands twisted his own sense of direction, and even the position of the sun became difficult to follow through the towering branches. He kept his attention on Chymmerlee, assisting her over deadfalls, around thick patches of brambles, and through copses of knotted branches.

Saviar also kept his ears attuned for sounds of a chase. Jeremilan had promised not to follow, at the risk of revealing the mages and losing his great granddaughter's life; but the Renshai could forgive the elder breaking that particular vow. Every tiny sound jarred Saviar, forcing him to analyze it. He found his back muscles tightening as he imagined some amorphous magic spearing through his back.

"Are we far enough now?" Saviar asked for the fifth time in as many hours.

Light as a dancer, Chymmerlee leaped over a decaying stump, avoiding the upright, jagged edges. "Not yet, my sweet. Not yet."

The forest gradually faded into darkness, and Saviar found himself straining his vision for hazards, twice tripping over roots and rocks rendered invisible by the encroaching twilight. The second time, he nearly pulled Chymmerlee down with him. He caught himself about to swear, cleaning up his language so as not to offend her.

Subikahn turned, but Saviar could not see his expression in the darkness. "Time to set camp?"

Saviar looked at Chymmerlee. "Is it safe to stop?"

Chymmerlee glanced through the brush. "I think so. If we don't draw attention to ourselves."

Subikahn grunted. "You mean, no fire."

"No fire," Chymmerlee agreed, clearly searching for something. Apparently frustrated, she mumbled incoherently, made a broad gesture, and a patch of light appeared in front of her. Though not particularly strong, it cut through the forest darkness like a knife, revealing the ground and all of its stumbling blocks. With movements of one hand, she caused it to roll across the ground like a brilliant fog. Finally, she let it sit on a relatively flat area without jutting roots, large branches, or stumps. She picked up a few errant rocks and branches, tossing them into the darkness. "There. That should be comfortable enough for sitting and sleeping."

Saviar and Subikahn only stared as she worked.

Subikahn regained his voice first. "Doesn't that sort of negate our . . . not building . . . a fire?"

Chymmerlee shook her head. "Not really, no. The light stops abruptly at the edges of the spell. You can't see it from a distance or smell it, like you can a fire. And it's only there for as long as we need it." The light disappeared abruptly, leaving Saviar half-blinded.

Saviar blinked his eyes rapidly, trying to regain his night vision. "Couldn't you have done that sooner? Maybe *before* I broke my toe and nearly hurled you into a tree?"

"I'm sorry." The light snapped back into existence. "Do you want me to try to heal your toe?"

Saviar closed his eyes, replaying the sudden flare on the backs of his eyelids. "Not necessary. It's not actually broken. I was exaggerating to make a point."

"Oh," Chymmerlee said, with a hint of confusion. Apparently, such a tactic did not exist in her culture. "So your toe's . . . all right?"

"Just a bit bruised, I'm sure."

Chymmerlee took Saviar's hand. "Why don't you let me check, just in case?"

Saviar smiled, staring into her soft, blue-gray eyes.

Subikahn snorted. He used a tone usually reserved for babies, "Poor widdle Savi. Did 'ou stub 'ou's widdle toe?" He grabbed Saviar's arm. "Come on. We need to practice." He called over his shoulder. "Chymmer, can you dig up some food? Your mages didn't exactly provision us for our trip."

"You could hardly expect them to, under the circumstances." Saviar shook free of Subikahn's grip. He waited until Chymmerlee left, killing her light, to add, "Very nice. Make me look like an infant in front of her."

Subikahn threw up his hands. "Don't attack the messenger. You were the one acting infantile; I just pointed it out."

"I'll remember that the next time you're trying to grab an intimate moment with Talamir."

Subikahn stopped, stiffening. "Shut up, Saviar." Darkness hid his expression, but his tone dripped warning.

Saviar drew *Motfrabelonning.* "You're begging for a spar, my brother."

Subikahn turned away. "Do your *svergelse* here. I'll find my own place." He started walking.

"What's wrong with a bit of sparring?" Saviar called after him, but Subikahn never paused, disappearing into the woodland darkness. *He probably left me next to a bunch of spearlike broken trees and massive patches of nettles.* Saviar stepped around the area to get a clearer feel. *Wants me to trip and skewer myself.* Saviar did not believe a word of his own thoughts. Renshai practiced in the best and worst of conditions, training for every contingency.

Saviar lunged into violent *svergelse,* his movements smooth and strong, his sword a perfect extension of his arm. It felt good to have his grace back, his quickness and his power. He had felt naked and helpless without them. Now, he entered a higher level of thought in which all of him became a glorious weapon, sheering through enemies with the ease of a knife cleaving butter. No one and nothing could stop him. He dedicated his competence and his life to Sif, the goddess of Renshai, and her son Modi, Wrath.

Saviar did not stop until he fairly collapsed with exhaustion, and Chymmerlee was there the instant the swordwork ended. "You're beautiful," she whispered.

"What?"

"You're beautiful," Chymmerlee repeated. "You move with the flawless elegance of a swan combined with the speed and power of a galloping horse. It's amazing to watch you and impossible not to."

It felt to Saviar as if he blushed from the roots of his hair to the bottoms of his feet. "I'm . . . nothing special. Just a soldier flailing around with a sword." Among Renshai, at least, it was essentially true. "Now you, Chymmerlee. You're beautiful."

"See if you still feel that way after you eat what I've found. I didn't want to range too far."

"I'm hungry enough to eat dirt." Saviar sheathed his sword. "I'm sure whatever you found will suit me." *So long as you found a lot of it.*

Chymmerlee led Saviar back to the place she had chosen, reactivating her light to reveal Subikahn sitting on a fallen log, stuffing his mouth with shoots. "These are really good," he said without bothering to swallow. "You should try them."

"I intend to," Saviar replied. "Assuming they're not all already in your mouth."

"There're plenty for everyone," Chymmerlee assured him, gesturing at piles of tender shoots, purple berries, and multicolored flowers. "I know you men prefer meat, but it's not safe to eat it raw. And my light doesn't give off any heat."

" 's all right," Subikahn said around another mouthful. "This is delicious. Very satisfying."

Saviar doubted he would find it equally so, given the enormous difference in size between his twin and himself. He wondered how

Chymmerlee had developed such a vast store of knowledge regarding wild foods. Surely the mages could magic-up their own sustenance, without need for scavenging. Saviar crouched beside his brother and forced himself not to bolt the food. He wanted to show Chymmerlee the best of his manners.

Chymmerlee addressed the unspoken question. "We can't create objects that don't already exist, so mages and elves have to gather or grow their food, just like anyone else. I have a knack for finding the good stuff; plus, I get sick of the caves. I don't look threatening, and I have magic enough to hide from bandits. So, I'd volunteer to fetch the water and foodstuffs as much as possible. Eventually, it became my job."

Subikahn finally swallowed. "That's what you were doing when we met you?"

"Yes." Chymmerlee hovered over Saviar. "Try this. Oh, and this."

Saviar intended to eat pretty much everything, with or without her directions.

"Have as much as you want. I've already eaten, your brother's almost done, and I can always fetch more."

Saviar finished chewing and swallowed before speaking. "Relax. I'm fine." He wished she would just let him eat. The more she flitted around him, the slower he filled his empty gut.

Subikahn came to Saviar's rescue by engaging Chymmerlee in conversation. "What if there's a blizzard?"

Chymmerlee shook her head, moonlight finding glimmers of copper in her dark hair. "Magic helps, but we don't like to use it outside near our home; it looks suspicious if snow heaps everywhere except in one cave-shaped area. We grow some crops inside, too, and keep a few small animals. That sustains us even through long patches of bad weather. It's become rare for anyone but me to leave the caves anymore, except Mennalo, who goes on occasional expeditions to try to find more auras. The more traffic in and out, the more likely someone might discover us; and Pawpaw is worried someone might use magic at the wrong place and time. He trusts my judgment; and he knows that if I don't get some freedom, I'll run away."

Saviar shoved a handful of food into his mouth while Chymmerlee's attention was fully on Subikahn. That might account for the extremeness of Jeremilan's reaction to helping Béarn. It would take extraordinary events to goad such hermits out of hiding. It also explained the apparent lack of pursuit and the mages' ignorance of the world in general.

Subikahn nodded thoughtfully. "In the morning, you need to go back to your people."

"No." The single word, unaccompanied by emotion, hung in the night air.

"No?" Subikahn repeated. "Why not?"

"Because we're not far enough yet. You're not safe from their magic."

The explanation made sense to Saviar, though it also made him uneasy. If the mages could still present clear danger a day's quick walk distant, what kinds of spells might Béarn's enemies harbor?

Subikahn frowned. "You're lying."

Saviar jerked his head to his brother. "That's not nice."

"No," Subikahn admitted, not backing down. "But it's true. If the mages could work dangerous magic from this far away, they wouldn't worry about losing men to the war."

Chymmerlee sighed, rose, and walked a few paces away. "You're right. I'm lying."

"Why?" Subikahn demanded.

"Because I didn't want to fight with you about . . . staying with you."

"No!" Saviar said, no longer caring that he had food in his mouth, a bit of which flew out with the shout. He paused to swallow. "I promised I would send you back."

Chymmerlee shook her head. "No, you didn't, Savi. You promised you would *release* me unharmed. And you've done that." She sat, cross-legged, on a bed she had created from fallen leaves in their absence. "You can't control what I choose to do afterward."

Saviar felt confident he could throw Chymmerlee over one shoulder and carry her back to Myrcidë. "Can't I?"

Chymmerlee studied him defiantly. "Nope. Because, if you haul me back, kicking and screaming the entire way, you'll lose a lot of time and put yourself exactly back in the position you were in before you kidnapped me."

"But I didn't kidnap—"

Chymmerlee did not allow Saviar to protest. "And, if you head for Béarn without me, I'll follow." She turned her gaze to Subikahn. "And if you try to lose me, you probably will. Then, I'll get completely lost, alone in the woods. Animals will eat me, and you will have broken your vow."

"Animals aren't going to—" Saviar saw no reason to finish the sentence. They all knew he would never leave her wandering aimlessly. "Your people will think we dishonored our word. They'll come after us."

"Good." Chymmerlee cocked her head. "That's what you want, right? Them to follow us to Béarn?"

Subikahn crouched beside her, biting his lip against a smile.

His twin's loyalty change caught Saviar off guard. "Have you both gone mad? The Myrcidians won't come to help; they'll come to pulverize me." He jabbed a hand toward Subikahn. "And you, too."

"If they come, I'll explain the situation to them," Chymmerlee promised. "That it was all my fault."

Saviar snorted and rolled his eyes. "Before or after they pulverize me?"

"They would find *me*, first. My aura's much easier to trace. I'll explain it all, and you'll have them where you want them."

Subikahn nodded. He had, apparently, figured out Chymmerlee's plan in advance.

Saviar still saw several flaws, but he doubted explaining them would make a difference. He could not help noticing Chymmerlee's cautious phrasing, "if they come," and "they *would* find me first". Obviously, she did not expect the mages to pursue them. Her previous explanation about her people's secretiveness and reclusiveness made clear the reason why, though Saviar had his doubts. If a man had stolen his daughter, he would hunt them to the ends of the world; yet he was also a skilled warrior raised by an extraordinarily honorable father. He had no real means to understand the mages' point of view. Only twenty-six of them remained. Perhaps they reasoned it wiser to abandon one than risk ten more or even the entire group. Maybe they trusted Chymmerlee to find her own escape, whenever it might come. She had surely told someone her feelings for Saviar. Given the mages' desperation for new blood, they might even hope she returned impregnated by himself or his brother.

That last thought brought a flush to Saviar's cheeks, and he turned away to hide it. No matter how her people reacted, Chymmerlee had her mind made up. And, if she was anything like their mother, no man could change it.

CHAPTER 40

Timing is everything. In battle, in life, in diplomacy. Everything
is timing.

—*General Santagithi*

THE OLDEST CHILD OF King Griff and third-Queen Xoraida,
Prince Barrindar stood on the sixth-floor balcony of Béarn Castle
and surveyed the city below him in the twilight. His entire world
for his sixteen years of life, Béarn had changed so completely in the
past few months that he scarcely recognized it. The castle remained
the central feature, carved from the very stone of the mountains; but
tents and temporary buildings had sprung up all around it, as if overnight. He could still recognize the occasional business and cottage,
but the people milling through the streets came in a larger variety of
dresses, colors, shapes, and sizes than he ever knew existed.

Barrindar's gaze swept the ocean, where the pirates massed in a
swarm of nearly identical ships. From a distance, they looked like
enormous birds, their brown triangular sails spilling wind as they
remained anchored in tight formation. No worldly ship had gotten through the harbor in more than a fortnight; the pirates owned
the open water. Three hundred ships, someone had estimated, with
crews of a hundred, more or less. Thirty thousand ferocious pirates
massed for nothing but slaughter.

In contrast, the many and varied peoples that had come to Béarn
seemed pitifully ragtag. Commanded by at least thirty different generals, it seemed impossible to keep them all simultaneously focused.
Many had little or no training; decades had passed with nothing more
serious than border skirmishes, feuds, and general rattling of sabers
for those outside of Béarn. Many of the alliances, strained in the best
of times, might fray or shatter in the fury and chaos of war.

Béarn had grown massively and far too quickly. In addition to
the cramped military camps, tent cities had sprung up around the

borders in vast semicircles that continued out to Erythane, Frist, and beyond. These housed Béarn's women and children, her elders, the tradesmen with no weapon training or skills who could better serve in professional capacities. Supply lines curved outward in every direction, far beyond the extent of Prince Barrindar's vision.

It occurred to him to wonder how the pirates kept themselves provisioned. Surely, their capture of merchant vessels, their killing of the crews and seizing of property were grossly inadequate to keep their bellies full, especially in the last month when no ships had dared to sail the waters and all trade came overland.

The lethal ocean. The thought raised memories of Prince Arturo's death and a flood of devastating sorrow. Only two months apart in age, the princes had played together since infancy, like twins. No two brothers had ever been closer, and the loss left a hole in Barrindar's heart he doubted anyone could ever fill. He felt alone, lost and betrayed by gods who had stolen his courageous half brother for no logical reason. A man like Prince Arturo, a good-hearted, able person who had seemed to Barrindar the most suitable to take over Béarn's throne, should never die without high purpose.

Barrindar wished he could fight the coming war in Arturo's place, hacking down enemies with the swift, strong strokes his half brother displayed in practice and Barrindar could only emulate. But he understood the practicalities that came with his position. He was sixteen, still a few years short of his full growth. His war skills were adequate at best, and the world could not spare the life of another Béarnian heir. With Arturo dead, Marisole slated for the bard's position, and Ivana barred from the lineage by her elfin blood, even if she possessed a full range of faculties, it left only Barrindar, his two little sisters, and Matrinka's youngest child in line for the throne. In the past, the staff-test, now the Pica Test, had failed dozens in the search for a proper king or queen. No one cared for the current remaining odds.

The prince's thoughts shifted from his own agonizing loss to those of the people around him. He wondered how many women sobbed quietly in their beds, how many children curled in helpless balls at the realization that their fathers, their mothers, and they themselves might die in hopeless, screaming terror. The coming war would claim many lives, and the unfairness of who it took had already reached Barrindar personally, with the loss of Arturo. If they won, they kept their land, filled with wailing widows and orphans. If they lost, every one of them died. Barrindar was not sure which was worse.

Light footsteps behind him could not rouse Barrindar from the torture his own thoughts inflicted. The bare thought of such misery cut him to the depths of his heart and soul. When he opened himself to the suffering of his people, it proved a burden he could scarcely bear. Tears filled his eyes, his chest squeezed shut, and the simple act of breathing became a laborious chore.

If the newcomer spoke to him, Barrindar did not know, too desperately lost in his misery. But, where no words or touch could penetrate, something else did. The light notes of a mandolin, soft but powerful, seemed to envelop him. And the sweet voice that followed drew him inexorably into another world.

She sang of war and pestilence, of grief and regret. The bittersweetness of Marisole's song came to him as emotion rather than words. Barrindar could not have recalled a single poetic lyric; he absorbed it as a thing inseparably whole, a heart-searing expression of reality. He surrendered to the sound, unable to escape it, drawn wherever it might take him.

Barrindar's ears rang with the clash of steel, and he became snared in a battle for his life. Though not a warrior himself, though he had never tasted real battle, the slash and parry still seemed strangely real. His powerful arms rose and fell with need. He knew only a courageous swell of patriotism, a need to protect his precious family and friends from the hordes of pirates that assailed them. Dragged to a mind-set Barrindar could never have found on his own, he discovered each victory brought a fresh wave of joy, an unshakeable certainty that he would survive. If his companions died, he would see to it they never, ever did so in vain.

Transformed into a valiant soldier, Barrindar found a song-world that turned battle into delight, that transformed desperation into driving courage. He would succeed because failure was unthinkable, impossible. These pirates were humans, albeit vicious ones, and they would fall to his blade like wheat to a scythe. The thrill of victory went from desire to reality. With the help of so many allies, Béarn won the war. Women embraced their triumphant warriors or consoled their hapless neighbors, regaling them with stories of fallen bravery.

Swept along by the song, Barrindar hurled himself into Marisole's arms. Impact knocked the mandolin to the ground, where it loosed a sour note. The song died instantly and, with it, the intensity of misplaced emotion it inspired. But Barrindar found himself lost in another. Marisole felt so fragile in his arms, a perfect porcelain doll that needed his protection. He held her close, suddenly excited in a new and more powerful way. Though blood sister to Arturo, Marisole had never seemed like a sibling to Barrindar as her brother always had.

He had considered her more like a beloved cousin, perhaps because she resembled her Erythanian blood father while Arturo favored their Béarnian mother, Matrinka.

Marisole broke free and rescued her mandolin. Examining it carefully, she smiled and leaned it solidly against the low granite railing. "I'm glad you liked my song."

Freed from its spell, Barrindar stared at Marisole. Though tall for a woman, she barely reached Barrindar's chin. Her dark-brown hair, a bit too light for a full-blooded Béarnide, fell in a thick cascade, clipped together at the back. Her nose and lips were generous, her eyes a deep hazel, and her face soft and youthful. She had, only recently, turned nineteen; and the grim anticipation of the coming war had utterly eclipsed the celebration. "Your song was marvelous, as always, Marisole. But, right now, I'm driven by something else." Difficult words came with surprising ease, "I just never before realized how stunningly beautiful you are." It was a lie. He had noticed her beauty every moment of every day since even before Arturo's death, but he had only just found the courage to say so.

Marisole flushed from the roots of her hair to the tip of her chin and allowed him to draw her into another tight embrace. She wrapped her arms around him as well, and her touch felt as light and gentle as butterflies. If Barrindar squeezed just a bit harder, he could break her in half.

Barrindar buried his face in her hair. It held a hint of musk, the sweet, natural odor of Marisole. He had always found it pleasant; now, it drove him wild. "And you smell wonderful."

"But I haven't bathed in two days," Marisole protested. "And I'm not wearing any perfume."

"I know." Barrindar could not keep a hint of lust from his voice. "I like it."

Marisole pushed him away. "Barri, cut it out. We're . . . we're . . . halfway . . . siblings." Her words faltered. "Aren't we?"

Rebuffed and ashamed, Barrindar released her. He turned away to look out over the city again, and the grief her song had stripped away began creeping over him again. "Bloodwise, we're farther apart than our father and your mother. And the populace *demanded* they marry."

The observation got no immediate reply. Just as Barrindar thought Marisole had sneaked away to save them further embarrassment, she spoke, "You're right."

Barrindar thought he heard a hint of joy and relief in her tone, but worried he had only imagined it. He started to turn, then froze,

afraid of the expression he might find on her face. Thoughts of courting women had come to him only in the last year, and Marisole had
risen to his mind near the first. He did not understand why her response had become so urgently important to him, especially given
the looming war. Or, perhaps, it was because of it. Insignificant as it
seemed in the grand scheme of the world, he did not want to die a
virgin.

"My father and mother are cousins." Oblivious to the turn of
Barrindar's current thoughts, Marisole worried the original problem.
"But my blood father isn't related to them at all. In fact, he's not even
a Béarnide, which bloodwise, makes us . . ."

Since Marisole seemed incapable of finishing, Barrindar filled in
the blank. ". . . *distant* cousins."

"Kissing cousins," Marisole added with a smile.

Now, Barrindar turned fully, unable to hide his own grin. Despite
all the madness going on below him, perhaps because of it, he had
discovered something important missing from his life. He reached
for her again, cautiously this time. "Marisole, if Béarn survives this,
if *we* survive it, maybe . . . ?"

"Maybe," she repeated, rushing to his arms, "we shouldn't wait
to find out."

Barrindar could not have agreed more.

Béarn's Strategy Room buzzed with conversations in several different tongues. Darris remained quietly at his king's right hand, trying to absorb every feature, every nuance of this historical moment.
Nowhere in his research could Darris find a time when all the countries of the continent had united in a common cause. The nearest
they had come was the so-called Great War, three centuries past,
where the armies of the West and North had come together to battle
the Eastlands. Now, even the Eastern king held a place of honor at
the table.

Darris had convinced Rantire to remain outside the Strategy
Room with the argument that a Renshai presence might antagonize
the Northern forces. Alone, she would not have accepted his argument; Darris often suspected that Rantire was the Renshai word for
"provocation." But King Griff had agreed with his bard/bodyguard
and relegated Rantire to distant rooms and hallways.

Currently, the Strategy Room held fifteen men, whittled down
from more than double that number. The room simply could not
hold any more, so King Griff had forced the armies to come together

under common generals and high commanders. Driven to information, Darris had managed to memorize them all under the guise of Griff's need. Some, he knew well: King Humfreet of Erythane; Knight-Captain Kedrin; the Aeri General Valr Magnus, who had slain Kevral in battle; and King Tae from the Eastlands, still gaunt and bruised from his imprisonment. Others, Darris knew by reputation: General Markanyin of Pudar and General Sutton of the town of Santagithi who commanded the forces from Santagithi, Greentree, and Porvada.

The others Darris had only just met. They included five other Northmen, each representing a different tribe, and two Western leaders from small conglomerates of towns. More were on the way. King Griff had promises from the last three Northern tribes, another group of central Westerners, and the army of the distant Eastlands had not yet arrived.

For the sake of international harmony, King Griff stuck meticulously to the formalities of the meeting, though Darris felt certain that most of the leaders, including Griff himself, would have preferred to dispense with them. Only Knight-Captain Kedrin clung to every word and gesture.

Finally, Griff requested the first suggestion, which came from General Sutton. A large, well-muscled man with shrewd eyes, the representative of the most eastern portion of the Westlands spoke in a clear and booming voice. "What have we learned about this enemy so far? What are their priorities and intentions?" He used the Common Trading tongue, the only one they all shared.

For now, Darris knew, King Griff had no intention of mentioning the *Kjempemagiska*. Other than the people in the room at the time of Tae's report, only Kedrin had become privy to the information. They had all agreed to fight one battle at a time, to not allow the future threat of magical enemies hamper soldiers in their current war. Once they defeated the self-called *alsona*, Béarn and her allies could start worrying about and strategizing for the bigger war. By Tae's calculation, the *Kjempemagiska* had placed their faith squarely on their *alsona*. It would take time for them to muster for another war, time enough for the allies to celebrate victory, revise strategy, and attempt to recruit the elves. But first, of course, they had to defeat the *alsona*. Though he kept the thought to himself, Darris was not at all sure that was possible.

Griff addressed the question directly. "They intend to slaughter every person in our world and claim every bit of our land."

A short murmur swept the room. General Markanyin of Pudar spoke next, "How do we know this?"

"One man has managed to speak with them," the king of Béarn explained.

The general's head listed slightly to the left, and his brows knitted. In size, he rivaled the Béarnian king, a surprising feat. Average size for the bearlike Béarnides was enormous by the standards of other cultures. "Why don't we engage them in parley? Surely, the right person could convince them of the folly of—"

Griff cut him off. "They won't parley."

Knight-Captain Kedrin requested the floor with an archaic gesture, and Griff relinquished it with a faint sigh of relief. Had he not sat so close, even Darris would have missed it.

Kedrin took over, his voice commanding even at the volume of normal speech. "I'm afraid they don't even acknowledge the conventions of parley. They've slaughtered every man who came within reach of their weapons, no matter his gestures or flag."

"Except this one the high king spoke of." General Markanyin acknowledged Griff with a bow and a glance.

The knight dipped his head. "The one His Majesty spoke of only succeeded because the pirates he addressed were prisoners, the only two we've managed to capture in our years at war." He forestalled the obvious question, "They fight to their last breath, no matter the odds."

Grunts were heard throughout the room. Darris watched Kedrin formally give up the floor in the grand and arcane manner only the Knights of Erythane still remembered.

A knock sounded at the door, then it edged open to reveal Sir Ra-khir, Kedrin's son, in pristine knight silks. He bowed deeply to each king in turn, including Tae, who rolled his eyes in response. Ra-khir saluted each general, entered the room fully, and closed the door behind him. "I apologize for interrupting, but I've only just arrived."

Darris turned his attention to Kedrin. The Knight-Captain seemed mightily displeased, his features taut and the corners of his mouth bowed grimly downward. Taking back the floor with every flourish, he addressed his wayward son. "Sir Ra-khir, this meeting is for generals only."

Ra-khir tipped his head to his father. "Again, I beg the pardon of every great man in this room, but I am in command of an army. Though not among the largest, it is not the smallest either." The look he gave his captain seemed just a bit pointed to Darris. The Knights of Erythane currently consisted of only twenty-four men. One less with Ra-khir not among them.

Knight-Captain Kedrin made a brisk and full gesture of apology. "My pardon, Sir Ra-khir. Who is at your command?"

Ra-khir turned stiffly toward King Griff. "Sire, they're outcasts; but finer warriors more dedicated to Béarn you could not find anywhere. In a crisis such as this, it seems prudent to accept every sword arm in our defense. What say you, Your Majesty? May we join the allies of the continent?"

Renshai. Darris got it in an instant, and he believed Kedrin did, too. He was less certain about Griff. Markanyin held a thoughtful expression, as did General Sutton and Valr Magnus, but the remainder of the Western and Northern leaders showed no obvious sign of recognition.

King Griff spoke carefully. "Does anyone have a problem with allowing these outcasts full status among us? If so, speak now."

Murmurs passed around the table. Only General Sutton spoke aloud, "So long as we're sure they'll fight for us and against the pirates, I see no reason to exclude anyone."

King Griff gave a heavy nod.

"Let's take a formal vote," Kedrin suggested. "Everyone for including the outcast unit signify by saying, 'Aye'. 'Nay,' if opposed."

Around the table, a chorus of "aye" sounded, without a single voice in opposition.

"It carries, then," Kedrin said. "Sir Ra-khir, do you have consent to represent these outcasts?"

"Fully."

Knight-Captain Kedrin indicated that King Griff should take the floor for a decree that must seem standard and obvious to the overly formal Kedrin.

Clearly flummoxed, King Griff covered smoothly. "You announce it, please, Knight-Captain."

Kedrin suppressed a grin and dutifully proclaimed, "Then, Sir Ra-khir, you are granted the equal status of general. And your followers are forgiven any crimes, including trespass, for the duration of this war." He turned to Griff and bowed nearly to the ground. "Is that correct, Your Majesty?"

King Griff nodded broadly. "Utterly. Thank you."

"And," Kedrin added in clear warning, "since you also represent the Knights of Erythane, and our Majesties King Griff and King Humfreet . . ." He bowed humbly to each in turn. ". . . I expect you to keep your wayward followers completely in line."

Ra-khir looked momentarily stricken, but swiftly regained face. "I'll do my best, Knight-Captain." He had about as much chance of keeping Renshai corralled as he did the myriad of palace cats.

With every chair at the table full, Darris rose and offered his own to Ra-khir. The knight graciously accepted his offer, and Darris took a position behind and beside Griff, where he could observe most of the leaders' expressions.

The tribal leader of Gelshnir spoke in his musical Northern accent. "What are the pirates doing now?"

"Massing their ships offshore," the high king explained. "We estimate three hundred, but it's only a guess. They've destroyed every vessel that's drawn near enough to count."

The Gelshni general continued, "What about scouts? What do they know?"

King Humfreet of Erythane finally spoke. "They're less than worthless. Even those who can sneak near without getting butchered don't understand a word of the pirates' gabble."

Darris saw a spark flash through several eyes, but General Markanyin got the question out first. "What about the 'one man' who spoke with our prisoners?"

King Griff's gaze went directly to Tae, and he paused a moment before answering, perhaps expecting the king of the Eastlands to save him the trouble. When Tae did not oblige, Griff accepted his burden. "He has an uncanny gift for languages and had the chance, because of the two prisoners, to immerse himself."

"Can he spy?" Markanyin asked hopefully.

Darris looked at Ra-khir and found him smiling. He had easily figured out the identity of their mystery language speaker.

"No," Griff said, more as a command than an answer. "We can't risk him. Not only do we need him for his talent, but he's too important to lose."

Finally, Tae spoke. What he lacked in volume, he made up for in intensity. "I'll do it."

Every eye jerked to the Eastern king.

Tae continued, "If we don't win this war, we all die. Women, children, no one will be spared. What's one life, any life, compared with that?"

Silence followed. Strategists and warriors filled the room, yet none had ever fought a war as significant and potentially deadly as this one.

General Sutton cleared his throat. "I'm certain His Highest Western Majesty meant no slight upon your courage, Your Eastern

Majesty." Obviously unaccustomed to royal titles, the leader of Santagithi, and her closest allies, attempted to mimic proper formality as well as to smooth ruffled feathers. "He merely made the point that your precious skill might serve us better than on a simple scouting mission."

Tae smiled. No king despised formality more than he did. "No offense was taken."

Darris knew innocent Griff could kick and spit on Tae, and the scrappy little Easterner would give him all the time he needed to explain.

Valr Magnus ignored the verbal exchanges, studying the massive map that covered most of the tabletop. "Do we even know where these pirates come from?"

"Here." Leaning forward, Tae jabbed a finger that thumped against the wooden table well off the southern edge of the map and directly across from Béarn.

Exclamations and discussions began immediately. Though he had initiated it, Tae did not join any of the conversations. He sat back, clearly relieved to allow others to take the floor from him.

Unlike most of the others, Valr Magnus did not allow the shock of an army from beyond the known world to derail him. "We need to concern ourselves with more than just the army massed in the Southern Sea." The Northman stood to reach the exact spot off the map that Tae had indicated. "What we need to worry about are ships breaking off to go here . . ." He made a gliding motion around the isthmus of islands south and west of Béarn to indicate a shore fall near the twin Western cities of Corpa Schaull and Frist. ". . . and here." He indicated another sea path eastward to land on the barren stretch of land known as the Western Plains and beyond to the Eastlands.

"If we have all our armies massed here . . ." Magnus circled Béarn and Erythane with his finger. ". . . we leave our civilians wide open for attack." He scratched his honey-colored beard. "Then the enemy could circle around here . . ." He cut through the westernmost Westlands to Erythane and from the Western Plains through the Southern Weathered Mountains to Béarn. Magnus looked up to find all of his colleagues peering over the map. "At least, that's what I'd do if I were the pirates."

"Which is why," the general from Gelshnir said, "our armies are stretched along the western coast." He indicated the Erdai general and one of the Westerners, the one representing the twin cities of Corpa Bikat and Oshtan.

Tae added his piece again, which surprised Darris. When they had traveled together as friends, Tae had spent most of his time in silent hiding. He still seemed uncomfortable when attention turned to him, but his nearly two decades as king had, apparently, boosted his confidence. "The Eastern armies, right now, are massed along the shores of the Western Plains. My father reports having found some expert mystery general to lead them." Tae rolled his eyes. Weile Kahn had a habit of hitting his son with unwelcome surprises. "My father is on his way with a team of scouts. They're competent, but they're limited by not knowing the language."

General Markanyin rose and paced in the small space the table, and its massed kings and generals, left him. "With our armies spread thin, the pirates don't need strategy. They could attack Béarn en masse." He stopped between Tae and General Sutton, hand falling to the arm of Tae's chair. "These scouts of your father's . . ."

Darris held his breath. Rumors about Weile Kahn's followers abounded, and only the worst of them were true. Tae's father had gathered criminals as followers and served as their lord for decades. Survival had daily required stronger and more convoluted security than kings saw in a lifetime. His enemies included all of the world's power, above and beneath the law. Tae's mother had paid for Weile's antics with her life; and Tae, himself, had been left for dead on more than one occasion.

". . . can they infiltrate the enemy?"

Tae shook his head. "Not without knowing the language, I'm afraid. I'm not even sure I could do that; many little things, most I don't even know about, would give me away. But, at least, I could spy on them and understand what they tell one another."

"Can you teach it to others?" the only Western general who had not yet spoken piped in. He was a small man, compared with the others, and the youngest in the room.

Tae's brows rose in increments. "Sure I could. Just give me students with a knack for both languages and stealth for two to three years."

"Two to three *years?* Is that how long it took you?"

"No," Tae admitted. "But I learned under rather unique circumstances." He glanced toward Griff, who was hanging on Tae's every word, even though he knew most of the answer. "From two native speakers." He switched from the ubiquitous Common Trading tongue to Western, then Northern, then Pudarian. Darris did not know Northern, but he did the other two. Even the accents were spot on. "I was exposed to innumerable languages from infancy, and I obviously have a god-granted knack that few share."

General Sutton looked around Markanyin to address Griff. "You're right, Your Majesty. That's a talent we dare not risk."

"Except," Tae added, "that the Pudarian general is quite correct. We need to know where to position our armies, because we don't have the numbers to spread them even as thin as we have." He sucked in a deep breath, let it out slowly, then proclaimed without allowing an opening for argument, "So, I'm going in."

CHAPTER 41

I gave up thinking a long time ago.
—*King Tae Kahn of Stalmize*

THE STEADY LAP OF WATER against ships' hulls, the watery sounds of leaping fish and bobbing wood, the sharp wind blowing across the ocean all became too familiar to Tae. He and Imorelda had spent three days paddling cautiously between the massed warships on a hunk of old ship wood meant to look like ancient flotsam to anyone glimpsing it from a distance. He kept the cat focused on the proper wavelength for the *alsona*'s communication. They had heard just enough of sailor orders and warrior commands to assure that all the pirates used the same pitch level of mental communication.

The arrangement had initially seemed bewildering to Tae; mental communication did not allow much leeway for whispering, shouting, or mishearing. He wondered how the *alsona* kept myriad conversations going without interfering with one another. The last couple of days afloat, however, had brought answers. Apparently, they used regular speech for close, intimate conversations and reserved the mind calls for times when distance or numbers required it. At first, that bothered Tae. All that came to him were coarse discourses between sailors regarding chores, minor problems, and issues with the riggings. He worried that he was missing all the important exchanges.

Over time, however, Tae gathered a bit more from the stray bits and conversations that wafted clearly through the mental connection. He located the flagship in the middle of the formation, larger than the others and carrying their highest commander, the only *Kjempemagiska* they had brought.

I'm cold, Imorelda lamented. *I'm cold and wet and hungry. And, worst of all, I'm wet.*

Tae hated to lose his ability to scan for enemy communications. He just knew the moments focused directly on the cat, instead of the pirates, would turn out to be the most revealing ones. Also, when Imorelda was helping him listen, she could not complain. *You said 'wet' twice.*

I hate wet. Wet's twice as bad as the others.

Though tired of Imorelda's whining, Tae could not help feeling responsible for her misery. She had perched upon his shoulders for so long, he had already passed the points of pain and numbness. *I really am sorry, Imorelda. You know that. I'd have left you at the castle if I could, warm and overfed. But I can't do this without you.*

I'm cold and wet and hungry.

And wet, Tae reminded.

Imorelda shivered suddenly, and Tae had to grab hold of the sides of his makeshift boat to keep from teetering into the water.

Get some food from the pack, Imorelda. Eat as much as you want. Tae knew he could moderate his own rations to make up for whatever extra she ate.

Imorelda snubbed Tae's offer as if only a fool would have made it. *I'm not hungry.*

Tae sighed and closed his eyes, seeing no need to argue. *Then crawl inside my cloak. It's warmer and relatively dry.*

Imorelda remained in position. Apparently, she preferred complaining to action.

Imorelda, please go back to scanning. I need you.

But I don't understand anything they're saying. Imorelda rearranged herself on Tae's shoulders, much to his relief. *And it's boring.*

I understand. Tae meant it and hoped his sincerity came through with his words. *Saving our world may seem boring to you, but it's survival to me and everyone we know and love.*

Like Subikahn?

Tae stiffened. He had managed to shove thoughts of his only son out of conscious memory for longer than he would have believed possible. *Can't afford distractions.* He put an emphasis just short of anger into his sending, *Just go back to scanning, Imorelda. If we lose this war, every human of our world will die. And these* alsona *don't seem to like cats much, either.*

Imorelda gave Tae just enough mental sending to demonstrate her displeasure with him, before going back into listening mode.

Tae found himself hopelessly entwined with thoughts of Subikahn. He remembered romping with his son, the boy's cherubic cheeks shining, and the day toddler Subikahn had discovered Imorelda's eyes. The poking had not endeared him to her, and it had taken six scratchings to teach Subikahn not to pull her tail or try to cut her whiskers. Imorelda did not like children; she had made that abundantly clear. Yet, once Subikahn turned six or seven, they had become close friends. She would chase him through the fields of Stalmize, finding him rodents and butterflies to capture and bring triumphantly home.

In later years, whenever Subikahn sneaked into the kitchen for snacks, much to the staff's chagrin, he always snagged a bit of meat or cheese for Imorelda. For her, Subikahn could do no wrong. And, once, it was the same for his father.

Violently, Tae drove the thought from his mind, forcing himself to absorb every nuance of communication with a single-mindedness that precluded other thought. When a mind-call finally did come through, the intensity of his concentration turned it into a shout that echoed painfully through his mind. *Firuz wants all second-level commanders in his quarters at sunrise.* Tae's heart rate doubled. The moment had come. The *Kjempemagiska* had called a strategy meeting. Now, Tae only had to figure out a way to be there when it happened.

Queen Matrinka paced the rooftop of Béarn Castle, peering down over the Southern Sea. She no longer noticed the bunched, gray warships or the squealing gulls overhead; and the salt wind whipping off the sea no longer bothered her. Her gaze could not pick out the tiny speck that represented Tae and his flotsam raft, and the mind-calls she sent repeatedly to Imorelda went unanswered. She had known their mental bond would not endure at such a distance; she had had to stay reasonably close to Mior to hear her, too. But Matrinka felt she had to try.

The hatch flopped opened. Accustomed to guardsmen coming and going, Matrinka paid it no heed until she recognized her oldest child, Marisole, poking her head through the opening. Gracefully, the nineteen-year-old swung up through it to join her mother on the rooftop. Placing a hand over her eyes to shade them, Marisole peered into the dingy daylight. "You can't see him from here, you know."

"Who?" Matrinka asked innocently.

"Who?" Marisole struck a distinctly adolescent pose, one hand on her hip, her brows arched. "Mama, if you could see King Tae from here, the folks on the ships could see him, too, couldn't they?"

Matrinka sighed. Years had passed since she could hide anything from Marisole.

"You love him, don't you, Mama?"

Matrinka tore her gaze from the ocean. She had long ago stopped really looking, only stared in mindless habit. "Of course, I love him, Marisole. He's been a close friend for many years, long before either of us became . . . rulers."

"So how come you and he never . . . ?" Marisole made a gesture that Matrinka could not fathom.

"Tae and I never . . . what?"

"Never courted. Never married." Marisole's dark eyes demonstrated a sincerity Matrinka would never have expected for such a foolish question. She had to remind herself that Marisole had not lived the youthful interactions between her parents and their companions, had no personal experience with love and true commitment. For all her knowledge and study, Marisole did not yet understand relationships.

Matrinka remained patient, as usual. "Marisole, I love Tae like a brother, never like a lover. He adored my closest friend, and I was in love with—"

"—my father," Marisole finished.

Matrinka would not lie. "No, not with your father. I didn't even know Griff, then."

"I'm sorry. That came out all wrong. I meant with my blood father," Marisole said matter-of-factly. "With Darris."

Matrinka stared as her blood grew gradually colder in her veins. She knew this day might come, but she had always hoped to avoid it. "Marisole," she said carefully, "why do you say that?"

Marisole raised one shoulder. "Because it's the truth, right? You loved Darris."

"I did," Matrinka admitted. "I still do. But why are you denouncing your wonderful father?" She took a closer look at her growing daughter. Marisole looked more like Darris with each passing day: the generous nose, the streak of green in her eyes, the full and sensuous lips.

"I'm not denouncing him," Marisole said defensively. "He's the best father in the world, and he's made some extraordinary children." A smile tugged the corners of her mouth. She tipped her head up to Matrinka, and she clearly wanted the truth, obviously needed it.

Over the decades, Matrinka had found peace in understanding Darris' drive to know everything, had come not only to accept his need to use song when imparting knowledge, but to revel in listening to it. Marisole, she knew, suffered the same affliction.

"But I've studied enough to know the bardic curse is passed through blood, from bard to oldest child, through eternity. I can't speak for Arturo . . ." Marisole choked on her brother's name. "Nor for Halika. But I know for an indisputable fact that I am the blood child of Bard Darris."

Matrinka said nothing.

Marisole pressed, "Aren't I?"

Matrinka could not lie to her daughter. "You are."

Marisole continued to study her mother, speaking slowly. "Have you and Papa ever . . . shared . . . a bed?"

Matrinka turned away. "That's an awfully personal question."

"Mama!" A hint of anger entered Marisole's tone. "I have a right to know."

Matrinka shook her head, not looking at her eldest daughter. "You have the right to know about your bloodline. Not about my . . . bedroom."

"Mama."

When Matrinka continued to ignore her, Marisole continued. "All right, then. Here's what I know and what I believe based on the facts I've studied. Papa's parents were exiled from Béarn because they had an illegal relationship. They were too closely blooded for marriage, but they had sex anyway."

Matrinka whipped back around. "Marisole, language!"

Undeterred, Marisole continued, "Papa's worried about that; he thinks he's flawed in his head. He's never had proper faith in his cleverness. He believes he's 'slow-witted,' and it's due to his close-blooded parents. So, when the populace demanded he marry his Cousin Matrinka, he was afraid to make babies because they'd be closer-blooded even than him. And they might turn out like . . . Ivana."

"Marisole!" Matrinka could not believe her daughter would dare say anything negative about Griff's unfortunate elfin daughter.

"Well, it's true." Marisole did not back down. "I love Ivana, Mama; I really do. But let's be honest. No one deliberately sets out to create a child like her, do they? I mean, no expectant mother in the history of the world ever said, 'I hope my baby is unintelligent, drooling, and incapable of speech.' It's not like Papa and Tem'aree'ay have tried to make more offspring."

Matrinka found it impossible to argue, though she still refused to support the point. "What are you trying to say?"

"I'm saying I believe Darris fathered Arturo, Halika, and me, with Papa's blessing." Marisole's stance softened. "That's right, Mama, isn't it?"

Matrinka finally understood Marisole's consternation. She did not want to think her mother was a wanton woman who had deceived and cheated on her father. "Every bit of it." Matrinka sighed. "But I wish you wouldn't tell your little sister yet. I'd rather she never knew, like . . ." Tears flooded Matrinka's eyes before she could stop them. She had not realized her grief remained so raw. She forced herself to choke out the name, ". . . Arturo."

Marisole wrapped her mother in a hug. "I didn't mean to bring that up."

Matrinka nodded, returning the embrace and trying to regain control. It came easier each time. "You didn't do anything wrong, Marisole."

"What about . . . Barrindar?"

Their closeness muffled Marisole's words, and she had also spoken unusually softly. Matrinka was not sure she had heard right. She released her eldest daughter and took a step backward. "You mean *Prince* Barrindar? Your brother?"

"He's not really my brother, is he?"

"Half brother," Matrinka conceded. "But that's close enough, isn't it? You're all siblings; halves shouldn't matter. I don't think you should treat him any differently than you did . . ." She still had to force out the name, ". . . Arturo."

Marisole pursed her lips. Apparently, she was not getting the answers she wanted. "Princess Xoraida wasn't consorting with the bard, too, was she?"

The coarseness of the question surprised Matrinka. She made a mental note to have a serious discussion with Marisole regarding her decorum, but not now. Matrinka did not want to stifle the current conversation; she suspected something important and not yet uncovered lay at the heart of it. "Of course not. But as far as anyone is concerned the king is your father. And Barri's, too."

Marisole's expression turned grim with frustration, and she blurted out, "But Mama, we're not siblings by blood at all. Not even half siblings."

Matrinka wondered why so many people placed such an importance on blood relations. Best friends often grew closer than siblings, and one's truest deepest love rarely shared any blood at all. In fact, the less the better. "Marisole, bloodline's not important. You love him like a brother, don't you?"

Marisole kicked at the stone flooring. Béarn Castle was carved from the very mountains against which it nestled. "No, Mother, I don't. Not . . . like a brother . . . exactly."

A light dawned suddenly, and Matrinka understood. She felt like a fool for taking so long to figure out her daughter's need. "You and Prince Barrindar? Barrindar—"

"—and me, yes, Mother."

The thought horrified Matrinka. "You haven't done anything—"

"—illegal? No. But we have . . . we've kissed. And we'd like permission to court."

Court? "Marisole, you're just too . . . just too . . . young." Matrinka realized she sounded ridiculous the moment the words left her mouth. The issue was not age; it was incest.

Taking her mother at her word, Marisole grinned. "When you were my age, you were married with a child."

"Yes . . . but . . ."

"But what?"

"I want a better life for you, Marisole."

For a moment, Marisole only stared. Then, she started laughing. It grew from a chuckle to a torrent in an instant, and even Matrinka could not help smiling.

At length, Marisole caught enough breath to speak. "All right, Mother. Let's say for a moment that the destruction of all mankind didn't lay at our feet right now. You're the queen of the most powerful country in the Westlands. You have two healthy daughters. And, while I'll grant you Arturo's death was a calamity, you can hardly blame that on the age at which you courted. The populace, the whole world, loves you. If my life was any happier than yours, I'd be in a constant state of delirium."

Matrinka's grin could not last. As it faded, she pulled Marisole into a much looser embrace and rocked her ever so slightly. "You're right, Marisole. Bloodwise, you're not that close, and Prince Barrindar is very sweet." She shook her head at the enormity of understanding behind that simple statement. "But getting my blessing's not enough. You still have to convince your father, Barri's mother, and the Council, which includes Bard Darris. Even then, you have to consider the populace; the price of being royalty is that you're both ruler of, and property of, your people. And, no matter what you've figured out about your bloodline, they believe you're half siblings."

Marisole allowed her mother the moments of babying. "We've thought of all of that. And more."

"More?" Matrinka cupped her daughter's face. A long time had passed since teenaged Marisole had allowed her this much contact.

"I'm the next bard," Marisole reminded. "That eventually makes me the bodyguard of the ruler of Béarn. What if the test chooses Barri? Would he let me guard him; or would he try to protect me instead?" Marisole's shoulders rose and fell in resignation. "Worse, what if the test picked me? Would I have to guard myself?"

Matrinka knew no similar situation had ever presented itself because the bard's line and the royal line had always remained distinctly separate. In fact, Darris was Pudarian on both sides of his family as far back as history recorded. "I know we seem old to you, but your parents are not yet decrepit. Griff could rule till he's a hundred, gods willing. Darris might guard him into his own dotage."

"That would make things easier for us," Marisole said plainly, responsibly. "But I'm trying to consider the worst possible cases; because if I prepare for them, I'm ready for anything." She turned serious. "Mother, it's possible that neither of them will survive this war. Or Barri, either."

"Oh, honey." Matrinka could barely contemplate the thought. She had heard Tae's report. She, and only a handful of others, knew the truth. If the continental allies lost this war, no one of their world would survive. The *alsona* would kill every last one of them: man, woman, or child. She would not burden Marisole with that knowledge, not now. She had enough for any adolescent to deal with. "Griff's not a fighting king. He'll remain behind the lines, and Darris is pledged to stay at his side. Prince Barrindar's not a warrior either; and he's too young and valuable to risk. The loss of even one life is a tragedy, but those three are more likely than most to survive."

Marisole forced a smile that looked more like a grimace. "You'll understand if I want to spend as much time as possible with Barri?"

Matrinka understood. The two could not present their case to the king or the Council until the war had ended; and, by then, one or both of them might die. *We all might die.* The thought became a dark, grim noose that she could barely contemplate. Matrinka could still recall the burning desire she had felt for Darris as a teen, a love that still flared inside her at the mere thought of him. The law prevented them from courting, from marrying, yet that had not stopped them. The flame was too hot, the need too great, to bow to laws and family. "Thanks for talking to me instead of sneaking around behind my back."

Marisole nodded and smiled hopefully.

"The intent of the royal incest law is to prevent the line of kings from becoming too inbred, just as other laws exist to keep it from straying from the god-blessed Béarnian blood that keeps the West in balance."

Marisole understood more than Matrinka expected. "You mean the law that kept you and Darris from marrying."

"Yes," Matrinka admitted. "Which is why it's unlikely the heir-test will select you or Halika."

"Or Ivana."

Matrinka bobbed her head. "The Council already decreed before Ivana's birth that no child born of an elf could take the throne."

"So, there's about a one-in-three chance that, if Barrindar and I are allowed to marry, Bard Darris will have to guard his own son-in-law-by-blood. Or I could be in the position of faithfully guarding my own husband." Marisole turned her mother a pleading look that spoke volumes.

Matrinka sighed. The queen understood so much more that Marisole had, apparently, not yet considered. To obtain permission for such a courtship meant announcing Matrinka's infidelity, which might violate significant law of its own. It might also subject Darris to serious, perhaps even capital, punishment. To protect them, Griff would have to admit his complicity, which could bring justice down upon his head as well.

All three had been very young when they spawned the agreement, the eldest only Marisole's current age. At the time, Matrinka had only wanted to dodge a loveless marriage, to couple with the man she truly loved. Although she had considered the danger and consequences since, the worst she had anticipated was the need to lie or to explain the deception to their children. It had never, in her wildest imaginings, occurred to her that her children might want to consort with siblings, like-blooded or not.

Nevertheless, Matrinka knew forbidding young love would only make it flare brighter, become infinitely more sure and desperate. Had Griff insisted on sharing her bed, she would have done her duty and never disgraced their marriage. However, she would have lived in the constant dark depths of depression, longing forever for her husband's bard bodyguard. Always tantalizingly in sight and always forbidden.

"Marisole, spend the time you have with the one you love; but you must keep it secret. I know some herbs that can help keep you . . . safer."

"Safer?"

Matrinka blushed, weighing her words.

As usual, Marisole blurted the ones Matrinka so cautiously tried to avoid. "To keep me from getting pregnant, you mean?"

Matrinka bit her lip. Now was not the time for pussyfooting or a lesson in manners. "You can*not*, under any circumstances, allow that to happen. Even I can't help you, then. Do you understand?"

"Yes." Marisole looked her mother full in the eyes. "I'll use your herbs. Faithfully, I promise."

That did not satisfy Matrinka. "They're not foolproof, Marisole. It's better if you don't take things that far." Under ordinary circumstances, Matrinka would have demanded abstinence. Good women did not have intercourse before marriage. Even she had waited, though she could hardly give lectures on marriage and bedroom protocol. While staring down annihilation, even the most moral citizens of the continent might choose to engage in one last act of love or lust. She doubted many soldiers, married or single, would go to war with their manhood unsated.

"We'll be careful," Marisole promised. "In every way."

Matrinka's gaze drifted back to the ocean, and her concerns for Tae resurfaced. She did not wish to discuss the matter further. "The Council, and your father, have enough to worry about right now. If we win the war, we'll talk more about this."

Marisole fairly danced. "Thank you, Mother."

"Don't thank me yet." Matrinka turned her attention back to the sea. "Your behavior over the next weeks or months will determine whether or not I continue to assist you. And, if you get caught, you're on your own."

"We'll be discreet," Marisole promised. "Secret and careful."

Matrinka bowed her head. The whole conversation seemed trivial when the fate of the entire world hung in the balance. Yet, for Marisole, she knew, it meant everything. If the prince and princess of Béarn were going to die young, they should at least do so in loving arms.

CHAPTER 42

A spy's job is to remain invisible and inaudible—to hold the ene-my's fate in his hands.
                                                              —*General Santagithi*

CROUCHED ON HIS BIT of ship wood in the shadows of the largest warship, Tae Kahn watched rowboats arrive from the other, clustered ships, each containing two or three men. One by one, their rowers called mentally for the lines. A team of sailors dropped hook-ended ropes that the newcomers fastened to giant iron eyelets on either end of their boats. The sailors hauled the occupants up the hull and over the gunwales, where they disappeared from Tae's sight. Moments later, the rowboats fluttered back down, minus an occupant. The man or men remaining freed their crafts and headed back toward their own ships.

When it became clear that the only mind-calls would come from rowboaters needing a lift, Imorelda dropped her coverage and spoke directly to Tae, *You're going to do something stupid, aren't you?* She stood beside him, lashing her tail.

Tae continued to watch, digging out the mahogany-colored wig from his supplies and placing it carefully on his head. *Don't I al-ways?* He counted five generals and no more approaching boats. He guessed each man might command ten thousand men. Assum-ing the *Kjempemagiska,* the one they called Firuz, did not directly control a unit of his own, the *alsona* army might consist of as many as fifty thousand men. *Fifty thousand.* Tae shook his head. The conti-nental armies might wind up with nearly as many by the time they all gathered, but under many divergent commanders and banners. The *alsona,* he felt sure, would act with an easy coordination the diverse-background allies could never match.

The cat's tail thrashed harder. *Well, don't expect me to risk my furry neck with you. You can be stupid all by yourself.*

Tae frowned, still calculating. When he put all his knowledge together, combined with logic, he guessed the ships would carry a half measure of sailors, led by the ship's captain, and a half measure of soldiers, led by a commander of some named rank. *All right, Imorelda. Don't come.*

The cat's head jerked toward him, and the tail grew even faster and more jagged in its movement. *You're not even going to try to talk me into it?*

Why would I? You're an intelligent creature; you can make your own decisions. Tae held out his arms. *Matrinka's been wanting a replacement for Mior, and I imagine one castle's the same as another for a cat.*

Imorelda paced a half circle to face Tae, then sat. Only the tip of her tail kept twitching. *What do you mean?*

Mean? Tae shrugged. *Isn't it obvious? If I attempt to interact with them but can't send or receive mind messages, they'll know I'm not one of them despite my brilliant disguise.* He adjusted the wig.

Imorelda stared.

Before they kill me, I'll try to send as much information to you as I can, assuming I can reach you. You take the information back to Matrinka and live the rest of your life with her. Tae tried to look all innocence. *And all her cats, of course. Oh, and your own darling kittens.*

The hair stood up on Imorelda's back, and she hissed. *You don't have to curse me. I'm coming.*

If you insist. Tae looked at the sky. A crescent moon hung, veiled behind a cottony network of clouds. At the horizon, a pink sky peeked through gossamer strands of blue. *For now, you can sit on my shoulders. Eventually, though, you'll have to stay hidden on their ship.* Tae tried to think of a safe place to put her, but he drew a blank. She made too big a bulge beneath his clothing, whether at the abdomen or back; and she would surely move and give herself away. *Can you do that?*

Imorelda licked a paw and used it to straighten her whiskers. *Can I do that?* Disgust radiated clearly through the words. If she had a speaking voice, she would certainly have mocked him. *A human asking a cat if she can hide. It's like me asking you if you can manage walking on your hind legs.* She turned her back on Tae again. *Cats have been the mistresses of stealth since long before humans existed. Cats twenty times my size would stalk and kill humans before they knew they were being hunted.* She snorted. *Can I hide?*

Tae had no idea where that information came from. He doubted cats had existed longer than humans, and he could not imagine one twenty times her size. *Big as a pony.* But Imorelda still had a worthwhile point. *Sorry, Mistress of Stealth. Just make sure you don't hide so well that I can't find you.*

You'll find me if I want you to find me. Imorelda clambered delicately up Tae's chest and arms to spread herself across his shoulders. *I'm not going to get wet, am I?*

Sensing genuine concern in the question, Tae did not joke. *I'll do my best to keep you dry. Just, please, don't panic if you take a splash or two.*

Tae felt her shudder. Imorelda did not like water in general, but she had taken a particular dislike to the salty variety. Or, perhaps, it had more to do with the vastness of the ocean. He imagined tumbling off a merchant ship into the dark and icy depths, watching the ship glide away, oblivious to her loss. Surrounded by water; nothing to drink. A world of fish; nothing to eat. A man would die of exposure or thirst or drowning long before he could swim to shore or find another ship. To a cat, it had to seem the worst death of all.

Looking out for boats, Tae paddled toward the stern. The first edge of sun was just touching the horizon. The meeting had likely not started yet, but he hoped the generals had settled into closed quarters rather than standing on the deck gabbing in the cold morning breeze. *Imorelda, please. I need you to focus again.*

Tae received no reply. Apparently, Imorelda was already scanning, but the *alsona* were mentally silent. An idea came to him, based on his previous thoughts. He prodded the cat with a finger.

She looked at him.

Uncertain whether Imorelda was set on his mind level, or theirs, he spoke aloud. "Can you bring my mind speech to a place where only one man can 'hear' me?"

Imorelda gave no reply.

Just as Tae assumed she had not heard him, and prepared to repeat the question, she finally answered. *Maybe I could. If he was the nearest of them and away from the others.*

Tae would have liked a more definitive answer, but doubted one was possible. Aside from the elves, Imorelda, Matrinka, and himself, no one on the continent had any experience with mental communication. He supposed he could have gone to Tem'aree'ay for advice, but he doubted Griff's elfin wife could have helped him much, if at all. Tae had already noticed significant differences between the *alsona*'s mind conversation and the elves' *khohlar*. *Good enough, Imorelda. It won't ruin everything if more than one sailor hears me. It'll just make things a bit more difficult.*

You mean 'make the incredibly stupid a bit more impossible?'

Tae smiled. *Exactly.* Then he became serious. His plan would require him to kill an innocent man, albeit an enemy, in cold blood. And, while fully justified by war, it still bothered him. Tae tried to shake the last modicum of guilt with the teachings of his father: "Thought is a man's greatest gift and also his most dangerous enemy. For, though it can save you from any situation, *any* situation, it can also paralyze you with fear or horror or guilt. Hesitation has killed many a killer and stolen many a thief."

No hesitation, Tae reminded himself. *Bold and sure.* Hoping Imorelda had gone back to scanning, he spoke to her directly. "Hang on. I'm going to need my hands to climb." Realizing the opening he had just given her, he clarified. "Try not to dig your claws through my neck veins, please. If I bleed to death, we're both plunging into the ocean."

Imorelda gave him a warning jab in the right shoulder but did not bother to reply.

Tae paddled flush to the lead ship's bow, but found nothing on which to hook his flotsam boat. He had no choice but to abandon it, and the pack with their remaining rations, which meant he would have to either find more debris or swim to shore. He believed he could make it, but Imorelda would have to balance on his back, despising and complaining every moment.

Tae nestled his fingers against the wood, pleased to find easy hand- and toeholds amid the barnacles and mollusks clinging to the sides. He moved quickly, concerned about putting his full weight on any bit for longer than an instant. Sailors cursed the job of cleaning the hull, but enough scraping broke even the most tenacious creatures free.

The hull curved outward, then inward, providing an uncomfortable shelf beneath the gunwale that allowed Tae a brief respite. He regrouped there, crouched below sight of the deck. The moon played through the riggings, turning the brown sails to iridescent bronze. When he craned his neck around the bulge above his shelf, Tae caught a glimpse of a sailor messing with the main sail shrouds. He found no one else in his line of vision.

Tae checked his pockets, already knowing what he ought to find. He always traveled light, more so when he could tumble into the ocean at any moment. Now, he carried the wig on his head, a knife, and a few coins seized from the two captured pirates. Those would give him an air of authenticity should he need it. His other pocket held a fist-sized gemstone that Matrinka had insisted he take. Tae knew the *alsona* would not allow him to buy his way out of anything;

if they wanted the gem, they would simply kill him and take it. If they didn't, they would kill him and leave it. Either way, it did him no earthly good.

Yet, now, Tae found a purpose for it. He smiled, clutching it in his fist. "Imorelda, listen."

I'm here, the cat said mournfully. *Where else could I be?*

Tae could feel the claws pressing through his clothing into his upper back. *Try to carry my voice just to that sailor near the main mast.*

Imorelda shifted position, and Tae lowered his center of gravity to keep from losing his balance. *I see one man. Near that rope tangle.*

Only Imorelda would see a perfectly woven ladderwork and consider it a "tangle." Tae knew they were probably looking at the same man. With the ships at anchor, the *alsona* only needed one sailor working at the mainsail before sunrise.

Tae nodded, still worried he might catch Imorelda in the wrong phase and accidentally broadcast conversations meant only for her. "If you're ready."

Imorelda loosened her claws long enough to pat his cheek in reply, then ratcheted them back into his flesh.

Man overboard! Tae tried to put panic into his sending. *Help!*

A worried voice entered Tae's head, *Where are you, friend?*

The flaw in Tae's plan became immediately clear. With Imorelda's aid, his sending might reach only one person; but the sailor's reply could possibly travel farther.

Starboard stern. Tae appreciated the days he had spent listening to dull sailor talk. It had given him the *alsona* vocabulary he needed. *Please hurry. I can't hold out much longer.* Rising, he gripped the gemstone tightly in his right fist.

Tae heard running footfalls on the deck. A head and torso appeared suddenly around the gunwale, looking into the water.

With all the strength he could muster, Tae rose up and slammed the gemstone against the sailor's left temple. Surprise registered in the man's dark eyes, then he collapsed across the railing.

That wasn't nice.

Tae ignored Imorelda. The gem crashed against the *alsona*'s head a second time with a sickening crack, stone against skull. Bracing for the weight, Tae slid the limp form over the railing to ease it, as gently as possible, onto his sloping ledge. Blood twined between Tae's fingers and made a sticky tangle in the other man's reddish hair.

Swiftly, Tae wiped his hand and the gemstone on the hem of his own shirt, then tore off a huge piece.

⋆What are you doing?⋆

⋆Get down, Imorelda.⋆ Tae barely waited for her to obey before whipping off his cloak. He secured the piece of fabric around the *alsona*'s head to cover the wound he had created.

Imorelda paced around them. *⋆What are you doing?⋆* She poked her furry face into the *alsona*'s. *⋆You've practically killed him, and now you're tending his wounds?⋆*

Tae did not want to lose his focus but knew he had to answer the cat or field an ever increasing number of questions. He still needed her to keep him tuned to the *alsona* or risk missing important announcements that might determine his knowledge or survival. *⋆I'm not tending anything. I'm just trying to keep blood off my new clothes.⋆* Tae refused to think of the *alsona* as human, only as an enemy. Even as he did, Tae realized the irony of the strategy, the same one the *alsona* used to justify slaughtering the people of the Westlands. *⋆Imorelda, stay on their level, for now. You need to keep in touch, so we don't lose each other, but I also have to make sure no one has noticed this man's absence.⋆*

Carefully, Tae worked to strip the man of his foreign clothing. The belt came off first, leather with several small, stitched pockets, each holding an item: a utility knife, a handkerchief, rolled twine, a smear of pitch folded into a thick scrap, a few copper coins, dull metal pins, and some small hooks. All things a sailor might use, stored in convenient locations. Tae made a mental note to see if his tailors could fashion something similar for the Eastern navy.

Aside from the belt, and deceptively light cloth shoes, the clothing came off in a single piece that covered the arms, legs, and torso; it fastened with hooks and eyelets in the front. The whole seemed more suitable for sleep than work, except for the fabric itself. It looked and felt like cotton but with a strange, diagonal double-weave that made it thick, tough, and resistant to tearing. Dyed indigo, it hid most stains, including whatever droplets of blood Tae might have missed. The bottom of the pants flared outward, which, Tae supposed, made them easy to doff in an emergency. It also allowed the wearer to roll them all the way above the knee should warm weather or wet conditions require it.

Matrinka had suggested Tae wear captured clothing from *alsona* killed in the shore skirmishes. Now, Tae was glad he had refused. As he expected, the sailor's garb little resembled the armor of the attacking soldiers, or even their underpadding. It would have taken him much longer to change, because he would have had to doff battle gear, soaked through and unfamiliar in its latching, before dressing.

Instead, it took him only a moment to switch clothing, even with his fingers stiff from cold.

The suit fit reasonably well, a bit generous in all parts, but surprisingly comfortable. The shoes molded to the shape of his feet, skimpy on the sides and top but thickly soled to protect them from riggings and loose bits of wood or metal on the deck. Tae had to add a hole to the belt to keep it from sliding off his hips. He finally glanced at the limp and naked *alsona*, seeing no signs of life. Imorelda had declared him "practically dead," and Tae trusted the cat's judgment. The wound was clearly lethal. Even if he had survived it, the impact with ocean would finish him, and he would sink like a stone without means to protect his airway.

Tae knew he had to work quickly. As the sun came fully up, his actions might become visible to the *alsona* aboard the other ships. Careful not to tip his own balance, he shoved the body into the sea. The plop of its landing disappeared beneath the normal creaks and splashes of anchored ships.

Tae motioned for Imorelda to climb back onto his shoulders, and she obeyed. He rechecked his wig, still firmly and properly in place. As he inched to the gunwale, wary of nearby soldiers or sailors who might see him emerge from nowhere, he whispered to the cat. "As soon as we're on board, secrete yourself. Don't let anyone see you, but stay near enough to funnel their mind-words to me. Also, be prepared to leave suddenly."

Without waiting for acknowledgment, Tae popped over the railing, dropped Imorelda to the deck, and tried to appear nonchalant.

Almost immediately, a guttural curse and a set of squeaky wheels broke over the normal sounds of the ship. Tae could hear the sailors' mental chatter, instinctively sifting out mood and content. They spoke of normal, mundane matters; if the general's meeting inconvenienced them in any way, they kept their grumblings private, softly spoken by mouth.

Heart pounding, Tae watched the approaching cart and sailor, wondering if he could truly pass himself off as one of them despite his limited vocabulary. If something went wrong, he would have to kill this man, too. With the sun nearly fully risen, and no good place to hide, it would prove a terrible risk.

The plump, red-faced sailor pushing the cart caught sight of Tae and stopped.

Tae held his breath.

"Do you mind giving me a hand?" The voice held just a hint of irritation, as if he had expected Tae to volunteer rather than wait for an invitation.

"Not at all." Tae mimicked the accent with practiced ease and headed toward the sailor. "Is it going to the generals' meeting?"

"Yeah." The sailor grunted as they both put their hands on the bar. "Can't discuss strategy without stuffing their faces with the best we've got."

Tae chuckled. The problem had less to do with the weight of the cart than its poor construction and maintenance. The wheels needed oil.

The *alsona* glanced over at Tae. "I've never seen you before. Did you come with one of the generals?"

Tae continued to read tone as well as words. The man seemed curious, not accusatory, but Tae still felt his chest squeeze. "Yes." He described one of the men he had seen coming in the rowboats. "Tall guy. Narrow face. Short beard."

"General Fallon?"

Tae sure hoped he wasn't being tested. "You know him?"

The plump man spit. "Know them all by now. It's not like there're a lot of them." He stopped pushing and motioned for Tae to do the same. "Thanks. Can you make sure it doesn't roll while I open the hatch?"

"Sure," Tae said. He got an idea. "In fact, I'll carry the food down for you, if you want to get back to doing other things."

Hand on the hatch ring, the sailor turned toward Tae. "Really? You'd do that."

"Why not? You're working, and I'm doing nothing but waiting."

"All right." The sailor smiled. "Thanks. That would be great." He hesitated. "Oh, hell. I'm going to be honest with you. They're hard to please."

Tae shrugged. "I'll deal with it."

"You're sure?"

"I'm sure. I'm used to serving General Fallon. I know how they think."

"Thanks." The sailor hauled on the hatch. Only faint mumbling emerged from below. Apparently, the generals conversed aloud to keep their discussion private. From Tae's experiences the last several days, he had expected that. This once, it would work to his advantage; he would not need Imorelda's help to eavesdrop. "I owe you."

Tae prepared to ease the basket of foodstuffs and wine from the cart.

"I can help you, at least," the sailor offered, still apparently feeling guilty.

Tae hesitated. He did not know exactly how to keep the generals talking with him in the room, aside from requests, demands, and complaints about the foodstuffs and his service. The only thought that came to him would involve an act Imorelda and Matrinka would call "exceedingly stupid"; but, first, he needed to learn a new phrase in the *alsona*'s language.

Tae hefted the basket, finding it heavier than he expected, and deliberately placed himself into the sailor's path. As he intended, the sailor bumped him. Tae exaggerated the impact, stumbling several steps and juggling the basket.

The sailor apologized, catching hold of the basket to steady it in Tae's grasp. Tae focused on the sailor's words and tone as he tried to make the simple act of catching his balance look difficult.

"That's all right." Tae glanced down the open hatch, eyes widening. "I probably only would have broken my neck."

The sailor gave a more profuse apology, bowing slightly as he did so. "I really am sorry. Why don't I just do it?"

Tae waved him off. "I've got it, and I'm fine. If you could just close the hatch behind me, please."

"Sure. Least I can do."

Tae took a solid grip on the basket. He moved confidently now, not wanting the sailor to insist on taking the job back. He now knew how to apologize, and he expected to do a whole lot of that in the next few moments. He edged down the ladder, placing his feet as carefully as possible. As his head went below the deck, the sailor gently and quietly closed the hatch.

As he did so, something soft brushed Tae's cheek. He stiffened for an instant before dismissing it as a wad of dust or a cobweb, a last breath of wind funneled through the closing hatch. Then, something scraped against his right ankle. Tae twisted away from it. The momentum of the basket threw off his usually impeccable timing. His foot touched down on empty air instead of the rung he expected. His free hand caught another too hard, slamming painfully against iron, and he felt himself starting to fall.

Instinctively, Tae let go of the basket to secure his hand- and toe-holds. Abruptly realizing he might garner a bit more sympathy and less rage if he went down with it, he went against every survival trick he ever knew and followed the plummeting basket. *Look out!* he tried to send in warning.

Bottled wine, bread, and crockery tumbled from the falling basket, bouncing from the iron rungs. Glass chimed against metal. Splashed with bits of glass and droplets of liquid, Tae covered his face and throat as he fell, hoping to land as nearly on his feet as possible.

Tae hit the ground hard, tumbling through a mess of butter, squashing a fine white loaf, and feeling hunks of glass pressing into his skin. He landed, face first, in the basket, which skidded across the floor.

A deafening silence followed.

Careful not to dislodge his wig, Tae freed himself from the basket to look at the generals. The nearest three had leaped from their seats, wine puddling at their feet. Four remained at a large table that contained three oil lamps and a large map of the southern, eastern, and western coasts of Tae's continent. Tae's gaze lingered longest on the being at the head of the table. Seated, he towered over the others, even the standing generals. Tae guessed he was at least half again as tall as King Griff. He had coarse features, his nose obscenely broad and bulbous, his ears as big as a man's hand, and his jaw as wide as the top of his head. He stared at Tae through narrowed dark eyes, his wide lips drawn tight in a frown.

Tae scrambled to his feet, apologizing at least twenty times as he bowed repeatedly, lower each time. He tried to simulate the sailor's most conciliatory tone and added at the end, "I couldn't possibly be more sorry, and I will clean up every bit of this mess immediately."

The giant, obviously Firuz the *Kjempemagiska* growled out, "What's your name, sailor?"

Tae swallowed hard, not having to feign fear. He knew from his conversations in the dungeon that the *Kjempemagiska* would not hesitate to tear an *alsona* in half, burn him alive, or roll him in a vat of scalding acid. He did not fully understand their conventions of naming. It seemed best to use a name he already knew was *alsona*. He kept his head low, dodging the giant's gaze. "Jaxon, my lord."

"Well, Jaxon. Perhaps after you've cleaned this mess and are prepared to bring us more food, you'll have the wisdom to make two trips."

That's it? The *Kjempemagiska* did not seem nearly as cruel as the imprisoned *alsona* had suggested. *I don't suppose they can punish every infraction with death. Otherwise, they would lose their servants: if not to murder, then to paralyzing fear, escape, or mutiny.* "Yes, my lord. Thank you, my lord. How wise of you, my lord."

Tae set to the task of cleaning, attempting to appear eagerly efficient while actually lingering over the task.

The standing generals retook their seats.

The *Kjempemagiska* went back to business. "They have armies on how many beachfronts currently?"

The general Tae now knew as Fallon responded. "We believe three, my lord. Two on the south coast, with mountains between them, and one on the west coast."

"None on the east?" someone asked incredulously.

Tae casually turned his head toward the table to see one of the generals tracing the coast of his own realm.

"It's wide open."

Another man spoke as Tae returned to picking up the largest shards of glass and laying them in the basket. He had known bringing the Eastern forces westward would open his coast to attack. The *alsona* could take the entire country with little resistance, but the same geographical concerns that kept the East separated from the West most times would come into play.

Another of the generals pointed out what Tae already knew. "Wide open, but essentially useless. This band of mountains cuts the eastern part of the continent off from every other place. There's only one workable pass, and that's guarded by a large force here."

Tae did not have to look to know where "here" was. The East's only connection to the remainder of their world was the pass onto the barren Western Plains, where the Eastern army now massed. He set to gathering the smaller shards of glass. He appreciated the cloth lining the basket; he would not need to go above decks looking for rags to sop up the spillage.

"That could also work as an advantage." A new voice this time. "If we take the eastern quarter of the continent, we can fortify it. So long as we protect that pass, we're safe. Then, once we have magical forces, we can go over the mountains and attack from every direction."

Firuz' voice was ice. "You're awfully free with the lives of your masters, Kalka."

Kalka apologized as profusely as Tae had. "You're right, of course, my lord. I wasn't thinking."

A tense silence settled over the group. Tae paid them no obvious attention, trying to look absolutely absorbed in his work. He could only guess at the details. Apparently, they intended for the *alsona* to fully front the battle, keeping the *Kjempemagiska* safely home until needed. That boded well for the allies, at least until the war reached that critical stage.

Apparently trying to defuse the situation, Fallon cleared his throat. "We haven't checked the northern shores, my lord. North of these mountains . . ."

Northern Weathered Range, Tae filled in, still on the floor working to clean up the mess.

". . . it's uninhabitably cold, by our reckoning."

Except to Northmen, Tae finished. *And they're just crazy.*

"Where, exactly, are the beachfronts?" someone asked. "Here, I assume, for one. And here."

Tae wished he could see where they indicated, but looking too often posed an unaffordable risk.

"Correct," Fallon said. "And the third one's here, on the west side. They have the largest army concentrated here."

Tae knew that corresponded to Béarn.

"They only have about a third as many men here and even fewer here."

The Western Plains and the open west coastline. Tae used the lining cloth, and the napkins, to mop up the spilled wine.

"I'm thinking," Fallon continued, "we could send a diversionary force toward their main body, then hit them hard on the west coast. It might take a week or so for their main force to reach us."

Tae dropped the soaked cloth into the basket, using the remaining napkins to dry up the last of the liquid and the tiniest pieces of glass. He glanced up in time to see Firuz' face locked in a tight grimace.

"No," the *Kjempemagiska* finally said. "We will attack them at their strongest point. If we can't best them there, we will never win this war. And, if we can, we will have won it in a single battle." He added with an actual hint of compassion, "And, in the long run, we will lose fewer soldiers by not splitting our ranks, diversionary or otherwise."

Tae tossed the butter crock and bread into the basket, on top of the sodden linens. If the *alsona* sailors were like his own people, Tae knew they would not worry about the condition of the ruined food, only about the taste. They would snack well on what the generals would no longer touch, so long as they avoided the glass shards.

The generals' conversation descended into strategic details involving the commanders and battalions; and, with his cleaning finished, Tae found it safest to leave. As the discussion became more finely honed, he understood fewer words, especially punctuated by given names, ship names, and titles.

Swiftly, Tae headed up the stairs, through the hatch, and onto the deck, quickly lowering the door behind him. The instant it closed, something bumped against it. Fear seized him. *Did they figure me out? Is someone coming after me?* He drew back into the shadows, watching and waiting, but no one came.

Tae set the basket down as his heart rate subsided to normal.

"Imorelda," he whispered, glad the cat had followed his orders to hide. She had been right to brag about her stealthiness; even in broad daylight, knowing she was aboard, he could not find her.

The cat did not reply, with presence or mental voice.

"Imorelda," Tae called, a bit louder.

A sailor appeared from around the mainmast and studied Tae quizzically. "Did you say something?"

Tae shook his head, frowning. "No. Did you hear something?"

The sailor did not reply, only studied Tae more carefully in the full sunlight. "Who are you?"

Tae thought it best to stick with as much of his story as possible. "Jaxon. I came with General Fallon." He peered about cautiously, hoping he would spot Imorelda, and the sailor would not. *Imorelda,* he mind-called carefully, worried she might still have him attuned to the *alsona*'s level. She would hear him, but they would also.

The sailor continued to stare. He did not seem to notice Tae's call. Yet, suddenly, his expression changed from curious to suspicious. He drew a wicked-looking knife from his belt, its blade curved and serrated. "Answer my question . . . Jaxon."

"I did," Tae insisted. "I told you—" It occurred to him abruptly that the man had asked something mentally. And he had not heard. Which meant Imorelda had dropped the *alsona*'s communication level, she had passed beyond range of their connection, or she was dead. *No.* Tae refused to accept the latter possibility. Then, little things came back to haunt him: the light touch as he descended to the captain's quarters, the lost footing, the bang against the hatch as he closed it. *She followed me down.* A worse realization struck him. *And she's still stuck there.*

Knife leading, the sailor lunged for Tae so suddenly he dodged more from instinct than intent. As he whirled to run, Tae seized the handle of the basket and hurled it toward the sailor. He did not pause to see if it hit. Though he had lost his mental connection, Tae could imagine the call of "intruder" touching every mind above decks.

A grunt reached him, then a cry, followed by the pounding of many footfalls on the deck. Tae risked a glance back as he rounded on the hatch. Men raced toward him from the fore, sailors with knives, soldiers with swords, and even a few dragging out small bowlike weapons to which they were fitting strange, metal arrows. He could scarcely believe they had mobilized so fast.

Tae thought he could make it to the rail, barely, if he did not slow; but he would not leave Imorelda behind. With hardly a thought to his own survival, he snatched at the hatch and jerked it open.

Imorelda emerged, puffed up and hissing. Her mind touched Tae's for an instant, then disappeared as she noticed the crowd bearing down upon them.

Saving her proved Tae's downfall. He twisted as he moved, trying to minimize himself as a target. A sword stroke meant to decapitate him gashed through his right shoulder and slammed against bone. The impact hurled him leftward, saving him from a skewering from a second blade but sending him tripping over the hatch, into an uncontrolled spin toward the port stern.

IMORELDA! Tae screamed, not caring if she had them on *alsona* level. Without solid wood between them, she should hear him. *Grab on, and don't panic!* Easy advice, impossible for either of them to obey. Another blade carved a crazy arc across Tae's back, partially protected by the resilience of the garment he wore.

Imorelda!

Appearing out of nowhere, the cat flung herself at Tae's chest. He caught her without slowing, flinging himself desperately toward the rail. The hammer of footfalls, the shouts of the soldiers and sailors, the lap of the ocean all blended into one indecipherable noise. Then, Tae found himself airborne, falling in a spray of salt water and his own blood. Arrows whizzed around him. One nicked his ear. Another crashed into his back, piercing deep through muscle and into his chest.

Got him! someone crowed.

I'm dead, Tae realized. The peace it brought put the world in slow motion. He heard nothing but a toneless buzz, saw only the vast blueness of the ocean rushing up to claim him, felt nothing but the cold kiss of sea air against his skin. Then, he hit the water with a slap that brought everything back into focus. A mass of arrows fell around him, slowed to a crawl by the thickness of the water, except for the one that pierced his left thigh.

Still clutching Imorelda, Tae dove, watching the water turn scarlet around him. The cat went crazy in his arms, clawing, biting, twisting in a berserk attempt to free herself from the enclosing depths. The more she fought, the tighter Tae winched her, forcing his legs to move. They had to come up in a different spot or risk another hail of arrows or worse. He hoped they would not be able to follow the blood trail. *They may not, but the sharks eventually will.*

In the shadow of the bow, Tae finally dared to surface, still grasping a sodden and deadly ball of fur.

Once she filled her lungs with air, Imorelda finally gained enough composure to speak. *You stupid, stupid two legs! You tried to drown me!*

Tae's every breath was agony. Bloody froth bubbled from his mouth, and his shoulder ached so badly he could barely move. He wanted nothing more than to close his eyes and surrender to darkness, to let death quietly take away the pain. *Imorelda*, he reminded himself. *You have to get her home.* The only thing firmly settled in Tae's mind was that he would not allow a loved one to die for his folly. Imorelda deserved to live, and Matrinka needed the cat for her sanity. *Imorelda, just listen.* Tae let his head sink backward, allowing the ocean to bear its weight. *Tell Matrinka they have five generals and one magical leader.*

Imorelda climbed onto Tae's uninjured shoulder, shaking out the water. *Tell her your damned self.*

Tae appreciated that the mental conversation did not require breathing. He could never have gasped out that many words. *Imorelda, just listen. Five generals and one magical leader. The whole force will come directly against Béarn. Can you tell her that?*

No, you cat drowner. I'm not telling her anything.

Imorelda. Tae did not have the energy to argue, even in his mind. He dared not move from beneath the bow for fear of another attack.

Quiet! Imorelda commanded.

Tae obeyed gladly, the cat balanced on his shoulder. Her wet fur seemed ten times heavier than normal.

A moment later, Imorelda reappeared in his mind. *They're convinced we're dead.*

Anyone who had seen the arrow pierce him, who noticed the sheer volume of blood in the water, could come to no other conclusion. *They're half right. I won't make it, but I'm going to get you home safely.* Tae kept that thought to himself. *Hang on, Imorelda. I have to tear these clothes. If I don't stop the bleeding, the sharks will come.* The prospect seemed impossible. Tae felt his consciousness fading, and the idea of getting devoured did not seem so bad. At least, the pain would disappear.

Imorelda jabbed Tae with a claw. *So start ripping already. What are you waiting for?*

"I can't," Tae whispered.

Imorelda swiped her paw across his face hard enough to feel like a slap, though she kept her claws sheathed.

Tae opened his eyes; he did not remember closing them.

Get that bleeding stopped. I don't want to be eaten.

As long as the sailors did not make a habit of shoveling fish entrails over the side, Tae knew he had a bit of time before the sharks found them. He just had to stay well away from the man he had killed to buy more time. *I have to do this. For Imorelda. I can't let Imorelda die.* Tae unfastened his one-piece garment and tried to tear it, without success. The sturdy, diagonal double-weave made it nearly impossible. He turned his attention to the shoulder area, where the soldier's sword had cut through the fabric. There, he found better leverage and managed to tear it in half. Cold ocean water seeped over every part of him, reviving and strangely soothing.

Maddeningly slowly, Tae managed to make long strips, which he first stuffed into the hole in his thigh. It felt like torture. Sharp pain racked his entire leg, but he finished the job before winding cloth around the wound to hold the pieces in place.

As he worked, Imorelda shifted around to keep from falling into the water. Apparently, she examined Tae as she did so. *Your shoulder looks like rats have been chewing on it. And there's an arrow sticking out of your back. Want me to try to pull it out?*

Tae could not answer quickly enough. *No! Don't touch it.* He knew what might happen. Moving the shaft could cause the tip to shift, possibly into his heart. He would die instantly. And, even if the worst did not occur, removing it would result in more blood than they might be able to staunch. *Is it bleeding at all?*

Imorelda shifted cautiously. *No.*

Better to leave it, then.

Imorelda finished the sentence, *Until trained healers can get to it?*

Tae nodded, without real consideration. It did not matter if they ever removed it; he was essentially already dead. He only had to survive long enough to get Imorelda to shore.

Your ear's bleeding, too; but not a lot. Want me to direct you?

Please. Tae set to the shoulder first, winding material around it in a bundle. Although the thick sturdiness of the cloth had made it difficult to tear, he now appreciated that it also did a better job of staunching and covering the bleeding. He moved delicately, as much to maintain consciousness as to accommodate the cat. *Have to get Imorelda home.* The thought became an inviolate chant, the only thing keeping him going long after he should have surrendered.

Now the ear, Imorelda prompted.

Tae wound his remaining strip of cloth around his head, binding the right ear tightly against his skull. As he did so, he started looking for pieces of wood, a bit of flotsam, anything to which he might cling. It did not take him long. The pirates had destroyed many Western ships, and hunks of broken hull haunted this part of the sea. Tae threw his arms over a generous hunk of nailed-together boards and steered them toward shore.

CHAPTER 43

Success is the product of the application of good sense to the circumstances of the moment.

—*General Santagithi*

TAE KAHN AWAKENED TO a sudden stabbing pain in his shoulder and a shout echoing through his head. *Wake up! Wake up! Wakeupwakeupwakeup!* Disoriented, he remained utterly still, trying to recall where he was and how he had gotten there. He lay slumped over a timber, floating in water. He had to force his eyelids open; and, when he did, salt stung them mercilessly. Surrounded by the steely grayness of dawn or twilight, he caught a blurry view of ocean and distant shore. *Shore!* *Imorelda, we're almost home.*

But Imorelda, he realized, was facing the other direction, her hackles raised and her claws still embedded in his wounded shoulder. *This way! Danger!*

Pain that racked his body kept Tae from moving quickly. Reluctantly, he turned his head to see a broad dorsal fin slicing the water behind him. It moved erratically, driving toward them, then backing away to return at a different angle. *Shark,* Tae realized, ransacking his brain for all the information he had ever absorbed about the creatures. *Don't panic.* Realizing Imorelda needed to know as well, he sent, *Don't panic.*

The cat minced backward, finally extracting her claws from Tae's wound, to his great relief. *Don't panic? Don't panic? There's a killer fish about to rip us to pieces, and I'm not supposed to panic? Fish aren't supposed to eat cats; cats are supposed to eat fish.* She paused an instant, breathing heavily. *I'm panicking, damn it. I'm panicking.*

Tae ignored her, watching the fin as it settled into a circular motion. Slowly, carefully, he pulled free his knife. Even that small movement hurt. His injuries seemed to have coalesced into one giant, overwhelming ache, and he kept his breathing shallow, to avoid the agony that came with the gasps his body sought. The bleeding from his throat had diminished, probably what had drawn the shark in the first place.

Imorelda, climb off me onto the boards.

The cat gave no notice of having heard him.

The fin dipped.

Imorelda, go!

The shark slammed against Tae and his makeshift float, knocking them apart. The weight of the cat on his shoulders disappeared, and water replaced the fur on the back of his neck. Tae grabbed wildly for support, and his hand scraped against something rougher than unsanded wood, abrading his fingers. *Sharkskin.* He swung the knife. Hilt and fist slammed against a nose hard as rock, and Tae found himself nearly on top of it, staring into a beady, black eye. Slowed by dizziness and exhaustion, Tae attempted to stab it in the eye but managed only to poke it with his fingers. The hilt jarred sideways against its hide, and the blade wrenched loose from Tae's fingers, sinking into the dark depths.

The creature's jaw opened, revealing a morass of teeth.

Certain it could outmaneuver him in water, Tae tried to do the unpredictable, lunging toward the shark rather than attempting escape. At the least, he might buy Imorelda some time. He tried not to think about the fact that she had always avoided water and might not be able to swim.

The shark also charged. Tae tried to grab it, fingers grating over the coarse skin to sink into the gill slits. He found himself nose-to-nose with the monster, only to realize it was, if anything, smaller than he was. This time, the shark fought, hurling its head up and down, gnashing its teeth, trying to free its head from Tae's ever-tightening grip. Weaponless and without even the use of his hands, Tae butted the creature repeatedly, hammering his skull against its rigid nose until his thoughts scrambled and his forehead felt ready to explode.

With a last twist, the shark tore away from Tae's grip. It turned tail, fleeing deep into the ocean, seeking easier prey.

A shiver ripped through Tae, so strong and extensive it reawakened the anguish of every wound. He savored the moment, *I wrestled a shark. And won.* He had never heard of anyone doing such a thing and vowed to add the sensitivity of the gill slits to the current body of knowledge on how to escape a hungry shark. Then, he remembered Imorelda.

Imorelda! Where are you?

I'm here.

Relief flooded Tae. He had no idea where "here" was, but at least he knew she had survived. *Where?* He made a cautious circle, concerned that fast movement might overwhelm his consciousness as well as draw more sharks. He finally found her, a soggy pile of indistinguishable fur huddled on top of the flotsam they had ridden.

Floating on the wood. Hurry. I'm cold, and I'm wet, and I need you.

You don't need me. Tae did not send the thought; it would only upset Imorelda. He reached out a hand to swim toward her, but it felt as heavy as an iron anchor. Air-starved and anguished, he only wanted to remain in place, to sink quietly to the bottom and allow the ocean to claim him. *She can't get to shore without me.* This time, the words scarcely motivated him. Each breath had become a burdensome chore. He had to force himself to move, every tiny tensing of muscle, each motion of joint, seemed as significant as life itself. Tae wondered how many years it might take to reach her.

Tae had somehow managed to span half the distance, when Imorelda's voice reached him. *They're coming.*

Tae did not believe his heart rate could increase; the effort of swimming already had it racing. *Who's coming, Imorelda? Sharks or alsona?*

Imorelda sat up, finally taking the shape of a drenched tabby cat. *People, silly. Our people are coming to rescue us!*

Tae looked toward shore. In his current condition, it seemed too far away to contemplate. On the beach, he could now see the massed armies, looking like vast herds of milling animals, and a few rafts taking to the water. Tae had come too far to let Imorelda die now. *Careful. They may think we're pirates.*

Imorelda gave Tae a scandalized look, at least as much as she could with her feline face and sodden body. *They know who we are. I found Queen Matrinka and talked to her.*

Smart cat. Tae rolled onto his back and settled into a float, no longer fighting toward Imorelda. *So clever.*

I've told you that many times. A hint of concern accompanied her sending, though she clearly tried to rein it. *You have to get saved, too. I don't remember what you told me to tell her. About the enemy.*

You remember. Tae felt his consciousness drifting. The sky grew darker, the ocean colder. Apparently, night was coming, and the blackness beckoned. *You remember . . .*

I don't remember! Imorelda stomped her paws and shook water from her fur. *I wasn't listening. I told you to tell them yourself, and I meant it.*

Can't, Tae thought dreamily.

You have to. I promised Matrinka you would. And I don't remember anything.

It seemed like too much effort to reply, even mentally. A long forgotten lullaby filled Tae's head. He wondered if his mother had once sung it to him, before his father's enemies had murdered her and left him, too, for dead. It came to him in a voice filled with love and sweetness.

Then, abruptly, rough hands plucked Tae from the ocean and jarred him onto a set of lashed together logs. Men speaking Béarnese forced him to sit up, pried open his jaws, and poured water into his mouth. Forced to swallow or drown, Tae drank. "Imorelda," he choked out. "Have to get my cat." A blanket fell on him, heavy enough to bear him down on the raft. Again, the men supported him back to a sitting position.

"Don't worry," one said in Common Trading tongue, though Tae knew Béarnese nearly as well. "They have your cat." Tae did not bother to follow his gesture. "Queen Matrinka would never let us forget a cat, even with the life of a king at stake."

Tae managed a weary smile. "This cat's special. She saved my life, at least twice in just the last few moments." Speaking proved too much effort. Tae slumped into the Béarnides' arms.

"He's badly hurt. We need to get him back quickly." Tae heard one man say. Safe, for the moment, he allowed himself to slip back into unconsciousness.

Tae awakened to exquisite pain piercing his chest and back like a white-hot sword. He screamed before he could gather his wits to bite it back. He attempted to roll, but something pinned him to the ground.

Someone swore. "Hold him still."

Fingers clamped down on Tae's arms and legs. Weights intensified across his sides and buttocks. The world fuzzed into blurry existence. Tae was lying prone on the beach, seeing sand and milling warriors to the extent of his vision. People massed closely around him. A striped paw appeared suddenly in his face and tapped his nose.

Be still, Imorelda commanded. *They're trying to help you.*

New pain seared Tae's spine. Every muscle stiffened, the world returned to a curtain of weaving black and white spots, and he grunted despite himself. *They're killing me.*

Imorelda carried Tae's mind to another plane. *He says it hurts a bit.*

Steeped in agony, Tae did not have the wherewithal to correct the understatement. He clung to consciousness, breathing in quick, short bursts that only intensified the pain.

A gentle hand wiped his brow, swept fingers through the tangles of his hair. "Hang on, Tae. It's almost over."

Tae recognized Matrinka's voice. *What's she doing on the beach? It's not safe for her here.* He managed to gather his thoughts. *Imorelda, tell her what I told you about the plans. Tell her to keep you safe, to keep herself safe. She needs to go back to the palace.*

Imorelda did not reply directly, but she took Tae with her again to address Matrinka. *He says he needs a soldier-man to explain what he heard.*

Assailed by anguish, Tae could not even muster his frustration. *Imorelda, that's not what I said. Tell her what I said.*

He also said do whatever you have to do. He can take it.

Not for the first time, Tae wanted to strangle the cat. *Listen, Imorelda.* He gasped. *Quit playing. This is important.*

Matrinka continued to stroke Tae's head. The pain seemed to lessen in intensity, but he still could not find the strength to speak aloud. *I'm dying, Imorelda. Grant me the dignity of coherent last words.*

Imorelda addressed Matrinka, *My idiot master thinks he's dying.*

Matrinka's hand stilled in Tae's hair. "Dying! Oh, no you don't!" She slapped him.

It was just enough to throw Tae over the edge. All thought and emotion, all sound and sensation disappeared. He seized a tiny shred of awareness, clinging to it, waiting for the rest to reappear. The instant it did, his head filled with Matrinka's angry words. "There's not a lethal wound here, Tae Kahn. Nothing I can't fix, do you hear me?" She grabbed both ears, sending more pain shooting through the injured one, and forced his face into her own. "You . . . are . . . not . . . dying!"

Imorelda, tell her if she doesn't stop manhandling me, she's going to be the thing that kills me.

Imorelda did not pass on the information, to Tae's knowledge, but Matrinka did not attack again. She whispered directly into his left ear. "Listen to me, Tae; and listen good. We can fix these wounds, every one of them. If you die, it's because you choose to. You, no one else. And I'm not going to lie to Subikahn about it. Dying of fatal injuries is one thing; but choosing to die when you don't have to is nothing but cowardice. Do you want me to have to tell Subikahn his father was a coward?"

Tae knew wounds. He had taken far more than his share, and the arrow through his chest had certainly seemed a mortal one. Yet he also knew few healers had Matrinka's experience or talent. Perhaps, in the excitement of the moment, he had misjudged the severity. Whatever else Subikahn did or was, he was always first a Renshai. Nothing would humiliate him more than his own, or his father's, surrendering to fear. He had wanted to toughen Subikahn, not break him. *Tell her, I'll fight to my last breath.*

This time, Imorelda relayed his words exactly.

Tae kept his eyes tightly closed, waiting for the arrival of a general and hoping the need to pass along information would distract him from the healers' excruciating ministrations. Matrinka was right about one thing: dying would be so much easier.

———

Saviar, Subikahn, and Chymmerlee reached Erythane in twilight, not wholly surprised to find a ring of alert guards at the border. They wore tabards emblazoned with Erythane's orange and black and held long spears as well as swords at their hips. Beyond them, Saviar could see the city the Renshai had once known well, had once called home. "Halt!" a guard called, his voice a monotone. He had clearly done this too many times over the last few weeks. "State your names and business."

To Saviar's surprise, Subikahn stepped forward to speak. Usually, he left the orations to his brother. "Saviar and Subikahn Rakhirsson. Our companion is called Chymmerlee. We come in defense of Béarn."

Subikahn Ra-khirsson? Saviar kept the question to himself, for the moment. Subikahn never did anything without reason, though sometimes those reasons confounded his twin.

"Enter." The guards stepped aside, a token gesture. The three newcomers could just as easily have passed between them. The guards' need to cover the entire border left them thinly spread.

As they entered Erythane, Saviar was assailed by a sudden rush of unexpected pleasure. *Home.* He shook away the thought; and, with it, all comfort. *Not home anymore.* Bitterness tinged his memories, and he tried to let all of them go. On the journey, they had decided to enter Béarn proper, from due north. Saviar did not want to veer toward the Road of Kings and despised the thought of even glimpsing the Fields of Wrath and its new occupants.

As they passed beyond the guards' earshot, Subikahn said softly, "That was remarkably easy."

Thoughts still on the Renshai's home for his entire life, Saviar did not grasp his brother's meaning. "What?"

"Anyone could say they've come to Béarn's aid. How did they know I was telling the truth?"

"You weren't," Saviar reminded. "You're not Ra-khir's son; I am."

"You mind?"

"Of course not. It just . . . surprised me." Saviar realized it should not have. Tae Kahn might have already reached Béarn with his Eastern army; and, if they knew Subikahn was his son, word would quickly reach the Eastern king. "Surely a war takes precedence over a family feud."

Subikahn shrugged. "I don't think I want to take that chance."

Saviar thought it best to change the subject before Chymmerlee started asking questions. He suspected there were other reasons Subikahn had lied, not the least of which was his hatred of fawning and attention. If the guards had realized they faced the prince of the Eastlands, they would have abandoned their posts to tend to Subikahn. "At least we know why they let us through so easily. They probably know my father . . . forgive me, *our* father as a knight."

Subikahn brow furrowed. "Maybe." He did not sound convinced. Abruptly, he laughed. "I've got it. We speak Western. The enemy doesn't. Not at all. It's as simple as that."

The three passed through city streets packed with strange tents in a gloom that seemed to smother Erythane. The houses had already gone quiet, shutters and doors tightly bolted. Though packed full, the taverns no longer echoed with raucous laughter; Saviar could hear signs creaking in the wind. The entire city appeared to be holding its breath, waiting for the moment the whole world exploded into violence. A shiver racked Saviar. It all seemed too controlled, too eerie. He took a solid hold on Chymmerlee's arm, and she leaned against him as they walked. She could know little or nothing of cities; yet she also, apparently, sensed the wrongness of it.

A full day and night of walking through Erythane brought them to the outskirts of Béarn, where a larger contingent of enormous warriors met them. Chymmerlee pressed more tightly against Saviar, clearly intimidated by the sheer size and number of Béarn's men. Saviar was a large man by most standards: a full head taller than the average and powerfully built. Yet, all of the massive Béarnides stood at least as tall as he did and outweighed him. Compared to them, Subikahn looked like a woman and Chymmerlee like a dainty child.

The guard who met them scarcely glanced in their direction. "Which unit are you with?"

Saviar turned to Subikahn, certain his quick-witted brother already had an answer. But Subikahn said nothing, only stared in fascination at the granite city beyond the guards.

"Uh . . ." Saviar started stupidly, not expecting the onus to fall on him. His mind started racing. He could hardly ask for the Renshai, and no Northern tribe would accept them. "Uh, how about . . ." *Erythane's infantry?* He stopped himself from speaking the words aloud. They were exiled from Erythane, from all of the West, actually. "How about . . . the Eastern one?"

Finally Subikahn's attention snapped back to Saviar, and the look he turned his brother virtually defined murder. The guard studied him quizzically. "You don't look Eastern." His gaze flicked to Subikahn. "Now, your friend there—"

"Brother," Saviar interrupted. "He's my brother. My *twin* brother."

The guard looked between them dubiously. Another voice punctuated the silence, the nearest guardsman chiming in. "Ruther, don't you recognize them? That's Knight-Captain Kedrin's grandson, there." He inclined his head toward Saviar. "And the brother, that's Prince Subikahn Taesson."

Chymmerlee stiffened against Saviar.

The first guard's jaw sagged. "It is?" He continued to study the trio in front of him. "They are?" He next turned his full attention upon his companion, as if worried to be made to look a fool.

The second guard beat him to it, bowing and gesturing. "Thank you for coming, Your Majesty. We're honored by your presence."

"Stop it, please." Subikahn's tone held a combination of graciousness and impatience. "I don't want anyone to know I'm here unless I tell them, all right?"

Seeing his friend making gestures of respect, the first guard joined him. "I'm sorry I didn't recognize you, Prince Subikahn."

Subikahn ignored him, directly addressing the guard who had recognized him. "Where's the Eastern army?"

"Last I heard, Sire, they were guarding the shores of the Western Plains."

"The Western Plains." Subikahn relaxed visibly. "So they're not here."

"No, Sire. Though it's rumored they're on their way."

"King Tae was here," the first guard piped in. "He arrived quite a while ago. I'm not sure if he's still here. There are rumors—"

"Ruther," the second guard said sharply. "We don't need to be bothering the prince with rumors."

"But—"

The look the second guard gave his companion was nearly as sharp as the one Subikahn had given Saviar when he had suggested joining the Eastern forces. Then, he looked directly at Saviar. "You're Sir Ra-khir's son, right?"

"Yes."

"Brave man, your father."

Saviar did not know what to say. "Th-thank you."

"He's commanding one of the smaller units, a band of outcasts he brought back from the East."

Saviar did not know which question to ask first. He had not known his father had traveled to the East, would not have believed Ra-khir capable of it given his own last encounter with the knight, overwhelmed by grief. Only an odd set of circumstances would put Ra-khir in charge of a unit, rather than guiding Erythane's cavalry, with the rest of the knights.

Subikahn broke in, unconcerned with his brother's considerations. "We'd like to join that unit, the one commanded by Sir Ra-khir." He did not wait for confirmation. "Where is it?"

"Front line, beach. Central east quadrant." The first guard seemed more at ease in his element, directing stragglers to their units. "East of the Santagithans and the Northern contingent from Erd. West of the Pudarians."

"Thank you." Subikahn dipped his head, which sent both guards scurrying into bows. The trio headed into Béarn, with more questions raised than answered.

Valr Magnus rode through the massed archers on the ridge, pleased to see them attentive and ready. Each had several arrows with rag-wrapped tips, saturated with oil. The nearby fire pots burned steadily through the twilight, like round and regular campfires. When the command came, they would follow orders, as always, with the fine precision Captain Sivaird had trained into them.

The captain walked over to greet his general, laying a hand on the saddle's pommel. "They're all ready, sir. One command."

"Yes." Magnus never doubted the efficiency of his captain, or his troops. "I know. You always do the finest work, Captain. It's not your men I'm worried about." He looked over the massed armies that spread across Béarn's beaches. Viewed from a distance, they seemed such a mismatched, ragtag lot, dragged together only by a common enemy. His men knew war. His captains were tough and experienced. Most of the Northern armies skirmished enough between themselves to remain in fighting condition, but the West had seen too much peacetime. They had grown dangerously soft. So many of their men came fresh from farms, shops, and apprenticeships. They were uncertain and, worse, unpredictable.

Apparently misunderstanding Magnus' concern, Captain Sivaird nodded. "There's a unit led by one of the Knights of Erythane, sir."

"Yes." Magnus knew what his captain wanted to say. "Commanded by Sir Ra-khir, who, I understand, once had the audacity to declare war on the entire kingdom of Pudar. Single-handed." He grinned at the thought, the savage courage it must have taken, and could not help feeling impressed.

"Our scouts say his band of outcasts includes a fair number of blonds who aren't Northmen, and as many women as men."

Magnus glared at his captain. "So, we're using scouts now to spy on our own army?"

Sivaird could not have looked more shocked if Magnus had asked him to transform into a kitten. "Well, sir . . . I . . ." He flushed. "There isn't much else for them to do, sir. And they're not exactly our 'own army,' sir. They're—"

"Renshai," Magnus finished. "Yes. All the generals already knew it."

The surprise remained indelibly etched on the captain's face. "But, sir. Don't the generals . . . I mean, shouldn't we . . ."

"Shouldn't we what, Captain? Fight amongst ourselves before we take on the enemy?"

"No, sir. But—"

"Ban some of the most competent swordsmen?" Magnus remained relentless. "Perhaps, if we do it right, we can drive them to the bosom of our enemy so we will have to fight pirates and Renshai simultaneously."

The captain seemed about to let the matter drop. Then, suddenly, he flexed his fingers and stiffened his jaw in clear resolve. "Sir, respectfully, should we allow demons to battle among us? Animals, perhaps? Bogeymen?"

General Magnus smiled. "If they're fighting on our side against a common enemy, why not? Perhaps bogeymen have necessary skills we don't possess. As to animals, even our own army has cavalry. We can always battle the demons after the war is over."

"Weakened and bloody."

Magnus made a throwaway gesture. "If necessary, yes. And remember, they're getting weakened and bloody alongside us. Better to fight a strong enemy together and a weak one afterward than to fight both at once at the top of their strength."

Captain Sivaird nodded. "I suppose you're right, sir, as always. But it feels so wrong to throw our lot in with . . ." He practically spat as he spoke the next word, ". . . Renshai, even temporarily."

"War can make for strange allies."

"Strange allies," Sivaird repeated, most thoughtfully. "General, sir. That reminds me of another concern."

Magnus gave his captain his full attention, though he knew what had to come next.

"Captain Alsmir is having trouble with those two younglings you picked up in the bar in Aerin."

Having heard exactly what he expected, Valr Magnus nodded.

"The younger one's clearly never been trained. We had to give him a weapon, then we took it back. He's more dangerous with it to himself, and to us, than to the enemy. Sir, to be utterly frank, he has the courage of a lion and the fighting ability of a turtle."

"A dangerous combination," Magnus had to admit. "I know the older one can fight."

"Judging from his sword forms, competently. But he's sullen, irritable, and oppositional."

"You mean, he's an adolescent."

"An adolescent who could do with a few solid spankings."

Magnus laughed. "I dare you. He'd sever your hands before they reached his bottom."

Captain Sivaird's look became one of outrage. "What are you saying?"

"I'm saying I've been watching him, too. And you've gravely underestimated his skill." *Something I can't afford to do.*

The captain grunted. "With all respect, sir, maybe you're underestimating *my* skill."

Magnus had not meant to offend his loyal captain. "You have many skills, Captain, and I appreciate all of them."

Sivaird bowed his head, silently acknowledging the compliment.

"But this boy's swordsmanship is peerless. I accepted him into my ranks even though he stated outright that he would follow orders only if they suited him."

Sivaird's brows whisked upward, and he opened his mouth; but no words emerged. "One such as that is very dangerous, sir. Not just for himself, but for every one around him."

"Yes." No one had to remind Valr Magnus of that fact. "Better in my command than another's, though, yes?"

Sivaird's frown suggested he did not agree, though his words spoke otherwise. "Yes, sir. If he turns coat, no one's better suited to bring him down, sir. But, his insolence does undermine Captain Alsmir's command."

"Then tell Alsmir not to command him. Tell the captain to leave the young man utterly and completely to me."

Captain Sivaird saluted. "It would be my pleasure."

Alsmir's, too, Magnus guessed. He sighed, feeling most sorry for Sir Ra-khir. One Renshai was bad enough. *What must it be like to command . . . to attempt to command . . . hundreds?*

CHAPTER 44

War is the only proper school of the healer.
—*Anonymous*

SAVIAR HAD NO DIFFICULTY finding his father's white charger, a beacon amidst the milling infantries on Béarn's southern beachfront. For the first time, it bothered him that the Knights of Erythane had chosen such a garish symbol of leadership. It made them easy to recognize among the peasantry, but it also branded his father the obvious target for every missile and sword.

As the three walked along the beach, struggling through scraggly weeds and clambering over heaps and dunes, it soon became clear that Ra-khir studied them as well. Silver Warrior faced in their direction. One of the knight's gloved hands sat squarely on his forehead, shading his eyes from the reflected glare. He clambered down from the horse long before details became clear. He could not yet have recognized their features, but he already seemed to know that he needed to greet these newcomers, that they headed toward his unit.

Apparently, Subikahn also noticed. "He knows it's us."

"You think so?" Saviar tightened his grip on Chymmerlee's hand to help her slog through a loose pile of sand. "How could he possibly know? I wouldn't have known it was him if the guard hadn't told me. He looks like any other knight."

Subikahn grinned. "They do try their best to appear identical, don't they? But if anyone's askew, it's always Ra-khir."

Saviar also smiled. It had become a family joke, one neither Ra-khir nor Kedrin appreciated. Ra-khir did spend the most time performing stable muckings, cleaning tabards, and mending hats. If a hair was out of place, it was a red one. If a sword angled slightly off-kilter, it was always Ra-khir's. Saviar did not know if his father truly had the worst eye for perfection or if his grandfather simply tended to expect more of him and thus focused on every tiny flaw.

They watched as Ra-khir handed his reins to a boy and started walking toward them.

"Oh, yes," Subikahn said confidently. "He's recognized us."

Saviar could not argue. It certainly seemed as though the knight intended to greet them warmly.

Then, suddenly, Ra-khir was running toward them, and Saviar felt a smile stretch across his face, his own feet moving without the need to guide them. And, a moment later, they fell into one another's arms, laughing, smiling, clinging.

"Papa," Ra-khir said into his father's neck. "You're all right."

"*I'm* all right?" Ra-khir laughed again. "I thought you were dead."

I was, practically. Saviar did not bother to share that information. Barely over his paralyzing grief, Ra-khir might see that as a reason to protect his oldest son mercilessly.

Ra-khir disengaged from Saviar to face Subikahn. The Eastern prince reached out a hand in greeting, but Ra-khir ignored it, catching his stepson into an embrace as loving as his son's. "I'm so glad you're back."

"Hey," Subikahn said breathlessly. "I'm little; I can actually break." As Ra-khir eased his powerful grip, the prince added in his normal voice, "You knew it was us long before you could see our faces. How?"

"Movement, mannerisms." Ra-khir studied them both as he talked. "A man knows his sons."

Subikahn jabbed a finger at Saviar. "Sons, see? I wasn't lying."

Ra-khir finally turned his attention to Chymmerlee, executing a grand bow. "Forgive my rudeness, beautiful lady. I'm Sir Ra-khir Kedrin's son, Knight of Erythane in the service of their Majesties, King Humfreet of Erythane and High King Griff of Béarn."

Chymmerlee curtsied nervously. "So I'd gathered. I've heard a lot about you, Sir Ra-khir. All of it very good."

Saviar supplied the one amenity she had missed, "Her name's Chymmerlee, Papa. She's a friend."

Curious faces watched the reunion from the beachfront, and Saviar suddenly recognized them. "Sif and Modi, Papa! You're commanding—"

"Sir!" Subikahn shouted over his twin, with a rudeness Ra-khir would never have tolerated from Saviar.

Ra-khir would usually haughtily refuse to acknowledge such a discourteous plea, but the volume and abruptness of the call apparently had him turning to Subikahn before he could think to stop himself.

Subikahn's cheeks reddened in tight circles. "Sorry, sir. I was just thinking the war could start any moment, and I really need to get Chymmerlee somewhere safe."

"Actually," Chymmerlee said, her voice seeming small and sweet in the wake of Subikahn's cry. "I need to stay within visual distance of the war."

Subikahn swiftly lost his embarrassment. "Is there someplace like that, Ra-khir? Someplace she can watch from a safe distance?"

Only then Saviar realized the mistake he had nearly made, the one Subikahn had covered with his abrupt rudeness. Saviar had been about to say "Renshai"—a word that would have shaken Chymmerlee terribly.

Ra-khir licked his lips, clearly weighing his words. "To be brutally honest . . ." He paused to glance in Saviar's direction, looking to him for clues on how much information Chymmerlee could handle.

Saviar nodded decisively. Chymmerlee had a purpose, and shielding her from the truth would not make the threat as clear. She, and her people, needed to know and understand the worst case scenario.

Thus encouraged, Ra-khir finished. ". . . our enemies are ruthless killers of men and women. No place in the world is safe." He made a broad gesture that encompassed the massed ships. "But, if I had to pick the most secure location from which to watch this war, it's the peak of Béarn Castle. Matrinka's there, the whole royal family." His gaze flicked toward the mountain castle. "But the guards certainly won't let just anyone join them."

Saviar took Chymmerlee's hand, a gesture that did not go unnoticed by his father. "I'll convince them."

"No," Subikahn chimed in. "It'll have to be me."

Saviar's brows furrowed, and he gave his twin a curious look. "Do you think you're more convincing than I am?"

"No," Subikahn said, smiling. "Definitely not. But . . ." He tipped his head to Ra-khir, allowing him to explain what apparently seemed obvious to Subikahn.

Ra-khir accepted the burden. "He's a prince, Saviar. His words, no matter how well or poorly spoken, carry a lot more weight than yours do in royal situations."

Subikahn turned his twin an irritating "I told you so" expression.

"But there's a more important reason why Subikahn should go instead of you."

Those words surprised both of the young men, and a note of unhappiness in Ra-khir's tone struck Saviar. He looked at Subikahn, who had dropped his sneer for an expression of innocent uncertainty. He, too, had detected something in Ra-khir's delivery.

"Subikahn, your father's at the castle."

Subikahn blinked. When he replied, he sounded suspicious, defensive. "Yeah? So?"

Ra-khir's brows lifted, and creases appeared in his forehead. "He's badly injured, Subikahn. I've talked to some of the healers. More than one thinks he's only lived this long because Matrinka's convinced him his lethal wounds . . . aren't."

Other than a slight trembling in his hands, Subikahn gave no reaction. Not a hint of emotion crossed his features. He took Chymmerlee's other arm, a gesture that did not go unnoticed by Saviar. Dutifully, wistfully, he released her to the care of his brother. Without another word, Subikahn headed toward the palace.

Saviar watched them go, startled by the drop of a heavy, gloved hand on his shoulder.

"There's something going on between you, isn't there?"

Saviar turned to his father, "Well, we are brothers."

Ra-khir chuckled. "Not you and Subikahn, you goose."

It was the first time Saviar could remember his father engaging in name-calling. He would have smiled if not for the burdensome news the knight had dropped just moments earlier. "Is King Tae really going to . . . die?"

Ra-khir shrugged. "Matrinka's a gifted healer, and she seems utterly convinced she can fix him. But he's also one of her closest friends. I'm not sure she's able to see his situation objectively."

Saviar could only nod. He could not imagine the world without Tae Kahn. Some of his fondest memories involved romping on the floor with a king who could switch from childlike to manly in an instant. At times, Saviar had envied Subikahn his father. He could scarcely imagine Ra-khir or Kevral wrestling in the dirt with them or playing seek and hide games involving windowsills, precious heirlooms, and swinging from chandeliers.

"Of course," Ra-khir added thoughtfully, "it wouldn't be the first time Tae surprised everyone. He won't talk about it, but his body is riddled with old wounds, the kind of scars that run deep. He's been stabbed and shot dozens of times. He once fell off Béarn Castle in the winter and got trapped under a solid layer of ice for only the gods know how long. And he's still here, Saviar. He's still here."

Saviar had seen some of those scars, including the one directly over Tae's heart. "He's ornery, Papa. Neither Valhalla nor Hel wants him, so they keep throwing him back."

Ra-khir laughed. "I hope you're right." He started back toward Silver Warrior. "So, are you going to tell me about this lady of yours?"

"Gladly." Saviar walked alongside his father. "What man doesn't relish the opportunity to talk about his . . ." Saviar paused to pick the right word. ". . . budding girlfriend."

"Budding?"

"Well, I haven't known her all that long," Saviar admitted. *And half of that time I was in a coma.* "Thialnir is set on me courting only Renshai, and his argument is a good one."

Ra-khir sighed. "Please don't take this as criticism, but Chymmerlee doesn't seem . . ."

Saviar waited out the pause.

". . . exactly the Renshai type."

The words confused more than offended. "What do you mean?"

"She seems . . . quiet. She's not carrying any obvious weapons. You just seem very . . . different. From one another, I mean."

Saviar could not help interjecting, "You mean, different? As opposed to you and Mama?"

Ra-khir stiffened only slightly. Apparently, he had gotten far enough past the grief to function normally, even when the conversation turned directly to Kevral. "Yes, we were different, all right. And it worked, but it wasn't easy. There were lots of problems to overcome, from inside and outside the marriage. Even to the very end." He managed a lopsided smile. "But I loved her like the stars love the sky. I would have dug to the world's core had she only asked." He gave Saviar a steady look. "Is that how you feel about Chymmerlee?"

"No," Saviar admitted. "Not yet, anyway. But I like her an awful lot, and I want to get to know her better."

"And your brother?"

"Well, of course I love him. Not sure I'd dig to the world's core for him, though."

Ra-khir stopped walking. "Are you being deliberately dense?"

"What?" Saviar came to a halt at his father's side. "No. What do you mean?"

"Tae and I were rivals for your mother's hand, you know. I'd hate for you boys to fall out over a girl."

"Oh." The idea seemed patently ludicrous now that Subikahn had shared his secret. "That's not a problem, Papa."

"You're sure."

"We've talked it out. Subikahn is not attracted to Chymmerlee."

"Good." Ra-khir continued, taking Silver Warrior's reins from the boy holding them. "Thank you, Darby. Mount up."

Only then, Saviar noticed the only other horse in the vicinity, a light brown chestnut. The boy scrambled to obey. *Darby? Who in Hel is Darby?*

Apparently noticing Saviar's consternation, Ra-khir made the introductions. "Saviar, this is Darby. My squire."

"Squire?" The word startled from Saviar's mouth; he had not meant to speak it aloud. But, once spoken, he had to continue, "As in, training him to become a Knight of Erythane?" Saviar felt suddenly hot all over. He had to bite down on the angry words taking shape in his head.

Ra-khir swung into his own saddle. "Yes, of course."

"But I . . . I was supposed to . . ." *Supposed to what?* Saviar had expressed interest in becoming a Knight of Erythane, but he had never followed up on it in any way. The Renshai training kept him too busy, then his work toward becoming Renshai leader, followed by the exile. He had left Ra-khir in the night, sleeping, without so much as a good-bye.

Darby dispersed the awkward moment with a happy greeting. "You must be Saviar. I'm so glad to finally meet you."

"I'd say the same." Saviar tried not to sound as grumpy as he felt. "But I didn't know you existed."

"Well, now you do." Ra-khir wheeled his mount. "Saviar, Thialnir and I need your help. Commanding Renshai is rather like taming volcanoes or herding butterflies. They seem to listen to you two, somewhat. Can you help?"

Saviar looked out over the ocean, where the enemy ships massed, then to the Renshai. They milled without pattern or structure, some sharpening weapons, others sparring, still more engaged in wild *svergelse*. Something much bigger than who squired his father lay at stake. "I'll help any way I can." He smiled blandly. "Just call me Saviar Ra-khirsson, volcano tamer."

⚔———

Subikahn could not open the door. He did not know how long he stood outside, his hand resting on the latch, his brain numb. Once the royal family had accepted responsibility for Chymmerlee and taken her to her quarters, he found himself incapable of clear and rational thought. She had served as a lovely distraction on which he could no longer depend. The moment he eased open that door, he had to face King Tae Kahn Weile's son. The very idea churned acid through his gut.

Subikahn heard someone approach from behind; his Renshai

training would not allow a potential threat to go unnoticed. Logic overruled instinct. No one currently in Béarn Castle would harm him, and it seemed like too much trouble and energy to turn.

Matrinka came up beside Subikahn and rested her hand on his. "It's all right, honey. He's going to be fine."

Subikahn turned to face her, glad to give his hand to her, any excuse to remove it from the latch. "Your Majesty—"

"Matrinka," she corrected, her features stern. "No formality between old friends."

At nineteen, Subikahn found it difficult to say he had any friendships he could consider long-standing. But he had known Matrinka nearly since birth. "I-I've heard a rumor."

"Yes?"

"That his injuries . . ." Subikahn wanted Matrinka to finish.

Matrinka did not oblige, but she did answer his actual question. "The other healers don't understand. They see a wound and pronounce it fatal for any man." She turned him a grin, lopsided from weariness and discomfort. "Your father, Subikahn, is not 'any man.' "

Subikahn held his breath, afraid of what he might hear. It would not surprise him to find out that animal blood ran through the veins of his paternal ancestors. *Are we demons? Sorcerers? We can't be god-blooded.* "What do you mean?"

Matrinka took Subikahn's other hand. "I mean, your father . . . he survived . . . what he survived in childhood, you know. And I don't know if he was born with an iron nature or acquired it through what happened when he was simply too young to know he should be dead; but I've seen him wounded worse than this before. I've pronounced him dead on at least one other occasion, yet he's still with us: then . . . and now."

Subikahn blinked. He had no idea what she was talking about. "Your Maj . . ." he started; then, remembering her admonishment, changed in mid word, ". . . trinka. What happened?"

"Sword cut and arrow shot," Matrinka explained, "a bad fall, a long float in the ocean, and a shark attack."

Subikahn went even stiller, if possible. He had meant his question to refer to the childhood incident, but the current information stunned him. "All of that?"

"I'm afraid so."

Subikahn swallowed hard. *How could anyone survive that?* The idea of walking through the door became even more difficult. "When you mentioned what he survived in childhood, is that where the scars came from?"

Matrinka was visibly startled. "You don't know? He's never told you?"

Subikahn hesitated, worried Matrinka would keep the confidences of her longtime friend she considered a brother. He thought about lying but doubted he could successfully pull it off and get the answers he had sought for as long as he could remember. "He always dodges the question. I want to know. Tell me."

Matrinka looked from the door to Subikahn, as if weighing her loyalties to father and to son. Finally, she sighed. "Enemies of your grandfather tortured and slaughtered your grandmother, stabbed your father at least a dozen times, and left him for dead. My understanding is that there was more blood on the floor than inside Tae when Weile found him."

Subikahn did not allow himself to cringe. He did not want to discourage Matrinka. The scars riddled Tae's chest; the assassins had clearly intended to kill him. Surely, Matrinka had nothing to add.

But the queen of Béarn continued talking. "And before he turned your age, Weile sent Tae out alone, experienced killers at his heels, to 'toughen him up.'" She snorted. "Toughen him up? He's the toughest son of a bastard in the kingdom, I'd guess. Maybe in the world. He hated his father for doing that to him, despised the entire world for a while, and vowed that he would keep his own child safe and close. Which is why, Subikahn, he's always been so sweet and loving with you."

Has he? Clearly, Tae had not told Matrinka of their falling out, how the king had exiled the son he had promised to keep safe and close. "So," Subikahn said without a hint of emotion. "He's going to recover?"

Matrinka heaved another, deeper sigh. "It's up to him, now, Subikahn. The salt water cleansed his wounds nicely, and I've given him potent herbs to keep infection at bay." She shrugged. "He's living from event to event, which is never a good thing. First, he was just going to drag on long enough to get Imorelda safely to me. Then, it was until he described his scouting mission to someone in authority. Now, he's waiting to settle things up with you."

Icy prickles passed along Subikahn's shoulders to his fingers. He could not help wondering how much Matrinka knew. "Settle things up?"

"You know, the father/son deathbed speech. Half promises, half pep talk. I've seen a number of them. Very inspiring, but also a perfect excuse to . . . surrender."

Subikahn guessed her point. "Surrender . . . to death, you mean?"

"Yes."

Subikahn stepped back, relieved. "So, the longer I delay this meeting, the longer he lives?"

"No." Matrinka would not let him off that easily. "Subikahn, you have to see him. No matter what I think, his wounds are serious. You may not get another chance, and we will both hate ourselves forever if you don't see him before he dies."

Or I die. Subikahn realized Tae's fate might prove less tenuous than his own once the battle began in earnest.

"Just . . . be sure you leave something undone or unsaid. Something significant that will obsess him until the wounds have more time to heal. Give him a new short-term goal to live toward."

Subikahn tried to ask casually, "And I suppose you don't want me to give him any . . . stress."

"Stress," Matrinka repeated thoughtfully. "A child in his second decade not giving his father stress?" She snorted. "If you start getting all sweet and sappy on him, he'll think he's dying for sure."

Subikahn could not help smiling. "All right, then." He took his hands from Matrinka and put one on the latch again. "If I can just remember how to open a door."

Without warning, Matrinka put her hand over Subikahn's, tripped the latch, and eased the panel open. She nudged him forward, and Subikahn stumbled just enough to allow her to close it gently behind him.

Thanks. Subikahn found himself in a large room furnished with enough chairs and benches to hold a small meeting. The bed took up the far corner, across from an open window that admitted flower-scented air in the occasional huffs of wind. Across from it, Tae leaned on a bunched and colorful blanket, two others spread across his legs and abdomen. His bare chest looked thin, sallow instead of its usual healthy olive, and the scars stood out in mute testimony to past hardships. Remembering the story Matrinka had told him, Subikahn could not help wincing at the sight of them.

Apparently noticing the direction of Subikahn's gaze, Tae pulled up one of the blankets.

Imorelda strolled across Tae from legs to abdomen, as if he were nothing more than furniture. She yawned and stretched each paw delicately.

"Hello there, Papa," Subikahn said cheerily, as if they had seen one another mere hours ago. "How's your life going?"

Using Tae as a launch site, Imorelda sprang at Subikahn. Suppressing the urge to dodge, Subikahn managed to catch the large cat, holding her as she rubbed her head all over his face in greeting.

"Bit tenuous at the moment, I'm afraid." Despite the warning in his words, Tae managed a smile. His features looked wan, older; but his dark eyes remained clear. His usually tangled hair had been combed to an ebon sheen.

Subikahn did not know what to say. "Papa, I know I wasn't supposed to see you for another year, and you told me not to run to Erythane. But under the circumstances—"

Tae nodded. "You did the right thing, Subikahn. Béarn needs everyone. Everyone. Especially talented swordsmen like you."

Subikahn saw no need to respond to the compliment. No Renshai would.

"I love you, Subikahn." The words seemed to come from nowhere. No thread of the conversation had brought Tae there.

Subikahn set the cat back down on the bed, absently stroking her head and back while she stretched and turned to bring the right places under his hand. Her purr filled the room. "Stop it, Papa. I talked to Matrinka. I know you're not dying."

Tae grimaced. "Matrinka's words do not determine the fate of the universe."

"No," Subikahn admitted, drawing a hard, wooden chair directly up to the bedside. "But you'd be hard-pressed to find a more skilled healer. If she says you're not dying, I believe her." He abandoned the cat to sit.

Imorelda continued purring.

"What if I told you I can feel my body decaying day by day? That each time I awaken, it's a painful and terrible surprise." Red-tinged froth bubbled from his lips as he spoke, and he wiped it away with the already stained corner of a blanket. "That it's a fight I want to quit now, a battle I just can't win."

Subikahn bit his lip. He would not lie, not this time. "I'd say you were a coward and a craven, misjudged by the Renshai. A man like that does not deserve to have his blood in the Renshai pool."

Tae lowered his head. "Matrinka said you'd say that."

"Matrinka's words," Subikahn said, "determine the fate of the universe."

Tae managed a laugh, though he cringed at the obvious pain it caused him. "If only that were so, there would never be another war." He wiped away more blood-tinged drool. "Subikahn." Tae's tone grew intent, serious. "When I sent you from the East, I had no idea the Renshai would become Western exiles."

"Barred from the North, West, and East." Subikahn shrugged. "Where was I supposed to go? Another world? A star? *Valhalla?*"

"I'd have found a way."

It was truth, Subikahn knew. He had heard enough stories of his father's exploits. "Yes, but you're a sneaky little sod who can eavesdrop on anyone. I wouldn't put it past you to have already picked up the enemy's language." He gestured in the general direction of the shore. "I'm not like you, Papa. I'm not tough as steel."

Tae's brows eeled upward. "You must have inherited that softness from your mother."

"Funny." Subikahn had never considered how an aggressive, uncompromising Renshai and a man with a constitution of iron had created a sensitive daisy like him. "Maybe Saviar shared some blood with me in the womb."

"Maybe." Tae did not seem convinced, or else he did not think it mattered. "Then perhaps I can blame Ra-khir for putting me in the position of . . ."

"Position of what?"

"Nearly having to execute you for being a—"

"*Bonta?*"

Tae looked away. "I was going to be more discreet."

"More discreet than *bonta?*"

A hint of command entered Tae's voice, weak but clearly there. "Stop saying that!"

"*Bonta, bonta, bonta!*" Subikahn continued to stare until Tae finally met his gaze again. "It's what I am, Papa. I'm a *bonta*. Your son, Prince Subikahn Taesson the *bonta*."

"Stop saying *bonta*."

"Why, Papa?" Subikahn would not relent. "Why should I stop saying *bonta?* What's wrong with *bonta?* I like the word *bonta*. *Bonta* just rolls off the tongue." He remembered his conversation with Saviar and could not help grinning. The more times he used the word, the less power it held over him.

"Because it's a derogatory term. Degrading. My son is not a *bonta*."

"I am, too."

Tae held up a hand. "He's a . . . a . . . lover of men."

Warmth flooded Subikahn. At least, his father seemed to have grasped the most important point, to have accepted the once unacceptable. "Fine, I'm a man-lover, a sodomist, a daisy. Call me what you want, but I'm done sleeping with women. It's . . ." He could not think of a suitable word, so he resorted to childish slang, ". . . bleffy."

"You tried?"

"I did, Papa. Many times." A terrible thought occurred to him. "You could have an illegitimate grandchild out there somewhere."

"And you're still . . ."

". . . a lover of men. Yes, Papa. It's not something I can change any more than I can my parentage. I'm stuck with you as a father, and you're stuck with me as a . . ."

". . . son?" Tae inserted.

"As a *bonta*."

"Stop saying that!"

Subikahn took the sober route this time. He had had enough fun at Tae's expense. "It's just a label, Papa. Like prince. Or Easterner."

"Except that label is punishable by execution."

Subikahn leaned forward. "As opposed to . . . Renshai? In some places, it's a crime just to *speak* the name. They consider us anathema, to be killed on sight."

"Not in the East, anymore. Weile repealed that law."

Subikahn stared at his father, wondering how long it would take Tae to see the obvious solution now that he had practically spoken it.

"I still think we can fix you, Subikahn."

"No, Papa. I'm not broken." Subikahn resorted to Kevral's words, "It's the way the gods made me." He noticed the cat staring at him, waving her tail fiercely, demanding more pets.

"The gods, Subikahn, are not infallible. They make babies without legs sometimes, with extra fingers. I once saw a stillborn with two heads."

"Fine." Subikahn saw no reason to argue the point. "Perhaps they made a mistake with me, but it's not something that needs 'fixing.' I like being a . . ."

Tae winced.

". . . lover of men. A lover of one man in particular." The image of Talamir sent a wave of comfort through Subikahn. He pictured the blond in his mind: strong, confident, handsome, with blue eyes a man could get lost in. "Papa, you know what it's like to be in love. The kind of love that overwhelms you, against which you measure every person, every emotion, that crosses your path. Imagine if Kevral had chosen to marry you. Talamir—"

Tae made a gasping sound that completely upended Subikahn's thoughts.

"What's wrong?"

All the color drained from Tae's face.

Subikahn sprang from his chair. "Are you choking? What can I do?"

"Talamir," Tae said. His voice sounded feeble, but not gravelly or breathless.

Subikahn tried to guess the source of Tae's abrupt discomfort. "He didn't rape me, Papa. I swear it. I initiated the . . . the contact. He was nothing but sweet and gentle and loving . . ."

Tae only looked more uncomfortable. Subikahn took several nervous steps backward. *He's going to die. He's going to die right in front of me.* "Matrinka's right outside the door. I'll get her."

"Just give me one last hug." The words came out hoarse, painful.

Matrinka's words echoed in Subikahn's head: ". . . be sure you leave something undone or unsaid . . ."

"The hug can wait." Subikahn started for the door. "I'm getting Matrinka."

Imorelda yowled and sprang from the bed.

"No," Tae said. "I'm not dying right now. At least not any faster than a moment ago. I need to tell you something; but, once I do, I won't have any right to request another hug. Ever."

Subikahn turned and studied his father. Tae looked awful: skin drawn over bones, sallow and sunken; but the eyes still contained plenty of life. The sound his father had made in his throat had nothing to do with breathing, only desperate concern that his son would judge him harshly. *About what?* Subikahn had a sudden, gripping feeling in his chest. He did not want to know, but he could stand the suspense even less. "What?" he asked carefully.

Tae gestured him closer, demanded the embrace.

Subikahn obliged, but he found it difficult to put much emotion into the gesture. If he squeezed too hard, he might worsen the injuries, and worry about the forthcoming news made him tentative. He stepped back. "Now, tell me."

"Subikahn." Tae's voice emerged surprisingly clear now, as if the embrace itself had cured him. "My one and only son."

Subikahn gritted his teeth but refused to speak. Words would only prolong the already interminable wait.

"Sentence was pronounced on Talamir."

All thought drained from Subikahn's head. "What?" The world seemed to disappear around him: sight, sound, touch. All that remained were the smells: blood and herbs, sickness and the aroma of flowers on the breeze from the windows. "Sentence . . . for what? What kind of sentence?"

"Talamir confessed to the rape, Subikahn. Freely and without coercion. In front of the entire court."

"Confessed?" The word confused Subikahn further. "But he

didn't—" Subikahn tried again. "Tally didn't rape anyone; he couldn't. Why would he . . . ?" Nothing made sense.

"Then, he mutilated two elite guardsmen and attempted to kill me. High treason, Subikahn. The sentence—"

Subikahn knew the obvious sentence, for either crime. What he could not grasp was Talamir admitting to having done such a thing, Talamir losing his sanity in the courtroom. Subikahn's mind drifted back to the fateful night that seemed so long ago. *"If your love is real and strong,"* Tae had said, *"it will survive two years of separation."* Subikahn clung to that. "But you promised, Papa. You said that I could come back to Tally in two years, if our love survived."

Tae sighed. His head seemed to collapse into the pillow. "I'm sorry, Subikahn. Talamir is—"

"No!" Subikahn could not bear to hear the last word. "No!" The agony that descended upon him was so raw it pained him worse than any physical wound. "No! No! No!" He whirled without thinking, wrenched open the door, and darted from the room, nearly colliding with Matrinka. Without so much as a mumbled apology, he burst through the hallways, down the staircases, in a blind, deaf fog of anguish. He did not stop running until he found himself outside, with no memory of opening any doors or facing any guardsmen. There, he threw himself into the grass, alternately sobbing and screaming, ranting and melting, until all understanding became buried in a dark morass of impenetrable grief.

CHAPTER 45

A reasonable plan executed now is better than a perfect one next week.

—General Santagithi

A SCARLET EDGE OF sun burst over the horizon, its color bleeding across the dawn sky and blending through the rainbow spectrum to a dense and savage blue. The blare of horns greeted the new day, their notes crisp and triumphant, a battle cry from the once silent ships.

A smile eased onto Subikahn's face, the first show of emotion Saviar had noticed since his twin's return that night. The swollen, red-rimmed eyes had said enough, and the desperate violence that characterized his *svergelse*. Renshai vented with sword strokes instead of blustering or shouting or tears. Tae, Saviar surmised, was not doing well; and Subikahn had the look of a man prepared to die in glorious combat, more eager than ever to find Valhalla.

Saviar would have liked to discuss the situation with his twin, but circumstances did not allow it. Subikahn had nothing to say, and Saviar found himself tied up trying to explain the generals' strategy well enough that the Renshai would not spoil it. It simply called for the infantrymen to pause long enough from engaging to allow the bowmen a few rounds at the enemy as they scrambled from their ships. But Ra-khir and Saviar both knew the futility of asking Renshai to hesitate in battle.

Saviar was not sure it mattered anyway. The Renshai had no bows, no cavalry per se, though they did keep some horses. They might foil the shots of the bowmen stationed in the armies on either side, but no arrows, bolts, or quarrels should spring from directly behind them. Saviar hoped that would work well enough. Ra-khir would have no more luck restraining Renshai than he would the wind itself. And Saviar the Volcano Tamer doubted he could do much better.

The Aeri soldier waited for the blare of horns to die to echoes before addressing Valr Magnus. The general stood at the back of his infantry, watching for Archer-Captain Sivaird to give the signal. "Sir, we found young Treysind bound hand and foot. Shall we release him?"

Magnus had to suppress a laugh. "Tied him up, did he? That's one way to keep a small brother safe."

"Sir?"

"Have someone nonessential take Treysind to whoever's guarding the children in Béarn." Magnus watched the enemy pour from their ships with astounding precision. They moved in an orderly fashion, perfectly coordinated. This did not bode well. "Have them tell the women in charge to keep both eyes on him. Otherwise, he's going to run to the thickest part of the battle, swamp his brother and others around them, and get his fool self hacked to bits."

"Yes, sir." The soldier rushed to obey.

Valr Magnus wondered why the archers had not yet fired. He trusted Captain Sivaird to know the precise moment, yet the sooner they did so, the more rounds they could get off before the infantry engaged. The various cavalries waited, bunched just behind the beachhead, to catch any pirates who scythed their way through the soldiers on foot.

Valr Magnus turned his attention back to the enemy, finally finding the reason for Sivaird's hesitation. From nearly every massed army on the shore, infantrymen charged the pirates, disobeying the commands of red-faced, screaming commanders. *Damn!* Magnus' own army held firm, aside from one man who stormed down the sand with the ferocity of a she-bear protecting cubs.

"General!" Captain Alsmir shouted.

Magnus did not need an explanation. He had weathered enough war to know this might happen. "I see them!" *The best laid plans are more often thwarted by inexperienced allies than enemies.*

"What do you want me to do?" the archer's captain called down from the ridge.

Captain Alsmir rode off to bunch his men, making sure that the remainder of his charges obeyed orders and did not break ranks to follow the one.

Valr Magnus looked from the growing battles on the beaches to Sivaird. He could order them to sacrifice the one disobedient man, to pepper Calistin with the same barrage as the enemy. He dismissed the thought the instant it arose; it was a cowards' way out, ethically and strategically wrong. "Use the Strikers." Magnus referred to the most competent archers, the specialists reserved for specific targets. "Take down the ships, if you can. Leave the shore-bound for the infantry. The reservists need to switch to handheld weapons, and the designated bowmen . . ." He could think of no specific use for them but hated wasting their skill. ". . . use your judgment. If you can get a clear shot without jeopardizing *any* of our men, take it."

Captain Sivaird saluted and rushed to reorganize. Flaming arrows flew toward the ships. Only three hit their targets, but all of the others crashed safely into the sea. Smoke rose from one of the ships, then burst brilliantly into flames. *One down.* One seemed so few. Yet, even that small triumph brought them one step nearer to victory. "Again," he said beneath his breath. And Sivaird complied. Another wave of flaming arrows flew from the ridge, accompanied by a tight barrage of quarrels over the heads of the massed infantry on the open portion of beach.

All up and down Béarn's beaches, of ringing steel, battle cries, grunts, and screams filled the air with the familiar sounds of war.

Another ship went up in flames, then another, and a few more up and down the ocean from other units. Then, the pirates swarmed the beach, and Captain Alsmir released the infantry. Valr Magnus freed his sword and raced to join his men, reminding himself not only to watch for the familiar uniforms of his unit but for the various and sundry other continental warriors, the random clothes of volunteers and conscripted soldiers, the homespun farmers. He need not have worried. To a man, the enemy sported the same leather armor, helmets, and shields; and it became easier to target them and protect every other.

Bodies fell around Valr Magnus, flesh yielding to his sword, steel slamming against his blocks and parries. Several of his own men had fallen amongst the enemy, each blood-splattered aqua-and-bronze uniform a painful reminder that not every man would return. He set his sights on allowing as few pirates past him as possible, easing the burden on the cavalry farther up the beach. They were the last resort for the women and children of Béarn, the city, the castle, and all the lands beyond.

Piles of bloody bodies formed on the beach, and Magnus found himself shifting slightly southward as he cleared the area around him. At length, he found an unexpected partner behind him, a man of such skill and ferocity that the general was incapable of not trusting that his flank was safe. Without intention or planning, the two men merged their personal strategies to become a single fighting unit. The dead all but surrounded them, and they had to move together across the beach to find opponents as the pirates deliberately avoided them.

All up and down the beach they fought without pause, no breaks for what felt like half a day or longer, their skin, clothing, and hair spattered with enemy gore. Valr Magnus felt fatigue press him, but he banished it through willpower. His arms and legs kept moving long past pain and weariness. He dared not stop, not break even for a moment, worried that doing so would allow exhaustion to finally catch him. Once stilled, he might not find the strength to move again. And, luckily, his partner remained with him.

It did not occur to Valr Magnus to wonder who fought the battle with him. Knowing the truth would ruin everything, would force him to contemplate an intolerable situation, would shatter any illusions left from centuries of stories, legends, and history. Subconsciously, Magnus knew his benefactor was the archest of nemeses, that he threw his lot in with a Renshai sworn to kill him. Yet, he would not allow that thought to come to the fore. He could not remember the last time he had fought a battle with such an aura of faith at his back, at the side of an ally who matched or exceeded his own talent. It was a joy he would not allow something as mundane as reality to destroy.

Ra-khir swiftly realized that it did not matter if he served as the Renshai's only cavalry. Nobody made it past the world's most skilled swordsmen. All up and down the beach, pirates slipped through the knots of infantries to the horsemen stationed beyond them. He could see the knights' white chargers plunging behind Erythane's infantry, saw one occasionally veer off to assist among the golds, browns, and grays of the other troops. He, alone, had no one to chase. It all seemed a cruel joke. *A battle of this magnitude, and I'm actually bored.*

Ra-khir did wander right or left at times to catch a charging pirate or assist other horsemen, but he did so at his own risk. The Western army to his south worked as a well-rehearsed team. To the north, he discovered more leeway, but he also found himself moving in that direction to back the Renshai. As the pirates fell or tried to find easier routes up the beachhead, the Renshai had to shift as well. And, like a golden tide, they rolled casually northward.

As Ra-khir rode the dunes for a better view of the battle, several things became clear. The abilities of the continental armies varied greatly, while those of the pirates seemed nearly identical. Early on, this favored the pirates, who could fall back on consistency and drive into the weaker areas of the allies' defenses. But, as the weakest and least experienced fighters fell, the pirates found themselves facing a tougher defense, with a higher percentage of trained soldiers who gradually learned to exploit their enemy's unwavering style.

Suddenly, two Renshai broke from the chaos to charge up the beach, as if fleeing the battle. Ra-khir knew better. No Renshai would ever display such cowardice. Those two had other reason for rushing toward him. *Saviar and Subikahn,* he assumed. *And they've seen something.*

Ra-khir reined Silver Warrior into their path and nudged him into a ground-eating canter. The looseness of the sand slowed the stallion into a rolling slog, but he soon met up with the twins. They looked frightful, their arms, hair, and clothing striped with blood and spotted with bits of unidentifiable gore. Their swords dripped crimson circles into the sand. Saviar's expression appeared worried, his pale eyes crinkled and his forehead lined; but Subikahn looked positively corpselike. His eyes had sunken into pools of pained darkness, his cheeks drawn.

"Papa," Saviar shouted as soon as they drew close enough to hear one another. "Look there." He used his sword to point toward the pirate ships.

Ra-khir had looked there a thousand times in the past several hours, but he dutifully followed Saviar's gesture. Most of the ships still remained at anchor off the coast, bobbing gently in swells that made a strange and peaceful contrast to the raging battle on the shore. He could see some bubbling and movement in the water where sharks had discovered bodies. Otherwise, nothing appeared to have changed. "You mean the sharks?" He wondered if the boys had some strategy that involved driving the pirates into the jaws of the savage fish. "Because I don't think anyone's going to let themselves—"

Saviar shoved the hilt of his sword against his father's fist, which startled Ra-khir. No Renshai, not even his son, ever willingly handed over his weapon to someone outside the tribe. Cautiously, he wrapped his fingers around it.

"Look again."

Ra-khir kept his eyes in the direction Saviar had indicated. At first, he saw nothing unusual. Then, a shimmer drew his attention slightly to the right where he discovered a ball of light that seemed to hover over the deck of the central ship. "What's that?"

"It's an aura," Saviar explained, snatching back his sword.
The glow disappeared, at least to Ra-khir's eyes.

"Someone's working magic. We need to find Chymmerlee."

Ra-khir did not fully understand, but he trusted the twins. "All right. What—?" The distant waves seemed to hesitate. Nearer the shore, the water sucked back from the edge. "The ocean . . . it's changing."

Subikahn grabbed Saviar's arm, but his attention went to Ra-khir. "Can we borrow your horse, sir?"

"What?" Ra-khir had never even allowed groomsmen to handle his steed, and he would have to bend his orders, and knightly law, to allow such a thing. Nevertheless, he dismounted. The water drew farther inward, like a string of drool sucked back into a large dog's mouth. He pointed toward his favorite vantage. "Meet me there, on that largest dune. The view is perfect."

Saviar nodded as he swung into the saddle, and Subikahn leaped into place behind him. Silver Warrior galloped toward the castle, Ra-khir cringing at every wallowing step. Speed was dangerous in sand for a massive animal with such slender legs. He vowed to give the boys a strongly-worded lecture on the proper treatment of animals when they returned, then discarded the thought. He trusted Saviar's wisdom and ability to weigh risk. The twins clearly saw a desperate need for speed that Ra-khir did not yet understand; and, while it seemed to him that one rider should have sufficed, especially since they would add Chymmerlee on their return, the boys had a reason for fetching her together. Saviar would not risk his father's precious charger without desperate need.

"Godspeed," he whispered beneath his breath. He could still feel the impression of the split leather hilt against his palm. It had been Kevral's sword Saviar had handed him, he realized. She had never allowed him to touch it. For Saviar to do so meant a critical situation that words and expressions couldn't explain. He looked back at the shoreline, where the water drew back farther and farther toward the anchored ships.

⊶⊢————

Though it seemed like hours to Ra-khir, only a few moments passed before he heard the familiar hoof falls and Silver Warrior came bounding through the sand. Three figures sat astride, one nearly as heavy as himself but the other two much lighter. Subikahn dismounted before the horse drew up, but Saviar waited and gently assisted Chymmerlee to the ground.

"It's a tidal wave," Ra-khir said in an awed whisper. "That's what he's preparing for. A massive wall of ocean that takes out all of our troops . . . and his as well." Ra-khir had heard about the two types of pirates, the one huge and magical, the other mortal and bound to their bidding. It made sense that the creatures that called themselves *Kjempemagiska* might care little for servant underlings, but the thought appalled Ra-khir. Even the greatest gods of their world did not treat humans as expendable playthings, at least not in such numbers. *We're all going to die,* Ra-khir realized with strangely little fear. *Even those as far away as the castle might not survive.*

Saviar's mouth set into a grim line. "Chymmerlee?"

The Myrcidian did not respond, only opened her arms wide and mumbled strings of harsh syllables. Ra-khir's attention flitted between her and the middle ship, where he had seen the glow while holding Saviar's sword. He did not bother to ask what Chymmerlee was doing. It was clearly magic, and he did not want to distract her with foolish questions. He did, however, look askance at his son.

Saviar complied softly. "She's a mage, Papa."

Ra-khir considered. The word made sense in a fairy-tale sort of way. The only known creatures with magic living on the world of men were elves. However, Ra-khir had seen enough of the home of the gods, and of other worlds, in his time to know things existed of which men knew little or nothing. Now, he understood why both boys had insisted on fetching her; she was valuable enough to deserve two Renshai bodyguards. "Elfin blood?" he guessed.

Saviar shook his head. "His aura just flared up," he informed those who could not see it.

Chymmerlee tossed her head suddenly.

The water rushed back toward shore in a large, tumbling mass that rocked the boats wildly and carried those closest to the shore into the sea. At least, the colossal behemoth of water the *Kjempemagiska* had apparently planned never made it to fruition.

"He knows he lost control of his spell," Chymmerlee explained breathlessly, "but he doesn't know why. He hasn't found me yet. He's convinced by centuries of spying that we have absolutely no magic here."

Centuries of spying? The thought astounded Ra-khir and sent a shiver stabbing through him. *They've been among us that long?* His mind shot instantly back to his studies, and he did manage to pull out a few oddities. There were references to mages in the distant past, and most people knew of the Cardinal Wizards in stories their parents' told. A few scattered references to giants and oversized weapons spotted the military history texts, and he remembered hearing of a detail about the Great War, hundreds of years past, where huge weapons left by a warrior from across the sea found their way into an armory. "Until the elves came to our world, that was essentially true."

"Essentially," Subikahn muttered.

"He's getting off the ship." Chymmerlee announced, though whether she knew from watching or feeling, Ra-khir did not know. Even he could see an enormous man stepping off a central ship and wading into the foam, apparently oblivious to the frenzy of sharks around him. Water that would have drowned a normal man came only to the middle of his chest. Although Ra-khir no longer saw the aura, he suspected that Chymmerlee and Saviar, who clutched the hilt of the magical sword, did.

As the *Kjempemagiska* came to shore, he was abruptly mobbed by continental soldiers, their weapons flying and weaving. The giant seemed not to notice. He drew his own massive sword with slow deliberateness and, with a single swipe, dropped ten or twenty men.

"Gods be damned," Ra-khir whispered.

Saviar started running toward the shore; but, before he could take a second step, Chymmerlee snagged his arm. "Wait!"

Saviar stopped so suddenly he had to back step to keep from falling.

"I need you, Saviar. And Subikahn. I need people here to protect me."

"That's what I'm trying to do," Saviar explained hurriedly. "If I keep him busy fighting, he can't harm you."

"True," Chymmerlee admitted. "But once he knows I'm the one constraining him, he'll send his entire army after me. I can't fight them and hinder him at the same time." She sized up her adversary and shook her head. "I'm not that strong, as mages go. One against one, he'd have me. So long as he has to fight your men, however, he can't come directly after me."

"We can't afford to lose her," Subikahn said.

Saviar glared. Clearly, he did not even need that possibility spoken aloud. "We'll stay and protect Chymmerlee. I'm sure the others will see him as their primary target."

Ra-khir looked worriedly at the shore. Men dove on the giant in droves, but he did not even seem to notice their blows. Every one of his strokes, however, effortlessly took down several defenders. At one point, he seemed to crackle with lightning, and warriors toppled in a piled up ring around him. The odor of ozone and charred flesh filled the air.

"No," Chymmerlee gasped. Closing her eyes, she raised her hands and started speaking in odd gutturals. Saviar and Subikahn crouched in front of her. Ra-khir remounted Silver Warrior and circled them warily, prepared to take down any pirate who dared come too close.

"What happened?" Saviar demanded suddenly.

Ra-khir studied the battle on the shore. The soldiers attacking had become more cautious and hesitant, but the bigger change came from the *Kjempemagiska*. He held his sword in one hand, the other raised as if to do something, and he looked wildly frustrated. His head jerked in all directions, then focused suddenly and intently on the dune.

"I . . . can . . . stem . . . his magic," Chymmerlee panted. "Or . . . I can . . . talk. Not both."

Sword readied, Saviar hovered over Chymmerlee while Subikahn crouched quietly in shadow. Ra-khir continued to watch around them. Suddenly, just as Chymmerlee predicted, pirates swarmed toward them.

Both young Renshai leaped into battle, and even Ra-khir found himself hard-pressed for the first time since the war began. Silver Warrior reared and bit while Ra-khir's sword flashed around him. They worked together like a team, well- and long-trained for battle. The sword never gashed the horse; the stallion never unbalanced its rider. Instead, they slashed and stabbed, danced and bit in a wild flurry of warfare. And left a trail of bodies in their wake.

Calistin cut down the last of his enemies with an easy gut slice, then whirled to face more that never materialized. The putrid reek of bowel and blood filled the air, obscuring the odors of sea wrack, death, and sweat. The dying man writhed at his feet; but, for the moment, the Renshai had no opponents. Clutching a dripping sword in each hand, he surveyed the beach. Something, he did not yet know what, had changed significantly. Nearby, Valr Magnus chopped down his own final pirate and found himself as strangely open as Calistin. He crouched, clearly also sensing that the tide of battle had become altered in a big way.

"There!" the general said suddenly, jabbing his sword southward.

Calistin turned to see a giant standing on the shore amid a haphazard pile of continental soldiers. He moved easily, clearly unconcerned about the men hurling themselves at him. A human wall of hacking blades left him without a scratch. He took them down without effort, his movements revealing only derision and contempt. At length, the soldiers dropped back to circle him warily, afraid to move within striking distance of his blade. The pirates' ranks on the shore had noticeably thinned. Either the continental armies had cut most of them down, or they had turned their attentions elsewhere.

No longer racing with exertion, Calistin's heart slowed to a steady pound, like war drums. A smile eased its way onto his face. Finally, it seemed, he had discovered an opponent worthy of his skill. Without hesitation, he charged, battle-screaming. His booted footfalls pounded the packed, wet sand, and his swords streamed lines of scarlet in his wake.

Men from both sides of the war scurried out of Calistin's way, and he found his route to the *Kjempemagiska* unbarred. As he plunged toward Firuz, he suddenly regretted his decision to run the entire distance. He threw himself into the combat with his legs taxed and his lungs winded, while Firuz only waited, with a curious expression, to receive him. As Calistin drew near, the *Kjempemagiska* raised his sword suddenly, intending for his crazed opponent to impale himself on the stop thrust.

Calistin dodged easily, closing under the sword and delivering a slash that cut a bloody line through Firuz' leggings and across his shin.

The *Kjempemagiska* roared, leaping back in surprise. His sword whipped down with shocking speed for one so large, and Calistin found himself hard-pressed to avoid it. He threw himself sideways, keeping his feet but missing his opening for another attack. The sword sped past him with such size and force that it overbalanced him. Even a few of the men standing back staggered in the gust of its passing.

A voice entered Calistin's head. *So you have a weapon imbued with magic, little man. Now that I know it, you will not touch me again.*

Calistin drove in, slashing with his mother's sword in his right fist, raising the left in defense. This time, he went for the knee, hoping to incapacitate. The giant moved with impressive speed. Calistin's blade barely skimmed his clothing, and the massive, curved sword slammed down hard on Calistin's left-hand blade. The attempt at a parry nearly proved Calistin's downfall. His blade shattered beneath the mighty blow; and, though the breaking steel absorbed most of the force, Calistin felt something snap in his forearm. Agony shot through his arm.

"Modi!" Calistin shouted, as much cursing his own incompetence as channeling the god of wrath. With no sword to honor, he dropped the useless hilt and forced himself to the attack. He threaded through a wild sweep of defense to bury the sword given to his mother by Colbey into the meaty part of Firuz' lower leg.

The giant roared and jerked. Sword trapped deeply in flesh, Calistin grasped the hilt like a lifeline. Firuz ripped the blade free, leaving Calistin staggering but armed. He managed to dodge the *Kjempemagiska*'s riposte, though it moved with impossible speed for one so massive. Whatever magic he had lost, the giant could still clearly keep his own movements stronger than humanity and quicker than liquid.

I need to get higher, Calistin realized; but the possibilities defeated him. They fought on flat shore, and the surrounding men made it impossible to lead the giant to the dunes, even if he bothered to follow. Calistin knew better than to jump, which would fully commit his momentum and rob him of the dexterity that was his only hope against the giant. He could not win this contest strength to strength. He reassessed his targets. Only two lethal areas seemed accessible: the massive arteries in the back of the thighs and the groin. Anything else was out of reach.

Calistin bore in, slashing, dancing, always moving. His sword scored several nicks against various parts of the giant's hands and legs. Firuz' own brutal attacks fell on empty air as Calistin remained in perpetual motion, anticipating the strikes and gliding through them. Then, abruptly, the side of Firuz' blade slammed across Calistin's cheek and neck with bruising force. The impact sent him airborne, crashing into the piled corpses, where he rolled down the opposite side, entangled with floppy arms and twitching legs. Bruised and aching, he rolled swiftly to his feet, but the giant had not followed. Firuz stood back, watching, a lopsided grin wreathing his massive face.

CHAPTER 46

The quality Valkyries seek is courage. Valhalla is the reward for any man who dies bravely in battle.

—Freya

THE WORLD DISAPPEARED into a red fog of battle, and Saviar saw nothing but targets and weapons. His arms and legs kept moving long after exhaustion overtook understanding, emotion, and most of his awareness. Hearing and smell, feeling and taste all lost meaning. Nothing remained but the sole concern of his current universe: anticipate, dodge or parry, and slash. Even the slam of his sword into flesh lost significance, except to create a hole where more enemies could flood in to meet him.

Saviar knew he had given up ground. He could sense Chymmerlee directly at his back, felt the swish of Silver Warrior and Ra-khir's sword at his left and the cut of Subikahn's to his right. They formed an unwavering triangle that seemed to remain in place more from habit and raw necessity than the skill and talent it once represented. They continued to fight because to do otherwise might mean the end of their world. They could not afford to collapse, to die, though Saviar secretly wished he dared. The promised rewards of Valhalla had never beckoned so strongly. Yet he kept fighting, kept hacking at his fresher, eager foes; and they continued to tumble back from his assault. Only to be replaced by more.

Saviar's arms had gone beyond aching to numbness. His thoughts wallowed through inertia as thick as pudding. His legs felt detached, though they continued to work in concert with his body. Eternally, his Renshai instincts, his constant and obsessive practices, came through; he chopped down enemies in singlets and pairs. Quitting was not an option, so onward Saviar went, buoyed beyond fatigue, beyond strained agony, nearly beyond consciousness itself by forces he could not name.

The triumphant blare of a horn managed to penetrate Saviar's thoughts, although its meaning eluded him.

Subikahn shouted breathlessly, "It's the East!"

The East. The words were insignificant sounds in Saviar's ears. *The.* He had to define it. *East.* Understanding seeped slowly through his brain. Then the sound of clamoring steel chimed across the beach and joined the echoes from the great mountains and buildings of Béarn. *The East!* It came to him like lightning through a crackling wall of dancing spots. The armies of the East had arrived, abandoning their previous station on the Western Plains. *Strong, untired reinforcements.* If he could have dredged up the energy, Saviar might have cheered.

Then, suddenly, Subikahn gasped.

The sound proved so compelling, Saviar could not help glancing toward his twin, even though it opened his defenses. Luckily, no one gaffed him through the hole. Subikahn remained standing, his motions as swift and graceful as ever, at least to Saviar's exhausted eye. Whatever had happened was not a deathblow. Subikahn stared out over the enemies to the newcomers; and something there held his gaze as much as any one thing could keep the focus of a man engaged in battle, hemmed in by enemies.

Though concentrating on his opponents, Saviar dared to look. The man at the head of the Eastern cavalry caught his eye like a golden beacon. Tall and blond, unarmored and unhelmeted, he stood out magnificently among the swarthy Easterners, which also made him an obvious target. Saviar's own resistance decreased noticeably as the pirates turned some of their attention to this new threat.

"It's Talamir," Subikahn said. Though he spoke barely above a whisper, Saviar heard him. "Talamir's . . . alive. He's alive."

For the moment. Hard-pressed to his own defense, Saviar did not speak aloud, even had he had something useful to say. The sight clearly galvanized Subikahn, whose strokes became as swift and vigorous as if he had newly joined the fight. Saviar did not try to match him. The sharp sting of small cuts and injuries seemed the only thing keeping him awake. He plunged back into a battle that, at least now, seemed to have a positive end.

<hr />

It took General Valr Magnus longer to clear a path along the beach, and he arrived just in time to see Calistin tumble down a pile of the dead and dying. Without a thought, he dove for Firuz, only to find himself unexpectedly jerked backward by his sword arm. He whirled, catching his balance, but unable to stop the movement from appearing awkward. He slashed blindly at the person or object that had stopped him, but his sword cut through empty air.

Magnus found himself staring at a warrior he had never seen before, clearly of the continental forces by his dress and a Northman by coloring. He wore no armor, jewelry, or adornments. His tunic and breeks, though simple, looked richly tailored; and he wore a sword at either hip. "Sheathe your weapon, Valr," the man commanded.

Affronted, Valr Magnus ignored the demand. "I'm not letting Calistin fight that abomination alone."

"Nor should you." With a movement so quick Magnus could not follow it, the stranger drew and flipped his own right-hand weapon so that the hilt faced the general. "But your blade can't hit him. Mine can."

Magnus blinked, uncertain. From the corner of his eye, he saw Calistin spin to his feet and fling himself at the monster again. There was no time for questioning. The offered weapon appeared finely polished, oiled and cared for. Dutifully, he slammed his sword into its sheath and closed his fingers around the other's hilt. For an instant, his touch met resistance, and the stranger looked distressed. Then, it came free in Valr Magnus' hand, and the extent of its fineness became abundantly clear. The balance awed him, a perfection he would not have believed any blacksmith could achieve. The blade glimmered, just heavy enough for solid momentum and steel integrity, yet light for speed. The split-leather haft fit his hand as if crafted especially for it. Whirling, he breathed out a grateful "Thank you," as he charged Firuz.

Calistin became a golden blur of motion, his sword slicing nicks into flesh that felt as thick and solid as wood. Firuz' attacks still came as swiftly and with the force of a galloping steed, but Calistin never held still long enough for the massive sword to touch him. A couple of times, it came dangerously close, rocking him in the wave of air that accompanied its passing. Always, that proved enough to dislodge Calistin and to steal any opening he might have for a dangerous riposte. His left arm ached excruciatingly, and his right felt heavy with exhaustion.

They both knew time favored the *Kjempemagiska*. Calistin's constant need for motion would become his undoing. Fatigue took even the gods, eventually; and both attack and defense required Calistin to make ten or twenty movements for every one of the giant's. It would only take one miscalculation, a single lucky swing, to remove Calistin permanently from the battle.

But Calistin refused to consider the odds. He defied them daily. Three to one, a hundred to one, a million to one; all that mattered was the one. He drove in again and again, hoping fortune would favor him with just enough time to jab in a lethal blow. All he needed was an opening. He would handle the rest.

And that opening did finally come, after what seemed like grim hours of dodge and slash, whirlwind grace and steel lethality. Calistin managed to stab his blade deeply into the giant's left leg.

Firuz let out a bellow of outrage and pain, stock-still for a moment in deadly stalemate. If he moved too quickly, he might dislodge the sword causing dangerous tearing or bleeding. But, if he remained still too long, he gave Calistin the opportunity to shove it deeper or jerk it loose with the same horrible consequences.

The moment lasted less than a small, grim fraction of a second. As Calistin wrestled to wrench the gouge into a tear, Firuz kicked him with his unharmed leg. Calistin sprang, but his hold on his own hilt limited his movement. The giant's shin caught him an off-balance blow with enough force to free sword and Renshai, sending them spinning in an awkward arch.

Then, another blade joined the battle, in the grip of Valr Magnus.

Twisting, trying to keep his steadying movements unpredictable, Calistin shouted a warning. "No, Valr! Your sword can't—"

But, miraculously, it did. The blade carved a line of leather from Firuz' sandal ties and kissed open a spot of blood just below his knee.

Calistin charged in again, with renewed vigor. The two men fell into a cooperative rhythm, as they had on the shore, two insidious mosquitoes assaulting their massive foe. Magnus had the great advantage of height and reach, but Calistin moved more quickly and with a fluid grace that seemed more liquid than human. Magnus demonstrated a great skill and quickness of his own, and his strength made Calistin's seem paltry.

Then, suddenly, laughter filled Calistin's head. *She's wavering.*

Calistin had no idea what Firuz meant, nor did he care. He knew better than to converse during a battle of this magnitude. A truly competent *torke* would sprawl him the moment he opened his mouth, a well-taught lesson. Yet, even without question, the answer came. With an abruptness Calistin had to attribute to magic, Firuz' movements accelerated. The change caught both men off guard, but Valr Magnus took the first blow. It caught him hard in the side, hurling

him into the air. Blood splashed Calistin, then he found himself too
hard-pressed to his own defense to worry about his companion.

Stand still, you gnat!

In comparison to Firuz' newfound speed, Calistin felt as if he
might have obeyed the command. He found himself pushed beyond
the limit to dodge the giant's wild blows, more by anticipation than
skill. Things made sudden sense. Whatever had curtailed the *Kjempemagiska*'s magic had started to fail. Calistin had no idea of the full
range of Firuz' abilities, but he knew he had better act swiftly. The
sooner he took the giant down, the less chance Firuz would have to
regather his power, to demonstrate the supernatural talents he was
gradually regaining.

Calistin bore in, sacrificing agility for speed. *The best defense is a
dead enemy.* He sprang for Firuz' thigh.

But the giant's superhuman speed defied even Calistin. Another
kick sent him sprawling, then the giant's sword screamed down on
the Renshai.

Battle-trained eyes knew death when they saw it, and Calistin
could not move quickly enough. *I'm dead.* Nevertheless, he flung
himself sideways, attempting to roll.

"No!" someone screamed. A small figure flew over Calistin. In
the instant it took the sword to skewer this new body, Calistin's roll
carried him free. His rescuer collapsed, run through by Firuz' blade,
flopping onto Calistin's trailing and injured left arm.

Agony burst through Calistin a second time. "Modi," he screamed,
to clear his head. "Modi!" He jerked free, pain whitewashing his vision, and stumbled toward his opponent. Despite the near-miss, despite the anguish chewing at his consciousness, Calistin had to claim
what might prove his only opening. In the instant it took the magically quickened giant to dislodge his blade from the corpse, Calistin
sprang through his defenses to bury Kevral's sword in the right side
of Firuz' groin.

The blade cut deeply into flesh. Ignoring all sight and sound
around him, with no regard to defense, Calistin ripped the blade
downward with all the strength remaining in his arm and body.

Blood shot from the wound with a force that sent Calistin tumbling, sword still gripped tightly in his fist. Like a wave, it encompassed him, salty and stinging, battering him helplessly until he
worried he would never breathe again. Then, Firuz' body toppled,
amid running screaming men. The torrent of arterial blood dropped
to a trickle, and Calistin sprang to his feet, spitting and dripping.

Only then, Calistin glanced at his savior, the one who had taken the blow that should have killed him. Treysind lay, still, on the sand, his chest torn open by the giant's massive blade. Shattered ribs poked through the opening, and blood dripped mercilessly onto the sand.

"No!" Calistin found himself seized with a sudden urge to tear apart anyone and anything in his reach. He threw himself on the boy, shaking until loops of bowel appeared at the wound. "No, Treysind! Wake up!" It was raw stupidity for a Renshai to act like an ignorant child who cannot tell that his mother has died. Calistin knew death better than anyone, knew a fatal wound when he saw one, and even an infant could see that no life remained in Treysind's body. "Get up, do you hear me! Get! Up!" He shook Treysind even more violently. "I told you not to help, you stupid child! You weren't supposed to be here!"

"Calistin," Valr Magnus said sternly, but even he knew better than to step within Calistin's reach.

Then, Calistin saw the Valkyrie, and his blood ran cold. Randgrithr, *Shieldbearer.* He knew her name just as he had Hildr's, the Valkyrie who had accompanied his mother to Valhalla. *For Valr Magnus?* Calistin thought he had heard the general's living voice, but the *Valkyrie* must have come for someone brave, someone who had died in glorious combat. He glanced past Treysind's body to the Aeri general. The Northman's mail hung in strips, revealing a heaving well-muscled chest, and the entire left side of his body was smeared scarlet. He stood in clear awe, his blue eyes wide, his jaw drooping, and his nostrils flared. Slowly, he collapsed to one knee, not from pain or fatigue, but in a gesture of overwhelming respect.

An insubstantial image of Treysind stood beside the boy's ravaged body, talking earnestly and softly with Randgrithr. Then, suddenly, they both turned toward Calistin.

Instinctively, Calistin raised his sword. He knew he looked a fright, covered from the tips of his hair to his toes in sticky, giant's blood and sweat, his left arm hanging uselessly at his side. Sparing him barely a glance, the *Valkyrie* turned back to Treysind's soul, her gestures broad and irate. Then, she let her hands fall in obvious defeat, sighed, and nodded.

Treysind's body remained where it had fallen, but the image of him at Randgrithr's side flew at Calistin like an angry wraith. Startled, Calistin kept his sword in battle position, but the image only dissipated like a loose sand sculpture in the wind. Warmth suffused Calistin, so vast and sudden he was seized with the urge to strip off his clothing and leap into the ocean. A new rush of sweat further slicked his every part. Then, as quickly as the fire had flared, it disappeared. A breeze from the ocean whipped his damp limbs into gooseflesh.

The *Valkyrie* raised her arms to leave, but Calistin caught one, jerking her to face him.

Randgrithr turned and glared at Calistin. "What do you want, Calistin Ra-khirsson?" She made a gesture to indicate the body-strewn beach. "A war of this magnitude is not enough for you? You want at me, too?"

Calistin did not seek a battle this time, but he would gladly fight her if she wished it or refused him the information he craved. "You came for Treysind?"

The *Valkyrie* regarded Calistin. "He died in brave and glorious combat. He gave himself for you. Twice." She shook her head. "I'm not at all sure you're worth it."

Calistin gritted his teeth at the insult but did not otherwise react. He could not imagine any *Einherjar* would prefer Treysind over him as an opponent. Yet the *Valkyries* clearly saw the world differently than their charges. Or, at least, this one did. "I saved his life, too."

The Valkyrie's brows rose over pale eyes, and a thick wad of yellow hair escaped her helmet. "Perhaps. But you did not give him . . . everything."

Startled, Calistin back stepped. "What?"

In that moment, Randgrithr raised her hands again and disappeared in a golden flash of light.

Valr Magnus rose, staring at the place where she had stood. "That . . . she . . ." He looked helplessly at Calistin. "Was that a . . ."

"*Valkyrie,* yes." Calistin kicked Treysind's body, wrestling a mass of emotions he could not handle. "You idiot child!" He hammered a toe against Treysind's ear, sending the bloodless face flopping sideways. Sand splashed, clinging to the sightless eyes.

"Stop that!" Magnus made a move as if to grab Calistin but stopped short of doing so. "He's your brother. Don't dishonor him like that."

Calistin bit his lower lip, wanting to continue until the head came fully free and he could send it flying into the surf. "That's not my brother. It's nothing but an empty container. He's dead, and his soul . . . his soul . . ." Calistin gazed into the sky. Multihued bands touched the western horizon in layers of color. Only a bare tip of the sun remained.

". . . found Valhalla," Magnus finished. "He's *Einherjar.* When your time comes, you'll see him again."

"No." Calistin understood the *Valkyrie*'s words in a way the general never could. "No. He refused her. He chose not to go."

Valr Magnus stiffened. No Northman could understand why anyone given the opportunity would not accept Valhalla. "Are you sure?"

Calistin nodded grimly. "He made the ultimate sacrifice," one the Renshai found himself incapable of imagining. In all the annals of history, in all the fairy tales of yore, no one had ever performed such an unselfish act, not even one lover for another. For Treysind, Calistin realized, had given up not only his life, but his afterlife. With Randgrithr's help, Treysind had donated his soul to the one living being who had none. *I'm not at all sure you're worth it,* the *Valkyrie* had said, and Calistin had to agree. It was a gift like no other; surely no man could ever live up to anything so singularly precious.

Galloping hoofbeats pulled Calistin from his thoughts, and a horse skidded to a stop in front of Valr Magnus, plowing up sand that clung to the drying blood on both men. The Béarnian rider called out, "General, there's an officers' meeting at Béarn Castle as soon as everyone can be gathered."

"Thank you." Valr Magnus waved the soldier off.

The Béarnide reined his horse and headed along the beach to inform the others.

Calistin found himself nearly incapable of thought. Every part of him ached, and his arm desperately needed the attention of a healer. He battled emotions he usually kept well-suppressed, and his thoughts scattered like the sand beneath the horse's hooves.

Valr Magnus cleared his throat. "So, Calistin. The war is essentially won. Do you want that battle now?"

Calistin glanced up. The general looked a fright, his helmet dented and askew, his mail sliced open, his every part smeared with blood. The Renshai knew he looked equally horrible: his arm broken, his body covered with bruises and slashes, fully steeped in Firuz' blood. He considered the general's offer for less than an instant. Magnus had killed his mother and exiled his people from the only home he knew. And, though that combat seemed grossly unfair, Magnus himself had fought with honor. The desperate urge to destroy Valr Magnus, once a burning and insatiable need, had died with Treysind. At the moment, Calistin felt nothing but overwhelming grief, sorrow, and fatigue.

Still, the challenge needed answering, his honor and that of his tribe depended on it. "Valr." Calistin's voice sounded strangely raspy, and he cleared his throat. "For the first time in my life, I saw a live

Renshai willingly give his sword to another." He granted the general a look intended to demonstrate, beyond a doubt, the significance and seriousness of that statement. "I can have no quarrel with a man so respected by the immortal and consummate Renshai, Colbey Calistinsson."

All remaining color drained from Magnus' face, making the blood still leaking from his side resemble fire. "Colbey Calistinsson?" He whirled toward the place where he had acquired his newest sword, though the stranger had long since disappeared. Valr Magnus muttered, clearly quoting, "Your blade can't hit him; mine can." A smile crossed his lips. "Colbey Calistinsson."

The moment was historic in so many ways—because of two enemies bonded against a magical foe, the pirates had lost their great leader and, soon, the war itself. Yet nothing cemented it more than the immortal being, dismissed by Northmen as a figment of foolish Renshai imagination, handing over his most prized possession to a Northman, a sworn enemy of Renshai, the very cause of their exile.

To Calistin's own surprise, a laugh escaped him.

Valr Magnus also smiled, then honest laughter rumbled from him to join with Calistin's own.

For several moments the two stood, dripping, on the beach, laughing at a joke only they understood.

"Come on," Magnus finally said, placing an arm across Calistin's shoulders. He reeked of blood and death, of sweat and steel, of salt and wind. "Let's wash up and get to that meeting."

"Meeting?" Calistin gave the Aeri general a sideways look. "I'm not an officer."

"Sure you are." Steel still clanged along the beach as the last battles raged to their foregone conclusion. Without the leadership of their only *Kjempemagiska*, the pirates seemed confused and uncertain. "You're the captain of . . ." Valr pursed his lips. "The captain of . . . my . . . Renshai."

Calistin's brows rose. It seemed petty to argue over the pronoun "my" when they had just laughed off a prearranged battle to the death. "So, basically, I command . . . myself." Calistin stopped there, not bothering to mention what they both already knew. Once the war in Béarn ended, they would have to go their separate ways, not only because Calistin already had a commitment to his own people, but because all Renshai were banned from the Northlands.

"Well, someone should. And I can't think of anyone else you'd listen to."

Deliberately keeping his thoughts off Treysind, Calistin forced a smile. For the moment he wanted to enjoy this one small alliance, a tiny victory in a crusade that spanned centuries.

The door to his sickroom eased open silently, yet the movement still awakened King Tae Kahn. Even a recovery from near-fatal injuries failed to steal the wariness ingrained in him nearly since birth. He remained still, as always, one eye open to a slit, just enough to catch the identity of the person who had disturbed him without revealing his awakening. He continued to breathe deeply, in the pattern of his previous sleep.

The newcomer wore the familiar black and silver of his Eastern army, without the bulk of mail or lacquered leather. Instead of the ornate helmets that served as a badge of honor for the Eastern leaders, he wore only a hat from which jutted the familiar five feathers of his highest general. By movement alone, through the slit of one eye, Tae could tell this was not General Halcone, the previous high commander of his armies. Apparently, Tae now faced Weile's acclaimed mystery general.

As the other man turned to quietly close the door, Tae opened both eyes and sat up in his bed.

The curtains to the open, fourth-story window fluttered in the breeze; then, as the door clicked closed, went dormant. Tae discerned as many details as possible in the moments before the man turned to face him. First, he was a bit shorter and far leaner than Halcone; and his movements demonstrated a grace and quickness that the former high general did not share. The visible flesh at his wrists and neck looked far too pale to fit the swarthy East, and the hair that feathered out from beneath his hat was short and brilliant yellow. *A Northman,* Tae realized, and that only confused him. *Why would Weile Kahn put a Northman at the head of our troops? Why would the men accept and follow him?*

Tae eased himself from the covers, though it seemed pointless. He did not yet have the strength to do much more than hurl himself out the window to his death.

The man in Eastern silver and black turned. He swept his hat from his head to his hand.

Tae recognized him instantly and found himself incapable of keeping that knowledge to himself, "Talamir?" Myriad questions sprang to mind, but he did not voice them.

"Yes, Sire." Talamir moved nearer and bowed.

Tae only stared. "But you're . . . you're . . ."

"Dead?" Talamir supplied.

It was the right word, but clearly stupid, so Tae discarded it. "Obviously not. You're . . . my . . . general?"

"Yes, Sire." Talamir came even closer, standing at the side of Tae's bed. He looked fresh and strong. If he had taken part in the long battle, he had suffered no injuries and cleaned up well. "I couldn't use the armor, of course, or the beautiful helmet."

"Of course." Tae knew the laws of Renshai well. The answer to all his questions came to him in a rush of logic. "This was my father's idea."

Talamir shuffled his feet, touched his hilt. "I'm not permitted to say, my lord."

"Of course not. Nothing Weile Kahn does is ever 'on the record.'" Tae forced a smile. He knew what had to come next but had spent too much time flirting with death to care. "Does Subikahn know . . . you're . . . alive?"

"Yes, Sire."

"Good."

Talamir's brows rose. "Is it?"

Tae suppressed a sigh and tried not to hesitate. "Yes, it's good. Subikahn will need someone to look after him, someone to love him, after I'm dead."

"Dead, Sire?" Talamir continued to stare at Tae, though he still avoided the king's eyes. "But the healers told me you're past the point of uncertainty. Your wounds are definitely healing, Sire."

Imorelda crawled out from under the bed, yawning widely and stretching each leg. *I told you.*

Tae ignored the cat. "True, but you've come to kill me, haven't you?"

Talamir back stepped. "Sire?"

Imorelda stopped in mid-stretch and jumped onto the bed, as if to defend her master. *Sire?* she repeated, equally surprised.

Tae merely studied Talamir, trying to catch the gaze that kept dodging his. The Renshai still saw him as an authority figure, one he obviously intended to obey.

Talamir cleared his throat. "Sire, I have no intention of committing regicide, even were you not the beloved father of my . . . my . . ." His voice faded into nothingness, clearly worried to offend by whatever word he chose.

"Beloved?" The word caused Tae physical pain, and his hand went to the agony still brewing in his lung. "Talamir, you must know by now. Subikahn hates me."

"Never, Sire."

"He hates me for what I did to you. To both of you." Tae closed his eyes. "And without my son, I have no reason to go on."

A claw dug through the blankets into Tae's leg, and Imorelda glided up to rest beneath his arm. *What about me? Aren't I worth something?*

Wincing, eyes flashing open, Tae took Imorelda into his arms. *Of course. You're worth your weight in fish heads, my darling; but Subikahn is my son.*

Talamir bit his lip, as if trying to contain words that burned his tongue. In the end, they slipped out, "I didn't rape him. I would never do that to anyone, but especially not to the one I love more than my own self."

Tae raised a hand to stem the tide. "I know. Subikahn convinced me, and I've had several days lying here with nothing to do but think. It took me a while to figure out why you confessed to a crime you never committed."

"I did it for Subikahn."

"Yes." For a long time, the Renshai's selflessness had defied Tae's understanding. "You did it to protect Subikahn, to save him from execution."

Talamir nodded. "I was dead either way, whether for rape or for consensual sodomy. But, in the latter case, you would have had to execute Prince Subikahn with me."

"I would never have done that."

Talamir looked directly at the floor now. "I couldn't take that chance."

Imorelda purred beneath Tae's touch.

"But that's not why I came to see you, Sire." Talamir continued to avoid Tae's gaze, clearly uncomfortable and needing to change the subject. "As your general, I came to inform you of the officers' meeting taking place in the Strategy Room. It's my job to either accompany you or represent you."

Tae considered. Matrinka had kept him apprised of the war as it progressed, and he knew this phase had all but ended. "With help, I think I can make it. Someone needs to tell them not to celebrate too quickly, that the next round we'll face more men and many more giants."

Talamir stiffened and finally looked toward Tae again. "Next round? You mean . . . it's not over?"

"Not nearly." Tae remembered the jumble of information he had taken from the pirates' minds. "They underestimated us once, but they will not do so again. They made a lot of assumptions and fatal mistakes, expecting us to have no magic, for example. Thinking they would find us as consistent as their *alsona*. They did not expect the Northmen, believing their lands uninhabitable. Though they had a bit of experience with Renshai, they did not anticipate them organized and in such numbers. Our enemy came at us cocky and overconfident, but the loss of one of their *Kjempemagiska* has taught them otherwise. Next time, they will attack in true force; and, without the elves and their magic, we will be overcome."

"Overcome? In battle? Never!" It was the only response a Renshai could give, yet it demonstrated the worst vice of the tribe.

Tae knew he had to attend the meeting. Talamir might be incapable of delivering the proper message. In addition to believing wholeheartedly in their own skill, Renshai had a tendency to blurt news that should be handled with subtlety and caution.

Talamir turned. "I'll see you in the Strategy Room, Sire."

Tae could not let him go, not yet. "Talamir?"

The Renshai looked back, hat still clutched in his hand. "Yes, Sire?"

"I'm sorry, Talamir. I made a huge mistake."

"Mistake, Sire?" Talamir turned around, and this time he met Tae's gaze. "Your reaction was completely understandable."

It was? Tae found himself incapable of blinking. Imorelda's purring died, and she went utterly still.

"And your strategy was brilliant. I could have saved myself a lot of pain and worry had I seen through it sooner."

Bewildered, Tae let Talamir speak.

"You had to test us. I mean, you had to make absolutely certain I loved Subikahn for himself, not for his wealth or power."

So far, Talamir spoke with eminent intelligence.

"Ye-es?" Tae encouraged.

"And you had to make sure I hadn't beguiled Subikahn, that he had entered the relationship of his own accord."

Tae saw where Talamir was going. And, though they both knew it was a game, he played along. "And that Subikahn had the fortitude to take my place someday."

"So," Talamir said, "you concocted this whole terrible scheme but made sure your father would give me the means to survive it." A slight smile played over Talamir's lips as he looked askance at Tae.

★You're making this up!★ Imorelda looked from man to man. *★You're making this all up!★*

"And," Tae added thoughtfully. "Had I directly asked you to lead my army, you would have refused, given your need to return to the Renshai. This way, I got you."

"How very clever," Talamir exclaimed a bit too eagerly. "I would have missed that part." He winked. "And when I'm finished explaining all of this to Prince Subikahn, I'm certain he will forgive you."

Tae grinned. He could think of nothing more important than reclaiming the love and respect of his son. "And after I've explained it all to Weile Kahn, I may disappear under mysterious circumstances." Despite his words, Tae reveled in the chance to actually appear as if he had conned his inhumanly clever father. He just had to be careful not to harm Weile's reputation while rescuing his relationship with his only son.

"Oh, I think you'll find he's proud of you. I suspect it's been many decades since anyone manipulated Weile Kahn. To have one's son finally surpass him, I'm told, is the secret dream of every father."

Tae looked over the Renshai in a new light and bestowed the greatest compliment he could think of at the moment. "Talamir, I never thought I'd say this to anyone, ever, given that I have no daughters. But, I'm proud to call you son-in-law."

Talamir fairly beamed. "I'll wait outside, Sire. Knock when you're ready, and we'll go to the strategy meeting together."

EPILOGUE

Hard-won friendships often have an intensity that regular relation-
ships never match.

> —*Bard Darris*

THE CLANG OF WEAPONRY lasted through the night and continued in small, scattered pockets into the morning. As the fresh
troops from the distant beaches faded, the soldiers who had managed
to sleep through the night took over. Acrid smoke floated over Béarn,
and Ra-khir could see flames blazing from the anchored ships, the
water glowing red as wine. Apparently, the continental allied archers
had performed the job they had failed at earlier, or scouts had braved
the sharks to torch the pirates' ships directly.

Ra-khir had no trouble leaving Thialnir to handle the Renshai.
The knight's job had technically ended the moment he won them
legitimacy for the course of the war, and the Renshai would fight
without strategy or pattern anyway. They seemed ideally suited for
cleaning up the chaotic remnants of the once-mighty pirates. Ra-khir
had a more pressing matter, one that he had arranged at the short
officers' meeting the previous evening.

When the last of the enemies fell, Béarn had promised a massive
feast: in the banquet hall for the commanders, civilian and military
leaders, and royalty; outside on the beach for the regular and volunteer soldiers. Then, the Knights of Erythane would serve another
purpose, maintaining suitable decorum and tradition. Tedious rituals
and long-winded speeches would rule the hours before and after the
food got served, interrupted at proper intervals by entertainers, animals, and bards. Though he had learned to respect the procedures,
Ra-khir had never learned to love them. He did not look forward to
the ceremony, other than the fact that its start would mean that he
had finished the business that faced him now.

Ra-khir found Saviar crumpled in the sand beyond the dunes,

where the battles had long finished, his clothing tattered and his skin striped with nicks and blood. The knight's heart rate quickened, a startled pounding in his ears. Then, he noticed Subikahn sitting calmly nearby, sword meticulously balanced across his knees. "Relax, Papa. He's only sleeping."

A cold rush of relief washed through Ra-khir, nearly as uncomfortable as the fear that had clutched him a moment earlier. "I've never seen anyone sleep like that." He gestured at Saviar.

"Apparently, you've never seen anyone fall asleep standing up."

"No," Ra-khir admitted. "What are you doing here?"

"Making sure no one uses his lifeless-looking body as a battle dummy." Subikahn yawned, his own exhaustion clear and understandable. "I can't believe you're still running around."

"I slept," Ra-khir admitted. "After the officers' meeting I couldn't keep my eyes open." He thought it better not to mention that he had caught himself slipping away twice at the meeting. Only Tae Kahn's grave pronouncement regarding the future war had finally shocked him enough to finish. "Your father was there, at the meeting. Out of bed."

"I know." Subikahn yawned again. "I talked to Talamir last night."

Ra-khir laughed.

Subikahn gave him a strange look.

"Sorry. I was just thinking of how odd things got. A Knight of Erythane as general of Renshai, and a Renshai as general of the Eastlands. The best seers in the land could never have predicted that."

Now, Subikahn also laughed. "Who was it that said, 'War makes for the strangest of alliances?'"

Ra-khir knew the answer, much to his chagrin. "That would be General Santagithi. And the full text continues, '... separates the incompetent from the skilled and the petty from the truly important.'"

Subikahn widened his eyes, clearly surprised. Apparently, no one in the past had known to whom to attribute the quotation.

"My father has taken an intense interest in that ancient general, especially now that Kedrin's actually met several people from the town named for him." Ra-khir rolled his eyes. King Griff had spent most of his life there, with his Santagithian stepfather, but Kedrin had never before met actual warriors from that Western nation. The Knight-Captain's excited chattering had broken into Ra-khir's precious resting time, and he had fallen asleep to war quotations. "Apparently, Santagithi's military studies are from a book written by him, and they're actually acclaimed for their strategies."

"And how is Chymmerlee?"

"Exhausted and starving, but apparently unhurt. Matrinka said she'd never seen a woman eat that much in a sitting. She's sleeping soundly in a private room, away from the wounded soldiers." Ra-khir looked pointedly at Subikahn. "I intended to present Chymmerlee to the Council as one of the war's greatest heroes, but she made me vow not to tell anyone what she did, never to speak of her magic."

Subikahn bobbed his head wearily. "Saviar made a similar promise. I didn't, but he'd kill me if I told you anything more."

Ra-khir did not press. He would never break a promise, nor cajole anyone else to do so either. "She did say that two elves had assisted her, enhancing her powers, from the top of Béarn Castle. Without them, she could not have lasted nearly as long. She asked me to thank them and do my best to swear them to secrecy as well."

Subikahn maintained eye contact, though his lids drooped over bloodshot whites. "And have you done so?"

"Tem'aree'ay had no difficulty agreeing, but she denied having a companion. She said Chymmerlee must have made a mistake; she alone strengthened the magic." Ra-khir tried to read something more than exhaustion from Subikahn's expression. "What do you think?"

Subikahn yawned. "I think . . . Chymmerlee must have been mistaken. Unless . . ." He dismissed his own suggestion with a doubtful shake.

"Unless?" Ra-khir encouraged.

"Unless . . . Ivana?"

Ivana had shown no signs of intelligence for eighteen years. Ra-khir hated to admit his thoughts had gone in the same direction before he dismissed them. "It seems unlikely."

"Unlikely," Subikahn echoed. He looked longingly at Saviar. "Can you take over as bodyguard? If I don't get some sleep soon, I'm going to keel over. Hopefully, enemies will mistake us both for corpses and won't bother to stab us full of holes."

Ra-khir appreciated Subikahn's loyalty to his brother and understood his current distraction. "I'll do better. I need to take Saviar to the castle for a meeting. Why don't you tag along, and we'll find you a safe bed?"

Subikahn did not argue. He closed his eyes while Ra-khir awakened Saviar, and the three men trudged across the sand together.

By the time Ra-khir and Saviar arrived at the Strategy Room, the others had already assembled. They opened the door to a rumble of speculative conversation that faded into questioning silence. King Griff sat in his place at the head of the table, Bard Darris to his left and Queen Matrinka to his right. King Humfreet of Erythane was seated beside Matrinka, Captain Erik Leifsson of Nordmir at his other side. Across from him sat General Valr Magnus of Aerin and, much to Ra-khir's surprise, Calistin. Two seats remained, the one beside the Nordmirian, which Saviar reluctantly took, and the one at the far end from the King of Béarn, which protocol indicated should belong to Ra-khir, who had assembled them.

Erik's teenaged son, Verdondi, sat on the floor outside the circle, along with a Béarnian page already hurriedly taking notes for the Sage. Recalling the time he had hauled a curious Saviar to a Council meeting, Ra-khir had had little trouble agreeing to let Verdondi observe. Destined to take his father's place someday, he should witness instances of diplomacy, even one as uncomfortable as this one threatened to become. To deny Erik's request, Ra-khir would have had to give a reason, one that might have raised suspicions in the mind of Nordmir's representative. Ra-khir wanted to see an honest, not a rehearsed, reaction.

Ra-khir glanced at Saviar to rebuke him for his rudeness, then bowed gallantly and properly to each guest in order of rank. Only when he had dispensed with the proper amenities did he take his own seat. "I apologize profusely for arriving late. I was searching for our last representative, still among the combatants, and he required some grooming.

Saviar put a hand over his mouth, presumably to hide a smile. Clearly, he appreciated that his father had not mentioned finding him in a crumpled heap.

Ra-khir mouthed all the meeting preliminaries, though he knew that, absent a Knight of Erythane, they might well have gotten skipped. At length, he reached his final prefacing announcement: "In the interests of full disclosure, I must mention that the man representing the Renshai, and the one serving as a captain of Aerin, are my sons."

Valr Magnus rose so suddenly, he had to grab his chair to keep it from toppling. He stared at Calistin. "Your father is a Knight of Erythane? But I thought—"

Calistin grinned, obviously amused by the general's consternation. "Calistin *Ra-khirsson*. I believe I mentioned that."

Magnus looked at Ra-khir, who dutifully bowed. "Sir Ra-khir Kedrin's son, Knight to their Majesties, King Humfreet of Erythane and High King Griff of Béarn."

The general had also heard that introduction before, but he had clearly not put together the Ra-khirsson of Calistin's name with the Sir Ra-khir of Erythane. He would not get fooled twice, however. "Kedrin's son. So your father is . . ."

Ra-khir gave Magnus the opportunity to finish.

". . . the knights' general."

"We use the title captain," Ra-khir explained. "My father is properly titled Knight-Captain Kedrin."

"Yes, well." Valr Magnus cleared his throat. "In the interest of full disclosure, then, I must proclaim that my Captain of . . ."

"Renshai," Calistin filled in, studying his chipped fingernails, which still had bits of blood beneath them.

The Aeri glared at Calistin. "My captain is, apparently, his son."

Now, Erik leaped to his feet. "Valr, are you saying your captain is a . . ." He looked from Calistin to Ra-khir and back, clearly trying to put together everything so far spoken. ". . . a . . ." His brow knitted. ". . . a Knight of Erythane?"

"Gods, no," Calistin said quickly, his voice even. "What a horrible thought."

Now, Ra-khir turned his searing gaze on Calistin. "Captain Erik, both of my sons are Renshai."

Erik kept his attention on Valr Magnus, his cheeks purpling and his eyes glaring.

Verdondi rose and placed a hand on Erik's shoulder. He stared nearly as intently at Saviar and whispered something into the Northman's ear.

King Humfreet took over. "Now that the additional introductions are out of the way, and all the family ties elucidated, why did you call us here?"

"I have one last introduction, with your leave, Your Majesty."

Griff nodded and gestured for Ra-khir to continue.

Ra-khir turned, opened the door, and addressed one of the guards. "Bring our guest here now, please."

The guard bowed, and Ra-khir shut the door again. "With your indulgence, I would like you to meet a man with some interesting information. Before we do, though, I must ask for immunity for him from all of you, as representatives of your respective peoples. Without it, I don't believe he will speak."

Erik's massive fist crashed to the table. "I'll make him speak."

Released from the Nordmirian's pinning stare, Magnus sat calmly.

Ra-khir sighed. By bringing Saviar instead of Thialnir, he had hoped to avoid theatrics. "Our guest has committed no crime himself. He has come to tell us what he knows, but he worries that some among us might hold him responsible for things his nephew has done."

Griff said softly, "Given that information, I have no trouble granting him immunity and protection, if he needs it."

"Granted here as well," King Humfreet added gruffly.

Valr Magnus went next, "Aerin does not punish innocent men, and I will not allow my men to exact vengeance on him either."

Still standing, Erik waved a gruff hand, obviously intended as a vow.

Ra-khir's gaze fell to Saviar, and the others followed. Suddenly the focus of every man's attention, Saviar slouched in his chair, clearly wishing he could disappear entirely. "Saviar," Ra-khir reminded. "You speak for the Renshai."

The cool look Saviar returned his father spoke of future retaliation, not against the visiting speaker but against the knight himself. "I can't . . . I mean I don't know . . ."

Ra-khir squared his jaw. He should have prepared Saviar more thoroughly, but their conversation had turned to other matters. "Saviar, I assure you that, without a vow from a Renshai leader, this man will not speak out. He fears the Renshai most of all."

Saviar sucked air through his lips, then let it out in a slow stream from his nose. "I promise not to harm this man for past crimes, and I will do everything I can to keep any individual Renshai from hurting him either."

Ra-khir nodded, satisfied. He knew as well as Saviar that no one could contain a Renshai bent on killing, but he trusted his son to do his best to present things to his tribe in the best possible light. He was not so sure, however, about Calistin.

The door edged open to admit a sheepish-looking, potbellied Erythanian dressed in foppish garb. His shoes were made of silk, and he wore a pointed hat with an enormous tassel. Clearly, he had not participated in the war.

Ra-khir held the door for the Erythanian, who sidled inside, studying the gathering at the table. He bowed several times, each one deeper than the one before.

"These men have granted you immunity in the name of Béarn, Erythane, Aerin, Nordmir, and the Renshai. You are safe to speak your piece."

The man bowed a few more times. His voice emerged as a frightened squeak. "My name is Georan, brother to Harveki and uncle to Frendon Harveki's son."

Murmurs traveled through the listeners as they recognized the name of the man who had turned the tide of battle between Valr Magnus and Kevral Tainharsdatter, the one who had fallen from the tree.

The man glanced at Ra-khir, his features scrunched and his expression needy.

Ra-khir reached into his pocket, retrieved the Northern coins he had bought back from the merchant in Dunford, and dumped them onto the table. The coins jangled together then plunked to the wooden top in an arrhythmic jumble, some rolling on edge before dropping flat. "Merchants in Dunford sold me these coins of Nordmirian mint, used by an Erythanian to buy luxuries. They described Georan, and his purchases, perfectly, down to that . . . rather unique headgear."

"And," Erik demanded, leaning forward.

Georan swallowed hard and caught Ra-khir's hand.

"You're safe," Ra-khir said, as much a command to the assemblage as a reassurance. "Please finish."

Georan lowered his head. "I spent that money in Dunford, not Erythane, at Frendon's request. He said he got it from Paradisians who paid him to make certain the Renshai lost their single combat."

"What!"

Ra-khir looked instinctively toward Erik, but it was Valr Magnus who had shouted as he sprang to his feet again. The blood rushed from a face already pale, making it appear entirely bloodless.

As if in direct contrast, Erik's cheeks appeared to gain all the color Magnus' lost, plus more. Arteries throbbed in his neck. "Are you calling us cheaters?" Erik demanded.

Georan shrank against Ra-khir, and the knight shielded him as the situation demanded.

"Sit down, Erik," King Humfreet demanded. "No one is saying you personally cheated."

Erik obeyed with obvious reluctance, but Magnus remained standing, still chalk white and looking as if he might vomit.

King Griff addressed the man cowering against Ra-khir. "Georan, did Frendon tell you exactly who paid him, by name?"

Georan shook his head.

Ra-khir felt more than saw it. "No, Sire. He believes they either swore Frendon to secrecy or never showed him their faces."

"He's lying!" Erik bobbed up again, clearly unable to keep his seat. "He's a confessed father of Renshai with every reason to lie."

"No!" King Humfreet also clambered to his feet, and everyone except Griff scrambled to do the same from etiquette. "My Knights of Erythane never lie. Never. Not even to save their own lives."

"But it was the Knights of Erythane who declared the battle results fair! They can't just turn around and negate that judgment."

King Humfreet took the words as proof of his own point. "The grandfather of Renshai banished his own. Sir Ra-khir, himself, once surrendered his own infant son rather than break a vow. The Knights of Erythane are above reproach."

Surprised, Ra-khir turned to the king of Erythane. No one should know the details of the vow he once made with Pudar. It was Weile Kahn who had rescued Calistin from becoming a Pudarian prince, in a deal whose fine points Ra-khir hoped he never learned.

Ra-khir answered the real question, "Captain Erik, when the knights verified the results of that battle, the information Georan just gave us was not available. When circumstances change, we have the right and the duty to change our minds.

Valr Magnus finally found his tongue. "I humbly apologize to Sir Ra-khir and his sons for taking the life of valiant Kevral Tainharsdatter in a battle that we now know was unfairly won." He nodded to Ra-khir, Saviar, and Calistin in turn. "Please believe me when I say I had no hand in, nor knowledge of, this deceit. And, no matter the determination of kings and captains, I refuse to acknowledge the ill-gotten title of Renshai-slayer. I will not claim victory, and the banishment of the Renshai from the West is withdrawn."

Captain Erik Leifsson sputtered. "You can't do that! You're merely our champion, not a signatory to the contract. You have no authority to undo an agreement to which you were never bound."

"But I was," King Humfreet said. "And I can." He pronounced loudly, deliberately repeating Magnus' exact words, "The banishment of the Renshai from the West is withdrawn."

Ra-khir's heart leaped, and he turned Saviar a warning glance. At this point, the Renshai's best strategy was silence.

King Humfreet continued, "The area of Erythane once called Paradise Plains will revert back to its previous name, the Fields of Wrath."

Erik's mouth worked for several moments without a word emerging. "Fine, so be it. We issue another challenge, our champion against the Renshai in single combat with the same end point."

Saviar smiled. "And we accept your challenge."

Caught behind Georan, Ra-khir could barely reach a kick to his son's unsuspecting shin.

Valr Magnus grinned. "You against Calistin, Erik? I'd pay money just to watch."

The corners of Erik's mouth drooped. His nostrils flared. "But you're our champion, Valr. You're the best swordsman in the North. We *need* you."

"As I understand it," Valr said coolly. "I was not a signatory and, so, never bound by the agreement."

Betrayed by his own words, Erik growled something Northern before shoving aside his chair with great violence and storming from the room. It was all Verdondi could do to scramble out of the way and rush after his father.

Silence reigned in the Nordmirians' wake. For now, Ra-khir realized, they had won the battle. But they could not afford to lose the war. The West still needed the North's ore, and its sword arms, against the threat of *Kjempemagiska*. Angering a man representing the high Northern kingdom seemed folly. Yet, for the moment, Ra-khir was ecstatic. As a Knight of Erythane, he had a dedication to justice and truth that transcended even such alliances.

Calistin stretched and rose, seemingly unfazed by the actions of those around him. "General Magnus, I'll take that handshake now." He offered his palm.

Valr Magnus took it and, not only shook, but pulled Calistin into an embrace.

For the first time in many years, Calistin did not stiffen or pull away from the contact. He seemed almost to relish it.

Surprised by a tiny pang of jealousy, Ra-khir still smiled. Something enormous, something he could not define, had gotten into Calistin. And maybe, just maybe, changed him for the better.

Appendices

WESTERNERS

Béarnides

Aerean (AIR-ee-an)—minister of internal affairs

Aranal (Ar-an-ALL)—a former king (deceased)

Aron (AHR-inn)—the current Sage

Arturo (Ahr-TOOR-oh)—a prince; second child of Griff and Matrinka

Barrindar (BAA-rinn-dar)—a prince; first child of Griff and Xoraida

Calitha (Kuh-LEE-tha)—a princess; second child of Griff and Xoraida

Chaveeshia (Sha-VEE-sha)—minister of local affairs

Davian (DAY-vee-an)—prime minister

Eldorin (Ell-DOOR-in)—a princess; third child of Griff and Xoraida

Franstaine (FRAN-stayn)—Minister of household affairs; in-law uncle of Helana

Griff (GRIFF)—the king

Halika (Huh-LEE-ka)—a princess; third child of Griff and Matrinka

Helana (Hell-AHN-a)—Griff's mother; Petrostan's wife

Ivana Shorith'na Cha-tella Tir Hya'sellirian Albar (Ee-VAH-nah): a princess; half-elfin, only child of Griff and Tem'aree'ay (see Outworlders)

Jhirban (JEER-bonn)—captain of the flagship *Seven* (deceased)

Kohleran (KOLL-er-in)—a previous king of Béarn (deceased); Matrinka's grandfather

Lazwald (LAHZ-wald)—a guardsman

Marisole (MAA-rih-soll)—a princess; first child of Griff and Matrinka; the bard's heir

Matrinka (Ma-TRINK-a)—the queen; Griff's senior wife; mother of Marisole, Arturo, and Halika

Morhane (MOOR-hayn)—an ancient king who usurped the throne from his twin brother, Valar (deceased)

Myrenex (My-RINN-ix)—a former king (deceased)

Petrostan (Peh-TROSS-tin)—King Kohleran's youngest son; Griff's father (deceased)

Richar (REE-shar):—minister of foreign affairs

Ruther (RA-ther)—a guardsman

The Sage—chronicler and keeper of Béarn's history and tomes

Saxanar (SAX-a-nar)—minister of courtroom procedure and affairs

Seiryn (SAIR-in)—captain of the guards

Sterrane (Stir-RAIN)—best-known ancient king (deceased)

Talamaine (TAL-a-mayn)—Matrinka's father (deceased)

Valar (VAY-lar)—Morhane's twin brother; Sterrane's father; a previous king murdered during his reign (deceased)

Walfron (WALL-fron)—supervisor of the kitchen staff

Xanranis (ZAN-ran-iss)—Sterrane's son; a former king (deceased)

Xoraida (Zor-AY-duh)—Griff's junior wife (third); mother of Barrindar, Calitha, and Eldorin

Yvalane (IV-a-layn)—Kohleran's father; a previous king (deceased)

Zapara (Za-PAR-a)—a guard

Zaysharn (ZAY-sharn)—overseer of the caretakers of livestock, gardens, and food

Zelshia (ZELL-sha)—a head maid

Zoenya (Zoh-ENN-ya)—a previous queen (deceased)

Erythanians

Arduwyn (AR-dwinn)—a legendary archer and friend of King Sterrane (deceased)

Avra (AHV-rah)—a street tough

Braison (BRAY-son)—a knight

Edwin (ED-winn)—a knight; the armsman

Esatoric (EE-sah-tor-ik)—a knight

Eshwin (ESH-winn)—a horse breeder; Tirro's neighbor

Frendon (FRENN-dinn)—interrupted battle between Kevral and Valr Magnus by falling or jumping from a tree (deceased)

Garvin (GAR-vinn)—a knight

Georan (JOR-inn)—brother to Harveki; uncle to Frendon

Harritin (HARR-ih-tin)—a knight
Harveki (Harr-VEK-ee)—father of Frendon; brother of Georan (deceased)
Humfreet (HUM-freet)—the king
Jakrusan (Jah-KROO-sin)—a knight
Kedrin (KEH-drinn)—captain of the knights; Ra-khir's father
Khirwith (KEER-with)—Ra-khir's stepfather (deceased)
Lakamorn (LACK-a-morn)—a knight
Oridan (OR-ih-den)—Shavasiay's father
Parmille (Par-MEEL)—a street tough
Ra-khir (Rah-KEER)—a knight; Kedrin's son; father of Saviar and Calistin (see Renshai)
Ramytan (RAM-ih-tin)—Kedrin's father (deceased)
Shavasiay (Shah-VASS-ee-ay)—a knight
Tirro (TEER-oh)—a farmer; Eshwin's neighbor
Treysind (TRAY-sind)—an orphan

Pudarians

Alenna (A-LENN-a)—Prince Leondis' wife; mother of second Severin
Boshkin (BAHSH-kinn)—Prince Leondis' steward and adviser
Cenna (SEH-na)—an ancient queen (deceased)
Chethid (CHETH-id)—one of three lieutenants
Cymion (KIGH-mee-on)—the king
Daizar (DYE-zahr)—Minister of visiting dignitaries
Darian (DAYR-ee-an)—one of three lieutenants
Darris (DAYR-iss)—the bard; Linndar's son; blood father of Marisole, Arturo, and Halika (see Béarnides)
DeShane (Dih-SHAYN)—a captain of the guards
Eudora (Yoo-DOOR-a)—the late queen; Severin and Leondis' mother (deceased)
Harlton (HAR-all-ton)—a captain of the King's guards
Horatiannon (Hor-ay-shee-AH-nun)—an ancient king (deceased)
Jahiran (Jah-HEER-in)—the first bard (deceased); initiated the bardic curse
Javonzir (Ja-VON-zeer)—the king's cousin and adviser
Larrin (LARR-inn)—a captain of the guards
Leondis (Lee-ON-diss)—the crown prince; second son of Cymion and Eudora
Linndar (LINN-dar)—a previous bard; Darris' mother (deceased)
Mar Lon (MAR-LONN)—a previous bard in the age of King Sterrane (deceased)

Markanyin (Marr-KANN-yinn)—the general of the army
Nellkoris (Nell-KORR-iss)—one of three lieutenants
Severin (SEV-rinn)—first son of Cymion and Eudora; previous heir to the throne (deceased)
Severin (SEV-rinn)—Leondis' son; named for his deceased uncle

Renshai

Ashavir (AH-sha-veer)—a boy
Asmiri (Az-MEER-ee)—a guardian of Prince Barrindar
Calistin the Bold (Ka-LEES-tinn)—Colbey's father (deceased)
Calistin Ra-khirsson (Ka-LEES-tinn)—youngest son of Ra-khir and Kevral
Colbey Calistinsson (KULL-bay)—legendary immortal Renshai now living among the gods
Elbirine (Ell-burr-EE-neh)—a guardian of Princess Halika; trained with Kevral
Episte Rachesson (Ep-PISS-teh)—an orphan raised by Colbey; later killed by Colbey after being driven mad by chaos (deceased)
Erlse (EARL-seh)—a man
Gareth Lasirsson (GARR-ith)—tested the worthiness of Ra-khir and Tae to sire Renshai; Kristel's father
Gunnhar (GUN-her)—a guardian of Arturo (deceased)
Kevralyn Balmirsdatter (KEV-ra-linn)—Kevralyn Tainharsdatter's namesake (deceased)
Kevralyn Tainharsdatter (KEV-ra-linn)—aka Kevral; Ra-khir's wife; mother of Saviar, Subikahn, and Calistin
Kwavirse (Kwah-VEER-seh)—a man
Kristel Garethsdatter (KRISS-tal)—a previous guardian of Queen Matrinka
Kyndig (KAWN-dee)—another name for Colbey Calistinsson; "Skilled One"
Kyntiri (Kawn-TEER-ee)—a torke of Saviar and Subikahn
Mitrian Santagithisdatter (MIH-tree-in)—foremother of the tribe of Tannin; Santagithi's daughter (deceased)
Modrey (MOH-dray)—forefather of the tribe of Modrey
Nirvina (Ner-VEE-nah)—a torke of Saviar
Nisse Nelsdatter (NEE-sah)—a previous guardian of Queen Matrinka
Pseubicon (Soo-bih-kahn)—an ancient Renshai; half-barbarian by blood (deceased)

Rache Garnsson (RACK-ee)—forefather of the tribe of Rache; son of Mitrian (deceased)

Rache Kallmirsson (RACK-ee)—Rache Garnsson's namesake; Episte's father (deceased)

Ranilda Battlemad (Ran-HEEL-da)—Colbey's mother (deceased)

Rantire Ulfinsdatter (Ran-TEER-ee)—Griff's bodyguard in Darris' absence; a dedicated guardian

Raska "Ravn" Colbeysson (RASS-ka; RAY-vinn)—only son of Colbey and Freya

Saviar Ra-khirsson (SAV-ee-ahr)—first son of Ra-khir and Kevral; Subikahn's twin

Sitari (Sih-TARR-ee)—Calistin's secret crush (deceased)

Subikahn Taesson (SOO-bih-kahn)—only son of Tae and Kevral; Saviar's twin

Sylva (SILL-va)—foremother of the tribe of Rache; an Erythanian; daughter of Arduwyn (deceased)

Tainhar (TAYN-har)—Kevral's father (deceased)

Talamir Edminsson (TAL-a-meer)—a torke of Subikahn

Tarah Randilsdatter (TAIR-a)—foremother of the tribe of Modrey; sister of Tannin (deceased)

Tannin Randilsson (TAN-inn)—forefather of the tribe of Tannin; Tarah's brother; Mitrian's husband (deceased)

Thialnir Thrudazisson (Thee-AHL-neer)—political representative

Trygg (TRIG)—a guardian of Arturo (deceased)

Santagithians

Herwin (HER-winn)—King Griff's stepfather

Mitrian (MIH-tree-inn)—Santagithi's daughter (see Renshai) (deceased)

Santagithi (San-TAG-ih-thigh)—legendary general for whom the town was named; main strategist of the Great War (deceased)

Sutton (SUTT-inn)—general of the army; current leader

Mages of Myrcidë

Chymmerlee (KIM-er-lee)—a young woman

Jeremilan (Jerr-ih-MY-lan)—the leader

Shadimar (SHAD-ih-mar)—legendary Eastern Wizard who returned King Sterrane to his throne (deceased)

Ainsvillers

Burnold (Burn-OLD)—the blacksmith
Karruno (Ka-ROON-oh)—a farmer (deceased)
Oscore (OSS-ker)—the bartender

Keatovillers

Darby (DAR-bee)—a boy
Keva (KEY-va)—Darby's younger sister
Tiega (Tee-AY-ga)—Darby's mother
Tiego (Tee-AY-go)—Tiega's father

Other Westlanders

Howall (HOW-ell)—Sheatonian; the guardsman
Khalen (KAY-linn)—New Lovénian; a fabric-seller
Lenn (LENN)—Dunforder; owner and barkeeper of only inn
Nat (NAT)—a highwayman
The Savage—New Lovénian; a brawly (deceased)

EASTERNERS

Alneezah (Al-NEE-zah)—a castle maid
Alsrusett (Al-RUSS-it)—one of Weile Kahn's bodyguards (with Daxan)
Chayl (SHAYL)—a follower of Weile Kahn; commander of Nighthawk sector
Curdeis (KER-tuss)—Weile Kahn's brother (deceased)
Daxan (DICK-sunn)—one of Weile Kahn's bodyguards (with Alsrusett)
Halcone (Hell-KAHN)—high general of the Eastern armies
Jeffrin (JEFF-rinn)—an informant working for Weile Kahn
Kinya (KEN-yah)—a long-time member of Weile Kahn's organization
Leightar (LAY-tar)—a follower of Weile Kahn
Midonner (May-DONN-er)—previous king of Stalmize; high king of the Eastlands (deceased)
Nacoma (Nah-KAH-mah)—a follower of Weile Kahn
Saydee (SAY-dee)—a server at the Dancing Dog
Shavoor (Shah-VOOR)—an informant working for Weile Kahn
Shaxcharal (SHACKS-krawl)—the last king of LaZar

Tae Kahn (TIGH KAHN)—the king of Stalmize; high king of the Eastlands; Weile Kahn's only son

Tisharo (Ta-SHAR-oh)—a con man working for Weile Kahn

Usyris (Yoo-SIGH-russ)—a follower of Weile Kahn; commander of Sparrowhawk sector

Weile Kahn (WAY-lee KAHN)—Tae's father; father of organized crime

NORTHERNERS

Alsmir (ALS-meer)—AERI; captain of Aerin's infantry

Andvari (And-VARR-ee)—NORDMIRIAN; warrior and diplomat

Avard (AV-ahrd)—AERI; a bartender in Aerin

Erik Leifsson (EH-rik)—NORDMIRIAN; captain of the *Sea Dragon,* a warship

Griselda (Gree-ZELL-da)—AERI; a server in the tavern in Aerin

Mundilnarvi (Munn-dill-NAR-vee)—NORDMIRIAN; *Einherjar* killed in the war against the Renshai

Olvaerr (OHL-eh-vair)—NORDMIRIAN; Valr Kirin's son (deceased)

Olvirn (OHL-eh-veern)—AERI; captain of Aerin's cavalry

Sivaird (SEE-vayrd)—AERI; captain of Aerin's archers

Tyrion (TEER-ee-on)—ASCAI; an inner court guard of Pudar

Valr Kirin (Vawl-KEER-inn)—NORDMIRIAN; an ancient enemy of Colbey's; Rache Kallmirsson's blood brother (deceased)

Valr Magnus (Vawl-MAG-nuss)—AERI; general of Aerin's army; the best swordsman in the North

Verdondi Eriksson (Ver-DONN-dee)—NORDMIRIAN; Erik's son

OUTWORLDERS

Arak'bar Tulamii Dhor (AHR-ok-barToo-LAHM-ee-igh ZHOOR)—eldest of the elves; aka He Who Has Forgotten His Name; aka The Captain

Arith'tinir Khy-loh'Shinaris Bal-ishi Sjörmann'taé Or (ARR-ith-tin-eer KIGH-loh-shin-ahr-iss Bal-EE-shee Syorr-mahn-TIGH Orr)—The Captain's given name

The Captain—the common name for Arak'bar Tulamii Dhor

Dillion (DILL-ee-yon)—a pirate

Firuz (Fa-ROOZ)—one of the *Kjempemagiska*

Fallon (FOUL-in)—a general of the *alsona*

Jaxon (JACKS-onn)—a pirate

Kalka (KOWL-kah)—a general of the *alsona*

Tem'aree'ay Donnev'ra Amal-yah Krish-anda Mal-satorian (Teh-MAR-ee-ay Donn-EV-er-a Ah-MAL-yah Kreesh-AND-ah Mahl-sah-TOR-ee-an); a healer; King Griff's junior wife (second)

ANIMALS

Clydin (KLY-dinn)—Darby's chestnut gelding

Frost Reaver—Colbey's white stallion

Imorelda (Ih-moor-ELL-dah)—Tae's silver tabby cat

Mior (Mee-ORR)—Matrinka's calico cat (deceased)

Silver Warrior—Ra-khir's white stallion

Snow Stormer—Kedrin's white stallion, replacement for the horse of the same name

GODS, WORLDS & LEGENDARY OBJECTS

Northern

Aegir (AHJ-eer)—Northern god of the sea; killed at the *Ragnarok*

Alfheim (ALF-highm)—the world of elves; destroyed during the *Ragnarok*

Asgard (AHSS-gard)—the world of the gods

Baldur (BALL-der)—Northern god of beauty and gentleness who rose from the dead after the *Ragnarok*

Beyla (BAY-lah)—Frey's human servant; wife of Byggvir

The Bifrost Bridge (BEE-frost)—the bridge between Asgard and man's world

Bragi (BRAH-gee)—Northern god of poetry; killed at the *Ragnarok*

Brysombolig (Briss-om-BOH-leeg)—Troublesome House; Loki's long-abandoned citadel

Byggvir (BEWGG-veer)—Frey's human servant; husband of Beyla

Colbey Calistinsson (KULL-bay)—legendary immortal Renshai; blood son of Thor and a mortal Renshai; husband of Freya

The Fenris Wolf (FEN-ris)—the Great Wolf; the evil son of Loki; also called Fenrir; killed at the *Ragnarok*

Frey (FRAY)—Northern god of rain, sunshine and fortune; father of the elves

Freya (FRAY-a)—Frey's sister; Northern goddess of battle

Frigg (FRIGG)—Odin's wife; Northern goddess of fate

Geirönul (Gay-EER-awn-ull)—Spear-bearer; a Valkyrie

Gladsheim (GLAD-shigm)—"Place of Joy"; sanctuary of the gods

Göll (GAWL)—Screaming; a Valkyrie

Hel (HEHL)—Northern goddess of the cold underrealm for those who do not die in valorous combat; killed at the *Ragnarok*

Hel (HEHL)—the underrealm ruled by the goddess Hel

Heimdall (HIGHM-dahl)—Northern god of vigilance and father of mankind; killed at the *Ragnarok*

Herfjötur (Herf-YOH-terr)—Host Fetter; a Valkyrie

Hildr (HEELD)—Warrior; a Valkyrie

Hlidskjalf (HLID-skyalf)—Odin's high seat from which he could survey the worlds

Hlökk (HLAWK)—Shrieking; a Valkyrie

Hod (HAHD)—Blind god, a son of Odin; returned with Baldur after the *Ragnarok*

Honir (HON-eer)—an indecisive god who survived the *Ragnarok*

Hrist (HRIST)—Shaker; a Valkyrie

Idunn (EE-dun)—Bragi's wife; keeper of the golden apples of youth

Ìfing (IFF-ing)—river between Asgard and Jötunheim

Jötunheim (YOH-tun-highm)—the world of the giants; destroyed during the *Ragnarok*

Kvasir (KWAH-seer)—a wise god, murdered by dwarves, whose blood was brewed into the mead of poetry

Loki (LOH-kee)—Northern god of fire and guile; a traitor to the gods and a champion of chaos; killed at the *Ragnarok*

Magni (MAG-nee)—Thor's and Sif's son; Northern god of might

Mana-garmr (MAH-nah garm)—Northern wolf destined to extinguish the sun with the blood of men at *Ragnarok*; killed in the *Ragnarok*

The Midgard Serpent—a massive, poisonous serpent destined to kill and be killed by Thor at the *Ragnarok*; Loki's son; killed in the *Ragnarok*

Mimir (MIM-eer)—wise god who was killed by gods; Odin preserved his head and used it as an adviser

Mist—Mist; a Valkyrie

Modi: (MOH-dee)—Thor's and Sif's son; Northern god of blood wrath

Nanna (NAH-nah)—Baldur's wife

Nidhogg (NID-hogg)—dragon who gnaws at the root of the World Tree in Niflheim

Niflheim (NIFF-ul-highm)—Misty Hel; the coldest part of Hel to which the worst of the dead are committed

Njord (NYORD)—Frey's and Freya's father; died in the *Ragnarok*

Norns—the keepers of past (Urdr), present (Verdandi), and future (Skuld)

Odin (OH-din)—Northern leader of the pantheon; father of the gods; killed in the *Ragnarok*; resurrected self by placing his soul in the empty Staff of Law prior to his slaying, then overtaking the leader of the elves (deceased)

Odrorir (ODD-dror-eer)—the cauldron containing the mead of poetry brewed from Kvasir's blood

The Ragnarok (RAN-yer-rok)—the massive war prophesied to destroy the gods, humans, and elves; partially thwarted by Colbey Calistinsson and Odin

Ran (RAHN)—wife of Aegir; killed in the *Ragnarok*

Randgrithr (RAWND-greeth)—Shieldbearer; a Valkyrie

Raska Colbeysson (RASS-ka)—son of Colbey and Freya, aka Ravn (RAY-vinn); see Renshai

Ratatosk (Rah-tah-TOSK)—a squirrel who relays insults between Nidhogg and the eagle at the top of Yggdrasill

Rathgrithr (RATH-greeth)—Plan-Destroyer; a Valkyrie

Reginleif (REGG-inn-leef)—God's Kin; a Valkyrie

Sif (SIFF)—Thor's wife; Northern goddess of fertility and fidelity

Sigyn (SEE-gihn)—Loki's wife

Skeggjöld (SKEG-yawld): Ax Time; a Valkyrie

Skögul (SKOH-gull)—Raging; a Valkyrie

Skoll (SKOHWL)—Northern wolf who was to swallow the sun at the *Ragnarok*

Skuld (SKULLD)—Being; the Norn who represents the future

Spring of Mimir—spring under the second root of Yggdrasill

Syn (SIN)—Northern goddess of justice and innocence

Surtr (SURT)—the king of fire giants; destined to kill Frey and destroy the worlds of elves and men with fire at the *Ragnarok*; killed in the *Ragnarok*

Thor—Northern god of storms, farmers, and law; killed in the *Ragnarok*

Thrudr (THRUD)—Thor's daughter; goddess of power

Tyr (TEER)—Northern one-handed god of war and faith; killed in the *Ragnarok*

Ugagnevangar (Oo-gag-nih-VANG-ahr)—Dark Plain of Misfortune; Loki's world on which sits Brysombolig

Urdr (ERD): Fate—the Norn who represents the past

Valaskjalf (Vahl-AS-skyalf)—Shelf of the Slain; Odin's citadel

Valhalla (VAWL-holl-a)—the heaven for the souls of dead warriors killed in valiant combat; at the *Ragnarok,* the souls in Valhalla (*Einherjar*) assisted the gods in battle

Vali (VAHL-ee)—Odin's son; survived the *Ragnarok*

The Valkyries (VAWL-ker-ees)—the Choosers of the Slain; warrior women who choose which souls go to Valhalla on the battlefield

Verdandi (Ver-DAN-dee)—Necessity; the Norn who represents the present

Vidar (VEE-dar)—son of Odin destined to avenge his father's death at the *Ragnarok* by slaying the Fenris Wolf; current leader of the gods

The Well of Urdr—body of water at the base of the first root of Yggdrasill

The Wolf Age—the sequence of events immediately preceding the *Ragnarok* during which Skoll swallows the sun, Hati mangles the moon, and the Fenris Wolf runs free

Yggdrasill (IGG-dra-zill)—the World Tree

Western

(now considered essentially defunct;
mostly studied for its historical significance)

Aphrikelle (Ah-frih-KELL)—Western goddess of spring

Cathan (KAY-than)—Western goddess of war, specifically hand-to-hand combat; twin to Kadrak

Dakoi (Dah-KOY)—Western god of death

The Faceless God—Western god of winter

Firfan (FEER-fan)—Western god of archers and hunters

Itu (EE-too)—Western goddess of knowledge and truth

Kadrak (KAD-drak)—Western god of war; twin to Cathan

Ruaidhri (Roo-AY-dree)—Western leader of the pantheon

Suman (SOO-mon)—Western god of farmers and peasants

Weese (WEESSS)—Western god of winds

Yvesen (IV-eh-sen)—Western god of steel and women

Zera'im (ZAIR-a-eem)—Western god of honor

Eastern

(though more common than the Western religion,
it is also considered essentially defunct)

Sheriva (Sha-REE-vah)—omnipotent, only god of the Eastlands

Outworld Gods

Ciacera (See-a-SAIR-a)—goddess of life on the sea floor who takes the form of an octopus

Mahaj (Ma-HAJ)—the god of dolphins

Morista (Moor-EES-tah)—the god of swimming creatures who takes the form of a seahorse

FOREIGN WORDS

a (AH)—EASTERN. "from"

ailar (IGH-LAR)—EASTERN. "to bring"

al (AIL)—EASTERN. the first person singular pronoun

alfen (ALF-in)—BÉARNESE. "elves"; new term created by elves to refer to themselves

alsona (al-SOH-na)—OUTWORLD. "person" or "people"

amythest-weed—TRADING. a specific type of wildflower

anem (ON-um)—BARBARIAN. "enemy"; usually used in reference to a specific race or tribe with whom the barbarian's tribe is at war

åndelig mannhimmel (AWN-deh-lee mahn-hee-mell)—RENSHAI. "spirit man of the sky"; an advanced Renshai sword maneuver

aristiri (ah-riss-TEER-ee)—TRADING. a breed of singing hawk

årvåkir (AWR-vaw-keer)—NORTHERN. "vigilant one"

baronshei (ba-RON-shigh)—TRADING. "bald"

bein (BAYN)—NORTHERN. "legs"

berserks (BAIR-sair)—NORTHERN. soldiers who fight without emotion, ignoring the safety of self and companions because of drugs or mental isolation; "crazy"

bha'fraktii (bhah-FROK-tee-igh)—ELFIN. "those who court their doom"; a *lysalf* term for *svartalf*

binyal (BIN-yall)—TRADING. a type of spindly tree

bleffy (BLEFF-ee)—WESTERN/TRADING. a child's euphemism for nauseating

bolboda (bawl-BOH-da)—NORTHERN. "evilbringer"

bonta (BONN-tah)—EASTERN. vulgar term for a male homosexual

brawly (BRAWL-ee)—WESTERN. street slang for gang-level protection racketeers

brigshigsa weed (brih-SHIG-sah)—WESTERN. a specific leafy weed with a translucent, red stem; a universal antidote to several common poisons brorin (BROAR-inn)—RENSHAI. "brother"

brunstil (BRUNN-steel)—NORTHERN. a stealth maneuver learned from barbarians by the Renshai; literally "brown and still"

butterflower—TRADING. a specific type of wild flower with a brilliant, yellow hue

chrisshius (KRISS-ee-us)—WESTERN. a specific type of wildflower

chroams (krohms)—WESTERN. a specific coinage of copper, silver, or gold

corpa (KOR-pah)—WESTERN. "brotherhood", "town"; literally "body"

cringers—EASTERN. gang slang for people who show fear

daimo (DIGH-moh)—EASTERN. slang term for Renshai

demon (DEE-mun)—ANCIENT TONGUE. a creature of magic

dero (DAYR-oh)—EASTERN. a type of winter fruit

djem (dee-YEM)—NORTHERN. "demon"

djevgullinhåri (dee-YEM-gull-in-HAWR-ee)—NORTHERN. "golden-haired devils"

djevskulka (dee-yev-SKOHL-ka)—NORTHERN. an expletive that essentially means "devil's play"

doranga (door-ANG-a)—TRADING. a type of tropical tree with serrated leaves and jutting rings of bark

drilstin (DRILL-stinn)—TRADING. an herb used by healers

dwar-freytii (dwar-FRAY-tee-igh)—ELFIN. "the chosen ones of Frey"; a *svartalf* name for themselves

Einherjar (IGHN-herr-yar)—NORTHERN. "the dead warriors in Vahalla"

ejenlyåndel (ay-YEN-lee-ON-dell)—ELFIN. "immortality echo"; a sense of infinality that is a part of every human and elf

eksil (EHK-seel)—NORTHERN. "exile"

erenspice (EH-ren-spighs)—EASTERN. a type of hot spice used in cooking

ernontris (err-NON-triss)—OUTWORLD. a specific gruesome and magical type of torture

fafra (FAH-fra)—TRADING. "to eat"

feflin (FEF-linn)—TRADING. "to hunt"

floyetsverd (floy-ETTS-wayrd)—RENSHAI. a disarming maneuver

formynder (for-MEWN-derr)—NORTHERN. "guardian", "teacher"

forrader (foh-RAY-der)—NORTHERN. "traitor"

forraderi (foh-reh-derr-EE)—NORTHERN. "treason"

forsvarir (fors-var-EER)—RENSHAI. a specific disarming maneuver

frey (FRAY)—NORTHERN. "lord"

freya (FRAY-a)—NORTHERN. "lady"

frichen-karboh (FRATCH-inn kayr-BOH)—EASTERN. widow; literally "manless woman, past usefulness"

frilka (FRAIL-kah)—EASTERN. the most formal title for a woman, elevating her nearly to the level of a man

fussling (FUSS-ling)—TRADING. slang for bothering

galn (GAHLN)—NORTHERN. "ferociously crazy"

ganim (GAH-neem)—RENSHAI. "a non-Renshai"

garlet (GAR-let)—WESTERN. a specific type of wildflower believed to have healing properties

garn (GARN)—NORTHERN. "yarn"

Gerlinr (gerr-LEEN)—RENSHAI. a specific aesthetic and difficult sword maneuver

granshy (GRANN-shigh)—WESTERN. "plump"

gullin (GULL-in)—NORTHERN. "golden"

gynurith (ga-NAR-ayth)—EASTERN. "excrement"

hacantha (ha-CAN-thah)—TRADING. a specific type of cultivated flower that comes in various hues

hadongo (hah-DONG-oh)—WESTERN. a twisted, hardwood tree

harval (harr-VALL)—ANCIENT TONGUE. "the gray blade"

Hastivillr (has-tih-VEEL)—RENSHAI. a sword maneuver

herbont (HER-bont)—TRADING. a specific type of gnarly tree that tends to grow with multiple trunks

jovinay arithanik (joh-VIN-ay ar-ih-THAN-ik)—ELFIN. "a joining of magic"; a gathering of elves for the purpose of amplifying and casting spells

jarfr (YAHR-fer)—OUTWORLD. a fierce predator akin to a wolverine.

jufinar (JOO-fin-ar)—TRADING. a specific type of bushlike tree that produces berries

kadlach (KOD-lok; the ch has a guttural sound)—TRADING. a vulgar term for a disobedient child; akin to brat

kathkral (KATH-krall)—ELFIN. a specific type of broad-leafed tree

kenya (KEN-ya)—WESTERN. "bird"

khohlar (KOH-lahr)—ELFIN. a mental magical concept that involves transmitting several words in an instantaneous concept

kjaelnabnir (kyahl-NAHB-neer)—RENSHAI. temporary name for a child until a hero's name becomes available

kinesthe (kin-ESS-teh)—NORTHERN. "strength"

kolbladnir (kol-BLAW-neer)—NORTHERN. "the cold-bladed"

krabbe (krab-EH)—NORTHERN. "the crab"; a Renshai sword maneuver kraell (kray-ELL)—ANCIENT TONGUE. a type of demon dwelling in the deepest region of chaos' realm

kyndig (KAWN-dee)—NORTHERN. "skilled one"

latense (lah-TEN-seh—RENSHAI. a sword maneuver

lav'rintir (lahv-rinn-TEER)—ELFIN. "destroyer of the peace"

lav'rintii (lahv-RINN-tee-igh)—ELFIN. "the followers of Lav'-rintir"

lessakit (LAYS-eh-kight)—EASTERN. "a message"

leuk (LUKE)—WESTERN. "white"

loki (LOH-kee)—NORTHERN. "fire"

lonriset (LON-rih-set)—WESTERN. a ten-stringed instrument

lynstriek (LEEN-strayk)—RENSHAI. a sword maneuver

lysalf (LEES-alf)—ELFIN. "light elf"

magni (MAG-nee)—NORTHERN. "might"

meirtrin (MAYR-trinn)—TRADING. a specific breed of nocturnal rodent

minkelik (min-KEL-ik)—ELFIN. "human"

mirack (merr-AK)—WESTERN. a specific type of hardwood tree with white bark

missy beetle—TRADING. a type of harmless, black beetle

mjollnir (MYOLL-neer)—NORTHERN. "mullicrusher"

modi (MOE-dee)—NORTHERN. "wrath"

Morshoch (MOOR-shok)—ANCIENT TONGUE. "sword of darkness"

Motfrabelonning (mot-frah-bell-ONN-ee)—NORTHERN. "reward of courage"

mulesl om natten (MYOO-sill-ohm-NOT-in)—RENSHAI. "the night mule"; a Renshai sword maneuver

musserënde (myoo-ser-EN-deh)—RENSHAI. "sparkling"; a Renshai sword maneuver

mynten (MIN-tin)—NORTHERN. a specific type of coin

nådenal (naw-deh-NAHL)—RENSHAI. "needle of mercy"; a silver, guardless, needle-shaped dagger constructed during a meticulous religious ceremony and used to end the life of an honored, suffering ally or enemy, then melted in the victim's pyre

nålogtråd (naw-LOG-trawd)—RENSHAI. "needle and thread"; a Renshai sword maneuver

noca (NOE-ka)—BÉARNESE. "grandfather"

odelhurtig (OD-ehl-HEWT-ih)—RENSHAI. a sword maneuver

oopey (OO-pee)—WESTERN/TRADING. a child's euphemism for an injury

orlorner (oor-LEERN-ar)—EASTERN. "to deliver to"

pen-fruit: WESTERN—an edible fruit that is the seed of the pen-fruit tree

perfrans (PURR-franz)—WESTERN. a specific scarlet wildflower

pike—NORTHERN. "mountain"

placeling (PLAYS-ling)—ANCIENT TONGUE. a creature with Outworld blood placed magically into a human womb

prins (PRINS)—NORTHERN. "prince"

ranweed—WESTERN. a specific type of wild plant

raynshee (RAYN-shee)—TRADING. "elder"

rexin (RAYKS-inn)—EASTERN. "king"

rhinsheh (ran-SHAY)—EASTERN. "morning"

richi (REE-chee)—WESTERN. a specific type of songbird

rintsha (RINT-shah)—WESTERN. "cat"

Ristoril (RISS-tor-rill)—ANCIENT TONGUE. "sword of tranquillity"

sangrit (SAN-grit)—BARBARIAN. "to form a blood bond"

sawgrass—WESTERN. a specific type of grass

shucara—(shoo-KAHR-a): TRADING. a specific type of medicinal root

skjald (SKYAWLD)—NORTHERN. "musician chronicler"

skulk i djevlir (SKOOLK ee dyev-LEER)—NORTHERN. "devils brutal fun"

skulkë i djeygullinhåhi (SKOOLK-eh EE djev-gull-inn-HARR-ee)—NORTHERN. "golden-haired devil's brutal fun

stjerne skytedel (STYARN-eh skih-TED-ell)—RENSHAI. "the shooting star"; a Renshai sword maneuver

svartalf (SWART-alf)—ELFIN. "dark elf"

svergelse (sverr-GELL-seh)—RENSHAI. "sword figures practiced alone"; katas

take—TRADING. a game children play

takudan (TOK-oo-don)—OUTWORLD. "sewer rat"

talvus (TAL-vuss)—WESTERN. "midday"

tåphresëlmordat (taw-FRESS-al-MOOR-dah)—RENSHAI. "brave suicide"; leaping into an unwinnable battle for the sole purpose of dying in glory for Valhalla rather than of illness or old age

thrudr (THRUDD)—NORTHERN. "power", "might"

tisis (TISS-iss)—NORTHERN. "retaliation"

torke (TOR-keh)—RENSHAI. "teacher", "sword instructor"

tre-ved-en (TREH-ved-enn)—RENSHAI. "Loki's cross"; a Renshai sword maneuver designed for battling three against one

trithray (TRITH-ray)—TRADING. a specific type of purple wildflower

tvinfri (TWINN-free)—RENSHAI. a specific disarming maneuver

ulvstikk (EWLV-steek)—RENSHAI. a specific sword maneuver
uvakt (oo-VAKT)—RENSHAI. "the unguarded"; a term for children whose *kjaelnabnir* becomes a permanent name
Valhalla (VAWL-holl-a)—NORTHERN. "hall of the slain"
valkyrie (VAWL-kerr-ee)—NORTHERN. "choser of the slain"
valr (VAWL)—NORTHERN. "slayer"
Vestan (VAYST-inn)—EASTERN. "The Westlands"
waterroot—TRADING. a specific edible sea plant
wertell (wer-TELL)—TRADING. a specific plant with an acid seed
used for medicinal purposes
wisule (WISS-ool)—TRADING. A foul-smelling, disease-carrying
breed of rodents that has many offspring because the adults will
abandon them when threatened
yarshimyan (yar-SHIM-yan)—ELFIN. a type of tree with bubblelike
fruit
yonha (YON-a)—OUTWORLD. "wild animal"
yrtventrig (eert-VEN-tree)—RENSHAI. a specific sword maneuver

PLACES

Northlands

The area north of the Weathered Mountains and west of the Great
Frenum Range. The Northmen live in nine tribes, each with its own
town surrounded by forest and farmland. The boundaries change.
Asci (ASS-kee)—home of the Ascai; Patron god: Bragi
Aerin (Ah-REEN)—home of the Aeri; Patron god: Aegir
Devil's Island—an island in the Amirannak. A home to the Renshai
after their exile. Currently part of Nordmir
Erd (URD)—home of the Erdai; Patron god: Freya
Gelshnir (GEELSH-neer)—home of the Gelshni; Patron god: Tyr
Gjar (GYAR)—home of the Gyar; Patron: Heimdall
Nordmir (NORD-meer)—the Northlands high kingdom, home of
the Nordmirians; Patron: Odin
Shamir (Sha-MEER)—home of the Shamirians; Patron: Freya
Skrytil (SKRY-teel)—home of the Skrytila; Patron: Thor
Talmir (TAHL-meer)—home of the Talmirians; Patron: Frey

Westlands

The Westlands are bounded by the Great Frenum Mountains to the
east, the Weathered Mountains to the north, and the sea to the west

and south. In general, the cities become larger and more civilized as the land sweeps westward. The central area is packed with tiny farm towns dwarfed by lush farm fields that, over time, have nearly coalesced. This area is known as the Fertile Oval. The easternmost portions of the Westlands are forested, with sparse towns and rare barbarian tribes. To the south lies an uninhabited tidal plain.

Almische (Ahl-mish-AY)—a small city

Béarn (Bay-ARN)—the high kingdom; a large mountain city

Bellenet Fields (Bell-eh-NAY)—a tourney field in Erythane

Corpa Bickat (KOR-pah Bih-KAY)—a large city

Corpa Schaull (KOR-pah SHAWL)—a medium-sized city; one of the "twin cities" (see Frist)

Dunford (DUNN-ferd)—a small village east of Erythane

Erythane (AIR-eh-thayn)—a large city closely allied with Béarn; famous for its knights

The Fields of Wrath—plains on the outskirts of Erythane; home to the Renshai

Frist (FRIST)—a medium-sized city; one of the "twin cities" (see Corpa Schaull)

Granite Hills—a small, low range of mountains

Great Frenum Mountains—(FRENN-um): towering, impaasable mountains that divide the Eastlands from the Westlands and Northlands

Greentree—a small town

Hopewell—a small town

Keatoville (KEY-toh-vill)—a small town east and south of Dunford

The Knight's Rest—a pricy tavern in Erythane

Myrcidë (Meer-see-DAY)—a town near the Weathered Mountains that consists entirely of magically hidden caves

New Lovén (Low-VENN)—a medium-sized city

Nualfheim (Noo-ALF-highm)—the elves' name for their island

The Off-Duty Tavern—a Pudarian tavern frequented by guardsmen

Oshtan (OSH-tan)—a small town

Paradise Plains—an Erythanian name for the Fields of Wrath

Porvada (Poor-VAH-da)—a medium-sized city

Pudar (Poo-DAR)—the largest city of the West; the great trade center

The Red Horse Inn—an inn in Pudar

The Road of Kings—the legendary route by which the Eastern Wizard is believed to have rescued the high king's heir after a bloody coup

Santagithi (San-TAG-ih-thigh)—a medium-sized town

Sheaton (SHAY-ton)—a small town northeast of Dunford
The Western Plains—a barren salt flat
Wynix (Why-NIX)—a medium-sized town

Eastlands

The area east of the Great Frenum Mountains, it is a vast, overpopu-
lated area filled with crowded cities and eroded fields. Little forest
remains.
Dunchart (DOON-shayrt)—a small city
Ixaphant (IGHCKS-font)—a large city
Gihabortch (GIGH-hah-bortch)—a city
LaZar (LAH-zar)—a small city
Lemnock (LAYM-nok)—a large city
Osporivat (As-poor-IGH-vet)—a large city
Prohathra (Pree-HATH-ra)—a large city
Rozmath (ROZZ-mith)—a medium-sized city
Stalmize (STAHL-meez)—the Eastern high kingdom

Bodies of Water

Amirannak Sea (A-MEER-an-nak)—the northernmost ocean
Brunn River (BRUN)—a muddy river in the Northlands
Conus River (KONE-uss)—a shared river of the Eastlands and
Westlands
Icy River—a cold, northern river
Jewel River—one of the rivers that flows to Trader's Lake
Perionyx River (Peh-ree-ON-ix)—a Western river
Southern Sea—the southernmost ocean
Trader's Lake—a harbor for trading boats in Pudar
Trader's River—the main route for overwater trade

Objects/Systems/Events

Bards, the—a familial curse passed to the oldest child, male or female,
of one specific family. The curse condemns the current bard to obsessive curiosity but allows him to impart his learning only in song. A
condition added by the Eastern Wizards compels each bard to serve
as the personal bodyguard to the current king of Béarn as well.
Cardinal Wizards, the—a system of balance created by Odin in the
beginning of time consisting of four, near-immortal, opposing
guards of evil, neutrality, and goodness who were tightly constrained by Odin's laws. Obsolete.

Great War, the—a massive war fought between the Eastland army and the combined forces of the Westlands

Harval—"the Gray Blade." the sword of balance imbued with the forces of law, chaos, good and evil. Obsolete

Knights of Erythane, the—an elite guardian unit for the king of Erythane that also serves the high king in Béarn in shifts. Steeped in rigid codes of dress, manner, conduct, and chivalry, they are famed throughout the world.

Kolbladnir—"the Cold-Bladed." a magic sword commissioned by Frey to combat Surtr at the *Ragnarok*

Mages of Myrcidë—a society of genetic human mages once feared and revered. The greatest and strongest of the Cardinal Wizards came from this society before the Renshai killed them all and left their dwellings in ruins. Always reclusive, after their destruction, they were all but erased from human memory

Mjollnir—"Mullicrusher." Thor's gold, short-handled hammer so heavy only he can lift it

Necklace of the Brisings, the—a necklace worn by the goddess Freya and forged by dwarves from "living gold"

Pica Stone, the—a clairsentient sapphire. One of the rare items with magical power. Once the province of the Mages of Myrcidë, it became the totem of Renshai, was returned to the "last" Myrcidian by the "last" Renshai, then was shattered. The shards were regathered, the stone remade, and it now tests the heirs of Béarn to assign the one worthy of rulership.

Ragnarok (RAN-yer-rok)—"the Destruction of the Powers" the prophesied time when men, elves, and nearly all the gods would die. Because of actions by Colbey Calistinsson and Odin, things did not go exactly as fated. The current flashpoint of religious differences comes in the form of those who believe the *Ragnarok* has already occurred and those who believe it is still to come.

Sea Seraph, the—a ship once owned by an elf known only as the Captain and used to transport the Cardinal Wizards. Obsolete.

Seven Tasks of Wizardry, the—a series of tasks designed by gods to test the power and worth of the Cardinal Wizards' chosen successors. Obsolete.

Trobok, the—"the Book of the Faithful" a scripture that guides the lives of Northmen. It is believed that daily reading from the book assists Odin in holding chaos at bay from the world of law.